D0961668

Dear Reader,

My friends Beverly and Linda and I have worked on the concept for these books for about four years. We've spent hours and hours discussing them, playing with ideas and laughing our heads off. Not that these books are funny, but after a while we'd get sort of punch-drunk and go off on tangents. One such tangent was limericks (*There was a young man from Paducah…*), which of course had nothing to do with the Raintree books.

We loved working out the mythology behind the Raintree, extraordinary people trying to live in the ordinary world without being found out. We loved the characters. They are all very human, and at the same time they are…more than human. I hope you enjoy them, too.

Linda Howard

# LINDA HOWARD
# BEVERLY BARTON
## LINDA WINSTEAD JONES

# RAINTREE

HQN™

**HQN**™

ISBN-13: 978-0-373-77342-8
ISBN-10:    0-373-77342-0

RAINTREE

Copyright © 2008 by Harlequin Books S.A.

The publisher acknowledges the copyright holders of the individual works as follows:

RAINTREE: INFERNO
Copyright © 2007 by Linda Howington

RAINTREE: HAUNTED
Copyright © 2007 by Linda Winstead Jones

RAINTREE: SANCTUARY
Copyright © 2007 by Beverly Beaver

www.HQNBooks.com

**Printed in U.S.A.**

THE RAINTREE TRILOGY NOW IN ONE EXCITING VOLUME

# LINDA HOWARD

# INFERNO

To Beverly Barton and Linda Winstead Jones,
for the years of friendship and all the fun we had planning
these books, and to Leslie Wainger, for being everything an
editor should be, as well as a friend.

# PROLOGUE

There have always been those among us who are more than human. At first they were few, but like always calls to like, and so it was from the beginning, when mankind was new and clumped together in fire-lit caves. Sometimes they were driven out by fear and fists wielding clubs. Sometimes they simply left, seeking others like them. And though they were few and the earth was large, they found each other, drawn by the very instinct and power and knowledge that set them apart from the very beginning—and by the will to survive, for only in numbers was there safety.

In time those numbers grew large, and there was strife between those who wanted to use their powers, their *otherness*, to take what they wanted from the weaker humans, and those who wanted to live in harmony with the Ungifted. Over seven thousand years ago they split into what became two tribes, and then two kingdoms: the Raintree and the Ansara.

The two kingdoms then locked into eternal war, and earth in all her dimensions became the battleground.

So it was, and so it is.

# ONE

*Sunday*

Dante Raintree stood with his arms crossed as he watched the woman on the monitor. The image was in black and white, to better show details; color distracted the brain. He focused on her hands, watching every move she made, but what struck him most was how uncommonly *still* she was. She didn't fidget, or play with her chips, or look around at the other players. She peeked once at her down card, then didn't touch it again, signaling for another hit by tapping a fingernail on the table. Just because she didn't seem to be paying attention to the other players, though, didn't mean she was as unaware as she seemed.

"What's her name?" he asked.

"Lorna Clay," replied his chief of security, Al Rayburn.

"Is that her real name?"

"It checks out."

If Al hadn't already investigated her, Dante would have been disappointed. He paid Al a lot of money to be efficient and thorough.

"At first I thought she was counting," said Al. "But she doesn't pay enough attention."

"She's paying attention, all right," Dante murmured. "You just don't see her doing it." A card counter had to remember every card played. Supposedly counting cards was impossible with the number of decks used by the casinos, but no casino wanted a card counter at its tables. There *were* those rare individuals who could calculate the odds even with multiple decks.

"I thought that, too," said Al. "But look at this piece of tape coming up. Someone she knows comes up to her and speaks, she looks around and starts chatting, completely misses the play of the people to her left—and doesn't look around even when the deal comes back to her, she just taps that finger. And damned if she didn't win. Again."

Dante watched the tape, rewound it, watched it again. Then he watched it a third time. There had to be something he was missing, because he couldn't pick out a single giveaway.

"If she's cheating," Al said with something like respect, "she's the best I've ever seen."

"What does your gut say?" Dante trusted his chief of security. Al had spent thirty years in the casino business, and some people swore he could spot cheats as soon as they walked in the door. If Al thought she was cheating, then Dante would take action—and he wouldn't be watching this tape now if something hadn't made Al uneasy.

Al scratched the side of his jaw, considering. He was a big, bulky man, but no one who observed him for any length of time would think he was slow, either physically or mentally. Finally he said, "If she isn't cheating, she's the luckiest person walking. She wins. Week in, week out, she wins. Never a huge amount, but I ran the numbers, and she's into us for about five grand a week. Hell, boss, on her way out of the casino she'll stop by a slot machine, feed a dollar in and walk away with at least fifty. It's never the same machine, either. I've had her watched, I've had her followed, I've even looked for the same faces in the casino every time she's in here, and I can't find a common denominator."

"Is she here now?"

"She came in about half an hour ago. She's playing black-jack, as usual."

"Who's the dealer?"

"Cindy."

Cindy Josephson was Dante's best dealer, almost as sharp at spotting a cheater as Al himself. She had been with him since he'd opened Inferno, and he trusted her to run an honest game. "Bring the woman to my office," Dante said, making a swift decision. "Don't make a scene."

"Got it," said Al, turning on his heel and leaving the security center, where banks of monitors displayed every angle of the casino.

Dante left, too, going up to his office. His face was calm. Normally he would leave it to Al to deal with a cheater, but he was curious. How was she doing it? There were a lot of bad cheaters, a few good ones, and every so often one would come along who was the stuff of which legends were made: the cheater who didn't get caught, even when people were alert and the camera was on him—or, in this case, her.

It was possible for people to simply be lucky, as most people understood luck. Chance could turn a habitual loser into a big-time winner. Casinos, in fact, thrived on that hope. But luck itself wasn't habitual, and he knew that what passed for luck was often something else: cheating. Then there was the other kind of luck, the kind he himself possessed, but since it depended not on chance but on who and what he was, he knew it was an innate power and not Dame Fortune's erratic smiles. Since his power was rare, the odds made it likely the woman he'd been watching was merely a very clever cheat.

Her skill could provide her with a very good living, he thought, doing some swift calculations in his head. Five grand a week equaled two hundred sixty thousand dollars a year, and that was just from his casino. She probably hit all of them, careful to keep the numbers relatively low so she stayed under the radar.

He wondered how long she'd been taking him, how long she'd been winning a little here, a little there, before Al noticed.

The curtains were still open on the wall-to-wall window in his office, giving the impression, when one first opened the door, of stepping out onto a covered balcony. The glazed window faced west, so he could catch the sunsets. The sun was low now, the sky painted in purple and gold. At his home in the mountains, most of the windows faced east, affording him views of the sunrise. Something in him needed both the greeting and the goodbye of the sun. He'd always been drawn to sunlight, maybe because fire was his element to call, to control.

He checked his internal time: four minutes until sundown. He knew exactly, without checking the tables every day, when the sun would slide behind the mountains. He didn't own an alarm clock. He didn't need one. He was so acutely attuned to the sun's position that he had only to check within himself to know the time. As for waking at a particular time, he was one of those people who could tell himself to wake at a certain time, and he did. That particular talent had nothing to do with being Raintree, so he didn't have to hide it; a lot of perfectly ordinary people had the same ability.

There were other talents and abilities, however, that did require careful shielding. The long days of summer instilled in him an almost sexual high, when he could feel contained power buzzing just beneath his skin. He had to be doubly careful not to cause candles to leap into flame just by his presence, or to start wildfires, with a glance, in the dry-as-tinder brush. He loved Reno; he didn't want to burn it down. He just felt so damn *alive* with all the sunshine pouring down that he wanted to let the energy pour through him instead of holding it inside.

This must be how his brother Gideon felt while pulling lightning, all that hot power searing through his muscles, his veins. They had this in common, the connection with raw power. All the members of the far-flung Raintree clan had some power, some heightened form of ability, but only members of the royal family could channel and control the earth's natural energies.

Dante wasn't just of the royal family; he was the Dranir, the leader of the entire clan. "Dranir" was synonymous with "king," but the position he held wasn't ceremonial, it was one of sheer power. He was the oldest son of the previous Dranir, but he would have been passed over for the position if he hadn't also inherited the power to hold it.

Gideon was second to him in power; if anything happened to Dante and he died without a child who had inherited his abilities, Gideon would become Dranir—a possibility that filled his brother with dread, hence the fertility charm currently lying on Dante's desk. It had arrived in the mail just that morning. Gideon regularly sent them, partly as a joke, but mainly because he was doing all he could to insure that Dante had offspring—thus upping the chances that *he* would never inherit the position. Whenever they managed to get together, Dante had to carefully search every nook and cranny, as well as all his clothing, to make certain Gideon hadn't left one of his clever little charms in a hidden place.

Gideon was getting better at making them, Dante mused. Practice made perfect, after all, and God knows he'd made plenty of the charms in the past few years. Not only were they more potent now, but he varied his approach. Some of them were obvious, silver pieces meant to be worn around the neck like an amulet—not that Dante was an amulet kind of guy. Others were tiny, subtle, like the one Gideon had embedded in the newest business card he'd sent, knowing Dante would likely tuck the card into his pocket. He'd erred only in that the very power of the charm gave it away; Dante had sensed the buzz of its power, though he'd had the devil's own time finding it.

Behind him came Al's distinctive *knock-knock* on the door. The outer office was empty, Dante's secretary having gone home hours before. "Come in," he called, not turning from his view of the sunset.

The door opened, and Al said, "Mr. Raintree, this is Lorna Clay."

Dante turned and looked at the woman, all his senses on alert. The first thing he noticed was the vibrant color of her hair—a rich, dark red that encompassed a multitude of shades from copper to burgundy. The warm amber light danced along the iridescent strands, and he felt a hard tug of sheer lust in his gut. Looking at her hair was almost like looking at fire, and he had the same reaction.

The second thing he noticed was that she was spitting mad.

# TWO

Several things happened so closely together that they might as well have been simultaneous. With his senses already so heightened, the quick lash of desire collided with Dante's visceral reaction to fire, sending explosions of sensation cascading along all his neural pathways, too fast for him to control. Across the room, he saw all the candles leap with fire, the wicks burning too fast, too wild, so that the multiple little flames flared larger and more brightly than they should. And on his desk, Gideon's damn little fertility charm began to buzz with power, as if it had an on/off switch that had suddenly been pressed.

What the hell...?

He didn't have time to dissect and analyze everything that was going on; he had to control himself, and fast, or the entire room would be ablaze. He hadn't suffered such a humiliating loss of control of his powers since he'd first entered puberty and his surging hormones had played hell with everything.

Ruthlessly, he began exerting his will on all that leaping power. It wasn't easy; though he held himself perfectly still, mentally he felt as if he were riding a big, nasty-tempered bull. The natural inclination of energy was to be free, and it resisted any effort to tame it, to wrestle it back inside his mental walls. His control was usually phenomenal. After all, *having* power wasn't what made a Dranir; having it and *controlling* it *was*. Lack of control led to devastation—and ultimately to exposure. The Raintree had survived the centuries due in large part to their ability to blend with normal people, so it wasn't a matter to be taken lightly.

Dante had trained all his life to master the power and energies that ran through him, and even though he knew that as the summer solstice drew near his control was always stretched a bit, he wasn't accustomed to this degree of difficulty. Grimly he concentrated, pulling back, clamping down, exerting his will over the very forces of nature. He could have extinguished the candles, but with an even greater force of will he left them burning, for to make the tiny flames wink out now might draw even more attention than lighting them in the first place.

The only thing that evaded his control was that damn fertility charm on his desk, buzzing and throbbing and all but sending out a strobe effect. Even though he knew Al and Ms. Clay couldn't pick up on the energy the thing was sending out, not glancing at it took all his self-control. Gideon had outdone himself with this one. Just wait until the next time he saw his little brother, Dante grimly promised himself. If Gideon thought this was funny, they would both see how funny it was when the tables were turned. Gideon wasn't the only one who could make fertility charms.

All the wildfires once more under control, he returned his attention to his guest.

Lorna once again tried to twist her arm away from the gorilla holding her, but his grip was just strong enough to hold without applying undue pressure. While a small part of her appreciated that he was actively trying not to hurt her, by far the largest part of her was so furious—and, yes, scared—that she wanted to lash out at him with all her strength, clawing and kicking and biting, doing anything she could to get free.

Then her survival instinct kicked into high gear and her hair all but stood on end as she realized the man standing so silent and still in front of the huge windows was a far greater threat to her than was the gorilla.

Her throat closed, a fist of fear tightening around her neck. She couldn't have said what it was about him that so alarmed her, but she had felt this way only once before, in a back alley in Chicago. She was accustomed to taking care of herself on the streets and had normally used the alley as a shortcut to her place—a shabby single room in a run-down building—but one night when she had started down the alley, alarm had prickled her scalp and she'd frozen, unable to take another step. She couldn't see anything suspicious, couldn't hear anything, but she could *not* move forward. Her heart had been hammering so hard in her chest she could barely breathe, and she had abruptly been sick with fear. Slowly she had backed out of the alley's entrance and fled down the street to take the long way home.

The next morning a prostitute's body had been found in the alley, brutally raped and mutilated. Lorna knew the dead woman could have been her, if not for the sudden hair-raising panic that had warned her away.

This was the same, like being body-slammed by a sense of danger. The man in front of her, whoever he was, was a threat to her. She doubted—at least on a rational level—that he would murder and mutilate her, but there were other dangers, other destructions she could suffer.

She felt as if she were smothering, her throat so tight very little air could get past the constriction. Pinpricks of light flared at the edges of her vision, and in silent horror she realized she might faint. She didn't dare lose consciousness; she would be completely helpless if she did.

"Miss Clay," he said in a calm, smooth-as-cream voice, as if her panic were completely invisible to him and no one else in the room knew she was on the verge of screaming. "Sit down, please."

The prosaic invitation/command had the blessed effect of snapping her out of the trap of panic. Somehow she managed to take a breath without audibly gasping, then another. Nothing was going to happen. She didn't need to panic. Yes, this was mildly alarming and she probably wouldn't be coming back to the Inferno to gamble, but she hadn't broken any laws or casino rules. She was safe.

Those pinpricks of light flared again. What...? Puzzled, she turned her head and found herself staring at two huge pillar candles, each of them easily two and a half feet tall, one on the floor and the other perched on a slab of white marble that served as a hearth. Flames danced around the candles' multiple wicks.

Candles. She hadn't been about to faint. The flickers of light at the edge of her vision had come from those candles. She hadn't noticed them when she'd been literally dragged into the room, but that was understandable.

The candlelights were dancing and swaying, as if they stood in a draft. That too was understandable. She didn't feel any noticeable movement of air, but this was summertime in Reno, and the air-conditioning would be running full blast. She always wore long sleeves when she went to a casino anyway; otherwise she was too cold.

With a start she realized she was staring at the candles and had neither moved nor replied to the invitation to sit. She jerked her attention back to the man standing at the window, trying to recall what the gorilla had called him. "Who are you?" she demanded sharply. Once more she jerked her arm, but the gorilla merely sighed as he held her. "Let go!"

"You can let her go," the man said, sounding faintly amused. "Thank you for bringing her here."

The gorilla instantly released her, said, "I'll be in the security center," and quietly let himself out of the office.

Instantly Lorna began assessing her chance of making a run for it, but for now she stood her ground. She didn't want to run; the casino had her name, her description. If she ran, she would be blacklisted—not just in the Inferno, but in every casino in Nevada.

"I'm Dante Raintree," the man said, then waited a beat to see if she gave any reaction to the name. It meant nothing to her, so she merely gave a slight, questioning lift of her brows. "I own the Inferno."

*Crap!* An owner carried serious weight with the gaming commission. She would have to tread very carefully, but she had the advantage. He couldn't prove she'd been cheating, because the simple fact was, she hadn't been.

"Dante. Inferno. I get it," she replied with a little edge of *so what?* in her tone. He was probably so rich he thought everyone should be awed in his presence. If he wanted to awe her, he would have to find something other than his wealth to do the job. She appreciated money as much as anyone; it certainly made life easier. Now that she had a little financial cushion, she was amazed at how much better she slept—what a relief it was not to worry where her next bite was coming from, or when. At the same time, she despised people who thought their wealth entitled them to special treatment.

Not only that, his name was ridiculous. Maybe his last name really was Raintree, but he'd probably chosen his first name for the drama and to fit the name of the casino. His real first name was probably something like Melvin or Fred.

"Please have a seat," he invited again, indicating the cream-colored leather sofa to her right. A jade coffee table sat between the sofa and two cushy-looking club chairs. She tried not to stare at the table as she took a seat in one of the chairs, which was just as cushy as it looked. Surely the table was just the color of jade and not actually made of the real stone, but it *looked* real, as if it were faintly translucent. Surely it was just glass. If so, the craftsmanship was superb.

Lorna didn't have a lot of experience with luxury items, but she did have a sort of sixth sense about her surroundings. She began to feel overwhelmed by the things around her. No, not overwhelmed; that wasn't the right word. She tried to nail down what she was feeling, but there was an alien, unknown quality to the very air around her that she couldn't describe. This was unfamiliar, and it definitely carried the edge of danger that had so alarmed her when she'd first become aware of it.

As Dante Raintree strolled closer, she realized that everything she was sensing centered on him. She'd been right; *he* was the danger.

He moved with indolent grace, but there was nothing slow or lazy about him. He was a tall man, about eight or nine inches taller than her own five foot five, and though his excellently tailored clothing gave him a lean look, there was no tailor skilled enough to completely disguise the power of the muscles beneath the fabric. Not a cheetah, then, but a tiger.

She realized she had avoided looking him full in the face, as if not having that knowledge would give her a small measure of safety. She knew better; ignorance was never a good defense, and Lorna had learned a long time ago not to hide her head in the sand and hope for the best.

He sat down across from her, and with an inward bracing she met his gaze full-on.

The bottom dropped out of her stomach.

She had a faint, dizzying sensation of falling; she barely restrained herself from gripping the arms of the chair to steady herself.

His hair was black. His eyes were green. Common colors, and yet nothing about him was common. His hair was sleek and glossy, falling to his shoulders. She didn't like long hair on men, but his looked clean and soft, and she wanted to bury her hands in it. She shoved *that* idea away and promptly became snagged by his gaze. His eyes weren't just green, they were *green,* so remarkably green that her first thought was that he was wearing colored contacts. A color that darkly rich and pure couldn't be real. They were just very realistic contacts, with tiny black striations in them like real eyes. She had seen ads for those in magazines. The only thing was, when the candles flared and his pupils briefly contracted, the color of his irises seemed to expand. Could contacts give that appearance?

He wasn't wearing contacts. Instinctively she knew that everything she saw, from the sleek blackness of his hair to that intense eye color, was real.

He was drawing her in. Some power she couldn't understand was tugging at her with an almost physical sensation. The candle flames were dancing wildly, brighter now that the sun had set and twilight was deepening outside the window. The candles were the only light in the now gloomy office, sending shadows slashing across the hard angles of his face, and yet his eyes seemed to glow brighter with color than they had only a few moments before.

They hadn't said a word since he'd sat down, yet she felt as if she were in a battle for her will, her force, her independent life. Deep inside, panic flared to candlelight life, dancing and leaping. *He knows,* she thought, and tensed herself to run. Forget the casinos, forget the very nice money she'd been reaping, forget everything except survival. *Run!*

Her body didn't obey. She continued to sit there, frozen...mesmerized.

"How are you doing it?" he finally asked, his tone still as calm and unruffled as if he were oblivious to the swirls and surges of power that were buffeting her.

Once again, his voice seemed to break through her inner turmoil and bring her back to reality. Bewildered, she stared at him. He thought *she* was doing all this weird stuff?

"I'm not," she blurted. "I thought you were."

She might have been mistaken, because in the dancing candlelight, reading an expression was tricky, but she thought he looked slightly stunned.

"Cheating," he said in clarification. "How are you stealing from me?"

# THREE

Maybe he didn't know.

His bluntness was a perverse relief. Lorna took a deep breath. At least now she was dealing with something she understood. Ignoring the strange undercurrents in the room, the almost physical sensation of being surrounded by...something...she lifted her chin, narrowed her eyes and gave him stare for stare. "I'm not cheating!" That was true—as far as it went, and in the normal understanding of the word.

"Of course you are. No one is as lucky as you seem to be unless he—excuse me, *she*—is cheating." His eyes were glittering now, but in her book glittering was way better than that weird glowing. Eyes didn't glow anyway. What was wrong with her? Had someone slipped a drug into her drink while her head was turned? She never drank alcohol while she was gambling, sticking to coffee or soft drinks, but that last cup of coffee had tasted bitter. At the time she'd thought she'd been unlucky enough to get the last cup in the pot, but now she wondered if it hadn't been pharmaceutically enhanced.

"I repeat. I'm not cheating." Lorna bit off the words, her jaw set.

"You've been coming here for a while. You walk away with about five grand every week. That's a cool quarter of a million a year—and that's just from my casino. How many others are you hitting?" His cool gaze raked her from head to foot, as if he wondered why she didn't dress better, taking in that kind of money.

Lorna felt her face getting hot, and that made her angry. She hadn't been embarrassed about anything in a very long time, embarrassment being a luxury she couldn't afford, but something about his assessment made her want to squirm. Okay, so she wasn't the best dresser in the world, but she was neat and clean, and that was what mattered. So what if she'd gotten her pants and short-sleeve blouse at Wal-Mart? She simply couldn't make herself spend a hundred dollars on a pair of shoes when a twelve-dollar pair fit her just as well. The eighty-eight dollar difference would buy a lot of food. And silk not only cost a lot, but it was difficult to care for; she would take a nice cotton/polyester blend, which didn't have to be ironed, over silk any day of the week.

"I said, how many other casinos are you hitting each week?"

"What I do isn't your business." She glared at him, glad for the anger and the surge of energy it gave her. Feeling angry was much better than feeling hurt. She wouldn't let this man's opinion matter enough to her that he could hurt her. Her clothes might be cheap, but they weren't ragged; she was clean, and she refused to be ashamed of them.

"On the contrary. I caught you. Therefore I should have Al warn the other security chiefs."

"You haven't *caught* me doing anything!" She was absolutely certain of that, because she hadn't *done* anything he could catch.

"You're lucky I'm the one in the driver's seat," he continued as if she hadn't spoken a word. "There's a certain element in Reno that thinks cheating is a crime deserving of capital punishment."

Her heartbeat stuttered. He was right, and she knew it. There were whispers on the street, tales of people who tried to tilt the odds their way—and who either disappeared completely or had assumed room temperature by the time they were found. She didn't have the blissful ignorance that would let her think he was merely exaggerating, because she had lived in the world where those things happened. She knew that world, knew the people who inhabited it. She had been careful to stay as invisible as possible, and she never used the ubiquitous players' cards that allowed the casinos to keep track of who was winning and who wasn't, but still she had done something wrong, something that called attention to herself. Her innocence wouldn't matter to some people; a word to the wrong person, and she was a dead woman.

Was he saying he didn't intend to turn her in, that he would keep the matter Inferno's private business?

Why would he do that? Only two possible reasons came to mind. One was the old sex-for-a-favor play: "Be nice to me, little girl, and I won't tell what I know." The other was that he might suspect her of cheating but had no evidence, and all he intended to do was maybe trick her into confessing or at the least bar her from the Inferno. If his reason was the former one, then he was a sleaze, and she knew how to deal with sleazes. If his reason was the latter, well, then he was a nice guy.

Which would be his tough luck.

He was watching her, really *watching* her, his complete attention focused on reading every flicker of emotion on her face. Lorna fought the urge to fidget, but being the center of that sort of concentration made her very uneasy. She preferred to blend in with the crowd, to stay in the background; anonymity meant safety.

"Relax. I'm not going to blackmail you into having sex with me—not that I'm not interested," he said, "but I don't need coercion to get sex when I want it."

She almost jumped. Either he'd read her mind, or she was getting really sloppy about guarding her expression. She knew she wasn't sloppy; for too long, her life had depended on staying sharp; the defensive habits of a lifetime were deeply ingrained. He'd read her mind. *Oh, God, he'd read her mind!*

Full-blown panic began to fog her mind; then it immediately dissipated, forced out by a sharply detailed image of the two of them having sex. For a disorienting moment she felt as if she were standing outside her own body, watching the two of them in bed—naked, their bodies sweaty from exertion, straining together. His muscled body bore her down, crushing her into the tangled sheets. Her arms and legs, pale against his olive-toned skin, were wrapped around him. She smelled the scents of sex and skin, felt the heat and weight of him on top of her as he pushed slickly inside, heard her own quick gasp as she lifted into his slow, controlled thrusts. She was about to climax, and so was he, his thrusts coming harder and faster—

She jerked herself away from the scenario, suddenly, horribly sure that if she let it carry on to the end she would humiliate herself by climaxing for real, right in front of him. She could barely keep herself in the present; the lure of even imagined pleasure was so strong that she wanted to go back, to lose herself in the dream, or hallucination, or whatever the hell it was.

Something was wrong. She wasn't in control of herself but instead was being tossed about by the weird eddies of power surging and retreating through the room. Neither could she get a handle on anything long enough to examine it; just when she thought she was grounded, she would get tossed into another reaction, another wild emotion bubbling to the surface.

He spoke again, seemingly oblivious to everything but his own thoughts. How could he not *feel* everything that was going on? Was she imagining everything? She clutched the arms of the chair, wondering if she was having some sort of mental break-down.

"You're precognitive." He tilted his head as if he were studying an interesting specimen, a slight smile on his lips. "You're also a sensitive, and maybe there's a little bit of tele-kinesis thrown in. Interesting."

"Are you crazy?" she blurted, horrified, and still struggling to concentrate. *Interesting?* He was either on the verge of de-stroying her life or she was going crazy, and he thought it was *interesting?*

"I don't believe so. No, I'm fairly certain I'm sane." Amuse-ment flickered in his eyes, warming them. "Go ahead, Lorna, make the leap. The only way I could know if you were a precog is...?" His voice trailed away on a questioning lilt, inviting her to finish the sentence.

She sat as if frozen, staring fixedly at him. Was he saying he really *could* read minds, or was he setting some trap she couldn't yet see?

A sudden, freezing cold swept through the room, so cold

she ached down to the bone, and with it came that same overwhelming sense of dread she'd felt when she'd first entered the room and seen him. Lorna hugged herself and set her teeth to keep them from chattering. She wanted to run and couldn't; her muscles simply wouldn't obey the instinct to flee.

Was he the source of this...this *turmoil* in the room? She couldn't put a better description to it than that, because she'd never felt quite this way before, as if reality had become layered with hallucinations.

"You can relax. There's no way I can prove it, so I can't charge you with cheating. But I knew what you are as soon as you said you thought I was 'doing it.' Doing what? You didn't say, but the statement was an intriguing one, because it meant you're sensitive to the currents in the room." He steepled his fingers and tapped them against his lips, regarding her over them with an unwavering gaze. "Normal people would never have felt a thing. A lot of times, one form of psi ability goes hand in hand with other forms, so it's obvious, now, how you win so consistently. You know what card will turn up, don't you? You know which slot machines will pay off. Maybe you can even manipulate the computer to give you three in a row."

The cold left the room as abruptly as it had entered. She had been tensed to resist it, and the sudden lessening of pressure made her feel as if she might fall out of the chair. Lorna clenched her jaw tight, afraid to say anything. She couldn't let herself be drawn into a discussion about paranormal abilities. For all she knew, he had this room wired for both video and audio and was recording everything. What if one of those weird hallucinations seized control of her again? She might say whatever he wanted her to say, admit to any wild charge.

Heck—everything she was feeling might be the result of some weird special effects he'd installed.

"I know you aren't Raintree," he continued softly. "I know my own. So the big question is…are you Ansara, or are you just a stray?"

Shock rescued her once again. "A *stray?*" she echoed, jerking back into a world that felt real. There was still an underlying sense of disorientation, but at least that sexually disturbing image was gone, the cold was gone, the dread was gone.

She took a deep breath and fought down the hot rush of anger. He'd just compared her to an unwanted mongrel. Beneath the anger, though, was the corrosive edge of old, bitter despair. *Unwanted*. She'd always been that. For a while, a wondrously sweet moment, she had thought that would change, but then even that last hope had been taken from her, and she didn't have the heart, the will, to try again. Something inside her had given up, but the pain hadn't dulled.

He made a dismissive gesture. "Not that kind of stray. We use it to describe a person of ability who is unaffiliated."

"Unaffiliated with *what?* What are you talking about?" Her bewilderment on this point, at least, was real.

"Someone who is neither Raintree nor Ansara."

His explanations were going in circles, and so were her thoughts. Frustrated, frightened, she made a sharp motion with her hand and snapped, "Who in hell is Aunt Sarah?"

Tilting his head back, he burst out laughing, the sound quick and easy, as if he did it a lot. The pit of her stomach fluttered. Imagining sex with him had lowered defenses she usually kept raised high, and the distant acknowledgment of his attractiveness had become a full-fledged awareness. Against her will she noticed the muscular lines of his throat, the sculpted line of his jaw. He was... *Handsome* was, in an odd way, too feminine a word to describe him. He was *striking*, his features altogether too compelling to be merely handsome. Nor were his looks the first thing she'd noticed about him; by far her first impression had been one of power.

"Not 'Aunt Sarah,' " he said, still laughing. "Ansara. A-N-S-A-R-A."

"I've never heard of them," she said warily, wondering if this was some type of mob thing he was talking about. She didn't suffer from the delusion that organized crime was restricted to the old Italian families in New York and Chicago.

"Haven't you?" He said it pleasantly enough, but with her nerve-endings stripped raw the way they were, she felt the doubt—and the inherent threat—as clearly as if he'd shouted at her.

She had to get her reactions under control. The weird stuff happening in this room had taken her by surprise, shocked her into a vulnerability she normally didn't allow, but now that she'd had a moment without any new assault on her senses, she began to get her composure back. Mentally she reassembled her internal barriers; it was a struggle, because concentration was difficult, but grimly she persisted. She might not know what was going on, but she knew protecting herself was vitally important.

He was waiting for her to respond to his rhetorical question, but she ignored him and focused on her shields—

Shields?

Where had that word come from? She never thought of herself as having shields. She thought of herself as strong, her heart weathered and toughened by hard times; she thought of herself as unemotional.

She never thought of herself as having *shields*.

Until now.

She was the most unshielded sensitive he'd ever seen, Dante thought as he watched her struggle against the flow and surge of power. She reacted like a complete novice to both his thoughts and his affinity for fire. He had his gift under strict control now, but to test her, he'd sent tiny blasts of it into the room, making the candles dance. She'd latched on to the arms of the chair as if she needed to anchor herself, her alarmed gaze darting around as if searching for monsters.

When he'd picked up on her expectation of being black-mailed for sex—which hadn't exactly been hard to guess—he'd allowed himself a brief, pleasant little fantasy, to which she'd responded as if he'd really had her naked in bed. Her mouth had gotten red and soft, her cheeks flushed, her eyes heavy-lidded, while beneath that cheap sweater her nipples had become so hard their shape had been visible even through her bra.

Damn. For a moment there, she'd been in real danger of the fantasy becoming fact.

She might be Ansara, but if she was, she was completely un-tutored. Either that or she was skilled enough to *appear* untu-tored. If she *was* Ansara, he would bet on the latter. Being Raintree had a lot of advantages and one big disadvantage: an implacable enemy. The hostility between the two clans had erupted into a huge pitched battle about two hundred years ago, and the Raintree had been victorious, the Ansara almost destroyed. The tattered remnants of the once-powerful clan were scattered around the world and had never recovered to the point that they could again make concerted war on the

Raintree, but that didn't mean that the occasional lone Ansara didn't try to make trouble for them.

Like the Raintree, the Ansara had different gifts of varying degrees of strength. The ones Dante had infrequently crossed paths with had all been trained as well as any Raintree, which meant none of them were to be taken lightly. While they weren't the threat they had been before, he was always aware that any one of them would love a chance to get at him in any way.

It would be just like an Ansara to get a kick out of stealing from him. There were bigger casinos in Reno, but stealing from the Inferno would be a huge feather in her cap—*if* she was Ansara.

He had some empathic ability—nothing in the same ballpark as his younger sister, Mercy, but enough that he could read most people as soon as he touched them. The exceptions, mainly, were the Ansara, because they had been trained to shield themselves in a way normal humans never were. Sensitives *had* to shield or be overwhelmed by the forces around them…much as Lorna Clay seemed to have been overwhelmed.

Maybe she was just a good actress.

The candlelight was magic on her skin, in her hair. She was a pretty woman, with finely molded bone structure, if a tad brittle and hostile in her attitude, but what the hell—if he'd been caught cheating, he would probably be hostile, too.

He wanted to touch her, to see if he could read anything.

She would probably run screaming from the room if he laid a hand on her, though. She was so tightly wound that she might throw herself backward in the chair if he said "Boo!" He thought about doing it, just for the amusement value.

He would have, if not for the very serious matter of cheating.

He leaned forward to hammer home a point, and—

A loud but not unpleasant tone sounded, followed by another, then another. A burst of adrenaline shot through his system, and he was on his feet, grabbing her arm and hauling her out of the chair before the recorded announcement could begin.

"What is it?" she cried, her face going white, but she didn't try to pull away from him.

"Fire," he said briefly, all but dragging her to the door. Once the fire alarm sounded all the elevators stopped responding to calls—and they were on the nineteenth floor.

# FOUR

Lorna stumbled and almost went down on one knee as he dragged her through the doorway. Her hip banged painfully into the door frame; then she regained her balance, lurched upward and hurtled through so fast that she immediately crashed into the wall on the other side. Her arm, held tight in his iron grip, was wrenched as he ruthlessly pulled her onward. She didn't say a word, didn't cry out, almost didn't even notice the pain, because the living nightmare she was in crowded out everything else.

Fire!

She saw him give her a searing, comprehensive look; then he released her arm and instead clamped his left arm around her waist, locking her to his side and holding her up as he ran toward the stairs. They were alone in the hallway, but as soon as he opened the door marked Exit, she could hear the thunder of footsteps below them as people stampeded down the stairs.

The air in the hallway had been clear, but as the door clanged shut behind them, she smelled it: the throat-burning stench of smoke. Her heartbeat stuttered. She was afraid of fire, always had been, and it wasn't just the caution of an intelligent person. If she had to pick the worst way on earth to die, it would be by fire. She had nightmares about being trapped behind a wall of flame, unable to get to someone—a child, maybe?—who was more important to her than her own life, or even to save herself. Just as the flames reached her and she felt her flesh begin to sear, she would wake, trembling and in tears from the horror.

She didn't like any open flame—candles, fireplaces, or even gas cooktops. Now Dante Raintree was carrying her down into the heart of the beast, when every instinct she had screamed for her to go up, up into fresh air, as far away from fire as she could get.

As they made the turn at the first landing, the mental chaos of panic began to strengthen and grab at her, and she fought it back. Logically she knew they had to go down, that jumping off the roof wasn't a viable option. Clenching her teeth together to keep them from chattering, she concentrated on keeping her balance, making sure her feet hit each step squarely, though the way he was holding her, she doubted she could stumble. She didn't want to impede him or, God forbid, cause both of them to fall.

They caught up with a knot of people also going down the stairs, but the passage was clogged, and people were shouting at others to move out of the way. The uproar was confusing; no one could make themselves understood, and some were coughing now as the smoke thickened.

"You can't go up!" Raintree thundered, his voice booming

over the pushing, yelling human logjam, and only then did Lorna realize that the uproar was caused by people trying to push their way up the stairs while others were just as focused on going down.

"Who the hell are you?" someone bellowed from below.

"The owner of the Inferno, that's who the hell I am," Raintree snapped. "I built this casino, and I know where I'm going. Now turn your ass around and go all the way down to the ground floor, that's the only way out."

"The smoke's worse that way!"

"Then take off your shirt and tie it over your nose and mouth. Everyone do that," he ordered, booming out the words again so all could hear him. He suited action to words, releasing Lorna to strip out of his expensive suit jacket. She stood numbly beside him, watching as he swiftly removed a knife from his pocket, flicked it open, and sliced the gray silk lining from the jacket. Then he just as swiftly ripped the lining into two oblong panels. Handing one panel to her, he said, "Use this," as he closed the knife and slipped it back into his pocket.

She expected some of the group to push on upstairs, regardless of what he said, but no one did. Instead, several men, the ones who wore jackets, were following his example and ripping out the garments' linings. Others were taking off their shirts, tearing them up and offering pieces to women who were reluctant to remove their blouses. Lorna hastily tied the silk over her nose and mouth, pulling it tight so it hugged her face like a surgical mask. Beside her, Raintree was doing the same.

"Go!" he ordered, and like obedient sheep, they did. The tangle of people began to unravel, then ribbon downward. Lorna found her own feet moving as if they weren't attached to her, taking her down, down, closer to whatever living,

crackling hell awaited them. Every cell in her body was screaming in protest, her breath was coming in strangled gasps, but
still she kept going down the stairs as if she had no will of her
own.

His hand put pressure on her waist, moving her to one side.
"Let us pass," he said. "I'll show you the way out." The people
in front of them all moved to one side, and though Lorna heard
several angry mutters, they were drowned out by others telling
the mutterers to shut up, that it was his place and he'd know
how to get out of the building.

More and more people were crowding into the stairwell ahead
of them as the floors emptied, but they pressed to the side as
Raintree moved Lorna and himself past them. The acrid smoke
stung her eyes, making them water, and she could feel the temperature rising as they went down. How many floors had they
descended? At the next landing she peered at the door and the
number painted on it, but the tears in her eyes blurred the figures.
Sixteen, maybe. Or fifteen. Was that all? Hadn't they gone farther
than that? She tried to remember how many landings they had
passed, but she had been too numb with terror to pay attention.

She was going to die in this building. She could feel the icy
breath of Death as it waited for her, just on the other side of
the flames that she couldn't see but could nevertheless feel, as
if they were a great force pulling at her. *This* was why she had
always been so afraid of fire; she had somehow known she was
destined to burn. Soon she would be gone, her life force seared
or choked away——

——and no one would miss her.

Dante kept everyone moving downward, the mind compulsion he was using forcing them into an orderly evacuation. He

had never tried this particular power, never even known he possessed it, and if they hadn't been so close to the summer solstice, he doubted he could have done it. Hell, he hadn't been sure he could make it work at all, much less on such a large group, but with fire threatening to destroy the casino he'd worked so hard to build, he'd poured all his will into the thought, into his words, and they had obeyed.

He could feel the flames singing their siren song, calling to him. Maybe they were even feeding his power, because the close proximity of fire was making his heart rate soar as adrenaline poured through him. Even though smoke was stinging his eyes and filtering through the silk tied over his nose and mouth, he felt so alive that his skin could barely contain him. He wanted to laugh, wanted to throw his arms wide and invite the fire to come to him, to do battle with him, so he could exert his will over it as he did over these people.

If it hadn't been for the level of concentration he needed to keep the mind compulsion in place, he would already have been mentally joined in battle. Everything in him yearned for the struggle. He *would* vanquish the flames, but first he had to get these people to safety.

Lorna kept pace beside him, but a quick glance at her face— what he could see of it above the gray silk—told him that only his will was keeping her going down the stairs. She was paper white, and her eyes were almost blank with terror. He pulled her closer to his side, wanting her within reach when they got to the ground floor, because otherwise her panic might be strong enough that she could break free of the compulsion and bolt. And he wasn't finished with her yet. In fact, with this damn fire, he thought he might have a good deal more to discuss with her than cheating at blackjack.

If she was Ansara, if she had somehow been involved in starting the fire, she would die. It was that simple.

He'd touched her, but he couldn't tell if she was Ansara or not. His empathic power was on the wimpy side anyway, and right now he couldn't really concentrate on reading her. Not picking up anything meant she was either a stray or she was Ansara, and strong enough to shield her real self from him. Either way, the matter would have to wait.

The smoke was getting thicker, but not drastically so. There was some talking, though for the most part people were saving their breath for getting down the stairs. There was, however, a steady barrage of coughing.

The fire, he sensed, was concentrated so far in the casino, but it was rapidly spreading toward the hotel portion of the building. Unlike most hotel/casinos, which were built in such a way that the guests were forced to walk through the casino on their way to anywhere else, thereby increasing the probability that they would stop and play, Dante had built Inferno with the guest rooms off to one side. There was a common area where the two joined and overlapped, but he also provided a bit of distance for the guest who wanted it. He'd been taking a chance, but the design had worked out. By concentrating on providing a level of elegance unmatched at any other hotel/casino in Reno, he'd made Inferno different and therefore desirable.

That offset design would save a lot of lives tonight. The guests who had been in the casino, though…he didn't know about them. Nor could he let himself dwell on them, or he might lose control of the people in the stairwell. He couldn't help the people in the casino, at least not now, so he let himself think only about his immediate charges. If these people panicked, if they started pushing and running, not only would some people fall and be trampled, but the crowd might well crush the exit bar and prevent the door from being opened. That had happened before, and would happen again—but not in his place, not if he could help it.

They reached another landing, and he peered through the smoke at the number on the door. Three. Just two more floors, thank God. The smoke was getting so thick that his lungs were burning. "We're almost there," he said, to keep the people behind him focused, and he heard people begin repeating the words to those stacked on the stairs above them.

He wrapped his arm around Lorna's waist and clamped her to his side, lifting her off her feet as he descended the remaining floors two steps at a time. The door opened not to the outside but into a corridor lined with offices. He held the door open with his body, and as people stumbled into the corridor, he said, "Turn right. Go through the double doors at the end of the hall, turn right again, and the door just past the soda machines will open onto the ground level of the parking deck. Go, go, go!"

They went, propelled by his will—stumbling and coughing, but moving nevertheless. The air here was thick and hot, his vision down to only a few feet, and the people who scrambled past him looked like ghosts and disappeared in seconds. Only their coughing and the sound of their footsteps marked their progress.

He felt Lorna move, trying to break his grip, trying to obey not only his mental command but the commands of her own panic-stricken brain. He tightened his hold on her. Maybe he could fine-tune the compulsion enough to exclude her right now.... No, it wasn't worth the risk. While he had them all under his control, he kept them there and kept them moving. All he had to do was hold Lorna to keep her from escaping.

He could feel the fire at his back. Not literally, but closer now, much closer. Everything in him yearned to turn and engage with the force of nature that was his to call and control, his to own. Not yet. *Not yet...*

Then no more smoke-shrouded figures were emerging from the stairwell, and with Lorna firmly in his grip he turned to the left—away from the parking deck and safety, and toward the roaring red demon.

"*Noooo.*"

The sound was little more than a moan, and she bucked like a wild thing in the circle of his arm. Hastily he gave one last mental shove at the stream of people headed toward the parking deck, then transferred the compulsion to a different command, this one directed solely at Lorna: "Stay with me."

Immediately she stopped struggling, though he could hear the strangled, panicked sounds she was making as he strode through the smoke to another door, one that opened into the lobby.

He threw the door open and stepped into hell, dragging her with him.

The sprinkler system was making a valiant effort, spraying water down on the lobby, but the heat was a monster furnace that evaporated the spray before it reached the floor. It blasted them like a shock wave, a physical blow, but he muttered a curse and pushed back. Because they were produced by the fire, were parts of the fire, he owned the heat and smoke as surely as he owned the flames. Now that he could concentrate, he deflected them, creating a protective bubble, a force field, around Lorna and himself that sent the smoke swirling and held the heat at bay, protecting them.

The casino was completely engaged. The flames were greedy tongues of red, great sheets of orange and black, transparent forks of gold, that danced and roared in their eagerness to consume everything within reach. Several of the elegant white columns had already ignited like huge torches, and the vast expanse of carpet was a sea of small fires, lit by the falling debris.

The columns were acting as candles, wicking the flames upward to the ceiling. He started there, pulling power from deep inside and using it to bend the fire to his will. Slowly, slowly, the flames licking up the columns began to die down, vanquished by a superior force.

Doing that much, while maintaining the bubble of protection around them, took every ounce of power he had. Something wasn't right. He realized that even as he concentrated on the columns, feeling the strain deep inside. His head began to hurt; killing the flames shouldn't take this much effort. They were slow in responding to his command, but he didn't let up even as he wondered if the energy he'd used on the group mind compulsion had somehow drained him. He didn't feel as if it had, but something was definitely wrong.

When only tendrils of smoke were coming from the columns, he switched his attention to the walls, pushing back, pushing back....

Out of the corner of his eye, he saw the columns burst into flame again.

With a roar of fury and disbelief, he blasted his will at the flames, and they subsided once again.

What the hell?

Windows exploded, sending shards of glass flying in all directions. Brutal streams of water poured through from the front, courtesy of the Reno Fire Department, but the flames seemed to give a hoarse laugh before roaring back brighter and hotter than before. One of the two huge, glittering crystal chandeliers pulled loose from the fire-weakened ceiling and crashed to the floor, throwing up a glittering spray of lethal glass splinters. They were far enough away that few of the splinters reached them, but one of the lovely crystal hornets stung his cheek, sending a rivulet of blood running down his face. Maybe they should have ducked, he thought with distant humor.

He could feel Lorna pressed against him, shaking convulsively and making little keening sounds of terror, but she was helpless to break the mind compulsion he'd put on her. Had any of the glass hit her? No time to check. With a great whoosh, a huge tongue of fire rolled across the ceiling overhead, consuming everything in its path as well as what felt like most of the available oxygen; then it began eating its way down the wall behind them, sealing off any escape.

Mentally, he pushed at the flames, willing them to retreat, calling on all his reserves of strength and power. He was the Dranir of the Raintree; the fire *would* obey him.

Except it didn't.

Instead it began crawling across the carpet, small fires combining into larger ones, and those joining with others until the floor was ablaze, getting closer, closer....

*He couldn't control it.* He had never before met a flame he couldn't bend to his will, but this was something beyond his power. Using the mind compulsion that way must have weakened him somehow; it wasn't something he'd done before, so he didn't know what the ramifications were. Well, yeah, he did; unless a miracle happened, the ramifications in this case were two deaths: his and Lorna's.

He refused to accept that. He'd never given up, never let a fire beat him; he wouldn't start with this one.

The bubble of protection wavered, letting smoke filter in. Lorna began coughing convulsively, struggling against his grip even though she wouldn't be able to run unless he released her from the compulsion. There was nowhere to run *to,* anyway.

Grimly, he faced the flames. He needed more power. He had thrown everything he had left at the fire, and it wasn't enough. If Gideon or Mercy were here, they could link with him, combine strengths, but that sort of partnership required close proximity, so he had only himself to rely on. There was no other source of power for him to tap—

—except for Lorna.

He didn't ask; he didn't take the time to warn her what he was going to do; he simply wrapped both arms around her from behind and blasted his way past her mental shields, ruthlessly taking what he needed. Relief poured through him at what he found. Yes, she had power, more than he'd expected. He didn't stop to analyze what kind of power she had, because it didn't matter; on this level, power was power, like electricity. Different machines could take the same power and do wildly different things, like vacuuming the floor or playing music. It was the same principle. She had power; he took it, and used it to bolster his own gift.

She gave a thin scream and bucked in his arms, then went rigid.

Furiously he attacked the flames, sending out a 360-degree mental blast that literally blew out the wall of fire behind him and took the physical wall with it, as well. The rush of renewed oxygen made the fire in front of him flare, so he gathered himself and did it again, pouring even more energy into the battle, feeling his own reserves well up, renewed, as he took every ounce of power and strength from Lorna and blended it with his own.

His entire body was tingling, his muscles burning with the effort it took to contain and focus. The invisible bubble of protection around them began to shimmer and took on a faint glow. Sweating, swearing, ignoring the pain in his head, he blasted the energy of his will at the fire again and again, beating it back even while he tried to calculate how long he'd been standing there, how much time he needed to give the people in the hotel to escape. There were multiple stairwells, and he was certain not all evacuations had been as orderly as the one he'd controlled. Was everyone out by now? What about disabled people? They would have to be helped down the flights of stairs. If he stopped, the fire would surge forward, engulfing the hotel—so he couldn't stop. Until the fire was controlled, he couldn't stop.

He couldn't put it out, not completely. For whatever reason, whether he was depleted or distracted or the fire itself was somehow different, he couldn't put it out. He accepted that now. All he could do was hold the flames at bay until the fire department had them under control.

That was what he concentrated on, controlling the fire instead of extinguishing it. That conserved his energy, and he needed every bit he had, because the fierceness of the fire never stopped pushing back, never stopped struggling for freedom. Time meant nothing, because no matter how long it took, no matter how his head hurt, he had to endure.

Somewhere along the way he lost the line of division between himself and the fire. It was an enemy, but it was beautiful in its destruction; it danced for him as always, magic in its movement and colors. He felt its beauty like molten lava running through his veins, felt his body respond with mindless lust until his erection strained painfully against his zipper. Lorna had to feel it, but there wasn't a damned thing he could do to make it go away. The best he could do, under the circumstances, was not grind it against her.

Finally, hoarse shouts intruded through the diminished roar of the beast. Turning his head slightly, Dante saw teams of firefighters advancing with their hoses. Quickly he let the bubble of protection dissolve, leaving him and Lorna exposed to the smoke and heat.

With his first breath, the hot smoke seared all the way down to his lungs. He choked, coughed, tried to draw another breath. Lorna sagged to her knees, and he dropped down beside her as the first firefighters reached them.

# FIVE

Lorna sat on the bumper of a fire-medic truck and clutched a scratchy blanket around her. The night was warm, but she was soaking wet, and she couldn't seem to stop shivering. She'd heard the fire medic say she wasn't in shock; though her blood pressure was a little high, which was understandable, her pulse rate was near normal. She was just chilled from being wet.

And, yet, everything around her seemed...muted, as if there were a glass wall between her and the rest of the world. Her mind felt numb, barely able to function. When the medic had asked her name, for the life of her, she hadn't been able to remember, much less articulate it. But she *had* remembered that she never brought a purse to a casino because of thieves and that she kept her money in one pocket and her driver's license in another, so she'd pulled out her license and showed it to him. It was a Missouri license, because she hadn't gotten a license here. To get a Nevada license, you had to be a resident and gainfully employed. It was the "gainfully employed" part that tripped her up.

"Are you Lorna Clay?" the medic had asked, and she'd nodded.

"Does your throat hurt?" he'd asked then, and that seemed as reasonable an explanation for her continued silence as any other, so she'd nodded again. He'd looked at her throat, seemed briefly puzzled, then given her oxygen to breathe. She should be checked out at the hospital, he'd said.

Yeah, right. She had no intention of going to a hospital. The only place she wanted to go was *away*.

And, yet, she remained right where she was while Raintree was checked out. There was blood on his face, but the cut turned out to be small. She heard him tell the medics he was fine, that, no, he didn't think he was burned anywhere, that they'd been very lucky.

Lucky, her ass. The thought was as clear as a bell, rising from the sluggish morass that was her brain. He'd held her there in the middle of that roaring hell for what felt like an eternity. They should be crispy critters. They should, at least, be gasping for breath through damaged airways, instead of being *fine*. She knew what fire did. She'd seen it, she'd smelled it, and it was ugly. It destroyed everything in its path. What it didn't do was dance all around and leave you unscathed.

Yet, here she was—unscathed. Relatively, anyway. She felt as if she'd been run over by a truck, but at least she wasn't burned.

She should have been burned. She should have been *dead*. Whenever she contemplated the fact that she not only wasn't dead, she wasn't even injured, her head ached so much she could barely stand to breathe, and the glass wall between her and reality got a little bit thicker. So she didn't think about being alive, or dead or anything else. She just sat there while the nightmarish scene revolved around her, lights flashing, crowds of people milling about, the firefighters still busy with their hoses putting out the remaining flames and making certain they didn't flare again. The fire engines rumbled so loudly that the noise wore on her, made her want to cover her ears, but she didn't do that, either. She just waited.

For what, she wasn't certain. She should leave. She thought a hundred times about just walking away into the night, but putting thought into action proved impossible. No matter how much she wanted to leave, she was bound by an inertia she couldn't seem to fight. All she could do was...sit.

Then Raintree stood, and, abruptly, she found herself standing, too, levered upward by some impulse she didn't understand. She just knew that if he was standing, she would stand. She was too mentally exhausted to come up with any reason that made more sense.

His face was so black with soot that only the whites of his eyes showed, so she figured she must look pretty much the same. Great. That meant she didn't have much chance of being able to slip away unnoticed. He took a cloth someone offered him and swiped it over his sooty face, which didn't do much good. Soot was oily; anything other than soap just sort of moved it around.

Determination in his stride, he moved toward a small clump of policemen, three uniforms and two plainclothes. Vague alarm rose in Lorna. Was he going to turn her in? Without any proof? She desperately wanted to hang back, but, instead, she found herself docilely following him.

Why was she doing this? Why wasn't she leaving? She struggled with the questions, trying to get her brain to function. He hadn't even glanced in her direction; he wouldn't have any idea where she'd gone if she dropped back now and sort of blended in with the crowd—as much as she could blend in anywhere, covered with soot the way she was. But others also showed the effects of the smoke; some of the casino employees, for instance, and the players. She probably could have slipped away, if she felt capable of making the effort.

Why was her brain so sluggish? On a very superficial level, her thought processes seemed to be normal, but below that was nothing but sludge. There was something important she should remember, something that briefly surfaced just long enough to cause a niggle of worry, then disappeared like a wisp of smoke. She frowned, trying to pull the memory out, but the effort only intensified the pain in her head, and she stopped.

Raintree approached the two plainclothes cops and introduced himself. Lorna tried to make herself inconspicuous, which might be a losing cause considering how she looked, plus the fact that she was standing only a few feet away. They all eyed her with the mixture of suspicion and curiosity cops just seemed to have. Her heart started pounding. What would she do if Raintree accused her of cheating? Run? Look at him as if he were an idiot? Maybe *she* was the idiot, standing there like a sacrificial lamb.

The image galvanized her as nothing else had. She would *not* be a willing victim. She tried to take a step away, but for some reason the action seemed beyond her. All she wanted to do was stay with him.

*Stay with me.*

The words resonated through her tired brain, making her

head ache. Wearily, she rubbed her forehead, wondering where she'd heard the words and why they mattered.

"Where were you when the fire started, Mr. Raintree?" one of the detectives asked. He and the other detective had introduced themselves, but their names had flown out of Lorna's head as soon as she'd heard them.

"In my office, talking to Ms. Clay." He indicated Lorna without really looking in her direction, as if he knew just where she was standing.

They looked at her more sharply now; then the detective who had been talking to Raintree said, "My partner will take her statement while I'm taking yours, so we can save time."

Sure, Lorna thought sarcastically. She had some beachfront property here in Reno she wanted to sell, too. The detectives wanted to separate her from Raintree so she couldn't hear what he said and they couldn't coordinate their statements. If a business was going down the tubes, sometimes the owner tried to minimize losses by burning it down and collecting on the insurance policy.

The other detective stepped to her side. Raintree glanced at her over his shoulder. "Don't go far. I don't want to lose you in this crowd."

What was he up to? she wondered. He'd made it sound as if they were in a relationship or something. But when the detective said, "Let's walk over here," Lorna obediently walked beside him for about twenty feet, then abruptly stopped as if she couldn't take one step more.

"Here," she said, surprised at how raspy and weak her voice was. She had coughed some, sure, but her voice sounded as if she'd been hacking for days. She was barely audible over all the noise from the fire engines.

"Sure." The detective looked around, casually positioning himself so that Lorna had to stand with her back to Raintree. "I'm Detective Harvey. Your name is…"

"Lorna Clay." At least she remembered her name this time, though for a horrible split second she hadn't been certain. She rubbed her forehead again, wishing this confounded headache would go away.

"Do you live here?"

"For the moment. I haven't decided if I'll stay." She knew she wouldn't. She never stayed in one place for very long. A few months, six at the most, and she moved on. He asked for her address, and she rattled it off. If he ran a check on her, he would find the most grievous thing against her was a speeding ticket she'd received three years ago. She'd paid the fine without argument; no problem there. So long as Raintree didn't bring a charge of cheating against her, she was fine. She wanted to look over her shoulder at him but knew better than to appear nervous or, even worse, as if she were checking with him on what answers to give.

"Where were you when the fire started?"

He'd just heard Raintree, when asked the identical question, say he'd been with her, but that was how cops operated. "I don't know when the fire started," she said, a tad irritably. "I was in Mr. Raintree's office when the alarm sounded."

"What time was that?"

"I don't have a watch on. I don't know. I wouldn't have thought to check the time, anyway. Fire scares the bejesus out of me."

One corner of his mouth twitched a little, but he disciplined it. He had a nice, lived-in sort of face, a little droopy at the jowls, wrinkly around the eyes. "That's okay. We can get the time from the security system. How long had you been with Mr. Raintree when the alarm sounded?"

Now, there was a question. Lorna thought back to the episodes of panic she'd experienced in that office, to the confusing hallucinations, or whatever the disconcerting sexual fantasy was. *Nothing* in that room had been normal, and though she usually had a good grasp of time, she found herself unable to even estimate. "I don't know. It was sunset when I went in. That's all I can tell you."

He made a note of her answer. God only knew what he thought they'd been doing, she thought wearily, but she couldn't bring herself to care.

"What did you do when the fire alarm sounded?"

"We ran for the stairs."

"What floor were you on?"

Now, that, she knew, because she'd watched the numbers on the ride up in the elevator. "The nineteenth."

He made a note of that, too. Lorna thought to herself that if she intended to burn a building down she wouldn't go to the nineteenth floor to wait for the alarm. Raintree hadn't had anything to do with whatever had caused the fire, but the cops had to check out everything or they wouldn't be doing their jobs. Though…did detectives normally go to the scene of a fire? A fire inspector or fire marshal, whichever Reno had, would have to determine that a fire was caused by arson before they treated it as a crime.

"What happened then?"

"There were a lot of people in the stairwell," she said slowly, trying to get the memory to form. "I remember…a lot of people. We could go only a couple of floors before everyone got jammed up, because some of the people from the lower floors were trying to go up." The smoke had been heavy, too, because visibility had been terrible, people passing by like ghosts... No. That had been later. There hadn't been a lot of smoke in the stairs right then. Later— She wasn't certain about later. The sequence of events was all jumbled up, and she couldn't seem to sort everything out.

"Go on," Detective Harvey prompted when she was silent for several moments.

"Mr. Raintree told them—the people coming up the stairs—they'd have to go back, there was no way out if they kept going up."

"Did they argue?"

"No, they all turned around. No one panicked." Except her. She'd barely been able to breathe, and it hadn't been because of the smoke. The memory was becoming clearer, and she was amazed at how orderly the evacuation had been. No one had pushed; no one had been running. People had been hurrying, of course, but not being so reckless that they risked a nasty fall. In retrospect, their behavior had been damned unnatural. How could everyone have been so calm? Didn't they know what fire *did?*

But she hadn't run, either, she realized. She hadn't pushed. She had gone at a steady pace, held to Raintree's side by his arm.

Wait. Had he been holding her then? She didn't think he had been. He'd touched her waist, sort of guiding her along, but she'd been free to run. So...why hadn't she?

She had trooped along like everyone else, in an orderly line. Inside she'd been screaming, but outwardly she'd been controlled.

Controlled... Not self-controlled, but controlled like a

puppet, as if she hadn't had a will of her own. Her mind had been screaming at her to run, but her body simply hadn't obeyed.

"Ms. Clay?"

Lorna felt her breath start coming faster as she relived those moments. Fire! Coming closer and closer, she didn't want to go, she wanted to run, but she couldn't. She was caught in one of those nightmares when you try to run but can't, when you try to scream but can't make a sound—

"Ms. Clay?"

"I— What?" Dazed, she stared up at him. From the mixture of impatience and concern on his face, she thought he must have called her name several times.

"What did you do when you got out?"

Shuddering, she gathered herself. "We didn't. I mean, we got to the ground floor and Mr. Raintree sent the others to the right, toward the parking deck. Then he...we..." Her voice faltered. She had been fighting him, trying to follow the others; she remembered that. Then he'd said, *"Stay with me,"* and she had, with no will to do otherwise, even though she'd been half mad with terror.

Stay with me.

When he'd sat, she'd sat. When he'd stood, she'd stood. When he'd moved, that was when she had moved. Until then, she had been incapable of taking a single step away from him.

Just moments ago he'd said, "Don't go far," and she'd been able to leave his side then—but she hadn't gone far before she'd stopped as if she'd hit a brick wall.

A horrible suspicion began to grow. He was controlling her somehow, maybe with some kind of posthypnotic suggestion, though when and how he'd hypnotized her, she had no idea.

All sorts of weird things had been happening in his office. Maybe those damn candles had actually given off some kind of gas that had drugged her.

"Go on," said Detective Harvey, breaking into her thoughts.

"We went to the left," she said, beginning to shake. She wrapped her arms around herself, hugging the blanket close in an effort to control her wayward muscles, but in seconds, she was trembling from head to foot. "Into the lobby. The fire——" The fire had leaped at them like a maddened beast, roaring with delight. The heat had been searing for the tiniest fraction of a second. She'd been choking on the smoke. Then...no smoke, no heat. Both had just gone away. She and Raintree should have been overcome in seconds, but they hadn't been. She'd been able to breathe. She hadn't felt the heat, even though she'd watched the tongues of fire hungrily lapping across the carpet toward her. "The fire sort of *w-whooshed* across the ceiling and got behind us, and we were trapped."

"Would you like to sit down?" he asked, interrupting his line of questioning, but considering how violently she was shaking, he probably thought sitting her down before she fell down was a good idea.

She might have thought so, too, if sitting down hadn't meant sitting on asphalt littered with the debris of a fire and running with streams of sooty water. He probably meant sit down somewhere else, which she would have liked, if she'd felt capable of moving a single step beyond where she was right now. She shook her head. "I'm okay, just wet and cold and shaken up some." If there was an award given out for massive understatement, she'd just won it.

He eyed her for a moment, then evidently decided she knew whether or not she needed to sit down. He'd tried, anyway, which relieved him of any obligation. "What did you do?"

Better not to tell him she'd felt surrounded by some sort of force field; this wasn't *Star Wars,* so he might not understand. Better not to tell him she'd felt a cool breeze in her hair. She must have been drugged; there was no other explanation.

"There wasn't anything we *could* do. We were trapped. I remember Mr. Raintree swearing a blue streak. I remember choking and being on the floor. Then the firefighters got to us and brought us out." In the interest of believability, she had heavily condensed the night's events as she remembered them, but, surely, they couldn't have been in the lobby for very long, no more than thirty seconds. An imaginary force field couldn't have held off real heat and smoke. The firefighters must have been close to them all along, but she'd been too panic-stricken to notice.

There was something else, probably that worrisome niggle of memory, that she couldn't quite grasp. Something else had happened. She knew it; she just couldn't think what it was. Maybe after she showered and washed her hair—several times—and got twenty or thirty hours of sleep, she might remember.

Detective Harvey glanced over her shoulder then flipped his little notebook shut. "You're lucky to be alive. Have you been checked for smoke inhalation?"

"Yes, I'm okay." The medic had been puzzled by her good condition, but she didn't tell the detective that.

"I imagine Mr. Raintree will be tied up here for quite a while, but you're free to go. Do you have a number where you can be reached if we have any further questions for you?"

She started to ask, *Like what?* but instead said, "Sure," and gave him her cell-phone number.

"That local?"

"It's my cell." Now that cell numbers could be transferred, she no longer bothered with a landline so long as she had cell-phone service wherever she temporarily settled.

"Got a local number?"

"No, that's it. Sorry. I didn't see any point in getting a landline unless I decided to stay."

"No problem. Thanks for your cooperation." He nodded a brief acknowledgment at her.

Because it seemed the thing to do, Lorna managed a faint smile for him as he strolled back to the other detective, but it quickly faded. She was exhausted and filthy. Her head hurt. Now that Detective Harvey had finished interviewing her, she was going home.

She tried. She made several attempts to walk away, but for some reason she couldn't make her feet move. Frustration grew in her. She had walked over here a few minutes ago, so there was no reason why she shouldn't be able to walk now. Just to see if she could move at all, without turning around, she stepped back, moving closer to Raintree. No problem. All her parts worked just as they should.

Experimentally, she took a step forward, and heaved a sigh of relief when her feet and legs actually obeyed. She was beyond exhausted if the simple act of walking had become so complicated. Sighing, she started to take another step.

And couldn't.

She couldn't go any farther. It was as if she'd reached the end of an invisible leash.

She went cold with disbelief. This was infuriating. He must have hypnotized her, but how? When? She couldn't remember him saying, *"You are getting sleepy,"* and she was pretty certain hypnosis didn't work that way, anyway. It was supposed to be a deep relaxation, not a do-things-against-your-will type of thing, regardless of how stage shows and movies portrayed it.

She wished she'd worn a watch, so she could have noticed any time discrepancy from when she'd gone into Raintree's office and when the fire alarm had sounded. She had to find out what time that had been, because she knew roughly what time sunset was. She'd been in his office for maybe half an hour…she thought. She couldn't be certain. Those disconcerting fantasies could have taken more time than she estimated.

Regardless of how he'd done it, he was controlling her movements. She knew it. When he said, "Stay with me," she'd stayed, even when faced with an inferno. When he said, "Don't go far," she had been able to go only so far and not a step farther.

She turned her head to look at him over her shoulder and found him standing more or less alone, evidently having finished answering whatever questions the other detective had asked. He was watching her, his expression grim. His lips moved. With all the background noise she couldn't hear what he was saying, but she read his lips plainly enough.

He said, "Come here."

# SIX

She went. She couldn't stop herself. Her scalp prickled, and chills ran over her, but she went, her feet moving automatically. Her eyes were wide with alarm. How was he doing this? Not that the "how" mattered; what mattered was *that* he was doing it. Being unable to control herself, to have *him* in control, could lead to some nasty situations.

She couldn't even ask for help, because no one would believe her. At best, people would think she was on drugs or was mentally unstable. All sympathy would be with him, because he'd just lost his casino, his livelihood; the last thing he needed was a nutcase accusing him of somehow controlling her movements. She could just see herself yelling, "Help! I'm walking, and I can't stop! He's making me do it!"

Yeah, right. That would work—*not*.

He gave her a grim, self-satisfied little smile as she neared, and that pissed her off. Being angry felt good; she didn't like being helpless in any way. Too street-savvy to telegraph her intentions, she kept her eyes wide, her expression alarmed, though how much of her face he could see through all the soot and grime was anyone's guess. She kept her right arm close to her side, her elbow bent a little, and tensed the muscles in her back and shoulder. When she was close, so close she could almost kiss him, she launched an uppercut toward his chin.

He never saw it coming, and her fist connected from below with a force that made his teeth snap together. Pain shot through her knuckles, but the satisfaction of punching him made it more than worthwhile. He staggered back half a step, then regained his balance with athletic grace, snaking out his hand to shackle her wrist with long fingers before she could hit him again. He used the grip to pull her against him.

"I deserved one punch," he said, holding her close as he bent his head to speak just loud enough for her to hear. "I won't take a second one."

"Let me go," she snapped. "And I don't mean just with your hand!"

"You've figured it out, then," he said coolly.

"I was a little slow on the uptake, but being shoved into the middle of a freaking, big-ass fire was distracting." She laid on the sarcasm as thickly as possible. "I don't know how you're doing it, or why——"

"The 'why,' at least, should be obvious."

"Then I must be oxygen-deprived from inhaling smoke—gee, I wonder whose fault that is—because it isn't obvious to me!"

"The little matter of your cheating me. Or did you think I'd forget about that in the excitement of watching my casino burn to the ground?"

"I haven't been— Wait a minute. Wait just a damn minute. You couldn't have hypnotized me while we were going down nineteen stories' worth of stairs, and if you did it while we were in your office, then that was before the fire even started. 'Splain that, Lucy!"

He grinned, his teeth flashing whitely in his soot-blackened face. "Am I supposed to say 'Oh, Ricky!'?"

"I don't care what you say. Just undo the voodoo, or the spell, or the hypnotism, or whatever it is you did. You can't hold me here like this."

"That's a ridiculous statement, when I obviously *am* holding you here like this."

Lorna thought steam might be coming out of her ears. She'd been angry many times in her life—she'd even been enraged a couple of times—but this was the most *infuriated* she'd ever felt. Until tonight, she would have said that the three terms meant the same thing, but now she knew that being infuriated carried a rich measure of frustration with it. She was helpless, and she hated being helpless. Her entire life was built around the premise of not being helpless, not being a victim ever again.

"Let. Me. Go." Her teeth were clenched, her tone almost guttural. She was holding on to her self-control by a gossamer thread, but only because she knew screaming would get her exactly nowhere with him and would make *her* look like an idiot.

"Not yet. We still have a few issues to discuss." Completely indifferent to her temper, he lifted his head to look around at the scene of destruction. The stench of smoke permeated everything, and the flashing red and blue lights of many different emergency vehicles created a strobe effect that felt like a spike being pounded into her forehead. Hot spots still flared to crimson life in the smoldering ruins, until the vigilant fire-fighters targeted them with their hoses. A milling crowd pressed against the tape the police had strung up to cordon off the area.

She saw the same details he saw, and the flashing lights reminded her of a ball of flame…no, not of flame…something else. She gasped as her head gave a violent throb.

"Then discuss them, already," she snapped, putting her hand to her head in an instinctive gesture to contain the pain.

"Not here." He glanced down at her again. "Are you okay?"

"I have a splitting headache. I could go home and lie down, if you weren't being such a jerk."

He gave her a considering look. "But I *am* being a jerk, so sue me. Now be quiet and stay here like a good girl. I'll be busy for a while. When I'm finished, we'll go to my house and have that talk."

Lorna fell silent, and when he walked off she remained rooted to the spot. Damn him, she thought as furious tears welled in her eyes and streaked down her filthy cheeks. She raised her hands and wiped the tears away. At least he'd left her with the use of her hands. She couldn't walk and she couldn't talk, but she could dry her face, and if God was really kind to her, she could punch Raintree again the next time he got within punching distance.

Then she went cold, goose bumps rising on her entire body. The brief heat of anger died away, destroyed by a sudden, mind-numbing fear.

What was he?

A man and a woman who had been standing behind the police cordon, watching the massive fire, finally turned and began trudging toward their car. "Crap," the woman said glumly. Her name was Elyn Campbell, and she was the most powerful fire-master in the Ansara clan, except for the Dranir. Everything they knew about Dante Raintree, and everything she knew about fire—aided by some very powerful spells— had been added together to form a plan that should have resulted in the Raintree Dranir's death and instead had accomplished nothing of their mission.

"Yeah." Ruben McWilliams shook his head. All their careful planning, their calculations, up in smoke—literally. "Why didn't it work?"

"I don't know. It *should* have worked. He isn't that strong. No one is, not even a Dranir. It was overkill."

"Then evidently he's the strongest Dranir anyone's ever seen—either that or the luckiest."

"Or he quit sooner than we anticipated. Maybe he chickened out and ran for cover instead of trying to control it."

Ruben heaved a sigh. "Maybe. I didn't see when they brought him out, so maybe he'd been standing somewhere out of sight for a while before I finally spotted him. All that damn equipment was in the way."

She looked up at the starry sky. "So we have two possible scenarios. The first is that he chickened out and ran. The second, and unfortunately the most likely, is that he's stronger than we expected. Cael won't be happy."

Ruben sighed again and faced the inevitable. "I guess we've put it off long enough. We have to call in." He pulled his cell phone from his pocket, but the woman put her hand on his sleeve.

"Don't use your cell phone, it isn't encrypted. Wait until we get back to the hotel, and use a landline."

"Good idea." Anything that delayed placing this call to Cael Ansara was a good idea. Cael was his cousin on his mother's side, but kinship wouldn't cut any ice with the bastard—and he meant "bastard" both figuratively and literally. Maybe this secret alignment with Cael against the current Dranir, Judah, wasn't the smartest thing he'd ever done. Even though he'd agreed with Cael that the Ansara were now strong enough, after two hundred years of rebuilding, to take on the Raintree and destroy them, maybe he'd been wrong. Maybe Cael was wrong.

He knew Cael would automatically go for the first scenario, that Dante Raintree had chickened out and run instead of trying to contain the fire, and completely dismiss the possibility that Raintree was stronger than any of them had imagined. But what if Raintree really *was* that powerful? The attempted coup Cael had planned would be a disaster, and the Ansara would be lucky to survive as a clan. It had taken two centuries to rebuild to their present strength after their last pitched battle with the Raintree.

Cael wouldn't be able to conceive of being wrong. If the plan failed—which it had—Cael would see only two possibilities: either Ruben and Elyn hadn't executed the plan correctly, or Raintree had revealed a cowardly streak. Ruben *knew* they hadn't made any mistakes. Everything had gone like clockwork—except for the outcome. Raintree was supposed to be consumed by a fire he couldn't control, a delicious irony, because fire-masters all had a strange love/hate relationship with the force that danced to their tune. Instead, he had emerged unscathed. Filthy, sooty, maybe singed a little, but essentially unhurt.

A bullet to the head would have been more efficient, but

Cael didn't want to do anything that would alert the Raintree clan, which an overt murder would certainly do. Everything had to be made to look accidental, which of course made guaranteeing the outcome more problematic. The royal family, the most powerful Raintrees, had to be taken out in such a way that no one suspected murder. A fire—they would think losing their Dranir in a fire was tragic and a bitter finale, but they would completely understand that he would fight to the end to save his casino and hotel, especially the hotel, with all the guests in residence there.

Cael, of course, wouldn't allow for the fact that setting up incidents that *didn't* point to the Ansara wasn't an exact science. Things could go wrong. Tonight, something had definitely gone wrong.

Dante Raintree was still alive. That was about as wrong as things could get.

The big assault on the Raintree homeplace, Sanctuary, was planned for the summer solstice, which was a week away. He and Elyn had a week to kill Dante Raintree—or Cael would kill *them*.

# SEVEN

Dante grimly walked back to where he'd left Lorna, reluctant to leave but knowing there was nothing else he could do here. Once the police were finished questioning him, his only thought had been to check on his employees to find out if there had been any fatalities. To his deep regret and fury, the answer to that last question was yes. One body had already been pulled from the smoldering ruins of the casino, and the cops were working with the crowd to establish if there were any missing friends or relatives, which would take time. There might not be a final count for a couple of days.

He'd found Al Rayburn, hoarse and coughing from smoke inhalation but refusing to go to a hospital, instead helping to keep order among the evacuated guests. The hotel staff was doing an admirable job. The hotel itself had suffered compara-tively little damage, and most of that was to the lobby area that connected the hotel and casino, where Dante had made his stand. Everyone in the hotel, guests and staff, had safely evacu-ated. There were some minor injuries, sprained ankles and the like, but nothing major. There was smoke damage, of course, and the entire hotel would have to be cleaned to remove the stench. The good news, what there was of it, was that the parking deck hadn't been damaged, and the hotel had no struc-tural damage. He could probably re-open the hotel within two weeks. The question was: why would anyone want to stay there without the casino?

The casino was a complete loss. About twenty vehicles in the parking lot outside the casino entrance had been damaged, and the parking lot itself was a mess right now. Twenty or thirty people had burns of varying degrees, and as many again were suffering from smoke inhalation; all of them had been transported to local hospitals.

The media had descended en masse, of course, their constant shouts and interruptions and requests/demands for interviews interfering with his attempts to organize his em-ployees, arrange other lodging for his hotel guests, and arrange with Al for the guests to retrieve their belongings and at the same time secure the hotel from thieves posing as guests. He had his insurance provider to deal with. He had to call Gideon and Mercy, to let them know about the fire and that he was all right, before they saw all this on the news. They were both in the Eastern Time Zone, meaning he'd better get in touch with them damn soon.

Finally he'd accepted that there was little more he could do tonight; his staff was excellent, and they had matters well in hand, plus he could always be reached by phone. He might as well go home and take a much-needed shower.

And that left the problem of Lorna.

Tonight was a night of firsts. Before tonight, he'd never used mind compulsion, never known he could. He had no idea what the parameters were. At first he'd thought his own sense of urgency had provided the impetus, but even after the evacuation was over, he'd been able to control Lorna just with the words and a nudge from his mind, so adrenaline wasn't the catalyst. He had stepped into new territory, and he had to tread lightly because this particular power could be easily abused. Hell, he'd already abused it, hadn't he? Lorna would definitely say yes to that——when he let her speak.

Tonight was also the first time he'd brutally overwhelmed someone else's mind and literally stolen all their available power. In the aftermath, she'd been dazed, lethargic, unable to remember even her name, all symptoms attributable to emotional shock. How extensive the amnesia was, and how temporary, was something that remained to be seen. She'd begun recovering fairly soon, but she still didn't remember vast portions of the experience——unless she'd recovered her memory in his absence, in which case he should probably find some body armor before he released her from the compulsion.

Was she Ansara? That was the burning question that had to be answered——and soon.

His thinking went both ways. Part of him said, no, she couldn't possibly be, or he wouldn't have been able to overpower her mind so easily, nor would she be so susceptible to mind compulsion. An Ansara, trained from birth to manage and control her unusual abilities, just as the Raintree were, would have automatically resisted mind compulsion. The power was rare, so rare that he'd never met anyone capable of exercising it, though the family history said that an aunt six generations back had been adept at it. Rare or not, because the power existed at all, he and every other Raintree had been taught how to construct mental shields. The Ansara basically mirrored the Raintree in their gifts, so undoubtedly they, too, taught their people how to shield, which meant that the completely unshielded Lorna could not be Ansara.

Unless...

Unless she was so gifted at shielding that he couldn't detect it. Unless she was merely pretending to be controlled by mind compulsion. He'd spoken his will aloud, so she knew what he wanted. If she also had the gift of controlling fire, she could have been bolstering the blaze, resurrecting the flames every time he managed to beat them down. No. He rejected that idea. If she'd been the one feeding the fire, he would have been able to extinguish it completely after he'd commandeered her power. Someone else must have been feeding the fire, but she could have been distracting him, deflecting some of his power.

Was she or wasn't she? He would know soon. If she wasn't...then he'd played some real hardball with a woman who might not be an innocent but was still far from being an enemy. He didn't know that he would have done anything differently, though. When he'd overwhelmed her mind, it had been an act of desperation, and he hadn't had the luxury of time to explain things to her. He might have to make amends, but he wasn't sorry he'd done it. He was just glad she'd been there, glad she was gifted and had a pool of mental energy for him to tap.

He rounded a fire engine, where the crew was laying out their hoses in preparation for recoiling them, and stepped up on a curb. Now he could see her. So far as he could tell, she was standing in the exact spot in which he'd left her, which at least was off to the side, so she wasn't in the way of any of the firefighters. She was filthy, her hair matted from the unhappy combination of smoke, soot and water, her posture shouting exhaustion. She still clutched a blanket around her, and she was literally swaying where she stood. He felt a quick spurt of impatience, mingled with sympathy. Why hadn't she sat down? He hadn't prevented her from doing that.

Looking at her, he gave a mental wince on behalf of his car seats, then immediately shrugged, because he was just as filthy. What did it matter, anyway? The leather could be cleaned.

When she saw him, pure temper flashed in her eyes, dispelling the fatigue. If he'd expected her to be cowed, he would have been disappointed. As it was, a little tinge of anticipation shot through him. Even after all she'd been through, she was still standing up for herself. Remembering the vast pool of power he'd found when he tapped her mind, he wondered if even she knew how strong she really was.

"Come with me," he said, and, obediently, she followed. There was nothing obedient about the way she grabbed his arm, though, pulling him around. She glared furiously up at him, indicating her mouth with a brief, impatient gesture. She wanted to talk; she probably had a lot of things memorized to say.

Dante started to release the compulsion, then stopped and grinned. "I think I'll enjoy the quiet for a little longer," he said, knowing that would really twist her drawers in a knot. "There's nothing you need to say that can't wait until we're alone."

Al had arranged for one of his security people to fetch Dante's car from the parking deck, where he had a reserved slot next to a private elevator. He'd been discreet about it, because some of the guests, the ones without identification, weren't being allowed to take their vehicles from the deck.

They were already sorting out that security problem for those guests who felt they absolutely had to have a car tonight, even though Dante was providing shuttles to take everyone to the various hotels where his people had found them lodging. He was doing everything possible to take care of his guests, but he knew there could still be a lot of resentment that formed over details like him getting his car when they couldn't.

The phantom-black Lotus Exige was idling, parking lights on, at the end of the huge casino parking lot, concealed from most of the crowd of onlookers by the huge knot of emergency vehicles with their flashing lights. Dante led Lorna along the edge of the lot; as they neared the car, the driver's door opened and one of the security men got out. "Here you go, Mr. Raintree."

"Thanks, Jose." Dante opened the passenger door. Lorna directed a lethal glare at him as she climbed into the car and somehow managed to dig an elbow into his ribs. He concealed a wince, then closed the door with a firm click and went around to the driver's side.

The Lotus was low-slung and not all that comfortable for his muscular six-two frame, but he loved driving it when he was in the mood for something with attitude. When he wanted more comfort, he drove his Jag. Tonight he would have liked to drive out into the desolate countryside and put the hammer down, to ease his anger and sharp edge of sorrow with sheer speed and aggression. The Lotus could go from zero to a hundred in eleven seconds, which was a rush. He needed to go a hundred miles an hour right now, needed to push the high-performance little machine to its limit.

Instead he drove calmly and deliberately, aware that he couldn't let go of the tight leash he was holding on his temper.

The fact that it was night helped, but the date was too close to the summer solstice for him to take any chances. Hell—could *he* have started the accursed fire? Was *he* responsible for the loss of at least one life?

The fire marshal said preliminary interviews indicated that it had started in the back, where the circuit breakers were, but the scene was still too hot for the investigators to get in there to check. If the fire had started from an electrical problem, then he had nothing to do with it, but he brooded over the possibility that the fire would turn out to have been started by something completely different. His control had wavered when he'd first seen Lorna, with the last rays of the setting sun turning her hair to rich fire. He'd lit the candles without even thinking about them; had he lit anything else?

No, he hadn't done it. He was sure of that. If he'd been the cause, things would have been bursting into flame all over the hotel and casino, rather than in one distant spot. He'd contained his power, brought it under control. The casino fire had been caused by something else; the timing was just coincidence.

Almost half an hour had elapsed before he opened his gate with a remote control and guided the Lotus up a twisting, curving drive to his tri-level house tucked into an eastern-facing fold of the Sierra Nevadas. Another button on the remote raised his garage door, and he put the Lotus in its slot like an astronaut docking a shuttle with the Space Station, then closed the garage door behind him. The silver Jag gleamed in its place beside the Lotus.

"Come on," he told Lorna, and she got out of the car. She stared straight ahead as he stepped aside to allow her to precede him into his gleaming kitchen. He punched his code into the security system to stop its warning beep, then paused. He briefly considered taking her back to town after he'd finished talking to her, then discarded that idea. He was tired. She could stay here, and if he had to——as he undoubtedly would——he would use a compulsion to keep her here and out of trouble. If she didn't like it, tough; the last couple of hours had been a bitch, and he didn't feel like making the drive.

With that in mind, he reset the alarm and turned to her. She was standing with her back to him, not four feet away, her shoulders stiff and, judging by the angle of her head, her chin up.

Regretting the imminent loss of silence, he said, "Okay, you can talk now."

She whirled to face him, and he braced himself for a flood of invective as her fists clenched at her sides.

"Bathroom!" she bellowed at him.

# EIGHT

The change in his expression would have been comical if Lorna had been in any mood to appreciate humor. His eyes rounded with comprehension, and he rapidly pointed to a short hallway. "First door on the right."

She took one frantic step, and then froze. Damn it, he was still holding her! The searing look she gave him should have accomplished what the casino fire hadn't, namely singe every hair from his head. "Don't go far," he snapped, realizing he hadn't amended the compulsion.

Lorna ran. She slammed the bathroom door but didn't take time to lock it. She barely made it in time, and the sense of relief was so acute she shook with involuntary shudders. A Tom Hanks scene from *A League of Their Own* ran through her mind, and she bit her lip to keep from groaning aloud.

Then she just sat there, eyes closed, trying to calm her jangled nerves. He'd brought her to his *home!* What did he intend to do? Whatever he was, however, he was controlling her, she was helpless to break free. The entire time he'd been gone, she had been willing herself over and over to take a single step, to speak a word—and she couldn't. She was scared half out of her mind, traumatized out of the other half, and on top of it all, she was so angry she thought she might have a screaming, out-of-control, foot-stomping temper tantrum just to relieve the pressure.

Opening her eyes, she started to flush, but she heard his voice and went still, straining to hear what he was saying. Was someone else here? Just as she began to relax just a fraction, she realized he was on the phone.

"Sorry to wake you." He paused briefly, then said, "There was a fire at the casino. Could be worse, but it's bad enough. I didn't want you to see it on the morning news and wonder. Call Mercy in a couple of hours and tell her I'm all right. I've got a feeling I'm going to have my hands full for the next few days."

Another pause. "Thanks, but no. You've got no business getting on an airplane this week, and everything here is fine. I just wanted to call you before I got so tied up in red tape I couldn't get to a phone."

The conversation continued for a minute, and he kept reassuring whoever was on the other end that no, he didn't need help; everything was fine—well, not fine, but under control. There had been at least one fatality. The casino was a total loss, but the hotel had suffered only minor damage.

He ended the call, and a moment later Lorna heard a savage, muttered curse, then a thud, as if he'd punched the wall.

He didn't seem like the wall-punching type, she thought. Then again, she didn't know him. He might be a serial wall-puncher. Or maybe he'd fainted or something, and the thud had been his body hitting the floor.

She liked that idea. She would seize the chance to kick him while he was down. Literally.

The only way to see if he was lying there unconscious was to leave the bathroom. Reluctantly, she flushed, then went to the vanity to wash her hands—a vanity with a dark, golden-brown granite top and gold fixtures. When she reached out to turn on the water, the contrast between the richness of the vanity and her absolutely filthy, black-sooted hand made her inwardly cringe as she lifted her head.

A grimy nightmare loomed in the mirror in front of her. Her hair was matted to her head with soot and water, and stank of smoke. Her face was so black only her eyes had any real defi-nition, and they were bloodshot. With her red eyes, she looked like some demon from hell.

She shuddered, remembering how close the flames had gotten. Given that, she couldn't imagine how she had any hair left on her head at all, so she shouldn't complain about it being matted. Shampoo—a lot of it—would take care of that. The soot would scrub off. Her clothes were ruined, but she had others. She was alive and unharmed, and she didn't know how.

As she soaped her grimy hands, rinsed, then soaped again, she tried to reconstruct an exact sequence of events. Her headache, which had subsided, roared back so fiercely she had to brace her soapy hands on the edge of the bowl.

Thoughts whirled, trying to connect in a coherent sequence, but then the segments would whirl out of touch again.

—she should have been burned—

—hair singed off—

—bubble—

—no smoke—

—agony—

Whimpering from the pain in her head, she sank to her knees.

Raintree cursing.

Something about that reminded her of something. Of being held in front of him, his arms locked around her, while his curses rang out over her head and his...his—

The memory was gone, eluding her grasp. Pain made her vision swim, and she stared at the soap bubbles on her hands, trying to summon the energy to stand. Was she having a stroke? The pain was so intense, burning, and it filled her head until she thought her skull might explode from the pressure.

Soap bubbles.

The shimmery bubbles...something about them reminded her...there had been something around her....

*A shimmering bubble.* The memory burst into her aching brain, so clear it brought tears to her eyes. She'd *seen* it, surrounding them, holding the heat and smoke at bay.

Her head had felt as if it really were exploding then. There had been an impact so huge she couldn't compare it to anything in her experience, but she imagined the sensation was the same as if she'd been run over by a train—or struck by a meteor. It was as if all the cellular walls in her brain had dissolved, as if everything she had been, was, and would be, had been sucked out, taken over and used. She'd been helpless, as completely helpless as a newborn, to resist the pain or the man who had ruthlessly taken everything.

With a crash, everything fell back into place, as if that memory had been the one piece she needed to put the puzzle together.

She remembered it all: every moment of unspeakable terror, her inability to act, the way he had used her.

Everything.

"You've had enough time," he called from the kitchen. "I heard you flush. Come here, Lorna."

Like a puppet, she got to her feet and walked out of the bathroom, soap still clinging to her hands and her temper flaring. He looked grim, standing there waiting for her. With every unwilling step she took, her temper soared into another level of the stratosphere.

"You *jerk!*" she shouted, and kicked his ankle as she walked by. She could go only a couple of steps past him before that invisible wall stopped her, so she whirled around and stalked past him again. "You *ass!*" She threw an elbow into his ribs.

She must not have hurt him very much because he looked more astonished than pained. That infuriated her even more, and when the wall forced her to turn around yet again, she reached a whole new level of temper as she began marching back and forth within the confines of his will.

"You made me go into *fire*——" A snake-fast pinch at his waist.

"I'm *terrified* of fire, but did you *care?*" Another kick, this one sideways into his knee.

"Oh, no, I had to *stand there* while you did your mumbo jumbo——" On that pass, she leveled a punch at his solar plexus.

"Then you *brain-raped* me, you jerk, you gorilla, you freakin' *witch doctor*——" On the return trip, she went for a kidney punch.

"Then, to top it all off, the whole time you were *grinding your hard-on against my butt!*" She was so incensed that she shrieked that last bit at him, and this time put everything she had into a punch straight to his chin.

He blocked it with a swift movement of his forearm, so she stomped on his foot instead.

"Ouch!" he yelped, but the jerk was *laughing,* damn him, and in another of his lightning moves, he captured her in his arms, pulling her solidly against him. She opened her mouth to screech at him, and he bent his head and kissed her.

In contrast to the strong-arm tactics he'd used against her all night, the kiss was soft and feather-light, almost sweet. "I'm sorry," he murmured, and kissed her again. He stank as much as she did, maybe even more, but the body beneath his ruined clothing was rock solid with muscle and very warm in the air-conditioned coolness of the house. "I know it hurt... I didn't have time to explain——" Between phrases, he kept on kissing her, each successive touch of his lips becoming a little deeper, lingering a little longer.

Shock held her still: shock that he would be kissing her; shock that she would *let* him kiss her, after all the antagonism between them; after he'd done everything he'd done to her; after she'd subjected him to that battery of drive-by attacks. He wasn't forcing her to let him kiss her; this was nothing like wanting to walk and not being able to. Her hands were on his muscled chest, but she wasn't making any effort to push him away, not even a mental one.

His mouth slid to the soft hollow beneath her ear, deposited a gentle bite on the site of her neck. "I'd much rather have been grinding my hard-on against your front," he said, and went back to her mouth for a kiss that had nothing light or sweet about it. His tongue swept in, acquainting him with her taste, while his right hand went down to her bottom, slid caressingly over the curves, then pressed her hips forward to meet his.

He was doing exactly what he'd said he would much rather have been doing.

Lorna didn't trust passion. From what she had seen, passion was selfish and self-centered. She wasn't immune to it, but she didn't trust it——didn't trust men, who in her experience would tell lies just to get laid. She didn't trust anyone else to care about her, to look out for her interests. She opened herself to passion slowly, warily, if at all.

If she hadn't been so tired, so stressed, so traumatized, she would have had complete control of herself, but she'd been off balance from the minute his chief of security had escorted her into his office. She was off balance now, as dizzy as if the kitchen were rotating around her, as if the floor had slanted beneath her feet. In contrast, he was solid and so very warm, his arms stronger than any that had ever held her before, and her body responded to him as if nothing else existed beyond the simple pleasure of the moment. Being held against him felt good. His incredible body heat felt good. The thick length of his erection, pushing against her lower belly, felt good——so good that she had gone on tiptoe to better accommodate it, and she didn't remember doing so.

Belatedly alarmed by the no-show of her usual caution, she pulled her mouth from his and pushed against his chest. "This is stupid," she muttered.

"Brainless," he agreed, his breath coming a little fast. He was slow to release her, so she pushed again, and, reluctantly, he let his arms drop.

He didn't step back, so she did, staring around her at the kitchen so she wouldn't have to look at him. As kitchens went, it was nice, she supposed. She didn't like cooking, so in the general scheme of things, kitchens were pretty much wasted on her.

"You kidnapped me," she charged, scowling at him.

He considered that, then gave a brief nod. "I did."

For some reason his agreement annoyed her more than if he'd argued with her assessment. "If you're going to charge me with cheating, then do it," she snapped. "You can't prove a thing, and we both know it, so the sooner you make a fool of yourself, the better, as far as I'm concerned, because then I can leave and not see you—"

"I'm not making any charges against you," he interrupted. "You're right. I can't prove anything."

His sudden admission stumped her. "Then why drag me all the way up here?"

"I said I can't prove you did it. That doesn't mean you're innocent." He gave her a narrow, assessing look. "In fact, you're guilty as hell. Using your paranormal gifts in a game of chance is cheating, pure and simple."

"I don't have—" Automatically, she started to deny that she was psychic, but he raised a hand to cut her off.

"That's why I did the 'brain-rape,' as you called it. I needed an extra reserve of power to hold off the fire, and I knew you were gifted—but I was surprised at *how* gifted. You can't tell me you didn't know. There was too much power there for you to pass yourself off as just being lucky."

Lorna hardly knew how to react. His cool acknowledgment of what he'd done to her raised her hackles all over again, but the charge that she was "gifted" made her so uneasy that she was already shaking her head before he finished speaking. "Numbers," she blurted. "I'm good with numbers."

"Bull."

"That's all it is! I don't tell fortunes or read tea leaves or anything like that! I didn't know 9/11 was going to happen—"

But the flight numbers of the downed flights had haunted her for days before the attack. If she tried to dial a phone number, the numbers she dialed were those flight numbers—in the order in which the planes had crashed.

That particular memory surfaced like a salmon leaping out of the water, and a chill shook her. She hadn't thought of the flight numbers since then. She had buried the memory deep, where it couldn't cause trouble.

"Go away," she whispered to the memory.

"I'm not going anywhere," he said. "And neither are you. At least, not right away." He sighed and gave her a regretful look. "Take off your clothes."

# NINE

"I will not!" Lorna yelped, backing as far away from him as she could get, which of course wasn't far.

"So will I, probably," he replied ironically, moving closer, looming over her. "Can't be helped. Look, I'm not going to assault you. Just take off your clothes and get it over with."

She retreated as he advanced, clutching at her blouse as if she were an outraged Victorian virgin and looking around for a weapon, any weapon. This was a kitchen, damn it; it was supposed to have knives sitting in a fancy block on the fancy countertop. Instead, there was nothing but a vast expanse of polished granite.

He took a deep breath, then heaved it out as if he were bored. "I can make you do it without even touching you. You know that, and I know that, so why do this the hard way?"

He was right, she thought impotently. Whatever it was that his mind did to her mind, he could make her do anything he wanted. "This isn't fair!" she shouted at him, curling her hands into fists. "How are you *doing* this to me?"

"I'm a freakin' witch doctor, remember?"

"Don't forget the rest of it! Jerk! Ass——"

"I know, I know. Now take off your clothes."

She shook her head, matted hair flying. Bitterly, she expected him to take control of her mind, but he didn't. He just inexorably advanced as she retreated, backing down the hallway past the powder room she'd used, through what she assumed was a very stylish den, though she didn't dare take her gaze from him long enough to look around.

He was herding her, she realized, as if she were a sheep, and she had no choice, but to do anything other than be herded. His bloodshot green eyes glittered in his grimy face, making him look completely uncivilized. Her heartbeat skittered wildly. Was he some sort of mad serial killer who left pieces of dismembered bodies scattered all over Nevada? A modern-day Rasputin? An escapee from some mental institution? He certainly didn't look or act like the millionaire owner of a top-notch casino/hotel. He acted like some sort of——of warlord, master of all he surveyed.

She backed into a door frame, briefly staggered off balance, then brought herself up short as she realized he'd maneuvered her into another bathroom, this one a full bath, and far more opulent than the half bath off the kitchen. No lights were on, but the illumination coming in the open door revealed their reflections in the gleaming mirror on her left.

He reached in and flipped on the lights, so bright and white that she lifted a hand to shield her eyes. "Now," he said, "no more stalling. Take off your clothes yourself, or we'll do this the hard way."

Lorna looked around. She was cornered. "Go to hell," she said, and did what cornered animals always do: she attacked.

For a short while he merely blocked her punches, deflected her kicks, avoided her bites, and the ease with which he did so made her that much angrier. She lost one shoe in the battle, the cheap sandal sailing across the room to clatter into the huge sunken tub. Then she felt a sudden wave of impatience emanating from him, and in three seconds flat he had her bent over the vanity with her hands pinned behind her.

He crowded in close, using his powerful legs to control her kicks, and gripped the neckline of her top. Three hard yanks brought the sound of several threads giving way, but the seams held. He cursed and yanked harder, and the left-side seam surrendered. Ruthlessly he tore at the garment until it was in rags, hanging from her right wrist. Her bra fastened in back, easy prey to the quick pinch of his fingers that released the hooks.

She squirmed like an eel, screaming until she was hoarse. He completely ignored everything she said, every insult and plea she hurled at him, silently and grimly concentrating on stripping her. She alternated between fury and sobs of panic as he opened the fastening of her pants, lowered the zipper, but stopped before pushing her pants and underwear down over her hips.

She went limp, sobbing, her face pressed against the cold stone of the vanity. He stopped pulling at her clothes, and instead the heat of his hand moved over her neck, lifting her matted hair aside for a moment, then tracing over her shoulders. He shifted his grip on her hands, instead pulling them up and over her head before resuming what felt like an inch-by-inch search of her skin. The sides of her breasts, her ribs, the indentation of her waist, the flare of her hips——he examined all of that, even pushing her pants lower to scrutinize the bottom curves of her buttocks. Mortified, she squirmed and sobbed, but he was inexorable.

Then he sighed and said, "I owe you another apology."

He released his grip on her hands and stepped back, freeing her from the pressure of his body. On his way out he said, "I'll bring you some clothes. Think about taking a shower, get your breath back and we'll talk afterward." He paused, added, "Don't leave this room," then quietly closed the door.

Sobbing, she slid from the vanity to the floor and curled in a vanquished heap. At first all she could do was cry and shake. After a while her temper resurrected itself and flashed over in a wordless shriek. She wept some more. Finally she sat up, wiped her face with the shreds of her blouse, yelled, "You bastard!" at the door, and felt marginally better for the invective.

Her eyes were swollen and her nose was clogged, but she felt calm enough to stand, though that wasn't easy with her pants around her knees. The indignity made her flush with humiliation, but there was no point in pulling them up. Instead she stripped completely naked and stood there in rare indecision.

The suggestion to take a shower, she discovered, had been just that: a suggestion. If she didn't want to, she didn't have to. She could take a long soak in the sunken tub, if she wished. She didn't have to bathe at all, though that was an option she immediately discarded.

Getting in the tub wouldn't be practical, because she would end up sitting in dirty water. A long——very long——hot shower was the only way to get clean.

The shower didn't have a door. The entrance was a curved wall of stone that led past a built-in shelf, stacked with thick, copper-colored towels, to three steps down into a five-foot-square stall with multiple showerheads. The controls were within easy reach, and when she turned the handle, water spurted out of three walls and from overhead. She waited until she felt the heat of the steam rising to her face, then stepped into the deluge.

Concentrating on getting clean, and nothing else, gave her nerves a much-needed respite. The hot water streaming over her body was a soothing, pulsating massage. She shampooed and rinsed, then did it again, and yet again, before her hair felt clean and untangled. She lathered and scrubbed with the fragrant bath gel, and found it didn't remove even half the soot and grime. A second scrubbing produced results that weren't much better, so she switched back to the shampoo; it had worked on her hair, so it should work on her skin.

Finally she realized that she'd been in the shower so long that her fingertips had wrinkled and the hot water should have long since been used up, though it wasn't—but enough was enough. She was waterlogged. Regretfully, she turned off the water, and the pulsating streams disappeared so suddenly that it was as if they'd been sucked back into the showerheads. Only the sounds of the vent fan overhead and the draining water came to her ears.

She hadn't turned on the vent fan. Unless it came on automatically when the humidity level reached a certain point, he'd come back into the bathroom.

Hurriedly, she went up the three steps, grabbed one of the fluffy towels and wrapped it around herself, then got another one and twisted it into a turban over her dripping hair. Following the curving wall, she moved until she could see into the main part of the bathroom. The mirrored wall behind the double sinks threw her reflection back at her, but hers was the only reflection. She was alone—now. The thick terry-cloth robe folded over the vanity stool told her that he *had* been there.

Lorna stared at the mirror. She looked pale, even to herself. The skin across her cheekbones was drawn tight, giving her a stark, shocked expression.

That was okay. She *felt* stark and shocked.

He'd said not to leave the bathroom. She was so soul-weary that she didn't even try, so she didn't know if that had been another suggestion or one of his weird mental orders that she couldn't disobey. At this point it didn't matter whether it was a suggestion or command. She was content to simply stay there, where there was nothing more complicated to do than dry her hair.

Rummaging in the drawers of the vanity, she found scented lotion, as well as a hair dryer and brush, which was all she needed right now. The shampoo had made her skin feel tight, so she rubbed in the lotion everywhere she could reach, then began the task of drying her hair.

Her motions with the brush became slower, then slower still. Exhaustion made her arms tremble. She was lucky that her hair was mostly straight, and had good body, because any attempt at styling it was beyond her. She just wanted her hair to be dry before she collapsed, that was all.

With that chore accomplished, she put on the robe, which was evidently his; the sleeves fell several inches past the tips of her fingers and the hem almost reached the floor. Funny, she thought fuzzily, he didn't seem like the robe-wearing type.

Then she waited, swaying on her feet, her bare toes clench-ing on the plush rug. She could have at least opened the door, but she wasn't in any rush to face him, or to find out that even with the door open, she was imprisoned in this room. Time enough for that. Time enough to engage the enemy again.

They would talk, he'd said. She didn't want to talk to him. She had nothing to say to him that didn't involve a lot of four-letter words. All she wanted was to go...well, not *home,* exactly, because she didn't have a home in that sense. She wanted to go back to where she was staying, to where her clothes were. That was close enough to home for her. For now, she just wanted to sleep in the bed she was accustomed to.

Without warning, the door opened and he stood there, tall and broad-shouldered, as vital as if the night hadn't been long and traumatic. He'd showered, too; his longish black hair, still damp, was brushed straight back to reveal every strong, faintly exotic line of his face. He'd shaved, too; his face had that freshly scraped look.

He was wearing a pair of very soft-looking pajama pants...and nothing else. Not even a smile.

His keen eyes searched her face, noting the white look of utter exhaustion. "We'll talk in the morning. I doubt you could form a coherent sentence right now. Come on, I'll show you where your room is."

She shrank back, and he looked at her with an unreadable expression. "*Your* room," he emphasized. "Not mine. I didn't make that a command, but I will if necessary. I don't think you'd be comfortable sleeping in the bathroom."

She was awake enough to retort, "You'll have to make it a command, otherwise I can't leave the bathroom, anyway."

She had decided that his command not to leave the bathroom had been meant to short-circuit her own will, and by his flash of irritation, she saw she'd been right.

"Come with me," he said curtly, a command that released her from the bathroom but sentenced her to follow him like a duckling.

He led her to a spacious bedroom with seven-foot windows that revealed the sparkling neon colors of Reno. "The private bath is through there," he said, indicating a door. "You're safe. I won't bother you. I won't hurt you. Don't leave this room." With that, he closed the door behind him and left her standing in the dimly lit bedroom.

He *would* remember to tack on that last sentence, damn him—not that she felt capable of making a run for it. Right now her capability was limited to climbing into the king-size bed, still wearing the oversize robe. She curled under the sheet and duvet, but still felt too exposed, so she pulled the sheet over her head and slept.

# TEN

*Monday*

"Are you okay?"

Lorna woke, as always, to a lingering sense of dread and fear. It wasn't the words that alarmed her, though, since she immediately recognized the voice. They were, however, far from welcome. Regardless of where she was, the dread was always there, within her, so much a part of her that it was as if it had been beaten into her very bones.

She couldn't see him, because the sheet was still over her head. She seldom moved in her sleep, so she was still in such a tight curl that the oversize robe hadn't been dislodged or even come untied.

"Are you okay?" he repeated, more insistently.

"Peachy keen," she growled, wishing he would just go away again.

"You were making a noise."

"I was snoring," she said flatly, keeping a tight grip on the sheet in case he tried to pull it down—like she could stop him if he really wanted to. She had learned the futility of that in the humiliating struggle last night.

He snorted. "Yeah, right." He paused. "How do you like your coffee?"

"I don't. I'm a tea drinker."

Silence greeted that for a moment; then he sighed. "I'll see what I can do. How do you drink your tea?"

"With friends."

She heard what sounded remarkably like a growl, then the bedroom door closed with more force than necessary. Had she sounded ungrateful? *Good!* After everything he'd done, if he thought the offer of coffee or tea would make up for it, he was so far off base he wasn't even in the ballpark.

Truth to tell, she wasn't much of a tea drinker, either. For most of her life she'd been able to afford only what was free, which meant she drank a lot of water. In the last few years she'd had the occasional cup of coffee or hot tea, to warm up in very cold weather, but she didn't really care for either of them.

She didn't want to get up. She didn't want to have that talk he seemed bent on, though what he thought they had to talk about, she couldn't imagine. He'd treated her horribly last night, and though he'd evidently realized he was wrong, he didn't seem inclined to go out of his way to make amends. He hadn't, for instance, taken her home last night. He'd imprisoned her in this room. He hadn't even fed the prisoner!

The empty ache in her stomach told her that she had to get out of bed if she wanted food. Getting out of bed didn't guarantee she would get fed, of course, but staying in bed certainly guaranteed she wouldn't. Reluctantly, she flipped the sheet back, and the first thing she saw was Dante Raintree, standing just inside the door. The bully hadn't left at all; he'd just pretended to.

He lifted one eyebrow in a silent, sardonic question.

Annoyed, she narrowed her eyes at him. "That's inhuman."

"What is?"

"Lifting just one eyebrow. Real people can't do that. Just demons."

"*I* can do it."

"Which proves my point."

He grinned—which annoyed her even more, because she didn't want to amuse him. "If you want to get up, this demon has washed your clothes—"

"What you didn't shred," she interjected sourly, to hide her alarm. Had he emptied her pockets first? She didn't ask, because if he hadn't, maybe her money and license were still there.

"—and loaned you one of his demon shirts. You'll probably have to throw your pants away, because the stains won't come out, but at least they're clean. They'll do for now. Your choices for breakfast are cereal and fruit, or a bagel and cream cheese. When you get dressed, come to the kitchen. We'll eat in there." He left then—really left, because she watched him go.

He was assuming she would share a meal with him. Unfortunately, he was right. She was starving, and if the only way she could get some food was to sit anywhere in his vicinity, then she would sit there. One of the first lessons she'd learned about life was that emotions didn't carry much weight when survival sat on the other end of the scale.

Slowly she sat up, feeling aches and twinges in every muscle.

Her newly washed, stained-beyond-redemption pants lay across the foot of the bed, as well as her underwear and a white shirt made out of some limp, slinky material. She grabbed for the pants and dug her hand into each pocket, and her heart sank. Not only was her money gone, but so was her license. He either had them, or they had fallen out in the wash, which meant she had to find the laundry room in this place and search the washer and dryer. Maybe he had someone working for him who did the laundry; maybe that person had taken her money and ID.

She got out of bed and hobbled to the bathroom. After taking care of her most urgent business, she looked in the drawers of the vanity, hoping he was a good host—even if he was a lousy person—and had stocked the bathroom with emergency supplies. She desperately needed a toothbrush.

He was a good host. She found everything she needed: a supply of toothbrushes still in their sealed plastic cases, toothpaste, mouthwash, the same scented lotion she'd used the night before, a small sewing kit, even new hairbrushes and disposable razors.

The toothbrush manufacturer had evidently not intended for anyone without a knife or scissors to be able to use their product. After struggling to tear the plastic case apart, first with her fingers and then with her teeth, she got the tiny pair of scissors from the sewing kit and laboriously stabbed, sawed and hacked until she had freed the incarcerated toothbrush. She regarded the scissors thoughtfully, then laid them on the vanity top. They were too small to be of much use, but...

After brushing her teeth and washing her face, she dragged a brush through her hair. Good enough. Even if she'd had her skimpy supply of makeup with her, she wouldn't have put any on for Raintree's benefit.

Going back into the bedroom, she locked the door just in case he decided to waltz in again, then removed the robe and began dressing. The precaution was useless, she thought bitterly, because if he wanted in, all he had to do was order her to unlock the door and she would do what he said, whether she wanted to or not. She *hated* that, and she hated *him*.

She didn't want to put on his shirt. She picked it up and turned it so she could see the tag. She didn't recognize the brand name, but that wasn't what she was looking for, anyway. The tag with the care instructions read 100% Silk—Dry-clean Only.

Maybe she could smear some jelly on the shirt. Accidentally, of course.

She started to slip her arms into the sleeves, then paused, remembering how he'd phrased his last statement: *When you're dressed, come to the kitchen*. Once she was dressed, she probably wouldn't have a choice about going to the kitchen, so anything she wanted to do, she should do before putting on that shirt.

She dropped the shirt back on the bed and retrieved the tiny scissors from the bathroom, slipping them into her right pocket. Then she systematically searched both the bathroom and bedroom, looking for anything she might use as a weapon or to help her somehow escape. If she saw any opening, however small, she had to be prepared to take it.

One big obstacle was that she didn't have any shoes. She doubted the ones she'd been wearing could be saved, but at least they would protect her feet. Raintree hadn't brought them to the bedroom, but they might still be in the bathroom she'd used last night. She didn't want to run barefoot through the countryside, though she would if she had to. How far would she have to run before she was free? How far out did Raintree's sphere of influence reach? There had to be a distance at which his mind tricks wouldn't work—didn't there? Did she have to hear him speak the command, or could he just *think* it at her?

Uneasily, she hoped he had somehow simply hypnotized her, because otherwise she was so deep in *The Twilight Zone* doo-doo she might never get the weird crap off her shoes.

Other than the scissors, neither the bath nor the bedroom supplied anything usable. There were no pistols in the built-in drawers, no stray hammer she could use to bash him in the head, not even any extra clothes in the huge closet that she could have used to suffocate him. Regretfully, with no other option left, she finally put on the silk shirt. As she was rolling up the too-long sleeves, she wondered when the command stuff would kick in. The slippery material didn't roll up very well, so she redid the sleeves several times before she gave up and let the rolls droop over her wrists. Even then, she didn't feel an irresistible urge to go to the kitchen.

She was on her own. He hadn't put the command mojo on her.

Tremendously annoyed that, under her own free will, she was doing what he'd told her to do anyway, she unlocked the bedroom door and stepped out into the hallway.

Two sets of stairs opened before her, the one on the right going up to the next floor and leading to what appeared to be a balcony. The set on the left went down, widening to a graceful fan at the bottom. She frowned, not remembering any stairs from the night before. Had she been that out of it? She definitely remembered arriving at the house, remembered noticing that it had three separate levels, so of course there were stairs—she just didn't remember them. Having this kind of hole in her memory was frightening, because what else did she not remember?

She took the down staircase, pausing when she got to the bottom. She was in a spectacular...living room? If so, it wasn't like any living room she'd ever seen. The arched ceiling soared three stories above her head. At one end was an enormous fireplace, while the wall at the other end was glass. Evidently he was fond of glass, because he had a lot of it. The view was literally breathtaking. But she didn't remember this, either. Any of it.

A hallway led off to the side, and cautiously she followed it. Something about this seemed familiar, at least, and she opened one door to discover the bathroom in which she'd showered last night—and in which he'd ripped off her clothes. Setting her jaw, she went in and looked around for her shoes. They weren't there. Resigned to being barefoot, she walked through the den, past the powder room she'd used and into the kitchen.

He was sitting at the bar, long legs hooked around a stool, a cup of coffee in one hand and the morning newspaper in the other. He looked up when she entered. "I found some tea, and the water is boiling."

"I'll drink water."

"Because tea is what you share with friends, right?" He put down the newspaper and got up, opening a cabinet door and taking down a water glass, which he filled from the faucet. "I hope you don't expect designer water, because I think it's a huge waste of money."

She shrugged. "Water's water."

He gave her the glass, then lifted his brows—both of them. "Cereal or bagel?"

"Bagel."

"Good choice."

Only then did she notice a small plate with his own bagel

on it, revealed when he'd put down the paper. Maybe it was petty of her, but she wished they weren't eating the same thing. She didn't wish it enough to eat cereal, though.

He put a plain bagel in the toaster and got the cream cheese from the refrigerator. While the bagel was toasting, she looked around. "What time is it? I haven't seen a clock anywhere."

"It's ten fifty-seven," he said, without turning around. "And I don't own a clock—well, except for the one on the oven behind you. And maybe one on the microwave. Yeah, I guess a microwave has to have a clock nowadays."

She looked behind her. The oven clock was digital, showing ten fifty-seven in blue numbers. The only thing was, she'd been blocking the oven from his view—and he hadn't turned around, anyway. He must have looked while he was getting the cream cheese.

"My cell phone has the time, too," he continued. "And my computers and cars have clocks. So I guess I do own clocks, but I don't have just *a* clock. All of them are attached to something else."

"If small talk is supposed to make me relax and forget I hate you, it isn't working."

"I didn't think it would." He glanced up, the green in his eyes so intense she almost fell back a step. "I needed to know if you were Ansara, and to get the answer I was rough in the way I handled you. I apologize."

Frustration boiled in her. Half of what he said made no sense to her at all, and she was tired of it. "Just who the hell are these Aunt Sarah people, and where the hell are my *shoes?*"

## ELEVEN

"The answer to the second part of your question is easy. I threw them away."

"Great," she muttered, looking down at her bare feet, toes curling on the cold stone tiles.

"I ordered a pair for you from Macy's. One of my employees is on the way with them."

Lorna frowned. She didn't like accepting anything from anyone, and she especially didn't like accepting anything from *him*—but it seemed she was having to do a lot of it no matter how she felt. On the other hand, he had thrown away her shoes and destroyed her blouse, so replacing them was the least he could do.

"And the Aunt Sarah people?" She knew he'd said "Ansara"—not that *that* made any more sense to her—but she hoped mangling the word would annoy him.

"That's a longer explanation. But after last night, you're

entitled to hear it." A little *ding* sounded, and the toaster spat up the bagel. Using the knife he'd got to spread the cream cheese, he flipped the two bagel halves out of the toaster slot and onto a small plate, then passed knife, plate and cream cheese to her.

She took the bar stool farthest from him and spread cream cheese on one slice of bagel. "So let's hear it," she said curtly.

"There are a few other things I'd like to get cleared out of the way. First——" He reached into the front pocket of his jeans, pulled out a wad of bills and slid them in front of her.

Lorna looked down. Her license was tucked amid the bills. "My money!" she said, grabbing both and putting them in her own pockets.

"*My* money, don't you mean?" he asked grimly, but he hadn't insisted on keeping it. "And don't tell me again that you didn't cheat, because I know you did. I'm just not sure even *you* know you cheated, or how you're doing it."

She focused her attention on her bagel, her expression shutting down. He was going off into *woo-woo* land again, but she didn't have to travel with him. "I didn't cheat," she said obstinately, because he'd told her not to.

"You don't know—— Hold on, my cell phone's vibrating." He pulled a small cell from his pocket, flipped it open and said, "Raintree... Yeah. I'll ask her." He looked at Lorna and said, "How much did you say your new shoes cost?"

"One twenty-eight ninety," she replied automatically, and took a bite of the bagel.

He flipped the phone shut and slid it back into his pocket.

After a few seconds the silence in the room made her look up. His eyes were such a brilliant green, they looked as if they were glowing. "There wasn't a call on my cell," he said.

"Then why did you ask——" She stopped, abruptly realizing what she'd said when he'd asked about the shoes, and what little color she'd regained washed out of her face. She opened her mouth to tell him that he must have mentioned the price of the shoes to her, then shut it again, because she knew he hadn't. She had a cold, sick feeling in the pit of her stomach, almost the same feeling she had every morning when she woke up. "I'm not a weirdo," she said in a thin, flat voice.

"The term is 'gifted.' You're gifted. I just proved it to you. I didn't need any proof, because I already knew. I'm even more gifted than you are."

"You're crazy, is what you are."

"I'm mildly empathic, just enough that I can read people very well, especially if I touch them, which is why I always shake hands when I go into a business meeting," he said, speaking over her as if she hadn't interrupted. "As you know very well, using just my mind, I can compel people to do things against their wishes. That's a new one on me, but what the hell. We *are* close to the summer solstice. That, added to the fire, probably triggered it. I can do a bunch of different things, but most of all, I'm a Class A Number One Fire-Master."

"Which means what?" she asked sarcastically, to cover the fact that she was shaken to the core. "That you moonlight at the circus as a fire-eater?"

He held out his hand, palm up, and a lovely little blue flame burst to life in the middle of his hand. He casually blew it out. "Can't do that for very long," he said, "or it burns."

"That's just a trick. Stunt people do that in movies all——"

Her bagel caught on fire.

She stared at it, frozen, as the thick bread burned and smoked. He picked up the plate and flicked the burning bagel into the sink, then ran water on it. "Don't want the fire alarm to go off," he explained, and slid the plate, with the other half of bagel on it, back in front of her.

Behind him, a candle flared to life. "I keep a lot of candles around," he said. "They're my equivalent of a canary in a coal mine."

A thought grew and grew until she couldn't hold it back. "You set the casino on fire!" she said in horror.

He shook his head as he slid back onto his stool and picked up his coffee. "My control is better than that, even this close to the solstice. It wasn't my fire."

"So you say. If you're a Class A Number One hotshot Fire-Master, why didn't you put it out?"

"That's the same question I've been asking myself."

"And the answer is...?"

"I don't know."

"Wow, that's enlightening."

His brilliant grin flashed across his face. "Has anyone ever told you you're a smart-ass?"

She barely kept herself from flinching back in automatic response. Yeah, she'd heard the comment before—many times, and always accompanied by, or even preceded by, a slap.

She didn't look up to see if he'd noted anything strange about her response, but concentrated on putting cream cheese on the remaining half of her bagel.

"Since I had never done mind control before last night, it's possible I drained myself of energy," he continued after a moment. She still refused to look up, but she could feel the intensity of his gaze on her face. "I didn't feel tired. Everything felt normal, but until I explore the parameters, I won't know what the effects of mind control are. Maybe I wasn't concentrating as much as I should have been. Maybe my attention was splintered. Hell, I *know* it was splintered. There were a lot of unusual factors last night."

"You honestly think you could have put out that fire?"

"I know I could have—normally. The fire marshal would have thought the sprinkler system did a great job. Instead—"

"Instead, you dragged me into the middle of a four-alarm fire and nearly killed both of us!"

"Are you burned?" he asked, sipping his coffee.

"No," she said grudgingly.

"Suffering from smoke inhalation?"

"No, damn it!"

"Don't you think you should have at least a few singed strands of hair?"

He was only saying everything she'd thought herself. She didn't understand what had happened during the fire, and she didn't understand anything that had happened since then. Desperately, she wanted to skate over the surface of everything, pretend nothing weird was going on, and leave this house with the pretense still intact, but he wasn't going to let that happen. She could feel his determination, like a force field emanating from him.

No! she told herself in despair. No force field, no emanating. Nothing like that.

"I threw a shield of protection around us. Then at the end, when I was using all your power combined with mine to beat back the fire, the shield solidified a bit. You saw it. I saw it. It shimmered, like a—"

"Soap bubble," she whispered.

"Ah," he said softly, after a moment of thought. "So that's what triggered your memory."

"Do you have any idea how **much that** *hurt,* what you did?"

"Taking over your power? **No, I** don't know, but I can imagine."

"No," she said flatly. "You can't." The pain had been beyond any true description. If she said it had felt as if an anvil had fallen on her head, that would be an understatement.

"Again, I'm sorry. I had no choice. It was either that, or we were both going to die, along with the people still evacuating the hotel."

"You have a way of apologizing that says you'd do the same thing again if the situation arose, so it's really hard to believe the 'sorry' part."

"That's because you're not only a precog, though an untrained one, you're also very sensitive to the paranormal energy around you."

Meaning he *would* do the same thing again, in the same circumstances. At least he wasn't a hypocrite.

"Yesterday, in my office," he continued, "you were reacting to energies you wouldn't have sensed at all if you weren't gifted."

"I thought you were evil," she said, and savagely bit into the bagel. "Nothing you've done since has changed my mind."

"Because you turned me on?" he asked softly. "I took one look at you, and every candle in the room lit up. I'm not usually that out of control, but I had to concentrate to rein everything in. Then I kept looking at you and thinking about having sex, and damned if you didn't hook into the fantasy."

Oh, God, he'd known *that?* She felt her face burn, and she turned her embarrassment into anger. "Are you coming on to me?" she asked incredulously. "Do you actually have the *nerve* to think I'd let you touch me with a ten-foot pole after what you did to me last night?"

"It isn't *that* long," he said, smiling a little.

Well, she'd walked into that one. She slapped the bagel onto the plate and slid off the stool. "I don't want to be in the same room with you. After I leave here, I never want to see your face again. You can take your tacky little fantasy and shove it, Raintree!"

"Dante," he corrected, as if she hadn't all but told him to drop dead. "And that brings us to the Ansara. I was looking for a birthmark. All Ansara have a blue crescent moon some-where on their backs."

She was so angry that a red mist fogged her vision. "And while you were looking for this birthmark on my *back* you decided to check out my ass, too, huh?"

"It's a fine ass, well worth checking out. But, no, I always intended to check it out. 'Back' is imprecise. Technically, 'back' could go from the top of your head all the way down to your heels. I've seen it below the waist before, and in the histories there are reports of, in rare cases, the birthmark being on the ass cheek. Given the seriousness of the fire, and the fact that I couldn't put it out, I had to make sure you hadn't been hin-dering me."

"Hindering you how?" she cried, not at all mollified by his explanation.

"If you had also been a fire-master, you could have been feeding the fire while I was trying to put it out. I've never seen a fire I couldn't control—until last night."

"But you said yourself you'd never used mind control before, so you don't know how it affected you! Why automatically assume I had to be one of these Ansara?"

"I didn't. I'm well aware of all the variables. I still had to eliminate the possibility that you might be Ansara."

"If you're so good at reading people when you touch them, then you should have known I wasn't," she charged.

"Very good," he acknowledged, as if he were a teacher and she his star pupil. "But Ansara are trained from birth to manage their gifts and to protect themselves, just as Raintree are. A powerful Ansara could conceivably have constructed a shield that I wouldn't be able to detect. Like I said, my empath abilities are mild."

She felt as if she were about to explode with frustration. "If I'd had one of these shields, you idiot, you wouldn't have been able to brain-rape me!"

He drummed his fingers lightly on top of the bar, studying her with narrowed eyes. "I really, *really* don't like that term."

"Tough. I really, *really* didn't like the brain-rape itself." She threw the words at him like knives and hoped they buried themselves deep in his flesh.

He considered that, then nodded. "Fair enough. Back to the subject of shields. You have them, but not the kind I'm talking about. The kind you have develop naturally, from life. You shield your emotions. I'm talking about a mental shield that's deliberately constructed to hide a part of your brain's energy. As for keeping me out—honey, there's only one other person, at least that I know of, who could possibly have blocked me from taking over his mind, and you aren't him."

"Ooooh, you're so scary-powerful then, huh?"

Slowly he nodded. "Yep."

"Then why aren't you, like, King of the World or something?"

"I'm king of the Raintree," he said, getting up and putting his plate in the dishwasher. "That's good enough for me."

Strange, but of all the really weird things he'd said to her, this struck her as the most unbelievable. She buried her head in her hands, wishing this day was over. She wanted to forget she'd ever met him. He was obviously a lunatic. No—she couldn't comfort herself with that delusion. She had been through fire with him, quite literally. He could do things she hadn't thought were possible. So maybe—just maybe—he really was some sort of leader, though "king" was stretching things a bit far.

"Okay, I'll bite," she said wearily. "Who are the Raintree, and who are the Ansara? Is this like two different countries but inhabited only by weirdos?"

His lips twitched as if he wanted to laugh. "Gifted. *Gifted*. We're two different clans—warring clans, if you want the bottom line. The enmity goes back thousands of years."

"You're the weirdo equivalent of the Hatfields and the McCoys?"

He did laugh then, white teeth flashing. "I've never thought of it that way, but…yeah. In a way. Except what's between the Raintree and the Ansara isn't a feud, it's a war. There's a difference."

"Between a war and a feud, yeah. But what's the difference between the Raintree clan and the Ansara clan?"

"An entire way of looking at life, I guess. They use their gifts to cheat, to do harm, for their personal gain. Raintree look at their abilities as true gifts and try to use them accordingly."

"You're the guys with the white hats."

"Within the spectrum of human nature—yes. Common sense tells me some Raintree aren't that far separated from some Ansara when it comes to their attitudes. But if they want to remain in the Raintree clan, they'll do as I order."

"So all the Ansara might not be totally bad, but if they want to stay in *their* clan, with their friends and families, they have to do as the Ansara king orders."

He dipped his head in acknowledgment. "That's about it."

"You admit you might be more alike than you're different."

"In some ways. In one big way, we're poles apart."

"Which is?"

"From the very beginning, if a Raintree and an Ansara cross-bred, the Ansara killed the child. No exceptions."

Lorna rubbed her forehead, which was beginning to ache again. Yeah, that was bad. Killing innocent children because of their heritage wasn't just an opportunistic outlook, it was bad with a capital *B*. Part of her own life philosophy was that there were some people who didn't deserve to live, and people who hurt children belonged in that group.

"I don't suppose there has been much intermarriage between the clans, has there?"

"Not in centuries. What Raintree would take the chance? Are you finished with that bagel?"

Thrown off track by the prosaic question, Lorna stared down at her bagel. She had eaten maybe half of it. Even though she'd been starving before, the breakfast conversation had effectively killed her appetite. "I guess," she said without interest, passing the plate to him.

He dumped the bagel remnants and put that plate in the dishwasher, too. "You need training," he said. "Your gifts are too strong for you to go around unprotected. An Ansara could use you—"

"Just the way you did?" She didn't even try to keep the bitterness out of her tone.

"Just the way I did," he agreed. "Only they would be feeding the fire instead of fighting it."

As she stood there debating the merits of what he'd said, she realized that gradually she had become more at ease with discussing these "gifts" and that somewhere during the course of the conversation she had been moved from denial to acceptance. Now she saw where he was going with all this, and her old deep-rooted panic bloomed again.

"Oh, no," she said, shaking her head as she backed a few steps away. "I'm not going to let you 'train' me in anything. Do I have 'stupid' engraved on my forehead or something?"

"You're asking for trouble if you don't get some training, and fast."

"Then I'll handle it, just like I always have. Besides, you have your own trouble to handle, don't you?"

"The next few weeks will be tough, but not as tough for me as they will be for the people who lost someone. Another body was pulled out just after dawn. That makes two fatalities." His expression went grim.

"I'm not talking about that. I'm talking about the cops. Something hinky is going on there, because otherwise, why would two detectives be interviewing people before the fire marshal had determined if the fire was arson or accidental?"

The expression in his eyes grew distant as he stared at her. That little detail had escaped his all-knowing, all-seeing gifts, she realized, but if there was one thing a hard life had taught her, it was how the law worked. The detectives shouldn't have been there until it was clear there was something for them to detect, and the fire marshal wouldn't make that determination until sometime today, probably.

"Damn it," he said very softly, and pulled out his phone. "Don't go anywhere. I have some calls to make."

He'd meant that very literally, Lorna discovered when she

tried to leave the kitchen. Her feet stopped working at the threshold.

"Damn you, Raintree!" she snarled, whirling on him.

"Dante," he corrected.

"Damn you, Dante!"

"Much better," he said, and winked at her.

# TWELVE

Dante began making calls, starting with Al Rayburn. Lorna was right: something hinky was going on, and he was pissed that she'd had to point it out to him. He should have thought of that detail himself. Instead of answering the detectives' questions, he should have been asking them his own, such as: What were they doing there? A fire scene wasn't a crime scene unless and until the cause was determined to be arson or at the very least suspicious. Uniformed officers should have been there for crowd control, traffic control, security—a lot of reasons—but not detectives.

He didn't come up with any answers to his questions, but he hadn't expected to. What he was doing now was reversing the flow of information, and that would take time. Now that questions were being asked—by Al, by a friend Dante had at city hall, by one of his own Raintree clan members who liked life a little on the rough side and thus had some interesting contacts—a lot of things would be viewed in a different light.

Whatever was going on, however those two detectives were involved, Dante intended to find out, even if he had to bring in Mercy, whose gift of telepathy was so strong that she had once, when she was ten and he was sixteen, jumped into his head at a very inopportune moment—he'd been with his current girlfriend—and said, "Eww! Gross!" which had so startled him he'd lost his concentration, his erection *and* his girlfriend. Sixteen-year-old girls, he'd learned, didn't deal well with anything they saw as an insult to their general desirability. That was the day when he'd started blocking Mercy from his head, which had infuriated her at the time. She'd even told their parents what he'd been doing, which had resulted in a very long, very serious talk with his father about the importance of being smart, using birth control and taking responsibility for his actions.

Faced with his father's stern assurance that Dante *would* marry any girl he got pregnant and stay married to her for the rest of his life, he had then become immensely more careful. The Raintree Dranir most definitely did *not* have a casual attitude about his heirs. A Raintree, any Raintree, was a genetic dominant; any children would inherit the Raintree gifts. The same was true of the Ansara, which was why the Ansara had immediately killed any child born of a Raintree and Ansara breeding. When two dominant strands blended, anything could be the result—and the result could be dangerous.

Mercy's gift had only gotten stronger as she got older. Dante didn't think her presence would be required, though; the Raintree had other telepaths he could call on. They might not be as strong as Mercy, but then, they wouldn't need to be. Mercy was most comfortable at Sanctuary, the homeplace of the Raintree clan, where she didn't have to almost shut down her gift because of the relentless emotional and mental assault by humans who had no idea how to shield. Occasionally she and Eve, her six-year-old daughter, would visit him or Gideon——Mercy was completely female in her love of shopping, and he and Gideon were always glad to keep Eve the Imp while her mother indulged in some retail therapy——but Mercy was the guardian of the homeplace. Sanctuary was her responsibility, hers to rule, and she loved it. He wouldn't call for her help if he had other options.

The whole time he was making calls, Lorna stood where he'd compelled her to stay, fuming and fussing and growing angrier by the minute, until he expected all that dark red hair to stand straight up from the pressure. He could have released her, at least within the confines of the house, but she would probably use that much freedom to attack him with something. As it was, he had to admit he rather enjoyed her fury and less-than-flattering commentary.

The fact was, he enjoyed *her*.

He'd never before been so charmed——or so touched. When he'd heard that pitiful little whimpering sound she made in her sleep, he'd felt his heart actually clench. What really, really got to him was that it was obvious she knew what sound she'd been making——she probably did it all the time——and yet she resolutely denied it. *Snoring* his ass.

She refused to be a victim. He liked that. Even when something bad happened to her——such as himself, for instance——she furiously rejected any sign of vulnerability, any hint of sympathy, any suggestion that she was, in any way, weaker than King Kong. She didn't bother defending herself; instead she attacked, with a ferocious valiance and sharp tongue, as well as the occasional uppercut.

He'd been rough on her—in more ways than one. Not only had he terrified her, mentally brutalized her, he'd humiliated and embarrassed her by tearing off her clothes and examining her the way he had. If she'd only cooperated... But she hadn't, and he couldn't blame her. Nothing he'd done last night would have inspired trust in her, not that trust appeared to come easily to her in any case. He couldn't even tell himself that he'd never intended her any harm. If the blue crescent birthmark of the Ansara had been on her back—well, her body would never have been found.

The sharpness of his relief at not finding the birthmark had taken him by surprise. He'd wanted to take her in his arms and comfort her, though unless he bound her with a compulsion not to harm him, she would likely have taken his eyeballs out with her fingernails, and as for his other balls—he didn't want to think what she would have done to them. By that time she hadn't wanted anything from him except his absence.

The way she'd been allowed to grow up was a disgrace. She should have been trained in how to control and develop her gifts, trained in how to protect herself. She had the largest pool of raw energy he'd ever seen in a stray, which meant there was enormous potential for her to abuse or to be abused.

Now that he thought about it, her gift probably wasn't pre-cognitive so much as it was claircognitive. She didn't have visions, like his cousin Echo; rather, she simply "knew" things—such as which card would be played next, whether a certain slot machine would pay off, how much her new shoes cost. Why she chose to play at casinos instead of buying a lottery ticket he couldn't say, unless she had instinctively chosen to stay as invisible as possible. Certainly she had the ability to win any amount of money she wanted, since her gift seemed to be slanted toward numbers.

Above all else, two sharp truths stood out:

She annoyed the hell out of him.

And he wanted her.

The two should have negated each other, but they didn't. Even when she annoyed him, which was often, she made him want to laugh. And he not only wanted her physically, he wanted her to accept her own uniqueness, accept him in all his differences, accept his protection, his guidance in learning how to shape and control her gift—all of which she rejected, which circled right back around to annoyance.

The doorbell rang, signaling the arrival of Lorna's shoes. Leaving her fuming, he went to the door, where one of his hotel staff waited, box in hand. "Sorry I'm late, Mr. Raintree," the young man said, wiping sweat from his forehead. "There was a wreck on the interstate that had traffic backed up—"

"No problem," he said, easing the young man's anxiety. "Thanks for bringing this out." Since he was continuing to pay his staff's salaries, he thought they might as well make themselves useful in whatever manner he needed.

He took the shoe box to the kitchen, where Lorna was still rooted to the spot. "Here you go, try them on," he said, handing the box to her.

She glared at him and refused to take it.

Guess he couldn't blame her.

He took the shoes from the box, the wads of tissue paper from the toes, and went down on one knee. He expected her to stubbornly refuse to pick up her foot, but she let him lift it, wipe his hand over her bare sole to remove any grit, and slide the buttery-soft black flat on her foot. He repeated the process with her other foot, then remained on one knee as he looked up at her. "Do they fit? Do they pinch anywhere?"

The shoes were much like her ruined ones, he knew: simple black flats. But that was where the resemblance ended. This pair was made of quality leather, with good arch support and good construction. Her other pair had had paper-thin soles, and the seams had been starting to fray. She'd been carrying over seven thousand dollars in her pocket, and wearing fifteen-dollar shoes. Whatever she was spending all that money on, clothing wasn't it.

"They feel okay," she said grudgingly. "But not a hundred and twenty-eight dollars worth of okay."

He laughed quietly as he rose to his feet and looked down at her face for a moment, charmed all over again by her stubbornness. She was one of those women whose personality made her prettier than she actually was, if one considered only her features. Not that she wasn't pretty; she was. Not flashy, not beautiful, just pleasant to look at. It was that attitude, that sarcastic, sassy mouth, the damn-you-to-hell-and-back eyes, that made her sparkle with vitality. The one way Lorna Clay would never be described was *restful*.

He should release her from the compulsion that kept her here, but if he did, she would leave—not just this house, but Reno. He knew it with a certainty that chilled him.

Dante functioned very well in the normal, human world, but he was the Raintree Dranir, and within his realm, he was obeyed. He had been Dranir for seventeen years now, since he was twenty, but even before that, he hadn't led an ordinary life. He was of the Raintree Royal Family. He had been Prince, Heir Apparent and then Dranir.

"No" wasn't a word he heard very often, nor did he care to hear it from Lorna.

"You may go anywhere you wish within this house," he said, and silently added a proviso that in case of danger, the compulsion was ended. If the house caught fire, he wanted her to be able to escape. After last night, such things were very much on his mind.

"Why can't I leave?" Her hazel green eyes were snapping with ire, but at least she didn't punch, pinch or kick him.

"Because you'll run."

She didn't deny it, instead narrowed her eyes at him. "So? I'm not wanted for any crimes."

"*So* I feel responsible for you. There's a lot you need to know about your gifts, and I can teach you." That was as good a reason as any, and sounded logical.

"I don't——" She started to deny she had any gifts, but stopped and drew a deep breath. There was no point in denying the obvious. When he had first broached the subject to her, in his office, her denial had been immediate and absolute. At least now she was beginning to accept what she was.

How had she come to so adamantly deny everything she was? He suspected he knew, but unless she was willing to talk about it, he wouldn't pry.

After a moment she said obstinately, "I'm responsible for myself. I don't want or need your charity."

"Charity, no. Knowledge, yes. I think I was wrong when I said you're precognitive." He watched relief flare on her face, then immediately die when he continued. "I think you may be claircognitive. Have you ever even heard of that?"

"No."

"How about *el-sike?*"

"That's an Arab name."

He grinned. *El-sike* was pronounced *el-see-kay*—and she was right, it did sound Arab. "It's a form of storm control. My brother Gideon has that gift. He can call lightning to him."

She gave him a pitying look. "It sounds like a form of brain damage. What fool wants to be near lightning?"

"Gideon. He feeds off electricity. He also has electrical psychokinesis, which in a nutshell means he plays hell with electronics. He explodes streetlights. He fries computers. It isn't safe for him to fly unless I send him a shielding charm."

Her interest was caught, however reluctantly. He saw the quicksilver gleam of it in her eyes. "Why doesn't he make his own shielding charms?"

"That's kind of along the same lines of precogs not being able to see their own futures. Only those in the royal family can gift charms, but never for themselves. He's a cop, a homicide detective, so I keep him stocked in protection charms, and if he has to fly, I send him a charm that shields his electrical energy so he won't fry all the plane's computers."

"Electrical psychokinesis," she said slowly, trying out the words. "Sounds kinky."

"So I've heard," he said dryly. He'd also heard that Gideon sometimes glowed after sex—or maybe that was before. Or during. Some things a brother just didn't ask too many questions about. But if Lorna was at last interested in learning about the whole range of paranormal abilities, he didn't mind using some of the more exotic gifts to keep her intrigued.

"Tell you what," he said, as if he'd just thought of the idea, when in fact he'd been considering something of the sort all morning. "Why don't you agree to a short trial period—say, a week—and let me teach you some basic stuff to protect yourself? You're so sensitive to every passing wave of energy that I'm surprised you're able to go out in public. I can also set up some simple tests, get a ballpark idea of how gifted you are in different areas."

He saw the instant repudiation of that idea in her expression, a quick flash, then her curiosity rose to counter it. Almost immediately, caution followed; she didn't easily put herself in anyone's hands. "What would I have to do?" she asked warily.

"You don't *have* to do anything. If you're absolutely dead set against the idea of learning more, then I'm not going to tie you to a chair and make you read lessons. But since you're going to be here for a few days anyway, you might as well use the time to learn something about yourself."

"I'll need my clothes," she said, which was as close to capitulation as he was likely to hear from her.

"Give me your address and I'll have them brought here."

"This is just for a few days. After that, I want your word you'll lift this stupid compulsion thing and let me go."

Dante considered that. He was the Dranir; he didn't, couldn't, give his word lightly. Finally he said, "After a week, I'll consider it. You're smart, you can learn a lot in a week. But I can't make a definite promise."

# THIRTEEN

"What, exactly, went wrong?"

Cael Ansara's tone was pleasant and even, which didn't fool Ruben McWilliams at all. Cousin or not, there had always been something about Cael that made Ruben tread very warily around him. When Cael was at his most pleasant, that was when it paid to be extra cautious. Ruben didn't like the son of a bitch, but there you go, rebellion made for strange bedfellows.

His intuition had told him to delay contacting Cael, so he hadn't called last night; instead, he'd put people in the field, asking questions, and his gamble had paid off—or at least provided an interesting variable. He didn't yet know exactly what they'd discovered, only that they'd found *something*.

"We don't know—not exactly. Everything went perfectly from our end. Elyn was connected to me, Stoffel and Pier, drawing our power and feeding the fire. She said they had

Raintree overmatched, that he was losing ground—and fast. Then…something happened. It's possible he saw he couldn't handle the fire and retreated. Or he's more powerful than we thought."

Cael was silent, and Ruben shifted uneasily on the motel bed. He'd expected Cael to leap on the juicy possibility that the mighty Dante Raintree had panicked and run from a fire, but as usual, Cael was unpredictable.

"What does Elyn say?" Cael finally asked. "If Raintree ran, if he stopped trying to fight the fire, without his resistance it would have flashed over. She'd have known that, right? She'd have felt the surge."

"She doesn't know." He and Elyn had discussed the events from beginning to end, trying to pinpoint what had gone wrong. She *should* have felt a surge, if one had happened—but she not only hadn't felt a surge, she hadn't felt the retreat when the fire department beat back the flames. There *had* to have been some sort of interference, but they were at a loss to explain it.

"Doesn't know? How can she not know? She's a Fire-Master, and that was her flame. She should know everything about it from conception on."

Cael's tone was sharp, but no sharper than their own tones had been when he and Elyn had dissected the events. Elyn hadn't wanted the finger of blame pointed at her, of course, but she'd been truly perplexed. "All she knows is, just as she was drawing the fire into the hotel, she lost touch with it. She could tell it was still there, but she didn't know what it was doing." He paused. "She's telling the truth. I was linked to her. I could feel her surprise. She thinks there had to be some sort of interference, maybe a protective shield."

"She's making excuses. Shields like that exist only at home-place. We've never detected anything like that on any of the other Raintree properties."

"I agree. Not about Elyn making excuses, but about the impossibility of there being a shield. She simply asked. I told her, no, I'd have known if one were there."

"Where were the other Raintree?"

"They were all accounted for." None of the other Raintree had been close enough for their Dranir to link to them and use their power to boost his own, as Elyn had done by linking to him and the others. They'd pulled in people to follow the various Raintree clan—members in Reno. There were only eight, not counting the Dranir, and none of them had been close to the Inferno.

"So, despite all your assurances to me, you failed, and you don't know why."

"Not yet." Ruben ever so slightly stressed the *yet*. "There's one other possibility. Another person, a woman, was with Raintree. None of us saw them being brought out because the fire engines blocked our view, but we've been posing as insurance adjusters and asking questions." They hadn't raised a single eyebrow; insurance adjusters were already swarming, and not just the ones representing Raintree's insurance provider. Multiple vehicles had been damaged. Casino patrons had lost personal property. There had been injuries, and two deaths. Add the personal injury lawyers to the mix, and there were a lot of people asking a lot of questions; no one noticed a few more people *or* questions, and no one checked credentials.

"What's her name?"

"Lorna Clay. One of the medics got her name and address.

She wasn't registered at the hotel, and the address on the paperwork was in Missouri. It isn't valid. I've already checked."

"Go on."

"She was evidently with Raintree from the beginning, in his office in the hotel, because they evacuated the building together. They were in the west stairwell with a lot of other people. He directed everyone else out, through the parking deck, but he and this woman went in the other direction. Several things are suspicious. One, she wasn't burned—at all. Two, neither was Raintree."

"Protective bubble. Judah can construct them, too." Cael's tone went flat when he said Judah's name—Judah was his *legitimate* half brother and the Ansara Dranir. Envy of Judah, bitterness that he was the Dranir instead of Cael, had eaten at Cael all his life.

Ruben was impressed by the bubble. Smoke? Smoke had a physical presence; any Fire-Master could shield from smoke. But heat was a different entity, part of the very air. Fire-Masters, even royal ones, still had to breathe. To somehow separate the heat from the air, to bring in one but hold the other at bay, was a feat that went way beyond controlling fire.

"The woman," Cael prompted sharply, pulling Ruben from his silent admiration.

"I've seen copies of the statement she gave afterward. It matches his, and neither is possible, given what we know of the timetable. I estimate he was engaged with the fire for at least half an hour." That was an eternity, in terms of survival.

"He should have been overwhelmed. He should have spent so much energy trying to control the fire that he couldn't maintain the bubble. He's the hero type," Cael said contemptuously. "He'd sacrifice himself to save the people in the hotel.

*This should have worked*. His people wouldn't have been suspicious. They would have expected him to do the brave and honorable thing. The woman has to be the key. She has to be gifted. He linked with her, and she fed him power."

"She isn't Raintree," said Ruben. "She has to be a stray, but they aren't that powerful. If there had been several of them, maybe there would have been enough energy for him to hold back the fire." He doubted it, though. After all, there had been four powerful Ansara, linked together, feeding it. As powerful as Dante undoubtedly was, adding the power of one stray, even a strong one, would be like adding a cup of water to a full bathtub.

"Follow your own logic," Cael said sharply. "Strays aren't that powerful, therefore she can't be a stray."

"She isn't Raintree," Ruben insisted.

"Or she isn't *official* Raintree." Cael didn't use the word "illegitimate." The old Dranir had recognized him as his son, but that hadn't given Cael precedence over Judah, even though he was the elder. The injustice had always eaten at him, like a corrosive acid. Everyone around Cael had learned never to suggest that maybe Judah was Dranir because of his power, not his birthright.

"She'd have to be of the royal bloodline to have enough power for him to hold the fire for that long against four of us," said Ruben dubiously, because that was impossible. The birth of a royal was taken far too seriously for one to go unnoticed. They were simply too powerful.

"So maybe she is. Even if the split occurred a thousand years ago, the inherited power would be undiminished."

As genetic dominants, even if a member of one of the clans bred with a human—which they often did—the offspring were completely either Ansara or Raintree. The royal families of both clans were the most powerful of the gifted, which was how they'd become royal in the first place; as dominants, their power was passed down intact. To Ruben's way of thinking, that only reinforced his argument that, no matter what, a royal birth wouldn't go unnoticed for any length of time, certainly not for a millennium.

"Regardless of what she is, where is she now?"

"At his house. He took her there last night, and she's still there."

Cael was silent, so Ruben simply waited while his cousin ran that through his convoluted brain.

"Okay," Cael said abruptly. "She has to be the key. Wherever it comes from, her power is strong enough that he held the four of you to a draw. But that's in the past. You can't use fire again without the bastard getting suspicious, so you'll have to think of something else that'll either look accidental or can't be linked to us. I don't care how you do it, just do it. The next time I hear your voice, you'd better be telling me that Dante Raintree is dead. And while you're at it, kill the woman, too."

Cael slammed down the phone. Ruben replaced the receiver more slowly, then pinched the bridge of his nose. Tactically, killing the royal Raintrees first was smart. If you cut off the head of a snake, taking care of the body was easy. The comparison wasn't completely accurate, because any Raintree was a force to be reckoned with, but so were the Ansara. With the royals all dead, the advantage would be theirs and the outcome inevitable.

The mistake they'd made two hundred years ago was in not taking care of the royal family first, a mistake that had had disastrous results. As a clan, the Ansara had almost been destroyed. The survivors had been banished to their Caribbean island, where most of them remained. But they had used those two hundred years to secretly rebuild in strength, and now they were strong enough to once more engage their enemy. Cael thought so, anyway, and so did Ruben. Only Judah had held them back, preaching caution. Judah was a *banker,* for God's sake; what did he know about taking risks?

Discontent in the Ansara ranks had been growing for years, and it had reached the crisis point. The Raintree had to die, and so did Judah. Cael would never let him live, even in exile.

Ruben's power was substantial. Because of that, and because he was Cael's cousin, he'd been given the task of eliminating the most powerful Raintree of all—a task made more difficult because Cael insisted the death look accidental. The last thing he wanted was all the Raintree swarming to the homeplace to protect it. The power of Sanctuary was almost mystical. How much of it was real and how much of it was perceived, Ruben didn't know and didn't care.

The plan was simple: kill the royals, breach the protective shields around Sanctuary and take the homeplace. After that, the rest of the Raintree would be considerably weakened. Destroying them would be child's play.

Not destroying the Ansara homeplace two centuries ago, not destroying every member of the clan, was the mistake the Raintree had made. The Ansara wouldn't return the favor.

Ruben sat for a long time, deep in thought. Getting to Raintree would be easier if he was distracted. He and the woman, Lorna Clay, were evidently lovers; otherwise, why take her home with him? She would be the easier of the two to take out, anyway—and if she were obviously the target rather than Raintree, that wouldn't raise the clan's alarm.

Cael's idea had been a good one: kill the woman.

# FOURTEEN

*Monday afternoon*

"What happens if you die?" Lorna asked him, scowling as, car keys in hand, he opened the door to the garage. "What if you have a blowout and drive off the side of the mountain? What if you have a pulmonary embolism? What if a chicken-hauler has brake failure and flattens that little roller skate you call a car? Am I stuck here? Does your little curse, or whatever, hold me here even if you're dead or unconscious?"

Dante paused halfway out the door, looking back at her with a half amused, half disbelieving expression. "Chicken-hauler? Can't you think of a more dignified way for me to die?"

She sniffed. "Dead is dead. What would you care?" Then something occurred to her, something that made her very uneasy. "Uh—you *can* die, can't you?" What if this situation was even weirder than she'd thought? What if, on the *woo-woo* scale of one to ten, he was a thirteen?

He laughed outright. "Now I have to wonder if you're planning to kill me."

"It's a thought," she said bluntly. "Well?"

He leaned against the door frame, negligent and relaxed, and so damned sexy she almost had to look away. She worked hard to ignore her physical response to him, and most of the time she succeeded, but sometimes, as now, his green eyes seemed to almost glow, and in her imagination she could feel the hard, muscled framework of his body against her once more. The fact that, twice now, she'd felt his erection against her when he was holding her only made her struggle that much more difficult. Mutual sexual desire was a potent magnet, but just because she felt the pull of attraction, that didn't mean she should act on it. Sometimes she wanted to run a traffic light, too, because it was there, because she didn't want to stop, because she could—but she never did, because doing so would be stupid. Having sex with Dante Raintree would fall into the same category: stupid.

"I'm as mortal as you—almost. Thank God. As much as mortality sucks, immortality would be even worse."

Lorna took a step back. "What do you mean, *almost?*"

"That's another conversation, and one I don't have time for right now. To answer your other question, I don't know. Maybe, maybe not."

She was almost swallowed by outrage. "What? *What?* You don't know whether or not I'll be stuck here if something happens to you, but you're going to go off and leave me here anyway?"

He gave it a brief thought, said, "Yeah," and went out the door.

Lorna leaped and caught the door before it closed. "Don't leave me here! Please." She hated to beg, and she hated him for making her beg, but she was suddenly alarmed beyond reason by the thought of being stuck here for the rest of her life.

He got into the Jaguar, called, "You'll be okay," and then the clatter of the garage door rising drowned out anything else she might have said. Furious, she slammed the kitchen door and, in a fit of pique, turned both the lock on the handle and the dead bolt. Locking him out of his own house was useless, since he had his keys with him, but the annoyance value was worth it.

She heard the Jag backing out; then the garage door began coming down.

Damn him, damn him, *damn him!* He'd really gone off and left her stranded here. No, not stranded—*chained.*

Her clothes had been delivered earlier, and she'd changed out of the ruined pants—and out of his too-big silk shirt—so he wouldn't have had to wait for her to get ready or anything. He had no reason for leaving her here, given that he could easily prevent her from escaping with one of his damnable mind commands.

Impotently, she glared around the kitchen. Being a drainer—king—whatever the hell he'd said—had made him too big for his britches. He pretty much did whatever he felt like doing, without worrying about what others wanted. It was obvious he'd never been married and likely never would be, because any woman worth her salt would—

Salt.

She looked around the kitchen and spotted the big stainless steel salt and pepper shakers sitting by the cooktop. She began opening doors until she found the pantry—and a very satisfy-ing supply of salt.

She'd noticed he put a spoonful of sugar in his coffee. Now she very carefully poured the salt out of the salt shaker, replaced it with sugar from the sugar bowl, then put the salt in the sugar bowl. He wouldn't much enjoy that first cup of coffee in the morning, and anything he salted would taste really off.

Then she got creative.

About an hour after he left, the phone rang. Lorna looked at the caller ID but didn't bother answering; she wasn't his sec-retary. Whoever was calling didn't leave a message.

She explored the house—well, searched the house. It was a big house for just one person. She had no frame of reference for estimating the square footage, but she counted six bedrooms and seven and a half baths. His bedroom took up the entire top floor, a vast expanse that covered more floor space than most families of four lived in. It was very much a man's room, with steel blue and light olive-green tones dominating, but here and there—in the artwork, in an unexpected deco-rative bowl, in a cushion—were splashes of deep, rich red.

There was a separate sitting area, with a big-screen televi-sion that popped out of a cabinet when a button was pushed and sank back into hiding afterward. She knew, because she found the remote and punched all the buttons, just to see what they would do. There was a wet bar with a small refrigerator and a coffeemaker in case he didn't want to bother going down-stairs to make his coffee or get something to eat. She'd replaced the sugar with salt there, too—*and* mixed dirt from the potted plants in with his coffee.

Then she sat in the middle of his king-size bed, on a mattress that felt like a dream, and thought.

As big and comfortable as the house was, it wasn't what she would call a mansion. It wasn't ostentatious. He liked his creature comforts, but the house still looked like a place to be lived in, rather than a showcase.

She knew he had money, and a lot of it—enough to afford a house ten times the size of this one. Throw in the fact that he lived here alone, with no daily staff to take care of him and his home, and she had to draw the obvious conclusion that his privacy was more important to him than being pampered. So why was he forcing her to stay here?

He'd said he felt responsible for her, but he could feel that way wherever she stayed, and because of that damned newly discovered talent of his for making people do whatever he wanted, she couldn't have left if he'd commanded her to stay. Maybe he was interested in her untrained "power" and wanted to see what he could make of it just to satisfy his curiosity. Again, she didn't have to stay here for him to give her lessons or conduct a few experiments on her.

He wanted to have sex with her, so maybe that was what motivated him. He could compel her to come to him, to have sex, but he wasn't a rapist. He was possibly a lunatic, definitely a bully, but he wasn't a rapist. He wanted her to be willing, truly willing. So was he keeping her here in order to seduce her? He couldn't do that if he went off somewhere and left her here, not to mention doing so made her mad at him.

Somehow the sex angle didn't feel right, either. If he wanted to get her in bed, making her a prisoner wasn't the right way to win her over. Not only that, she wasn't a femme fatale; she simply couldn't see anyone going to such extraordinary lengths to have sex with her.

He had to have another reason, but damned if she could

figure out what it was. And until she knew…well, there wasn't anything she could do, regardless. Unless she could somehow knock him out and escape, she was stuck here until he was ready to let her leave.

Last night, from the moment the gorilla had "escorted" her away from the blackjack table and manhandled her up to Raintree's office, had been a pure nightmare. One shock had followed so closely on the heels of another—each somehow worse than the one before—that she felt as if she'd lost touch with reality somewhere along the way.

Yesterday at this time she had been anonymous, and she liked it that way. Oh, people would come up and talk to her, the way they did to winners, and she was okay with that, but being alone was okay, too. In fact, being alone was better than okay; it was *safe*.

Raintree didn't know what he was asking of her, staying here, learning how to be "gifted." Not that he was asking—he wasn't giving her a choice.

He'd tricked her into admitting that she had a certain talent with numbers, but he didn't know how nauseated she got at the thought of coming out of the paranormal closet. She would rather remain a metaphysical garment bag, hanging in the very back.

He had grown up in an underground culture where paranormal talents were the norm, where they were encouraged, celebrated, trained. He had grown up a *prince*, for God's sake. A prince of weird, but a prince nonetheless. He had no idea what it had been like growing up in slums, skinny and unwanted and different. There hadn't been a father in her picture, just an endless parade of her mother's "boyfriends." He'd never been slapped away from the table, literally slapped out of her chair, for saying anything her mother could construe as weird.

As a child, she hadn't understood why what she said was weird. What was so wrong with saying the bus her mother took across town to her job in a bar would be six minutes and twenty-three seconds late? She had thought her mother would want to know. Instead she'd been backhanded out of her seat.

Numbers were her thing. If anything had a number in it, she knew what that number was. She remembered starting first grade—no kindergarten for her, her mother had said kindergarten was a stupid-ass waste of time—and the relief she'd felt when someone finally explained numbers to her, as if a huge part of herself had finally clicked into place. Now she had names for the shapes, meanings for the names. All her life she'd been fascinated with numbers, whether they were on a house, a billboard, a taxicab or anywhere else, but it was as if they were a foreign language she couldn't grasp. Odd, to have such an affinity for them but no understanding. She had thought she was as stupid as her mother had told her she was, until she'd gone to school and found the key.

By the time she was ten, her mother had been deep into booze and drugs, and the slaps had progressed to almost daily beatings. If her mother staggered in at night and decided she didn't like something Lorna had done that day or the day before—or the week before, it didn't matter—she would grab whatever was handy and lay into Lorna wherever she was. A lot of times Lorna's transition from sleep to wakefulness had been a blow—to her face, her head, wherever her mother could hit her. She had learned to sleep in a state of quiet terror.

Whenever she thought of her childhood, what she remembered most was cold and darkness and fear. She had been afraid her mother would kill her, and even more afraid her mother might not bother to come home some night. If there was one thing Lorna knew beyond doubt, it was that her mother hadn't wanted her before she was born and sure as hell didn't want her *after*. She knew because that had been the background music of her life.

She had learned to hide what numbers meant to her. The only time she'd ever told anyone—*ever*—had been in the ninth grade, when she had developed a crush on a boy in her class. He'd been sweet, a little shy, not one of the popular kids. His parents were very religious, and he was never allowed to attend any school parties, or learn how to dance, anything like that, which was okay with Lorna, because she never did any of that stuff, either.

They had talked a lot, held hands some, kissed a little. Then Lorna, summoning up the nerve, had shared her deepest secret with him: sometimes she knew things before they happened.

She still remembered the look of absolute disgust that had come over his face. "Satan!" he'd spat at her, and then he'd never spoken to her again. At least he hadn't told anyone, but that was probably because he didn't seem to have any buddies he *could* tell.

She'd been sixteen when her mother really did walk out and not bothered to come back. Lorna had come home from school—"home" changed locations fairly often, usually when rent was overdue—to find her mother's stuff cleared out, the locks changed and her own meager collection of clothes dumped in the trash.

Without a place to live, she had done the only thing she could do: she had contacted the city officials herself and entered the foster system.

Living in foster homes for two years hadn't been great, but it hadn't been as bad as her life had been before. At least she got to finish high school. None of her foster parents had beaten or abused her. None of them ever seemed to like her very much, either, but then, her mother had told her she wasn't likeable.

She coped. After she was eighteen, she was out of the system and on her own. In the thirteen years since then—for her entire life, actually—she had done what she could to stay below the radar, to avoid being noticed, to never, ever be a victim. No one could reject her if she didn't offer herself.

She had stumbled into gambling in a small way, in a little casino on the Seminole reservation in Florida. She had won, not a whole lot, but a couple hundred dollars meant a lot to her. Later on she'd gone in some of the casinos on the Mississippi River and won some more. Small casinos were everywhere. She'd gone to Atlantic City but hadn't liked it. Las Vegas was okay, but too *too*: too much neon, too many people, too hot, too gaudy. Reno suited her better. Smaller, but not too small. Better climate. Eight years after that first small win in Florida, she regularly won five to ten thousand dollars a week.

That kind of money was a burden, because she couldn't bring herself to spend much more than she had always spent. She didn't go hungry now, or cold. She had a car if she wanted to pack up and leave, but never a new one. She had bank accounts all over the place, plus she usually carried a lot of cash—dangerous, she knew, but she felt more secure if she had enough cash with her to take care of whatever she might need. Unless and until she settled somewhere, the money was a problem, because how many savings books and checkbooks could she be expected to cart around the country?

That was her life. Dante Raintree thought all he had to do was educate her a little on her talent with numbers, and—well, what *did* he expect to happen? He knew nothing about her life, so he couldn't have any specific changes in mind. Was she supposed to become Little Mary Sunshine? Find other people like her, maybe develop their own little gated community, where, if you ran out of charcoal lighter fluid at the neighborhood barbecue, one of the neighbors could breathe fire on the briquettes to light them? Maybe she could blog about her experiences, or do talk radio.

Uh-uh. She would rather eat ground glass. She liked living alone, being alone and depending only on herself.

The phone rang again, startling her. She scrambled across the bed to look at the caller ID, though why she bothered, she had no idea; she wouldn't recognize the number of anyone calling Dante Raintree, anyway. She didn't answer that call, either.

She had sat on the bed, thinking, for so long that the afternoon shadows were beginning to lengthen, and she was drowsy. Thank goodness for that phone call, or she might have fallen asleep on his bed, and wouldn't that have been an interesting situation when he got home? She had no intention of playing Goldilocks.

But she *was* sleepy, as well as hungry. After a late breakfast, she hadn't had lunch. Why not eat a light dinner now and go to bed early? She couldn't think of any reason why she should wait for Raintree, since he hadn't had the courtesy to tell her when he might be back.

The least he could do was call—not that she would answer the phone, but he could always leave a message.

Definitely no point in waiting for him. She raided the refrigerator and made a sandwich of cold cuts, then looked at all

the books in his bookshelves—he had a lot of books on paranormal stuff, but she chose a suspense novel instead—and
settled down in the den to read for a while. By eight o'clock
she was nodding over her book, which evidently wasn't sus-
penseful enough to keep her awake. The sun hadn't quite set
yet, but she didn't care; she was still tired from the night
before.

Fifteen minutes and one shower later, she was in bed, curled
in a warm ball, with the sheet pulled over her head.

The flare of a lamp being turned on woke her. She endured
the usual grinding fear, the panic, knowing that her mother
wasn't there even though, all these years later, her subconscious
still hadn't gotten the message. Before she could relax enough
to pull the sheet from over her head, the covers were lifted and
a very warm, mostly naked Dante Raintree slid into bed with
her.

"What the hell are you doing?" she sputtered sleepily, glaring
at him over the edge of the sheet.

He settled himself beside her and stretched one long,
muscled arm to turn out the lamp. "There appears to be sand
in my bed, so I'm sleeping here."

# FIFTEEN

"Don't be silly. I couldn't leave the house, so how would I get sand? It's salt." Maybe he expected her to deny any involvement, but that *would* be silly, given that she'd been the only person in the house after he left. Maybe he also expected her to get all indignant and starchy because he was in bed with her, but for some reason, she wasn't alarmed. Annoyed at being awakened, yes, but not alarmed.

"I stand corrected." He used his superior muscle and weight to shove her over in the bed. "Move over. I need more room."

He had already forced her out of her nice warm spot, which annoyed her even more. "Then why didn't you get in on the other side, instead of making me move?" she grumbled as she scooted to the other side of the bed, which was king-size, like every other bed in the house.

"You're the one who put salt in my bed."

The sheets were cold around her, making her curl in a

tighter ball than usual. Even the pillow was cold. Lorna lifted her head and pulled the pillow from beneath her, tossing it on top of him. "Give me my pillow. This one's cold."

He made a grumbling sound, but pushed the warm pillow toward her and tucked the other pillow under his head. She snuggled down into the warmth; the soft fabric already had his scent on it, which wasn't a bad thing, she discovered. She had known him only a short time, but a lot of it had been spent in close contact with him. The primitive part of her brain recognized his scent and was comforted.

"What time is it?" she asked drowsily, already drifting back to sleep.

"You know what time it is. It's a number. Think about it." He sounded drowsy himself.

She had never thought of time as a number, but as soon as she did, the image of three numbers popped into her head. "One-oh-four."

"Bingo."

Mildly pleased, she went to sleep.

She woke before he did, which wasn't surprising, given how early she'd gone to bed and how late he'd gotten in. She lay there through the tense expectation of being hit, then slowly relaxed. The bed was toasty warm; he gave off so much heat that she could feel the warmth even though they weren't touching.

Sleepily curious to see if the time thing worked again, she thought of time as a series of numbers and immediately saw a four, a five and a one. She pulled the sheet from over her head; the room was getting a little brighter. Without any way to check—short of getting out of bed and going down to the kitchen, which she wasn't willing to do—she supposed four fifty-one was close enough. How handy was that, to not need a clock?

Dante was lying on his side, facing her, one arm bent under his head, his breathing slow and deep. The room was still too dim for her to make out many details, but that was okay, because she wasn't ready for details yet; the general impression was sexy enough as things were.

What was a woman supposed to think when a healthy, heterosexual man slept with her for the first time and didn't even try to cop a feel? That something was wrong with her? That he wasn't attracted to her?

She thought he was dangerously intelligent and intuitive.

Sex was definitely part of their relationship, if knowing someone for roughly thirty-six hours could be described as a relationship. Some of those thirty-six hours had seemed years long, especially the first four or five. She couldn't say that their time together had been quality time, either. On the other hand, since she hadn't seen him at his best, she thought she might know him better than someone who had known him for a much longer time but only in a social setting, so she wasn't surprised that he hadn't made a pass at her during the night.

She wasn't ready for sex with him, might never be ready, and he knew that. If he'd tried to storm the barricades, as it were, she would have stiffened her resistance. By simply sleeping with her and not making any overtly sexual moves, he was, in a way, counteracting those first terrible hours together and making sex a possibility, at least.

He wasn't even naked, though the boxers he'd worn to bed didn't cover much. She wasn't naked, either; he'd had *all* her clothes brought to her, so she was sleeping in her usual cotton pajamas. Perversely, because he *hadn't* tried to have sex, she began to wonder what it would be like if they did—then suspected that he'd known that would be her reaction.

Sex wasn't easy for her. She didn't trust easily; she didn't arouse easily. Voluntarily giving up her personal sense of privacy was difficult, and the payback was usually not worth the cost. She liked the feel of sex, and when she thought about it in the abstract, she wanted it. The reality, though, was that the execution didn't live up to the expectation. Regardless of what she was doing, she seldom relaxed completely, which she thought good sex probably required.

The thing was, she was more relaxed with Dante than she'd been in a long, long time. He knew what she was, knew she was different, and he didn't care—because he was even more different than she was. She didn't have to hide anything with him, because she didn't care if he liked her or not. She certainly hadn't tried to hide her temper or sweeten her tart tongue. Likewise, she had no soft-focus ideas about his character. She knew he was ruthless, but she also knew he wasn't mean. She knew he was autocratic, but that he tried to be considerate.

So maybe she could let herself go and really enjoy sex with him. She didn't have to worry about his ego; if he started going too fast, she could tell him to slow down, and if he didn't like that...tough. She wouldn't have to worry about his pleasure; he would see to that himself.

She wondered if he took his time, or if he liked to get down to business.

She wondered how big he was.

*Maybe* she could relax enough to enjoy it, and even if she didn't, at least she could satisfy her curiosity.

With a suddenness that startled her, he threw back the

covers and got out of bed. "Where are you going?" she asked, surprised when he headed toward the door instead of the bathroom.

"It's sunrise," was all he said.

And? The sun rose every day. Did he mean he always got up at this time, even when he'd had only four hours' sleep? Or did he have an early appointment?

She didn't follow him. She had her own appointment— with the bathroom. She also wanted to give him enough time to have that first cup of coffee.

When she left her room forty-five minutes later, after having made the bed and put away her clothes, she went to the kitchen but found it empty. A pot of coffee had been made, however, and she smiled with satisfaction.

Where was he? In the shower?

She didn't intend to stand around waiting for him to make an appearance. She was in the living room, heading toward her bedroom, when he appeared on the balcony two floors above.

"Come up here," he called down. "I'll be outside."

His bedroom had a deck—or was it a balcony, too?—that faced east. She had looked at it yesterday, but hadn't gone out, because his damn command had kept her from stepping outside. There were two comfortable-looking chairs and a small table out there, and she'd thought it must be a comfortable place to sit in the afternoon when the sun had passed its apex and that side of the house was shaded.

She went up the two flights of stairs to his bedroom. His bed, she noticed, had been stripped; that gave her a sense of satisfaction. She could see him sitting in one of the chairs outside, so she went to the open French door. Coffee cup in hand, he sat with his head tilted back a little, his eyes almost closed against the brilliance of the bright morning sun, the expression on his face almost...blissful.

"You're handy with the salt, aren't you?" he said neutrally, sipping the coffee, but she sensed he wasn't angry. Of course, the coffee from the kitchen wasn't dirt-flavored. When he made the next pot of coffee in here, he might not be as sanguine about things.

"Payback."

"I guessed."

He didn't say anything else, and after a moment she shifted her weight. "Was that all you wanted, just to say that?"

He looked around, as if he'd drifted off into a reverie and was faintly surprised by her presence. "Don't just stand there, come out here and sit down."

Just thinking about doing so gave her the sense of running into a wall. "I can't."

That got a quick smile from him as he realized she was still housebound. He didn't say anything, but immediately the mental wall disappeared.

"Crap," she said, stepping outside and going to sit beside him. "What?"

"You didn't say anything, you just thought it. I'd hoped you had to speak the command out loud, that I had to *hear* it, before it would work."

"Sorry. All I have to do is think it. I was tempted to use the gift yesterday afternoon and tell a few people to go jump in the lake, but I restrained myself."

"You're a saint among men," she said dryly, and he gave her a quick grin.

"I was dealing with the media, so, considering the level of temptation, I tend to agree with you."

Media, huh? No wonder he had refused to take her with him.

"I called last night to tell you I wouldn't make it back until late, but you didn't answer the phone."

"Why would I? I'm not your secretary."

"The call was for *you*."

"I didn't know that, did I?"

"I left a message for you."

"I didn't hear it." The answering machine was in the kitchen; she'd been in his bedroom when the last phone call came in, which must have been him calling her.

"That's because you didn't bother to play it back." He sounded annoyed now.

"Why would I? I'm not—"

"My secretary. I know. You're a pain in the ass, you know that?"

"I try," she said, giving him a smile that was more a baring of her teeth than anything related to humor.

He grunted and sipped coffee for a while. Lorna pulled her bare feet up in the chair and looked out over the mountains and broad valleys, enjoying being outside after an entire day cooped up in the house. The morning was cool enough to make her wish she had on socks, but not so cool that she was forced to go inside.

"Do you want to go with me today?" he finally asked, with obvious reluctance.

"Depends. What are you doing?"

"Overseeing cleanup, talking to insurance adjusters, and I still don't have an answer to why two detectives were asking questions immediately after the fire, so I'm pursuing that by going directly to the source."

"Sounds like fun."

"I'm glad someone thinks so," he said wryly. "Get ready and we'll eat breakfast out. For some reason, I don't trust the food here."

# SIXTEEN

*Tuesday morning, 7:30 a.m.*

The man sitting concealed behind some scrub brush had been in place since before dawn, when he had relieved the unlucky fool who had been on surveillance duty all night. When he saw the garage door sliding up, he grabbed the binoculars hanging by a strap around his neck and trained them on the house. Red brake lights glowed in the dimness of the garage; then a sleek Jaguar began backing out.

He picked up a radio and keyed the microphone. "He's leaving now."

"Is he alone?"

"I can't tell—no, the woman is with him."

"Ten-four. I'll be ready."

His job done for the moment, he let the binoculars fall

before the light glinting on the lenses gave him away. He could relax now. Following Raintree wasn't his job.


"Has the fire marshal said yet how the fire started?" Lorna asked as they drove down the steep, winding road. The air was very clear, the sky a deep blue bowl. The shadows thrown by the morning sun sharply delineated every bush, every boulder.

"Only that it started around a utility closet."

She settled the shoulder strap of the seat belt so the nylon wasn't rubbing against her neck. "So have one of your mind readers take a peek and tell you what the fire marshal thinks."

Dante had to laugh. "You seem to think there are a lot of us, that I have an army of gifted people I can call on."

"Well, don't you?"

"Scattered around the world. Here in Reno, there are nine, including myself. None of them are gifted with telepathy."

"You mean you can't call your strongest telepath, tell him—"

"Her."

"—*her* the fire marshal's name, and she could do it from wherever she is?"

"The telepath is my sister, Mercy, and she could do it only if she already knew the fire marshal. If she were meeting him in person, she could do it. But a cold reading, at a distance of roughly twenty-five hundred miles, on a stranger? Doesn't work that way."

"I guess that's good—well, unless you need a stranger's mind read from a few thousand miles away. I suppose this means mind reading isn't one of your talents." She hoped not, anyway. If he'd read her mind that morning...

"I can communicate telepathically with Gideon and Mercy,

if we deliberately lower our shields, but we're more comfortable with the shields in place. Mercy was a nosy little kid. Then, when she got older, she wanted to make sure we couldn't pop into her head without warning, so she armored up, too."

"What all *can* you do? Other than play with fire and this mind-control thing."

"Languages. I can understand any language, which comes in handy when I travel. That's called xenoglossy. Um...you know I have a mild empathic gift. Something that's fun is that I can make cold light, psycholuminescence. That's usually called witch light."

"Bet that comes in handy when the electricity goes off."

"It has on occasion," he admitted, smiling. "It was especially fun when I was a kid, and Mom made me turn out the light and go to bed."

That sort of home life was as alien to her as if he'd grown up on Mars, and it made her feel vaguely uneasy. To get away from the subject, she asked, "Anything else?"

"Not to any great degree."

She lapsed into silence, mulling over all that information. There was so much she didn't know about this stuff. From the way Dante talked about himself and his family, their gifts had evolved with age, and their skills had grown like any other skill, through constant use. If she began learning more about what she could do, would she find more abilities within her power? She wasn't certain she wanted that. In fact, she was almost certain she didn't. Enough was enough.

Now that she was away from his house, she felt exposed and vulnerable. Though his autocratic way of keeping her there had been maddening, maybe he'd had the right idea. She had been insulated from the world there, able to more calmly think about being one of the gifted—albeit a lowly "stray" rather than a Raintree or Ansara, which she likened to being a Volkswagen as compared to, well, a Jaguar—because she hadn't had to guard herself. With every minute they drew closer to Reno, and with every minute she grew more and more anxious. By the time he sent the Jaguar prowling up the on-ramp to the interstate and they joined with heavy traffic, she was almost in a panic.

Old habits and patterns were very hard to break. A lifetime of caution and secrecy couldn't be easily changed. What was easy enough to contemplate while in seclusion seemed entirely different in the real world. Lorna's mother hadn't been the only person in her life to react so negatively to her ability. Dante could call it a gift all he wanted, but in her life it had been more of a curse.

She felt suddenly dizzy and sick at just the thought of getting deeper into this new world than she already was. Nothing would change. If she let anyone know, she would be leaving herself open for exploitation at the best, ridicule or persecution at the worst.

"What's wrong?" Dante asked sharply, glancing over at her. "You're almost hyperventilating."

"I don't want to do this," she said, teeth chattering from sudden cold. "I don't want to be part of this. I don't want to learn how to do more."

He muttered a curse, gave a quick look over his shoulder to check traffic, and slotted the Jaguar between a semi and a frozen-pizza truck. At the next exit, he peeled off the interstate. "Take a deep breath and hold it," he said, as he pulled into the parking lot of a McDonald's. "Damn it, I should have thought—this is why you need training. I told you that you're a sensitive. You're picking up all the energy patterns around you—has to be all the traffic—and it's throwing you into overload. How in *hell* did you ever function? How did you survive in a casino, of all places?"

Obedient to his earlier suggestion, Lorna sucked in the deepest breath she could and held it. *Was* she hyperventilating? she wondered dimly. She supposed she was. But she was cold, so cold, the way she'd been in Dante's office before the fire.

He put a calming hand on her bare arm, frowning a little when he felt how icy her skin was. "Focus," he said. "Think of your sensitivity as this shining, faceted crystal, picking up the sun and throwing rainbows all around you. Envision it. Or if you don't like crystals, make it something else fragile and breakable. Are you doing that? Can you see it in your imagination?"

She struggled to concentrate. "What shape crystal? Hexagonal? How many sides does it have?"

"What difference does it—never mind. It's round. The crystal is round and faceted. Got it?"

She formed a mental picture of a round crystal, only hers was mirrored. It didn't throw rainbows, it threw reflections. She didn't mention that, though. Concentrating helped dispel that debilitating coldness, so she was willing to think of crystals all day. "Got it."

"Okay. A hailstorm is coming. The crystal will be shattered unless you build a shelter around it. Later you can come back and build a really strong shelter around it, but right now you have to use whatever materials you have at hand. Look around. What do you see that you can use to protect the crystal?"

In her mind she looked around, but no handy bricks and mortar were nearby. There were some bushes, but they weren't sturdy. Maybe she could find some flat rocks and start stacking them in layers to form a barrier.

"Hurry," he said. "You only have a few minutes."

"There are some rocks here, but not enough of them."

"Then think of something else. The hailstones are the size of golf balls. They'll knock the rocks down."

In her mind she glared at him; then, desperate and unable to think of anything else, she mentally dropped to her knees and began scooping a hole in the sandy dirt. The sides of the hole were soft and kept caving in, so she scooped some more. She could hear the storm approaching with a thunderous roar as the hail battered everything in its path. She had to get under shelter herself. Was the hole deep enough? She put the crystal in the hole, and hurriedly began raking dirt around and over it. No, it was too shallow; the crystal ball wasn't completely underground. She began raking dirt from a wider circle, piling it on top of the crystal. The first hailstone hit her shoulder, a blow like a fist, and she knew the dirt wasn't going to do the job. With no time left and no other choice, she threw her own body over the dirt mounded over the crystal, protecting it with her life.

She shook herself out of the image and glared at him. "Well, that didn't work," she snapped.

He was leaning very close, his green eyes intent on her face, his hand still on her arm. "What did you do?"

"I threw myself on the hand grenade, so to speak."

"What?"

"I was trying to bury the damn crystal but I couldn't get it deep enough, so I threw myself on top of it and the hailstones beat me to death. No offense, but your imagery sucks."

He snorted and released her arm, sitting back in his seat. "That wasn't my imagery, it was yours."

"You thought of the stupid crystal."

"Yeah. It worked, too, didn't it?"

"What did?"

"The imagery. Are you still feeling—I don't know how you were feeling, but I'd guess it was as if you were being attacked from all sides."

Lorna paused. "No," she said thoughtfully. "I'm not feeling that now. But it wasn't as if I were being attacked. It was more of an anxious feeling, a sense of doom. Then I got so cold, just the way I did in your office before the fire."

"Only then? You've never felt overwhelmed like that except in my office?" He considered the idea, frowning a little.

She rubbed the back of her neck, feeling the knots of tension. "Contrary to what you seem to think, I could pretty much go anywhere and do anything without feeling all those swirls and currents, or like the world was coming to an end. I thought you were the one doing all of it, remember?" Whatever this new stuff was, she didn't like it at all. She wasn't a happy-go-lucky person, never had been—it was tough to be Little Miss Sunshine when you were getting slapped every time you opened your mouth—but neither had she felt hopeless, overwhelmed by a dark despair that went way beyond depression.

"I'm not a sensitive," he said. "I've never felt what you're describing. I know I give off a force field of energy, because other sensitives have picked up on it, but no one has ever said I made them feel as if the world was coming to an end."

"Maybe they didn't know you the way I do," she said sweetly.

"You're right about that," he replied, smiling a little, and just that fast the air between them became heavy and hot, as if a summer thunderstorm were approaching. His gaze dipped down to her breasts, stroked over the curves with an almost physical sensation. He'd never touched her breasts, hadn't touched her sexually at all unless she counted the times she'd been able to feel his erection against her. Come to think of it, that was pretty damn sexual. With a jolt of self-honesty, she realized she'd liked knowing she could make him hard; thinking of how he'd felt made her abdominal muscles clench, low in her belly.

How could he do that, make her respond so fast? Her nipples beaded, so that every breath she took scraped them against her bra, which made them even harder. She almost hunched her shoulders to relieve the pressure, but she knew that would be a dead giveaway. Her bra was substantial enough that he couldn't see her excitement, which was a good thing. He might suspect, from the heightened color she could feel in her cheeks, but he couldn't *know*.

His gaze flashed up, caught hers. Slowly, but not at all hesitantly, he lifted his hand and rubbed the back of one finger over her left nipple, letting her know that she'd been wrong: he *knew*. Her cheeks got hotter, and she felt that delicious clenching again, the softening deep inside. If she hadn't been thinking about having sex with him...if she hadn't been thinking just a couple of hours ago about seeing him naked...maybe she wouldn't have responded so readily. But she had been, and she did.

"When you're ready," he said, holding her gaze a moment longer. Then he dropped his hand and nodded toward the fast-food restaurant. "Let's go get breakfast."

He had his door open and was getting out when, in tones of astonishment, she said, "You brought me to get breakfast at *McDonald's?*"

"It's those golden arches," he said. "They get to me every time."

# SEVENTEEN

"They're going into McDonald's," one of the Ansara watchers reported.

"Sit tight," said Ruben McWilliams, sitting on the bed in his motel room. Why the hell didn't motels put the damn phone on the stupid little table so a man could sit in a chair when he talked on the phone, instead of sitting hunched over on an uncomfortable mattress? "Keep them in sight, but don't get any closer. Something spooked him. Let me know when they leave."

Something had prompted Raintree to abruptly cut across two lanes of traffic and take the exit ramp at seventy miles an hour, but Ruben doubted it was a sudden urge for a McMuffin. It wasn't as if he couldn't have gone another couple of exits and found another McDonald's, without the dangerous maneuver.

He didn't think it was anything his people had done that had caused the aberrant behavior, but he wasn't on-site, so he couldn't be certain. His people were supposed to watch and follow, that was all. Raintree wasn't a clairvoyant, so he shouldn't have picked up any warning that way, but he could have had a premonition. Premonition was such a common ability, even ordinary humans had it. Raintree might have felt a twinge of uneasiness, but because he was one of the gifted, he would never dismiss the warning; he would act on it, where most ordinary humans would not.

Since there had been no immediate danger—that would come later—maybe he'd sensed an accident in his immediate future if he stayed on the interstate, so he'd gotten off at the next exit. That was possible. There were always variables.

Staging the planned incident hadn't been possible on such short notice. They hadn't known when Raintree would leave his house, or where he would go when he did. Now that they had a tail on him, they could direct the *amigos* to him wherever he was; then they would fall back and let the *amigos* do their job.

Over a McMuffin, Dante said, "Tell me exactly what you felt when you were in my office."

Lorna sipped her coffee, thinking. After the weird feelings she'd had in the car, she'd wanted something hot to drink, even though Dante had dispelled all the physical chill. The heat of the coffee couldn't touch the remnant of mental chill she still felt, but it was comforting anyway.

She searched through her memory. It was normally excellent anyway, but everything had happened so recently that the details were still fresh in her mind. "You scared the crap out of me," she finally replied.

"Because you'd been caught cheating?" he prompted when she didn't immediately go on.

"I didn't cheat," she insisted, scowling at him. "Knowing something isn't the same as cheating. But, no, it wasn't that. Once, in Chicago, I was going home one night and was about to take a shortcut through an alley. I used the alley a lot—so did a bunch of people. But that night, I couldn't. I froze. Have you ever felt a fear so intense it made you sick? It was like that. I backed out of the alley and took another way home. The next morning a woman's mutilated body was found in that alley."

"Presentiment," he said. "A gift that saved your life."

"I felt the same way when I saw you." She saw by his expression that he didn't like that at all, but he'd asked, so she told him. "I felt as if this huge force just...*slammed* into me. I couldn't breathe. I was afraid I'd pass out. But then you said something, and the panic went away."

He sat back in the booth, frowning. "You weren't in any danger from me. Why would you have such a strong reaction?"

"You're the expert. You tell me."

"*My* first reaction to *you* was that I wanted you naked. Unless you're terrified of sex, and I don't think you are—" he gave her a hooded look that had her nipples tightening again "—you weren't picking up anything from me that would cause you to feel that way."

Heat again pooled low in her belly, and it wasn't from the coffee. Because they were in McDonald's and there was a four-year-old sitting in the booth behind her, she looked away and forcibly removed her thoughts from going to bed with him. "At least part of it was from you," she insisted. "I remember thinking that even the air felt different, alien, something I'd never felt before. When you got closer, I could tell the feeling came from you. You're a dangerous man, Raintree."

He just watched her, waiting for her to continue, because he couldn't accurately deny that particular charge.

"I could feel you," she said, her voice low as she became mired in the memory. "Pulling at me, almost like a touch. The candles were going wild. I wanted to run, but I couldn't move."

"I *was* touching you," he said. "In my imagination, anyway."

Remembering how she'd been snagged by his sexual fantasy, drawn in, stole her breath. "I knew something was wrong," she whispered. "I wasn't in control. I felt as if I'd been caught in a power surge that kept blinking out, and then coming back, pushing me off balance. Then I got so *cold,* just like in the car. Not a normal cold, with chill bumps and shivering, but something so intense it made my bones hurt. Then that feeling of dread came back, the same feeling I had in the alley. You were talking about how I was sensitive to the currents in the room—"

"I was talking about sexual currents," he said wryly. "The summer solstice is in a few days, and control is more difficult when there's so much sunshine. That's why the candles were dancing. I was turned on, and my power kept flaring."

Lorna thought about that. She'd been attracted to him from the first moment she'd looked him in the eyes. Regardless of the fear and panic she'd felt at first, when she had met his gaze, she'd fallen headlong into lust. The debilitating coldness had come afterward and hadn't affected her physical response to him, because when the coldness left, the attraction remained—unchanged.

"The cold went away," she said. "Like something had been pressing me into the chair and then suddenly was gone. I thought I might fall out of the chair, because I'd been pushing back so hard, and all of a sudden the pressure was gone. That was it. We talked some more, and then the fire alarm went off. End of scene, beginning of even more weirdness."

"And you felt the same thing in the car?"

She nodded. "Exactly the same. Except for the sex. The farther we got from the house, the more anxious and depressed I felt, as if I were really exposed and vulnerable. Then I got really cold."

"You were definitely picking up on external negative energies, probably from the traffic around us. You never know who's in the car beside you. Could be someone you wouldn't want to meet even on a crowded street at high noon. What puzzles me is why you felt the same way in my office." He shook his head. "Unless you sensed the fire that was about to burn down the casino, which is possible, if you have some precognitive ability."

"I think I might, but only as things relate to numbers." She told him about the 9/11 flight numbers, and the fact that she hadn't had any visions of airplane crashes or buildings burning, just the flight numbers interjecting themselves into her subconscious. "What I felt before the fire was *different*. Maybe it's because I'm—"

She stopped and glared at him. He raised his eyebrows. "You're...what?"

"I have a hang-up about fire." He waited, and, exasperated, she finally said, "I'm afraid of it, okay?"

"Anyone with any intelligence is cautious of fire. *I'm* cautious with it."

"It isn't caution. I'm *afraid* of it. As in terrified. I have nightmares about being trapped in a burning building." He might be cautious with fire, she thought, but it still turned him on. He would make a jim-dandy firebug. Standing in the burning casino, she had felt his fascination and appreciation for the flames, felt his excitement, because he had expressed it very physically. "Anyway, maybe that's why I felt so panicked then, and so anxious. But why would I feel that way today—unless you're going to force me into another burning building in the next hour or so, in which case tell me now, so I can kill you."

He laughed as he gathered up the debris of their meal, loading it on the plastic tray. She slid from the booth, walking ahead of him as they left the restaurant. "Where to now?"

"The hotel."

They were back on the interstate within a minute. Dante slanted a glance at her. "Feeling okay?"

"I feel fine. I don't know what was going on."

She *did* feel fine. She was riding around in a Jag with the most unusual man she'd ever met, and she was thinking about going to bed with him. She glanced over at him, thinking of how he'd looked wearing just those boxers, and feeling the pleasant warmth of anticipation.

She liked watching him drive. Sunday night, going to his house, she hadn't been in any shape to appreciate the smoothness, the economy of motion, with which he handled a car. Good driving was very sexy, she thought. The play of muscles in his forearms, bared by the short-sleeved polo shirt he was wearing, was incredibly sexy. He had to work out somewhere, on a regular basis, to keep that fit.

They were cruising in the middle lane. A car with a loud muffler was coming up from the right, and she saw him glance in the rearview mirror. "Idiots," he muttered, smoothly accelerating into the left lane. Lorna turned her head to see what he was talking about. A battered white Dodge, gray smoke belching from its exhaust, was coming up fast. She could see several people inside it. What had prompted Dante to move over and give them plenty of room was the blue Nissan right on the bumper of the Dodge.

"That's an accident waiting to happen," she said, just as the blue Nissan swung into the middle lane, the one they had just vacated, and shot forward until it was even with the white Dodge. The Nissan swerved toward the Dodge, and the driver of the Dodge slammed on his brakes, setting off a chain reaction of squealing brakes and smoking tires behind him. The Nissan's motor was screaming as the car drew even with Dante and Lorna. Inside, she could see four or five Hispanics, laughing and pointing back at the Dodge.

Traffic on the interstate was fairly heavy, as usual, but not so heavy that the driver of the white Dodge wasn't now rapidly gaining on them.

"Gangs," Dante said in a clipped voice, braking to let the rolling disaster that was unfolding get ahead of him. He couldn't go faster, because there was a car ahead of him; he couldn't get around the car, because the blue Nissan was right beside them, boxing him in. No one in the Nissan seemed to be paying attention to them; they were all watching the Dodge. If anything, the Nissan's driver let up on the gas pedal, as if he *wanted* the Dodge to catch up.

"Shit!" Dante swerved as far as he could to the left as the Dodge pulled even with the Nissan. Lorna saw a blur as the left rear passenger in the Dodge rolled down his window and stuck out a gun; then Dante's right hand closed over her shoulder in a grip that seemed to go to the bone, and he yanked her forward and down as the window beside her head shattered in a thousand pieces. There were several deep, flat booms, punctuated by lighter, more rapid cracks, then a soul-jarring impact as Dante spun the steering wheel and sent them skidding into the concrete barrier.

# EIGHTEEN

Somehow Dante had pulled her shoulder free of the seat belt's shoulder strap, but the lap belt tightened with a jerk. Something grazed the right side of her head and hit her right shoulder so hard and fast it slammed her backward, and she ended up facedown, with her upper body lying across the console and twisted between the bucket seats. All the horrible screeching noises of tires and crushed metal had stopped, and a strange silence filled the car. Lorna opened her eyes, but her vision was blurred, so she closed them again.

She'd never been in a car accident before. The sheer speed and violence of it stunned her. She didn't feel hurt, just…numb, as if a giant had picked her up and body-slammed her to the ground. The hurting part would probably arrive soon enough, she thought fuzzily. The impact had been so ferocious that she was vaguely surprised she was alive.

Dante! What about Dante?

Spurred by that urgent thought, she opened her eyes again, but the blurriness persisted and she couldn't see him. Nothing looked familiar. There was no steering wheel, no dashboard....

She blinked and slowly realized that she was staring at the back seat. And the blurriness was...fog? No—*smoke*. She heaved upward in abrupt panic, or tried to, but she couldn't seem to get any leverage.

"Lorna?"

His voice was strained and harsh, as if he were having difficulty speaking, but it was Dante. It came from somewhere behind and above her, which made no sense.

"Fire," she managed to say, trying to kick her legs. For some reason she could move only her feet, which was reassuring anyway since they were the farthest away; if they could move, everything between there and her spine must be okay.

"Not fire—air bags. Are you hurt?"

If anyone would know whether or not there was a fire, Dante was that person. Lorna took a deep breath, relaxing a little. "I don't think so. You?"

"I'm okay."

She was in such an awkward position that pain was shooting through her back muscles. Squirming, she managed to work her left arm from beneath her and push with her hand against the back floorboard, trying to lift herself up and around so she could slide back into her seat. "Wait," Dante said, grabbing her arm. "There's glass everywhere. You'll cut yourself to shreds."

"I have to move. This position is murder on my back." But she stopped, because the mental image of what sliding across broken glass would do to her skin wasn't a good one.

There were shouts from outside, coming nearer, as passersby stopped and ran to their aid. Someone beat on Dante's window. "Hey, man! You okay?"

"Yeah." Dante raised his voice so he could be heard. She felt his hand against her side as he tried to release his seat belt. The latch was jammed; he gave a lurid curse, then tried once more. On the third try, it popped open. Freed from its restraint, he shifted around, and she felt his hands running down her legs. "Your right foot's tangled in the air bag. Can you move . . ." His hand closed over her ankle. "Move your knee toward me and your foot toward your window."

Easier said than done, she thought, because she could scarcely maneuver at all. She managed to shift her right knee just a little.

The man outside Dante's window grabbed the door handle and tried to pull it open, shaking the car, but the door was jammed. "Try the other side!" she heard Dante yell.

"This window's busted out," said another man, leaning in the front passenger window—or where it had been—and asking urgently, "Are you guys hurt?"

"We're okay," Dante said, leaning over her and pushing on her right ankle while he turned her foot.

The trap holding her foot relaxed a little, which let her move her knee a bit more. "This proves one thing," she said, panting from the effort of that small shift.

"Point your toes like a ballerina. What does it prove?"

"I'm definitely—ouch!—not precognitive. I didn't see *this* coming."

"I think it's safe to say neither of us is a precog." He grunted, then said, "Here you go." With one last tug, her foot was free. To the man leaning in the window he said, "Can you find a blanket or something to throw over this glass so you can pull her out?"

"I don't need pulling," Lorna grumbled. "If I can shift around, I'll be able to climb out."

"Just be patient," Dante said, turning so he could slide his right arm under her chest and shoulders and support her weight a little to give her muscles some rest.

They could hear sirens blasting through the dry air, but still some distance away.

A new face, red and perspiring, and belonging to a burly guy wearing a Caterpillar cap, appeared in the broken window. "Had a blanket in my sleeper," he said, leaning in to arrange the fabric over the seat, then folding the excess into a thick pad to cover the shards of glass still stuck in the broken window.

"Thank you," Lorna said fervently as Dante began levering her upright into the seat. Her muscles were screaming from the strain, and the relief of being in a more natural position was so intense that she almost groaned.

"Here you go," said the truck driver, reaching through once more and grasping her under the arms, hauling her out through the broken window before she could do it under her own steam.

She thanked him and everyone else who had reached out to help, then turned and got her first look at the car as Dante came out with the lithe grace of a race car driver, as if exiting through a window was something he did every day.

But as cool and sexy as he made his exit look, what stunned her to silence was the car.

The elegant Jaguar was nothing but crumpled and torn sheet metal. It had skidded almost halfway around, the front end crushed against the concrete barrier, the driver's side almost at a T to the oncoming traffic. If another car had plowed into them after they hit the barrier, Dante would be dead. She didn't know why no other vehicle had smashed into them; traffic had been heavy enough that it was nothing short of a miracle. She looked at the snarled pileup of cars and trucks and SUVs stopped at all angles, as if people had been locking down their brakes and skidding. There was a three-car fender bender in the right lane, about fifty yards down, but the people were out of their vehicles examining the damage, so they were okay.

*She* wasn't okay. The bottom had dropped out of her stomach, and her heart felt as if someone had punched her in the chest. She had a very clear memory of Dante spinning the steering wheel, sending the Jaguar into a controlled skid— turning the passenger side away from the spew of bullets and his side toward the oncoming traffic.

She was going to kill him.

He had no right to take that sort of risk for her. None. They weren't lovers. They'd met less than forty-eight hours before, under really terrible circumstances, and for most of that time she would gladly have pushed him into traffic herself.

How dare he be a hero? She didn't want him to be a hero. She wanted him to be someone whose absence wouldn't hurt her. She wanted to be able to walk away from him, whole and content unto herself. She didn't want to think about him after- ward. She didn't want to dream about him.

Her father hadn't cared enough to stick around, assuming he'd even known about her. She had no real idea who he was— and neither had her mother. Her mother certainly wouldn't have risked a nail, much less her life, to save Lorna from any- thing. So what was this…this *stranger* doing, putting his own life in danger to protect her? She hated him for doing this to her, for making himself someone whose footprint would always be on her heart.

What was she supposed to do now?

She turned her head, searching for him. He was only a few feet away, which she supposed made sense, because if he'd moved any farther away than that she would have been compelled to follow him. He wouldn't lift that damned mind control he used to shackle her, but he'd risk his life for her—the jerk.

He normally kept his longish black hair brushed back, but now it was falling around his face. There was a thin line of blood penciling down his left cheek from a small, puffy cut high on his cheekbone. The skin around the wound was swelling and turning dark. His left arm looked bruised, too; the span from his wrist almost to his elbow was a dark red. He wasn't cradling his arm or swiping at his cheek, any of the things people instinctively did when they were hurt. His injuries might as well not exist for all the attention he paid them.

He looked in complete command of himself and the situation.

Lorna thought she might be sick, she was so angry. What he'd done wasn't fair—not that he'd seemed concerned about fairness before now anyway.

As if he were attuned to her thoughts, his head turned sharply and his gaze zeroed in on her. With two swift strides he was beside her, taking her arm. "You don't have any color at all in your face. You should sit down."

"I'm fine," she said automatically. A sudden breeze blew a curtain of hair across her face, and she lifted her hand to push it back. Two RPD patrol cars were approaching on the other side of the highway, sirens blaring, and she almost had to shout to make herself heard. "I'm not hurt."

"No, but you've had a shock." He raised his voice, too,

turning his head to watch the patrol cars come to a stop on the other side of the barrier. The sirens died, but other emergency vehicles were approaching, and the din was getting louder again.

"I'm *okay!*" she insisted, and she was—physically, at least.

His hand closed on her arm, moving her toward the concrete barrier. "Come on, sit down. I'll feel better if you do."

"I'm not the one bleeding," she pointed out.

He touched his cheek, as if he'd forgotten all about the cut, or maybe had never noticed it in the first place. "Then come sit down with me and keep me company."

As it happened, neither of them got to sit down. The cops were trying to find out what had happened, get traffic straightened out and moving again, albeit very slowly, and get any injured people transported to a hospital to be checked out. Soon a total of seven patrol cars were on the scene, along with a fire engine and three medic trucks. The drivers of the damaged cars that were still drivable were instructed to move their vehicles to the shoulder.

There were several witnesses to what had happened. No one knew whether road rage had caused the shooting or if the whole thing had been a conflict between rival gangs, but everyone had an opinion and a slightly different version of events. The one thing they all agreed on was that the people in the white Dodge had been shooting at the Nissan, and the people in the Nissan had been shooting back.

"Did anyone get the plate number of either vehicle?" a patrolman asked.

Dante immediately looked at Lorna. "Numbers?"

She thought of the white Dodge and three numbers came into sharp focus. "The Dodge is 873." Nevada plates were three digits followed by three letters.

"Did you get the letters?" the patrolman asked, pen at the ready.

Lorna shook her head. "I just remember the numbers."

"This will narrow the search considerably. What about the Nissan?"

"Hmm...612."

He jotted that down, too, then turned away as he got on the radio.

Dante's cell phone rang. He fished it from the front pocket of his jeans and checked the caller ID. "It's Gideon," he said, flipping the phone open. "What's up?" He listened a moment, then said, "Royally screwed."

A brief pause. "I remember."

They talked for less than a minute when Lorna heard him say, "A glimpse of the future," which made her wonder what was going on. He had just laughed at something his brother said when she suddenly shivered, wrapping her arms around herself even though the temperature was rapidly climbing toward the nineties. That awful, bone-aching chill had seized her as suddenly as if she'd been dropped into a pool of ice water.

Dante's gaze sharpened, and he abruptly ended the call, tucking the phone back into his pocket.

"What's wrong?" he asked, keeping his tone low as he pulled her to the side.

She fought waves of dizziness, brought on by the intense cold. "I think the depraved serial killer must have followed us," she said.

# NINETEEN

Dante put his arms around her, pulling her against the heat of his body. His body temperature was always high, she thought, as if he had a permanent fever. That heat felt wonderful now, warming her chilled skin.

"Focus," he said, bending his head so no one else could hear him. "Think of building that shelter."

"I don't want to build a damn shelter," she said fretfully. "This didn't happen before I met you, and I want it to stop."

He rubbed his cheek against her hair, and she felt his lips move as he smiled. "I'll see what I can do. In the meantime, if you don't want to build shelters, see if you can tell what's causing the problem. Close your eyes, mentally search around us, and tell me if you're picking up anything, like any changes in energy patterns from a particular area."

That suggestion seemed a lot more practical to her than building imaginary shelters for imaginary mirrored crystals.

She would rather be doing something to stop these sudden sick feelings instead of merely learning how to handle them. She did as he said, leaning into him and letting him support part of her weight while she closed her eyes and began mentally searching for something weird. She didn't know what she was doing, or what she was "looking" for, but she felt better for doing it.

"Is this really supposed to work?" she asked against his shoulder. "Or are you just distracting me?"

"It should work. Everyone has a personal energy field, but some are stronger than others. A sensitive has a heightened awareness of these energy fields. You should be able to tell where a strong one is coming from, sort of like being able to tell from which direction the wind is blowing."

That made sense to her, put it in terms she could understand. The thing was, *if* she was a sensitive, why didn't she sense stuff like this on a regular basis? Other than the time in Chicago when she'd been suddenly terrified of what lurked in that alley, she'd never been aware of anything unusual.

*Some are stronger than others,* Dante had said. Maybe she had been around mostly normal people all her life. If so, these feelings must mean that there were now people near her who weren't normal and had very strong energy fields.

The strongest of all was holding her in his arms. Concentrating like this, she decided to use him as a sort of standard, a pattern, against which she could measure anything else she detected. She could physically *feel* the energy of his gifts, almost like static electricity surrounding her entire body. The sensation was too strong to call pleasant, but it wasn't *un*pleasant. Rather, it was exciting and sexual, like tiny pinpoints of fire reaching deep into her body.

Keeping a part of the feeling in the forefront of her consciousness, she began widening her awareness, looking for the places that had stronger currents. It was, she thought, like trout fishing.

At first there was nothing other than a normal flow of energy, albeit from many different people. She and Dante were surrounded by police officers, firemen, medics, people who had come to their aid. Their energy flow was warm and comforting, concerned, protective. These were good people; they all had their quirks, but their baseline was good.

She expanded her mental circle. The pattern here was slightly different. These were the onlookers, the rubberneckers, the ones who were curious but weren't moved to help. They wanted to talk about seeing the accident, about being stuck in traffic for X number of hours, as if it were a great hardship to endure, but they didn't want to put out any effort. They—

*There!*

She started, a little alarmed by what she felt.

"Where is it?" Dante whispered against her hair, his arms tightening. Probably the people around them thought he was comforting her, or that they were clinging to each other in gratitude that they'd been spared any harm.

She didn't open her eyes. "To my left. About…I don't know…a hundred yards out, maybe. Off to the side, as if he's pulled onto the shoulder."

"He?"

"He," she replied, very definitely.

"Our friends missed completely," the Ansara follower said in disgust, lowering the binoculars he held in one hand to concentrate on the phone call. "He wrecked the car, but they aren't hurt."

Ruben cursed under his breath. He guessed this just proved the old adage: *If you want something done right, do it yourself.*

"Call off surveillance," he said. "I have something else in mind."

Their plans had been too complex. The best plan was the simplest plan. There were fewer details that could go wrong, fewer people to screw things up, less chance of the target being warned.

Instead of trying to make Raintree's death look like an accident, the easiest thing to do was wait until the last minute, when it was too late for the clan to rally to Sanctuary, then simply put a bullet through his head.

Simple was always best.


"I see who you're talking about," Dante said, "but I can't tell anything from this distance. He doesn't seem to be doing anything, just standing outside his car like a bunch of other people."

"Watching," Lorna said. "He's watching us."

"Can you tell anything about his energy field?"

"He's sending out a lot of waves. He's stronger than anything else I'm sensing out there, but, um, I'd say nowhere near as strong as you." She lifted her head and opened her eyes. "He's the only unusual one as far as I can tell. Are you sure I'm not just imagining this?"

"I'm sure. You need to start trusting your senses. He's probably just—"

"Mr. Raintree," one of the policemen called, beckoning Dante over.

He gave Lorna a quick kiss on the mouth, then released her and strode over to the cop. Willy-nilly, Lorna followed, though she stopped as soon as she was able, when the compulsion was no longer tugging her forward.

The accident scene was beginning to clear up; witnesses had given their statements, and more and more people were managing to maneuver their vehicles around the demolished Jag, the remains of the fender bender and all the rescue vehicles. Two wreckers had arrived, one to tow Dante's Jaguar, the other to get the center car in the fender bender, because it had a ruptured radiator. Before his poor car was taken away, Dante was getting his registration and insurance card from the glove compartment, as well as the garage door opener. Given how mangled the car was, finding anything and getting to it was a major undertaking.

From what Lorna could tell, he wasn't upset at all about the Jaguar. He didn't like the inconvenience, but the car itself didn't mean anything to him. He had already made arrangements for a rental car to be waiting for him at the hotel, and one of his many employees was on the way to the accident site to pick them up. As she had always suspected, money smoothed out many of life's bumps.

Thinking of money prompted her to casually brush her hand against her left front pocket. Her money was still there, and her driver's license and the tiny pair of scissors were in her right pocket. She had no idea what good those scissors would do in any truly dangerous situation, but she had them anyway.

She noticed she was feeling much better, that the ugly, cold sensation had gone away. She turned and looked over to where the watcher had been parked. He wasn't there any longer, and neither was his car. Coincidence, she wondered, or cause and effect?

And wasn't it odd that she'd had that sickening cold feeling both right before the casino fire, and right before she almost got mowed down in the crossfire of a gang shooting? Maybe she wasn't reacting to a person at all but to something that was about to happen. Maybe that coldness was a warning. Of course, she'd also gotten the feeling right before Dante fed her a McMuffin for breakfast, but the principle could still be holding true: Warning! McMuffin ahead!

She had almost come to terms with the claircognizance thing, because even though she'd spent a lifetime insisting she was simply good with numbers, she had always *known* it was more than that. She didn't want to discover yet another talent, particularly one that seemed to be useless. A warning was all well and good if you knew what you were being warned about. Otherwise, why bother?

"Our ride's here," Dante said, coming up behind her and resting his hand on the curve of her waist. "Do you want to go to the hotel with me, or go back home?"

Home? He was referring to his house as her home? She looked up, ready to nail him on his mistake, and the words died on her lips. He was watching her with a steady, burning intent; that hadn't been a slip of the tongue but a warning of a different kind.

"We both know where we're going with this," he said. "I have a suite at the hotel, and the electricians got the power back on yesterday, so it's functional. You can come with me to the hotel or go home, but either way, you're going to be under me. The only difference is that going home will give you a little more time, if you need it."

She needed more than time, but standing on the side of the interstate wasn't the place to have the showdown she knew was coming.

"I haven't decided yet whether or not to sleep with you, and I'll make the decision on my timetable, not yours," she said. "I'll come to the hotel with you because I don't want to spend another day cooped up in that house, so don't get too cocky, Raintree."

The expression of intense focus faded, to be replaced by wryness. Looking down at himself, he said, "Too late."

# TWENTY

Lorna was too restless to just sit in Dante's suite while he was literally all over the hotel, directing the cleaning and repairs, touring with insurance adjusters, meeting with contractors. She dogged his steps, listening but not joining in. The behind-the-scenes details of a luxury hotel were fascinating. The place was hopping, too. Rather than wait until the insurance companies ponied up, he'd brought the adjusters in to take pictures; then he got on with the repairs using his own money.

That he was able to do so told her that he was seriously wealthy, which made his lifestyle even more of a statement about him. He didn't have an army of servants waiting on him. He lived in a big, gorgeous home, but it wasn't a mansion. He drove expensive cars, but he drove himself. He made his own breakfast, loaded his own dishwasher. He liked luxury but was comfortable with far less.

When it came to the hotel, though, he was unbending. Everything had to be top notch, from the toilet paper in the bath-rooms to the sheets on the beds. A room that was smoke-damaged couldn't be cleaned and described as "good enough." It had to be perfect. It had to be better than it had been before the fire. If the smell of smoke wouldn't come out of the curtains, the curtains were discarded; likewise the miles of carpet.

Lorna found out that the day before had been a madhouse, with guests being allowed to go to their rooms and retrieve their belongings. Because the destroyed casino was attached to the hotel, for liability purposes guests had to be escorted to make certain their curiosity didn't lead them where they shouldn't go.

A casino existed for one reason only, and that reason was money. In a rare moment when he had time to talk, he told Lorna that over six million dollars a day had to go through the casino just for him to break even, and since the whole point of a casino was its generous profit margin, the amount of cash he actually dealt with on a daily basis was mind-boggling.

The acre of melted and charred slot machines held thousands upon thousands of dollars, so the ruins had to have around-the-clock security until the machines could be transported and as much as possible of their contents was salvaged. About half the machines had spewed printed tickets instead of belching out quarters, which saved both time and money. The coin vaults and the master vault were fireproof, thus saving that huge amount of cash, and his cashiers in the cages had refused to evacuate until they secured the money, which had been very loyal of them but not smart: the two fatalities had been from their ranks.

The fire marshal was wrapping up his investigation, so Dante cornered him. "Was it arson?" he demanded bluntly.

"All indications are that it was electrical in nature, Mr.

Raintree. I haven't found any trace of accelerants at the source of the fire. The flames reached unusually high temperatures, so I was suspicious, I admit."

"So was I—when detectives were here questioning me immediately after the fire on Sunday night, when you hadn't even begun your investigation. This wasn't a crime scene."

The fire marshal rubbed his nose. "They didn't tell you? A call came in about the time the fire started. Some nutcase claimed he was burning down the casino. When they tracked him down, turns out he'd been eating in one of the restaurants, and when the fire alarm went off, he pulled out his trusty cell phone and made a grab for glory. He'd had one too many adult beverages." He shook his head. "Some people are nuts."

Dante met Lorna's gaze; both were rueful. "We'd wondered what was going on. I was beginning to feel like a conspiracy theorist," he said.

"Weird things happen in fires. One of them is how you two are alive. You had no protection at all, but the heat and smoke didn't get to you. Amazing."

"I felt as if the smoke got to us," Dante said in a dry tone. "I thought I was coughing up my lungs."

"But your airways had no significant damage. I've seen people die who faced less smoke than you two dealt with."

Lorna wondered what he would think if he could see what was left of Dante's Jaguar, since the two of them were walking around without even a bruise.

No, that wasn't right. Frowning, she looked at Dante, really looked. He'd had a cut on his face where the impact of the air bag had literally split open the skin over his cheekbone. His cheekbone had been bruised and was swelling, and his left arm had been bruised.

Just a few hours later, his cheek looked fine. She couldn't see the cut at all. There was no swelling, no bruising. She knew she hadn't imagined it, because there had been blood on his shirt, and he had gone to his suite to change; instead of the polo shirt, he now wore a white dress shirt with his jeans, the sleeves rolled up to expose his unbruised left forearm.

She didn't have any bruises, either. After the way she'd been slammed around, she should at least have some stiff and sore muscles, but she felt fine. *What was going on?*

"That was a dead end," he remarked after the fire marshal had left and he was inspecting the damage done to the landscaping. "The stupidity of some people is mind-boggling."

"I know," she said absently, still mentally chasing the mystery of the vanishing cut. Was there any way to diplomatically ask a man, *Are you human?*

But what about her own lack of bruises? She knew *she* was human. Was this part of his repertoire? Had he somehow kept her from being injured?

"The cut on your face," she blurted, too troubled to keep the words in. "What happened to it?"

"I'm a fast healer."

"Don't pull that crap on me," she said, more annoyed than was called for. "Your cheekbone was bruised and swollen, and the skin was split open just a few hours ago. Now there isn't a single mark."

He gave her expression a lightning fast assessment, then said, "Let's go up to the suite so we can talk. There are a few things I haven't mentioned."

"No joke," she muttered as they went through the hotel offices to his private elevator, which went only to his suite. His office was on the same floor, but it was separate from the suite, on the other side of the hotel. When his chief of security had dragged her up here, he had used one of the public elevators. No wonder there hadn't been any other people on the floor when they evacuated, she thought; the entire floor was his.

The three-thousand-square-foot suite felt and looked like any luxury hotel suite: completely impersonal. He'd said the only time he spent the night there was if some complication kept him at the casino so late that driving home was ridiculous. The rooms were large and comfortable, but there was nothing of him there except the changes of clothing he kept for emergencies.

It was strange, she thought, that she already knew his taste in furnishings, his color choices, artwork he had personally chosen. Some interior designer specializing in hotels, not in homes, had decorated this suite.

He strolled down the two steps to the sunken living room and over to the windows. He had an affinity for windows, she'd noticed. He liked glass, and lots of it—but he liked being outside even more, which was why the suite had a sundrenched balcony large enough to hold a table and chairs for alfresco dining.

"Okay," she said, "now tell me how bruises and cuts went away in just a few hours. And while you're at it, tell me why I'm not bruised, too. I'm not even sore!"

"That one's easy," he said, pulling a silver charm from his pocket and draping the cord over his hand so the charm lay flat on his palm. "This was in the console."

The little charm was some sort of bird in flight, maybe an eagle. She shook her head. "I don't get it."

"It's a protection charm. I told you about them. I keep

Gideon supplied with them. He usually sends me fertility charms——"

Lorna jerked back, making a cross with her fingers as if to ward off a vampire. "Keep that thing away from me!"

He chuckled. "I said it's a protection charm, not a fertility charm."

"You mean it's like a rubber you hang around your neck instead of putting on your penis?"

"Not that kind of protection. This kind prevents physical harm——or minimizes the damage."

"You think that's why we weren't injured today?"

"I know it is. Since he's a cop, Gideon wears one all the time. This one came in the mail on Saturday, which means he'd just made it. I don't know why he made a protection charm instead of a fertility charm, unless he now has a diabolical plot to eventually disguise a fertility charm as a protection charm, but this one is the real deal. This close to the solstice, his gifts can get away from him, just like mine sometimes do. He must have breathed one hell of a charm," he said admiringly. "I didn't wear it. I just put it in the glove box and forgot about it. Normally the charms are for specific individuals, but when neither of us was injured today...I guess it must affect anyone within a certain distance. It's the only explanation."

Actually, that was kind of cool. She even liked the way he'd phrased it: *Breathed one hell of a charm.* "Does it make you heal faster, too?"

Dante shook his head as he slipped the charm back in his pocket. "No, that's just part of being Raintree. When I say I'm a fast healer, I mean really, really fast. A little cut like that—— it was nothing. A deeper cut might take all night."

"How terrible for you," she said, scowling at him. "What other unfair advantages do you have?"

"We live longer than most humans. Not a lot longer, but our average life expectancy is about ninety to a hundred years. They're usually good years, too. We tend to stay really healthy. For instance, I've never had a cold. We're immune to viruses. Bacterial infections can still lay us low, but viruses basically don't recognize our cellular composition."

Of all the things he'd told her, not ever having a cold seemed the most wonderful. That also meant never having the flu, and—"You can't get AIDS!"

"That's right. We run hotter than humans, too. My temperature is usually at or above a hundred degrees. The weather has to get really, really cold before I get uncomfortable."

"That's so unfair," she complained. "I want to be immune to colds and AIDS, too."

"No measles," he murmured. "No chicken pox. No shingles. No cold sores." His eyes were dancing with merriment. "If you really want to be Raintree and never have a stuffy nose again, there's a way."

"How? Bury a chicken by the dark of the moon and run backward around a stump seven times?"

He paused, arrested by the image. "You have the strangest imagination."

"Tell me! How does someone become Raintree? What's the initiation ritual?"

"It's an old one. You've heard of it."

"The chicken one is the only one I know. C'mon, what is it?"

His smile was slow and heated. "Have my baby."

# TWENTY-ONE

Lorna went white, then red, then white again. "That isn't funny," she said in a stifled tone, getting up to prowl restlessly around the room. She picked up a pillow and fluffed it, but instead of placing it back on the sofa, she stood with it clasped to her chest, her head bowed over it.

"I'm not joking."

"You don't...you shouldn't have babies as a means to an end. People who don't want babies for themselves should never, never have them."

"Agreed," he said softly, leaving his spot by the windows and strolling toward her as unhurriedly as if he had no destination, no agenda.

"It's nothing to be taken lightly." That was a dirty game of pool he was playing, saying *Have my baby* as if he meant it. He couldn't mean it. They had known each other two days. That was something men said to seduce women, because hundreds of centuries ago some cunning bastard had figured out most women were pushovers for babies.

"I'm taking this very seriously, I promise." His tone was gentle as he touched her shoulder, curving his palm over the slope before sliding his hand over her back. She felt the heat transferring from his skin to hers, burning through her clothes. His fingertips sought out her spine, stroking downward, gently rubbing out the tension thrumming beneath her skin.

She hadn't known she was so tense, or that the gentle massage would turn her to butter. She let him urge her against him, let her head nestle into his shoulder, because everything about what he was doing felt so good. Still... She looked up at him with narrowed eyes. "Don't think I haven't noticed how close that hand's getting to my butt."

"I'd be disappointed if you hadn't." A smile curved his mouth as he pressed a warm kiss, then another, to her temple.

"Don't let it get any lower," she warned.

"Are you sure?" Beginning at the waistband of her jeans, he traced a finger down the center seam—down, down, pressing lightly, while his hot palm massaged her bottom. That finger left a trail of fire in its wake, made her squirm and shudder and begin, at least ten times, to say *No*. He would stop if she said it; the decision to continue or not was hers—but the security of knowing that was what kept the single word unsaid. Instead, all she did was gasp with agonized anticipation, and arch, and cling—waiting, waiting, focusing entirely on the slow progression of the caress, as his hand slowly slid down to dip between her legs from behind. He pressed harder then, his fingers rubbing against her entrance through her jeans, so that the friction of the seam lightly abraded flesh that was soft and yielding.

He had been bringing her to this point for two days, since that first kiss in his kitchen, patiently feeding the spark of desire until it became a small flame, then keeping the flame going with fleeting touches and something even harder to resist: his open desire for her. She could recognize what he was doing, see the subtle progressions, and even appreciate the mastery of his restraint. Getting into bed with her last night—and then not touching her—had been diabolically intelligent. Since the moment they'd met, he had forced her to do a lot of things, but not once had he tried to force her response. She would have shut him down cold if he had. The spark would have gone out, and she wouldn't have let it be resurrected.

His warm mouth moved along the line of her jaw, leisurely nipping and tasting, as if he wanted nothing more than this and had all the time in the world in which to savor her. Only the rock-hard bulge in his jeans betrayed any urgency, and she was pressed so tightly to him that she could feel every twitch, every throb, that invited her to part her legs and let him get even closer.

Then his mouth closed over hers and the last shred of re-straint dissolved. The kiss was hard and deep and hungry, his tongue taking her mouth. Desire sizzled along her nerves, turned her warm and yielding and boneless. His free hand moved to her breasts, found her nipples through the layers of cloth, gently pinched them awake. He had her now; she wasn't restraining him from any caress, and the clothing that kept his body from hers was suddenly maddening. She wanted the rest of it, all he had to give her, and with a burst of clarity, she knew she had to say what she wanted to say *now*. A minute from now would be too late.

The proof of how far gone she was came in the amount of

willpower it took for her to tear her mouth from his. "We need to talk," she said, her voice strained and husky.

He groaned and laughed at the same time. "Oh, God," he muttered, frustration raw in his tone. "The four words guaranteed to strike fear in any man. Can't it wait?"

"No—it's about this. Us. Now."

He heaved a sigh and pressed his forehead against hers. "Your timing is sadistic, you know that?"

Lorna slid her hands into the black silk of his hair, feeling the coolness of the strands, the heat of his scalp. "Your fault. I almost forgot." Her tongue felt a little thick, her speech slower than normal. Yes, this was definitely his fault, all of it.

"Let's have it, then." Resignation lay heavy in the words, the resignation of a simple male who just wanted to have sex. She would have laughed, if not for the heavy pull of desire that threatened to overwhelm everything else.

She swallowed, struggled to get the words lined up in her head so she could say them coherently. "My answer...to whether or not we do this...depends on you."

"I vote yes," he replied, biting her earlobe.

"This mind-control thing...you have to stop. I can be your prisoner or your lover, but I won't be both."

He lifted his head then, his gaze going cool and sharp. "There's no compulsion involved in this. I'm not forcing you." Anger clipped his words.

"I know," she said, drawing a shuddering breath. "I can tell the difference, believe me. It's... I have to have the choice, whether to stay or go. The freedom has to be there. You can't keep moving me around like a puppet."

"It was necessary."

"At first. I hated it then, I hate it now, but you did have valid reasons *at first*. You don't now. I think you're too used to having your way in everything, *Dranir*."

"You would have run," he said flatly.

"My choice." She couldn't bend on this. Dante Raintree was a force of nature; dealing with him in a relationship would be challenging enough even without his ability to chain her with a thought. He had to bow to her free will or their only relationship could be jailer and prisoner. "We're equals...or we're nothing."

Reading him wasn't easy, but she could see he didn't like relinquishing control at all. Intuitively, she grasped his dilemma. On a purely intellectual basis, he understood. On a more primitive level, he didn't want to lose her, and he was prepared to be as autocratic and heavy-handed as necessary.

"All or nothing." She met his gaze, squaring up with him like fighters in a boxing ring. "You can't use mind control on me *ever again*. I'm not your enemy. At some point you have to trust me, and that point is now. Or were you planning to keep me pinned forever?"

"Not forever." He ground out the words. "Just until—"

"Until what?"

"Until you wanted to stay."

She smiled at that rough admission and gripped both hands in his hair. "I want to stay," she said simply, and kissed his chin. "But at some point I may want to go. You have to take that chance, and if that day does come, you have to let me go. I'm taking the same chance with you, that one day you may not want me around. I want your word. Promise me you'll never use mind control on me again."

She saw his fury and frustration, saw his jaw work as he ground his teeth. She knew what she was asking of him; giving up a power went against every instinct he had, as both a man and a Dranir. He lived in two worlds, both the normal and the paranormal, and in both he was boss. As understated as he kept things, he was still boss. If he hadn't been the Raintree Dranir, his natural dominance would have been reined in more, but reality was what it was, and he was a king in that world.

Abruptly he dropped his arms from around her and stepped back. His eyes were narrowed and fierce. "You may go."

Lorna barely controlled a protest at the loss of his touch, his heat. What was he saying? "Are you giving me your permission—or an order?"

"A promise."

Breathing was abruptly difficult. Her lips trembled, and she firmed them, started to speak, but he lifted a hand to stop her. "One thing."

"What?"

The green of his eyes almost glowed, they were so intent. "If you stay...the brakes are off."

Fair warning, she thought dizzily, shivering a little in anticipation. "I'm staying," she managed to say, taking half a step forward.

A half step was all she had time to take before he moved, an explosion of pent-up power that was now released from all constraint. If she was free, then so was he. He swung her off her feet and carried her into the bedroom, moving so fast her head swam. The slow, careful seduction was over, and all that was left was raw desire. He tossed her on the bed and followed her down, pulling at her clothes, his movements rough with urgency, even though she helped him, her own hands shaking as she dealt with buttons and zippers, hooks and laces. He jerked her shoes and jeans off as she fought to unbutton his shirt, peeled her underwear down her legs while she struggled to lower his zipper, hampered by the thrust of his erection.

He shoved his jeans and boxers down, and kicked them away. Lorna tried to reach for him, tried to stroke him, but he was a tidal wave that flattened her on the bed and crushed her under his heavy weight. His penetration wasn't careful, it was hard and fast and powerful, taking him deep.

She gave a choked cry, her body shocked by the impact even as she rose to meet it. His heat burned her, inside and out. He pulled out, thrust in again, then again. Her brain stuttered a warning of what that heat meant, and she managed to say, "Condom."

He swore, pulled out, and jerked open a drawer in the bedside table. He tore the first condom, rolling it on. Swearing even more, he slowed down, took more care with the second one. When he was safely sheathed, he pushed into her again, then held her crushed to him, their bodies straining together as relief shuddered through them. Tears rolled down her face. This wasn't an orgasm, it was...pure relief, as if unrelenting pain had suddenly vanished. It was completion—not a sexual one, but something that went deeper, as if some part of her had been missing and suddenly was there.

It was being filled, when she hadn't realized how empty she was; fed, when she hadn't known she was hungry.

He rose, supporting his weight on his arms as he pulled back, then eased forward in a slow, deep thrust. "Don't cry," he murmured, kissing the tears from her wet face.

"I'm not," she said. "It's just leakage."

"Ah."

He said it as if he understood, and maybe he did. He snagged her gaze and held it as he moved in and out, drawing her response to him, going deep to find more. She was both relaxed and tense at the same time: relaxed because she knew he wasn't going to leave her behind, and tense from the building pleasure.

It happened faster than she'd thought possible. Instead of hovering just out of reach, building slowly, she came hard in a rush of sensation that roared through her entire body. Dante slipped his own leash, driving fast and deep, and followed.

When she was able to breathe again, able to open her eyes, the first thing she saw was fire. Every candle in the room was flaming.

"Tell me why you denied your gift."

They were lying entwined, her head on his shoulder, barely recovered from what had felt so cataclysmic that neither of them had spoken for a long time. Instead they had been slowly stroking each other, touch replacing words, touches of reassurance and comfort, of silent joy.

She sighed, for the first time in her life feeling a little distance from the unhappiness of her childhood. "I think you already know. It's not an original story, or an interesting one."

"Probably not. Tell me anyway."

She smiled against his shoulder, glad he wasn't making any big deal of it, though the smile faded almost as fast as it had bloomed. Talking about her mother was difficult, even though it had been fifteen years since she'd last seen her. Maybe it would never be easy, but at least the pain and fear were less immediate.

"As bad as it was, a lot of kids have it worse. The only reason she didn't abort me was so she could get that monthly check. She told me that every month when it came. She'd shake the envelope at me and say, 'This is the only reason you're alive, you freak.' That check helped keep her in drugs and booze."

He didn't say anything, though his mouth tightened.

Her head found a more comfortable resting spot on his shoulder, and she nestled against him, soaking up his heat. She'd known he felt hot, but it was nice to know she hadn't been imagining things. "It was constant slaps, and she'd throw things at me—cups, empty wine bottles, a can opener. Whatever was near. Once she threw a can of chicken noodle soup, hit me in the head, and knocked me out. I had a headache for days. And she wouldn't let me have any of the soup."

"How old were you?"

"That time...six, I think. I'd started school and discovered numbers. Sometimes I was so excited I'd have to tell someone what I'd learned about the numbers that day, and she was the only someone I had. She told my teacher I'd fallen and hit my head on the curb."

"You'd have been better off in foster care," he growled.

"I ended up there when I was sixteen. She took off one day and never came back. I remember... even though she'd made it plain how much she hated me, when she left it was as if part of me was missing, because she was what I knew. By that time I wasn't helpless, but when I was little...no matter how bad it is, little kids will do anything to hold on to what passes for a family, you know?" She sighed. "I know I overreacted about the baby thing. I'm sorry. You said 'baby,' and that's one of my triggers."

A little smile curved his mouth. "Don't get upset again, but I wasn't joking. When a human mother gives birth to a Raintree baby, she becomes Raintree. No, I don't understand the science of it. Something to do with hormones and the mixing of blood, and the baby being a genetic dominant. I'm not sure there *is* any science to explain it. Magic doesn't need to be logical."

The explanation intrigued her. Everything she'd learned about the Raintree intrigued her. It was such a different world, a different experience, and yet they existed normally within the regular world—not that the regular world knew about them, because if that ever came about, then their existence would not only not be normal but they might cease to exist at all. Lorna had few illusions about the world she lived in. "What about human men who have babies with Raintree women? What changes them?"

"Nothing," Dante said. "They stay human."

That didn't seem fair, and she said so. Dante shrugged. "Life isn't perfect. You deal with it."

Wasn't that the truth. She knew about dealing. She also knew that, right now, she was very happy.

The dozen or so candles in the room were putting out enough heat that she was beginning to be uncomfortable. Looking around at them, she realized that Dante and fire went hand in hand. She didn't like fire, would always be afraid of it, but…life wasn't perfect. You dealt with it.

"Can you put out those candles?" she asked.

He lifted his head from the pillow and looked at them, as if he hadn't realized they were burning. "Damn. Yeah, no problem." Just like that, they went out, the wicks gently smoking.

Lorna climbed on top of him and kissed him, smiling as she felt a leap of interest against her inner thigh. "Now, big boy, let's see if you can light them again."

# TWENTY-TWO

*Sunday morning*

She had stayed.

Dante came back into the bedroom from the balcony where he'd met the sunrise, intense satisfaction filling him as he saw Lorna still peacefully asleep in his bed. Only the top half of her head was visible, dark red hair vivid against the white pillow, but he was acutely aware of what it meant for even that much to not be covered by the sheet.

She was feeling safer. Not completely safe, not yet, but safer. When he was in the bed with her, she slept stretched out, relaxed, cuddled against him. When he left the bed, though, within five minutes she was curled in a tight, protective ball. One day—maybe not this week or this month, or even this year, but one day—he hoped he could see her sprawled in sleep, head uncovered, maybe no covers at all. Then he would know she felt safe.

And when the day came that he didn't feel the need to constantly check on her whereabouts, he would know that he felt safe, too.

He *didn't* constantly check on her; his pride refused to let him do that to either her or himself, but the need, the anxiety, was always there.

On Wednesday she hadn't gone with him. He'd called the Jaguar dealership and had a new car sent over, and she had stayed there to accept it. The salesman had called his cell phone to let him know delivery had been made, but Dante had expected Lorna to also call and let him know. She hadn't. Since he had also had her own car—a dinged-up, slightly rusty red Corolla—delivered that morning, he'd been acutely aware that she was free, she had wheels, and she had cash in her pocket. If she wanted to leave, he couldn't stop her. He'd given his word.

He'd wanted to call, just to reassure himself that she was still there, but he hadn't. She could walk out as soon as the call ended, so talking to her at any given time was useless. The only thing he could do, *would* do, was hope. And pray.

He hadn't cut his work short. No matter what happened, whether she stayed or left, the work had to be done. Consequently, it was almost sunset when he drove up to see her car still parked in his garage, with his brand-new Jaguar sitting outside, exposed to the sun and blowing grit. As he'd zoomed the Lotus into its slot, all he'd been aware of was a relief so intense that he'd almost been weak with it. Let the Jaguar sit out; seeing her Corolla still there was worth more to him than any car, no matter how expensive.

She'd met him at the kitchen door, wearing a pair of cutoffs and one of his silk shirts, a scowl on her face. "It's eight-thirty.

I'm starving. Do you work this late on a regular basis? Got any idea what we're going to do for dinner?"

He'd laughed and pounced, and showed her exactly what he wanted to eat for dinner. She hadn't said another word about food until after ten.

On Thursday, she'd gone to the hotel with him. Work was continuing at a frantic pace. He'd gotten the okay to bulldoze the charred ruins of the casino so he could begin rebuilding, and things were so hectic he'd actually delegated some authority to her, because he couldn't be in two places at once. On a perverse level, he'd enjoyed watching her give orders to Al Franklin. Al, being Al, was sanguine about everything, but Lorna got a great deal of satisfaction from the arrangement, and he'd got a great deal of enjoyment from her satisfaction.

At lunch, they'd gone to his suite and lit candles. Twice.

On Friday, she didn't go with him, and he'd sweated through that day, too. When he got home, his relief at seeing her car still there had been as acute as it had been on Wednesday, and that was when he faced the truth.

He loved her. This wasn't just sex, just a brief affair, or *just* anything. It was the real deal. He loved her courage, her gallantry, her grumpiness. He loved the snarky comments, the stubbornness and the vulnerability she hated for anyone to see.

Gideon would laugh his ass off when he found out, not just because Dante had fallen so far, but out of sheer relief that at long last, and if the angels smiled, he might soon lose his position as heir apparent.

The bottom dropped out of Dante's stomach and his gut clenched. Last night he'd been rolling on a condom when abruptly he knew that he didn't want to wear protection.

Lorna had been watching him, waiting, and she'd noticed his long hesitation. Finally, without a word, he'd pulled off the condom and tossed it aside, then steadily met her gaze. If she wanted him to put on another one, he would; the choice was hers.

She had reached out and pulled him down and into her. Just remembering the intense half hour that had followed turned him on so much that the candle beside the bed flared to life.

Today was the solstice, and he felt as if he could set the world on fire, as if his skin would burst from all the power boiling inside him. He wanted to pull her under him and ride her until he was completely empty, until she had taken everything he had to give. First, though, they had to have a very serious talk. Last night they'd done something that was too important for them to let drift along.

As he sat down on the edge of the bed, he extinguished the candle, because a candle that was already lit was useless as a barometer of his control. This conversation might be emotionally charged, so he would have to be very careful.

He slid his hand under the sheet and touched her bare thigh. "Lorna. Wake up."

He felt her tense, as always; then she relaxed, and one sleepy hazel eye blinked open and glared at him over the edge of the sheet. "Why? It's Sunday, the day of rest. I'm resting. Go away."

He tugged the sheet down. "Wake up. Breakfast is ready."

"It is not. You're lying. You've been on the balcony." She grabbed the sheet and pulled it over her head.

"How do you know that, if you've been asleep?"

"I didn't say I was sleeping, I said I was resting."

"Eating isn't considered work. Come on. I have fresh

orange juice, coffee, the bagels are already toasted, and the sunrise is great."

"To *you,* maybe, but it's *five-thirty* on Sunday morning, and I don't want to eat breakfast this early. I want one day a week when you don't drag me out of bed at the crack of dark-thirty."

"Next Sunday you can sleep, I promise." Rather than fight her for custody of the sheet, he slid his hand under the covers, found her thigh again and swiftly reached upward to pinch her ass.

She squeaked and bolted out of bed, rubbing her backside. "Payback will be hell," she warned, as she pushed her disheveled hair out of her face and stalked off to the bathroom.

He imagined it would be. Dante grinned as he returned to the balcony.

She came out five minutes later, wrapped in his thick robe and still scowling. She wasn't wearing anything under the robe, so he enjoyed glimpses as she plopped into a chair across from him. It also gaped at the neck, revealing the gold chain from which hung the protection charm he'd given her on Wednesday night. He'd made it specifically for her, out here on the balcony, and let her watch. She'd been enthralled at the way he cupped the charm and held it up so his breath warmed it as he murmured a few words in Gaelic. The charm had taken on a gentle green glow that quickly faded. When he slipped the chain over her head she had fingered the charm, looking as if she might cry. She hadn't taken it off since.

As grumpy as she was when she first woke, she didn't stay that way for long. By the time she'd had her second bite of bagel she was looking much more cheerful. Still, he waited until she'd finished the bagel and her juice glass was empty before he said, "Will you marry me?"

She had much the same reaction as when he'd mentioned a

baby. She paled, then turned red, then jumped out of her chair and went to stand at the railing with her back to him. Dante knew a lot about women, but more specifically, he knew Lorna, so he didn't leave her standing there alone. He caged her with his arms, putting his hands on top of hers on the railing, not holding her tightly but giving her his warmth. "Is the question that hard to answer?"

He felt her shoulders heave. Alarmed, he turned her around. Tears were streaking down her face. "Lorna?"

She wasn't sobbing, but her lips were trembling. "I'm sorry," she said, swiping at her face. "I know this is silly. It's just—no one has ever wanted me before."

"I doubt that. Probably you just didn't notice them wanting you. I wanted you the minute I saw you."

"Not that kind of wanting." Another tear leaked down. "The other kind, the staying-around kind."

"I love you," he said gently, mentally cursing the bitch who had given birth to her for not nurturing the sense of security that every child should have, the knowledge that, no matter what, someone loved her and wanted her.

"I know. I believe you." She gulped. "I sort of figured it out when you deliberately wrecked your Jaguar to protect me."

"I knew I could buy another car," he said simply.

"That's when I knew that you'd ruined me, that I wouldn't be able to leave unless you threw me out. I kept hoping it was just old-fashioned lust I was feeling, but I knew better, and it scared me to death." She gave a shaky laugh, despite the slow roll of yet another tear. "In just two days, you'd ruined me."

He rubbed the side of his nose. "We hadn't had much time together, but it was quality time."

"Quality!" She gaped at him, mouth open. Indignation dried

her tears. "You manhandled me, dragged me into a fire, tore open my head and smashed my brain flat, tore off my clothes and kept me a prisoner!"

"I didn't say it was good quality. You have a way with words, you know that? 'Tore open your head,' my ass."

"You don't like it when I call it 'brain-rape,'" she said sourly. "And I think I have a better grasp of how it felt than you do."

"I guess you do, at that. When you voluntarily link with someone, it doesn't—"

"Good God." She looked horrified. "Some of you actually do that *willingly?*"

"I told you, it doesn't hurt when it's done right. If someone needs to boost their power, they find someone else who is willing to link. Every so often Gideon and I go home to Sanctuary, and we link with Mercy to perform a protection spell over the homeplace. Doing it right takes time, but it doesn't hurt. Will you answer the—"

"I hope you have some kind of law against doing it without permission."

"Uh—no."

She looked horrified. "You mean you Raintree people can just go around breaking into people's heads, and nobody does anything about it?"

He was beginning to feel frustrated. Would the woman never answer his question? "I didn't say that. Very few of us are strong enough to overpower someone else's brain unless they cooperate."

"And you're one of those few," she said sarcastically. "Right. Lucky me."

"Specifically, only the royal family. Which I've asked you to join, I'd like to point out, if you'll answer the damn question!"

She smiled, and it was like a ray of sunshine breaking across her lively, mobile face. "Of course I will. Did you really doubt it?"

"I never know which way you'll jump. I thought you might love me, because you stayed. Then, last night——" He flicked a finger over her chin. "Not telling me to wear a condom was a dead giveaway."

She stared at him, a peculiar expression stealing over her face.

He straightened, instantly alert. "What's wrong?" Just that quickly she looked sick, as if she were going to throw up.

She rubbed her arms, frowning. "I'm cold. It's that same——" She broke off, her eyes widening with horror, and before he could react she threw herself bodily at him, catching him unprepared for the impact of her weight. He caught her, staggering back, then lurching to the side as he tried to catch his balance and failed. They fell to the floor of the balcony in a tangle of arms, legs and bathrobe as the French door behind him shattered. Hard on the explosion of glass came a sharp, flat retort that echoed through the mountains.

Rifle fire.

Dante wrapped his arms around Lorna, got his feet under him and lunged through the shattered door just as another shot spatted into the side of the house where they had been. Then he rolled with her, getting her away from the wall, before finally lunging to his feet and dragging her out into the hall. "Stay down!" he yelled at her when she tried to stand, pushing her flat again.

His mind was racing. The fire. The gang shooting when he and Lorna so conveniently happened to be boxed in the kill zone. Now someone was shooting at him again. These weren't a series of accidents; they were all related. The fire marshal hadn't found any evidence of arson, which meant—

A Fire-Master didn't need accelerants to start a fire, or to keep it going. Someone, or several someones, had been feeding the fire; that was why he hadn't been able to extinguish it. If he hadn't used mind control for the first time just minutes before trying to control the fire and hadn't known how it would affect him, if he hadn't suspected Lorna might be Ansara, he would have figured it out right away.

Ansara! He snarled his rage. It had to be them. Several of them must have gotten together and decided to try burning him out. They'd known he would engage the fire, that he wouldn't give up until it overwhelmed him. If Lorna hadn't been there, the plan would have worked, too, but they hadn't counted on her.

The cold, sick feeling she kept getting—that was when any Ansara were nearby.

"There was a red dot on your forehead," she said, though her teeth were chattering so hard she could barely speak, or maybe that was because he was practically kneeling on her back to keep her down.

A laser targeting system, then. This wasn't simply seizing an opportunity, but actively planning and pursuing.

The sniper had failed. What would they try next? He had to assume there was more than one Ansara out there, had to assume there was a back-up plan. They wouldn't try to burn him out again, since the first effort had failed; they would think he had sufficient power to handle any flame they could muster. But what *would* they do?

Whatever it was, he couldn't let them succeed, not with Lorna here.

"Stay here," he commanded, getting to his feet.

She scrambled after him. The woman didn't obey worth a damn. "I said stay here!" he roared, whirling back and catching her arm, pushing her down once more. He started to stick her ass to the floor with a mental command, but he'd promised her—damn it, he'd *promised* her—and he couldn't do it.

"I was going to call the cops!" she shouted at him, so furious at his rough handling that she was practically levitating.

"Don't bother. This isn't something the cops can handle. Stay here, Lorna. I don't want you caught between us."

"Who is *us?*" she yelled at his back as he charged down the stairs. "What are you going to do?"

"Fight fire with fire," he said grimly.

Dante had a tremendous advantage. This was his home, his property, and he knew every inch of it. Because he was Raintree, because he was the Dranir and took precautions, he went out through the tunnel he'd built under his house. He knew where he'd been standing when the laser scope had settled the telltale dot on his forehead, so he had a good idea where the shooter had been standing, too.

There was only one. He hadn't found signs of any others.

He had no intention of trying to capture the bastard or engaging him in any sort of face-to-face battle. He prowled up the ravine like a big cat, death in his eyes. The shooter's position must have been just around this cut, maybe in that big cluster of rocks. A sniper needed a stable shooting platform, and those rocks would be convenient. This ravine provided good cover, too, for approaching.

And for leaving.

Dante slid around the cut and came face-to-face with a man

wearing desert camo and toting a rifle. He didn't hesitate at all. The man had barely moved, bringing the rifle up to fire, when Dante set him aflame.

The screams were raw and terrified. The man dropped the rifle and threw himself to the ground, frantically rolling, but Dante ruthlessly kept the fire going. This bastard had come close to killing Lorna, and there was no mercy in his heart for anyone who harmed her. In seconds the screams became howls, taking on an inhuman quality—and then silence.

Dante extinguished the flame.

The man lay smoldering, barely recognizable as human.

Dante used his foot to roll the man onto his back. Incredibly, hate-filled eyes glared up at him from the charred face. The hole that had been the man's mouth worked, and a ghostly sound tore from a throat that shouldn't have worked.

"Toooo late. Toooo late."

Then he died, massive shock stopping his heart. Dante stood frozen, his thoughts working furiously.

Too late? Too late for what?

He'd touched the Ansara. The man had been in agony, his hate projected like a force field, and Dante had read him.

Too late.

He could warn Mercy, but it would be too late.

"Oh, shit," he said softly, and ran.

Lorna had obeyed him, and stayed put. She was in the kitchen, crouched by the refrigerator, when he charged in and grabbed the nearest phone. His first phone call was to Mercy. His second was to Gideon, who could get to Mercy much faster than he could.

Because it was the solstice, because Gideon's personal

electrical field played hell with all electronics, when Gideon answered the phone almost all Dante could hear was static.

"Get to Mercy!" he roared, hoping Gideon would understand anyway. "The Ansara are attacking Sanctuary!" Then he slammed down the phone and tore open the door to the garage, his mind racing.

The corporate jet would get him to the airport nearest Sanctuary in about four hours. He could try Gideon again from the plane.

Two hundred years ago the Ansara had tried to destroy the Raintree and had failed. Now they were trying again, and, damn it, this time they might succeed in destroying Sanctuary—where Mercy was, with Eve.

"Where are you going?" Lorna shrieked as he got in the Lotus.

"Stay here!" he ordered one last time, and reversed out of the garage. He didn't want Lorna anywhere near Sanctuary. He didn't know if he would make it back alive, but no matter what, he had to know she was safe.

"I don't think so," Lorna muttered furiously as she changed clothes. Dante Raintree wasn't the only person who knew how to get things done. If he thought he could leave her behind while he went to fight some sort of supernatural battle, well, he would soon find out he was wrong.

* * * * *

# LINDA WINSTEAD JONES

## HAUNTED

With special thanks to Louis Goodrum, for the tour of Wilmington and the valuable insight.

For Linda and Beverly. What a trip this has been!

And for Leslie Wainger. Here's to butterfly years and (thankfully) missed camera moments.

# GIDEON

I am Raintree. It's more than a last name, more than a notation on a family tree. It's a quirk in my DNA.

It's a mark of destiny.

Long story short, magic is real. It's not only real, it exists all around us, but most people never open their eyes wide enough to see. My eyes have always been wide open. Magic is in my blood. My ancestors were called wizards, magicians and witches. They were also called demons and devils. Is it any wonder the family decided years ago to hide our gifts? *Hide,* I said, not *bury.* There's a difference. Power is a responsibility not to be denied in order to make life simple.

Each family member has a specific gift. Some are strong and some are weak; some have gifts that are more useful than others. Each Raintree has an otherworldly talent. Mine is electrical energy. I can harness the electricity that exists all around us. I can even create my own special surge of voltage.

Yeah, I have a tendency to fry computers and destroy fluorescent lights, but that comes with the territory and I've learned to deal with it.

I also speak to ghosts, who are simply a form of electrical energy we don't yet fully understand. This talent comes in handy in my current profession.

I am Gideon Raintree, and I'm Wilmington, North Carolina's one and only homicide detective.

# PROLOGUE

*Sunday—Midnight*

The adrenaline was pumping so hard and fast that Tabby couldn't make herself stand entirely still. Even the quick climb to this third floor walkup hadn't dimmed her excitement. She wrinkled her nose in disdain as she studied the green apartment door and anxiously rose up onto her toes, then dropped down again. The paint on the door was peeling badly; the wood was warped; the number was crooked. What self-respecting Raintree would live in a dump like this one?

Tabby had been waiting for this moment for so long. Forever, it sometimes seemed. She hadn't waited *patiently,* but she had waited. Everything had to be perfect before the assault began; that had been stressed to her on more than one occasion. Finally it was time. She balanced the pizza box in her left hand as she knocked again with her right, harder and faster than she had before. A giddiness rose within her, and she savored it. She'd trained for this moment, had been practicing for almost a year, but finally the time was here.

"Who is it?" an obviously annoyed woman asked from the other side of the weathered green door.

"Pizza delivery," Tabby answered.

She listened as the security chain was undone with the slide of metal on metal and the rattle of sturdy links. A dead bolt turned, and finally—*finally*—the lock in the doorknob clicked and the door swung open.

Tabby took quick stock of the woman before her. Twenty-two years old, five foot four, green eyes, short pink hair. *Her.*

"I think there's been a mistake, unless..." the pink-haired woman began. She didn't get the chance to say another word.

Tabby forced her way into the apartment, pushing the Raintree woman back into the shabby living room and slamming the door behind her. She dropped the empty pizza box, revealing the knife she held in her left hand. "Scream and I'll kill you," she said before Echo had a chance to make a sound.

The girl's eyes got big. Funny, but Tabby had expected the Raintree eyes to be more striking. She'd heard so much about them. Echo's eyes were an average, unexciting blue-gray-green, not at all special.

One swipe and this job would be done, but Tabby didn't want it to be over too soon. Her gift was one of empathy, but rather than experiencing others' emotions, she craved their fear. Hate and horror tasted sweet when Tabby allowed her gift free rein. The dark sensations she drank in made her stronger. At this moment she fed off Echo Raintree's terror, and it felt good. It made her strong, physically and mentally. That terror fed the giddiness.

"I don't have much money," Echo said, pathetic and whining, and growing more and more afraid with every second that passed. "Whatever you want..."

"Whatever I want," Tabby repeated as she forced Echo away until her back was against the wall. Literally. What she really wanted was this girl's power. Prophecy. There was power in prophecy, properly used, though judging by this crappy apartment, Echo had not made the best of her talents. What a shame that something so extraordinary had to be wasted on this trembling doormat.

Tabby sometimes dreamed that when she killed, she absorbed the powers of her victim. It should be possible, should be an extension of her gift, but so far she hadn't been able to make it happen. One day, when her power was properly nourished as it should be, she would find the dark magic to take the next step in her own evolution.

Wishing the gift of prophecy could somehow fly from this Raintree's soul into her own, Tabby touched the girl's slender, pale throat with the tip of her knife. She made a small cut, and the girl gasped, and oh, the rush of fear that filled the air was tasty, and very, very strong.

She could play with Echo Raintree all night, but Cael wanted the job done quickly and efficiently. He'd stressed that to Tabby more than once, when she'd received her assignment. This was not the time to play but to be a soldier. A warrior. Much as she would love to stay here a while and amuse herself with the Raintree, Tabby definitely didn't want to end up on Cael's bad side.

She smiled and drew the knife very slightly away from the drop of blood on the girl's pale throat. Echo looked slightly relieved, and Tabby let the frightened woman believe, for that moment, that this was a simple robbery that would soon be over.

Nothing was over. It had just begun.

# ONE

*Monday—3:37 a.m.*

When Gideon's phone rang in the middle of the night, it meant someone was dead. "Raintree," he answered, his voice rumbling with the edges of sleep.

"Sorry to wake you."

Surprised to hear his brother Dante's voice, Gideon came instantly awake. "What's wrong?"

"There's a fire at the casino. Could be worse," Dante added before Gideon could ask, "but it's bad enough. I didn't want you to see it on the morning news without some warning. Call Mercy in a couple of hours and tell her I'm all right. I'd call her myself, but I'm going to have my hands full for the next few days."

Gideon sat up, wide awake. "If you need me, I'm there."

"No, thanks. You've got no business getting on an airplane

this week, and everything here is fine. I just wanted to call you before I got so tied up in red tape I couldn't get to a phone."

Gideon ran his fingers through his hair. Outside his window, the waves of the Atlantic crashed and rolled. He offered again to go to Reno and help. He could drive, if necessary. But once again Dante told him everything was fine, and they ended the call. Gideon reset his alarm for five-thirty. He would call Mercy before she started her day. The fire must have been a bad one for Dante to be so certain it would make the national news.

Alarm reset, Gideon fell back onto the bed. Maybe he'd sleep, maybe not. He listened to the ocean waves and let his mind wander. With the solstice coming in less than a week, his normal electric abnormalities were really out of whack. The surges usually spiraled out of control only when a ghost was nearby, but for the past few days, and for the week to come, it didn't take the addition of an electrically charged spirit to make appliances and electronics in his path go haywire. There was nothing he could do but be cautious. Maybe he should take a few days off, stay away from the station altogether and lie low. He closed his eyes and fell back asleep.

She appeared without warning, floating over the end of the bed and smiling down at him, as she always did. Tonight she wore a plain white dress that touched her bare ankles, and her long dark hair was unbound. Emma, as she said she would one day be called, always came to him in the form of a child. She was very much unlike the ghosts who haunted him. This child came only in dreams and was untainted by the pain of life's hardships. She carried with her no need for justice, no heartbreak, no gnawing deed left undone. Instead, she brought with her light and love, and a sense of peace. And she insisted on calling him Daddy.

"Good morning, Daddy."

Gideon sighed and sat up. He'd first seen this particular spirit three months ago, but lately her visits had become more and more frequent. More and more real. Who knew? Maybe he had been her father in another life, but he wasn't going to be anyone's daddy in this one.

"Good morning, Emma."

The spirit of the little girl drifted down to stand on the foot of the bed. "I'm so excited." She laughed, and the sound was oddly familiar. Gideon liked that laugh. It made his heart do strange things. He convinced himself that the sense of warm familiarity meant nothing. Nothing at all.

"Why are you excited?"

"I'm coming to you soon, Daddy."

He closed his eyes and sighed. "Emma, honey, I've told you a hundred times, I'm not going to have kids in this lifetime, so you can stop calling me Daddy."

She just laughed again. "Don't be silly, Daddy. You always have me."

The spirit who had told him that her name would be Emma in this lifetime did have the Raintree eyes, his own dark brown hair and a touch of honey in her skin. But he knew better than to trust what he saw. After all, she only showed up in dreams. He was going to have to stop eating nachos before going to bed.

"I hate to tell you this, sweetheart, but in order to make a baby there has to be a mommy as well as a daddy. I'm not getting married and I'm not having kids, so you'll just have to choose someone else to be your daddy this time around."

Emma was not at all perturbed. "You're always so stubborn. I *am* coming to you, Daddy, I *am*. I'm coming to you in a moonbeam."

Gideon had tried romantic relationships before, and they never worked. He had to hide so much of himself from the women in his life; it would never do to have someone that close. And a wife and kid? Forget it. He already had to answer to the new chief, his family and a never-ending stream of ghosts. He wasn't about to put himself in a position where he would be obligated to answer to anyone else. Women came and went, but he made sure none ever got too close or stayed too long.

It was Dante's job to reproduce, not his. Gideon glanced toward the dresser, where the latest fertility charm sat ready to be packaged up and mailed. Once Dante had kids of his own, Gideon would no longer be next in line for the position of Dranir, head of the Raintree family. He couldn't think of anything worse than being Dranir, except maybe getting married and having kids of his own.

Big brother had his hands full at the moment, though, so maybe he would hold off a few days before mailing that charm. Maybe.

"Be careful," Emma said as she floated a bit closer. "She's very bad, Daddy. Very bad. You have to be careful."

"Don't call me Daddy," Gideon said. As an afterthought he added, "Who's very bad?"

"You'll know soon. Take care of my moonbeam, Daddy."

"In a moonbeam," he said softly. "What a load of..."

"It's just begun," Emma said, her voice and her body fading away.

The alarm went off, and Gideon woke with a start. He hated that freakin' dream. He glanced toward the dresser where Dante's fertility charm sat, and then he looked up, almost as if he expected to see Emma floating there. The dreams that were touched with reality were always hardest to shake.

He left the bed and the dreams behind, feeling his body and his mind come awake as he walked slowly to the French doors that opened onto a small private deck. He tossed open the drapes to reveal the ocean, drawing strength from the water as he always did. There were times when he was certain the breaking of the waves came in time with his heartbeat, and there was so much electricity in the ocean that he could smell it, taste it.

He needed to call Mercy and tell her what had happened at Dante's casino, and he would get that taken care of as soon as he had the coffee percolating. He dreaded telling her what had happened. Even though Dante was fine, she would worry.

After he made the call he would head for the office. He knew without a doubt that Frank Stiles had murdered Johnny Ray Black, but he didn't have the evidence just yet. He would, though, in time. He thought again about taking a few days off, just until the summer solstice passed. If everything was quiet at the station, he could bring the case files home and work from here.

Then Emma's final words rang in his ears, as if she were whispering to him still. "It's just begun."

# TWO

The small apartment had been trashed. Broken glass sparkled on anonymous beige carpet; books and carefully chosen knick-knacks had been raked from the shelf to the floor; an empty pizza box lay discarded on the floor; and someone had taken a sharp blade to the old red leather sofa that sat in the middle of the room. Had the sofa been mutilated with the same knife that had killed Sherry Bishop? He didn't know. Not yet.

Gideon kept his eyes on Bishop's body while the woman behind him talked, her voice quick and high. "I thought maybe Echo was on her way home early and had ordered a pizza on her cell, you know? She does like to eat late at night, so I didn't even think..." She snorted. "Stupid. My mother will kill me when she finds out I let a wacko into the apartment."

Gideon glanced up and back. Was that an expression Sherry

Bishop had used a hundred times before and automatically called upon now? Or did she not yet realize that she was dead? *My mother will kill me...*

She looked almost solid, perched on the chair behind him. As usual, she wore a faded pair of hip-hugger jeans and a T-shirt with the hem ripped to display her belly button and the piercing there. The hairdo was new.

Echo had found the body earlier this morning, after returning from a weekend trip to Charlotte. She'd immediately called him instead of dialing 911. So much for taking the week off. Gideon had made the necessary calls by cell phone, while on his way to the scene. After he'd arrived, he'd talked to Echo in the hallway. He'd calmed her down as best he could, and he'd been here to stop the first patrolmen who arrived from entering and possibly contaminating the crime scene. The uniforms stood in the hallway still, peering into the apartment like kids who weren't allowed into the candy store. Had he ever been that young?

They were all watching, but he couldn't worry about that. He already had a reputation as being odd; that was the least of his worries.

"Did you know him?" he asked softly.

"Her," Sherry said.

A woman? Gideon glanced at the body again, then at the mess the attacker had made of the apartment. *She's very bad, Daddy. Very bad.* When Emma had appeared to him in the dream, Sherry Bishop had been dead for hours. Not only dead, but mutilated. The index finger of her right hand was missing, cut off after death, judging by the small amount of blood that had been shed. A neat square of her scalp, as well as a portion of blond and pink hair, had also been taken. He had a hard time comprehending that a woman had done this, but by now he should know that anything and everything was possible.

"Did you know her?"

The specter shook her head. She looked almost real, except that she wasn't entirely solid. It was as if she were manufactured entirely of a thick mist. Her pink-and-blond spiked hair, the jeans and T-shirt she wore, her pale skin. It was all slightly less than substantial. "I opened the door, she rushed in and said she wouldn't hurt me if I didn't scream, and then she hit me on my neck and..." She laid a hand over her throat and looked past Gideon to the body. Her body. "That bitch killed me, didn't she?"

"I'm afraid so. Anything you can tell me about her would be helpful."

Sherry looked at the body and gasped. "She cut off my finger? How am I supposed to play the drums with..." The ghost fell back against the couch. "Yeah, I know," she sighed. "Dead."

"Detective Raintree?" One of the patrolmen stuck his head in the room. "Are you, uh, okay?"

Gideon lifted a hand without looking at the officer. "I'm fine."

"I heard you, uh, talking."

This time Gideon did look at the kid. Hard. "I'm talking to myself. Let me know when the crime scene techs arrive."

He heard Echo start to cry again, and the officers turned to comfort her. His cousin was distracting them so he could work in peace, he knew. There wasn't a man alive who would mind comforting Echo Raintree.

The ghost of Sherry Bishop sighed again, and her form vibrated. "They can't see me, can they?"

"No," Gideon whispered.

"But you can."

He nodded.

"Why is that?"

Blood. Genetics. A curse. A gift. Electrons. "We don't have time to talk about me." He didn't know how long Sherry Bishop would remain earthbound. Maybe a few minutes more, maybe an hour, maybe a couple of days. Perhaps she would demand justice and hang around until his job was done, but he couldn't be sure. He could never be sure. Ghosts were damned unreliable. "Tell me everything you remember about the woman who attacked you."

Detective Hope Malory rushed up the stairs of the old apartment building, slowing her step as she approached the third floor. Half a dozen cops and a handful of neighbors were milling around in the hallway outside the victim's apartment, all of them trying to peer inside as if there were a show going on. All but one petite young woman with short blond hair shot with liberal hot pink streaks. She hung back, almost as if she were afraid to see what was happening inside.

Hope took a deep breath and smoothed her navy-blue jacket as she approached. This morning she'd dressed professionally, as always, in trousers and a jacket like any other detective. Her pistol was housed in a holster at her waist, and her badge hung around her neck, so everyone could see it plainly.

The only concessions she made to her femininity were a touch of makeup and the two-inch heels. She wanted to make a good impression, since this was her first day on the job. From everything she'd heard, no matter what she said or did, her new partner was *not* going to be happy to see her.

She made her way past a couple of the officers to the

doorway. One of them whispered to her, "You can't go in there." She stopped for a moment and watched Detective Gideon Raintree at work.

She'd studied his file extensively in preparation for this assignment. The man was not only a good cop, he had a solution rate that boggled the mind. Right now he was down on his haunches, studying the body and talking to himself in a low voice. Behind him, a lamp on an end table directed light on to his tightly-wound body in an odd way, as if he were caught in the spotlight. All the blinds were closed, so the room was almost dark. Everything was as he'd found it, she knew.

The photograph in Gideon Raintree's file didn't do him justice, Hope could tell that from where she stood, even though she didn't have a clear view of his face. He was a very good-looking man with a great body—the perfectly cut suit couldn't hide that—and the fact that he needed a haircut didn't make him any less attractive. She'd always been a sucker for longish hair on a man, and very dark brown hair with just a touch of a wave hung a tad too long on Raintree's neck. No matter how conservatively he dressed, he would never completely pull off a conventional look.

The suit he wore was expensive; he hadn't bought that on a cop's salary, not unless he'd been living on macaroni and cheese for the past year. It was dark gray, perfectly fitted, and would never dare to wrinkle. The shoes were expensive, too, made of good quality leather. He had a neatly trimmed mustache and goatee, very hip, very roguish. If not for the gun and badge, Raintree wouldn't look at all like a cop.

She stepped into the room, against the whispered advice of the officer behind her. Raintree's head snapped up. "I told you…" he began, but he didn't finish his sentence. He stared at her with intense green eyes that were surprised and intelligent, and Hope got her first really good look at Gideon Raintree's face. Cheekbones and eyelashes like that on a man really should be illegal, and the way he stared at her with those narrowed eyes...

The lightbulb in the lamp behind him exploded.

"Sorry," he said, as if he had somehow made the lightbulb explode. "I'm not ready for the crime scene techs. Give me a few more minutes and I'll be out of your way." His tone was dismissive, and that rankled.

"I'm not with the Crime Scene Division," Hope said as she took a careful step forward.

His head snapped up, and he glared at her again, not so politely this time. "Then get out."

Hope shook her head. Normally she would offer her hand for a professional greeting when she got close enough, but Raintree was wearing white gloves, so she would be keeping her hands to herself. The firm businesslike handshake she usually offered the men she worked with would have to wait. "I'm Detective Hope Malory," she said. "Your new partner."

He didn't hesitate before answering with confidence, "My partner retired five months ago, and I don't need another one. Don't touch anything on your way out."

She was dismissed, and Raintree returned his attention to the body on the floor, even though he now had less light to study it by. The overhead light was dim, but she supposed it cast enough illumination over the scene. Hope had tried not to actually look at the body, but as she continued to stand her ground, she made herself take in the scene before her. It was the hair that caught her attention first. Like the woman in the hall, this victim's hair was a mixture of pale blond and bright pink. She was dressed in well-worn blue jeans and a once-white T-shirt that advertised a local music festival. She had four gold earrings in one ear and one in the other, and wore a total of five rings—a mixture of gold and silver—on her slender fingers. All nine of them. Hope's stomach flipped. One finger had been removed, and there was a horrible bloody wound on the top of the victim's head, as if someone had tried to scalp her.

The same someone who had sliced her throat.

Hope took a deep breath to compose herself, then decided that wasn't a good idea. Death wasn't pretty, and it didn't smell nice, either. She had, of course, seen bodies before. But they hadn't been quite this *fresh,* or this mangled. It was impossible not to be affected by the sight.

Raintree sighed. "You're not going away, are you?"

Hope shook her head, and tried to casually cover her nose and mouth with one hand.

"Fine," Raintree said sharply. "Sherry Bishop, twenty-two years old. She was single and had no significant relationship at the time of her murder. Money was tight, so robbery is unlikely as a motive. Bishop was a drummer with a local band and also waitressed at a coffee shop downtown to make ends meet."

"If she was in a band, maybe a stalker fixated on her," Hope suggested.

The man who continued to squat on the floor by the body shook his head. "She was killed by a left-handed woman with long blond hair."

"How did you come up with all that information in the past, what, twenty minutes?"

"Fifteen." Gideon Raintree stood slowly.

He was over six feet tall—six-one, to be exact, according

to his file—so Hope had to crane her neck to look him in the eye. His skin was warm, kissed by the sun, and this close, the green of his eyes was downright remarkable. The goatee and moustache gave him an almost devilish appearance, and somehow it suited him. When his eyes were narrowed and watchful, as they were now, he looked incredibly hard, as if he possessed no more heart than the murderers he pursued. Feeling more than a little like a coward, Hope dropped her gaze to his blue silk tie.

"From the angle of the wound, it appears that the attacker held the knife in her left hand," he explained. "The coroner will confirm that, I'm sure."

From what she'd heard, Gideon Raintree was always sure of himself. And always right. "You said *her*. How can you know the killer was a woman?"

Gideon nodded. "There's a single long blond hair on the victim's clothing. Hair that length on a man is possible, but unlikely. Again, the coroner will have to confirm."

All right, he was observant. He had done this before. He was good. "How could you possibly know the personal details of her life?" Hope asked. Drummer. No significant other. Waitress in a coffee shop. She quickly scanned the room for clues and saw none.

"Sherry Bishop was my cousin Echo's roommate."

Hope nodded. She tried to remain unaffected, but the smell was making her queasy.

Raintree stared right through her with those odd eyes of his. "This is your first homicide, isn't it?"

Again Hope nodded.

"If you're going to throw up, do it in the hallway. I won't have you contaminating my crime scene."

How thoughtful. "I'm not going to contaminate your crime scene."

"Good. If you insist on sticking around, interview the neighbors and see if they heard anything last night or early this morning."

Gladly. Hope nodded yet again, then turned to escape from the room, leaving Gideon Raintree alone with the victim. She was quite certain that he was more comfortable with the dead woman than he was with her.

His new partner was intently interviewing a nosy neighbor, and the crime scene techs were doing their thing inside the apartment. Gideon sat beside Echo on the steps that led to the fourth floor.

"Is she here?" Echo asked softly.

No one was paying them any attention at the moment. Gideon didn't expect that would last long. "She's sitting behind us."

Even though Echo knew she wouldn't see anything, she glanced over her shoulder to the deserted steps. "I'm sorry. I should've known."

Like Bishop, Echo was a young twenty-two. She was incredibly talented—as a guitar player and as a seer—but she had little or no control over her gift of prophecy. Calling her psychic wasn't quite right. She couldn't tell you where you'd left your wallet or whether or not you would marry within the next year, but she did see disasters. She dreamed of floods and earthquakes. Her nightmares came true.

Gideon had a touch of pre-cog ability, but not enough to make a significant difference. His instincts were just a hair sharper than was normal, but he didn't dream about catastrophes and experience them as if he were there—there and unable to do anything to stop what was coming. Compared to Echo's power, he considered talking to dead people a walk in the park.

"It was painless," Gideon said as he put his arm around Echo's shoulder. "She didn't even know what happened."

"What a load of bull," Sherry muttered, her voice sour. "It hurt like hell!"

Fortunately, no one but Gideon heard her.

"Why would anyone kill Sherry?" Echo asked. The tears hadn't stopped, but they were softer now. Constant but gentle. "Everyone liked her."

"I don't know." Something Gideon didn't like niggled at his brain. Bishop hadn't recognized her killer. She'd never suspected that her life was in danger. There was no logical reason for her to be dead, much less savagely mutilated. In every case he'd had since moving to Wilmington four years ago, the victim had known the name of the killer. Drugs were the usual motive, but there had been a few crimes of misdirected passion. Murder by stranger was a rare thing. With a few notable exceptions, it took a personal connection for murder to occur.

He didn't want to scare his cousin, but there was one possibility he couldn't ignore. "Have you had any visions lately that might've put you in danger?"

Echo didn't need to be asked twice. "Do you think the person who killed Sherry was after *me?*"

"Son of a bitch!" Sherry said softly. "I never should've dyed my hair blond and pink like Echo's. We thought it would be such a good thing for the band, you know? A trademark. A…a *thing…*" She pouted. "I thought it was so cute."

"It's just a possibility," Gideon said softly. "Look, you won't be able to stay here for a while anyway, so I want you to find yourself a quiet place to crash, and I want you to stay there until I figure this out. Where are your folks?"

"St. Moritz."

Figures. "I don't want you going that far." Besides, Echo's parents were all but useless in a crisis. "You can stay at my place for a few days."

Echo sighed and rested her head on her hands. "We have a gig next weekend, so I'm cool until then. I can call the coffee shop and tell them I won't be in this week, and then I can go to Charlotte and stay with Dewey until Friday."

Dewey. Great. The guy was a rail-thin goofy-looking saxophone player who had the hots for Echo, even though she insisted they were just friends. Still, a few days with Dewey would be better than staying around here if there was any chance the murderer had been after Echo and not Sherry. "Call me before you come back to town. You may have to cancel your gig."

Echo didn't protest, as he'd thought she might. "Maybe we should just cancel everything. We'll never find a drummer to take Sherry's place. And even if we do, it won't be the same."

Gideon didn't see Echo often. He was twelve years older than she was, and they had no common interests. In fact, his little cousin had a wild streak that put his teeth on edge. Not that he'd always been a saint. But they were family, and he checked in on her now and then. He had even been to a smoky club to see her band play a couple of times. The music had been too loud and too angry to suit him, but the girls had all seemed to have a good time.

She was right. It would never be the same.

"You look tired."

Echo shrugged her thin shoulders. "I'm supposed to work this afternoon—you know, at the coffee shop—so I stayed up all night instead of driving home last night or trying to get up early this morning to drive back. You know how I hate to get up early."

"Yeah, I know."

"It just made more sense to stay up and drive back to grab something to eat before I had to..." Her voice hitched. "I guess I should call Mark and tell him I won't be in today, and that Sherry won't...you know."

It was difficult to say aloud. Sherry Bishop wouldn't be going back to work. Ever.

Gideon took his house key from his pocket and handed it to Echo. "Get a couple of hours sleep at my place before you head to Charlotte. You shouldn't be on the road in your condition." She nodded and slipped the key into her front pocket. "Keep your cell on," Gideon added.

None of the Raintrees advertised their gifts, but perhaps someone who had discovered Echo's ability had wanted to silence her. Because of something she'd seen or might possibly see? And why take the finger and a segment of the scalp? That alone took this case beyond anything he had ever worked, but it didn't help him. All he had were questions. Theories. More questions.

When he walked down the steps, Sherry Bishop followed. "You *are* going to find out who did this to me, aren't you?" she asked.

"I'm going to try."

"This is just so freakin' unfair. I had plans for my life, you know. Big plans. I was kinda hopin' you'd ask me out one day. I mean, you're older and all, but you're really hot anyway."

"Gee, thanks," Gideon mumbled.

Sherry gasped. "I never got a chance to wear my new boots! They were really kickin', and I got them on sale." She sighed. "Crap. Tell Echo she can have them."

"I'll tell her."

Gideon stopped at the foot of the stairs and watched his new partner as she interviewed an older woman with frizzy gray hair. He liked to work alone. It made speaking to the victims so much easier. His last partner had finally decided to believe that Gideon talked to himself and had great hunches on a regular basis. Hope Malory didn't look as if she would make things that easy for him. She didn't look at all accepting of things she did not understand.

He appreciated women. He had no plans to marry or even get involved in a serious relationship, ever, but that didn't mean he lived like a monk. Most women were attractive in some way; they all had a feature or two that could catch and hold a man's attention for a while. Hope Malory was much more than attractive. She had a classic beauty. Black hair, cut chin length, hung around her face thick and silky. Her skin was creamy pale and flawless, her eyes a serene dark blue, her lips full and rosy. She was tall, long-legged and slender, yet rounded in all the right places. She had the face of an angel, a body that wouldn't quit, and she carried a gun like she knew how to use it. Did that make her the perfect woman?

A shimmer of pure electricity ran through his body. The lights in the hallway flickered, causing everyone who was lingering in the hall to look up. At least this time nothing exploded.

"You're going to catch her, right?" Sherry Bishop pressed.

He watched Hope Malory take a few furious notes, then ask

another question of the neighbor. "Catch her? Right now I'm not even planning to chase her. She's pretty, but she's not my type, and it's never a good idea to mix business with pleasure."

"Get your mind out of your pants, Raintree," Sherry said sharply. "I'm not talking about your new partner, I'm talking about the woman who killed me."

He didn't take his eyes off Malory as he answered, "I'm going to try."

"Echo says you're the best," Sherry said more kindly.

"Does she?" Hope Malory glanced his way, caught his eye, then quickly returned her attention to the neighbor.

"Yeah. And you'd better hurry, Raintree."

Gideon turned to look at Sherry Bishop. She'd faded considerably since they'd left the apartment. Soon she would move on, go home, be at peace. That was as it should be, but once that happened he would have a much harder time communicating with her. It might be possible, but it certainly wouldn't be this easy.

Malory made her way toward him with long, easy strides that spoke of confidence and grace. Her notes had been dutifully taken, and he was sure they would be complete.

"Nothing," she said softly as she came near. "Mrs. Tarleton, who lives right next door, is practically deaf, and the other neighbor was out until early this morning. No one heard anything. Everyone liked the victim and your cousin, even though they were, as Mrs. Tarleton said, young and a bit wild." She looked past Gideon to the stairway. "Maybe I should talk to your cousin."

"No."

She looked him in the eye and lifted her eyebrows slightly. "No?"

"I've already talked to Echo."

"You're her cousin, which means you're too close to her to be objective. Besides, you're a man."

"You make that sound like a bad thing."

"It can be. The point is, she might tell me things she wouldn't tell you."

"I doubt it."

The woman got her hackles up. "Should you even be working this case? After all, you have a personal connection here."

"I met Sherry Bishop one time. Maybe twice. There's no reason——"

"I'm not talking about your relationship to the victim, Raintree. Until we eliminate her, your cousin is a natural suspect."

"Echo wouldn't hurt anyone."

"You tell her, Gideon," Sherry Bishop said in an irate voice. "How dare she insinuate that Echo would do this to me?"

"You're not objective," Malory insisted.

Gideon did his best to ignore Sherry's ramblings, which had nothing at all to do with her death. "We'll establish my cousin's alibi first thing, if it'll make you feel better. Once she's eliminated from your list of suspects maybe it'll be okay with you if I do my job."

"There's no reason to get snippy."

Gideon leaned down slightly and lowered his voice. "Detective Malory, if you're determined to be my new partner I don't guess there's much I can do about it. Not at the moment, anyway. But do us both a favor and act like a detective, not a little girl."

Her nostrils flared. Ah, he'd hit a nerve. "I am not a *girl*, Raintree, you——"

"Snippy," he interrupted. "A word not used by real men anywhere."

"Fine," she said with unnecessary sharpness. "I'll just grunt a lot and scratch my ass now and then, and maybe I'll fit in."

Sherry grimaced. "I'll bet a chick like her never scratches her ass."

The truth of the matter was that Gideon knew it didn't matter what Hope Malory did or said. She was going to get under his skin big time. Like it or not, she was already there, and she was going to stay until he found a way to get rid of her. Out of sight, out of mind, right? It wasn't as if she was the only pretty woman in Wilmington.

He didn't need a partner; he didn't want one; it would never work. And in the end, it wouldn't matter.

Malory wouldn't last long.

# THREE

"Lunch?" Gideon glanced at his new partner briefly as he negotiated a turn in the road. The wind blew Malory's carefully styled sleek hair into her face. He could have put the top up, he supposed. Then again, why make this easy on her? She'd insisted on coming along, and he'd insisted on driving. She didn't want to know what could happen to her new, electronically handicapped car if he was too near it at the wrong moment.

"I thought you wanted to talk to that club owner," she shouted to be heard above the wind.

"He won't be in until four or later." They'd already spoken to the manager at the coffee shop where Bishop and Echo had both worked for the past seven months. Mark Nelson knew nothing of interest, but Gideon wanted to go back tonight and have a look around. Maybe the killer would be there, watching for a reaction to the news of Sherry Bishop's death.

"Okay," Malory said reluctantly. "I could eat something, I suppose."

She sounded less than enthusiastic, but Gideon figured she would never admit that the murder scene had dampened her appetite.

He made a couple of turns on narrow downtown streets and pulled into the parking lot of Mama Tanya's Café. It was late enough in the afternoon that the lunch rush was over. The gravel parking lot was practically deserted.

"Where are we, Raintree?" Malory asked suspiciously, eyeing the small concrete block building that could use a coat of paint and a bucket of spackle. And maybe a window or two.

"Mama Tanya's," he said, opening his door and stepping out. "Best soul food in town."

She followed him, her heels crunching in the gravel. "If you're trying to scare me off…" she muttered.

Gideon ignored her and stepped into the dimly lit, windowless restaurant. He hadn't been kidding when he'd said this was the best place in town for soul food. It was also a good place, filled with good people. Even the ghosts who dropped in here were happy.

"Detective Raintree." Tanya herself greeted him with a smile that deepened the wrinkles on her serene face. "The usual?"

"Yep." He grabbed his regular booth.

Tanya looked at Malory and raised her eyebrows slightly. "And for you, young lady?"

"I'll just have a salad. Vinaigrette on the side."

The order was met with silent surprise. Gideon glanced back at Tanya as Malory joined him. "Just bring her what I'm having."

Malory started to argue, then thought better of it.

"What if I don't like what you're having?" she asked when Tanya was out of hearing distance.

"You'll like it," he said.

It was the first time all day they'd been in a quiet place, alone, and he took the opportunity to study Hope Malory critically. Her hair was mussed from the ride in his convertible. She'd smoothed it with her hands but hadn't run to the ladies' room to make more extensive repairs. Her cheeks were flushed, her eyes smart. Take-no-prisoners smart. Man, she was gorgeous.

And she was pissed.

"So what are you doing here?" he asked.

"I just wanted a salad," she said softly.

"In Wilmington," he clarified. "This is a relatively small department. I know the detectives from the other divisions, and I know the uniforms. You're not one of them, so how did you end up with this ill-advised and temporary assignment as my partner?"

She didn't take the bait. "I transferred in from Raleigh. I worked vice there for the past two years."

He was surprised. She looked too young to have been a detective for two years. "How old are you?"

She didn't seem to be offended by the question, as some women might have been. "Twenty-nine."

So she was on the fast track. Ambitious, smart, maybe even a little bit greedy. "Why the move?"

"My mother lives here in Wilmington. She needs family close by, so I decided it was time to come back home."

"Is she sick?"

"No." Malory squirmed a little, obviously getting uncomfortable with the personal nature of the discussion. "She fell last year. It wasn't anything serious. She sprained her ankle and hobbled for a couple of weeks."

"But it worried you," he said. Of course it did. Malory was so earnest, so relentlessly dedicated and serious. If anything had happened to her mother, she would see it as somehow being her fault. And so here she was.

"It worried me a little," she confessed. "What about you?" she asked quickly, turning the subject of the conversation around. "Do you have family close by? Other than Echo, that is."

People who asked too many questions always made him nervous. Why did she need to know about his family? Of course, he *had* started this personal discussion. Turnabout was fair play, he supposed. "I have a sister and a niece who live in the western part of the state, a few hours away, a brother in Nevada and cousins everywhere I turn."

That last bit got a small smile out of her. Nice. Maybe she wasn't entirely earnest, after all.

"What about your parents?" she asked.

"They're dead."

Her smile faded quickly. "Sorry."

"They were murdered when I was seventeen," he said without emotion. "Anything else you want to know?"

"I didn't mean to pry."

Of course she hadn't, but his blunt answer had killed the conversation, just as he had hoped. This woman could play hell with his life on so many levels if she made even half an effort. Scary notion.

Tanya placed two very full plates on the table, along with two tall glasses of iced tea.

"Raintree," Malory said in a lowered voice, after Tanya

walked away. "Everything on my plate but the turnip greens is fried."

"Yep," he answered as he dug in. "Good stuff."

They both turned their attention to eating, Hope slightly less enthusiastic than Gideon about the fare, though after a few bites she relaxed and started to enjoy the meal. Gideon was glad for the silence, but it also made him nervous, because there was a level of comfort in it.

He didn't need or want a partner. He'd tolerated Leon for three and a half years, and in the end they'd made a pretty good team. Gideon solved the cases; Leon did the paperwork and handled the bullshit. At the end of the day they both looked good and everyone was happy. Hope Malory did not look like a happy person.

"I think she's killed before," a soft voice called.

Gideon turned his head to glance into the unoccupied booth behind him. Well, it *had* been unoccupied—until Sherry Bishop arrived. She looked less solid than she had back at the apartment, but it was definitely her. "What?" he asked softly.

"Raintree," Malory began, "are you all…"

He silenced his new partner with a lifted hand but never took his eyes from Sherry.

"The woman who killed me," the ghost said. "She wasn't at all afraid or even nervous, just anxious. Wound up, the way Echo and I always were before a gig. I think she liked it. I think she enjoyed killing me."

"Raintree," Malory said again, her voice sharper than before.

Gideon lifted his hand once more, this time with a raised finger to indicate silence.

"Shake that finger at me again and I'll break it off."

Sherry Bishop disappeared, and Gideon turned around to face an angry and confused Detective Malory.

"Sorry," he said. "I was just thinking."

"You have an odd way of *thinking*."

"I've heard that before."

Something in her expression changed. Her eyes grew softer, her lips fuller, and something worse than anger appeared. Curiosity. "But apparently it works," she said. "How do you do it?"

"Think?" He knew what she was asking; he just didn't want to go there.

"I've never known a detective with a record like yours. Except for that one case last year, your record is flawless."

"I know Stiles did it, I just can't prove it. Yet."

"How?" she whispered. "How do you know?"

It was easiest to pretend that he was like everyone else when the question came up. He had a gift for seeing small things that others missed; he had an eye for detail; he saw patterns; he was dedicated to solving each and every case. All those things were true, but they weren't the reason for his almost flawless record.

"I talk to dead people."

Malory's response was immediate and not at all unexpected. She laughed out loud. The laugh did great things to her face. Her eyes sparkled; her cheeks grew pink; her lips turned up at the corners. It struck Gideon sharply that he felt much too comfortable with Hope Malory. That laugh was nicely familiar. He could get used to this…and he couldn't allow that to happen.


Hope drove slowly past Raintree's house, and the sight of his house didn't allay her suspicions at all.

The three-story pale gray Carolina-style house right on Wrightsville Beach hadn't been bought on a cop's salary, that was for sure. This was one of the nicest areas along the strip, and he owned one of the nicest houses. She'd already done some investigating, and she knew what he'd paid for the place when he'd moved in four years ago.

There was a three-car garage at the end of a short paved driveway. She knew, even though the garage doors were down, that every bay was filled. Raintree owned a black '66 Mustang, the convertible he'd driven today; a '57 Chevy Bel Air, turquoise and cream; and a '74 Dodge Challenger in rally-red, whatever that was.

Money aside, no one was as good a cop as Gideon Raintree seemed to be. Most of the murders he'd solved were drug related, which meant he could very well be connected to someone in the community of dealers. Someone high enough up to be able to buy his own cop. Was her new partner involved with the criminal element in Wilmington?

*I talk to dead people* my ass.

The houses on this strip of the beach were impressive, but space was at a premium, and they had been built very close together. One colorful house after another lined this street, and Raintree's tastefully painted gray was one of the finest. Why hadn't anyone ever questioned his lifestyle?

Every detective she knew wanted to work homicide. It was high-profile; it was important. And yet five months after his partner's retirement, Raintree was still working alone—or had been, until she'd come along. The new chief had told her the other detectives weren't interested in working with Raintree. They didn't want to get lost in the shuffle, always being second man on the team, or else they knew Raintree liked to work alone and didn't want to be the one to rock the boat. In other words, if it ain't broke, don't fix it.

Hope had never minded rocking the boat.

Maybe there were completely reasonable answers to all her questions about Raintree, but then again, maybe not. She had to know, before she got herself in too deep. Before she trusted him, before she accepted him.

She knew in her gut that Raintree was a liar. Of course he lied on a regular basis: He had a penis. The question was, how deep did the lies go?

Hope parked her blue Toyota down the street, where someone was having a gathering and an extra car wouldn't stand out, and walked back to Raintree's house. It was unlikely she would see anything this late at night, but she was so curious and wound up that she couldn't possibly sleep. Since her mother never went to bed before 2:00 a.m. and the apartment over the shop was small, sleep wasn't all that easy to come by, anyway.

The house, the expensive suits, the cars...Raintree was definitely into something.

The recently retired partner, Leon Franklin, came off as clean as a whistle when she looked into his background. Franklin had a little money in the bank, but not too much. A nice house, but not too nice. And everyone she'd talked to said Gideon Raintree was the brains of the operation. He got every homicide case in Wilmington, and he solved them all. It just wasn't natural.

Hope slipped into the darkness between Raintree's house and the less subtle yellow house next door. She'd dressed in black for this outing, so she blended into the shadows. She wasn't going to peek through a window and catch Raintree red-handed, but the more she knew about this guy, the better off she would be. There wasn't any harm in just looking around his place a bit.

Movement on the beach caught her attention, and she turned her head in that direction. Speak of the devil. Gideon Raintree was coming in from a swim, too-long hair slicked back, water dripping from his chest. He stepped from the sand onto his own private boardwalk and into more direct lighting. When the light from his deck hit him, she held her breath for a moment. He wore old, holey jeans that had been cut off just above the knees and that hung too low on his waist, thanks to the weight of the water. He wore nothing else, except a small silver charm that hung from a black cord around his neck.

"Gideon," a singsong voice called from the yellow house next to his. He stopped on the boardwalk and lifted his head, then smiled at the blonde who was leaning over her own balcony. Hope hadn't seen so much as a hint of a smile like that one all day. Yeah, the guy was definitely trouble.

"Hi, Honey." Raintree leaned against the boardwalk railing and looked up.

"We're having a party Saturday night," Honey said. "Wanna come?"

"Thanks, but probably not. I'm working a case."

"That girl I saw on the news?" Honey said, her smile fading. "Yeah."

Another woman, a brunette this time, joined Honey at the balcony railing. "You'll have the case solved by Saturday," she said confidently.

"If I do, I'll drop by."

Both women leaned over the railing. They were wearing skimpy bathing suits, as any self-respecting beach bum would be on a warm June night. They practically preened for their neighbor's benefit.

Raintree was the kind of man a shallow woman might go for,

Hope imagined. He had the looks and the bank account, and an obvious kind of charm that came with self-confidence. With those eyes and cheekbones, and the way he looked in those cutoffs, he might make a silly woman's heart race.

Hope had never been silly.

"Why don't you come on up now and have a drink with us?" Honey asked, as if the idea had just popped into her head, though she'd probably been planning to ask her studly neighbor up from the moment she'd seen him on the beach.

"Sorry. Can't do it." Raintree turned toward his own house—and Hope—and it seemed to her that he actually looked directly at her. "I have company."

Hope held her breath. He couldn't possibly see her there. Someone else was coming over, or else he was making an excuse to be polite. As if any red-blooded male would turn down "drinks" with Honey and the brunette bimbo.

"Company?" Honey whined.

"Yeah." Raintree leaned against the walkway railing again and stared into the dark space between the two houses. "My new partner stopped by."

Hope muttered a few soft curse words she almost never used, and Raintree smiled as if he could hear her. That was impossible, of course. As impossible as him seeing her standing in the shadows.

"Bring him on up," the brunette said. "The more the merrier."

"Her," Raintree responded without glancing up to his neighbors. "My new partner is a girl."

He'd said "girl" just to rile her, Hope knew, so she did her best not to react to the gibe.

"Oh." Honey sighed. "Well, you can bring her. I guess." She sounded decidedly less enthusiastic, all of a sudden.

"Thanks, but we'll pass. We have work to discuss. Isn't that right, Detective Malory?"

Busted. Hope took a few steps so that she was caught in the soft light cast from both decks. It was apparently too late to hide. Was Raintree dangerous? Maybe he was. He looked dangerous enough. Then again, she was armed and knew how to defend herself, if it came to that. Somehow, she didn't think it would.

"That's right," she said, as she walked through sand and tall sea grass to the boardwalk.

"How long have you been down there?" Honey asked.

"Just a few minutes."

"You sure were quiet."

"I was just admiring the view."

The brunette sighed. "We certainly do understand that."

Hope felt herself blush. She'd meant the *beach,* of course, but from the tone of the bimbo's voice they thought she meant… Oh, no. She did not want Raintree thinking she enjoyed looking at *him.* Even if she did. "I love the water."

"Me, too," Gideon said.

Hope bounded easily over the railing to join him.

"Come on inside," he said, turning his back on her and leading the way. "I guess you're here to talk about the Bishop case."

"Yeah," she said brightly. "I hope you don't mind me dropping by this way."

He glanced over his shoulder and smiled, wickedly amused. "Not at all, Detective Malory. Not at all."

She was up to something. Pretty Detective Hope Malory was so wound up, so filled with an electricity of her own kind, that if he laid his hands on her, they would probably both explode. Not necessarily a bad idea.

"I'm going to change." Gideon gestured toward the kitchen. "Help yourself to something to drink and I'll be right back."

Echo had slept here for a few hours and then driven to Charlotte. He'd talked to her on the phone, before heading out for a quick swim. She was still upset, but the panic had faded somewhat. Whether he liked it or not, Dewey was actually helping with the difficult situation.

It didn't take Gideon five minutes to put on dry clothes and towel dry his hair, and the entire time he kept asking himself, *Why is Malory here? What does she want?* If there were early results from the crime scene techs' study of the murder scene, they would call him, not her. If she had a theory—and that was all she could possibly have at this point—it could have been communicated by telephone. The owner of the club where Echo's band often played hadn't been any help at all. So why was Malory *here?*

He found out pretty quickly, right after stepping into the living room to find his new partner sitting in a leather chair with a glass of cold soda in one hand. "Nice place, Raintree," she said as her eyes scanned the walls almost casually. "How do you manage this on a cop's salary?"

So that was it. She thought he was dirty, and she was here to find out *how* dirty. Did she want to join him in profitable corruption or toss his ass in jail? He would guess she was the ass-tossing sort, but he'd been wrong about women before. "My family has money." He headed for the kitchen. "I'm going to make myself something to drink."

She nodded to the opposite side of the room, where a glass of soda much like hers sat on a coaster. "I already fixed you a drink."

"How do you know what I want? Psychic?"

Again that fleeting but brilliant smile. "Your fridge was full of the stuff. I took a shot."

Gideon lowered himself into a chair. Was it coincidence that she had placed his glass as far away from her chair as possible? No. Not a coincidence at all. Malory liked to look tough, but now and then he saw a hint of the skittish beneath her skin. When she'd talked about her mother falling and how she might need her daughter, when he'd looked her in the eye…he'd seen the vulnerability in her.

She had certainly done her best to look tough tonight, in her black jeans and black T-shirt and pistol. "Family money," she said, prompting him to continue.

"Yeah."

"What kind of family money?"

"My parents and my grandparents, as well as their parents and grandparents, were all successful. And lucky."

She looked him dead in the eye in that oddly annoying way she had. "I saw Echo's apartment this morning. Is she from the poor side of the family?"

"Echo is a rebel," he explained. "Her parents very happily live off the family money. They travel, they sleep, they drink, they party. That's about it. Echo wants to earn her own way. I admire that in her, even if she does sometimes cut off her nose to spite her face."

"Are you lucky?"

He looked her over appreciatively and smiled. "Not tonight, I'm guessing."

She didn't respond to the comment, not even to bristle. "You're definitely lucky as a detective. I've seen your file."

"Goody for you. I'd like to have a look at yours."

"I'll see what I can do."

She took a drink of her soda, and he played with the condensation on his glass with one finger. If Malory got too nosy, if she asked too many damn questions, he would have to move. Dammit, he liked it here. He liked his house, and the men he worked with—most of them—and he loved being near the ocean. He had come to need it in a way he had never expected. For years he'd moved from department to department, always going to the place where he thought he was needed most. Sadly enough, his talents were called for just about everywhere, so he'd finally decided to settle down here.

If Detective Malory started investigating him and uncovered more than she should, he wouldn't be able to stay here much longer. So much for settling down. So much for home.

He was either going to have to make Hope Malory a friend or get rid of her. She didn't seem like the kind of woman who was easy to get rid of once she dug in her heels, and he wasn't sure he could make her his friend. She didn't seem to be the friendly type.

Again Malory studied the living room with critical eyes. "There's something odd about this place," she said thoughtfully. "Don't get me wrong, it's very pleasant. You have comfortable furnishings, and nice paintings on the walls. Everything matches well enough, and the lamps didn't come from a discount store or a yard sale...."

"But?" Gideon prodded.

She looked at him, then, with those curious blue eyes of hers. "The television is small and cheap, and the phone is an old landline. Most single men of a certain age who have a disposable income own a decent stereo. You have a boom box that any self-respecting fifteen-year-old would be embarrassed to carry onto the beach. Run of bad luck?"

Luck again. How could he tell her that his electronic devices had a nasty habit of exploding without warning? He owned two more small televisions, which were stored in a spare bedroom, ready for the time when this one went, and he'd never had any luck with cordless phones or digital clocks. He couldn't get too close to a vehicle that relied on computer chips, which was why he drove older models. On the rare occasions when he'd been on an airplane, he'd worn a powerful shielding charm that only Dante could fashion. He went through cell phones the way other people went through Kleenex.

"I don't watch much TV. Don't listen to much music, either. Cordless phones aren't secure."

"And you need your phone calls to be secure because...?"

Enough was enough. Gideon rose slowly to his feet. He left his drink behind and crossed the room to stand near her. "Why don't you just ask me?" he said softly.

"Ask you what?"

"Ask me if I'm dirty."

The alarm in her eyes was vivid, and he could almost see her assessing the situation. He wasn't armed, at least as far as she could tell. She was. He had a small advantage, standing over her this way, but she had the gun handy.

"Ask," he said again.

Her eyes caught and held his. "Are you?"

"No."

Her alarm faded gradually. "Something here stinks to high heaven. I just haven't figured out what, yet."

"It's the money. People can't believe that anyone would be a cop if they have any other choice."

"It's more than the money, Raintree. You're good. You're *too* good."

He leaned slightly forward, and she didn't shrink away. She smelled good. She smelled clean and sweet and tempting. She smelled comfortable and familiar. His fingers curled, as he resisted the temptation to reach out and touch her. Just a finger on her cheek or a tracing of her jaw, that was all he wanted. He kept his hands to himself.

"I made my choice a long time ago. I don't do this job because I have to. I have enough money in the bank to be a beach bum, if it suits me. I could get a job in my brother's casino—" as long as he stayed far, far away from the slot machines "—or live at the homeplace, or just do nothing at all. But when my parents were murdered, it was a couple of detectives and a handful of deputies who caught the killer and put him away. This job is important, and I do it because I can."

*He did this job because he had no choice.*

Her expression told him nothing. Nothing at all.

*She's bad, Daddy. Very, very bad.* Had Emma been warning him about Sherry Bishop's killer? Or his new partner?

# FOUR

She'd killed the wrong woman.

Tabby was sitting in the back corner of the coffee shop, but she didn't watch the riverfront beyond the wide window, which was busy on this warm summer night; instead she kept her eyes on the patrons and the employees inside. She wouldn't have thought a place that sold coffee and cookies would be so crowded this late on a Monday night, but the small tables were filled with a mixture of both tourists and regulars, who drank decaf and munched on giant-sized cookies. Many of the regular patrons and the two young waitresses on duty sniffled as they reminisced about the deceased Sherry Bishop. Okay, so she'd made a mistake. At least she had the pleasure of soaking in the pain and fear in the coffee shop for her trouble. Last night's exercise hadn't been a complete waste of time.

Until Tabby had seen the evening news, she'd had no idea that she'd killed the wrong woman. Satisfied and coming down off her natural high, she'd slept most of the day. When she'd awakened, she'd spent some time studying her newest souvenirs. One day she would learn of a way to use those mementos in a powerful working of magic that would give her the powers of those she'd killed. At the time she'd thought her newest victim was Raintree and therefore more powerful than the others, and so she'd touched what she'd taken with reverence and, yes, even glee. Everyone possessed some talent that could be taken, some gift that was wasted or ignored or undiscovered, but this was *Raintree*.

And then she'd turned on the television to watch the evening news, only to discover that what she'd taken had not been Raintree at all.

Who would have thought there would be two pink-haired women living in the same apartment? She sipped at her cooling coffee. Cael was going to kill her when he found out, unless she fixed her mistake, pronto. She'd been hoping Echo Raintree would be here tonight, so she could follow the girl to wherever she was staying and finish the job. But no such luck, at least not so far. The murder of both girls would raise a few eyebrows, she knew that, but what choice did she have? None.

So far Echo hadn't made an appearance. Not tonight. Maybe she was off somewhere crying about her roommate's death, but surely she wouldn't stay away all week. If nothing else, the funeral would take place in a matter of days. Tabby didn't know the details of the arrangements, but that info would be public soon enough. There was no way Echo could stay away from her roommate's funeral. It just had to happen *this week*.

If Echo Raintree had a vision about what was to come and

she warned her family, things would not go as smoothly as planned.

The door opened, and Tabby automatically turned her head to watch the couple enter the coffee shop. Her heart skipped a beat. Holy crap. Gideon Raintree. Her mouth practically watered. She wanted Gideon much more than she'd ever wanted Echo, but orders were to wait. Killing a cop would cause too much commotion, Cael said; it would raise too many questions. Later in the week, when it was almost time, then she could kill Gideon. But not tonight.

Tabby didn't think anyone had seen her near the scene of the crime last night, but she was doubly glad she'd decided to wear the short brunette wig tonight. Her head was hot, and it already itched, but at least she didn't have to worry about anyone recognizing her. She could relax, sit back and watch.

Gideon and the woman who was with him took a seat in the corner, where they could see everyone and everything in the restaurant. They were dressed casually, the woman all in black, Raintree in jeans and a faded T-shirt. Both of them were armed, though not openly. Ankle holsters for both; no badges visible. Was this an official visit? Of course it was. They were searching for Sherry Bishop's killer.

Out of the corner of her eye, Tabby studied the woman with Raintree. Cael had ordered her not to take out Gideon just yet, but what about the woman? Was she a girlfriend? Cop? Judging by the ankle holster, she would have to say cop, but maybe the woman was both colleague and bed buddy. Something was going on. No fear or sadness radiated from the couple on the opposite side of the room, but there was energy. Sexual, slightly acrimonious, uncertain energy. Whatever the relationship might be, killing the woman would definitely sidetrack Raintree if he got too close too soon. It would raise a stink, though, which Cael definitely didn't want just yet.

Tabby got antsy sitting and watching. Knowing she'd made a mistake did take some of the pleasure out of last night's outing, and she wanted more. She always wanted more. She'd already screwed up this job, so what did it matter if she killed a cop who wasn't a part of her original assignment? Getting rid of the woman would distract Gideon, and she needed him to be distracted. She needed his attention diverted to something besides Echo and the wrong damn dead woman.

Since everything had already gone wrong and Tabby didn't dare contact Cael until the job was done, his instructions didn't matter quite so much. As long as Echo and Gideon were both dead by the end of the week, she would be forgiven for any mistakes that happened along the way. She could shoot the female cop and Gideon from a distance at almost any time, but that wasn't what she wanted. Tabby didn't much care how she took out the woman, but Gideon was another matter entirely.

Gideon Raintree was a member of the royal family, next in line for Dranir, powerful in a way she could not entirely imagine. When she killed him, she wanted to be close. She wanted to be touching him when she thrust the knife that had taken Sherry Bishop's life into his heart. She wanted his blood on her hands, and a souvenir or two for her collection.

Even though she had not yet discovered a way to take the gifts she longed to steal, she did draw energy from the keepsakes she collected. Properly treated and dried, stored in a special leather bag that grew heavier with each passing year, those mementos fed her power when she was, by necessity, subdued. Cael insisted that she curb her enthusiasm, that she be cautious and not draw attention to herself and her gifts. Not yet. Not until they had taken that which was rightfully theirs. She had been very subtle and cautious in the games she played, but all that was about to change.

Yes, she could take out her target from a distance, but killing Gideon Raintree would be a powerful and delicious moment, and she wasn't yet ready to give up that moment in the name of expediency.

*Tuesday—7:40 a.m.*

Breakfast at the Hilton buffet, Raintree had informed her last night. It was a Tuesday morning tradition with the Wilmington PD detectives. Hope parked her Toyota in the lot and walked toward the restaurant, unconsciously smoothing a wrinkle out of her black pants and adjusting her jacket over her hips as she walked quickly toward the entrance. She was ten minutes late, but her mother had been talking her ear off as she'd left the shop, and it hadn't been easy to get away.

The group she'd been invited to join was easy to spot. A round table in the center of the restaurant was occupied by nine men, all of them in suits, all of them Wilmington detectives. Raintree stood out, even in this crowd of similarly dressed men who held jobs much like his own. He might as well have a spotlight trained on him, the way he drew the eye. The men talked to and over one another as they drank coffee, and consumed eggs and bacon and biscuits. Hope held her head high as she walked in their direction. It wasn't long before a few heads turned. Eyebrows rose. Jaws dropped.

Hope was accustomed to the initial reaction she usually aroused. She didn't look like a cop, and in the beginning there was always resentment, along with an unspoken question. Had she slept her way to the top? And if she hadn't, would she? She had to be more businesslike, more distant, more dedicated, than any man in this profession. She never would have left Raleigh and started this process all over again if not for her mother. Nothing else could have made her go through this uncomfortable initiation period for a second time.

The only vacant chair at the table was next to Raintree. She took it, and he introduced her to the other detectives. After the initial round of questions and open interest, the men returned to their discussion: Where to meet for lunch tomorrow.

Eventually the conversation turned from food to cases currently under investigation, including—but not exclusively— Sherry Bishop's murder. Through a number of outlets, state and federal, Raintree had requested the files of all unsolved murders of the same kind over the past six months, and by this afternoon he would have the majority of those files on his desk—and hers. As they talked about the case, a few important things quickly became clear. Gideon Raintree was a good cop, and the men he worked with respected and liked him.

Hope allowed herself to relax a little. Surely if Raintree was crooked, the others would know or at least suspect that something was wrong, and be mistrustful or distant or curious. She saw nothing like that at the table. Last night she'd been so certain that Raintree was somehow involved in the crimes he'd solved. Now she wasn't so sure. Did she want to believe he was a straight arrow because he was charming and good-looking as well as infuriating? She didn't want to be that shallow; she didn't want to be like those women who judged men by their looks and their well-planned words, without ever looking inside to find what was real. It was impossible to tell what a man was like from the outside, and getting to know them well enough to learn the truth was too painful. At least, it had been for her.

Eventually the detectives finished eating and peeled away from the table to start their day. Hope and Raintree left together, stepping from the restaurant into a sunny, warm morning.

"What's the plan?" Hope asked as they walked into the crowded parking lot. Her heels clicked on the asphalt. Gideon's steps were slower, steady and rhythmic.

"I want to go back to the apartment and have a look around. Maybe you can work on organizing the paperwork before the case files I requested start coming in. The neighbors' interviews need to be typed up. It'll be a day or two before we get a report from the crime lab, but you could give 'em a call and try to hurry it along."

Hope tried—very hard—not to get riled. "I'm not your secretary, Raintree."

"I didn't say you were."

"You want me to take care of the paperwork while you investigate."

"Leon didn't mind."

"I'm not Leon."

He stopped a few feet from his car and looked pointedly down at her. "I'm very well aware of that, Detective Malory."

"I'll drive today," she said.

"I'd better—"

"I'll drive," she said again, more slowly this time. She refused to allow him to dominate this partnership. Best to show him right now that she wasn't going to be pushed around.

There was a flash of something in Raintree's green eyes.

Amusement, maybe. It definitely wasn't surrender. Still, all he said was, "Okay. If you insist."

Her Toyota was parked just a few spaces down from his Mustang. "Do you want to put the top up?" she asked, pointing to his convertible.

"It'll be all right," he answered casually.

She slipped her keys from the side pocket of her purse and unlocked the doors with the remote on her key chain. She opened the driver's side door while Raintree paused to look over her vehicle.

He casually placed one hand on the hood and said, "Nice car. Does it get good gas mileage?"

She almost laughed. "Significantly better than your gas guzzler."

He straightened away from the car and coolly took his place in the passenger seat, seeming perfectly at ease. Yesterday he had been insistent about driving, but today he seemed to accept his role as passenger quite well. Maybe this partnership would work out after all. Hope buckled her seat belt and turned the key in the ignition. Nothing happened.

She tried again. There was a dead-sounding click, and nothing more.

"Sounds like your starter's on the fritz," Raintree said evenly as he opened the passenger door and stepped out. "I know a guy," he said as he snagged his own car keys from his pocket and headed for his convertible. "I'll give you his number, and you can catch up with me when—"

"Oh no." Hope locked her car and followed Raintree, her own strides shorter than his but no less firm. "I'll take care of the car later. You're not leaving me here."

He glanced over his shoulder. "You're very dedicated, Detective Malory."

With the harsh sunlight on Raintree's face, she could see the faint lines around his eyes. He had probably been a pretty boy in his youth, and just enough of the pretty remained to make him interesting. He wasn't a kid anymore, though. Neither was she.

"I'm stubborn," she said. "Get used to it."

He grinned as he opened the passenger side car door for her and waited for her to step inside. She did, and then she looked up at him. "Don't do that again," she said softly.

"Don't do what?"

"Treat me like we're on a date. I'm your *partner,* Raintree. Did you ever open the door for Leon?"

"No, but he was ugly as sin and had fat, hairy legs."

She glared at him and didn't respond.

"Fine," he said as he rounded the car. "You're one of the guys. Just another cop, just another partner."

"That's right." She was still annoyed about her car, but she wasn't about to stand there waiting for a mechanic while Raintree went to the crime scene and tried to piece together any clues he might have missed yesterday.

Hope no longer believed to the pit of her soul that Gideon Raintree was crooked, but she had no proof one way or another, and she didn't know him well enough to entirely trust what her instincts told her. She'd been burned more than once by a man who hadn't been what he'd claimed to be. It wouldn't happen again.

As he pulled his car out of the parking lot, Raintree said, "Leon called me Gideon. If you're determined to hang with me until we get this whole partner thing straightened out, you might as well do the same."

Calling him by his first name felt so personal. So friendly.

How could she be *friendly* with Raintree when she still suspected, however uncertainly, that he might be corrupt?

Maybe he really was just a good cop. Maybe she would discover that he was as great a detective as he appeared to be, and his motives were nothing but noble. If that were the case, she would work with him, and learn how and why he was so good.

In truth, more than that was causing her hesitation. In spite of her down-to-earth personality and her dedication to her career, she had the very worst luck with men. She always picked the wrong guy. If there were twenty nice guys in a room and one stinker, she picked the stinker every time. She'd felt an unwanted but undeniable attraction to Gideon Raintree from the moment she'd laid eyes on him, and the last thing she needed right now was to get involved with another stinker.

"Okay, Gideon it is," she said. "I guess you might as well call me Hope."

The half smile that crossed his face made him look as if he knew something she didn't, as if he was in on a secret joke and she wasn't. "You sound so enthusiastic about the prospect, how can I refuse?"

The apartment didn't look any different than it had yesterday. It was just quieter. Deader. Sherry Bishop wasn't hanging over his shoulder, wailing about the injustice of being dead and not getting to wear her new boots. There weren't cops and neighbors hanging around in the hallway, watching. It was just him and Malory trying to piece together a very bizarre crime.

His new partner stood near the door, studying the crime scene through her own calculating eyes. She was quiet, as if she understood that he needed silence and space to do his thing.

At first she had been a distraction, but he was already accustomed to her presence. It had taken him almost a year to get this comfortable with Leon.

The blinds were open to let the morning's natural light shine into the apartment. The ripped couch, the bloodstains and the wanton destruction looked obscene in the light of day, out of place and evil and *wrong*.

Standing in the quiet apartment, Gideon could almost see the progression of events. The doorbell had rung late in the evening. A woman's voice had informed Sherry Bishop that there was a pizza delivery. She opened the door, the woman rushed in and...

"There was something odd about the knife."

Gideon turned around and saw a very faint image of Sherry sitting on the couch as she had when she'd been living. Only now the couch was in shreds, and she was dead.

"The knife," he whispered as he dropped to his haunches so he was face-to-face with her. From this vantage point, she looked a little more solid.

"What?" Hope took a single step toward him.

He silenced his new partner with a raised hand. She hated that, he knew, but he didn't want to scare Sherry off. He couldn't even afford to look away, because if he did, he might lose her. The ghost before him wouldn't last long, not in her present state. "I'm thinking out loud," Gideon said without looking at Hope.

"Oh."

"What about the knife?" he asked softly.

"It was antique looking, you know?" Bishop said. "I think maybe it was silver, and there was something fancy on the handle."

"Fancy how?"

"I couldn't see the whole grip, because that psycho bitch was holding it, but there was an engraving. Words, I think."

"What did it say?"

The ghost shrugged. "I don't know. It wasn't English, I don't think. I wasn't exactly trying to *read* at that moment." Already she was starting to fade. "She was really angry. Why was she so angry? I never did anything to—"

Sherry didn't fade away; she disappeared in an instant. Gideon remained there before the sofa, hunkered down and thinking. She'd seemed certain the killer had done this before. This afternoon, when he sat down with the files he'd requested, maybe he would be able to figure out if that was true or not. They not only had the type of weapon and wound to match, but there was the matter of the missing finger and piece of scalp. This killer took souvenirs, and that was the key that would lead him to previous victims, if there were any.

It was unusual for a serial killer to be a woman, but it wasn't impossible. What had drawn the killer to Sherry Bishop? What had caught her eye and brought her here?

He heard and felt Hope crossing the room. She moved smoothly, silently, but he was in tune with her energy, and that was what he felt as she moved closer.

"Okay, you're spooking me a little," she said as she stopped behind him.

"Sorry." Gideon stood and turned to face her. "I want the uniforms to scour the surrounding area searching for the knife."

"They did that yesterday."

"I want them to do it again. Odds are the killer's still got it on her, but we can't take any chances. We need the murder weapon."

"It could be in the river, for all we know," she argued.

"I hope you're wrong." Sherry hadn't recognized her killer, so there was no name to go by, just a vague description, the mutilation...and that knife.

Hope's eyes softened a little. "You're taking this case kinda personally. Did you know Sherry Bishop better than you're letting on?"

"I take all my cases personally," he said.

Hope studied him carefully, as if she were trying to figure out what made him tick. Good luck.

Suddenly Emma, the wannabe daughter of his dreams, appeared, floating hazily behind Hope. Her eyes widened and she glanced toward the window and seemed to swipe at Hope with flailing hands, as if she were trying to push her. "Get down!"

Without hesitation, without even stopping to wonder at the fact that Emma had appeared while he was awake, Gideon tackled Hope and threw them both to the floor. They fell into and through Emma's image, before the girl disappeared. For a split second he was chilled by direct contact with the child who claimed to be his daughter. He and Hope landed hard, just as the window shattered and a bullet slammed into the wall. They lay there for a moment, his body covering and crushing hers.

A current of electricity shimmered through his arms and legs and torso. Not everywhere, but wherever he touched Hope there was definitely a flicker of unusual voltage that he couldn't control. She felt it, too; he knew by the way she reacted with a jolt.

After the gunshot all was silent, until they heard the shouts of an alarmed neighbor from two floors down.

Gideon rolled off Hope, drew his gun and edged toward the shattered window. She was right behind him, pistol in hand. He peered cautiously through the window, trying to see where the shot had originated. A window on the building next door was open, faded curtains ruffling slightly with the breeze. "Stay here and stay down," he ordered as he popped up and ran for the door.

"Like hell."

Hope was right behind him, and he didn't have time to stop and argue with her. Not now. She wanted to be treated like a real partner? Fine. "Third floor, fourth window from the south. I'm going up. You make the call and watch the front entrance. Nobody gets out."

For once she didn't argue with him.

Hope stood by the front door of the apartment building while Gideon ran for the stairwell. Anyone leaving would either come through this door or around the side of the building, a few feet away. Unless the shooter had already left the building, he was trapped. She made a phone call reporting shots fired at this location, and then she waited. Waiting had never been her strong suit, but sometimes it was required. Unfortunately, it gave her time to think about what had just happened, and at the moment she didn't want to think.

Had Raintree seen sunlight flashing on a muzzle? Had he heard something out of the ordinary that alarmed him? He'd tackled her a fraction of a second *before* the shot was fired, so he must have seen or heard something. Problem was, he'd been facing the wall at the time, not the window, so he couldn't have seen anything. The window had been shut, so hearing anything from across the alley would have been almost impossible. Instinct? No, instinct was too much like psychic ability, and she refused to go down that path. Two flakes in the family were quite enough.

Extraordinary intuition wasn't all she had to think about. When Gideon Raintree had landed on top of her, something odd had happened. She'd heard of chemistry, of course; she'd even experienced it a time or two. She'd certainly heard sexual attraction referred to as a spark before.

But she had never before felt an actual *spark*. A popping, charged spark. When Gideon had landed on top of her, it was as if she'd put her finger in a light socket. An electric charge had literally run through her body, from her toes to the top of her head. She'd felt it, as if lightning had danced through her blood. For a moment she'd had to fight the urge to reach out and hold on to the man above her with everything she had, not to fight the electricity off but to take it in and beg for more.

She tried to brush the memory off as imagination, but her imagination wasn't that potent. She'd felt *something;* she just didn't know what to call it.

Hope very much wanted to follow Gideon to the third floor, but until there was another officer available to guard this entrance, she wasn't going anywhere. She couldn't help but wonder what Raintree would find. Was the shooter still up there, just waiting?

A man with a solution rate like his had surely made enemies over the years. There was one open case he was continuing to investigate, many months after the fact. Had Frank Stiles, Gideon's suspect, fired that shot? Was Gideon getting too close? Or was the shooter connected to the Bishop murder? There were too many possibilities, and now was not the time for baseless theories.

A patrol car arrived, and Hope assigned the two uniformed officers to take her place on guard duty. She ran into the apartment building and to the stairwell, just as Gideon had minutes ago. She'd had partners before, and some of them had become friends. She'd lost a couple to retirement or promotion, but she'd never lost one to a bullet. Now was not the time to start.

She met Gideon on the second floor landing. "Apartment's empty," he said. "No one answering my knock at the others. Who's on the door?"

"Two uniforms, with orders not to let anyone in or out."

They took the second floor apartments, Gideon starting at one end, Hope at the other. No one had seen anything, though they had all heard the shots. Too many apartments were empty, the doors locked. Other officers arrived, the building manager was located, and in less than forty-five minutes they'd been through the entire building, floor by floor, apartment by apartment. They searched the narrow back alley. Twice. Either the shooter had escaped before they reached the building, or he was a regular tenant and they'd looked him in the eye without knowing who he was.

When the search was done, Gideon sat on the front stoop and stared out at the street, thinking. She hated to interrupt him when he was so deep in thought, but there were too many questions to leave unasked. Besides, she'd waited long enough.

She sat beside him, close but not too close. "So, who wants you dead?"

He turned his head to look at her. "What makes you think you weren't the target?"

She managed a tense smile. "I've been on the job here less than two days. I haven't had time to make any serious enemies yet. You, on the other hand..."

Gideon turned his gaze to the street again. "Yeah."

Hope leaned back slightly. "So how did you know?"

"How did I know what?"

"You tackled me before the shot was fired, Raintree," she said. "Not by much, but somehow you knew."

He was quiet for a moment. "Complaining?"

"No, but I'm definitely curious."

"Dangerous stuff, curiosity."

She wanted to ask about the sparks she'd felt, but what if that response had been one-sided? Maybe she really had imagined the lightning bolt, and it had just been surprise and maybe even her reluctant physical attraction that had made her tingle from head to toe. Then again, maybe she'd felt sparks when Gideon landed on her because it had been two years since any man had touched her.

"I live for danger," she said, half-serious.

"Let's save this conversation for later."

Even though she hated saving *anything* for later, she nodded and left him alone. She owed him that much, she supposed. "Okay. Now what?"

Gideon looked up and down the sidewalk. "Someone saw something. It's broad daylight, middle of the day, and if the shooter got out, he must've left here at a run. Somebody saw." He looked at her, and damned if she couldn't feel that lightning again, even though they were nowhere close to touching. "Let's find out who."

# FIVE

Gideon walked down the block from the apartment building where the shots had been fired, his new partner right beside him on the sidewalk. Today was the first time he'd seen Emma outside a dream. Her appearance had told him that she was indeed more than a fantasy. The little phantom had saved his life, or Hope's, or both. He wasn't sure who would have been hit if Emma hadn't warned him to get down and flailed vainly at Hope, as if she were trying to push the woman out of the way.

She wasn't a ghost. He was convinced that she was exactly what she'd claimed to be all along: an entity that had not yet come into this world, a spirit between lives. The amount of energy it had taken to appear to him as she had was considerable, and he could no longer write Emma off to bad dreams of a life he didn't dare to ask for. She was Raintree, all right, or one day would be.

They passed by the doorway to a corner bookstore. An older woman stood behind the counter near the window, her curious gaze turned to the street. If the shooter had come this way, she would have seen him. Gideon nodded through the glass to the nosy woman. "Why don't you ask that sales clerk if she saw anything?"

Hope, who'd been thoughtfully quiet since they'd left the building, said, "You don't want to question her yourself?"

"I need to make a phone call. Family stuff," he added, so this partner he didn't want would know he wasn't trying to leave her out of the loop. She hesitated, but finally went into the bookstore and left him standing on the sidewalk alone. He snagged his cell and hit the speed dial.

Dante answered on the second ring.

"How's everything?" Gideon asked—loudly, since there was a lot of static to talk over. Damn cell phones.

"Royally screwed," his brother answered.

"I can sympathize, trust me. I won't keep you, but I have to know. About three months ago you sent me a piece of turquoise."

"I remember."

"The blasted thing was gifted, wasn't it?" Unconsciously, he fingered the cord that hung around his neck. It was hidden by his dress shirt and tie, at the moment, but he was always aware of the power of the talisman. The silver charm that hung there carried the gift of protection, a blessing from his brother. A newly gifted charm arrived every nine days by overnight carrier. Big brother insisted, since Gideon's job came with potential dangers. The turquoise that was sitting on his bedroom dresser had obviously carried another kind of power.

Dante laughed. "I'm surprised it took you this long to figure out."

"What was the gift, exactly?"

"A glimpse of the future."

"Near future or distant?"

"It wasn't specific."

Gideon leaned against the bookstore's brick wall and cursed succinctly. Dante had made the gift nonspecific time-wise, but Emma was an entity waiting to come into this world, and she said she was coming soon.

Not necessarily. He was in control here. He made his own decisions. If he didn't want a family, then he wouldn't have one. In spite of everything he'd been taught in his life, he could not believe that he had no choice in such an important matter.

"What did you see?" Dante asked.

"None of your damn business."

Dante laughed again, then ended the conversation abruptly, as if someone had interrupted him.

Hope opened the bookstore door and stuck her head out. "Raintree, I think you're gonna want to hear this."

Tabby paced her recently rented apartment, the adrenaline still pumping amidst the faded and dusty furnishings. She'd had the woman in her sights, and it would have been an easy enough shot from the deserted apartment on the other side of the alleyway from Echo Raintree's place. Aim. Pull trigger. Watch the target fall. Run. It was a good, simple plan. Not the way she preferred to work, but still, a good enough plan to throw Raintree for a loop.

And then Gideon had knocked the target to the floor, and the bullet had been wasted. Tabby didn't know what all of Gideon's talents were, but apparently he had some kind of psychic power as well as the ability to see ghosts. He'd knocked his partner to the ground a split second *before* she'd pulled the trigger.

Tabby hated hotel rooms. There was no privacy in such places, and she needed to know that no one else had access to her things. No matter where she went, she was able to find a cheap apartment to rent, like this one. She paid a month in advance and was always long gone before the month was done. She avoided her neighbors and never *ever* brought her work home with her.

On the small kitchen table of this shabby, furnished apartment, the newly taken finger and hank of bloody hair had been treated and were drying. She sat before them and drank in the sensations they recalled so vividly. She wished for more, wished to be able to absorb the life power of her victims, but in a way she was satisfied that these things were now hers. There was such a wonderful dark mojo in her keepsakes; they soothed her even when everything else was going wrong. And at the moment it seemed that everything truly *was* going wrong.

Echo was still nowhere to be found, and that was a problem. Cael's orders had been specific. Echo was to die *first*. Tabby knew that if she called her cousin and told him what had happened, he would order her home, and then he would send someone else to finish the job she'd failed to accomplish. Her life wouldn't be worth spit if that happened. She had to finish the task she'd been given, and she had to finish it herself. Echo first, Gideon later in the week, and preferably at a time and place where she could get close enough to appreciate the experience.

Mulling over the possibilities, she reached out and barely touched a strand of spiked, pink and bloodied hair. She'd hit a couple of road bumps, but soon the Raintrees she'd been assigned to kill would be dead, and that was all that mattered. As for the woman cop, Tabby now wanted her dead on principle alone. She hated to miss.

The older lady at the bookstore had seen a woman with long blond hair walking very briskly—just short of running—away from the apartment building at exactly the right time. The long blond hair and the timing were enough to at least loosely tie the shooting to Sherry Bishop's murder. But what lay behind the crimes? It was a question Hope had no answer for.

"Sorry about your car," Gideon said. "It'll be safe in the Hilton parking lot until morning. We'll get someone out there then."

The shooting and the resulting investigation, and then a couple of hours spent in the office they shared scanning unsolved murders outside the Wilmington area that were similar to Sherry Bishop's, had delayed them until it was too late to call a mechanic. Gideon Raintree was driving her to her mother's place. He had a thin stack of files he was taking home with him to look over later. He was hoping he would see something new if he had a fresh look.

Hope had to admit that Raintree certainly appeared to be motivated by something other than greed. Was it possible that he was truly as devoted to his job as he appeared to be? Maybe his parents' murders had inspired him and there were no secrets waiting to be uncovered. No betrayal waiting to surprise her.

Meanwhile, she was exhausted and happy to be headed home, which at the moment was her mother's apartment over The Silver Chalice, a New Age shop Rainbow Malory owned and operated in downtown Wilmington. Of course, Rainbow was not the name Hope's mother had been given at birth. Her real name was Mary. A nice, solid, normal name, Mary. But at the age of sixteen Mary had become Rainbow, and Rainbow she remained.

To Hope's horror, Gideon parked at the curb and killed the engine.

"Thanks," Hope said, exiting the Mustang quickly and doing her best to dismiss her partner. Gideon Raintree was not easily dismissed. He left the driver's seat and followed her. Luckily The Silver Chalice was two blocks from the parking space Gideon had found. "We had this discussion, Raintree," she said sharply. "Would you have walked Leon home?"

"If someone shot at him, yes," he responded.

"Someone was shooting at *you,* not me."

"Prove it."

True enough, she couldn't prove anything. As her mother's shop grew nearer, she straightened her spine and sighed. "This is fine. Thanks."

"Is the shop still open?"

Hope glanced at her watch. In the summertime, the shop's hours were extended to suit the tourists. "Yeah, but I can't imagine there's anything in the store that would interest you."

"You don't have any idea what might interest me."

She had spent two days in this man's company, and she didn't know him at all, she realized. Hope reached the shop entrance and placed her hand on the door handle. "Don't tell my mother that someone shot at us," she said softly as she opened the door and the bell above her head chimed.

The Silver Chalice sold crystals and incense and jewelry made by local artisans. There was a display of tarot cards and runes for sale, as well as a collection of colorful silk scarves and hand-carved wooden boxes. The jewelry kept The Silver Chalice in business, but it was the New Age items that Rainbow Malory embraced. Strange, slightly off-key singing—meditation music, her mother called it—drifted from speakers overhead as Hope entered.

Rainbow looked up from her place at the counter and grinned widely. She was still very attractive at fifty-seven, though the streaks of gray in her dark hair gave away her age, as did the gentle smile lines in her face. She didn't color her hair or wear any makeup. Or a bra.

"Who's your friend?" Rainbow asked as she stepped from behind the counter. Her full, colorful skirt hung to the floor, the hem dancing around comfortable sandals.

"This is my partner, Gideon Raintree," Hope said. "He wanted to look around, but he can't stay."

Hope watched as her mother became as entranced as every other woman who discovered Gideon for the first time. Her back got a little straighter. Her smile brightened. And then she said, "You have the most beautiful aura I've ever seen."

Hope closed her eyes in utter embarrassment. She would never hear the end of this. Gideon would tell the other detectives over breakfast that Hope Malory's mother was into auras and crystals and tarot cards. She waited for the laughter to start, but instead of laughing, Gideon said, "Thank you."

Hope opened her eyes and glanced up at him. He didn't look as if he was kidding. In fact, he looked quite serious and at home here, as he began to study the merchandise on the shelves. "This is nice," he said. "Interesting products, pleasant atmosphere…"

"Atmosphere is so important. I try to fill my shop with positive energy at all times," Rainbow said.

Again Hope wanted to shrink away, but her partner didn't seem at all put off or amused. "I'll bet the tourists love this shop," he said. "It's a peaceful place."

"Why, thank you," Rainbow responded. "That's so astute of you. Of course, I knew as soon as I saw your aura..."

Not auras again. "Mom, don't talk Raintree's ear off. He has to go, anyway. He's got things to do tonight."

"Not really," he said casually. "I want to take another look at those files, but I need a little time away from them first."

She glared at him, but he ignored her as he continued to study the merchandise. If they were going to be partners, he would have to learn to take a hint.

"Join us for supper," Rainbow said, a new excitement in her voice. "I'll be closing up in twenty minutes, and there's stew in the Crock-Pot. There's more than enough for the three of us. You look hungry," she added in a motherly tone of voice.

To Hope's absolute horror, Gideon accepted her mother's invitation.

No two women could be more dissimilar. Where Hope was openly wary and more often than not tied up in knots, her mother was open and relaxed. They looked a little alike, as mothers and daughters often did, but beyond that, it was hard to believe that they'd ever lived in the same house, much less shared DNA.

Dinner was thick beef stew and homemade bread. Simple, but tasty. Gideon steered clear of the television set in the living room, and took the chair that placed him as far away from the stove and microwave as possible. He did his best to keep any electrical surges low and controlled.

Obviously Hope wanted him to eat and get out as quickly

as possible. She fidgeted; she cast decidedly uncomfortable glances his way. She was clearly embarrassed by her mother's beliefs and openness. What would his new partner say if she knew that Gideon believed in everything her mother embraced? And more. He could make her suffer and stay on after the meal was done, but Gideon did Hope a favor and declined dessert and coffee when they were offered. He said thanks and good-night, to his partner's obvious relief.

Rainbow remained in her little apartment, humming and cleaning the kitchen, and Hope walked with Gideon down the stairs.

"Sorry," she said softly when they were halfway down the stairway. "Mom's a little flaky, I know. She means well, but she never outgrew her hippie phase."

"Don't apologize. I like her. She's different, but she's also very nice." Man, did he know about being odd man out. "Different isn't always a bad thing."

"Yeah," Hope said with an audible scoff. "Try to believe that when your mother shows up for career day to talk about selling crystals and incense, and ends up heckling the CEO dad for ruining the environment and selling out to the corporate man."

Gideon couldn't help himself. He laughed.

"Trust me, you wouldn't think it was so funny if she told your first real boyfriend that he had a muddy aura and really needed to meditate in order to boost his positive energy."

"Positive energy is a good thing," Gideon said as they reached the shop, where the lights had been dimmed when Rainbow locked the door for the night.

"You don't have to patronize me," Hope said sharply. "I know my mother is odd and flaky and just plain… weird."

Gideon didn't head directly for the door. He wasn't ready

to go home—not yet. He studied the crystals and jewelry in the display case, then fingered a collection of silver charms that hung suspended from a display rack. He choose one—a plain Celtic knot suspended from a black satin cord—and slipped it from the rack with one finger.

He turned his back to Hope, cupped the charm in both hands and whispered a few words. The faint gleam of green light escaped from between his fingers. The light didn't last long; neither did the words he spoke.

"What are you doing?" Hope asked, circling to face him just as the glow faded.

He slipped the charm over her head before she knew what he was planning to do. "Do me a favor and wear this for a few days."

She lifted the charm and glanced at it. "Why?"

Gideon had gifted the charm with protection. Only members of the royal family—Dante and Mercy in addition to himself—could gift charms, and they used the power sparingly. They could not bestow blessings on themselves, only others, and it was not an ability they advertised. Like everything else, it was a hidden talent that had to be carefully guarded. He didn't know if this afternoon's bullet had been meant for Hope or for him, but in either case, he would rest easier if she were protected. Nothing would shield her from everything, but the gifted charm would give her an edge. It would shield her with the positive energy she scoffed at for a few days, at least. Nine days, to be precise.

"Indulge me," he said calmly.

Hope studied the charm skeptically. "I haven't known you long enough to even consider that I should indulge your eccentricities."

"We've been shot at. That means we bond quickly as partners and you indulge me in all my eccentricities."

She was still uncertain, skeptical and wound so tight she was about to pop. The woman needed to have a little fun more than anyone he'd ever met.

While Hope was studying the Celtic knot, Gideon moved in on her. He backed her against the counter so she was trapped between his arms and the glass case. This close, he was reminded how tiny she was, how fragile. She tried so hard to be one of the guys, to be tough and independent and hard. But she was a woman, first and foremost, and she wasn't hard. She was soft, and she wasn't going anywhere, not until he was ready to let her go.

"Wear it for me," he said, his voice low. "Wear it because it'll make me feel better to know you have this lucky silver hanging around your neck."

"It's silly," she protested, obviously bothered by the fact that she was trapped. "Besides, you don't wear such a—"

He slipped a finger beneath his collar, snagged the leather cord and drew out the talisman Dante had sent him late last week. In the light cast from the streetlamps outside her mother's shop and in the blue flashing light of the café across the street, she clearly saw the charm he wore around his neck.

"Oh," she said softly. "I did see that...once."

"Just because you can't see or feel or touch something, that doesn't mean it doesn't exist." He had never tried to explain himself to anyone, much less a woman he hadn't even known two days. Life was too short, and he didn't care what people he barely knew thought of him. But Hope was surrounded by everyday magic, through her mother, and still she rejected it. That bothered him.

"So," she said, her voice no more warm than it had been before, "do you see auras, too? Am I glowing in the dark, Raintree?"

"I don't see auras."

Was it a trick of the light, or was she relieved?

"That doesn't mean I don't believe I have one."

He wanted her transferred, for her own good as much as his own. It was safer for him to work alone, and Hope was better suited to robbery or fraud or juvenile crimes. Anything but homicide. Any partner but him. She turned her head, and her throat caught the light from the street. Her neck was pale, slender and long enough to make him wonder what it would taste like. If Hope were renting a house on the beach for a week or two, if she were a tourist or a secretary or a sales clerk, he would gladly pick her up and take her home for an evening or two.

But she was his freakin' partner, for God's sake.

Not for long.

He leaned down and pressed his mouth against her neck. She gasped as he slipped his hand between their bodies and laid his palm against her belly, lower than was proper for partners, acquaintances or friends. Her body tensed; she was about to defend herself. She was going to push him away, or knee him where it would hurt the most.

Much of the body's response was electrical, though few people seemed to realize that simple fact. Gideon understood the power of electricity very well. He'd lived with it all his life. Even now, with the solstice approaching and his abilities slightly out of whack, he had enough control to do what had to be done.

His hand fit snugly against Hope's warm belly, pressed there as if he had the right to touch her in such a way. He reached inside Hope with the electric charge he'd harnessed. Through the thick fabric of her conservative trousers, through what was probably ordinary underwear—or would she surprise him with a slip of red silk and lace?—through her skin, he touched her and made her insides quicken and pulse. He made her orgasm with a touch of his hand and a sharing of his energy.

Hope gasped, twitched and shuddered. The hand that had been about to push him away grabbed at his jacket instead and clutched the fabric tightly in a small, strong fist. She made an involuntary noise deep in her throat and stopped breathing for a moment. Just for a moment. Her thighs parted slightly; her heart beat in an irregular rhythm. He had to hold her up to keep her from falling to the floor when her knees wobbled. The response to the electricity coursing through Hope's body wasn't ordinary or conventional. She moaned; she lurched. And then she went still.

He was hard, no surprise, and they were standing so close that she was surely aware of that fact. If she kneed him now, she would do serious damage. He slowly dropped his hands and backed away.

"What did you...?" Hope didn't finish her question.

Gideon reached into his back pocket, withdrew his wallet and slipped out a ten-dollar bill. "For the charm," he said, tossing the bill onto the counter and ignoring what had just happened. "Want me to pick you up in the morning? Breakfast at the Hilton again? We'll see about getting someone out there to look at your car."

He waited for her to tell him to go to hell. She could bring him up on charges of sexual harassment, but who would believe her? *We were both fully dressed. It happened so fast. He laid a hand on me, and I came like a woman who hadn't been with a man in ten years.*

She couldn't do that. No one would ever believe her. Her only option was to tell him to go to hell and ask for another partner, to request another, more suitable, assignment.

"I think I'll skip breakfast," she said, her voice still displaying the breathless evidence of her orgasm.

Gideon smiled. Maybe it was going to be easier to scare her off than he'd thought it would be. That hope didn't last long. Still breathless, she said, "Pick me up when you're done."

After she locked the door behind Raintree, Hope rushed to the stairway and sat on the bottom step, all but crumpling there. Her knees were weak; her thighs trembled; she still couldn't breathe; her mind was spinning. What had happened, exactly?

Granted, it had been a long time since any man had touched her. And she did find Gideon attractive. He had that roguish charm that both intrigued and annoyed her. But to orgasm simply because he laid a hand on her and kissed her neck? It was impossible. Right?

Unlikely, unheard of, but apparently *not* impossible.

She leaned against the wall, hiding in the shadows, her insides still quaking a little. Her knees continued to shake, and she felt a growing dampness that told her that she wasn't finished with the man who'd aroused her and made her come in a matter of seconds. Well, mentally she was most definitely finished with him, but her body felt differently.

Gideon could hurt her so much. He could be the wrong man all over again. She couldn't do it; she simply could not take that chance. So why did she still remember the way his mustache had tickled her neck and wonder how it would feel against her mouth?

She began to fiddle with the silver doodad that hung around her neck. What she should do was rip the damn thing off and throw it away. What she should do was file charges against the SOB for daring to put his hands on her. Of course, that was probably just what he wanted and expected her to do.

What she was going to do was meet him tomorrow morning and pretend that nothing had happened. There was more to Gideon Raintree than met the eye, and she was going to find out what that *more* was.

This time of year the storms came frequently. Gideon loved storms. Most of all, he loved the lightning. Midnight had passed. He stood on the beach wearing his cutoff jeans and Dante's protection charm, and lifted his face and his palms to the clouds. Electrons filled the air. He could taste them; he could feel them.

He could still feel and taste her, too. Normally nothing distracted him when there was electricity in the air, but he still felt Hope reeling against him, clutching at his clothes, moaning and wobbling and coming more intensely than he'd expected. He could still taste her throat on his tongue. It had been an exercise meant to distract her, and instead here he was, hopelessly distracted himself, hours after he'd walked away and left her trembling and confused.

He couldn't afford to be distracted. Not now, not ever. It was the reason he always sent Emma away, the reason he mailed Dante fertility charms on a regular basis. Someone had to carry on the Raintree name, and it wouldn't be him.

What normal woman would accept who and what he was?

Like it or not, there were moments when that was what he wanted more than anything. Not to be normal, not to deny who and what he was and give up his gifts. Not that, never that. But some days he craved a touch of normal in his life. Just a touch. And he couldn't have it. Nothing about his life ever had been or ever would be normal.

Hope was normal. If she knew what he was and what he could do, he would never again get close enough to touch her.

The first crack of lightning split the sky and lit the night. The bolt danced across the black sky, beautiful and bright and powerful, splintering like veins of power. He felt it under his skin, in his blood. The next bolt was closer and more powerful. It was drawn to him, as he was drawn to it. He and the lightning fed one another. He drew the energy closer; he drank it in.

The next bolt of lightning came to him. It shot through his body, danced in his blood. His eyes rolled up and back, and his feet left the sand so that he floated a few inches off the ground. He never felt more powerful than he did at moments like these, with the night cloaking him, the waves lapping close by, and the lightning running through his blood.

Gideon didn't just love the storm, he *was* the storm. Caught in the lightning show, an integral part of it, he drank in the power and the beauty. He gave back, as well, feeding the storm as it fed him. With the summer solstice coming, he didn't need the extra jolt of power the storm provided, but he wanted it. Craved it. Standing on the beach alone, fortifying his body with the power he shared with explosive nature, he could not deny who he was.

Raintree.

The next thunderbolt hit Gideon directly and blew him

back several feet. He felt not as if he had been thrown but as if he were flying. Flying or not, he landed in the sand on his ass, breathless and energized and invigorated. His heartbeat raced; his breath came hard. As the storm moved on, small slivers of lightning remained with Gideon, crackling off his skin in a way that was startlingly obvious in the darkness of night. White and green and blue, the electricity danced across and inside him. He lifted a hand to the night sky and watched the fading sparks his skin generated.

Normal wasn't his thing, and it never would be. Best not to waste his time wishing for things that would never happen, impossible things like being inside Hope the next time she lurched and trembled.

If she scoffed at auras and crystals and lucky tokens, what would she think of *him?*

# SIX

Gideon half expected Hope to be far, far away from her mother's shop by the time he arrived at The Silver Chalice to pick her up. She'd had time to think about last night. She could be downtown, filing a report against him or requesting a transfer. Maybe she was on her way back to Raleigh, though to be honest, she didn't look like a runner. Still, it was unlikely that she would continue on as if nothing had happened.

Again she surprised him. She was waiting out front, outwardly casual, a coffee cup in one hand. As usual, she was dressed conservatively, in a gray pantsuit and white tailored blouse that would look plain on any other woman but looked incredibly hot on Hope Malory. Did she know that those tailored trousers she thought made her look professional only advertised how long and slender her legs were? And with those heels she wore—heels that were probably intended to make her look even taller than she already was—she was a knockout. If she was wearing the charm he'd given her last night, it was well hidden, just as his was.

"You shouldn't be standing out in the open," he said as he reached across and threw open the passenger side door.

"Good morning to you, too," Hope said distantly as she took her seat. "What's the plan?" If she'd had the guts to actually look him in the eye, he wouldn't have believed she was human.

"I culled out four homicides, all of them in the Southeast, that share some similarities with the Bishop murder."

"All women?"

He shook his head. "Three women, one man."

"Commonality?"

"Similar weapon and souvenirs taken. Not always fingers and hair, but souvenirs in themselves are unusual enough to make them worth looking at. There were no witnesses, and no evidence to speak of. All the victims were single. Not just un-married, but unattached romantically and without family living close by. That could be coincidence, but…"

"I don't believe in coincidence," Hope said coolly.

"Neither do I."

He hadn't seen Sherry Bishop's ghost since yesterday, which didn't mean anything. She might show up at any moment to feed him another tidbit of useful—or not so useful—information. Or he might never see her again, in which case he was on his own.

He glanced at Hope. Not as *on his own* as he would like to be. Pretty and intriguing and smart as Hope Malory was, he didn't need or want a partner. Why was she still here? In forty-eight hours he'd tried to antagonize her and then to make her his friend. He'd disabled her car, saved her life and made her come. She should either love him or hate him, and yet here she was, cool as ever.

What would it take to rattle her?

"I called a mechanic about your car. He's going to meet us at the Hilton in ten minutes."

"Thanks," she said coolly.

"The lab analysis on Sherry Bishop should be in early this afternoon. Most of it, anyway. Once your car is taken care of, I figure we can go to the office and make some phone calls about these other murders while we wait for the report to come in."

"Fine with me. If we have the time I'd like a look at the file on Stiles, if you don't mind. He could be behind yesterday's shooting, and the blonde the bookstore clerk saw might have nothing to do with the case."

"Possible," Gideon agreed. "If we do have a serial killer on our hands, she hasn't done *this* before. She's never stuck around and targeted the investigators."

"Maybe she's scared because you're so *good.*"

"Do I detect a hint of sarcasm?"

"Ah, you really are a star detective."

So...she wasn't quite as cool and distant as she pretended to be.

When they pulled into the Hilton parking lot, the mechanic was already there, waiting. Gideon parked close to Hope's Toyota and killed the engine. As he started to leave the car, she said softly, "One more thing, Raintree, before the day gets under way. Lay a hand on me again and I'll shoot you."

He hesitated with his hand on the door handle. "You mean you'll file charges against me, right?"

She looked him in the eye then, squarely and strongly. Yeah, she was entirely human, not altogether pleased with him, and more than a little rattled.

"No, I mean I'll shoot you. I handle my own problems, so if you thought you were going to send me crying to the boss asking for justice and a transfer, you were mistaken."

And how.

"I don't know how you did it, and I don't care," she continued, her voice low but strong. "Well, not much. I *am* curious, but not nearly curious enough to let this slide. From here on out, keep your hands to yourself if you want to keep them." She opened the door and stepped out, dismissing him and effectively ending the conversation.

Damn. Apparently he had himself a new partner.

Tabby took long strides along the riverfront, anxious and twitchy and unhappy. Sherry Bishop's funeral wouldn't be held until Saturday, and even then, it was being held in Indiana. Freakin' Indiana! What was she supposed to do, travel all that way on the *chance* that Echo would be there? No, she had to be here on Sunday. Here and finished with her part of the preparations.

Time to be realistic. Time to look beyond what she wanted and concentrate on what had to be done. It was too late to get Echo first. If the Raintree prophet was going to see that something was about to happen, she'd already seen it. Maybe Echo wasn't as powerful as advertised.

Tabby had to focus on what she could do here and now, and dismiss what she couldn't. Echo was nowhere to be found, at least not at the present time, but Gideon Raintree was right here in Wilmington, so close she could almost taste him.

Raintree's neighbors were too close and too nosy. There was

always someone on the beach or on a nearby deck. Taking him at home would never work. She needed privacy for what she had planned. Privacy and just a little bit of time. She wouldn't have all the time she wanted, but she definitely planned to have minutes with Raintree instead of seconds. Hours would be better, but she would take what she could get.

Raintree and his partner had been in the police station most of the day, and she wasn't stupid enough to try to take them there. Besides, she didn't want this to be quick. She wanted to be looking into Gideon's green Raintree eyes when she killed him. She wanted to be close enough to absorb any energy he emitted when he drew his last breath, and she certainly wanted a memento or two.

Fortunately, she knew exactly how to draw him out of the safety of the police station and well away from home.

The boardwalk by the river was crowded with tourists and a few locals. She scanned them all, one at a time. Someone here had to be alone. Not just by themselves at the moment, but truly and completely *alone*. Miserably isolated. Tabby scanned people quickly, dismissing one after another as inadequate for her purposes. And then her gaze fell on the person she'd been searching for.

Alone, scared, separated from her loved ones. Uncertain, vulnerable, needy. *Perfect*.

Tabaet Ansara smiled as she focused on the redhead's shapely back and wondered if the woman had any inkling that she was about to die.

*Wednesday—3:29 p.m.*

"What do you mean, the computer chip is fried?" Hope all but shouted into the phone. "It's practically a new car!" Just out of warranty, in fact.

She listened to the mechanic's explanation, which was in truth no explanation at all. He didn't know what had happened. He only knew that a very expensive computer chip had to be replaced. Naturally, he didn't have the part on hand. It would take a few days to get the new chip in and have it installed.

She banged the phone down with a vengeance, and Raintree lifted his head slowly to look at her. "Bad news?"

"I'm without a car for a few days." She began to leaf through the yellow pages on her desk. "Who would you recommend I call about a rental?"

"You don't need a rental car," Raintree said.

"I'm not going to let you chauffeur me around town for days," she argued. And her mother's mode of transportation was an embarrassment. The car did get good gas mileage, but it was only slightly larger than a cigar box, and had a nasty habit of dying at stop signs and red lights.

"How are you with a stick?"

"Excuse me?"

"Standard transmission," he said, lifting his gaze to her once again. "Can you handle it?"

"Yes," she said tersely.

Raintree had taken her seriously this morning, she supposed, since he hadn't touched her all day. Not inappropriately, not casually, not at all. That was what she wanted, right? So why was she still so on edge in his presence that she wanted to scream?

"I'll loan you my Challenger," he said. "We'll run by the house tonight and I'll get you a set of keys." When she hesitated, he added, "If Leon was without a car, I'd make the same offer to him."

A part of her wanted to refuse, but she didn't. It would just be for a few days, after all. "Sure. Thanks."

Raintree sat well away from his computer, studying the thick file in his hands. They had the initial crime scene report from the Sherry Bishop case, such as it was, and were awaiting the coroner's report at any moment. Another detective, Charlie Newsom, stuck his head in the office Raintree and Hope shared—at least for the moment. He looked at Hope, openly interested with those sparkling eyes and that killer smile. Charlie was probably one of the nice guys, not a stinker at all. He didn't put her on edge in the least. "I ran that check on Stiles. He was locked up in the county jail last week for drunk and disorderly."

"He bonded out?" Gideon asked.

Charlie shook his head. "Nope. He's still there."

Which meant he couldn't possibly have been the one to take a shot at Raintree—or her—yesterday.

Gideon ran his fingers over the top photo of a woman killed in a rural part of the state four months ago. There were others just like it beneath, some with poor lighting, some from less gruesome angles, but this was the photo that spoke to him.

Marcia Cordell had very little in common with Sherry Bishop. Marcia had been a thirty-six-year-old schoolteacher in a small county school. At the time of her death she'd been wearing a loose-fitting brown dress that might have been purposely chosen to hide whatever figure she had. She wouldn't have been caught dead—or alive—with pink hair or a belly button ring. She'd lived not in an apartment but in a small house off a country road, a house she had inherited from her father when he'd passed on five years ago.

What she and Sherry did have in common was that they were both single. Instead of filling her lonely nights with music and a job at a coffee shop, Marcia Cordell had filled her emptiness with other people's children, two fat cats, and—judging by the photo on his desk—an impressive collection of snow globes from places she had never been. They'd also both been murdered with a knife that left a similar wound. Sherry had been killed by a slash to her throat, but Marcia had been stabbed half a dozen times before her throat had been cut. The angle and depth of the final wound was the same in both cases, though, and there was destruction at both scenes, as if the murderer had gone into a frenzy once the murders were done.

And one of Marcia Cordell's ears had been severed and taken.

Investigations in understaffed jurisdictions were often shoddy and incomplete, but the sheriff's office had done a fairly good job with this one. The case file was slim, but the sheriff was still actively pursuing the case and had been very cooperative over the phone. He'd invited Gideon to visit the crime scene, which had been well preserved, as Cordell had no immediate family and had left no provisions for her little house. Not that anyone was likely to want it after what had happened there.

Was it possible that Marcia Cordell's ghost was still there in that house, waiting for justice? Possible, but not necessarily likely. Still, this had been a particularly grisly murder, maybe even grisly enough to keep Marcia's spirit around for a while. If Marcia Cordell knew he was determined to find the woman who'd killed her, would she be able to rest in peace?

The stack of files on Gideon's desk was disheartening. If he had the time, he could solve them all. He could find the bad guys, put them away, send the spirits of those who had been murdered to a better place. But dammit, there was so much darkness he couldn't keep up with it all. One man couldn't possibly fix the ills of the entire world. It was a world he couldn't possibly bring a child into. He couldn't fix it all, not for a child…not for Sherry Bishop and Marcia Cordell.

"You okay, Raintree?"

He hadn't even heard Hope enter the office. "No," he said. "I'm not okay. I think we have a serial killer."

*Wednesday—11:17 p.m.*

Gideon hunkered down beside the body that lay atop the cheap carpet in a semirespectable hotel room. The victim's red hair covered most of her face, but he could see more than enough. Like Sherry Bishop, this woman had been killed with a knife. Unlike Sherry Bishop, this woman's death had not been quick. The scene looked more like the photos from the Marcia Cordell homicide.

Lily Clark. According to her driver's license she was thirty-one years old and had traveled here from a small town in Georgia for a week's vacation. She'd checked in with a male friend on Saturday, but according to the man at the front desk, that man hadn't been seen since Sunday afternoon. Clark had been seen in tears more than once since that time. Hope, of course, had immediately pegged the boyfriend as a suspect. Gideon already knew better.

Two murder victims in three days was unusual for Wilmington. The fact that this one was a tourist was going to cause a ruckus.

"She said my life wasn't worth a nickel," the ghost said softly. "And she was right. I didn't live the way I should've. I existed, scared of something or other more often than not. I never even thought to be afraid of something like this."

"She was trying to torment you, Lily," Gideon said gently.

"Don't let her continue hurting you now. Let everything she said to you go."

Lily Clark's ghost shook her head in denial, unable to let *anything* go. "No, she was right. She said I was ugly even before she cut my face, and she said that death was best for me because no man would ever be able to love me." The spirit of the dead woman sat on the side of the bed, her hands clasped primly in her lap, her lower lip quivering. Her form was more substantial than Sherry Bishop's had ever been. She was likely to stick around for a while. "She was right," the wraith whispered.

Hope was interviewing the hotel manager, and uniformed officers were keeping everyone else out. For the moment, at least, Gideon and the ghost were alone. "No, Lily, she wasn't right. Now, I want you to forget everything she said and concentrate on what you can tell me that will help me find her. Tell me about the woman who did this to you so I can get her off the streets. Tall and blond, you said. What can you tell me about the knife she used?"

"It was old, I think. The blade was sharp, and the handle was silver. Did you see?" She pointed. "She cut off my little finger!"

And this time she hadn't waited until after death.

"Was there an engraving on the handle?"

"Yeah," Clark said, a vague touch of enthusiasm in her voice. "I couldn't tell what it said, though. It wasn't English. When she was sitting on my chest and pointing the tip of the knife at my nose, I saw some old squiggly letters." Her red hair swayed slightly. "They didn't make any sense."

"And you never saw her before today?" Gideon said, repeating something Lily had told him when he'd first arrived on the scene.

"I was such an idiot," she wailed. "First I come here with

Jerry, only to find out that he's *married,* and then I let that awful woman into my hotel room. Of course, I didn't know she was awful when I asked her in. She seemed so sweet when we met on the riverfront. We ran into each other, literally, and I spilled my lemonade all over her. I thought she'd be mad, but she just laughed. We got to talking. You know how it is. She was having boyfriend troubles, too, and we were going to go out tonight and have a few drinks and…" The ghost went still and looked at Gideon with a puzzled expression on her face. "Wait a minute. Is your name Raintree? Gideon Raintree?"

Gideon nodded, wondering with a sinking stomach how the woman knew his name.

"I almost forgot. I have a message for you."

A shiver danced down his spine. "A message?"

She nodded her head. "The woman who killed me, she said you're to meet her at midnight on the riverfront, just down from the coffee shop where the other woman she killed used to work. She said you'd know where that was. Go alone. If you don't, she'll kill someone else. I don't think she cares who, just someone like me. Someone who won't be missed."

His sinking stomach didn't improve. Somehow the killer knew what he could do. Did she have psychic abilities herself, or had she hired a weak seer who'd just gotten lucky? The *how* didn't much matter, not now. The serial killer he was looking for had tortured and murdered this poor woman just so she would be strong enough to stick around and give him a message.

Lily Clark might never move on as she should. "Everyone is missed," he said. Lily was shaking her head, but he continued. "Everyone leaves a hole in the universe when they're taken too soon."

Her form fluttered, as if she had just become a little less substantial. "I won't," she whispered. "My first husband sure won't miss me, and my parents are just going to be angry because I never gave them grandchildren. I work with computers all day, and you know *they* won't miss me."

"I'll miss you," Gideon said, glancing down at the body and then up at the spirit on the bed. It was easier than looking at what was left of her physical form.

"Why?"

"Because if I had caught the woman who did this to you yesterday, you'd still be alive."

Lily reached out a hand as if she wanted to comfort him. Her fingers were cold, but he felt her touch very clearly. "I don't blame you."

"I blame myself."

"Do you always do that?"

Gideon's head snapped around. Hope stood in the doorway. How long had she been there, watching and listening? "Do what?"

"Blame yourself," she said, an unexpected trace of sympathy in her voice.

"The killer wasn't the boyfriend," he said. "It's the same woman who murdered Sherry Bishop."

Hope shook her head. "I know we have the…the severed finger, but other than that, this is a completely different MO. Bishop was killed with a quick swipe. Clark was…" Her gaze flitted to the body but didn't remain there long. "She was tortured, Gideon. This was personal."

"No, this was sick." He stood. "And very much like the unsolved murder in Hale County. It's the same woman, Hope. I know it. I want an analysis on the weapon ASAP. I'd bet my job that the same knife that killed Sherry Bishop and Marcia Cordell was also used to kill Lily Clark." When he took a step toward Hope, she flinched slightly, but she didn't step back. Somehow he had to get rid of his new partner before he went to the boardwalk to meet with the killer. He couldn't tell her how he knew the psycho who had murdered two women in three days would be there, and he didn't want to put Hope in danger.

The last thing he needed was a partner he had to worry about.

"It's too late to accomplish anything tonight," he said, the weariness in his voice real enough. "We'll let the crime scene techs do their thing, and then we'll get a fresh start in the morning."

Hope cocked her head slightly, openly confused. "In the morning?"

"Yeah. In the morning. I'm tired. Let's get out of here."

For a moment all was silent but for the ghost on the bed, who continued to chatter about how stupid she had been where people were concerned. She wasn't going anywhere soon. Not tonight, in any case. As far as he knew, Sherry had already moved on, but this woman would clearly remain earthbound for a while longer.

"You go on," Hope said. "I'll stick around here for a while, just in case anything comes up."

He would feel better if he knew she was home, doors locked behind her, but that wasn't his concern. Besides, he'd spotted the cord around her neck peeking out a time or two today. She was wearing the protection charm he'd given her.

"See you in the morning," he said, turning his back on Hope

and Lily Clark and the crime scene team that was waiting to go inside the bloody hotel room.

Wait until morning? No way. Two days—no, three —and she already knew that wasn't Gideon Raintree's style. Hope left the crime scene techs and trailed discreetly after Gideon. His mind was definitely elsewhere as he climbed into his Mustang and started the engine.

If she followed him in that huge and noisy red Challenger he'd loaned her, he would spot her before he got out of the parking lot. She turned to the closest person, the night manager of the hotel. "Can I borrow your car?"

"What?" he asked, confused and suspicious.

"Your vehicle," Hope said, offering her hand palm up for the keys. "I'll have it back as soon as possible, and I'll fill it up with gas."

The portly man was still less than certain.

"What am I going to do?" Hope snapped. "Steal it? I'm a cop."

He pulled his keys out of his pants pocket and reluctantly handed them over. "It's the gray pickup truck."

"Thanks." She ran to the truck, watching Raintree's taillights as he turned onto Market Street. That was *not* the way toward home.

This time of night, the streets were all but deserted. There were a few tourists still out and about, enjoying the clubs and the music in the downtown area, but trailing Raintree was easy enough to be problematic. She tried to stay back so he wouldn't know he was being followed, but she was definitely taking a chance.

There were a few possible scenarios to explain his quick exit from the hotel. He really could just be tired, but in that case he would be driving in the other direction, *toward* Wrightsville Beach. Maybe he had a date. That was probably it. He had a midnight rendezvous with some bimbo like his neighbor Honey. They were likely all *Honey* to him. Then again, maybe this was the proof she'd been waiting to find. He was meeting a drug dealer for a payoff. Maybe Lily Clark's death was connected to the other drug murders Gideon had solved in his time in the Wilmington PD, and he'd found something at the scene that alerted him to the identity of the killer.

It wasn't part of the plan to like Raintree, so why did she hope so desperately that he was going to meet some airhead for drinks and dancing and a little recreational sex? She didn't much like the idea, even though she had no claim on him and never would, but it was preferable to finding out that her initial instincts about him had been right and he was crooked. She didn't want him to be crooked. As he parked his car at the curb, she tried to come up with another scenario. One that didn't make him crooked *or* horny.

Hope drove past Raintree as he exited his Mustang, turning her head slightly so he wouldn't get a look at her face. He was so distracted, he didn't even glance at her. She turned a corner and parked in front of a closed gift shop, waiting until she saw Gideon in the rearview mirror before she left the truck.

He was headed for the riverfront. Hope stayed a good distance behind him, but close enough that she could always see the back of his head. Even though this area was well lit at night, there were plenty of shadows for her to conceal herself within. Raintree walked slowly, but with purpose and his own special brand of grace, and when he reached a particular section of the boardwalk, he stopped and leaned over the wood railing, looking down over the river.

Here was her most favorable scenario: Gideon wanted a little time alone to ponder the two murders. He was thinking in that odd way he had, winding down, putting together the pieces of the puzzle and not waiting for a Honey *or* a drug dealer. Hope stayed in the shadows and watched. One older couple passed him but didn't slow down or acknowledge him in any way other than a quick glance. Gideon continued to stare out over the river, motionless. She began to think this was a perfectly innocent evening…

And then he checked his watch. He was waiting for something. No, *someone*. Her heart sank, even though she knew she shouldn't care why he was there or who he had come to meet.

A few minutes later the tall blonde stepped out of the shadows, walking toward Raintree with a purpose of her own. He lifted his head as if he knew she was there long before he could have heard her step.

A woman. She should have known. Men like Raintree didn't live without female companionship, no matter how dedicated they might be to their jobs. She'd heard him talking to the victim back at the hotel, dragging his eyes away from the body to tell the woman who could no longer hear him that her life mattered, promising to find justice for her. And yet here he was, slipping away from a fresh investigation for a *date?* It didn't make sense, but then, what man ever did what was expected of him?

Hope was ready to slip away quietly and return the hotel manager's pickup without Raintree ever knowing that she'd once again stooped to spying on him when a niggle of warning stopped her.

The woman walking toward Raintree… Her blond hair was long and straight, matching the single strand that had been found on Sherry Bishop's body. She was taller than average, and moved in a way that advertised that she had muscles and knew how to use them.

And with her left hand she reached inside the jacket she wore and withdrew a long, wicked-looking knife.

# SEVEN

"That's her! That's her!" Lily Clark jumped up and down and pointed a shaking finger as she flailed and issued her warning. The ghost looked surprisingly solid to Gideon's eyes, but the blonde didn't seem to see her latest victim at all.

"I know," Gideon said softly.

"Shoot her," Lily instructed.

"Not yet." He wanted to discover what the blonde knew—and how. Besides, even though he knew this woman to be a murderer, shooting suspects on the riverfront was definitely frowned upon.

The blonde smiled and made sure he could see the knife in her hand. Anyone sitting in the coffee shop not too far away wouldn't see anything suspicious if they glanced in this direction, because the way the woman held her jacket shielded the weapon from their view. Most of the customers weren't looking this way, anyway. Through the window he could see that they were engrossed in their own conversations, their own lives. They had no idea that a monster walked a few feet away.

"I'm here," he said, holding his hands palm up so she could see he didn't hold a weapon of his own.

"I knew you would be, Raintree," the knife-wielding blonde said as she came closer.

"You know my name. What's yours?"

Her smile widened a little. "Tabby."

Gideon suspected she was telling the truth; she didn't expect him to be around long enough to share that information with anyone else.

"What do you want, Tabby?"

"I want to talk."

"That's what she said to me," Lily said indignantly. "Don't listen to her. You're a cop. You have a gun. Shoot her!"

"Not yet," he said softly.

"What do you mean...?" Tabby began, and then she hesitated. "You're not talking to me, are you? Which one is here?" She glanced around, but her eyes never fell on Lily. "Both, maybe. No, it's got to be that whiny Clark woman. Trust me, before long you'll be more than ready to be rid of her. She just about talked my ears off before I gagged her."

In a rage, Lily threw herself at Tabby, passing right through the tall woman's body. Maybe Tabby felt something, a chill, or a bit of wind. Her step faltered a little; her smile faded.

Thanks to the torture, physical and psychological, Tabby had made Lily more substantial than most spirits. She was tied to this plane in a way most spirits weren't. With a little concentration, maybe a *lot* of concentration, Lily could affect the physical in this world she'd left behind. Maybe.

Tabby stopped less than three feet away. The place was too

public for him to toss a surge of electricity her way, but when she got closer, if he could touch her and send a surge to her heart, the effect would be the same.

"You have two choices, Raintree. You can come with me without incident so we can discuss the situation privately for a while, or you can give me a hard time, and after you're dead, I'll take it out on the innocent citizens and tourists of this town you call home. You'll still be around to watch, I imagine, as a ghost who can't lift a finger to stop me." She grinned widely. "That would be very cool."

"I have a feeling it would be dangerous to go anywhere with you. Why don't we talk right here?"

"It would be very dangerous for you not to do as I say," she countered, her voice flat and her eyes hard. The grip on the knife in her left hand changed, tightening and growing more secure, more...ready. Gideon felt the tingle of electricity in his fingertips. If he had no other choice...

A young couple neared, arm in arm and oblivious to the rest of the world. Tabby moved closer. "Make a move and I'll stick 'em both before you can say boo."

Gideon remained still, sure that Tabby would do exactly as she threatened if she had the chance. The twosome passed, unaware of the danger that was so close. When they were out of earshot, Tabby smiled once again. "Are you going to come with me or not?"

"I'm going to arrest you or kill you. Your choice."

She didn't look at all afraid, not of him, not of anything. Her grin grew wide again for a split second, and then her head turned sharply and the smile disappeared altogether, with a swiftness that transformed her face. "I told you to come alone."

Gideon reached for her while she was distracted, intent on

grabbing her wrist and sending a jolt to her heart. He'd never killed anyone before, but he knew it was possible, and if ever a monster deserved to die... But before he could get a grip on her, she lifted the hand that didn't hold a knife and tossed a few grains of powder into his face. The grains fell into his eyes and onto his lips and everywhere else, and he was immediately half-blinded and dizzy. He missed her, and she swung out with the knife. It wasn't a wild swing but a well-planned maneuver that slipped past his guard and took him by surprise. With a minimum of wasted motion, Tabby thrust the knife deep into his thigh.

Gideon's leg gave out from under him, and he dropped to the boardwalk with a thud. Tabby took another swipe at his hand, this one wild and unplanned. Gideon shifted his hand. The tip of the knife barely grazed his flesh, drawing a small welt of blood rather than the finger she'd no doubt wanted to collect. Her head snapped up, she cursed, and then she ran.

Half-lying, half-sitting on the boardwalk, Gideon took aim. He hesitated. His vision swam. He blinked hard. Sending a bolt of electricity into her back was possible, but had the ruckus garnered the attention of the people in the café? He wondered if he could stop her without killing her. If he killed Tabby, he would never know how she had discovered his ability to talk with the dead...how many people she'd killed...why...?

He couldn't let her get away. His hand lifted, and he called up more power than he had ever directed at another person, one who could not absorb the energy as he did.

But he didn't fire. His thinking was usually so clear, so crisp, but at this moment it was anything but. Someone familiar called his name. *Raintree!* Somewhere in those shadows ahead stood the couple that had recently walked by. He couldn't see them well, but they were there. Sure enough, the surprised and curious young man stepped into Tabby's wake and directly into Gideon's sights, and again his vision swam.

Hope, her own pistol in her hand, passed Gideon at a run. "Are you all right?"

"Yeah," he said as she cut between him and the man who'd foolishly placed himself in front of Gideon's target. "No, not really," he added, even though she was already too far away to hear his low words. "What the hell are you doing here?" He shouldn't be surprised to see Hope here; he shouldn't be surprised that she so easily gave chase. The woman was everywhere she shouldn't be.

"Call for backup!" she yelled as she kept running.

Gideon lowered his hand and leaned against the boardwalk railing, glancing down at his torn trousers. He healed quickly, but he didn't heal immediately. The scratch in his hand was already fading away, but his thigh was another matter, and whatever Tabby had tossed into his face still had him reeling. The knife had gone deep, and he tamed the flow of blood by pressing his hand to the wound. At any other time of the year he would head to the ER for stitches, but not in any week approaching an equinox or a solstice. His presence would play hell with the hospital equipment.

He pressed against the wound and did his best to concentrate, to remain lucid. A serial killer who knew what he could do. It was a nightmare. Tabby wouldn't go from town to town, not anymore. She would send him ghost after ghost after ghost, each one of them begging him for justice. She would play this game of hers until one of them was dead. Gideon's thinking grew more and more muddled. He hadn't lost that much blood, yet he felt weaker now than he had when the knife had cut into his flesh. It hadn't been sand she'd tossed into his eyes, hoping to blind him, but some kind of drug that was stealing his reason. He pressed his hand against the wound with more force. He wished for numbness, but the deep gash hurt like hell.

The lights of the coffee shop whirled, and he blinked against the oddly shifting brightness. The streetlamps above grew oblong and faded and fuzzy, and his heart wasn't pumping right. It was off beat, out of tune. In the back of his mind, Gideon knew he should be trying to get up, but more than the pain in his leg kept him immobile. His entire body was heavy, and he couldn't manage to focus on anything for more than a split second. He could think just clearly enough to know that this was bad. Very bad.

A moment later Hope was headed back toward him, moving a little more slowly than she'd been when she'd first chased after Tabby, but still moving fast. She didn't maintain her shape any better than the lights above, and he blinked against the misty vision. How on earth was she able to run in those heels?

"I lost her," she said breathlessly. "Shit, she was right *there,* and I…" She shook off her frustration and dropped down to her haunches beside him. "You look terrible. You called for backup and an ambulance, right?"

"No." His lips felt numb and heavy as he answered.

She reached for her cell phone. "You didn't call this in? Dammit, Raintree…"

He placed his hand on her wrist before she could dial. "No hospital. No backup. I just need you to drive me home."

"Home!" She moved his hand and peeled aside a portion of sliced fabric, then grimaced at his injury. "I don't think so." She pressed her surprisingly strong hand over the wound. "You need a doctor."

He shook his head. "I can't."

"You're going to have to tell her," Lily Clark said with a shake of her red head.

"I can't," he answered.

"You already said that." Hope lifted her hand slightly and looked again at the gash in his leg, what she could see past the torn trousers. "You're not thinking straight."

"She'll understand," Lily said, almost kindly.

"No, she won't," Gideon said. He was feeling the loss of blood, as well as...something else. "No one ever understands."

"Understands what?" Hope asked. "Raintree, don't lose it on me." She tried to regain control of her cell phone so she could call 911, but Gideon still had enough strength to hold her off.

Maybe Lily was right. He hadn't trusted anyone with his secret in a long time. A very long time. Tabby knew. Did that mean the secret was out? Or soon would be? He glanced to the side to study the ghost's pale face, a face only he could see. "Maybe you're right," he said. "Maybe I can tell her the truth."

Lily nodded and smiled.

"She's going to think I'm crazy," he said.

The redhead laid a hand on his forehead, and he felt her cold touch very distinctly. He saw ghosts every day, talked to them frequently, but they rarely touched him in any way. Never like this. "Don't be like me, Gideon," Lily said. "Don't hold yourself back so much. Live well, and leave a big hole when the time comes for you to go."

He shook his head.

"Tell her."

"It's not a good idea."

"Dammit, Raintree, you're scaring the crap out of me," Hope said softly, and he could hear the concern in her voice.

Gideon turned his head to look up at Hope Malory. His head reeled. His leg didn't hurt that badly anymore, and though Hope's image was foggy, he could see that she was worried. He could see that she cared, even though she didn't want to care about him or anyone else. He hadn't told anyone what he could do in such a long time, and the last time...the last time it hadn't worked out too well.

"I didn't mean to scare you," he said. "I was just talking to Lily Clark."

Hope leaned slightly toward him. "Raintree, Lily Clark is dead."

"Yeah, I know."

Someone from the coffee shop had finally noticed the excitement on the boardwalk, and a few curious people walked toward him. He didn't have much time. "Remember when I told you I talk to dead people?"

"Yeah," Hope said.

"It was the truth."

Raintree was suffering from hallucinations. That was it.

Hope pressed against his injury harder. Hallucinations from a nasty but relatively minor knife wound to the thigh? It didn't make sense.

"That's not possible. I'm going to call 911 now..."

"There's no time to argue. I can't go to a hospital this week."

*This week?* "Raintree..."

"Watch this," he said tersely, then turned his gaze toward the nearest streetlamp. In an instant the light exploded in a shower of sparks. The people who were approaching from the coffee shop stuttered and stepped back. "And the next," Raintree said softly. Another streetlamp exploded. "The next?"

"Not necessary," she said softly, turning toward the other people, who were approaching once again. She mustered a smile for them.

"Should I call an ambulance?" the burly man in the lead called. He looked like he was in charge, but this wasn't the manager they'd spoken to earlier in the week.

"No, thanks," Hope said, sounding calm. "My friend here had a little bit too much to drink and fell, and I think he got a splinter or something in his leg. If you've got a towel or some bandages or something, I'll patch him up and take him home."

It was an uninteresting explanation, and the other onlookers turned away. "Sure," the man said, sounding disappointed. "I have a first aid kit with plenty of bandages."

"Cool," Hope said gratefully.

"Cool," Raintree echoed when the man from the coffee shop had walked away to fetch the bandages. "So you believe me?"

"Of course not," she said sternly.

"But you—"

"I believe something is up. I just haven't figured out what yet."

"I told you…" Suddenly Raintree turned his head and looked at a large expanse of air. "Yeah, she's pretty, but she's also stubborn as all get out."

"Talking to Lily Clark's ghost again?" Hope snapped.

Gideon leaned toward her. "She thinks you should be more open-minded."

"Oh, she does?"

"Yeah." Gideon looked puzzled for a moment, and then he added, "I haven't lost enough blood to feel this woozy. She tossed something in my face. A drug of some kind. Maybe even poison. This isn't good. I need to get out of here."

"You *need* a hospital."

"No. Lily says you'll take good care of me."

"That don't look like a splinter to me."

Hope's head snapped up, and she saw the man from the coffee shop staring down, suspicion in his eyes.

"Big splinter," Hope said as she took the bandages from him.

"Are you sure...?"

Hope flashed her badge at the big guy, and he held up his hands in surrender. "Never mind. None of my business."

"I'll get replacements for these bandages to you as soon as I get the chance," Hope promised.

"No problem," the man said as he backed away. "Don't worry about it." He clearly didn't quite believe her story, but he wasn't going to stir up trouble and maybe even bring some of that trouble to his own door.

Hope quickly bandaged Raintree's thigh, padding it thickly and then tying the dressing tight. He was definitely hallucinating, and he needed more care than she could give him. She quickly explained away the exploding streetlamps. He had a secret gizmo hidden somewhere, and he'd used it to short out the electrical connection somehow. Maybe it had even been a coincidence. He'd seen the lights flickering, played the long shot, and won. He certainly hadn't made the lights explode simply by looking at them. Common sense dictated that she lead Gideon out of here, put him in his Mustang and drive him to the ER.

"You still don't believe me," he said, his voice growing thicker. Was it possible that he really had been drugged? She would let a doctor figure that out. She certainly wasn't a doctor. Hell, she wasn't even a halfway decent babysitter. In years past she'd proven time and again that she couldn't even keep a goldfish alive.

"I'm sorry, Raintree," she said as she helped him up. It wasn't easy, since he was heavy and unsteady, but they managed. With her support, they should be able to get to the car and from there to the hospital. Their progress was slow, as they took one careful step and then another. To the small crowd who watched from the coffee shop, he probably did look drunk. Just as well. It was an easier explanation than the truth—whatever that might be.

Raintree muttered something low and indistinct.

"What?" Hope asked.

"I wasn't talking to you," he said gruffly.

"Of course you weren't," she answered.

A few more steps, and Raintree spoke again. "Touch her," he commanded. "You can, you know. Most ghosts can't affect the physical, but you're different, Lily. Your energy is more bound to this earth than most spirits, and if you concentrate and really, really try..."

"Cut it out, Raintree," Hope snapped. "This isn't funny anymore." Her steps faltered when it felt as if a sliver of ice brushed past her cheek, barely chilling her with its touch.

"She touched you," Raintree said as he took a small, pained step. He looked down at Hope and smiled. "Your cheek. The left one, just beneath the cheekbone."

Hope's heart stuttered much as her step had done a moment earlier. The iciness touched her stomach, as if an invisible finger had reached through her clothes.

"Stomach," Raintree said, the single word oddly heavy.

Hope licked her lips. "I don't know how you're doing that..."

The coldness wrapped itself around her ears. Both of them.

"Ears," Raintree muttered.

They walked beneath a streetlamp. The bulb didn't explode, but it did flicker a few times and then go out. Raintree turned his head back and looked up. "I can't control the energy right now. If I go into a hospital, stuff attached to sick people is going to start blowing up." He sounded a little drunk. No, he sounded a *lot* drunk. "Take me home, partner. Trust me."

Hope Malory didn't trust anyone, not anymore. She especially didn't trust cheesy parlor tricks and unbelievable explanations. But after she put Gideon into the passenger seat of the Mustang and pulled onto the road, she didn't head to the hospital. She drove toward Wrightsville Beach.

Whatever Tabby had tossed into his face was beginning to wear off. It hadn't been a lethal poison or he would be getting worse instead of better. But it *had* been a drug of some kind, meant to dull his senses. He would wonder why, but he'd seen Lily Clark's body and he knew damn well the why of it. She'd wanted to distract him, and she had.

More than that, she'd wanted time with him. She'd wanted the opportunity to torture him.

Gideon slipped the protection charm from beneath his shirt and fingered it gently. Hope would probably say the charm hadn't protected him at all, but he knew better. The knife could have hit an artery. Tabby could have decided to shoot him instead of taking a stab at his leg. He could be missing a finger right about now.

Hope might not have been behind him, literally watching his back.

"What were you doing there?" he asked.

She muttered a mild curse and kept her eyes on the road,

which was deserted at this late hour. The beach was quiet. The houses that lined it were dark.

"I'm just curious," he added after a few moments of silence.

"That crap about waiting until morning before continuing with the investigation? It just didn't ring true."

"So you followed me."

"Yeah. Complaining?"

"Not at the moment."

Lily wasn't with them as they drove toward his beach house, but she was still earthbound; he knew that much. Where was she? Watching the crime scene techs study her motel room for evidence? Standing by while the coroner examined her body? Tabby had done a number on the poor woman, and convincing her spirit to move on wouldn't be easy.

"Once I get you settled, I'm calling a doctor," Hope said as she pulled into his driveway and hit the remote to open the garage door.

"No," he said.

"Dammit, Raintree!"

"I don't need a doctor."

"I saw the wound," she said stubbornly as she parked the car. "It's too deep for you to treat on your own, and I sure as hell can't take care of it. I shouldn't have humored you by bringing you home, I know, but..."

"You're already forgetting how it felt when she touched you," he said. "And you're forgetting that I saw where she touched you."

"Nice trick, Raintree," she said as she rounded the car. "One day you'll have to tell me how you do that."

"It's not a trick," he said as she opened his car door and bent down to help him stand. She kept her arm around him as they headed for the stairs that led to a door off the kitchen. The trip up those stairs would be slow, but with Hope's assistance he would make it. He hated knowing he needed anyone, but right now…right now she was his partner.

"All life is electrical," he said as they climbed, one slow step at a time. "Electricity keeps your heart beating, makes your brain work, keeps the spirit here even after the body is dead. Do you really want a technical explanation? Sorry, I don't feel up to that right now. Takes too long. Electrons, another vibrational level, does any of that make sense to you?"

"It's not plausible," she said sensibly.

"Electricity can also cause muscles and organs like the uterus to convulse, often with interesting and even pleasurable results."

"I warned you, Raintree…"

"Gideon," he said as they stepped into the kitchen and Hope switched on the lights. "If you still don't believe me, I'd be happy to provide another demonstration."

"No!" She drew away from him a little but didn't let him go. Good thing, since he wasn't sure he could stand on his own just yet. "That won't be necessary."

He smiled at her, but he knew the effort was weak. He should be glad she still didn't believe him. If he left her alone she would eventually find a way to explain it all away. Everyone did, when confronted with things they found implausible.

"I've always seen ghosts," he said as they walked toward his bedroom. "When I was little, I didn't understand that everyone didn't see them like I did. The electrical surges came later. I was twelve the first time I blew up a television. From then to fifteen, those were interesting years. But I learned how to control the power, how to harness it and use it. Still, the weeks closest to a solstice or an equinox are unpredictable. The summer solstice is almost here. Sunday." He looked down at her. "I disabled your car."

"You did not…"

"I did it, and I'll pay for the repairs. I've already made arrangements with the mechanic. I just can't take the chance of getting stranded somewhere in one of those freakin' cars with the computer chips in them. Whose idea was that, anyway? Computers have no business in a vehicle."

In his bedroom, he unbuckled his belt, and removed his weapon and badge. Hope turned on the light as he tossed off his jacket and sat on the side of the bed. "Thanks," he said as he fell back onto the mattress. "You can go home, now."

His eyes closed, and his last thought before darkness claimed him was that Hope wasn't leaving. Stubborn woman.


Tabby huddled behind the deserted storefront for a long time before she dared to leave her hiding place. She'd run and run until she couldn't run anymore, until her lungs were burning and her legs wouldn't move. If Raintree and his partner had called in help, the cops were searching way off the mark. All was silent and undisturbed. She hadn't even heard any sirens.

Maybe they hadn't called. After all, Gideon didn't want anyone to know what he could do, so how could he explain the confrontation away? He was freakish enough, but if his talents were common knowledge, he would never know any rest. Half the world would brand him a nutcase; the other half would want to use him.

She'd gotten one good stab at him, but she knew it hadn't been enough. A little to the left and she would have sliced the artery, and he would have bled to death before his pretty partner could get help. But at the last moment her hand had slipped. At least he was undoubtedly having vivid nightmares at the moment. The drug she'd blinded him with had not only given her an advantage, the effects would linger for a while. What sort of nightmares did a Raintree have? she wondered.

The partner had come out of nowhere, damn her, and she'd ruined everything. Time was running out. No more games. No more attempts at finesse. Tabby didn't do finesse well.

By Saturday night Gideon and Echo Raintree both had to be dead. If they weren't, by Sunday morning it would be Tabby who was in the ground...or in the river, or in the ocean. She didn't think Cael would bother with anything resembling a proper funeral.

A few drops of Raintree blood stained her knife and her hand. Sitting in the dark, Tabby pulled both to her face and inhaled. She closed her eyes and imagined the power she could not yet take into her own body. This was Raintree blood. It wasn't as powerful as a finger or an ear or even a tiny slice of skin, but still...*Raintree*. She'd been so close, so very close.

It was time to sit back, think on the situation and come up with a foolproof plan. She wouldn't have her time alone with Gideon, more's the pity, but he would be well dead before the end of the week.

And he wouldn't be going alone.

# EIGHT

For a long while Hope sat in a chair by Gideon Raintree's bed and watched him sleep. He tossed and turned, and then finally fell into a sleep so deep it was like death. The motionless silence scared her far more than his restlessness or the rambling or the gash in his leg.

After he'd fallen to the bed and passed out, she'd removed the bandage from his thigh, intent on calling someone if it looked half as bad as she remembered. Somehow it didn't. It was a nasty cut, no argument, but she was no longer convinced that he needed professional doctoring. It was odd, though, to see an obviously strong and healthy body laid low so completely.

She'd removed his trousers, and then she'd cleaned the wound and rebandaged it. Through the entire ordeal, Raintree barely stirred. It had been a bit tougher to take off his shirt and tie, but she'd managed. She'd left his underwear in place. Her dedication only went so far.

With a damp washcloth, she'd wiped grains of what appeared to be sand from his face. Whatever it was, there wasn't much of it. A few specks had stuck to his goatee and his cheek, and she gently wiped away a granule that had settled near the corner of his eye. She didn't think there was enough of the substance to get any kind of analysis on, but she saved the washcloth, just in case.

She'd never actually undressed an unconscious man, and Gideon Raintree was most definitely all man. There was a dusting of hair on his chest, and his limbs were heavy and well-shaped with muscle. He had strong arms that were nicely muscled without being bulky. There was something about a man's forearms and hands, when they were built just so, that could make any woman's thoughts wander.

Besides, she couldn't look at those hands without remembering when he'd touched her. They'd both been fully dressed, and it had happened so quickly, and yet it had been intimate. Unexpected and powerful—and *intimate*.

Hope didn't want to think about that moment, not the particulars or the whys or the hows, so she attempted to concentrate on Gideon's health and well-being and put everything else in the past. This time of the night, a generous five o'clock shadow was growing in around his neatly trimmed goatee and mustache, making him look a tad grungy. It was almost a relief to realize that he could be less than perfect.

Through all her ministrations, she'd left the charm he wore beneath his suit around his neck. Since she didn't believe in lucky tokens or anything of the sort, she wasn't sure why she left the doodad alone; it just didn't seem right for her to remove it, since he believed it had some sort of power. Then again, she also couldn't explain why she was wearing the charm he had given her last night. It wasn't like her to believe in such nonsense.

When her initial round of totally inept doctoring was done, Hope sat in an uncomfortable chair she'd dragged from the corner of the room. She didn't want to leave Gideon alone or be too far away. What if he needed her? Silly thought, but still...she didn't leave.

He didn't have a modern digital clock by his bed but instead used a vintage windup alarm clock that was probably older than he was. The bedroom phone was another landline. All his talk of electricity and ghosts...she didn't believe him, but obviously *he* believed. She'd seriously considered that he was dirty; it had never so much as crossed her mind that he might be mentally unstable.

She'd used his bedside phone to call her mother, and also to call the very irate motel manager in order to tell him where she'd left his truck. He did have a spare set of keys in the motel office, thank goodness, and an officer who was still on the scene had agreed to give him a ride to his vehicle.

Hope fidgeted as she watched Gideon sleep. His story was ridiculous. It didn't make any sense at all. Ghosts. What a crock. Harnessing electrical energy? Also too fantastic to buy. She should be able to completely dismiss everything he said as impossible or continue to go with that "mentally unstable" possibility, but there were a few other things to consider.

His record as a homicide detective.

The old cars he drove and the odd way her car had malfunctioned.

His lack of decent electrical toys and televisions and phones.

The exploding streetlamps on the riverfront.

The way he'd knocked her out of a bullet's path *before* it had been fired.

The unexpected orgasm.

Hope no longer believed in things she couldn't see with her own eyes or touch with her own hands. Her mother was partly to blame. Growing up with crystals and incense and chanting and auras had been embarrassing for Hope on more than one occasion. She'd made an effort every day of her life to remain firmly grounded in reality.

But her mother wasn't entirely to blame. Jody Landers had been the one to finally and completely blow her orderly world to pieces.

She'd loved him. Love was yet another elusive thing that could not be held or touched or smelled. Yet her love for Jody had seemed so real for a time. It had filled her world and made her happy. And it had been a lie. Turned out Jody had targeted her from day one. Their meeting had not been chance; his love had not been real. He'd been a low-level drug dealer who'd wanted a cop in his pocket as he moved up the chain of command. When she finally caught him and discovered what he'd been up to, he'd claimed that he had come to love her. But she didn't believe him, not then and not now, four years later.

She'd eventually been promoted to detective in spite of the embarrassment. Jody was in prison and would be there for some time to come, but there were still people in Raleigh who believed that she'd known all along what kind of man he was. She hated to admit it, but it wasn't only her mother's welfare that had brought her home. She'd grown tired of the suspicious looks, the whispers that would never die.

She couldn't allow herself to be tainted again by association with the wrong kind of person, the wrong kind of *man*. She was not going to be a gullible patsy ever again. So what the hell was she doing here? She didn't owe Gideon Raintree anything. Not her time or her faith or her loyalty.

Watching him sleep began to get under her skin in a way she couldn't explain away. She squirmed a little in her uncomfortable chair. This was his bed, his house, and watching him was so personal, as if she were once again spying on him, trying to discover what made him tick so she wouldn't get caught in the cross fire.

Gideon seemed to be sleeping well enough. His breathing was even and steady, his heartbeat—which she'd checked a time or two—was strong. With that in mind, Hope shook off her inexplicable need to stand guard and left the bedroom. She was thirsty, and she was hungry. She was tired, too, but she didn't think she would be getting any sleep tonight. In the kitchen she noted the old propane stove, rather than the electric stove he should have had. No microwave. Cheap toaster. She opened a few cabinets, searching for something to eat, and found one deep storage space that held two additional cheap toasters, as well as an assortment of blenders and at least three coffeepots. Her heart crawled into her throat, and she settled for toast and peanut butter and a glass of milk, all of which were consumed at the kitchen table, where she could look out over the deserted beach. In the darkness she could barely see the waves crashing onto the sand, but they did catch the moonlight as they danced to shore. It was almost mesmerizing.

She should leave now. Go home, get some sleep, drop by in the morning to pick Raintree up and either take him to the doctor or make arrangements to collect his Challenger from the motel parking lot. He probably wouldn't be able to drive for a couple of days, but they would think of some way to get his car back here where it belonged.

Movement beyond the window caught her attention. Given that someone had recently stabbed Gideon, she paid close attention and concentrated, trying to discern what had caught her eye. A glare on the windowpanes made it difficult for her to see as well as she wanted to, so she turned out the kitchen light and focused on the beach while her eyes adjusted to the darkness.

The indistinct figure of a man was walking toward the water. He moved slowly, his feet all but dragging. The night had been clear thus far, but suddenly lightning flashed in the distance. Quickly, too quickly, clouds drifted before the moon, robbing the night of the light Hope needed to see who was out there at this hour.

The thunder and lightning moved closer, a jagged bolt flashing across the sky, giving off just enough light for Hope to see what she needed to. The man on the beach was near naked, wearing only a bathing suit or a pair of shorts—or boxers. His hair was a little too long, his broad shoulders were tired, his legs were long...and his left thigh was bandaged.

Hope ran first to the bedroom. The bed she'd left Gideon sleeping in was empty. The curtains covering the large window that overlooked the ocean had been drawn back, and she realized that it wasn't just a window but French doors that opened onto an elaborate deck.

Hope ran onto the deck, certain that she could *not* have seen what she thought she'd seen. Raintree must be sleepwalking, or maybe hallucinating. If he collapsed onto the sand, she would never be able to get him back here alone. And if he walked into the ocean… Dammit, she should have insisted on taking him to the hospital! She ran down the stairs that led to the boardwalk and then to the beach, her steps uneasy once she reached the sand. She stopped to remove her pumps and tossed them aside as another bolt of lightning lit the sky and thunder rumbled.

A stroke of lightning flashed straight down and hit Gideon, and instead of a rumble the thunder was a loud, dangerous pop. Hope stumbled in the sand, her breath stolen away, fear coloring her entire world for that split second.

"Gideon!" She waited for him to fall to the ground or burst into flame, but he didn't. He stood there, arms outstretched, and yet another bolt hit him. The thunder was an earsplitting crack, and this time the lightning that found Gideon seemed to stay connected to him, until sparks generated from the blast were dancing on his skin.

Hope didn't call Gideon's name again, but she continued to run toward him. This wasn't possible, was it? A man couldn't walk onto the beach and be hit by lightning again and again and just *stand* there. As she watched the electricity dance on his skin, she remembered what her mother had said after Raintree had left the apartment Tuesday night. Hope had still been shaking from the orgasm he'd triggered with his touch, and her mother had mused with a smile, "His aura positively sparkles. I've never seen anything quite like it."

"Stop," he commanded without turning to face her. "It's not safe for you to get too close."

Hope stuttered to a halt several feet behind him. The moon had disappeared behind clouds, dimming the night, but she could see him well enough. She could see him well because he was glowing gently.

He turned to face her as the storm that had come out of nowhere rolled away, fading and suddenly not at all threatening. But Hope didn't have eyes for the storm; her gaze was riveted to the man before her. Electricity popped and swayed on his skin, a gentle glow radiating from him. He'd shaved, she noticed, doing away with his goatee and mustache. And his eyes…did they glow, or was it a trick of the light?

It couldn't be a trick of the light. There was no light except for that he himself created.

A part of her wanted to turn and run. She was not the kind of woman who would gladly and openly embrace the impossible. But her feet were rooted in the sand, and she didn't run. "I was watching from the kitchen window," she said, her voice weaker than she would have liked.

Gideon stepped toward her, and tiny sparks swirled where his bare feet sank into the sand. "I know."

Nightmares—vivid dreams of his parents and Lily Clark and all the people in between that he hadn't been able to save— had sent Gideon to the water, where he'd drawn in the lightning to feed his body and his soul, and wipe the last vestiges of the drug from his system. He hadn't walked far onto the beach before he'd realized that Hope was watching. He didn't care. Maybe it was right that she know; maybe she needed to know.

She stood a few feet away, uneasy and unsteady in the soft sand. "Are you all right?" she asked in a soft, suspicious voice.

"Yeah."

The unspoken *how?* remained between them, silent but powerful. She'd seen the streetlamps explode, been touched by a ghost's cold fingers, and still she remained skeptical. But there was no explaining this away.

Her gaze dropped to his thigh, where the electricity was working upon his damaged flesh with a ferocity she couldn't begin to understand.

"You, uh, glow in the dark, Raintree." She tried for a light-hearted tone but fell far short.

"Only when I'm turned on." He stepped toward her, and she moved out of the way. Not running, but definitely avoiding being too close.

"Very funny," she said, as they walked back toward the house.

Actually, it wasn't funny at all. The fact that he wanted this woman naked in his bed was nothing to laugh about. She was his partner, and she was one of those staunch women who questioned everything endlessly. Why? How? When? That made her a great detective, but where he was concerned, such attributes led to disaster. He'd always tried to avoid overly curious women.

He'd never been caught before. Sure, there had been times when his neighbors, awakened by the storms he drew, later asked, *Didn't I see you on the beach?* He always denied it, and they always wrote off what they'd seen to a dream or a trick of the light. After all, what he did, what he *was,* was impossible to comprehend.

"You're walking better," Hope said as they neared the wooden steps that led to his bedroom.

"I think the drug affected me more strongly than the actual wound. It's wearing off." What remained after the nightmares had passed had been washed away by the lightning.

"Good." For a moment Hope didn't say more, and then she fidgeted and said, "Okay, you have some kind of weird electrical thing going on. I'm sure there's a perfectly logical medical explanation for everything."

"Why does it have to be perfectly logical?"

"It just does."

"Nothing is perfect, and logic is subjective."

"Logic is not subjective," she argued.

He tried to usher her up the deck stairs ahead of him, but she wasn't about to let him out of her sight; she didn't want him behind her, where she couldn't see him. So he ascended first, after watching Hope collect her shoes. At least she followed him, instead of fleeing into the night. Gideon stepped into the darkened bedroom from the deck. He did glow in the dark. A little.

Hope closed the French doors behind her but left the drapes open, so they could see the waves not so far away. The sound of the surf was muted but still filled the room as it had all night. It was a comforting sound; it was the sound of home.

Gideon stood near the end of the bed, drained by the storm as well as being rejuvenated by the electrical charge that continued to dance through his body. "The logical explanation is that my family is different. More different than you can imagine."

"That's not—"

*Possible,* she was going to say. He didn't let her get that far. "My brother controls fire, among other things. He's Dranir, leader of the Raintree family. My sister is an empath and a talented healer, and her little girl is showing amazing promise in a number of fields. Echo is a prophet. I talk to ghosts. Should I go on?"

"That's not necessary," Hope said coolly.

"You still don't believe me."

In the near-dark room, he saw Hope shake her head. He could drop the subject, let it lie. She would request her transfer, as he'd wished for just yesterday, and he could go on about his business. She wouldn't tell anyone what she'd seen and heard here tonight, because she didn't want to appear foolish in any way. Surely she knew that no one would believe her.

But he didn't want to let her go. There was something here that he couldn't explain. He wanted Hope; of course he did. She was beautiful and smart and ran in high heels. But beneath that, there was something *more,* though he did his best to ignore it. If he slept with her, she would have to request a transfer. She wasn't fond of breaking the rules. In fact, it was probably a safe bet that she never broke the rules.

He slowly unwrapped the bandage at his thigh. At last Hope moved closer to him. "You really shouldn't do that. Not..." Her voice died away as he removed the last of the bandage and revealed the scratch there. "Yet," she finished weakly. She reached out cautiously and laid her fingers over the nearly healed wound. She licked her lips, cocked her head, and uttered a succinct word he had never expected to hear from that sweet mouth.

"How...?" She drew her fingers away, and he immediately missed them. "What did you...?"

"I'm Raintree," he said. "If you want a more detailed explanation than that, we're going to have to make a pot of coffee."

They didn't sit on opposite sides of the room this time. Gideon sat beside her on the couch, and they each held a mug steaming with hot coffee. By the light of the living room lamps she couldn't tell if he was still glowing or not. A part of her wanted to insist that what she thought she'd seen had been her usually dismal imagination running amok, but she couldn't lie to herself that way.

"You're telling me that everything my mother told me all my life is *true?*"

"I can't say, since I don't know everything she told you." Gideon leaned back and propped his bare feet on the coffee table. He'd pulled jeans on, covering the impossibly healed wound on his thigh. Those jeans were all he wore, along with the green boxers and that silver talisman that rested against his chest, hanging there from a black leather cord and as much a part of him as the color of his eyes or the way his dark hair curled by the ears.

"Auras," she threw out. That was, after all, a bone of contention between her and her mother.

"I don't see them, but they do exist," he answered plainly. "It's another energy thing. In order to see them, you have to be clairsentient."

"Yours apparently sparkles," she said grudgingly.

Gideon just gave a half-interested hum that sounded almost bored.

"Ghosts."

"Those I can attest to without question," he said, casting a glance her way.

Hope leaned her head back against the leather couch. She'd removed her jacket and her shoes but otherwise was still completely and professionally dressed. What she wouldn't give to get out of this bra and into something comfortable....

She should be running for the hills; she should be terrified of what she'd seen and heard here tonight. And here she was worrying instead about the way her bra cut into her shoulders and the flesh beneath her breasts. It was going on four forty-five in the morning, and no woman was meant to wear a bra for twenty-two hours.

"Afterlife?"

"Yes," Gideon answered almost reverently.

Hope closed her eyes. There had been times when she had convinced herself that life could not possibly go beyond the physical boundaries she could see and touch. It was easier that way, most days. Believing we were here, then, one day, we were gone. No expectations, no disappointments. Listening to Gideon's simple answers...she believed him, and it felt unexpectedly good. "What's it like?"

"I don't know."

She laughed lightly. "What do you mean, you don't know? Don't the ghosts tell you anything?"

"Some things we're not meant to understand."

She nodded, oddly accepting. This conversation shouldn't seem so normal. Shouldn't she laugh? Or cry? Dance, or close herself away from the world that had just changed forever? Instead, this seemed very, very natural.

"Signs from above," she said next.

"Be more specific."

Hope lifted one hand and gestured in a casual way. "You see a rabbit cross the road, in a place where you've never seen a rabbit before. Maybe seeing a rabbit at a certain time of the day in a particular place is a sign. It's good luck or bad luck, or an indication that you're going to win the lottery or get hit by a bus."

"You really haven't studied this at all, have you?" Gideon teased.

"No. But I still want an answer." She took a long sip of coffee and waited for one.

"There are signs all around us, but we don't usually see them."

She squirmed a little, trying to get more comfortable. "Not even you?"

"Not even me. We overlook miracles every day. Then again…" Gideon shrugged slightly. "Sometimes a rabbit is just a rabbit."

The length of the day and waning adrenaline was making Hope's eyelids heavy. They drooped, but she wasn't ready to stop. Not yet. "Reincarnation."

"Definitely."

"You sound so sure."

"That's why I used the word *definitely*."

She slapped him lightly and too comfortably on the arm. "Don't tease me. I'm tired, and this is all new, and I still…" No, she couldn't say she still wasn't sure. She'd seen too much tonight not to be. Her hand remained on his arm, and it felt natural. Gideon was warm, and strong, and she liked the feel of his flesh right there, at least for now. It was soothing and spine-tingling at the same time. "If we come back again and again, and we meet the same people over and over, why don't we remember?"

"Where's the fun in that?"

"Fun?" Had he lost his mind? Life wasn't fun. Oh, there were occasional amusing moments, but for the most part, life was hard work.

"Yeah," Gideon said. "Fun. We get to make mistakes, learn how to survive, discover beauty, discover the thrill of taking a risk. We experience emotions fresh, with new eyes that haven't already been tainted or jaded by time. We face wonders with the excitement of something new and unknown, and fall in love with hearts that haven't yet been broken and battered."

"Talk about a risk," she said. Hearing Gideon talk about falling in love made her antsy. She leaned forward, placed her mug on the coffee table, reached beneath the back of her blouse, muttered a low "excuse me," unsnapped her bra and slid it off through her left sleeve.

"If you need help, all you have to do is ask," Gideon said.

"I'm fine," she said, wiggling back into place on the couch. *And ever so much more comfortable.* "Angels."

Gideon leaned back and settled in, much as she had. "Yep."

"Fairies?"

"I've never seen one, but that doesn't mean they don't exist somewhere. I'm not really sure."

She reached out a finger to touch the silver talisman on Gideon's chest. "Lucky charms?" she said softly.

He looked her in the eye, and her heart stuttered. Gideon did have amazing eyes. If she were in the market for a man, which she most certainly was not, he would do quite nicely. Not only was he beautiful in an entirely masculine way, he cared about his job. He fought for people who could no longer fight for themselves. He was justice and strength and sex…and occasionally he glowed in the dark.

"Sometimes," he finally answered.

She removed her hand from his chest and flicked her own charm out from beneath her blouse. "When I was getting ready this morning, I felt like this thing was staring at me. I'm still not entirely sure why I put it on."

"Do me a favor," Gideon said gently. "Don't take it off."

Hope nodded, then returned to her previous and very comfy position. Everything she had ever dismissed as fantasy was apparently all real. She should be screaming in denial, but instead she felt oddly calm.

"You say the Raintrees have been around for a long time."

"Yeah."

"When your ancestors married normal people, why weren't the…the… Crap, I don't know what to call it. I don't believe in magic, but for lack of a better word, it'll do. If your family has some kind of genetic magic, why hasn't it been phased out as you've bred with the common folk?"

Something about the word *bred* made them both squirm. From the beginning there had been sexual energy between them, even when she hadn't been entirely sure he was a good guy. Still, it was too soon for energy of this sort. She never should have leaned close and touched that charm on his chest, and he never should have looked her in the eye that way.

"Raintree genes are dominant," Gideon explained.

"So, if you have kids…" She opened her eyes and turned her head to look at him, curious once again. "Do you?" she asked. "Are there little Gideon Raintrees out there somewhere drawing in lightning and talking to dead people?"

"I don't have any children," he said, his voice more solemn than before.

"But when you do…"

He was shaking his head before she had a chance to finish the sentence. "No. It's hard enough to raise a kid in this world without teaching her that a part of who she is has to be hidden away. I won't do that to a child."

"Her," Hope repeated, closing her eyes again.

"What?"

"You said her. Not it, not him. Her."

He hesitated, briefly. "I have a niece. She's the only kid I've been around for a while. That's why I said *her*."

She didn't believe him, but there wasn't any real reason for her reservations. Just instinct. But she didn't believe in instinct, did she? She believed in fact. Concrete, undisputed proof. *That* had been pretty much blown away tonight.

"You shaved," she said, turning the conversation in an absurdly normal direction.

"I woke up feeling like the drug Tabby used was still there. It wouldn't wash away."

She should've heard him moving around in the bathroom, but the house was so big…and she'd been so distracted… "I like it."

He snorted, and she smiled.

"I'm gonna sleep now," she said, her mind and her body falling toward oblivion. She was much too tired to even think about driving home, and if she did, she would only get there in time to take a quick shower, grab a bite to eat and start a new day. Here, she could sleep for an hour or two. "We'll have to get up in a couple of hours and start the Clark investigation."

"It was Tabby," Gideon said. "The blonde who killed Sherry Bishop and stabbed me."

"Yeah," Hope answered, her speech slightly slurred. "I believe you." And she did believe him. Every word he said was true. What a kick in the pants that was. "Tomorrow we have to find a way to prove it."

# NINE

Gideon lifted a sleeping Hope gently, and she didn't even stir. He could leave her on the couch, he supposed, but the leather wouldn't be pleasant to sleep on for very long. He laid her in his bed, instead, and she immediately rolled onto her side, grabbed a pillow and sighed.

She could sleep in her clothes, but, like the couch... not very comfortable. He unfastened her trousers, waiting with each second that passed for her to wake up and slap him. But she was a deep sleeper, or else the day's events had exhausted her. She slept on, barely moving while he removed her once-crisp gray trousers and tossed them aside.

The blouse would have to stay. He really wasn't up to getting her completely naked and then turning away. Without the bra, which still sat on the living room couch, she would be comfortable enough.

When Hope was down to blouse and panties, he covered her

with the sheet and walked on bare feet to the window. Before closing the drapes, he stood there for a few minutes and watched the waves crash onto the beach.

He'd told her more than he'd ever told anyone else. One woman had seen a glimpse—a tiny *glimpse*—of what he could do, and she hadn't been able to get away from him fast enough. That had been a long time ago. He'd run into her once, a couple of years after the split, and she had apparently forgotten all about the reason for their breakup. People did that. If they couldn't explain what they saw, they simply forgot. It was an amnesia meant to protect the mind from things that could not be accepted, he imagined, no different than forgetting the details of a car crash or any other traumatic event. Happened all the time.

Would Hope forget everything come morning? Maybe. She was a no-nonsense woman who wasn't given to believing in anything that rocked her neat little world. He could most definitely rock her world—in more ways than one.

He finally closed the drapes and returned to the bed, crawling in beside Hope. Her warmth and softness called him closer, and he answered that call. All along he'd known that if he slept with her, she would have to request a transfer, but that didn't have anything to do with the way he wanted her.

There was a double bed in the spare bedroom on the third floor, and that was it as far as alternate sleeping arrangements were concerned. The room was used for storage, mostly, but Echo stayed here infrequently, and Mercy had visited with Eve on rare occasions, so he did keep it ready for guests. Only a glutton for punishment would fill a beach house with a selection of comfortable and welcoming guest rooms, and since Gideon preferred solitude, his lack of accommodations made perfect sense.

The single guest bed was without sheets at the moment since Echo had stripped the bed Monday before leaving for Charlotte, and it was also piled high with the files he'd brought home about the unsolved murders. He didn't feel like taking the time to clean off the bed in the name of being gentlemanly. His own bed was warm and soft, and he was drawn to Hope the way a man is drawn to his woman.

His woman. Hope was many things, but she was most definitely not his. And still he draped his arm across her waist and pulled her close before he fell asleep.

She'd slept so deeply that she didn't remember so much as a sliver of a dream. Hope burrowed into the soft mattress, trying to escape the chill. The air conditioner must be turned up high. Unusual, since her mother was usually such a stickler about conserving electricity.

The air was chilly, but she felt oddly and comfortably warm. The alarm hadn't gone off yet, which meant she could sleep a little while longer. A few more precious minutes.

Then, with a suddenness that made her twitch, she remembered where she was. Raintree's house. She'd fallen asleep on the couch, but this was no couch. It was Raintree's *bed*. She very carefully rolled over to face the man she'd been sleeping with. The reason she was so warm was that Gideon's mostly bare body was all but pressed against hers.

Still half asleep, she remained as still as possible while she studied him. They were close, closer than she'd ever thought to be with this man she had initially suspected of possible criminal misconduct. Now she knew he wasn't a dirty cop. He was just different. Very, *very* different.

He looked fine in the morning, none the worse for wear

after being wounded and drugged last night. In sleep he was a little rough around the edges, unguarded, and beautiful in the special way only a handsome man could be. But if Gideon knew he was beautiful, he didn't act that way, not like some men she knew. He just *was*.

Moving cautiously so as not to wake him, she lifted the sheet that covered them both and peeked beneath. His thigh was almost healed. Last night it had been sliced deep, and now all that remained was a nasty-looking scratch. She shouldn't be surprised. Nothing connected with this man should ever surprise her again.

"Don't worry," a gruff voice rumbled. "Nothing happened."

Hope lifted her head slightly to see that Gideon's eyes were trained unerringly on her. They were sleepy still, hooded and sexy and electric.

"I was checking your *wound*," she said primly.

"I thought you were checking to see if I had my drawers on."

She slapped the sheet down, and started to roll away and leave the bed, mainly so Gideon wouldn't see how she was blushing. Her cheeks actually grew hot, and it was such a girlie reaction.

Before she could roll away, Gideon snagged her with one strong arm and pulled her back against his chest. "Don't go anywhere just yet," he said, his voice still sleepy and gruff and sexy as hell. Hope knew she could escape easily, with a gentle shove and a roll. Gideon's grasp on her wasn't binding; it was simply persuasive. Heavy and warm and comfortable. She didn't shove or roll. Instead, she laid her head on the pillow and stared away from Raintree while he held her close.

Jody hadn't often slept over at her apartment. Twice, maybe. And even then, it had been a mistake on his part. He'd fallen asleep and awakened early in the morning to make his escape. But she remembered liking this part. She very much enjoyed being held, flesh to flesh, the connection sexual and yet also much more. This was what she missed by living alone, by dedicating herself to her career and always looking at every man who so much as smiled at her as if he might turn into an ogre and bite her in the next instant.

She didn't think Gideon would bite her, but that was a potentially dangerous supposition on her part. He was a man like any other, a fact that was quickly becoming evident as he held her close.

Now was the time to leave the bed, if she was going to make her escape. If she stayed here, in his bed, if she didn't leave *right now,* she knew darn well what was going to happen. She was a fully grown woman of sound mind, twenty-nine years old and unattached. And at this moment, with her world still spinning out of control thanks to all she'd learned last night, she wanted to be held. Not just by any man, but by this one. Gideon Raintree, who talked to ghosts and inhaled lightning and occasionally glowed in the dark.

He shifted her hair aside and laid his mouth on her neck. A decided shiver worked its way through her body. Was it electricity or just *him* that made her tingle? Something paranormal or something extraordinarily *normal?* She couldn't make herself care, at the moment. This felt so good....

"I want you," he said softly.

Hope licked her lips. *I know. I want you, too.* The words danced in her head, but nothing came out.

"I'm not sure that's such a good idea, but there you have it." His hand slipped beneath her blouse to caress her bare skin, and she closed her eyes and melted. Her brain told her this was a *very bad* idea. But her body disagreed. Her body wanted the same thing Gideon wanted, though her wanting wasn't as obvious as his. Physically, at least.

Could he feel her shiver? She hadn't let a man touch her this way in a very long time, so long that this felt new and exciting and powerful.

Eyes closed and body trembling, she drank in Gideon's warmth and imagined what might be yet to come, if she allowed it. If she wanted it. She didn't have to say a word. She just had to turn in his arms, lay her mouth on his and kiss him. That was all the answer he needed, and all she was capable of giving.

His hand raked down her belly and came to rest over the soft flesh beneath her belly button, just as it had in her mother's shop when he'd pressed her against the counter and taken her by surprise. Knowing what he was about to do, she grabbed his wrist and pulled his hand slightly away.

Hope felt the disappointment in him, felt his resignation. She turned slowly so that she was facing him, his wrist still grasped in her hand. "No cheating this time," she whispered. And then she kissed him.

She should have known that he would be a great kisser. One touch, one sway of his lips over hers, and she lost the last of her doubts. She threaded her fingers in his hair and pulled him closer as her lips parted wider and she flicked her tongue against his. There were a hundred reasons why they shouldn't be here. She barely knew him; he was her partner; she'd distrusted him from day one; he was who he was.

But none of that mattered. She wanted him to kiss her, longer and more completely and with the abandon she felt unraveling inside her.

He unbuttoned her blouse while they kissed, and together they discarded it. Now she could hold him and truly be skin to skin. It was such a wonderful sensation that she couldn't help but remember what he'd said last night about discovering new and wonderful things in life. This was new. The way she wanted him, the way she spiraled out of control, the way her body was drawn to his...it was all new and beautiful.

Gideon gently rolled her onto her back, and she lay against the mattress, yearning and oddly content for someone whose heart and blood were pounding so hard they pushed away everything else. He took a nipple into his mouth and drew it deep, and she almost came off the mattress, the pleasure was so intense. Inside, she clenched, *ready* in a way she had never been before. She grabbed at Gideon, held on while he moved his attentions to the other breast. He moved as if they had all the time in the world, but she could tell that he was as close to spinning out of control as she was.

They couldn't afford to lose control completely. "Do you have a condom?" she asked hoarsely. If he said no...he couldn't say no. Surely he wouldn't say no.

"Yes," he answered, and she breathed a sigh of relief.

"Good."

Gideon had such wonderful hands. They were masculine, well-shaped and strong. His fingers were long, and like everything else about this man, they were beautiful. His hands were tanned, too, thanks to hours spent on the beach. She didn't see the sun often. Her fair skin had a tendency to burn, and besides, tanning meant leisure time, and when was the last time she'd taken a real vacation? She couldn't even remember.

Gideon's sun-kissed hand skimmed over her pale flesh, and she watched him, fascinated and aroused by such a simple sight. He touched her as if she were made of porcelain, learning her curves as he went, learning the feel of her skin and inflaming her senses until she felt as if she were floating above the bed, soaring and grasping and wrapped in magic.

He snagged her panties and quickly pushed them down and off. Just like that, she was naked but for the protection charm he had made for her and insisted she wear. She slid her trembling fingers into the waistband of his boxers and pushed them down. Down and eventually off, leaving him wearing no more than she.

Before he covered himself, she wanted to touch him. She wanted to feel him in her hand, and she did. She wasn't shy, and neither was he. Not about this.

They kissed again, and this time Gideon spread her thighs and touched her while their mouths met and danced. A deep trembling had settled into her body, and nothing could stop it but the finale of this dance. There was only one possible end, only one acceptable conclusion, and that was Gideon inside her and the release they both needed. Her hands rested easily but insistently on his bare hips, her fingers gently rocking in much the way that her hips did.

He took his mouth from hers and reached for the bedside table, fumbling around and finally delving into the back of the messy drawer to snag a condom. It was a necessary but annoying delay, like stopping for gas when you were just five miles from your destination. But soon he was back, touching her again, slipping his fingers inside her and circling his thumb against her in a way that made her gasp and lurch. She had never wanted anything as much as she wanted him inside her. Now. And then he was there, pushing into her, stretching her slowly until she was accustomed to his size. She almost gasped at the sensation. Nothing had ever felt this good; no moment in her life had ever made her want to cry with the beauty of it.

Gideon made love the same way he did everything else: with complete dedication and an extraordinary level of skill. Hope closed her eyes and let him love her. He filled her body and took her to that place where she was on the edge, and he kept her there. Ribbons of pleasure danced inside her, strong and promising and demanding. Just when she was about to come, he backed away and slowed his pace, then started again.

She opened her eyes and whispered, "You're torturing me."

"Just a little."

The room was dark, thanks to the thickness of the drapes that covered the picture window and the French doors. If it hadn't been so dark, she never would have noticed the hint of a glow that rimmed the green irises of Gideon's eyes.

"You're glowing again." Oddly enough, she didn't find that fact at all disconcerting.

"Am I?"

"It's beautiful." She shifted her legs so that they were wrapped around his hips, lifted her body to his and pulled him to her, until he was buried fully inside her. He didn't draw back this time but plunged deeper and harder, faster and more completely, until she came with a cry. The release racked her body and went on even after she was sure it would end, unlike anything she had ever known before. She cried out again and grasped at Gideon's shoulders. He came with her, shuddering above and inside her.

Eventually he slowed, and so did she, and then he lay down on top of her and continued to hold her close while he remained cradled inside her. When he finally lifted his head to look down at her, she flinched a little in surprise.

"You give a whole new meaning to the word afterglow, Gideon."

He was indeed glowing a little. His eyes shone with that unnatural green light, and there was a hint of sparkling luminescence around his body.

"Is this...normal?"

He withdrew, physically and mentally, and rolled away from her. "It's happened a time or two. I wouldn't exactly call it normal."

She reached out to touch him, to stop him, to tell him that she wasn't complaining. Quite the contrary. But he moved faster than she did and left the bed before she could touch him, heading for the bathroom.

*Heart, body and soul.* Gideon didn't remember exactly how he knew that all three had to be involved for the literal afterglow to happen, but he did. He took an extra minute in the bathroom to wash his face, again, and brush his teeth—again. Normally he would have done those things before, not after, but nothing about this morning had been normal.

He barely knew Hope Malory. So she was gorgeous, so she was hot, so she'd seen what he could do and hadn't fled as if a monster was on her heels. Yet. Beyond that...shit, there couldn't be anything beyond that.

She was an interesting diversion, that was all, and sleeping with her would bring an end to the unwanted partnership. She would have to ask for a transfer now, like it or not, and that was what he wanted more than anything else. So why the damn glow?

An aberration, that was the answer. Next time, if there was a next time, nothing out of the ordinary would happen, and eventually Hope would convince herself that what she'd seen had been a trick of the light or the simple aftereffect of coming so hard that she'd temporarily screwed up her own eyesight.

And she *had* come hard. What was a woman like that doing alone? She was alone in the same way he was. He knew it, the same way he knew his heart, body and soul had to be involved for what had happened to happen.

No big deal. He'd thought himself in love once before. The woman in question had seen a small hint of who he really was, and that had been the end of that. That short relationship had really screwed up his ideas of having anything normal in his life. In the end, he'd gotten over her well enough, and he would get over Hope, too.

"It's Emma who's got my head all twisted around," he muttered to the mirror, studying his too-bare chin. "Dante and his damned turquoise."

All of a sudden he saw Emma's reflection in the mirror and instinctively grabbed a towel to wrap himself in before he turned. Appearing maybe five years old today, she was floating above the tub, dressed all in white again. Her dark hair curled a bit and was fashioned into two long pigtails.

"Hi, Daddy. Did you call me?"

"No, I didn't call you."

"I heard you say my name," she protested, with all the innocence and persistence of a stubborn little girl.

A horrifying thought crossed his mind. "Were you just here?"

"No," she said, wide-eyed and growing more and more substantial as he watched. "I was waiting, and then I heard you call my name."

"Waiting for what?"

Emma smiled. "Be careful, Daddy," she said as she began to fade away. "She's very bad. Very, *very* bad."

"Who's very...?" Before he could finish the question, Emma was gone. Surely she was warning him about Tabby. A warning last night before he'd gone to the riverfront would have been nice. Not that it would have stopped him from going.

By the time he returned to the bedroom, Hope was gone. He heard her moving around in the guest bathroom down the hall. After a few minutes the bathroom door opened and she shouted, "Raintree, you wouldn't happen to have an extra toothbrush, would you?"

"Second drawer to the left," he answered.

Gideon chastised himself as he pulled his clothes for the day from the closet. At least Hope wasn't being emotional about this. She recognized this morning for what it was: fun, in a world where there wasn't nearly enough fun. Release for two adult, apparently neglected, bodies that needed it. Just another day in a long line of days.

Yeah, Hope was hot; she was gorgeous; she was brave. But he couldn't love her, and this couldn't last.

"You must have more clothes around here that would fit me. I'd rather wear something of yours than *this!*"

"My clothes are too big for you," Gideon said sensibly. "Echo's fit just fine."

"That's a matter of opinion," Hope grumbled as she tugged on the hem of the cutoff T-shirt that revealed her belly button. She was a good three inches taller than Echo Raintree, so it was a miracle anything the other woman had left here would fit.

They'd both showered and changed clothes, but then she'd

been stuck with choosing between the wrinkled blouse she'd slept in and the even more wrinkled trousers Raintree had thrown on the floor last night, or something from the drawer of clothes his cousin had left here on one of her infrequent visits.

The man didn't own an iron, or so he said. Everyone owned an iron! Hope thought as she tried to tug up the waistband of the hip-hugger jeans. Gideon claimed the dry cleaner took care of all his ironing.

Her choices were a couple of bikinis, two T-shirts with the hems ripped out to display a belly button ring Hope did not have, and either a pair of cut-off shorts that would allow the cheeks of her butt to hang out or the tight pair of faded and ripped jeans she would normally have tossed in the garbage. For today the jeans were the lesser of two evils. They must have dragged on the ground when Echo wore them, given the frayed ends, but they were better than the cutoffs.

And not only would wearing the same clothes she'd worn yesterday be inappropriate and their hopelessly wrinkled state raise questions she didn't want to answer, this morning she'd discovered more than one spot of blood on the sleeve of her blouse and on the trousers. She didn't have a proper explanation for that, either, so she had no real choice but to make do with Echo's clothes.

At least Gideon had dressed casually, to keep her from feeling like a complete fool. His jeans actually looked good on him, and so did the T-shirt that entirely covered *his* belly button.

"We'll stop by your place later and you can change clothes," he said, turning his back on her to pour a cup of coffee.

"We'll stop by there *first,*" she said.

"Maybe not," Gideon said thoughtfully. "Someone must've seen Tabby hanging around the club where Echo's band played, or at the coffee shop, or checking out the apartment building. She hasn't been invisible. The suits put some people off. People get defensive and just want to get rid of us as soon as possible, so we end up with squat. We'll go in more relaxed today, just following up with a few more questions."

Judging by the way Gideon was acting, a casual observer would have thought nothing out of the ordinary had happened this morning. He wasn't distant, but he wasn't exactly warm and cuddly, either. He was all business, and he hadn't touched her at all since he'd left the bed this morning.

Maybe having incredible casual sex with a partner he barely knew wasn't out of the ordinary for Gideon. It was certainly out of the ordinary for *her,* but she didn't necessarily want him to know that. Not if he thought what had happened was casual and unimportant.

The plan for the day was to get one of the other detectives—probably Charlie Newsom—busy collecting mug shots of anyone who matched Tabby's general description, while she and Gideon interviewed Sherry Bishop's friends, coworkers and neighbors once again. Maybe one of them had seen Tabby in the days preceding Sherry's death. Maybe one of them knew her last name. Unless they were very lucky, they wouldn't get far with nothing but "Tabby" to go on. This afternoon Gideon was meeting with a sketch artist. She wasn't sure how he would explain how he knew what the killer looked like, but somehow he would manage. She also had the washcloth she'd used to wipe away whatever Tabby had used to drug him. It was a long shot, but she planned to get that washcloth to the state lab. Unfortunately it would take weeks to get the results, and they didn't have weeks.

"My sister's coming in later today," she said. "She makes jewelry for the shop, and she has some new pieces to deliver."

Gideon lifted his head and looked at her. "You have a sister?"

Yet more evidence that they didn't know one another nearly well enough for what had happened this morning to happen. "Yeah."

"If you want to take some time and spend it with her while she's in town, I don't mind."

Of course he didn't mind. He would probably be relieved to be rid of her. "No. We see each other fairly often." *And besides, I'm the odd man out when Mom and Sunny get together.*

"Is she anything like you?" he asked, half teasing, half curious.

"No. She's two years older than me, has three little boys, and is every bit as flaky as my mother."

"So you've always been the 'normal' one?"

For a while she'd thought that to be true. She'd been so sure that she was not only normal but *right* in her skepticism. Gideon had pretty much blown that theory out of the water. "Normal is relative."

He didn't continue with the conversation. "Let's go. We're running late."

Hope grabbed her purse and followed Gideon to the stairs that led to his garage. She recognized what he was doing; she just didn't know why. He was ignoring what had happened in the hope that it would go away. He had become professional Gideon Raintree again, his mind completely on the case.

Maybe if she followed his lead and pretended that nothing had changed, they would be able to work together. They could be partners and maybe even friends. He was a good cop, and she could learn a lot working with him.

On second thought, Hope wasn't sure she could do that. The change between them was too deep to ignore. Should she take a chance and tell Gideon that she couldn't be just his partner and his friend? She was a woman who wanted all or nothing, and she had decided in the last couple of years that her only option was nothing. Maybe it would be better if she just played it safe, let Gideon back away and pretend nothing had happened.

Fortunately for both of them, she didn't have to make that decision this morning. Tabby was out there, and gut instinct told Hope that the woman was nowhere near finished.

# TEN

If Tabby was local, she'd never been arrested. Not as Tabby or
Tabitha, at least. There was no way to be sure that was her real
name, of course. Could be a nickname. Maybe her name was
Catherine and it had been shortened to Cat, and then someone
had started calling her Tabby and it stuck. It might be an alias,
with no connection to her real name, in which case it did them
no good at all. For whatever reason, the initial search on Tabby
and her physical description had turned up nothing. It hadn't
taken Gideon fifteen minutes to very carefully study everything
Charlie had come up with. A couple of new detectives were
checking out hotels in the area, in case Tabby was a visitor and
not a resident. Charlie and another detective were now checking
federal databases, and that would likely take a while. Hope had
insisted on sending the particles of the drug Tabby had used on
him to the state lab, insisting they could explain the details of
how they came by the drug later, if an identification was made.

There was no way he could officially explain away what had happened last night. There was no sign of the wound in his thigh, and he couldn't reveal how he'd known to be in that place at that time without revealing that he'd spoken to Lily Clark's ghost. Somehow he didn't think the new chief or his coworkers would buy that explanation as easily as Hope had—not that he wanted them to know what he could do. To go public with his talents would not only be unwise, it was forbidden.

His current partner might be uncomfortable in Echo's clothes, but she looked great. Elegant and sleazy at the same time. The heels that barely peeked out from the frayed hem of the jeans only made the look more fetching. When they'd interviewed Sherry Bishop's friends, the men had all opened up to Hope in a way they hadn't during the first round of interviews. Unfortunately, none of them had anything startling or helpful to offer.

Right now Hope was rounding up coffee for both of them—her idea, not his—and Gideon was taking a moment's well-deserved rest in the office they shared in the police station on Red Cross Street. Now what? Tabby—for lack of a better name, that would have to do—had killed Sherry Bishop. Why? Chance? Bishop's bad luck? No. It couldn't be coincidence that all the victims were single. No one was going to come home at an inopportune time and interrupt Tabby while she was working. Tabby had tortured and killed Lily Clark just to get a message to him, and then she'd tried to add him to her list of victims.

He'd called the sheriff who'd handled the Marcia Cordell case, and they had an appointment for tomorrow afternoon. He hated the idea of leaving Wilmington even for a few hours while Tabby was on the loose, but if Marcia Cordell's ghost was hanging around that house, he not only needed to try to send her on, it was possible she might be able to add something new to what little he knew about Tabby.

Somehow he would have to find a way to leave Hope behind. She wouldn't like it if she knew what he was up to. She had accepted what he'd told her last night, but what would she think when he actually started using his gift? Would she freak out? Likely. He didn't want to leave her unguarded, but it wouldn't do for him to get too comfortable with his new partner, and that was where things were headed. Comfortable. Which meant that, deep down, he was more worried that she *would* accept what he could do.

They couldn't sleep together *and* work together; that was just asking for trouble. Truth be told, he would much rather sleep with Hope on a regular basis than accept her as a partner, but it wasn't likely that she would gently and obediently transfer to another division. Was she ever gentle or obedient? Not that he'd witnessed.

Hope entered the office with two disposable cups of steaming coffee. Seeing her was much too much of a relief, as if she'd been gone for hours, not minutes. And that was the problem. Getting involved with her simply wasn't going to work. It was going to complicate everything. Problem was, they were already involved, things were already complicated, and he wasn't ready to let this end.

Someone had taken a shot at one of them, and if he was right, she was in danger just because she was close to him. It was too late to undo their connection. Trying to separate himself from her now would be like locking the barn door after the horses had bolted.

She set both coffee cups on his desk. "Some idiot uniform

just made a pass at me. I swear, I think these clothes scream *party girl* and give off some kind of weird hormone thing. You'd think I was starring in a video of *Cops GoneWild*. I cannot wait to get out of your cousin's clothes and into some of my own."

An unwanted anger rose up in Gideon. "Did he touch you?"

"What?" She looked at him oddly, as if she didn't understand his very simple question.

"The uniform who made a pass. Did he *touch* you?"

She sighed. "No. He just leered at my belly button and asked me what I was doing after my shift was over."

"Get his name?"

Her eyes widened, and then she shook her head. "Oh no, Raintree. We're not going there."

"Not going where?"

"You know damn well where we're not going."

"Enlighten me."

She leaned back against her own desk, which was much neater than his. Of course, she hadn't been there long enough to mess it up. "Okay, fine. If we're going to be…whatever, and I'm not sure yet that we are or we aren't, but if we *are,* there will be boundaries."

"Boundaries," Gideon repeated, half-sitting on his own desk.

"I want to be your partner, and I think I can be. I understand and accept what you can do, and I can contribute. I can be a good partner for you, Raintree, but some things are going to have to be separate. There can be no chasing after crude men who make passes at me, no staking your claim like we're cavemen and you're marking your territory, no sex on the desk or stolen kisses by the water cooler. When I'm in your bed, *if* I'm ever in your bed again, things can be different. But here in this office, I have to be your partner and nothing else. Can we do that?" she asked, as if she wasn't quite sure.

"I don't know," he said honestly. "It would be easier if you worked with someone else."

She squirmed a little, though he was sure the thought must have crossed her mind at some point that day. "I don't want to work with anyone else. I want to work homicide, and I know I can learn a lot from you. Maybe we should just write this morning off as a mistake and forget the whole thing."

Forget. Literally? A flash of anger rose up in Gideon, hot and electric. The lights overhead flickered but didn't go out. "Go ahead and forget. I don't know that I can."

Hope swallowed hard. Did she think he wouldn't see that response? he wondered.

"We're almost done here. We can go to the motel and I'll pick up the Challenger, and then I'll go home and——"

"No," he said.

"No?" Her eyebrows lifted slightly.

"I can't be sure you're safe there."

"See?" She pointed a finger at him. "This is exactly the kind of macho posturing I was trying to avoid. Would you have treated Leon this way?"

"I never fucked Leon."

Her face went red and then pale, and she pushed away from her desk and stalked out of the office. He wanted to chase her, catch her and drag her back into the office to finish this, but others were watching. And he had to admit, it was a momentarily and insanely tempting thought, to have a partner who knew what he could do and wasn't frightened by it. Someone he could count on to help with the investigation, even if they had to work it backward and upside down and inside out to get the bad guy.

So much for his determination to scare her off.

He did follow her, but at a distance. He stayed well behind Hope until they were in the parking lot, and then he easily caught up with her.

"If you're here to apologize…" she began tightly.

"I'm not," he said honestly.

She glanced at him, surprised and angry.

"I'm not apologizing for what happened, and I'm not apologizing for telling the truth just now. You're not one of the guys, Hope, and you'll never be the same kind of partner Leon was." She stopped short when he opened the passenger door for her and waited for her to get into the car.

Eventually she climbed into the passenger seat, still angry, but a little less so.

Gideon got into the driver's seat but didn't crank the engine. "You can't go home tonight because, like it or not, you're in the circle. If Tabby can't get to me, she might try to get to you. Your mother and your sister would be right there in the cross fire."

"That makes sense, I suppose," she said tightly. "I'd still like to go by the apartment and pick up a few things."

"Sure," he said, pulling out of the parking lot and heading toward The Silver Chalice. The Challenger could wait; he wasn't about to let Hope out of his sight.

As they turned off Red Cross Street, he said, "No sex on the desk, huh? Bummer."

Sunny Malory Stanton was the perfect daughter for Rainbow Malory. Her hair was a dark blond, like their father's, but other than that, she was Rainbow made over. Big smile, bigger heart. Comfy sandals, long skirt, dangling earrings. No bra.

Sunny smiled when Hope and Gideon walked through the door. She didn't even notice that her little sister's attire was totally out of character.

If Sunny showed up wearing a suit, Hope would certainly notice.

Her mother and sister were rearranging the display of new jewelry. They were having fun, chatting away about the grand-children, who had been left at home with their father. It would do Rainbow a world of good to spend some time with her eldest daughter.

Now to explain away spending the next few days at Gideon's beach house. Hope had been trying to come up with a good explanation since leaving the station, though she knew her mother would require no explanation at all. She would just figure that her youngest daughter had finally decided to embrace the old free love concept, and since Rainbow already liked Gideon...

No explanation was called for. Rainbow Malory looked Hope up and down, quickly took in Gideon's casual attire, and whispered, "Undercover?" as if there were a dozen people around to hear.

When Gideon opened his mouth, probably to say, "No," Hope stepped in front of him and said, "Yes," loudly enough to cover his answer. "I just need to pack a few things, and then we have to go." She didn't like to think that her family might be in danger simply because she was near, so the faster she got out of there, the better off they all would be.

She hated leaving Gideon alone with her family, but she couldn't very well ask him to come upstairs and help her pack. So she left him perusing the merchandise while she ran to the apartment above, intent on packing as quickly as she could.

Not that she could possibly be quick enough, of course. She

gathered clothes, underwear, toothbrush, toothpaste, makeup. All the things she would need to make herself at home in Gideon's house.

Hope walked downstairs to find the three of them with their heads together, laughing as if someone had an old baby picture of her naked and was showing it off. Laughing as if Sunny had just told one of her embarrassing "Remember when?" stories about her little sister.

"We can go now," Hope said, her voice almost harsh.

They all three turned to look at her, and she got the feeling they knew something she didn't. She'd felt that way all her life, as if she were living on the outside looking in, as if she were missing out on some universal truth that was hidden from her and no one else.

"Yeah, okay," Gideon said, walking toward her, his eyes raking over her hungrily.

She was twenty-nine years old. She'd been involved with men before. Romantically, sexually, emotionally. And none of them had ever looked at her this way. None of them had ever looked into her with eyes that made her knees wobble.

None of them had been Gideon Raintree.

"I'm cooking Saturday night," Sunny called. "If y'all are finished with your undercover thingie, come by after the shop closes. I make a mean peach cobbler."

They said goodbye and left the shop just as three tourists— mother and daughters, judging by their similar round faces— entered, drawn there by a colorful display of wrapped stones in the window.

Hope tossed her bag into the back seat of Gideon's Mustang. She couldn't help but remember driving him home last night. He'd been so out of it that she'd been sure he would be in bed for days. She'd been certain he needed to be in the hospital. And here he was, looking as if nothing out of the ordinary had happened.

"Are they safe there?" she asked before Gideon had a chance to fire up the engine. She had seen what Tabby could do, and while she wasn't afraid for herself, the idea of a woman like that going near her family made her stomach and her heart turn.

"If I didn't think so, they wouldn't be there," Gideon answered. "They're under constant surveillance, just in case."

"How did you manage that without telling the chief everything you know?" And how did he know that was just what she needed to hear to maintain her peace of mind? Rainbow and Sunny might be flakes, but they were *her* flakes.

"I didn't tell the chief anything." He pointed to the storefront across the street, not to the busy café but to the upstairs window. "I hired a private team to keep an eye on your family, at least until Tabby is caught. Though I don't believe it's necessary," he added crisply. "Tabby wants me, and she might want you. I don't think your family's even a blip on her radar."

Twenty-four-hour surveillance didn't come cheap; she knew that. She could complain because her new partner had taken such a move without discussing it with her first, and she could offer to pay, since this was, after all, her family they were talking about. But instead she just said, "Thank you." And she meant it.

*Thursday——8:37 p.m.*

He wasn't surprised that Hope's bathing suit was a modest black one-piece. She looked great in it, but what he wouldn't give to see her in a skimpy bikini like the ones Echo wore when she was here. Something tiny and insubstantial, and maybe red. Beneath the conservative suits she wore to work, Hope Malory had a great body.

They'd studied the files over sandwiches and soda, but eventually they'd both started to lose what energy they had left, after last night. Words began to blur. They started making mistakes. Gideon's response to that kind of weariness was always the water.

The waves were ferocious, and night was coming, so they didn't go far from the shore. Churning salt water pummeled them both. They didn't stay close together. There was no holding hands or laughing in the surf. How could there be? He didn't yet know what they were. Partners yes, but probably not for long. Friends? No, Hope Malory was many things, but she was *not* his friend. Lovers? Maybe. It was too soon to say. One tryst did not a lover make.

As darkness crept up on them, they left the ocean and walked toward the house, a few feet of sand and an air of uncertainty separating them.

"Hi, Gideon!"

Honey, his blond next-door neighbor, leaned over her balcony and waved. He'd never once seen her in the ocean. He'd asked her about it once, and she'd said she didn't want to mess up her hair. With her hair slicked back and water dripping off her nose, Hope looked more beautiful than any other woman he'd ever seen. It was a realization he could have done without.

"Hi," he answered, his voice decidedly less enthusiastic than hers.

"Don't forget about the party Saturday night." Her eyes flitted quickly to Hope. "Are you going to be around?"

He shook his head. "Sorry, no."

"How about supper tomorrow night? We can cook out."

"I have to go out of town for the day. I'm not sure when I'll get back."

Hope glanced back at him and raised her eyebrows slightly. She was probably wondering if he was running out on her or telling Honey an out-and-out lie.

"Well, if you do get a chance on Saturday, stop by."

"Sure," he said, noncommittal and less than enthusiastic in his response.

He and Hope both reached the spigot at the foot of the stairway that led to his bedroom at the same time. They rinsed the sand off their feet.

"So where are you going tomorrow?"

"Hale County. The Cordell murder scene."

Her foot brushed against his, and she instinctively drew back. "Think it'll do any good?"

"I don't know. Maybe the ghost will still be there and can help in some way."

"After all this time?" Her question reminded her that she knew next to nothing about what he did.

"Some ghosts hang around for hundreds of years, stuck where they don't belong because they were so traumatized by life or their deaths that they can't move on. Four months is nothing."

"Do you do what you do to catch the killers, or do you try to send the ghosts of the victims to wherever it is they're supposed to be?"

"Both," he confessed.

He turned off the water, and they climbed the stairs, Hope in front, him lagging a few feet behind. What next? He wanted her, but he knew he shouldn't have her. Not couldn't, *shouldn't*.

In the end, she made the first move. At the top of the stairs she waited, and when he got there, she laid her hand on his arm, rose up on her toes and kissed him. It wasn't a sexual kiss—at least, not blatantly. It was a simple touch of her mouth to his, a hesitant, stirring kiss.

"You're a good man, Gideon. I'm sorry I suspected you of being crooked."

"That's all right," he muttered.

"No, it's not. You hide so much of yourself, and there's no way you can tell people what it is that you do. And yet you do it anyway, never taking credit, never asking for money or fame or even thanks."

"I'm a little surprised you're accepting this so easily," he said, leaning down for another kiss, because she was there and he could.

"Yeah," she whispered just before his lips touched hers again. "So am I."

The ocean had washed away Hope's worries, at least for a while, and once she'd let everything go she couldn't stop thinking about Gideon and what had happened that morning. Together they stripped off their wet bathing suits and stepped toward the master bathroom. She was sandy and salty, and she tasted Gideon on her mouth. Work was done, at least for a while, and for the moment she wasn't worried about anything but getting into the bed and staying there for a while. She felt almost wanton, which was unlike her.

Hope Malory was cautious where men were concerned, and though she'd always tried to be just like the males in her profession, she had never been aggressive in the bedroom. It was the one place where she was truly shy, where she sometimes felt reserved to the point of prim. She didn't feel at all prim now, as she gently pushed Gideon into the shower and followed him inside, stepping under the warm spray and letting it wash the last of the salt water from her skin and her hair.

"Do you ever get tired of living here?" she asked.

He ran a hand over her wet breast, almost casual and definitely familiar. There was such warmth in that hand, and she wanted more. She had a feeling she could never get enough of this man.

"Only when I get too much company," he answered. "When that happens, I just toss a few grains of sand into the bed each night, and eventually they go home."

She moved her body closer to his, unable to stop herself, not wanting to stop. "If I overstay my welcome, are you going to toss sand in my bed?" she teased.

"Not likely," he said, his voice soft and uncertain.

She wanted to ask him, *What are we, Raintree? A couple? Coworkers who have sex on the side? Friends?* But she didn't want to ask questions she knew he didn't have answers for. He kissed her under the shower's spray, and his hands wandered. So did hers. She wanted him here and now, but there was no condom nearby, and she wasn't about to let go of him, not yet. This felt too good, the spray of the water, Gideon's mouth and his hands, and the way her body responded to both. It didn't matter what they called themselves, not yet. Maybe one day it would matter, but for now, this was enough.

She closed her eyes while Gideon spread her legs and touched her intimately. She could have sworn a spark entered her body, teasing her, arousing her, fluttering through her like a little bolt of lightning. Maybe it did. At this point, nothing seemed impossible.

Her body began to quiver, she wanted Gideon so much.

Instead of leading her from the shower, he pressed his palm against her belly, low, where she felt empty and shuddery.

"I'm gonna cheat," he whispered into her ear.

"Okay," Hope whispered breathlessly, eyes closed as everything she had was focused on touch, and touch alone.

She cried out as the orgasm washed through her with an unexpected intensity, and if Gideon hadn't been holding her up, she probably would have fallen to the shower floor. But he did hold her up. He held her wet, slick body against his, as release whipped through her like lightning.

As the orgasm faded, Gideon whispered, "Open your eyes."

She did so, slowly. There was an odd glow in the shower, and it didn't come from Gideon. It came from her. Her aura, a literal afterglow, danced along her skin with little sparks of electricity. Gideon's eyes shone with a touch of green light, just a touch. The rest of the glow came from her.

He smiled. "Water is a great conductor."

He had been tempted to take Hope in the shower, condom or no condom, but Emma's frequent appearances and promises of coming soon had made him opt for another method, at least for now.

Besides, it wasn't as if they were finished.

They dried one another with a fat gray towel, then walked toward the bedroom and the bed that awaited. Hope's skin still glowed, but the luminescence was quickly fading. She didn't have the power to keep the electricity fed, as he did.

He tossed her onto the bed, and she laughed as he crawled onto the mattress to join her. She stretched beneath him, naked and damp and touched with magic.

"So," she said, reaching out to caress his face with gentle fingers. "What do girls normally say when you turn them into your own personal flashlights?"

He stroked her throat with the back of his hand. "I don't know. I've never done it before."

Her smile faded.

"I usually have to hide everything, remember?" He didn't tell her that the glow was special, that she was different, that she was so unlike other women she stunned him.

Hope shifted her body, making herself more comfortable against him. There was something most definitely different about the way his naked flesh and hers came together, something he didn't want to think about. He didn't want to *think* with her. He wanted sex. A few laughs, maybe.

"Don't hide anything from me," she said.

It was such an unexpected and startling thought, that any woman could know everything about him and stay, that Gideon almost flinched. He couldn't bare himself in every sense to anyone. Bare bodies, yes. Bare souls? Never.

He didn't want to talk about anything beyond the physical, so he spread Hope's thighs and stroked. She sighed and wrapped her fingers around him, gently, but not too gently. She caressed, and he closed his eyes and left everything behind to get lost in sensation. This was sex. It was good and right and powerful, but it was still only sex.

By the time he reached for the bedside drawer, neither of them were thinking about explanations for what this might be. It just was.

Sometimes a rabbit is just a rabbit.

# ELEVEN

She should have been able to sleep like a baby, but that hadn't happened. Not yet. Her mind was spinning with a thousand questions. When Hope became so restless that she began to worry about waking Gideon, she left him sleeping in his bed while she quietly roamed the half-dark bedroom.

Moonlight from the uncovered window and a hint of illumination from a night-light in the bathroom made it easy enough to see. Gideon was a bit of a minimalist, without a lot of unnecessary stuff in his house. There were family pictures on the walls here and there, but no flower arrangements or useless knickknacks on tabletops. She ran her hands over the dresser in his bedroom. Carelessly discarded on the surface was a ceramic dish for coins, a silk tie he'd dropped in a heap, a small piece of turquoise and what she recognized as another protection charm. She ran her fingers over the small silver charm attached to the slim leather cord. A week ago, if someone had told her that something so innocent and unimportant as a piece of silver could carry the power to protect, she never would have believed it. Now she knew that many of the things she'd once believed were wrong. She lifted the charm and placed it around her neck, where it lay close to the one Gideon had given her. Tabby was out there somewhere, and besides, her heart needed all the protection it could get at the moment. Was that kind of protection even possible? Or was it too late for her?

She grabbed a T-shirt Gideon had dropped onto a chair near the dresser, pulled it over her head and very quietly walked onto the deck that overlooked the Atlantic. The sound of the surf, together with the gentle light of the moon, soothed her, and she definitely needed soothing tonight.

It wasn't like her to get deeply involved with anyone or anything so quickly. She studied all new enterprises from every angle before committing herself in any way. She always remained coldly and totally detached from any situation until she knew without doubt that a move was the right one. She'd been that way since the age of eleven, maybe even longer. She didn't make rash decisions. Not anymore.

And here she was, deeply involved with Gideon Raintree. Through the sex, his secrets and the case they were working together, she was involved to the pit of her soul.

She heard the door behind her open but didn't turn to look at Gideon. His bare feet padded toward her, and a moment later his arms encircled her. Those arms were warm and strong and wonderfully embracing. It was a nice feeling, to be held this way. She liked it. Maybe too much.

"I didn't mean to wake you," she whispered.

"Two nights together, and I wake up because you're not

where you're supposed to be," he responded with a touch of displeasure in his voice.

She leaned her head back and relaxed against him. "I'm not exactly accustomed to needing anyone, either."

He slipped his hands beneath the oversized shirt she wore, raked his palms against her bare skin and cupped her breasts with familiarity. His fingers teased the sensitive nipples until she closed her eyes and swayed against him, her body responding quickly and entirely. She shouldn't want him now. She should most definitely not need him this way, with an intensity that drove away everything else. But she did.

His hands feathered over her breasts. Was that a touch of unnatural electricity that seeped through her skin and shot to her very core? Or was what she felt so intensely simply the response of a woman to a man? Gideon had such nice hands, charged or not, and he touched her as if he owned her, as if he knew exactly how to make her his in every way. He leaned down and kissed the side of her neck, familiarly and gently and amazingly arousingly. Her body quivered.

She turned in Gideon's arms, lifted her face and kissed him. Her mouth against his, she slipped her hands around his waist. He'd walked onto the deck naked—not that anyone would be on the beach to see them at this time of night, in this near-dark—and she boldly ran her fingers against his back, his hip, his thigh. If it was true that he could make her his, then it was just as true that *she* possessed a part of *him,* at least for tonight.

He kissed her deeply, arousing her and demanding more with his lips and his tongue and his hands. Her body clenched and unclenched, quivered, and quickly spiraled out of control. So did Gideon's. She felt it in every caress of his hands; she tasted it in his kiss. Moaning low in what sounded like frustration or maybe impatience, he easily lifted her off her feet. Her legs wrapped around his waist. He was close, so close.

"Don't you need a——" she began breathlessly.

"Already thought of that," he said, his voice husky.

She shifted her body to bring him closer, to guide him into her. "You came out here wearing a condom? Pretty sure of yourself, weren't you?" she teased.

"I was overcome by optimism."

The tip of his erection teased her entrance, and she began to lower herself onto him, anxious and wanting in a way that still surprised her. She'd had more sex in the past twenty-four hours than she'd had in the past five years. And she had *never* had sex like this before, all-consuming and powerful and beautiful, without awkwardness or disappointment. She had never felt a moment's disappointment in Gideon's arms.

"I'm glad you woke up," she whispered, her mouth resting against his ear. "I've never made love in the moonlight before."

Gideon went still. His entire body tensed, muscles tightening. "Moonlight."

He lifted her away from the railing she was partially balanced against, and carried her into the deep shadows against the house. No moonlight touched them there, and there was no railing to lean against. Gideon held her; she held him. The wall was against her back, and she felt grounded and afloat at the same time.

They were lost in complete and utter darkness when he pushed inside her, deep and hard. Hope didn't care where they were. Moonlight or daylight, darkness or sunshine. Under the covers or beneath nothing but the moon and the stars. As long as Gideon was with her, as long as he was holding her, she didn't care where they were. Instinct called her to him, but there was more than instinct here, more than intense physical need.

She hadn't thought herself in love for a very long time. Her mother, her sister, her nephews, that kind of love was all she dared to believe in. Romantic love was filled with pitfalls. She not only didn't wish for that emotion, she did her best to avoid it. Love was a trap, heartache just waiting to happen. This unexpected rush of emotion she felt for Gideon right now, while he held her and filled her and brought her closer to release, surely it was just the power of sex.

But as he made love to her, with her back to the wall and her arms and legs wrapped completely around him, she couldn't imagine any other man but Gideon making her feel this way. She could love him. She could wrap her entire world around this man and change who and what she was, who she had become. Ghosts, light shows and all, she could love him. Scary stuff.

They came together with a cry and a moan that were lost in a deep kiss. With the sounds of the surf in their ears and the moonlight inches away, with her body trembling, there was a moment of perfection when those words crossed her mind again. *I could love you.* Lost in darkness, the gentle glow of Gideon made her smile. *I love you* tugged at her lips, but she bit the words back. It was too soon for such a confession. It was also too risky.

He carried her inside the house and placed her gently on the bed. After disposing of the condom, he returned to the bed to lie beside her. She kept his T-shirt on. She liked the way it felt against her skin, this worn cotton that still smelled vaguely of Gideon.

"I'm going to get up in the morning and go to the Cordell

crime scene to have a look around," he said, his voice like gravel and silk.

"You mean *we,* right?"

He hesitated. "I want you to stay here."

She rose slightly. If she hadn't just been thoroughly exhausted and satisfied, if *I love you* weren't still niggling at the edge of her brain, his words might have made her angry. Instead she smiled. "No way."

"There are other case files that need to be examined. I need you here."

"Put the top up and I'll read the files in the car."

He wrapped an arm around her waist and pulled her body against his. "Can we argue about this tomorrow?"

"Sure." Her eyes drifted closed. Maybe now she could sleep. "I like arguing with you," she said beneath her breath. "You're really cute when you get mad."

Gideon snorted, and then he laughed. "You're one of a kind, Hope Malory."

"So are you, Gideon Raintree." It was as close to *I love you* as either of them were willing to get.

Gideon woke not long after sunrise, which was normal for him. Waking with his arms around a beautiful woman was not so normal.

His sexual relationships in the past had been brief. Even in those that lasted a few weeks or even a few months, he maintained a certain distance. He didn't spend the night elsewhere or ask women to spend the night here. It was too dangerous.

Sleeping with Hope didn't feel at all dangerous. It felt right and good and natural, as if they had been sleeping together for a thousand years. And that was truly dangerous. It was so dangerous that last night he had almost forgotten Emma's words and taken Hope right there in the moonlight. He'd been wearing a condom, but no kind of protection was a hundred percent effective. Moving into the shadows before he'd buried himself inside her had simply been a precaution.

He lifted her shirt, his shirt, and laid his mouth on her flat stomach. Damn, she tasted good. She felt good, so warm and silky. He kissed her there, drawing the essence of her into his mouth, trailing the tip of his tongue up and down, sucking against her skin until he felt her hand settle in his hair.

"Good morning," she murmured, her voice sleepy and satisfied.

He answered by lifting the shirt a bit higher and pushing his hand beneath the soft cotton. The chill of her protection charm brushed against his hand as he uncovered one breast and took the nipple deep into his mouth. Hope's fingers threaded more thoroughly into his hair, and he suckled her deeper. He tasted her and savored her until one of those little moans caught in her throat.

This morning he wasn't in any hurry. He would make her come a time or two, make love to her long and hard and then leave her sleeping soundly. When she woke up and found that he was well on his way to the Cordell crime scene, she might be pissed for a while, but she would forgive him. He knew exactly how to make her forgive him.

He spread her legs and ran one finger along the tender skin of her inner thigh. Her skin was soft, the muscle of her thigh gently shaped and utterly feminine. "You have the longest legs," he said as he lifted one and laid his mouth behind the knee. She shuddered and wrapped that leg around him as his mouth moved higher. Her leg hadn't seen much sun. It was as creamy

pale as any skin he had ever seen, and it fascinated him. He ran
a finger up from her knee, allowing a little bit of electricity to
escape. Hope laughed and twitched.

"That tickles."

"Does it?"

"Yes," she said with a sigh.

He wasn't anywhere near finished with this woman. Would
he ever be? While the morning came alive, he tasted her everywhere. He made her quiver and lurch; he made her moan.
After she came against his mouth, she all but threw him onto
his back, determined to have her way with him, as well. Determined to make him moan. And she did. With her mouth
and her hands, she studied every inch of him.

Knowing that he was as ready as a man could possibly get,
Hope pulled away from him and drew the T-shirt over her
head. Gideon reached for the drawer where he kept the
condoms. He would have to stop by the drugstore on the way
home tonight. He was almost out. And no matter how much
he liked Hope, no matter how right and close and true she felt,
no matter that she made him glow in the dark, he wasn't ready
to go any further than this. They had great sex, but there was
no guarantee that it would last. Not much in this world was
truly lasting.

Hope sat on the bed, smiling and flushed and breathing hard
all over again. Her black hair was mussed around her face.
Perfect Hope, so carefully put together, was utterly gorgeous
when she was mussed.

Mussed and naked…and wearing two charms around her
neck.

Gideon dropped the wrapped condom to the bed. He forgot
about pushing inside Hope and ending this torment. He forgot

about everything else but those pieces of silver. "Where did you get this?" he asked as he lifted one of the charms. The one he had *not* given her.

She lifted the charm and studied it absently. "I almost forgot about this one. I found it on your dresser last night."

Gideon jumped from the bed and turned toward the dresser in question. Sure enough, Dante's fertility charm was gone. No, not *gone*. Hope was wearing it around her pretty neck. "Were you wearing that last night when we were on the deck?"

"I think so." She pushed her hair back, combing it with long, pale fingers. "Yeah, I was. I picked it up and put it on before I went outside."

He turned and stared down at her. "Why?"

"I don't know. It's pretty." She removed the charm that had not been made for her, drawing the cord over her head and ruffling her mussed hair further in the process. Not that it mattered. It was too late. Much too late. "I guess I felt the need for a little extra protection last night." She offered the talisman to him with an outstretched hand. He didn't take it. "I'm sorry if I wasn't supposed to touch. Take it and come back to bed."

"All the protection in the world won't undo..." He stopped. One time, that was all, and he had been wearing a condom and they hadn't been in the moonlight. Maybe, just maybe... He rushed into the bathroom and slammed the door.

"Gideon?" Hope called through the closed door. "Are you all right?"

*Not even a little.* "Fine," he answered tersely.

*Fine?* What a lie. He'd been this close to another moment of absolute perfection inside Hope Malory, and then he'd seen that charm lying against her chest. Wanting someone to distraction physically was one thing. Making a baby together was another thing entirely.

Maybe everything *was* fine. He'd been thinking clearly enough to move Hope out of the moonlight last night before having sex with her. That one fact might have changed everything. Emma couldn't come to him in a moonbeam if there was no moonbeam in which to travel.

"Emma," he whispered. "Show yourself."

He waited for the spirit who claimed to be his daughter to drop in to say hello. After all, she'd shown up before when he'd called her name. But the bathroom remained silent and free of spirits of all kinds.

"You're sure you're all right?" Hope called. She was closer now, standing just on the other side of the door.

"I'm *fine!*" Gideon snapped.

She moved away, and a moment later he heard the water running in the guest bathroom. For a moment he leaned over the sink and studied his sour, bristly-cheeked reflection. He didn't look like a father; he didn't feel like a father. "Come on, Emma," he said, a bit louder than before. "This isn't funny. It isn't nice to tease. You're going to give Daddy heart failure if you don't show yourself."

The bathroom remained silent but for his own labored breathing.

Hope was special; he couldn't deny that. There was the continuing and annoying glow that told him his heart and soul were as involved as his body. Maybe, a few years down the line, if they continued to have great sex and they worked out the whole partner thing, then *maybe* he could consider the possibility that Hope was going to be a permanent fixture in his life.

But *now?*

"Come on, Emma. Sweetheart," he added. "There's no need to be hasty about this. A couple of years, maybe ten, and then I might be ready to have kids." It was a lie, and Emma likely knew it. The world wasn't fit for the innocence of a child; he saw that for himself every day.

She was pulling his leg. After all, he had moved Hope away from the early-morning moonbeams, and he'd used a condom faithfully.

And Hope had been wearing that damned fertility charm, which very well could have trumped everything.

Gideon took a quick shower, shaking off the feeling of impending doom as he toweled dry and then wrapped the towel around his waist. He found Hope in the kitchen, making coffee and scrounging around the cupboards looking for a breakfast of some sort.

She gave him a wary glance. "Are you sure you're all right?"

"Yeah." He looked at her. Most specifically, he looked at her stomach. "Come on, Emma," he whispered as Hope turned her attentions to the refrigerator. "Talk to me."

"What did you say?" Hope asked as she came out with a half gallon of milk.

"Nothing."

"Oh, I thought you said Emma." She placed the milk on the counter, beside a box of cereal. "That's my grandmother's name."

He almost groaned but caught himself just in time.

Hope reached for the bowls. She already knew her way around the kitchen pretty well. "My mother has her heart set on a grand-daughter named Emma," she said, "but Sunny has three boys, and I'm not planning to have kids any time soon, so she's outta luck."

"Wanna bet?" Gideon asked beneath his breath.

Hope left everything she'd gathered on the counter and turned to glare at him. "Maybe I should call you Rainman instead of Raintree. You're making no sense at all this morning."

Gideon pointed to the fertility charm Hope had put around her neck once again, after he'd refused to take it from her palm. It had been meant for Dante, a brotherly joke, a push to get the Dranir busy reproducing, but it would be just as effective on Hope.

"That talisman you lifted from the dresser last night," he said, as he continued to point a censuring finger, "is a fertility charm."

"A *what?*" Hope took a step away from him and yanked the thing from around her neck as if it might burn her. "What kind of sick person would make a fertility charm and leave it lying around!"

Gideon raised his empty hand. "This sick person. It was meant for my brother, not you."

Hope flung the charm at him, putting all her muscle behind it. "You really are sick," she said sharply as he caught the charm in midair. "What did your brother ever do to you to deserve that?" She looked around her immediate vicinity for something else to throw, found nothing handy and finally sat down at the kitchen table. "It didn't work," she said sensibly. "I'm sure it didn't work. That charm wasn't made for me, and we were careful. We were always careful. It's not like you have some kind of super sperm."

"Yeah," Gideon agreed, hoping she was right. If fertility charms worked without fail, Dante would have populated his own village by now. "I even moved you out of the moonlight."

"What does that have to do with anything?" she snapped.

He figured he might as well tell her everything. "For the past three months I've been dreaming about this little girl. Thanks to Dante," he added. "So don't feel too sorry for him just because I occasionally send him something he doesn't want."

"He sent you some kind of dream?"

"There have been a couple of times when I've seen Emma outside a dream. She was the one who told me to get down when Tabby took a shot at us."

"What does that have to do with moonlight, Raintree?" Hope was frustrated and irritated and maybe even a little scared. She tried to smooth her hair with agitated fingers.

"Emma told me that she's coming to me in a moonbeam."

Hope went pale. Deathly, scarily, white. As white as the milk she'd taken from the fridge. "You should have told me that before now." She grabbed the saltshaker off the table and threw it at him, but there wasn't as much anger in the motion as before, and he caught it easily. Some of the salt escaped and fell to the floor. Out of habit, he picked up a pinch and tossed it over his left shoulder.

"Why?" Gideon asked as he set the saltshaker aside. "I didn't believe her. We make our own choices in life, and I choose not to have kids. Besides, it's just some kind of poetic nonsense. And we weren't in a moonbeam last—"

"Shut up, Raintree." Hope stood and looked longingly at the pepper shaker, but she walked away without throwing it at him. "You were in a moonbeam last night," she said without turning to look at him. "You were most definitely in a moonbeam."

"Where are you going?"

She lifted a hand. "I'll be right back. Don't go anywhere."

A few seconds later Hope was in the kitchen again, purse in

hand, face no less pale. She sat at the table, took a slim black wallet from her purse, slid her driver's license from its designated slot and tossed it to Gideon. It sailed between them like a Frisbee, hit him in the chest and landed on the floor by his feet. "Read it and weep," she said weakly.

Gideon scooped the driver's license from the floor. The picture was less than flattering, like all such photos, and still...not too bad. It was the name on the license that caught and held his attention. He gripped the license tightly and said a word not fit for little Emma's ears as he read the name again and again.

Moonbeam Hope Malory.

# TWELVE

She'd thought about having her name legally changed a thousand times, but every time she so much as mentioned it to her mother there was hell to pay. Sunshine Faith and Moonbeam Hope, those were Rainbow's daughters. They had been Sunny and Moonie for years, until Hope had grown old enough to insist that she be called by her middle name.

Gideon drove too fast, but Hope didn't say a word about him speeding. Since he'd put the top of the convertible up, she was able to leaf through the case files. That way they didn't have to talk. Or look at each other.

Several of the files were from unsolved murders that probably weren't connected to the latest killings. Most were grisly but without the connection of the missing body parts. Gathering this much information hadn't been easy. There were a number of different jurisdictions and investigators involved. Still, she saw enough similarities in a number of cases to make her uneasy.

If Tabby was a serial killer, and that was definitely possible, then why had she targeted Gideon? Why had she tried to kill him on the riverfront? It didn't fit in several ways. Unlike her other crimes, it had been attempted in a public place, and Gideon was unlike her other victims. Wasn't he? He had been alone before taking up with her. Was he still a loner, emotionally? Of course he was. What they had was just sex, which didn't exactly qualify them to be a happy couple—this morning's odd developments aside.

Hope did her best not to think about those developments. Studying the disturbing cases before her was much easier on her heart, horrifying as they were.

The file on the victim in Hale County was thin but far from shoddy. It wasn't a lack of concern that caused the file to be thin. According to Gideon, the sheriff was anxious to talk to anyone who might be able to shed light on the schoolteacher's murder, and had seemed relieved that someone had taken an interest in the case.

"Why this one?" she asked when they'd been on the road more than an hour. "There are others that fit the profile, and at least one that's closer."

"It's less than three hours away, and more important, the crime scene is intact," Gideon answered in a businesslike voice.

"How could it be intact after four months?"

"It's been cleaned," he explained, "but no one's moved into the house. My best shot of speaking to the victim and maybe even spotting a real clue is with this case."

He hadn't wanted her to come along today, but he hadn't argued long when she'd insisted. Was that why he was so unhappy, or was he wound tightly for more personal reasons? He sure as hell didn't want her to be pregnant. She'd never seen a man react so strongly to the very prospect. Not that she had exactly embraced the idea of parenthood with a surge of joy and giggles.

He seemed so sure that Emma was a done deal. Hope wasn't, though all his talk of moonbeams and that damned fertility charm had given her more than a moment's pause. Gideon made her look at the impossible in a whole new way. He made her want to open her eyes and her heart in a way she had refused to do in the past. But really, a *fertility* charm?

She stared out the passenger window and watched the leafy green landscape blur. It wasn't like her to meet a man on Monday and end up in his bed on Wednesday. She'd obviously hit an invisible and unexpected sexual peak of some kind, because where Gideon was concerned, she hadn't been able to control herself. That was also very much not like her. Control was her middle name. Of course, Hope Control Malory was preferable to Moonbeam Hope Malory any day.

Could've been worse. Her mother could have named her Moonbeam Chastity. Then where would she be?

They were another hour down the road, perhaps half an hour from their destination, when Gideon said, "I'm sorry if I overreacted."

"A grown man tearing out his hair, cursing and screaming at my stomach, you call that overreacting?" she asked without emotion.

Gideon shifted his broad shoulders, fidgeting as if the car had suddenly become too small to contain him. "At least I didn't throw anything at you."

"I'm not the one who made a fertility charm and left it lying around in the bedroom for anyone to pick up."

"I said I was sorry."

She really didn't want to argue right now. In fact, she didn't want to think about the possibilities Gideon had presented to her. "Why don't we wait a while and see if there's really anything to be sorry about?"

Another awkward moment passed, and he said, "If you want to request another partner, I'll understand."

Hope almost snorted. "Is that what this is about?" she snapped. "You don't want a partner, so you go to extreme lengths to make sure—"

"No," he interrupted, then after a pause that lasted a few seconds too long, he added, "It's true. I don't want a partner."

"Then go to the chief and tell him you don't want me as a partner. Don't expect me to quit. I don't quit, Raintree. Not ever."

"He'd just assign me another one," Gideon grumbled.

She would never admit it out loud, but it hurt that Gideon didn't want to work with her. Not because they'd slept together and she felt there could be so much more, but because she'd worked so hard to get where she was, and she was damned tired of being dismissed by men who thought she couldn't do her job. She couldn't tamp her anger down. "It might be difficult to pretend to be devastated because you thought you knocked up Mike or Charlie."

Gideon didn't respond, so she glanced in his direction. He was almost smiling.

"I don't think I'm pregnant," she said sensibly, her anger fading. "We were careful. A piece of silver and a dream won't undo that." Super sperm aside.

"Maybe you're right," he said, though he didn't sound as if he believed there was a chance in hell she was.

"Even if I am...pregnant..." Damn, it was hard to say that

word out loud. "That doesn't mean we have to get married or anything." The *M* word was even more difficult than *pregnant*. "You don't have to concern yourself with whatever happens to me." She said the words, but her heart did a little flip. Single and pregnant, raising a child alone, pretending she hadn't almost said *I love you* to this man who was terrified of being tied to her by a child.

"Emma's Raintree," Gideon said. "I will most definitely be concerned."

"Actually, Emma is *Malory*," she responded. "If there *is* an Emma," she added.

"A woman who gives birth to a Raintree *becomes* Raintree, in many ways," Gideon said tersely.

"I don't think so," she responded, wondering at his statement but afraid to ask. . . .

"You've seen what I can do," Gideon said, his voice lowered, as if someone else out here in the middle of nowhere might hear. "Emma will have her own gifts, and there's no way I can walk away and not *concern* myself with what happens to her."

They hadn't known one another long enough for Hope to be hurt because none of his concern was for her. "Maybe this time will be different. Maybe Raintree genes won't be dominant in this case." Shoot, she was talking about this kid as if it was a done deal. "If I'm pregnant. Which I'm not."

"You're pregnant," he said sourly.

"*If* I'm pregnant," she said again, "is it really such a disaster?" Her heart flipped again. Her stomach, too. Of course it was a disaster! Maybe she did think she was in love with Gideon, but they'd just met, and she had career plans, and she was pretty sure he didn't love her back.

"Yes!"

Hope turned her gaze to the blurred landscape again, so Gideon wouldn't see her face. She had no right to be devastated because he didn't want her to be pregnant. It was such a girlie reaction, to get teary-eyed over a rejection from a man she barely knew.

Maybe growing up different had been so difficult for him that he couldn't bear to watch a child go through the same struggles. But he'd turned out okay. He had a nice life, and he helped people—the living and the dead—and he had made the most of his abilities. Maybe he did have to hide a lot of himself from the world, but he hadn't hidden himself from her.

He cut the Mustang sharply onto the grassy shoulder of the road, startling Hope so that she snapped her head around to glare at him. "What are you doing?"

Gideon put the car in Park, and with the engine still running, he reached into her lap and grabbed a file. "Which one is this?" he asked, leafing through the pages and photos. "Doesn't matter, does it?" He randomly grabbed a photo and held it up. The woman in the picture was lying half-on and half-off a faded sofa, blood soaking the front of her dress and her head all but severed. "There are people in the world who do things like this," he said in a lowered voice. "If there were just a handful of the bastards, maybe I wouldn't feel sick at the very idea of exposing an innocent child to a life where this happens every day. Every day, Hope. What if Emma's like me and she's faced with the horrors of death every day of her life? What if she's like Echo and she dreams of disasters she can't do anything about? What if—" His lips snapped closed. He couldn't even finish his final thought.

How could she stay angry with him? He wasn't being petty or selfish. His panic was rooted in a fear and concern for the child he claimed he didn't want. Hope lifted her hand and touched Gideon's cheek. Her thumb brushed against his smooth chin. He didn't pull away from her, as she'd thought he might. "You've been doing this too long."

"What choice do I have? I have an ability that allows me to put the bad guys away. If I don't, some of them will get away with it. Some of the victims will be stuck here, caught between life and death." He looked her in the eye. "What do you say when a little girl asks if there are monsters in the world? *Yes* is terrifying. *No* is a lie."

She stroked his cheek. "When was the last time you had a vacation, Raintree?"

"I don't remember."

"When we catch Tabby and put her away for good, we're taking a long vacation. I like the mountains."

Gideon didn't agree that a vacation was a fine idea, but he didn't disagree, either. He placed one hand over her stomach, and that hand was gentle. "I don't like the idea of having something so important to lose," he said softly.

"Emma?" she whispered.

He lifted his head and looked her in the eye. "And you, Moonbeam Hope. Dammit, where the hell did you come from?"

She smiled at his bewilderment. "Call me Moonbeam again and I'll shoot you."

He smiled for the first time that day, and then he leaned in and kissed her quickly. "Let's get this over with. The sheriff is waiting for us."

The living room where Marcia Cordell had been murdered looked like an old lady's parlor. There were doilies on the tables, dusty silk flower arrangements that had been neglected in the four months since her death, antique furnishings that didn't match and yet somehow did. There was also a large dried bloodstain in the center of the rug in the middle of the room.

Gideon squatted down by the bloodstain, while Hope and an anxious sheriff hovered nearby. The sheriff worked the brim of his hat with meaty, nervous hands.

"I really hope you can help us out here," the man said. "Miss Cordell was a right popular teacher. Everybody loved her. Well, we thought everybody loved her. Takes a lot of hate to do what was done to her. Did you see the pictures? God-awful scene. I'll never forget it."

The man went on and on, chattering endlessly. The sheriff was nervous, and he desperately wanted help on this case. He wanted it closed. He wanted proof that someone from outside the community had done this terrible thing, so he didn't have to imagine that a man or woman he knew was capable of this kind of violence.

The ghost of Marcia Cordell was in the room, but she lurked in a corner, watchful and afraid. Still afraid.

"What kind of a man would do such a thing?" the sheriff continued. "To…to violate and murder such a sweet woman…"

Gideon's head snapped around. *Violate?* "She was sexually assaulted?"

The sheriff nodded and worked harder at the brim of his hat.

So much for the connection to Tabby. There had been no sign of sexual activity of any kind at the other scenes. "It would've been nice if that information had been included in the report you sent me."

"Miss Cordell was a decent woman. Wasn't no reason to broadcast such unpleasantness about her after she was gone. Besides, we're keeping that part of the investigation under wraps. No need to broadcast all the details to the world."

"DNA?" Hope asked crisply.

The sheriff shook his head. "No. The man who did this wore a prophylactic, the coroner said."

"Detective Malory," Gideon said in a measured and calm voice. "Would you take Sheriff Webster outside and see if he can fill in some of the blanks in the Cordell file?"

"Excellent idea," Hope said. The sheriff didn't want to leave, but when Hope took his arm and headed for the front door, he went along like a well-trained puppy.

Alone in the eerie room, Gideon turned his eyes to the far corner, where Marcia Cordell's ghost waited in a ball of unformed light. He wasn't too angry with the sheriff, even though this trip meant a day away from his current investigation, time wasted in his pursuit of Tabby. If he was here, it was for a reason. "Talk to me, Marcia," he said softly. "Tell me what happened to you."

She took form gradually, the ball of light shifting, color and shape growing more defined. Marcia Cordell had been a plump and pretty woman. She was barely five feet tall, and her long brown hair was pulled back into a bun. She suited this old-fashioned room.

"You see me," she said, her voice shaking.

"Yes, I do." Gideon remained calm and still, so he wouldn't scare her away. "Marcia, do you know you're dead?"

She nodded her head. "I saw them come and take my body away. I screamed at them to help me, but no one heard."

"I hear you."

Marcia drifted toward him, slow and openly suspicious. One wrong move and she would disappear. She wasn't angry like Sherry and Lily. She was terrified.

"Would you tell me what happened here?" Gideon asked gently.

"I let him in, never knowing what he intended."

*Him.* Not Tabby, just as he'd suspected when he heard that she had been violated. Still, he could find out who'd raped and killed her, and then he could send her spirit to a better place. In that sense, his trip here had not been wasted.

Marcia Cordell's spirit sighed and drifted down to sit on a flowery sofa, her pose proper. "Dennis was always such an odd boy, but—"

"Dennis. You knew him?"

Miss Cordell gave Gideon a withering glance. It was a glance she had no doubt silenced students with over the years. "Young man, you asked me to tell you what happened, and I'm trying to do just that."

He didn't point out that he was just a couple of years younger than she had been at the time of her death, hardly a young man. She had the spirit of an older woman, as if she'd carried something into this life too strongly from another. "Sorry, ma'am," he said contritely. "Please continue."

She nodded her head. "Dennis Floyd is a neighbor. The Floyd family has been living in that house going on twenty years. Dennis was in elementary school when they moved in, and he was a pupil in my English class several years ago. He was not a good student," she said with reproach. "He stopped by that night and asked to use the phone. He said their phone was out. Of course I said yes." Her mouth thinned. "I didn't see the danger coming until he grabbed me and threw me to the floor like a…like a…" she sputtered, and her face grew red. Even in death, she could blush.

"I'm going to see that he goes away for what he did to you," Gideon said. "He'll be punished, in this life and in the next."

She nodded, obviously relieved. "Dennis needs to be punished for what he did to me. So does she."

The hairs on the back of Gideon's neck prickled. "She?"

"The woman who was with Dennis, the one who urged him on. I didn't see her, not at first. I would have had reservations about allowing a stranger into my home so late in the evening. Dennis knocked me down. He bound my arms and legs with duct tape, and left me lying on the floor while he went to the door to invite her inside." She seemed to be as incensed at having a stranger in her home as she was at being murdered.

"You didn't know this woman."

Miss Cordell shook her head. "No. Dennis called her…" She wrinkled her nose in thought. "Kitty, I think, or…"

"Tabby," Gideon said softly.

"That's it." Marcia Cordell pointed a fading and shaking finger. "She sat in that chair over there and watched while Dennis did unspeakable things to me. She smiled, and when I screamed for help she told me that no one would hear me way out here, so far away from everyone and everything else." Her figure trembled, and she almost disappeared, as if she wanted to hide from the telling of her death. "When I cried, she asked me if I liked it. She asked me if I had always fantasized about having a young stud show up at my door to make a real woman out of me."

"She's going to pay, too," Gideon said. "I'll see to it."

Miss Cordell nodded her head. "She's the one who killed me."

"I know."

"I thought it was finally over, and then that horrible woman leaned over my body and put a knife to my belly. She...she cut me, and she enjoyed it. When she was tired of cutting, she started stabbing me and..."

Gideon listened, while Marcia Cordell told him every last detail of the way Dennis and Tabby had tortured and finally killed her. He didn't want to listen to the details, but Miss Cordell needed to tell the tale to someone who could hear her.

He listened, and then he asked, "Is there anything you can tell me about the woman? You said Dennis called her Tabby. Did he ever use a last name? Did you see what kind of vehicle she was driving? Was there anything you remember that might help me find her?"

Miss Cordell shook her head. "They left together, Dennis and that awful woman."

Which meant Dennis was likely dead, too. He couldn't imagine Tabby leaving a witness behind. "Time to go, Miss Cordell," Gideon said as he stood and looked down at her. "I promise you, I'll make sure they pay for what they did. I'll take care of them for you. Move on to the next phase of your existence and find peace. You deserve it."

"So do you," Miss Cordell whispered before she faded to nothing.

Gideon left the crime scene behind. If Dennis was still alive—unlikely, but not impossible—maybe he held the key to finding Tabby. If ever there was concrete proof that this world wasn't fit for a child, this was it.

Sheriff Webster stood by his patrol car, still working the brim of that battered hat. Gideon glanced around the overgrown yard. "Where's Detective Malory?"

"She decided to interview some of the neighbors while we

were waiting for you." He nodded to a small white house down the road. It was almost a quarter of a mile away but still the closest house to Marcia Cordell's. "Detective Malory seemed to think maybe they might've seen something that night. We interviewed them all and didn't get squat, but..."

A knot of unease settled into Gideon's gut.

"Dennis Floyd drove by while we were talking and..."

The sheriff didn't get any further. Gideon turned toward the little white house and ran.

Hope glanced back toward the Cordell house. The sheriff continued to lean against his patrol car, obeying her instructions not to bother Raintree. There was no telling how long Gideon might be inside, talking to the ghost. Odd, how naturally those words came to her mind. *Talking to the ghost.*

If she could find something, any small detail, to add to what he learned, it might help. Maybe a neighbor had seen a car that night. That kind of information should have been in the report, but sometimes important facts were missed the first time around. Even if Gideon could find out who had killed the woman, they would need evidence in order to get a conviction.

"Come on in and I'll fix us some tea." Dennis Floyd was in his mid-twenties, at a guess. He was a rail-thin young man, with thinning blond hair and small, pale blue eyes. His car and his clothing had seen better years, but the house itself seemed to be well maintained. The front porch was clean, and a number of flowering plants in clay pots brightened the place considerably.

"My folks are at work," he said as he opened the screen door for her. "I used to have my own place," he added, apparently trying to impress her. "But when I was between jobs, I moved back in here. I'm workin' steady now, but the folks need a little help with the yardwork and such, so I'm doing them a favor by stayin' on."

Hope stepped into his cool, semi-dark living room. It was clean but musty, as if years of stale odors had seeped into the walls and would never wash out. There was too much clutter for her taste. The room housed too many knickknacks and ashtrays and dusty flower arrangements.

"You're investigating Miss Cordell's murder, aren't you?" Dennis asked as he walked past her.

"Yes."

He headed for the kitchen, and Hope followed. The kitchen windows were uncovered, letting in enough light to make the room cheerier than the dismal living room.

"The sheriff said the killer was some perv from out of town."

"Really? How does he know that?"

Dennis made himself busy, fetching glasses from the cupboard, filling them with ice, then taking a pitcher of tea from the fridge.

"No one around here could do such a terrible thing," he said in a lowered voice as he poured two tall glasses of iced tea. "Why, we all loved Miss Cordell."

"Did you see anything unusual that night?"

Dennis handed her a glass of tea, then leaned against the counter with his own glass in hand. "No, I don't believe I did. The sheriff asked, of course, but I didn't remember a thing that might help. Still don't, I'm afraid."

"A car that didn't belong, perhaps, or a stranger on the road?" Dennis shook his head, and Hope placed her untouched tea on the kitchen table. There was nothing of interest here, and still the hairs on the back of her neck were dancing. "Thank you for your time, Mr. Floyd. If you remember anything…"

"You know," Dennis said, straightening sharply and setting his own tea aside. "Maybe there *was* a car, now that I think about it. It passed by here, oh, about eleven o'clock or so. It was movin' real slow."

"What kind of car?"

"Fancy car, as I remember. One of them sporty cars. It was green."

Hope smiled. Dennis was lying. So she would stay a while longer? He had been leering at her, but why lie? Did he just crave the attention? Or was he curious to find out what she already knew?

Not only was this information brand-new, with no street-lamps on the narrow road, how had he been able to distinguish a color at eleven o'clock at night?

"Where were you standing," she asked, "when you saw the car on the road?"

Dennis had to take a moment to think, and to Hope's mind that proved he was lying.

"I had stepped outside to have a cigarette," he said.

Did he think she hadn't noticed the ashtrays in the living room? It wasn't necessary for him to step outside to smoke, and she knew it. But she played along. "You were in the front yard," she said.

"Yeah." He nodded. "I was in the front yard having a smoke."

"So if the green sports car had turned into Miss Cordell's driveway, you would've seen it."

He swallowed hard. "Maybe it did turn into her driveway. I can't rightly remember."

"A woman was brutally murdered, and the next morning

you didn't remember that maybe you saw a car pull into her driveway?" Hope snapped.

"It was a traumatic experience," Dennis explained. "To hear that one of my favorite teachers from high school, a neighbor, had been raped and sliced up by some stranger—"

Hope very subtly moved her hand to her pistol. Sheriff Webster hadn't even told Gideon that Marcia Cordell had been sexually assaulted until they were here. He hadn't put that detail in the official report or told the newspapers, and given how protective he was of the woman's memory, odds were he hadn't started any gossip about that night, either.

With a start, Dennis realized what he'd done. He cursed, then took his glass of tea and threw it at Hope's head. She simultaneously ducked and drew her weapon. The glass flew past her head and shattered against the doorjamb behind her. Bits of broken glass, cold tea and ice cubes exploded around her.

Instead of running to the back door to escape, which was what she'd expected him to do, Dennis charged her, knocking her gun hand aside just as she fired. He grabbed her, and they both slipped on the tea and broken glass.

Hope landed on the floor hard, a struggling Dennis on top of her. She tried to bring the gun up and around, but he grabbed her wrist and pushed it away. They struggled for control of the weapon, and he was winning that struggle. For a skinny man, Dennis was strong. There were muscles in those ropey arms, and he was desperate. Only a desperate and dangerous man would do what he'd done to Marcia Cordell.

She thought of the protection charm she wore beneath her blouse, and as she fought for control, she wondered if it would do her any good at all in this particular situation.

"Did she send you after me?" Dennis asked breathlessly as he tried to take the pistol.

Was it possible that Dennis knew what Gideon could do? Did he think Marcia Cordell's ghost had given them his name?

Dennis pinned Hope to the floor with his knee and ripped the gun from her hand. One word popped into her mind, unexpected and powerful.

*Emma.*

## THIRTEEN

Gideon was halfway to the white house, running as fast as he could, when he heard the gunshot. His heart jumped into his throat.

It was hard enough to talk to the ghosts of complete strangers, people he had never seen alive, never touched, never cared about. As difficult as it was to be visited by the shells of murder victims, he'd never had to confront the battered and weary spirit of a friend—or a lover. Last night and this morning Hope had been his in a way he'd thought impossible. She knew who he was, and still she stayed. She was probably carrying his child. Probably, hell. Dante's "gift" had worked too well; it was impossible to dismiss Emma as imagination.

He didn't want to be haunted by Hope; it was too soon to lose her.

Would Emma haunt him, too?

He jumped onto the porch and burst through the front door,

pistol in hand. Sounds of a struggle in the back of the house drew him there, and still at a run, he glanced into the kitchen to see a man on top of Hope. Her gun was in his hand, and he was doing his damnedest to turn it on her.

Gideon had his pistol ready, but no clear shot. Hope was holding her own, but that meant his target wasn't steady. He was rushing for Floyd in order to knock the gun away and pull him off Hope when she executed a well-planned and impressive move that simultaneously pushed the man off her and wrested the gun from his hand as her elbow slammed into his face. The entire maneuver took a few seconds, no more. With a whoosh of air and a grunt, Dennis Floyd ended up on his back, unarmed and bloody-nosed. A panting and red-faced Hope pinned him to the floor with her knee.

She lifted her head and looked at Gideon, her chest heaving with deep, quick breaths, her hair not as sleek as usual, her eyes strong and angry but also afraid. Outside, the sheriff's car pulled into the yard, and heavy footsteps sounded as the lawman made his way to the scene.

Gideon couldn't take his eyes off of Hope's face, and his heart hadn't yet slowed to a healthy pace and rhythm. He had come *this close* to losing her and Emma. He had come *this close* to being forced to bury them.

He was *this close* to asking Hope to marry him and never again leave his sight when the clumsy sheriff blundered into the house.

Hope rose, and Gideon gladly took charge of Dennis. He hauled the little man to his feet and slammed the skinny bastard against a wall.

"Ow. Be careful of my nose," the man said, squirming. "I think she broke it."

It took all the self-control Gideon possessed to read Dennis his rights. Since he was well out of his jurisdiction, he asked the sheriff to repeat the process. At this point Dennis hadn't been charged with anything, but Gideon was taking no chance that this little man—this little monster—might get off on a technicality.

"I know what you did," Gideon said in a lowered voice.

"I...I didn't do anything," Dennis blustered.

"I don't care about you, you little pissant." Gideon pressed Dennis more forcefully against the wall. "The sheriff will take good care of you after I'm gone. I want Tabby."

Dennis swallowed hard a couple of times before answering. "I don't know anyone named Tabby." He was a very bad liar.

"Fine. Don't talk. When she finds out I've been here—and she *will* find out—I imagine she'll pay you a visit. You've seen her work, so you know what to expect when she gets her hands on you." He leaned in until his mouth was close to Dennis's ear, and he whispered, "She likes that knife of hers, doesn't she? I've run across plenty of killers who prefer a blade to a gun, but I don't think I've ever met anyone who enjoys what they do as much as Tabby does. I wonder what sort of keepsake she'll take from you, little man? What body part will she take to remember you by?"

"I just met her that day," Dennis said, his voice high and quick. "I was at the gas station, filling up and getting something cold to drink, and this woman walks up to me and says she knows what I'm thinking. I hadn't been thinking anything," Dennis said. "She put them ideas into my head."

"Bad ideas," Gideon said as he backed slightly away.

Dennis nodded. "It's true, I always did think Miss Cordell was kinda uppity, thinking she was better than everyone else...."

"You wanted to put her in her place, didn't you?" Gideon pressed Dennis harder against the wall again. "You wanted to show her who's boss."

Dennis tried to nod, but with Gideon's arm against his throat, it wasn't easy. He wanted to kill this man with his bare hands, and he could. With Hope and the sheriff watching, he could shoot the bastard or break his neck or, even better, fry his ass until there was nothing left but dust. All he had to do was allow his anger to manifest itself in a powerful jolt of electricity. He was always so careful to hide what he could do, to contain himself whenever anyone was watching. That caution had kept him from stopping Tabby when he could have, and it had kept him from using his talents on more than one murderer when they were finally in his hands. Right now, with his heart still pumping hard and the unthinkable possibilities still too real in his mind, he didn't feel at all cautious. Gideon allowed a small shock to escape and shoot through Dennis's body.

"Ouch! What was...?"

He did it again, and Dennis began to shiver. As wound up as Gideon was, he could easily smoke this no-good waste of space and air. For Marcia Cordell. For Hope and Emma. But he didn't. Tempting as the idea was at this moment, he refused to let his anger turn him into the kind of man he'd spent his entire adult life hunting. The sheriff and the system would take good care of Dennis. And if they didn't, he could always come back.

"Tell me everything you remember about Tabby," he ordered.

The drive home had been quiet except for a few phone calls. Gideon got terrible reception on his cell, thanks to a combination of a weak signal here in the boonies and his unpredictable electrical charges, so he finally handed the phone to Hope, and she made the calls. Charlie was going to run a check on the type of car Dennis said Tabby had been driving. They still didn't have a last name for her, but maybe they could find her through the vehicle.

Hope had begun to accept that maybe, just maybe, she really was pregnant. In that moment when she'd thought she might die, when she'd expected to be shot with her own gun, the baby—or at least the possibility of the baby—had seemed very real. She'd realized she would do anything to protect Emma. What a kick in the pants that was. Hope Malory didn't have a maternal bone in her body! She liked being an aunt well enough, because she could visit her nephews and then leave when they got too rowdy or whiny. But to be a mother… She hadn't thought she was anywhere near ready, but maybe she was. Maybe.

It was after dark when they reached Gideon's house. There'd been no word from Charlie on Tabby's car, but since all they had was a make and a first name that might or might not be real, it was going to take a while. Gideon pulled into the garage and killed the engine as the garage door slowly closed behind them. He didn't immediately leave the Mustang but sat there with his gaze straight ahead and his hand resting on the steering wheel.

Hope stayed in place, too. "Do you want me to pack my stuff and leave? I know it's not a good idea for me to move back into Mom's apartment just yet, but I could—"

Gideon reached past the stick shift, grabbed the back of her head and pulled her in for a kiss. He didn't kiss her like a man who wanted her to leave. In fact, she was quite sure he had never kissed her quite this way, as if he wanted to consume her gently but entirely. When he pulled his mouth away, he did not drop his hand. "Marcia Cordell told me every vile thing that bastard did to her. At first she didn't want to talk about how she'd died, but once she got started, it seemed to do her good to get it out. She told me everything, every sick detail, and then I walk outside and the sheriff says, 'Oh, Detective Malory's down there over yonder, talking to Dennis Floyd.'"

Gideon called upon a deep and not entirely inaccurate drawl when impersonating the sheriff, and Hope laughed lightly. But she didn't laugh long.

"And I couldn't run fast enough," he said, his voice deep and soft.

"I'm not hurt." A few bruises, a lot of scary, but she wasn't really hurt.

"Not this time," he said. His thumb brushed her cheek. "But there's going to be a next time. There's going to be another Dennis, another struggle, another gunshot that makes my heart fly out of my chest. The protection charms will help, they give you an edge, and I can make sure you always have a fresh one to wear around your pretty neck. But they're not bulletproof shields, and they don't make bad guys like Dennis Floyd disappear. Dammit, Hope, I wish you'd be content to stay home and make cookies and lie on the deck under the sun and have babies and—"

"*Babies?*" she interrupted. "As in more than one?"

"If we're going to get married we might as well—"

"What happened to the world being too nasty to bring a child into?" she asked, only slightly panicked by the picture Gideon was painting.

"We can't go back and undo what's already done. Might as well give Emma brothers and sisters."

"Wait just a minute…"

"I didn't ask you to marry me yet, did I?" His thumb continued to caress her cheek.

"No, you didn't," she whispered.

"Marry me."

Hope licked her lips. "That's not exactly a question. It sounds more like an order."

A frustrated little moan escaped from deep in Gideon's throat. She knew this wasn't easy for him, but it wasn't easy for her, either. He was talking about marriage and children and forever. And she hadn't known him a week.

"Fine," he said. "We'll do this your way. *Will* you marry me?"

"Can I have a little time to think it over?" she asked, terrified and excited and stunned. "This is just too fast for me."

"No. You might as well learn now that I can be very impatient. I want an answer now."

It would be too easy to get caught up in this, in the way Gideon made her feel, inside and out. In the kissing and the touching and the promise of more to come. In the idea of him and Emma and babies—plural. "I never really planned to, you know, settle down and have kids and do the whole mommy thing."

"So make new plans."

If what he said about her *becoming* Raintree was true—and she had no reason to think it wasn't—she was definitely going to need a new plan.

He didn't move away but stayed close. Too close. That hand at the back of her neck was warm and strong and comforting, but she couldn't help but remember that just a few hours ago he'd been horrified at the idea of the life he was now presenting as a done deal. "If I actually said yes, you'd probably have a panic attack."

"If you say yes, I'm going to make love to you right here and now."

"In the car."

"Yep."

"With bucket seats."

He murmured in the affirmative.

Hope wrapped her arms around Gideon's neck and barely touched her lips to his. "This I gotta see."

"I think I broke something," Gideon said as he nuzzled Hope's neck. She laughed at him. He loved it when she laughed at him.

"Sex among the bucket seats was your idea, not mine."

"This is better." *This* was his bed, his woman and no clothes. It was softness and passion, boldness and demure exploration. It was a quiver and a gasp. It was the way Hope swayed and moaned when he touched her. It was the way she touched him, the way she wanted him.

He spread Hope's thighs and filled her gently. But not *too* gently.

"Nothing *seems* to be broken," she said dreamily, eyes closed and back arched.

Since he was convinced Hope was already pregnant, they hadn't bothered with a condom. Not in the car, not now. They were bare, heart and soul and body, and they were connected in a way he had never expected. Hope wanted to be his partner, and she was. In more ways than one. In all ways. In ways he had never dreamed to know.

Emma had said she was always his, in every lifetime. Maybe the same could be said of Hope. Was that why he'd felt such an undeniable and immediate pull toward her? Was that why she did not feel at all new or unknown to him?

They came together, and Hope pulled him deeper. The contractions of her body pumped him, squeezed him, and as everything slowed, she continued to sway her hips against his and hold him close.

"I love you," she said, her voice displaying exhaustion and confusion, as well as the affection she had not expected.

The words were on his lips, but he held back. He could love her this way; he could protect her as best he could and give her babies and make sure she never wanted for anything. Yes, she was undeniably his, but that didn't mean he was ready to lay it all on the line. He wasn't even sure he knew what love was anymore, but he did know that this was right. That was enough. For now.

While he was still searching for something semi-appropriate to say, he heard a trill of childish ethereal laughter. A girlish giggle, followed by a sigh and a very soft, "Told you so, Daddy." If Hope heard it, she didn't react.

He should be outraged, or at the very least surprised. But he wasn't.

"I think we've been tricked by our daughter," he said, raking a strand of black hair out of Hope's face.

Her eyes drifted open. "Tricked how?"

"You didn't get pregnant last night," he said, feeling oddly forgiving of Emma at the moment. Maybe because he was still inside Hope, satisfied and grateful and happy.

"I didn't?"

"No. You got pregnant now. Right now. Well, soon. Conception doesn't happen right away...."

Hope threaded her fingers through his hair and pulled him down for a deep, long kiss. Apparently she was feeling forgiving at the moment, too. "I know how it works, Raintree."

"Still wanna marry me?"

Without hesitation, she answered, "Yeah, I do."

*Still love me?* He didn't ask that question aloud. He should probably tell her that he loved her, too, or at least toss out a casual "ditto." But he didn't. The time would come when the words felt right.

Hope stroked his hair and wrapped one long leg around his, twining their limbs much as they had been earlier. She ran her foot up and down his leg.

He rose up to look down at her. "I don't want us to screw this up."

She closed her eyes and held him close. "Than let's not. Please."

There wasn't a lot to say, so they lay there, connected and touching and content. He was so rarely content.

"What you said earlier today," Hope said, her voice quick and a little shy. "I've been thinking about that."

"What did I say?" *So much...not enough...*

She raked her fingers along his neck. "Monsters."

"Oh." Not what he wanted to talk about at the moment.

"If there are monsters in the world—"

"There are, and you know it," he interrupted.

"*If* there are," she said again.

Gideon nuzzled her throat and kissed it. Now was not the time to argue.

"My mother's always talking about balance. Balance of nature, of male and female, even of good and evil. I used to dismiss that along with everything else, but she's beginning to make sense, darn it. And when you talk about monsters, I think...if the good gives up, then where will we be?"

"What's so good?"

"You," she answered without hesitation. "Us. Emma. Love. I think that's worth fighting for. I think maybe it's worth the occasional battle with a monster."

He fought monsters because it was his calling. His destiny. He didn't want his family to have to fight with him, but it was apparently the price he would have to pay in order to keep them.

Tabby sat in her apartment and carefully studied the package on the counter in the kitchenette. She disliked bombs. Not only were they unpredictable, they made it impossible for her to be close enough to drink in the fear of her victims. One minute they were alive, the next they were gone. No power, no souvenirs.

But she couldn't be picky at the moment. Time was running out.

She couldn't fail. Maybe she'd missed Echo, but Gideon was the one Cael thought of as most important to her mission. He was next in line for Dranir, a member of the royal family. He was a powerful Raintree, and his execution was necessary. Echo would be hers soon enough.

This bomb wouldn't kill Raintree, but it would draw him into the open. She would be waiting.

It was possible that Cael would still consider her mission a failure, since she hadn't killed Echo first, as planned. If her cousin were anyone else in the world, she would simply run from him when the time came. She could change her looks, change her name and take up where she'd left off. Training for this assignment had been more pleasurable than she'd imagined. It was a big country, filled with lonely people who would not be missed and sadistic little men who never dared to act on their own but were wonderfully violent when prodded.

She had become very good at prodding. If Cael didn't kill her for missing Echo, she would continue with her work after the battle was over. Maybe he would be so pleased by the act she was about to commit that he would even forgive her.

As long as she delivered Gideon Raintree's head to Cael— figuratively speaking, unfortunately—all would be well.

When she woke in Gideon's bed alone, Hope thought for a moment that it had all been a dream. Emma, Dennis, bucket seats and her foolishly uttered *I love you.* None of it was real.

But she realized soon enough that none of it had been a dream. The drapes were open, which meant Gideon was on the deck or the beach. Since it was morning, there wouldn't be a light show of any kind. Pity.

She went to the bathroom, brushed her teeth and pulled on one of Gideon's old T-shirts. It hung almost to her knees. He'd already made coffee—a quarter of the pot was gone— so she poured herself a cup and joined him on the deck. A few people were already on the beach, walking along the sand and getting their feet wet in the gentle waves.

Gideon was standing at the railing, looking out to the ocean as if he drew strength from it. Maybe he did. There was so much she didn't know about the man she had fallen in love with. Last night in bed they had laughed and made love, but this morning Gideon was serious again. His face looked as if it could be set in stone, it was so hard and unforgiving.

She knew the heart beneath that hard exterior. Hard? Sometimes. Unforgiving? Yes, when forgiveness wasn't appropriate. Nonexistent? Never.

"What's wrong?" she asked, leaning on the rail beside him.

He didn't dance around the issue. "I want you to quit work, and I don't think you will."

"You're right," she said. "At least, not any time soon. I need a little time to adjust to all this. Things have happened pretty fast."

"That's an understatement."

She leaned her head against his arm and rested there, her eyes on the ocean. "I'm a cop—just like you, Gideon. I'm not giving it up to have babies and knit and make cookies and wait at home while you do what you do. Cops have kids just like everyone else. We'll make it work."

"You'll distract me."

"So learn to deal with it."

"Why should I learn to deal with it when I have more than enough money for you to quit?"

"If money had anything to do with it, you wouldn't be doing the job, either. What we do is about more than a paycheck."

His lips thinned slightly, and then he said, "I know you think you're like every other cop, but you're not. You're mine, and I don't want to lose you."

"I'm tough," she said.

"You're fragile."

"I am not," she argued.

"Precious things are always fragile."

She didn't have an immediate response, since he'd stolen her breath away with that statement. *Precious* was not a word she'd thought he could ever speak, and yet he'd used it, however reluctantly.

He added, as if to turn her mind away from the subject, "In the beginning, I slept with you so you'd request a transfer."

"I know," she said without rancor.

"We've just upped the ante, Moonbeam. You can't be my partner anymore, and I don't trust you with anyone else."

Hope took a sip of her coffee. "Let's don't fight, not today."

His stony expression relaxed just a bit. "I thought you said I was cute when I got mad."

She laughed. "You are. I still don't want to fight with you today."

"Why not?"

The truth. Nothing but the truth. "Right now I feel too good, and I don't want to spoil it."

He wrapped an arm around her. "There are gifts that come with giving birth to a Raintree baby, gifts that are a part of being Raintree. You'll heal faster, live longer, be healthier. You and whatever children we make will have protection charms, I'll see to that. And still, if I could, I would lock you up in a place where you'd always be safe. A place where no one could ever hurt you or Emma."

"Exactly where is that place, Gideon?"

He didn't answer, because there *was* no answer; there was no such place.

"Besides," she said, "I have to help you put Frank Stiles away. Knowing is fine, but we need evidence."

He seemed perfectly willing to turn the conversation toward business. His business of stopping monsters. "There's not any. He burned the house down after he killed Johnny Ray Black. We've got no evidence."

"Then we need a confession or a witness."

"I haven't been able to obtain either."

She smiled at him. "You haven't given me a chance to try yet. I'm very good at getting confessions."

He almost smiled. "I just bet you are."

She stared out at the ocean, drinking in the beauty of it as if she, too, could literally absorb its power through her skin. How could this place already feel like home? Not the house, not the beach. Gideon. Gideon Raintree was home.

It was an oddly comforting and frightening thought, very much like the prospect of motherhood and all that would come with it.

# FOURTEEN

*Saturday—Noon*

They were getting nowhere fast with the info on the vehicle Tabby had been driving four months ago. Gideon had left Charlie following up that information, trying to wring something useful from it, and then he'd headed here.

The motel room where Lily Clark had been killed had been sealed off. No one but the crime scene investigators had been in this room since she'd been murdered. Her spirit stood in the corner of the room, solid and angry.

Hope insisted that she didn't have any unnatural powers of any sort, and yet she stood back and rubbed her arms as if warding off a chill on this warm day. She sensed the anger and sadness here; she still felt the violence.

"You said you were going to get her," Lily said, so furious that her image flickered.

"I'm working on it," Gideon said softly.

Hope stood behind him, just a few feet away, listening. He had to admit that it was nice not to have to hide what he could do. It was nice to be able to talk to Lily without tricking his partner into leaving the room or pretending to be talking to himself.

"Tabby was in this room for a long time," Hope said gently. "Knowing she killed Lily Clark is one thing, but we need physical evidence. There has to be something. She must've left some kind of clue behind."

"She's careful," Gideon said as he paced at the end of the bed.

"She left a hair at the Sherry Bishop scene. She left a *witness* at the Marcia Cordell site, and that's downright sloppy. There must be something here as well." Hope walked deeper into the room. "All the crime scene techs found were a few fibers that could have been here for days. Weeks, even. This isn't exactly the cleanest motel in town. Tabby must have touched a surface she forgot to wipe down or left something behind or..."

"She took a shower after I was dead," Lily said gently, her anger fading. "She had to, because my blood was all over her. On her face and in her hair and on her clothes...I think she liked it...."

"What did she do with her bloody clothes?" Gideon asked.

"I don't know."

Gideon nodded to Hope. "My cell phone is all but useless to me today." Tomorrow was the summer solstice, and his electrical surges were coming more frequently than usual. "Call Charlie and have him get the crime scene techs in here to check the shower drain. Today," he added forcefully.

Hope pulled out her own cell phone and made the call, and

Gideon walked closer to Lily Clark's much-too-solid image. "You can find those clothes for us," he said. "Your blood, a part of you, is there, and if you concentrate, you can find them. I can't guarantee that the clothes will lead us to the woman who killed you, but it's a possibility."

"I don't know how to do that," the ghost whispered.

"You can see so much more now, if you try. Think about that night. Remember what happened after. You watched Tabby walk out that door."

"Yes," Lily whispered. "I screamed at her, but she didn't hear me. I tried to stop her, but I couldn't do anything."

"Did she have the clothes with her? Were they wadded up or stuffed in a bag or——"

"She was wearing my favorite dress," Clark whined. She seemed to view that as just another indignity. "What nerve."

"What about the clothes she was wearing when she killed you? Did she have them with her when she left?"

Lily cocked her head and turned her mind back to that night, even though she undoubtedly wanted nothing more than to forget. Maybe when this was done and she moved on she *would* forget. No one should carry such painful memories with them for eternity. "No," she said thoughtfully. "All she was carrying was her purse. The knife was in it, freshly washed and wrapped in one of my nightgowns, and there wasn't room in that purse for her clothes, too. She loved that knife," the spirit added. "She touched it like it was alive."

Gideon turned to Hope, who had just ended her phone call. "The clothes are here somewhere."

"The room was searched," she said.

Gideon walked into the bathroom. "Lily, did Tabby ever

carry those bloody clothes out of this bathroom? After she had that shower, did she bring the clothes back out?"

The ghost shook her head, and Gideon glanced up at the tiles in the ceiling.

It would take a few days to get solid evidence from the clothes and the towel Gideon had found hidden above the ceiling tiles, but it was a step. They didn't expect Tabby would have her name and address stitched into the clothes she'd worn, but at least they had something concrete, and there was bound to be recoverable DNA. All they needed was Tabby in custody so a match could be made.

They'd hit a dead end with the vehicle, which was all they'd gotten out of Dennis Floyd—who was locked up in a Hale County jail, still terrified that Tabby would find him, somehow. No blue Taurus in North Carolina was registered to anyone named Tabby or Tabitha, and none of the Catherines were a match. They would now begin searching all females, but damn, it was a long list.

Hope didn't think they had that kind of time before Tabby struck again.

Gideon pulled the Mustang to the curb in front of The Silver Chalice, and Hope leaned over to kiss him briefly. "Be here by seven, if you can," she said, and then she smiled. "Sunny is a better cook than I am, so you're going to have to learn to grab a good meal when you get the chance."

"Are we going to tell them the news over peach cobbler?" Gideon asked.

"Not yet." Hope wasn't sure how to tell her mother and her sister that she was going to marry this man she'd met on Monday. And as for Emma, there was no logical explanation. Not that her mother had ever required logic for anything.

Gideon nodded, visibly relieved. Maybe he wasn't ready for explanations, either. "I'll be back by seven." He was going to the station to help Charlie with the vehicle search, unable to give up just yet. Unable to rest. She supposed that was something she would have to learn to live with.

"Sure you don't want me to tag along?"

"It's Saturday, and you need some time to visit with your sister before she heads for home."

"Yeah, partners or not, it's not like we're joined at the hip or anything." So why did she hate the very idea of watching him drive away? Tabby had been quiet for a couple of days. It was possible, even probable, that she'd left town after she'd stabbed Gideon. If she had a brain in her head, she'd run that very night. Gideon had seen her, and so had Hope. Hope wasn't so sure Tabby's brain worked in any logical manner; however, anything was possible.

Even if Tabby was still around, Raintree could take care of himself. So could she. They both had protection charms, weapons and better-than-average instincts. Her eyes flitted to the building across the street.

"They're still there," Gideon said.

"For how long?"

"Until we catch Tabby or have proof that she's out of the picture."

"I'd rather catch her."

"Me, too."

He kissed her again, and she exited the Mustang. The Silver Chalice was busy, as it often was on a Saturday afternoon. Tourists and regulars perused the items for sale, and there was a class of some kind going on in a back room. Meditation, vibrational healing…things Hope had always dismissed as nonsense.

She was able to look at the people in her mother's shop with new eyes today. Maybe they knew something she didn't. Maybe they saw or heard or touched things that had always been invisible to her, the way Gideon did.

An upside-down world wasn't as unsettling as she'd imagined it might be. In fact, she was finding it more comforting than she'd thought possible.

Tabby slung the big purse off her shoulder and set it down behind a display of copper bells, partially hidden behind a book rack. This corner of the store was crowded with merchandise and was also unoccupied at the moment.

Normally she wouldn't spend a second longer than was necessary in this place. The people here sought positive energy and were, for the most part, peaceful and calm. There was no power for Tabby in being in their company. She took no joy in this place, and in fact, it made her a little antsy. Still, she could hardly run into the shop, drop off the bomb and run out again, so she pretended to be interested in the merchandise.

She glanced up when the door opened with the jingling of a bell and smiled when she saw Raintree's woman walk in. Well, this would be a nice bonus.

Even though the cop had chased her down the riverfront, Tabby didn't fear being spotted here today. She was wearing a short dark wig and a baggy dress that disguised her shape. She stooped to diminish her height. There would be nothing familiar about her even if the cop noticed her. In any case, the woman wasn't even suspicious. At the moment the detective was happy to the point of distraction.

Tabby felt that happiness the same way she was able to feel fear and horror, but she took no pleasure or strength from it.

She did, however, take pleasure in knowing that happiness would be short-lived.

She walked away, leaving her oversized purse behind.

It was tough to help when getting too near the computer wasn't wise, but Gideon tried. He looked at the vehicular records Charlie had printed out, and he scanned driver's license photos until the faces all started to blur. Maybe Tabby's name wasn't Tabby after all. Maybe the car had been stolen from another state and the tags switched, and had been recovered or burned by now. Whatever the reason, he was getting nowhere.

He sent Charlie home with thanks and the promise of a get-together at the beach house, and sat down with the files of the unsolved murders that might or might not be Tabby's work. Some cases came together quickly. Murderers weren't usually the brightest colors in the box, and they left massive amounts of evidence behind. Tabby, if that was indeed her name, didn't. She wiped down doorknobs; she cleaned up after herself. Dennis Floyd and the bloody clothes from the hotel and a couple of hairs were all they had. And none of those would do any good unless—until—they caught her. When they *did* catch her, all that evidence would be enough to put her away forever.

His cell phone rang, and since there was no one else around to answer for him, he did it himself. The caller ID listed a Charlotte number, which meant it was likely Echo. She probably wanted to know if it was safe for her to come home. She was going to have a fit when he told her no.

There was so much static on the line that he could barely hear her. She was frantic, that much was clear, and he heard one word clearly. *Dream.* He told her to call him again on the landline in his office. Obviously she'd had a prophetic dream that alarmed her. He'd calmed her down a hundred times, after disturbing prophecies.

He couldn't help but feel sorry for her. At least he could do something with his abilities. There were many times when it seemed as if it would never be enough, but he did make a difference. Echo couldn't, not without advertising what she could do to the public. The Raintree *never* advertised their abilities. Besides, how did you stop a disaster when the warning always came so close to the event? Minutes, sometimes. No more than an hour in most cases. Maybe, if she worked at honing her skills, the warnings would come with more lead time, but Echo was determined *not* to hone her skills.

If Emma's talents took such a sad turn, would he want her to practice so that every dream was filled with horror?

The phone on his desk rang, and he answered, "Raintree."

"I took a nap," Echo said without preamble. "I just... fell asleep on the couch, you know, and I had this dream. I don't understand this one, Gideon. It's not like the others."

"Tell me about it," he said, remaining calm.

"There was an explosion. I couldn't see where it was, but there were people," she said in a low, shaking voice. "Lots of people. They didn't know it was coming. One minute they were happy and laughing, and then... There was so much blood, and there was fire, and people were screaming...."

The odds were that it was already too late to help anyone, but he had to try. "Calm yourself and think back. There had to be a hint in the dream as to where this explosion took place. Just take a deep breath and go there, Echo. You can do it." Whether she wanted to or not, she *could* do it.

He heard her take that deep breath. "It doesn't make sense," she said, only slightly calmer. "It wasn't just people, Gideon. I mean, there were lots of people, and they were cut and burned. But the sun exploded, a big bright rainbow faded into nothing and disappeared, and the moon broke apart into a million tiny pieces...."

"I know what that means!" Gideon slammed down the phone, lifted it again and dialed The Silver Chalice. Normally he would call on the run, but his damned cell phone wouldn't do for this call. Not today. He couldn't take the chance that he would get cut off, or that Hope wouldn't be able to understand. Rainbow answered, and his heart almost returned to a normal rhythm. He wasn't too late. "This is Gideon. I need to talk to Hope."

"Hope's around here somewhere," Rainbow Malory said casually. "I just saw her looking at some new..."

"This is an emergency," Gideon interrupted. "I want you to get everyone out of the shop."

"But—"

"Now."

He hated to do this, but he had no choice. "There's a bomb in your store." Then he slammed down the phone and ran out of the office. He had other phone calls to make, but he would have to make do with the cell, interference or not.

From her seat by the window at the café across the street from The Silver Chalice, Tabby muttered a curse word as people began to stream out of the shop. Even from here, she could tell they were afraid and confused. She saw *and* felt it. Someone had found the bomb.

That didn't mean it wouldn't go off, or that she wouldn't

still have Gideon Raintree right where she wanted him, but it would have been nice to have a few fireworks to enjoy before things got under way. Panic was always so lovely to enjoy, and the terror of hearing *bomb* as opposed to the terror that came from actually experiencing it were very different sensations.

She studied the people who streamed from the shop, waiting for the female cop to show. The stream of people turned into a trickle, and the woman wasn't among them. Tabby heard sirens in the near distance. Gideon Raintree was no doubt right behind the responding emergency vehicles. He might even get here before them.

Tabby took more than enough cash to pay for her coffee from the deep pocket of her oversized dress and placed it on the table. Then, with the tabletop shielding her hands from view, she removed the knife from the leather scabbard at her thigh and slipped it into her pocket, where it would be handy. Not that she was likely to need it. Much as she loved to work with her blade, she had a much more efficient weapon stashed in the back stairwell of the building across the street.

Ready for Raintree once again, determined to complete her task here and now, Tabby stood and headed outside.

The woman who owned The Silver Chalice stood on her tiptoes and searched the crowd, no doubt looking for her daughter. Tabby smiled. Maybe she would get that bonus after all.

Hope had intended just to change clothes, but her bed had looked so good that she'd fallen into it for a quick nap. After all, she hadn't exactly had lots of sleep this week. She fell asleep easily, snug in her familiar bed, warmed to her bones in a way she hadn't been warmed in a very long time.

She dreamed of Gideon and the beach, and of a dark-haired little girl who had a really great laugh. They were pleasant dreams, untouched by the stress of her job or any uncertainty about the future. There were no monsters here, not of the human variety, not of any variety.

*Precious.* Gideon thought she was precious. Whether he said so or not, that was love.

A door slammed, interrupting her pleasant dream of sand and laughter, and she heard Gideon calling her name. His voice was unnecessarily sharp, and it took her a moment to realize that what she heard wasn't a part of her dream.

Hope opened her eyes as he rushed into the room. "Is it seven already?" she asked as she sat up and stretched her arms over her head.

"I think there's a bomb downstairs," he said crisply. "Let's go." He didn't wait for her to respond but half lifted and half dragged her from the bed.

"I need my shoes," she protested, still muddled from sleep.

"No time," he responded, leading her toward the door that opened onto the stairway to the shop.

She was half-asleep, still fuzzy-brained and confused, and she wanted to collect her shoes and her purse and maybe an answer or two. "What do you mean, you *think* there's a bomb?" That didn't make any sense at all. There either was a bomb or there wasn't.

"Echo had a dream." Gideon's jaw clenched, and a muscle twitched there.

"I wondered how you found out about the bomb so fast."

They both spun to face the woman who stood by the kitchen door. She held a semiautomatic pistol in one hand, and with the other she removed a dark wig and shook out the long blond strands of her hair. Tabby was armed differently today, and she didn't look at all inclined to run.

Gideon had one hand on the doorknob to the stairwell, the other gripping Hope's arm. He smoothly placed his body in front of hers.

"Gideon Raintree," Tabby said with a crooked smile. "This isn't exactly what I'd planned, but I can't say I'm disappointed. When I saw the bomb squad arrive I was disappointed, because I'd hoped to have a little time with your girlfriend before you showed up. Still, I suppose this will do."

Gideon dropped Hope's arm and pushed her aside as he smoothly drew his weapon. Her own weapon was in the other room, resting on the bedside table. She'd never thought she might need it here, and in an instant she understood the violation Sherry Bishop and Marcia Cordell and all the other victims had felt when Tabby had entered their homes.

Tabby's aim never wavered. Her smile barely faded as she glanced at Gideon's weapon. "Shoot me and you'll never find out where the second bomb is, or when it's scheduled to go boom."

# FIFTEEN

"What do you want?" Gideon tried to ease Hope toward the door, doing his best to place himself between the two women.

"First thing, I want you and your girlfriend away from that door."

"She's my partner, not my girlfriend," Gideon said, knowing a close connection to him was a very bad idea at this particular moment.

"Liar," Tabby said. "I can feel the connection rolling off both of you like the tide outside your window."

Apparently the blonde had seen him and Hope together. She knew where he lived, too, which was more than a little disturbing. "You don't need her," Gideon said as he took a step toward Tabby.

"You don't know what I need, Raintree," Tabby snapped. "If your girl tries to leave before I say she can go, not only will I shoot her, I'll make sure you don't know where the second bomb is until it's too late."

He took another step toward the woman with the gun. "I'll ask you one more time. What do you want?"

"I want both of you dead by the end of the day, and I want Echo. Where the hell is she?"

"You want Echo?" Gideon said calmly. "Is that all? Give me the location of the second bomb and we'll talk."

Tabby held the gun as if she were comfortable with it, as if she'd been in this very position many times before. "You'd give up your cousin so easily?"

He needed her to believe that he would trade his cousin's life in order to save many others, so he remained calm as he answered, "Yes. For the bomb and Hope, you can have her."

"You're cold," Tabby said. "Sensible and predictably noble, but cold. Stop right there, and very carefully put that gun on the floor."

Lily Clark took shape beside Tabby and swiped vainly at the woman who had killed her. "There's not another bomb. Don't listen to her, Gideon! She's trying to trick you. She tricked me, and she tricked other people, too. I know that now. Don't let her trick you."

Did Lily know something he didn't, or was it a guess? Maybe there wasn't another bomb, but he couldn't be sure.

"None of this will make any difference if we don't hurry up," Gideon said as he dipped down to place his pistol on the floor. "How long before the bomb downstairs goes off?" He wanted to know how much time he had to get Hope out of here, if the bomb squad didn't get the device neutralized. They were in the building working on the bomb at this very moment; he heard male voices and the hum of motorized equipment downstairs.

"We have a few minutes," Tabby said, flipping her hair in a caricature of girlishness. "Long enough for us to finish our business. Much as I would love to spend a little time with you and your girl, I need to hurry. I have a party to go to tonight, and I want to make myself extra special pretty."

Gideon knew there was a rarely used back stairway that was kept locked, except when Rainbow took the trash to the Dumpster in the alleyway. Obviously Tabby had entered the building that way. She could have shot them both in the back when she'd come out of the kitchen. They wouldn't have known she was there until it was too late. Why hadn't she? Why was she so intent on dragging out the confrontation?

And where the hell was the team he'd hired to keep an eye on this place? Dammit, someone should know Tabby was here. They should have been watching all the entrances to the building, locked or not.

The fact remained: if Tabby simply wanted him dead, he would already be dead.

"Let's finish our business, then." He could take Tabby down with one motion; he just needed her to move the weapon aside so Hope wouldn't take a bullet if the automatic weapon the blonde was holding went off when she went down.

The psycho reached into the roomy pocket of her dress and drew out the knife she'd used to kill Sherry Bishop and Lily Clark and so many others. So that was the way of it. She wanted him dead, but not quickly and not from a distance. He could use that to get himself closer, to make sure Hope wasn't harmed in any way.

"Tell me why," Gideon said as he took a step forward. Since he was unarmed and she had two weapons, Tabby didn't feel threatened, and she didn't tell him to step back or stop moving forward.

"Who cares why?" Lily Clark said frantically, jumping up and down. "Just kill her! Don't let her get away with this."

Gideon turned his gaze to the ghost. Lily was strong. She had the power to affect this reality if she tried hard enough. If she wanted it badly enough. "I need you to move that weapon aside."

"I'm not moving anything," Tabby said, not yet realizing that Gideon wasn't speaking to her. Lily didn't realize it yet, either.

"I need you to shift the barrel of that gun away from me and Hope."

Clark's eyes went wide, and her figure shimmered. "Me?"

"Yes, you."

Tabby finally put two and two together. "You're not talking to me, are you? Well, good luck. I've killed a lot of people. I've even felt like maybe their ghosts were watching me. But none of them ever laid a hand on me. You know why? They can't. They're *dead*. All that's left when I'm done is a pitiful spit of energy that can't do anything but moan and cry to you. They're pathetic."

Lily's misty hand reached for Tabby's gun and wafted through it without creating so much as a wobble.

"I don't feel anyone trying to move my gun," Tabby said, brandishing the weapon almost wildly. "See? I'm in control here. No ghost is going to touch me *or* my weapon." She quit jiggling the pistol and took aim at Hope. "I want to feel you die in my hands, Raintree. I don't care about her. She can die right here and now."

Gideon threw himself between Hope and the gun just as Lily finally made contact. The ghost's misty hand grabbed the barrel and shoved upward. A surprised Tabby lost control of the weapon. It swung wildly up and then to the side, and a bullet slammed harmlessly and loudly into the ceiling before Lily managed to knock the weapon from Tabby's hand.

The pistol hit the floor and skittered away, coming to rest half beneath the sofa. Hope ran toward the weapon to retrieve it, while Gideon lifted his hand and directed a bolt of electricity at Tabby before she could reach for the pistol she'd lost. He could fry her heart from this distance, but he didn't want her dead. Not yet.

Was there a second bomb or not? He had to know. The bolt he let loose knocked Tabby backward and to the floor, where she landed hard. But she didn't lose her grip on the knife.

"What the hell was that?" she asked breathlessly as she looked up at Gideon. "They didn't tell me you could do that."

"Who's *they,* Tabby?" If she wasn't working alone, then this wasn't over by a long shot.

"Wouldn't you like to know?"

Gideon dragged the blonde to her feet and wrested the knife out of her hand, tossing it away. She tried to fight but was weakened by the electricity he'd called upon to stop her. Hope held on to Tabby's weapon and fetched her own pistol. She stood more beside than behind him, her own pistol pointed unwaveringly at Tabby.

"Where's the other bomb?" he asked.

Tabby just smiled, and he gave her a small jolt to remind her of what he could do. "I can stop your heart with one jolt," he said quietly. "I can pop you with more electricity than your brain can handle. Don't think I won't."

"Go ahead. I have worse waiting for me if I walk out of here and leave you alive. Besides, we're going up in a big boom any minute now. Tick-tock. Tick-tock." She grinned at him. "Afraid?" She closed her eyes and took a long, deep breath, inhaling deeply and holding it.

"Hope, check on the bomb squad," Gideon said without

turning to look at her. "If they don't have the device neutralized, get out of the building."

She edged to the door. "I'll get a status report, but I'm not walking out of here without you."

"Don't be stupid."

Hope left the room without responding, leaving Gideon alone with Tabby. "How touching," she whispered, opening her eyes once again. "What are you planning to do, Raintree? Get married and make little freaks? Settle down and pretend you're just any old cop? Good luck. Even if...well, let's just say it's never gonna happen, and we both know it."

He ignored her attempt to distract him. "Where's the other bomb?"

"Wouldn't you like to know?"

"It's in your best interest to cooperate, Tabby. Is that your real name?" he asked almost casually. "Tabby?"

The woman didn't answer. She worked her mouth oddly, and before Gideon realized what she was up to, she bit into something she'd had hidden in her mouth. Instantly her body bucked and her eyes rolled back in her head. A few seconds later, she went slack.

Gideon muttered every foul word he knew as he dragged Tabby from the room. Hope met him on the stairs. "The bomb was a simple mechanism, and it's already been disabled. What happened?"

"Tabby had some kind of poison hidden in her mouth, and when she realized she wasn't going to get away, she bit into it. Dammit!" Considering the almost paralyzing dust she'd thrown into his face, he should have seen this coming. He needed to know about the other bomb. He also wanted to know what she'd meant when she talked about "them." Were there others out there who knew what he could do? For all he knew, there was someone around the corner waiting to take her place.

"Is she dead?"

"Not yet." If she was dead, her spirit would be here, hounding him still.

"Did she tell you where the second bomb was?"

"No. I don't know when or where, or even if the bomb is real."

An ambulance was already on the scene, and the paramedics rushed forward as the three of them hurried from the building. Gideon didn't know what Tabby had taken, so he couldn't be much help. He did warn the EMTs to keep her restrained, in case she did come to. Anyone in her path was likely to end up dead if she woke up.

Gideon spotted one of the private security guards he'd hired to watch The Silver Chalice and the apartment above. He made his way roughly through the crowd of cops and onlookers, and grabbed the man by the collar, slamming him against the wall. "Where the hell were you?"

The kid didn't put up a fight. "While everyone was rushing out of the store, a woman's purse got snatched. She screamed, and people were running and talking about a bomb. It was a mess, and I was distracted. I'm sorry."

"Where's the other guard?" Gideon asked. "I specifically asked for *two* people to be on duty at all times."

The kid—and he really was just a kid—paled. "Joe went to the hospital in the first ambulance. He was checking the perimeter of the building, and a woman out back stabbed him in the gut. He was hurting, but he was able to tell the officers what happened before the ambulance left. The paramedics said he'll be all right."

Gideon released the boy and shook off his anger, running agitated fingers through his hair and turning away. Hope was talking to her mother, maybe making explanations or offering daughterly, calming words. When their eyes met, she placed a hand on her mother's arm, patted it gently and then walked away, heading for Gideon.

He wrapped his arms around her and held on as they met, not caring who was watching or what they thought.

"I love you," he whispered.

"Love you, too," she said comfortably, as if she'd already accepted everything. Their love, Emma, who and what he was, who and what she would become. Amazing, for a woman who just a few days ago had admitted without reservation that she didn't believe in anything she couldn't see or touch.

"Let's go home," she said as she smoothed a wayward strand of hair from his cheek. "We can leave word for the hospital to call us if Tabby wakes up. Or if she doesn't. I just want to go home."

There was such longing in her voice as she said the word. Home. His house. Their house. "Yeah. I just have one thing to do first."

He released Hope and turned to face what was left of Lily Clark's ghost. She was fading at last. "Thanks."

The spirit smiled at him, almost shyly. "I did help, didn't I?"

"I couldn't have done it without you."

The justice she'd demanded had been done, but Lily wasn't quite ready to go. Her smile faded. "If she dies, will she be there? Where I'm going? Will I have to face her all over again?"

Gideon didn't have to ask who *she* was. "No. Tabby's going to another place." He didn't know where or how, and didn't want to, but he knew for sure that Lily wouldn't be seeing her killer again.

Lily glanced up as she began to fade away. "They're so proud of you," she said, her voice growing distant.

"Who?"

"Your mom and dad. They're so..." Lily Clark didn't fade. She simply disappeared with a small and distinct pop that only Gideon heard.

How odd, that this house was home. Not her mother's apartment, not the house she'd grown up in, not her Raleigh apartment where she'd lived for years. Here.

The hospital had called not five minutes after they'd walked into the house. Tabby was dead. They knew from the remains of the capsule in her mouth and the way she'd died that it was a poison of some kind that had killed her, but they hadn't yet identified the toxin. It could be days before they knew exactly what it was.

Hope planned to call the lab on Monday morning and harass them about the dust Tabby had thrown into Gideon's face. Maybe the two drugs were related somehow.

Gideon was distracted. He'd undressed her slowly and made love to her without saying a word. Tonight he didn't cheat. He didn't arouse her with caresses colored with lightning or make her come with a touch of his hand. He just pushed inside her body and stroked until she climaxed hard, and then he found his own release in her. He did still glow in the dark a little, though, her own personal flashlight.

Eventually the warm glow faded, and he pulled her body against his and held on tight. If not for his breathing and the way one hand occasionally caressed her, she would have thought he had fallen asleep. But he hadn't. He was nowhere near sleep. She felt it; she knew it because she knew *him*.

"You can tell me anything, Gideon," she whispered. "What are you thinking about right now?"

At first she thought he was going to ignore her, and then he answered, "I never saw my parents."

"What do you...?"

"After they died. I never saw their ghosts. Everywhere I turned, there were spirits, but not theirs. Never theirs. I was so mad at them for not coming back. For a while I was mad at everybody."

She stroked his face with her fingertips.

"I started to get into trouble not long after they were murdered." He lifted his hands, studying them as if they weren't his at all but those of a stranger, hands he didn't know or understand. "Think about it. No security system or lock is going to stop me from getting to what I want. No jail is going to hold me. With enough lightning I can pop any lock. I would make a fine thief, and for a while I was so furious with the world that I almost went there."

He might not know that such a thing never would have happened, but she did. Gideon was one of the good guys. Heart and soul. "What stopped you?"

"My brother. My sister. Knowing that maybe, just maybe, even though I couldn't see my parents, they could still see me."

"You made that choice a long time ago, Gideon. Why are you thinking about it now?"

"Something Lily Clark said before she moved on, about my parents being proud of me, as if...as if she'd spoken to them. Maybe she did. And you. You have me thinking about things I haven't faced yet. Emma...I don't even know where to start there."

Hope led his hand to her bare stomach, where it rested comfortably. "You're going to teach our daughter everything your parents taught you. Whatever she can do, whatever her gifts, you will always know the right way to teach her." She grinned. "And I'm going to teach her how to shoot a gun, along with a vast repertoire of self-defense maneuvers."

Gideon kissed her. In the deep silence, music drifted into the room. Honey and the brunette bimbo next door were having a party tonight, and they had their stereo cranked up high. They could hear bursts of laughter, too, as the party got more earnestly under way.

Gideon pulled his mouth from hers and sat up quickly. "Party. Tabby said she was going to a party tonight. You don't think…"

"It's Saturday night, Gideon. There are lots of parties going on." So far they hadn't had word of another explosion. Maybe there wasn't another bomb and Tabby *had* been bluffing.

Gideon slid from the bed and reached for his clothes. "I'm going to walk over there and look around, just in case. She mentioned the surf outside my window, so I have to believe she knew all along where I live. If Tabby did plant a bomb there earlier in the day, it would probably be under the house."

"I'll come with you."

"No." He leaned over and kissed her. "You stay here. I'll be right back." He exited by way of the bedroom door, stepping onto the deck and into the moonlight.

Hope fell back against the pillows and closed her eyes, but there was no way she could possibly sleep. After a few minutes she left the bed and pulled on one of Gideon's T-shirts, then stepped out onto the deck herself. Leaning against the rail, she looked across the way to the crowded deck next door, which was well lit by the fading sun and the colorful lanterns the women had strung across the deck. It was very festive, and very foreign. Hope had never been a party girl. She'd always been too serious, too concerned about what was right and proper.

Young and beautiful members of both sexes, most of them in bathing suits even though they didn't look to be going anywhere near the water, drank beer and danced and laughed on the crowded deck. Hope couldn't see Gideon from here, but then, she could only see a small portion of the house from this vantage point. She couldn't see the front of the house, or the entrance to the area under it where Gideon would check for a bomb—just in case Tabby hadn't been bluffing.

Honey had one arm wrapped around a too-thin young man with longish blond hair and a killer tan. The brunette bimbo was similarly engaged. She and her young man were dancing. They were tanned and dressed in bright colors, and they'd probably spent hours on their seemingly casual hairstyles.

The life those women led was entirely alien to Hope. Had she ever been so young? Had she ever smiled that way, without a thought beyond which CD to play next? No. Never. Most of the people on the deck were the same way. They smiled as if they didn't have a care in the world. They danced and touched and kissed and laughed.

She'd never had that before, but in an unexpected way she had it now. Maybe her party was just a party of two—or perhaps three—but Gideon Raintree made her laugh. There were moments when he made her feel absolutely giddy. He made her truly happy, for the first time in her adult life.

Hope studied the partygoers as she waited for Gideon to return. One blond woman, wearing a short, colorful dress well-suited for the beach, stood alone by the rail, much as Hope did, and turned toward Gideon's house as if she knew she was being watched. Seeing Hope, the woman lifted her hand and waved, fluttering her fingers. Hope's heart stuttered, and her knees went weak.

*Tabby.*

# SIXTEEN

If a bomb had been planted at Honey's house, it was likely either under the house—perhaps under the deck—or in the garage. Gideon walked around the house, checked out the garage, then opened the hatch that led under the house through a half door. It didn't take fifteen minutes to discern that there was nothing out of the ordinary here. Maybe Lily Clark had been right and Tabby's talk of a second bomb had been nothing but a bluff.

Gideon didn't head straight for home but walked toward the ocean. Sunset and the brief period of half light that followed was a beautiful time of day, peaceful and powerful. If not for the thirty or so people crowded onto Honey's deck, he would reenergize himself here and now. He would reach for the power that was uniquely his and drink it in. Even though many of the partygoers were already drunk, it was a chance he couldn't take. Someone might see, and that was risky.

Maybe one day he would buy himself an island and build a

house for his family, a house so isolated that he could recharge whenever he felt like it, and no monsters would dare to come near him or Hope or Emma. In many ways it was a comforting idea, but could he do that? Could he literally hide away?

No, he couldn't, and neither could Hope. Somehow they were going to have to make it work in the real world, with bad guys and heartbreak and uncertainty.

He turned toward home, and Honey—dressed in a bikini top and a scarf worn like a skirt—waved at him. "Come on over!" she called.

Gideon shook his head. "I can't. Sorry."

She gave him an exaggerated pout, and someone else on the crowded deck began to wave at him. Another blonde. Tabby's ghost.

Crap, she looked solid and real. Did that mean she would stick around for a while? Did that mean she was going to be everywhere he turned? He'd been sending sad spirits on for years, but he'd never gotten himself stuck with a malevolent ghost.

The ghost stopped waving, turned and walked toward the stairs. She actually wove around the party guests, as if she was afraid she would bump into them. Did Tabby think she was still alive? Gideon stopped, his feet digging into the sand, and waited for her. Somehow he was going to have to get rid of her once and for all, but he had no idea how to send on a dark spirit who didn't want to leave.

Tabby walked toward him, smiling that sick, confident smile of hers. If Lily Clark had been able to affect this world, what could a spirit as dark as Tabby's do? He knew how to handle sad spirits and monstrous bad guys, but this was a new situation, one he didn't know how to handle.

As she moved closer, Gideon got a sick feeling in his stomach. Tabby looked too real, too solid. Her feet left impressions in the sand.

This was no ghost.

She pulled a small revolver from her pocket. The knife she preferred was locked away in evidence, but she seemed familiar enough with the gun. "Surprised to see me?"

"Yeah. I heard you were dead."

"Not really. I just appeared to be for a while. Imagine the coroner's surprise when he goes to the morgue to perform an autopsy and finds the body missing."

"Where's the bomb?"

Tabby nodded toward the deck. "Right up there with the dancers. Waiting."

He didn't think she was bluffing. She took too much pleasure from the pain of others not to take advantage of the opportunity. "Waiting for how long?"

"Not long."

Gideon had left his weapon sitting on the dresser, so he was basically a sitting duck. He didn't wear his weapon when he walked on the beach, or when he sat on the deck at the end of the day and listened to the waves, or when he met the night storms and traded energy. He didn't want to get to the point where he was always on guard, always waiting for someone like Tabby to come along.

"You could shock me again, I guess," she said. "But how will you explain that to the people who are watching? And they *are* watching, Raintree. They're curious and bored, and that one blonde, she really wants you to jump her bones. She'll settle for any other man who comes along, for the time being, but she really wants *you*. She's sad that your new partner has been hanging around so much. Sad and jealous, spiteful and envious."

"What do you want?"

Tabby cocked her head. "I want the same thing your neighbor wants, but in a very different way." She lifted her weapon and fired. Gideon saw the move coming and jumped to the side. A bullet creased his shoulder before he landed hard and rolled through the sand. His shoulder stung, but he was able to rise to his feet and run. He didn't run away from Tabby but toward her. She aimed the gun again.

He had to get close enough to shock and incapacitate her without creating a light show that would have everyone on the beach and on Honey's deck pointing at him. It was risky not to immediately take his shot, but he had to believe that his protection charm would give him an edge, as it always did. A few feet closer and he would be able to stop her without revealing his ability to those who were watching. Another step or two…

"Gideon!"

He and Tabby both turned sharply toward the sound. Hope was bounding from the boardwalk onto the sand, her long legs bare beneath one of his T-shirts. The gun was steady in her hand. "Drop it!" she ordered.

Tabby spun, took aim and fired in anger. Not at Gideon this time, but at Hope. Hope didn't fall; she fired back. Twice. It was Tabby who dropped onto the sand, one shot to the forehead, the other to the dead center of her chest. Gideon rushed forward and moved the revolver Tabby had dropped when she fell, tossing it away from the body as Hope reached them.

"Come back from that, bitch," Hope said softly. Then she looked at Gideon and said, with less venom, "You're bleeding."

Gideon turned and ran. "The bomb's on Honey's deck."

Hope was right behind him. "I'll call the bomb squad."

"No time."

Gideon ran up the deck stairs that led to the party. The music was still playing loudly, but there was no more laughter or dancing. The guests were somber; none of them had ever seen anyone shot before.

"I called the cops," one young guy said.

"Good," Gideon replied. He found Honey in the crowd. "That woman, did she leave anything up here?"

"Like what? She said she was a friend of yours, and that you'd come over later. What was she—"

"Did she leave anything here?" Gideon repeated more tersely.

Honey glanced around the deck. "She was carrying a big purse. I guess she might've left..." She raised her hand and pointed. "That's it, over there by the beer."

Gideon rushed past the subdued partygoers, grabbed the purse and ran from the deck.

"Hey!" Honey shouted. "You're bleeding!"

Gideon ran toward the water, the heavy purse dangling from one hand. Hope was still standing near Tabby's body, watching, her eyes alternately on him and on the bag. "Get back to the house!" he shouted.

"No way, Raintree."

He looked her dead in the eye as he passed her at a run. "For Emma, not for me."

Hope reluctantly did as he asked, hurrying away from the shore as he ran into the water. While the surf crashed around his calves he gave the purse a mighty heave. It flew through the air, tumbling and sailing. He prayed the bomb was no more powerful or complicated than the one Tabby had planted at The Silver Chalice. If that was the case, then he was far enough away. Hope and the people at Honey's were more than far enough away. If not...

He couldn't allow a live bomb to float out into the ocean or perhaps wash up somewhere else into innocent hands. With his body shielding what he had to do as much as possible, Gideon let loose a stream of electricity as the bomb landed in the water. It exploded when the spark hit the bag. The force of the blast knocked Gideon back, out of the water and into the wet sand. In an instant it was over, and all that was left were bits and pieces of debris floating on the waves.

Less than a minute later, Hope was there. She didn't help him to his feet but instead dropped to sit beside him in the sand.

"You're a good shot," he said as he placed his arm around her.

"Don't sound surprised."

"That's relief, not surprise."

Hope rested her head on his uninjured shoulder. In the distance, sirens approached. "For a second tonight, just a second, I thought I was seeing ghosts." She scooted closer. "It's not a whole helluva lotta fun."

"Nope."

"I thought my heart was going to come through my chest."

He threaded his fingers through her hair. "You didn't panic."

"No. I only panic when I find unexpected fertility charms hanging around my neck," she teased. "I called it in, grabbed my gun and walked outside just in time to see her following you onto the beach."

Night was falling quickly, but the lanterns on Honey's deck lit the beach well enough.

"You're going to make a good partner."

"I've been trying to tell you that all along."

"The chief will try to split us up once we're married. Annoying rules and all."

"Rules are made to be broken. We'll find a way." Hope stood and offered him her hand, as paramedics and two uniforms ran onto the beach. "Come on, Raintree. Let's go inside and have a look at that shoulder before you blow up the paramedics' equipment."

The police and the paramedics and Tabby's positively dead body had been taken away, and explanations had been made to the neighbors—which wasn't easy, since a couple of young men swore they'd seen lightning jump out of Gideon's fingers before the bomb exploded. Fortunately they'd been drinking heavily, and no one gave their account much credence.

Hope was still shaking a little. She'd never fired her weapon in any situation that wasn't controlled. Target practice, training and testing, that was it. But when she'd seen Tabby shoot at Gideon, she hadn't had any choice. She hadn't been thinking about Emma or marriage or special gifts—or nights on the deck, making love in the moonlight.

That psycho was shooting at her partner.

All the officials were gone, and the party at Honey's was over. Hope locked the doors and led Gideon into the bathroom, undressing him and herself as they went. She let her fingers trail over the bandage at his shoulder. It was just a scratch. Would he heal it anyway, with a tickle of lightning or a surge of electricity? Or would he leave it alone and let it heal on its own?

"A couple of those kids saw me, didn't they?" he asked, sounding unconcerned.

"Yes. I convinced them they were too drunk to see anything clearly, and I think they believed it by the time I was done."

"You're very convincing."

"Thank you."

They were mostly undressed when she leaned against Gideon's bare chest and tipped her face up to look him in the eye. "I have an appointment to interview Frank Stiles Monday afternoon."

"You're going to make him confess, is that it?"

Hope nodded. "Yeah. You did your part, now I'll do mine."

She was good at getting criminals to confess. She and Gideon hadn't been working together long enough for him to know that about her, but he would learn. Soon enough.

"What makes you so good at getting confessions?" Gideon teased as he brushed back a strand of hair that had fallen across her cheek. "You think just because you're prettier than all the other detectives, the bad guys are going to give it up for you?"

"No. I'm actually an excellent poker player, Raintree. I'm very good at bluffing my way to a confession. You give me enough information so I can bluff well, and I'll charm a confession right out of Stiles."

"Poor guy doesn't have a chance."

"Yeah, well, life's not fair."

Gideon held her, and she melted into him. It felt good to be embraced with love and passion and unexpected tenderness. She'd never known it would be so good to have a place to rest at the end of the day, a special person to rest with.

"I was so worried about you," she confessed. "When I saw Tabby point that gun at you and fire, and you fell…"

"I'm fine," Gideon said.

"I know, but…" The words caught in her throat. With the good came the bad. With the happiness, the worry.

Gideon leaned Hope back a little and kissed her throat. "Since you're feeling vulnerable, partner, maybe we should re-negotiate that sex on the desk ban...."

*Sunday—11:36 a.m.*

"At least she didn't get up and walk away from us this time," the coroner said as he walked around Tabby's covered body.

Gideon had tried to convince Hope to stay at home this morning, but she wouldn't have it. She'd insisted on coming with him. One of these days he was going to have to quit pro-tecting her so diligently. She didn't like it much.

But he wasn't going to quit today.

"It was the shot to the head that killed her," the coroner said without emotion. "The bullet that hit her torso missed the heart and lodged in the spine. That alone wouldn't have killed her. Would've stopped her cold, though."

Hope, who had never killed anyone before last night, paled a little. She'd been the one to pull the trigger and stop Tabby; she'd done what had to be done. Neither of them felt one iota of guilt. Tabby was one of the most evil people he'd ever met, and she didn't deserve a place on this earth.

"What was it you wanted me to see?" Gideon asked. He hated this place. He could live down here for years and never find a way to send all the ghosts to a peaceful place.

With help from an assistant, the coroner uncovered the body on the slab and gently rolled it over. "I've never seen anything quite like this. I thought it was a tattoo at first, but it's actually a birthmark. I know some birthmarks are shaped in such a way as to resemble something else, but this crescent moon on the corpse's shoulder blade is absolutely perfect. And it's such an unusual color. I thought it might be helpful in identifying her."

Gideon stared at the blue birthmark of a crescent moon. It was, as the coroner had already observed, perfect in shape and color.

"Oh, shit," he said softly.

"What is it?" Hope asked.

Gideon ran for the door as he reached for his cell phone, and Hope followed him. "Tabby said *they*," he muttered. "And she was afraid for her own life if she missed killing me. Of course she was afraid. She wanted Echo, too. She said so at your mother's apartment."

"Raintree." Hope followed him up the stairs at a run. "What are you talking about?"

He couldn't get a signal, so he cursed at the phone as they burst from the building and stepped into the sunshine. "Her name is Tabby Ansara. We thought they were down. Defeated and powerless and...dammit. This changes everything."

While he was moving away from the corner of the building in an attempt to get a decent signal, the phone rang. Instead of giving Hope the phone, as he often had in days past, he answered himself and got an earful of static.

It was Dante. Gideon couldn't make out every word, but he very clearly heard the two he most needed to hear.

Ansara.

Home.

Gideon turned to Hope. He loved her, and even though she didn't like it much when he tried to protect her, he wouldn't put her in the middle of what was coming. Wouldn't and couldn't. "I have to go home. The Raintree homeplace."

Concern was clear on her face, startling in her brilliant blue eyes. Had he ever told her that he loved her eyes? Not yet. When he got back, he would make sure to tell her. He had so much to tell her.

"I'm going with you," she insisted.

"No."

Her eyes widened. "What do you mean, *no?*"

"There's trouble at the homeplace, or soon will be." Trouble of an unimaginable sort. Trouble she wouldn't understand even if he tried to explain it. "I want you and Emma safe."

"I have a gun," she said. "I know how to use it."

How could he explain to her that a gun blazing in each hand wouldn't be enough in the battle to come? "Stay here," he insisted. "Please."

Hope sighed and accepted his order, but she didn't accept it easily. Would she ever? "Call me when you get there."

"I will." *If I can.*

"I still don't see why I can't go with you," she grumbled. "I already know about your family, so it's not like there's anything left to hide." He saw the unspoken *Is there?* in her eyes.

He took Hope's face in his hands. "I love you. I love you so much that it terrifies me. I didn't expect to ever care about anyone the way I care about you, and it happened so fast my head is still spinning. It's important, and I want us to have a real chance. One day I will take you to the homeplace, I promise," he said. "But not today."

"I don't understand," she said softly.

"I know, and I'm sorry."

He kissed her, long, but not nearly as long as he wanted to, and then he jumped into the Mustang. "Call Charlie and have him take you home. I'll call as soon as I can."

Gideon left a confused Hope standing in the parking lot. She wasn't a woman accustomed to waiting, he knew, but she would wait for him. He didn't have a doubt in his mind.

Today was the summer solstice; that wasn't a coincidence. Tabby's attempts to kill him and Echo in the past several days, also not a coincidence. The Ansara wanted the homeplace, they wanted the sanctuary and the power it harnessed, and they always had.

They weren't going to get it.

One day his wife and his daughter would discover the beauty and power of the land the Raintrees had always called sanctuary. It was Gideon's duty to protect the Raintree sanctuary, just as it was his duty to protect Hope and Emma and any other little Raintrees that came along in years to come. It was his duty and his honor to protect what was *his,* and if that privilege came with ghosts and electrical surges and the occasion battle, then so be it.

Gideon drove as fast as the Mustang would allow once he reached the highway. The wind whipped his hair, and the homeplace grew closer with every second that passed, and when the unexpected storm approached from the south and gathered in the darkening skies over the car, there was no one for miles around to see.

* * * * *

# BEVERLY BARTON

# SANCTUARY

To my dear friend Leslie Wainger, an extraordinary, insightful editor who appreciates unique ideas, encourages individual creativity and inspires her writers to learn, grow and spread their wings.

To my Raintree cocreators, Linda Winstead Jones and Linda Howard, two of the most talented writers I know and friends not only of the heart but also of the soul.

# PROLOGUE

*Sunday, 9:00 a.m.*

On this extraordinary June day, only a week away from the summer solstice, Cael Ansara watched and waited as the conclave gathered in their private meeting chambers here at Beauport. He and he alone knew just how momentous this day would be for the Ansara and the future of their people. Two hundred years ago, his clan had lost *The Battle* with their sworn enemy and been all but annihilated. The few who survived had found solace here on the island of Terrebonne and, generation by generation, had grown in strength and numbers. Like the proverbial Phoenix, the Ansara had risen from the ashes, stronger and more powerful than ever.

One by one, the members of the high council came together this Sunday morning as they did once a month, speaking quietly among themselves, comparing notes on the family's various widespread enterprises as they waited for the Dranir to arrive. Judah Ansara, the all-powerful ruler who was respected and feared in equal measure, had inherited his title from his father. From *their* father.

What would the noble council say, what would they think, how would they react, when they learned that the Dranir of the Ansara was dead? As soon as word came in that Judah had been killed, Cael knew he would have to act fast in order to take control and secure what was rightfully his. Naturally, he would pretend to be as shocked as everyone else, and would make a great show of mourning his younger half brother's brutal murder.

*I will even swear vengeance on Judah's behalf, promising to hunt down and kill the person responsible for his death.*

Cael smiled, the corners of his mouth curving ever so slightly. Even if several members of the clan suspected him of being behind Judah's murder, no one would ever be able to prove that he had sent a skilled warrior to eliminate the only obstacle in his path to ultimate power. Nor would they be able to prove that he had been the one to bestow a spell of ultimate strength and cunning on that warrior so that he would be equal, if not superior, to his opponent. All would soon learn that Judah the Invincible had been defeated.

At long last, after a lifetime of being the bastard son, of waiting and plotting and planning, he would soon take his place as the Dranir. Was he not the elder son of Dranir Hadar? Was he not as powerful as his younger brother, Judah, perhaps even more so? Was he not better suited to lead the great Ansara clan? Was it not his destiny to destroy their enemy, to wipe every single Raintree from the face of the earth?

Judah claimed that the time was not right for an attack, for all-out war, that the Ansara clan was not ready. At the last council meeting, Cael had confronted his brother.

"We are a mighty people, our powers strong. Why do we wait? Are you afraid to face the Raintree, my brother?" Cael had asked. "If so, step aside and I will lead our people to victory."

At the very moment he had confronted his brother, Cael had already made his plans and had been preparing assignments for the Ansara who looked to him for guidance. He had endowed each young warrior with protective spells. First, the most fearsome of his followers—Stein—would kill Judah. Then Greynell would strike a deadly blow to the very heart of the Raintree, in their home place, the land that had been the family's sanctuary for generations. After that, Tabby would eliminate the Raintree seer, Echo, to prevent her from "seeing" what devastating tragedies awaited her clan.

Unfortunately, only one member of the council had agreed with Cael. One of twelve. Alexandria, the most beautiful and powerful female member of the royal family and third in line for the throne, was his first cousin. She had once been Judah's faithful supporter, but when Cael promised her a place at his side if he were to become the Dranir, she had secretly switched allegiances. What did it matter that he had no intention of sharing his power with anyone, not even Alexandria? Once he ruled the Ansara, no one would dare defy him.

"It is unlike Judah to be late," Alexandria said to the others now.

"I am sure there is a good reason." Claude Ansara, another cousin, had been Judah's closest confidant since they were boys. Claude was second in line to the throne, right after Cael himself, his now deceased father a younger brother to Cael and Judah's father.

Rumblings rose from the others, some concerned by Judah's tardiness, others speculating that undoubtedly there had been an emergency of some sort of which they were not aware. The Dranir had never been late for a council meeting.

*Why has there been no telephone call?* Cael wondered. *Why hasn't the news of Judah's death been made known?* Stein had been given orders to disappear immediately after killing Judah, and not to resurface until Cael was irrefutably in charge of the Ansara and could give him permission to return to fight the Raintree. Soon. On the day of the summer solstice.

Once the Raintree had been destroyed, the Ansara would rule the world. And *he* would rule the Ansara.

Suddenly the chamber doors burst open as if a mighty wind had ripped them from their golden hinges. A dark, snarling creature, his icy gray eyes surveying the room, stormed into their midst. Clad in black boots, black pants, a bloodstained white shirt and ripped black vest, Judah Ansara arrived, growling like the ferocious beast he was. The wall of windows facing the ocean rattled from the force of his rage.

Cael felt the blood drain from his face, and his heart stopped for one terrifying moment when he realized that Judah had survived the assassination attempt. He had been able to defeat a warrior fighting under a spell created by Cael's incredibly powerful magic, which meant that Judah's powers were undoubtedly far greater than Cael had realized. But that wasn't of key importance right now. Even the fact that Stein was dead was unimportant in the wake of a far greater concern. What Cael needed to know was whether Stein had lived long enough to betray him?

"Lord Judah." Alexandria rushed to his side but stopped

short of touching him. "What has happened? You look as if you've been in a battle."

Whirling to face her, Judah narrowed his gaze and glared at her through sharp, shadowed slits. "Someone within my own clan wishes me dead." His voice reverberated with the throaty intensity of a man barely controlling his anger. "The warrior Stein came into my bedchambers at dawn and attempted to murder me in my sleep. The woman who shared my bed was his accomplice and had thought to drug me last night. But they were both fools to think I would not sense danger and act accordingly, despite the strong magical spell that had been placed on Stein. I switched drinks with the lady, so she was the one sleeping soundly, while I was dressed and ready for battle when Stein slipped in through the secret passage to my quarters that only you, the council, even know exists."

Cael realized that he must speak, must react with outrage, lest suspicion fall immediately upon him. "Are you implying that someone on the council...?"

"I imply nothing." Judah speared Cael with his deadly glare. "But rest assured, brother, that I will discover the identity of the person who sent Stein to do his dirty work, and when the time is right, I will have my revenge." As Judah rubbed his bloody shoulder, a fresh red stain appeared on his shirt.

"My God, you're still bleeding." Claude went to Judah, his gaze thoroughly scanning Judah's big body for signs of other injuries.

"A few knife wounds. Nothing more," Judah said. "Stein was a remarkable opponent. Whoever chose him, chose well. Only a handful of Ansara warriors have battle skills that equal mine. Stein came close."

"No one has your level of abilities," Councilman Bartholomew said, as he and the other council members surrounded Judah. "You are superior in every way."

"If your battle with Stein was at dawn, why are you still bloody and disheveled?" Alexandria asked. "Couldn't you have bathed and changed clothes before the meeting?"

Judah laughed, the sound deep, coarse and mirthless. "Once my men disposed of Stein's body and the body of his accomplice, the whore Drusilla, I intended to bathe and make myself presentable, but a telephone call from the United States—from North Carolina—interrupted my plans. What I learned from the conversation required immediate action. I spoke directly with Varian, the head of the Ansara team assigned to monitor the Raintree sanctuary."

The council members murmured loudly, and then elderly Councilwoman Sidra spoke for the others. "Tell us, my lord, was the call concerning the Raintree?"

Judah nodded; then again cast his gaze directly on Cael. "Your protégé, Greynell, is in North Carolina."

"I swear to you—"

"Do not swear a lie!"

Cael trembled with fear, all the while hating himself for cowering in the wake of his brother's fury. Squaring his shoulders and looking Judah directly in the eyes, Cael faced the Dranir's wrath. He reminded himself that he was an equal, that he was the elder son and deserved to rule the Ansara, that the failure of his most recent plot to dethrone his brother did not mean that he was not destined to rule. Regardless of what Judah said or did, he could not stop the inevitable. Not now. It was too late.

"Did you know that Greynell had gone to North Carolina?" Judah demanded.

"I knew," Cael admitted. "But I didn't send him. He acted on his own."

Judah growled. "And you know what his mission is, don't you?"

Cael wished that he could destroy his brother here and now and be done with it. But he dared not act. When Judah died, his blood should not be on Cael's hands.

"Yes, my lord, I know that some of the young warriors grow restless. They don't want to wait to wage war on the Raintree. A few have taken it upon themselves to act now instead of waiting until you tell them the time is right."

Judah swore vehemently. The windows shivered and cracked. Fireballs rained down from the ceiling. The marble floor beneath their feet shook, and the walls trembled.

Claude placed his meaty hand on Judah's shoulder and spoke softly to him. The shaking council chambers settled suddenly, the fires burning throughout the room died down, and the broken glass windowpanes jangled loudly as they fell out and hit the floor.

Judah breathed heavily. "Greynell is on a mission to penetrate the Raintree home place, their sanctuary."

Cael swallowed hard.

"Who is his target?" Judah demanded.

Did he lie and swear he did not know? Or did he confess? Cael could feel Judah probing his mind, searching for a way to penetrate the barrier he barely managed to keep in place. If he himself were not so powerful, he could never withstand his brother's brutal psychic force.

"Mercy Raintree." Cael spoke the name with reverence. The woman might be a Raintree, but her abilities were legendary among the Ansara as well as her own people. She was the most powerful empath living today.

Judah's nostrils flared. "Mercy Raintree," he said, his voice deadly calm and chillingly restrained, "is mine. I claimed her. She is my kill."

# ONE

Sidonia busied herself with breakfast preparations as she did every morning, moving slowly about the big kitchen. Like the other rooms in the old house, the kitchen had been constructed two hundred years ago, when the Raintree first settled in the hills of North Carolina. Shortly after *The Battle*. Dante and Ancelin Raintree had claimed nine hundred and ninety-nine acres of wilderness, establishing a home place for the Raintree clan, a safe haven where they could recuperate and rebuild after the ravaging war with the Ansara. Over the years, the house had been remodeled numerous times, but some things never changed around here, such as honor, duty and the love of family.

The main house sat atop one of the foothills, surrounded by the forest, with spring-fed streams, ancient trees and an abundance of wildlife. Originally built of wood and rock, the house had been bricked a hundred years ago and wings added to the original structure. Two dozen cottages dotted the landscape within the boundaries of the safe haven, some occupied by relatives, many empty a good part of the time but kept ready for visiting members of the Raintree clan. Family was always welcome.

Sidonia, a distant relative of the royal family, had come to work for them when she'd been a girl of eighteen, brought into the household of Dranir Julian when his wife, Vivienne, was carrying their first child. Young Prince Michael had been an only child for many years, and he had bonded with Sidonia so much that she became like a second mother to him. It was only natural that when he grew to manhood, married and became a father, he chose her to be the nanny for his own children. And when her Michael and his beloved Catherine had been brutally murdered seventeen years ago, it had fallen to her to look after the royal siblings——Dante, Gideon and Mercy.

Dante now lived in Reno, Nevada, owned a gambling casino and was still single, despite knowing full well he was expected to produce an heir. As the Dranir, he oversaw the Raintree clan and handled the clan's finances, having almost doubled the family's vast wealth during the past ten years. His younger brother, Gideon, lived in Wilmington and worked as a police detective. Gideon, too, was single and had made it perfectly clear to one and all that he did not intend to marry and most certainly would never father a child. Mercy remained at the Sanctuary as its keeper. Like her great-aunt Gillian before her, Mercy had been born a powerful empath, and so it fell to her to be the family's guardian, the caretaker of all things Raintree.

The nine hundred and ninety-nine acre refuge lay on a fault

line, and whenever there were any shifts in the earth, any small
tremors or minor earthquakes, those forces of nature simply
spread out and went around the shielded sanctuary. But the
Raintree absorbed the energy produced by the earth's
numerous little hiccups. Long ago, a triad of royal Raintrees
had placed a cloak of protection about the land, and, yearly,
Mercy and her brothers renewed that ancient spell on the day
of the Vernal Equinox in early spring. Only someone possessing magic power equal to or greater than the Raintree royals
could ever penetrate the invisible barrier that shielded the
sanctuary from outsiders.

Sidonia shivered as she recalled the frightening tales of the
Ansara and the legend of *The Battle* that had wiped the evil
warrior clan from the face of the earth. All except a handful
who had escaped, never to be heard from again.

Rolling out biscuit dough, Sidonia pretended not to see the
small child tiptoeing into the room. Perhaps it was the weakness
of approaching old age—after all, she was eighty-five now—but
she loved this little girl with a devotion that was almost sinful.
Princess Eve Raintree, a beautiful, charming, precocious imp, had
stolen Sidonia's heart the first moment she laid eyes on her.
Princess Mercy had given birth at home, in her bedroom
upstairs, only she and Sidonia present, as Mercy had wished. Her
labor had been hard, but not difficult. Her child had come into
the world a perfect specimen of feminine beauty, with her
mother's golden hair and delicate features. And with the bewitching green Raintree eyes, a dominant hereditary characteristic that
marked the ones who possessed such eyes as true Raintrees.

Sidonia refused to think about that other small but significant hereditary mark the child possessed, a mark known only
to her and to Mercy. That one detail set Eve apart from all

others and made her special in a way that must be kept secret, even from Dante and Gideon.

Eve crept up behind Sidonia, who held her breath, waiting to see what devilish trick the little one would conjure up this morning. Suddenly the rolling pin flew out of Sidonia's hands and danced through the air, landing with a thud in the middle of the kitchen floor. Gasping as if she were truly startled, Sidonia whipped around and held her hand over her heart.

"You scared me half to death, little princess."

Eve giggled, the sound like sweet music. "It's something new I've just learned to do. Mother says it's called lev-i-ta-tion. I think I will be very good at it, don't you?"

After wiping off her hands on her floral apron, Sidonia reached down and tapped Eve on the nose. "I believe you will be very good at many things, but you must learn to control your powers and always use them wisely."

"That's what Mother says."

"Your mother is a very wise woman." Yes, Mercy *was* wise. And good and kind and loving. And the most powerful empath in the world. She could feel another's pain, remove it from them and heal them. But the price she paid in personal agony often depleted her energy for hours, even days.

"She's very pretty, too," Eve said. "And so am I."

Sidonia chuckled. It was not a bad thing to know your strong points. "Yes, you and your mother are both beautiful."

Mercy was as beautiful inside as out, but Sidonia feared that might not be true of her precious little Eve. She was a good child, with a good heart, but there had been a few times when her temper had flared uncontrollably, and it was at those times Sidonia and Mercy had witnessed the incredible, untutored power Eve possessed.

"Where is Mother? Isn't she eating breakfast with me this morning?" Eve asked as she crawled up onto a stool at the granite-topped bar separating the kitchen from the breakfast room.

"She has gone up to Amadahy Pointe to meditate. I expect her home soon." Sidonia returned to her task. She picked up the rolling pin, washed it off, then used it to spread the dough into a half-inch-thick circle.

"Is something bothering my mother? Is something wrong?" Eve asked, with a wisdom far beyond her years.

Sidonia hesitated, then, knowing Eve had the ability to read her thoughts if she chose to do so, said, "To my knowledge, nothing is wrong. Mercy simply felt the need to meditate."

Sidonia cut the dough and placed each raw biscuit in the rectangular pan, then popped them into the hot oven to bake.

"May I have a glass of apple juice while I wait for Mother?" Eve glanced at the refrigerator.

"Yes, of course you may."

Suddenly the refrigerator door swung open, and the pitcher of juice lifted up and floated out of the refrigerator and across the room. Eve's tinkling girlish giggles jingled about the room.

Sidonia grabbed the pitcher midair and set it on the bar. "You're a little showoff."

"Mother said that practice makes perfect, and that if I don't practice my skills, I won't master them." Eve sighed heavily. Dramatically. The child had a flair for melodrama. "Mother frowned when she told me that. I believe she worries about me. She thinks I have amazing powers."

"Yes, we know, your mother and I. And we both worry, because you are so young and unable to direct your powers. That is why Mercy told you that you must practice. It was no different with your mother and your uncles. They had to learn to control their powers."

"But I am different. I'm not like Mother and Uncle Dante and Uncle Gideon."

Sidonia gasped. Was it possible the child knew the secret of her conception? Sidonia shook her head to dislodge such foolish thoughts. Eve might be talented far beyond any of the other Raintree children, might excel in talents even adults in the clan would envy, but she was still only a child. She might read other people's thoughts, but she did not always understand the words she heard inside her little head.

"Of course, you're different. You're a member of the royal family. Your uncle is the Dranir, and your mother is the greatest empath in the world."

Eve shook her head. Her long blond curls danced about her shoulders. "I am more than Raintree."

A shiver of pure, unadulterated fear quivered through Sidonia. The child sensed the truth, even if she did not know what that truth was. Sidonia removed a glass from the cupboard, lifted the pitcher and poured the apple juice for Eve. She set the glass in front of the child. "Yes, you are more than Raintree. You are very, very special, my precious."

*More special than you will ever know, if your mother and I can protect you by keeping your secret.*

Mercy Raintree sat on the firm, grassy ground, her eyes closed, her hands resting in her lap. Whenever she was troubled, she came to Amadahy Pointe to meditate, to collect her thoughts and renew her strength. The sunshine covered her like an invisible robe, wrapping her in light and warmth. The spring breeze caressed her tenderly, like a lover's soft touch. With her eyes closed and her soul open to the positive energy she drew from this holy place, this sanctuary within a sanctuary, she focused on what was most important to her.

Family.

Mercy sensed impending danger. But from whom or from what, she did not know. Although her greatest talents lay in being an empath and a healer, she possessed latent precognitive powers, less erratic than her cousin Echo's, but not as strong. She had also been cursed with the ability to sense the emotional and physical condition of others from a distance. *Clairempathy*. As a child, she'd found her various empathic talents maddening, but gradually, year by year, she had learned to control them. And now, despite both Dante and Gideon blocking her from intercepting their thoughts and emotions, she could still manage to pick up something on the outer fringes of each brother's individual consciousness.

Dante and Gideon were in trouble. But she did not know why. Perhaps it was nothing more than stress from their chosen professions. Or it could even be problems in their personal lives.

If her brothers thought she could help them, they would ask her to intervene. This knowledge reassured her that their problems were within the realm of human reality and not of a supernatural nature. Her brothers were, as they had pointed out to her on numerous occasions, grown men, perfectly capable of taking care of themselves without the assistance of their baby sister.

Past experience had taught her that when their souls needed replenishing, their spirits nurtured, her brothers came home, here to the Raintree land, deep in the North Carolina mountains. The home place was protected by a powerful magic that

had been established by their ancestors two centuries ago after
*The Battle*. Within the boundaries of these secure acres, no
living creature could intrude without alerting the resident
guardian. Mercy Raintree was that guardian, protector of the
home place, as her great-aunt Gillian had been until her death
at a hundred and nineteen, and like Gillian's mother, Vesta, the
first keeper of the sanctuary in the early eighteen hundreds.

Taking a deep, cleansing breath, Mercy opened her eyes and
looked at the valley below, spread out before her like a banquet
feast. Late springtime in the mountains. An endless blue sky
that went on forever. Towering green trees, the ancient, the
old and the young growing together, reaching heavenward.
Verdant life, thick and rich and sweet to the senses. A multitude of wild flowers blooming in abundance, their perfume
tantalizing, their colors pleasing to the eye.

Mercy wasn't sure exactly what was wrong with her, but she
felt a nagging sense of unease that had nothing to do with her
brothers or with anyone in the Raintree tribe. No, the restlessness was within her, a yearning she was forced to control
because of who she was, because of her duty to her family and
to her people. Whenever these strange emotions unsettled her,
she climbed the mountain to this sacred peak and mediated
until the uncertainty subsided. But today, for some unknown
reason, the anxiety clung to her.

Was it a warning?

Seven years ago, she had allowed that hunger inside her to
lead her into dangerous territory, into a world she had been
ill prepared for, into a relationship that had altered her life. She
would not—could not—succumb to fear. And except for brief
visits to Dante and Gideon, she would not leave the safety of
the Raintree sanctuary. Not ever again.

* * *

Pax Greynell knew no fear. Why should he? He was young, strong, brave. A highly trained warrior. And he was an Ansara. The blood of the royal family flowed in his veins, as it did in Cael's, and like the true Ansara Dranir, he, too, had been born out of wedlock. He was a cousin to Cael and Judah. All his life, he had been loyal to the clan and, since Judah had been crowned their leader, loyal to Judah. But in the past year, he, like several of the young warriors, had grown tired of waiting, tired of being told the time was not right, that the Ansara were not ready to do battle with the Raintree.

Cael whispered in their ears, promising them a new order, one in which they would become members of his council. He also implied that Judah was afraid to face the Raintree, whereas he, Cael, was not. Although Pax believed in Cael and would stand at his side in any battle, he knew Judah Ansara was not afraid of anything or anyone.

That thought would have unnerved Greynell if he hadn't been protected by a magic spell cast upon him by Cael. He would be invincible for the next forty-eight hours. No one could harm him. Only Cael or another Ansara of his equal could penetrate the invisible forcefield surrounding him. Twenty-four hours would be more than enough time for him to accomplish his mission and escape without being captured. Afterward, he would wait for word from Cael, and then he would join his master and the others for the final battle.

Greynell adjusted his binoculars and watched while Mercy Raintree rose from the ground with the fluid grace of a ballet dancer, her long blond hair shimmering in the morning sunlight. She was beautiful. And if she were a mere mortal woman, he would rape her before he killed her. But she was not mortal, no more than he was. He dared not risk compromising his mission for a taste of her, no matter how great the temptation.

He kept the binoculars trained on her as she stood there alone, so close, yet beyond his reach. Cael had warned him not to try to enter the Raintree sanctuary, had instructed him to find a way to lure Mercy outside, away from the protection of the home place.

Smiling at his own cleverness, he drank in the sight of this delectable Raintree princess and fantasized about ravaging her before he ended her life. She, like her brothers and her cousin Echo, had been marked for death. Destroy the royal family first, eliminate the most powerful, and the rest would follow.

*Sunday, 3:15 p.m.*

The Ansara private jet had landed in Asheville, North Carolina, half an hour ago. A prearranged rental car had awaited Judah, so he'd been able to get on the road almost immediately. He didn't know how much time he had before Greynell struck, wasn't sure he could save Mercy Raintree. He had known his foolish young cousin was a loose cannon and, like several of the other young warriors, was eager for battle. But he had not realized the extent of Cael's power over the boy and just how unbalanced Greynell had become.

Judah knew that Cael would try to contact Greynell and warn him. But by now, Cael must have realized that his telepathic powers had been imprisoned, that he had been temporarily put out of commission. Had he also figured out that he had underestimated Judah's powers? Like the egotistical bastard he was, Cael believed himself superior to Judah, actually thought he was more powerful. Idiot. Perhaps realizing that Judah had temporarily frozen his telepathic powers would prove to Cael just who the superior brother actually was.

The only reason Judah had not called Cael out and challenged him to a Death Duel was because they were brothers. But once he had taken care of Greynell—either before or after the young warrior killed the Raintree's most revered empath— Judah would have to face his half brother in combat, once and for all ending Cael's quest to dethrone him. There was little doubt in Judah's mind as to who had been behind the assassination attempt on his life this morning, although he could not prove his suspicions.

Judah stayed on Highway 74, heading southwest, toward the eastern foothills of the Great Smoky Mountains. The Raintree sanctuary bordered the Eastern Cherokee Indian Reservation. Several members of the Raintree clan had intermarried with the Cherokee before the Trail of Tears over a hundred and seventy years ago, and the family had provided assistance to the Cherokee who had escaped from the soldiers and taken refuge in the mountains.

From childhood, Judah had made a study of the Ansara's powerful enemy, knowing that it was his destiny to one day seek revenge for the Ansara defeat in *The Battle* two centuries ago and wipe every single member of the Raintree clan from the face of the earth. But the time was not right. Not yet. Cael was overeager, he and his followers. If they went up against the Raintree too soon, they would be doomed to failure. But he could not make his brother understand the importance of patience. Wait. Soon. But not now.

It was a pity that Mercy Raintree would have to die, along with her brothers and others of their kind. But despite the pleasure he might derive in keeping her alive, in making her his slave, he could not allow one single member of the Raintree clan to live. Not even Mercy.

But Greynell had no right to the kill. Every member of the Ansara clan knew that Mercy Raintree belonged to Judah. She was his kill, as was Dante Raintree. The powers she and her elder brother possessed were Judah's to absorb upon their deaths. And the other brother, Gideon, belonged to Claude. Cael had been furious when Judah had given Claude the right to kill the third Raintree royal.

Cael had been a thorn in Judah's side for far too long. He had indulged his brother, forgiven him his sins again and again, but no longer. Cael had become extremely dangerous, not only to Judah but to the Ansara. He could no longer put off dealing with his power-hungry sibling.

The call came in at seven-forty-two Sunday evening, while Mercy, Eve and Sidonia were sitting on the expansive back porch, Sidonia in her rocking chair, Eve resting her head in Mercy's lap in the swing. An orange slice of twilight sun nestled low on the western horizon, multicolored clouds feathering out on either side like pink and lavender cottony down. Summertime insects chirped, and tree frogs croaked contentedly, as nighttime approached, here in the foothills.

Serenity. Peace.

Mercy had sensed something was wrong, had felt uneasy the entire day. And now that she had received the call, she understood why she'd been concerned. She seldom left the Sanctuary for extended periods of time. Not any longer. As the years passed and her empathic abilities grew stronger, she found it difficult to be in a crowd. Simply walking down the street in

Waynesville proved difficult. Other people's thoughts and emotions bombarded her if she so much as made eye contact with them. And heaven help her if someone accidentally brushed against her. She heard their thoughts, sensed their pain, experienced their joy. And any protective spell she used had its limits and its drawbacks, so she used one only when necessary.

As a teenager, after her parents were murdered, she had longed to become a doctor, to save people as the doctors in Asheville had tried so valiantly to save her parents. She had foolishly believed that her inherited, innate empathic abilities would actually help make her a better doctor. She'd been wrong. Dr. Huxley, the oldest physician in the area and a friend of Mercy's father, had tutored Mercy and even arranged for her to accompany him on emergency calls where her empathic abilities often meant the difference between life and death for his patients. Dr. Huxley had grown up near the sanctuary and understood what a special people the Raintree were and how remarkable Mercey's talent was, even among her tribe. The Raintree trusted Dr. Huxley as they did few other humans, instinctively knowing he would never betray them. But then, after being homeschooled, she had left the mountains at eighteen to attend college. The University of Tennessee had been exciting, but also frightening, because of the dense population. With the help of her family—Dante had arranged for several Raintree clansmen to attend the same college—Mercy had managed to graduate. But living away from the sanctuary had shown her that she could never pursue her dream of becoming a doctor. Her empathic skills were as much a curse as a blessing.

Now, only on rare occasions did Dr. Huxley contact her for

assistance. Tonight was one of those occasions. There had been a wreck on the back roads, not far from the home place, and Dr. Huxley knew she would be able to reach the scene before anyone else because of the location—within a mile of the Raintree boundaries.

"You be careful," Sidonia said as she stood beside Mercy's white Escalade, Eve at her hip. "Are you sure you don't want me to call Brenna and have her stay with Eve so I can go with you?"

Mercy caressed Sidonia's wrinkled cheek. "You worry too much. I'll be fine. Dr. Huxley is on his way with the police, and the county rescue squad should reach the accident site very soon. I won't be there alone for long."

"Don't overdo. You know how weak—"

"If anything goes wrong, Dr. Huxley will take care of me and see that I get home safe and sound."

Mercy slipped behind the wheel of her new SUV, a present from Dante. As she backed out of the driveway, she glanced in the rearview mirror and saw Sidonia and Eve waving goodbye. Focusing on the road ahead, she pressed her foot against the accelerator, knowing that the accident victims' lives might well be in her hands.

Less than five minutes away from the sanctuary's boundaries, she came upon two mutilated vehicles that had apparently crashed headlong into each other. How could that have happened, on a clear evening, with no fog, no rain and on a relatively straight stretch of highway? Had one of the drivers been drinking or taking drugs? Mercy pulled off to the side of the road, opened the door and got out, her heart racing maddeningly as she hurried toward the nearest vehicle, a red sports car that had been crushed almost beyond recognition. Without even touching the driver's bloody body, she knew he was dead.

She wished his soul a safe journey into the afterlife. That was all she could do for him. But she sensed life inside the other vehicle, a silver truck. As she approached the smoking Ford, she heard moans and cries coming from within. She had to work quickly and do her best to free this couple. The driver, a middle-aged man, was trapped by the steering wheel, which had crushed his chest. The woman beside him was the one whimpering and groaning, her pale face streaked with blood— her own and the man's.

Using both hands, Mercy reached inside through the shattered passenger window and touched the female. The frightened woman screamed, then suddenly grew very still as Mercy connected with her and began drawing the pain from her mangled body. Without saying a word, Mercy communicated with the woman, doing her best to reassure her as well as comfort her.

"My name is Mercy, and I'm here to help you."

The woman finally managed to speak. "I'm Darlene and— oh, God, my husband. Keary…"

Lifting one hand away from Darlene, Mercy reached farther into the truck cab and ran her fingertips over Keary's right shoulder. She sensed no life. The man had died.

Returning to the task of healing Darlene, of keeping her from going into shock and from bleeding to death, Mercy concentrated completely on sustaining life, on taking the pain and suffering into her own body.

Mercy trembled as sheer agony surged through her, pain almost beyond bearing. No matter what, she must manage to remain conscious. Drawing on her inner personal strength and the powerful Raintree gifts with which she'd been blessed, she worked her magic.

\* \* \*

Judah had picked up on Greynell's scent twenty miles away, but he had known his whereabouts from the moment he got off the Ansara jet in Asheville. He could have pinpointed the warrior's exact location sooner if he had chosen to use his clairvoyant powers, but being gifted himself, Greynell would have known someone was intruding into his thoughts. The last thing Judah wanted to do was give his opponent any advance warning. He had no doubt that he could easily defeat his cousin if they did battle. But he had already fought to the death once today and preferred to dispose of Greynell more easily.

After parking his rental car some distance from where Greynell waited and watched, Judah crept into the forest. He let his prey's scent guide him into a wooded area adjacent to the back road only a few miles from Raintree land.

Suddenly, without any warning, Judah felt a forceful jolt of awareness, a recognition so strong that it momentarily halted him mid-step. Had Cael managed to break free from the spell Judah had cast over him, and was he now trying to get his attention? No, that wasn't it at all. The compelling connection was not with Cael but with a female. One nearby. And not an Ansara. No, that all-powerful magic came from his sworn enemy, Mercy Raintree.

He felt her deep inside him, as if she were a part of him. She was close, as close as Greynell. And she was in the throes of a potent healing. Mercy was not your average empath. She possessed the rare gift of *namapathy*. True psychic healing. And for whatever reason, she was now using all her power to save a human life.

Why she would bother with a mere mortal was beyond him. She was draining her strength and depleting her power, unknowingly making herself vulnerable to Greynell. But that was what the young warrior had wanted, why he had created the accident that had called Mercy from the safety of the Raintree sanctuary.

Unable to shake off the incredible energy Mercy emitted, Judah simply absorbed it. Flashes of her gentleness, her kindness and her tender touch bombarded him. She was far more powerful now than she had been seven years ago. At twenty-three she had been no match for him. Today, she was possibly the only woman on earth who came anywhere close to being his equal.

Cloaking himself with a spell of invisibility, blocking both his physical and psychic presence, Judah proceeded deeper into the forest. The trained warrior within him took over completely as he neared his destination. He paused as Pax Greynell crept up behind Mercy and wrapped a dark cord around her slender neck. She had been too deep into an empathic trance to sense her attacker's presence. Grasping the cord, she struggled to loosen it, but to no avail.

Judah ran with lightning speed, removing his dagger from the jewel-crested sheath inside his jacket as he raced to save the life of a woman who belonged to him in a way no other woman ever had or ever would. She was his and his alone. Only he, Dranir Judah Ansara, had the right to kill her.

Just as Mercy had been taken by surprise by her attacker, so was Greynell. Judah shoved the dagger deep into his back, puncturing a kidney, killing him without a second thought. Mercy gasped for air when the cord around her neck loosened. Her assailant's body dropped onto the pavement at her feet, crumpling into a dead heap.

Hurriedly, Judah blasted Greynell's body with an energy bolt, crushing it to dust.

Judah had accomplished his mission. It was time for him to leave. But he hesitated. For only a split second, but it was long enough to sense that Mercy was in trouble. Weakened by the healing miracle she had performed on the accident victim, Mercy was not only dangerously weak, but because of fighting Greynell with what little strength she'd had left, she was quickly fading into an unconscious state from which she might not recover.

Acting purely on possessive instinct, Judah grabbed Mercy before she fainted. The woman in the truck was still alive, healed by Mercy's magic. She slept peacefully at her dead husband's side.

The shrill cries of multiple sirens warned Judah to escape. But he could not leave Mercy. If he did, she might die. He, and he alone, could revive her.

Sidonia decided that if Mercy had not returned by midnight, she would call Dante. Dr. Huxley had phoned two hours ago to ask if Mercy had gotten home all right.

"I know she'd been to the site of the accident, because the only survivor told me that Mercy saved her life," Dr. Huxley had said. "I don't understand why she didn't wait for me. She knows I would have made sure someone saw her safely home if she was too weak to drive herself."

"You're worried about my mother, aren't you?" Eve said.

Sidonia gasped, then turned and faced the six-year-old, who was standing in the doorway between the foyer and the front parlor. "I thought I put you to bed hours ago. Did something wake you?"

"I haven't been asleep."

Intending to take Eve back to her bedroom, Sidonia

marched toward her. "It's past eleven, and time for all good little girls to be fast asleep."

"I'm not a good little girl. I am Raintree." Eve narrowed her expressive green eyes. "I am more than Raintree."

A foreboding chill rippled up Sidonia's spine. "So you have said, and I have agreed. So let's not talk about it again. Not at this late hour." She grasped Eve's hand. "Now come along. Your mother will be upset with both of us if, when she comes home, you aren't in bed."

"She will come home," Eve said. "Soon. Before midnight."

Sidonia lifted an inquisitive eyebrow. "Is that right? And you'd know that because…?"

"Because I can see her. She's asleep. But she will wake up soon."

Was Mercy out there somewhere, alone and weak to the point of unconsciousness? Was that what Eve saw? "Do you know where she is? Can you tell me exactly where I can find her?"

"She's in her car, the one Uncle Dante gave her," Eve said. "It's parked somewhere dark. But she's all right. He's with her. Touching her. Taking care of her. Giving her some of his strength."

"Who…?" Sidonia's voice quivered. "Who is with your mother? Who is giving her some of his strength?"

Eve smiled, the gesture equally sweet and impish. "Why, my daddy, of course."

# TWO

Mercy Raintree was even more beautiful than she'd been in her early twenties and far more dangerous. Despite her present weak state, Judah sensed the tremendous power within her. She was, as he had suspected, a woman who was now his equal. Odd that he, her rightful destroyer, had saved her from one of his own clan, that at this very moment he was restoring her strength when he could easily break her neck or drain the very life from her with a mere thought. And he *would* kill her—when the time was right. When the Ansara attacked the Raintree and annihilated their entire tribe. Unlike the Raintree, the Ansara would leave no one alive, not a single man, woman or child. But he would be merciful to his beautiful Mercy and take her life quickly, with as little pain as possible.

While she lay in his arms unconscious, he probed her mind but found it impossible to gain entrance. She had placed a block between her and the outside world, a shield to prevent anyone from listening to her private thoughts. If he tried harder, he could possibly destroy the barrier, but why should he bother? It wasn't as if he needed information from her. If not for Greynell's foolish actions, he would never have been here with her. Hell, he wouldn't be within a thousand miles of her. For the past seven years, he had made certain their paths never crossed, that he stayed far away from the North Carolina mountains and the Raintree home place.

Her eyelids flickered, consciousness fighting for dominance, her mind trying to come out of the shadows. But Judah knew she would not awaken fully for many hours. After the combination of such an arduous healing and her struggle for her life, her mind and body could not recover without rest, not even with the surge of strength with which he had infused her. She lay in his arms, helpless, completely vulnerable. But she was not without her weapons, protection far more potent than the psychic barrier that safeguarded her private thoughts.

If Greynell had succeeded in killing her, all hell would have broken loose. Literally. The death of a Raintree princess would have played havoc with the senses of all who were Raintree, especially Dante and Gideon. A host of her clansmen would have swarmed home, to the sanctuary. What if the Raintree Dranir and his younger brother suspected the fatal blow had come from an Ansara? He dared not risk even the slightest possibility that Mercy's premature death could warn the Raintree of the Ansaras' resurgence.

Judah looked down at her. She was resting peacefully against him as he sat with her in his lap on the passenger side of her vehicle. Her head nestled on his shoulder, her slender arms limp at her sides, her full, round breasts rising and falling with each breath she took.

He skimmed her cheek with the back of his hand.

Memories he had forced from his mind by sheer willpower years ago broke free and reminded him of another time, another place, when he had held this woman in his arms. When he had touched her, had tutored her, had taught her...

He had known who she was when they first met, and the very fact that she was a Raintree princess had whetted his appetite for her. She'd had no idea of his true identity, and the fact that she'd succumbed to his charms so easily had amused him. She had been practically an open book to him, unable to completely shield herself, her abilities still immature and only partly tamed. He, on the other hand, had protected himself, deliberately keeping his true identity and nature from her. They had spent less than twenty-four hours together, but in that short period of time she had become like a fever in his blood. No matter how many times he'd taken her, he had still wanted her.

"You were a bewitching little virgin," Judah told the sleeping Mercy. "Sweet. Luscious. Ripe for the picking."

Caressing her long, slender neck, he allowed his fingertips to linger on her pulse.

*Judah...Judah...*

Hearing Mercy telepathically whispering his name stunned him. He tightened his hold about her neck, then suddenly realized what he was doing and eased his hand away from her.

On some level, she sensed his presence. That was not good. How could he explain what he was doing here, why he had just happened to be on a back road in the North Carolina mountains at the exact moment some madman tried to kill her?

He had to take her home and leave her in safe hands before she awakened. If she recalled anything about him, perhaps she would believe she had simply dreamed of him.

Did she ever dream of him? Or was he nothing more than a vague memory?

*Why should I care? This woman means nothing to me. She didn't then. She doesn't now. She was only a fleeting amusement for me.*

An amusement that had haunted him for far too long after their one day and night together. He had been unable to forget awakening from a deep sleep and finding her gone, his bed empty. He'd been angry that she had run away and curious as to why. But common sense had cautioned him not to follow her. And for many months afterward, he had wondered if she had somehow realized who he was—her deadly enemy—and had fled to warn her brothers of a mighty Ansara Dranir's existence. But neither Dante nor Gideon had hunted him down and sought revenge for taking their sister's innocence.

*She did not know who I was.*

Judah gently maneuvered Mercy so that she sat in the SUV's passenger seat. He lowered the back of the seat until she was half reclining; then he fastened her seat belt. She whimpered. His stomach muscles knotted painfully. He hated the fact that after seven years, he could still remember the sound of her sweet, feminine whimpers when he had taken her the first time. And the second time. And the third…

After starting the Cadillac's engine, Judah shifted gears, turned the vehicle around and headed back up the country road. He would take Mercy home, leave her there and return to Asheville. He had no desire to stay in the United States any longer than necessary. His place was at Terrebonne, the home of the Ansara for the past two hundred years. Once the jet had landed on the island, he would call a special council meeting. Cael and his followers had to be stopped before their foolish actions endangered the Ansara and destroyed Judah's future plans to annihilate the Raintree.

Cael wanted to be the Dranir. Everyone knew that his older half brother believed he had been cheated out of the title by a mere chance of birth. Cael was first in line to the throne, a fact that greatly concerned Judah, who by now should have married and fathered a child. But while he could easily protect himself from Cael's evil machinations, he hesitated to put an innocent child's life in peril. Once Cael had been dealt with and the Raintree eliminated, Judah would choose an appropriate Dranira and procreate.

Within five minutes of following his instincts and driving toward his destination, the high iron gates protecting the entrance to the Raintree sanctuary came into view. Judah slowed the SUV, then hit the button inside the vehicle that opened the massive gates. Before driving through, he spoke quietly, reciting ancient words, conjuring up a potent magic. With Mercy asleep at his side, he drove onto the private road that wound around and around up the foothills, all the way to the top of the highest hill, where the royal family's house presided over the valley below, like a king on his high throne.

Lights from the veranda welcomed them, informing Judah that someone inside was waiting for Mercy, possibly concerned for her well-being. A husband? Had she married another from the Raintree clan, or had she chosen a mere human as her mate?

What did it matter? Whoever was now a part of her life— lover or husband or even children—they would all become Ansara targets and would die with Mercy on that fateful day. Judah parked the SUV, got out and rounded the hood. After opening the passenger door, he lifted Mercy up and into his arms. She nestled against him, her actions seeming to be instinctive, as if she believed herself safe and protected.

Judah hardened his heart. He would not allow this beguiling creature to tempt him. She was only a woman, one like so many others. He had bedded her, as he had bedded countless women. She was no better. No different.

*Liar,* an unwelcome inner voice taunted him.

Cael cursed violently as he tore apart his living room in the seaside villa in Beauport, a place he had called home since Dranir Hadar had acknowledged him as his son. His unwanted, illegitimate son. He was the bastard from an affair the Dranir had had before he'd wed the beloved Dranira Seana. Judah's sainted mother had died in childbirth, after suffering several miscarriages. Miscarriages caused by a curse put upon Seana by Cael's mother, Nusi, an enchanting sorceress. Upon learning of her wicked little spells, Hadar had ordered his former mistress's death—a public execution.

Cael clenched his teeth, anger from his childhood and from the present situation consuming him, his rage threatening to explode from within. How was it possible that Judah had frozen his telepathic abilities? How dare he do such a thing! His brother was far more dangerous than Cael had suspected, his powers far greater. If Judah could control Cael's inherited talents, then he had to find a way to protect himself from his younger brother's machinations.

Growling like a wounded bear, Cael shoved his fist through the wall, tearing apart plaster that shredded as if it were tissue paper.

"Temper, temper," Alexandria said, her voice mocking.

Cael whipped around and glared at her as she stood in the open double doors leading to the patio. "You're like a snake, Cousin, slithering silently about, sneaking up on unsuspecting victims."

Alexandria laughed, the sound even deeper and more throaty than her gruff voice. "You're not my victim, but from the way you're acting, I believe you must be the victim of some vile magic the Dranir has conjured up to prevent you from warning Greynell."

Cael stormed across the room toward his cousin. "What do you know?"

"Oh, dear, dear. Judah really did freeze your powers, didn't he?"

"He did not!"

"Perhaps only your psychic powers were affected, especially the telepathic ones. You weren't able to warn Greynell, were you?"

"Have you spoken to Judah?"

"No, I haven't spoken to him," Alexandria said. "And there is no official word from him. But Claude received a telepathic message from our revered Dranir, and I just happened to be with him at the time."

Cael paused, a good three feet separating him from his uninvited guest. "You never just happen to be anywhere."

Her lips curved in a closed-mouth smile. "I made a point of staying near Claude because I knew that if Judah contacted any one of us, it would be our dear cousin."

"If you expect me to beg you for the information—"

"Don't fret. I expect nothing from you now. But when you are Dranir, I expect to rule at your side."

"As you will." He closed the gap between them, reached out, circled her neck with one hand and drew her close. Close enough that his lips brushed hers. "You will be my Dranira."

Sighing contentedly, Alexandria wrapped her arms around Cael's neck. "Greynell is dead. Judah killed him to prevent him from disposing of Mercy Raintree."

"Fool. Son of a bitch fool. He destroyed one of his own to save a Raintree. The council will——"

"The council will be called into a special meeting once Judah returns."

Cael sucked in a hard, agitated breath. "For what purpose? To investigate the assassination attempt on his life? He will learn nothing. There is no trail leading back to me."

"Claude told me that we, the council members, must band together with Judah to stop the renegade factions within the Ansara clan. Judah truly believes we are not ready to fight the Raintree." She looked directly into Cael's eyes. "Are you sure we *are* ready, that we can win if we go to war on the day of this year's summer solstice?"

Snarling, Cael tightened his hold at the back of her neck. "There is nothing Judah can do to stop us. Not now. There are warriors in place, ready to strike. Even if Judah managed to stop Greynell, he cannot stop the others. Even he cannot be in two places at once."

"Just what do you have up your sleeve?" Alexandria's heart-beat accelerated. Cael sensed her excitement.

"Tabby is in Wilmington taking care of Echo Raintree. And then, on my command, she will eliminate Gideon."

"Tabby is a wild card. What if you can't control her? She takes perverse pleasure in killing. She could easily draw atten-tion to herself."

"Tabby knows what I will do to her if she fails me."

"Our success might well depend upon removing the Raintree royal siblings before the great battle, yet all three are still alive and well."

"But not for long." Cael grinned. "Dante is in for quite a surprise tonight. And once Judah returns to Terrebonne and is consumed with other matters, I will send another warrior to take care of Mercy."

Sidonia heard the car drive up and park. She had taken Eve back to her room and tucked her in for a second time, warning the little imp to stay put, but she doubted the child was asleep. Eve was concerned about Mercy, just as she herself was.

Pausing at the front door, Sidonia, peered through the left sidelight and gasped when she saw a large, dark man walking toward the veranda, an unconscious Mercy in his arms. The only vehicle in sight was Mercy's Escalade, so who was this stranger and why was he with Mercy?

Closing her eyes, Sidonia called for her animal helpers to awaken and come to her. Within minutes, by the time the stranger set foot on the veranda, Magnus and Rufus, her fiercely faithful Rottweilers, appeared in the yard, one on the right, the other on the left, flanking the veranda.

Sidonia opened the front door, took one step over the threshold and faced the stranger. He paused as if he'd been expecting her, and his gaze connected with hers. He was not Raintree. His eyes were steel gray. Hard and cold, with no sign of emotion.

"I've brought your mistress home, old woman," the man told her, his voice a deep, commanding baritone.

No, he was not Raintree, but neither was he a mere mortal.

A tremor of unease jangled Sidonia's nerves. If he was not Raintree and he was not human, that meant...

"You assume correctly," he said. "I am Ansara."

Sensing Sidonia's fear, Magnus and Rufus growled.

The man—the Ansara man—stared first at Rufus and then at Magnus. They quieted instantly. Sidonia hazarded quick glances to her right and left. Both large animals stood frozen like marble statues.

"What have you done to—"

"They're unharmed. In an hour, they will be as they were and return to their sleep."

"What are you doing with Mercy? Did you harm her? If you have, the wrath of the Raintree will—"

"Be quiet, old woman, and show me where to place your mistress so she can rest and recover from her ordeal. She healed a dying woman tonight."

Confused by this Ansara's concern for Mercy, Sidonia hesitated, then backed up to allow him entrance. He was a handsome devil. Wide shouldered, at least six-two, with flowing black hair that hung in a single braid down his back, and chiseled features that made him look as if he'd been cut from stone.

"Her room is upstairs, but I think it best if you—"

Ignoring Sidonia, the man headed for the staircase.

"Wait!"

He did not wait; instead, he took the stairs two at a time, Sidonia following as quickly as her old legs would carry her. By the time she reached the second floor, he already had the door to Mercy's bedroom open, apparently being guided by his instinct.

Scurrying down the hall, Sidonia came up behind the Ansara just as he laid Mercy on her bed. From the doorway, she watched him as he stared at Mercy for a full minute, then turned and walked toward the door.

"Who are you? What is your name?" Sidonia demanded. *He couldn't be* that *Ansara, could he? Surely not.*

"I am Judah Ansara."

Sidonia gasped.

He smiled wickedly. "I once wondered if Mercy might have suspected I was an Ansara, and if that was the reason she fled from me so quickly that long ago morning."

"Stop reading my mind!" Heaven help her, she had to do something to prevent this Ansara demon from listening to her thoughts. He mustn't find out—shut up, you old fool, she told herself. Then she closed her eyes and recited an ancient spell, one that should protect her from this wicked Ansara's mental probing.

"Don't trouble yourself, Sidonia," Judah told her. "I will leave your thoughts private. But when I leave, I'm afraid I must erase from your mind all memory of my visit here tonight."

"Don't you touch my mind again, you evil beast."

Judah laughed.

"You find me amusing, do you? Don't think because I am well past eighty that my skills are not as sharp as they ever were."

"I would never insult you by underestimating your powers."

"Why are you with Mercy?" Sidonia demanded. "What are you doing here on Raintree land? How did you—"

"Why I'm here doesn't matter. I found Mercy in an unconscious state and brought her home. You should be grateful to me."

"Grateful to Ansara scum like you? Never!"

"Does Mercy feel about me the way you do? Does she hate me?"

"Of course she hates you. She is Raintree. You are Ansara."

He glanced at the bed where Mercy rested. Tempted to probe the old woman's mind for answers, Judah snorted, disgusted with himself for allowing his curiosity about Mercy's feelings to concern him.

"You can't stay here," Sidonia said. "You must leave. Immediately."

"I have no plans to remain here," Judah told her. "I leave your mistress in your capable hands."

"Yes, yes. Leave now, and go quickly."

When Judah turned to leave, his mind centered on a spell that would erase Sidonia's memories of his visit, he spotted a small shadow behind and to the side of the old woman. He paused and waited, suspecting the Raintree nanny might have conjured up some deadly little spirit to escort him out of the house. But suddenly the shadow moved from behind Sidonia and came into the room, the light from the hallway backlighting the figure, making it appear a golden white, like the glow of moonlight. The shadow was a child, a girl child, he realized.

Judah stared at the little one and saw that her eyes were a true Raintree green, and her pale blond hair flowed in long, shimmering curls to her waist. If his eyesight had not told him that Mercy was the child's mother, his inner vision would have.

So Mercy had married and had children. At least one child. This remarkably lovely little girl was so like her mother, and yet...

What was it about the child that puzzled him? She was a Raintree child, no doubt of that. But she was different.

Sidonia grabbed the girl and tried to shove the little beauty behind her, but the child wiggled free of the old nanny's hold and walked fearlessly toward Judah.

"No, child, don't!" Sidonia cried. "Stay away from him. He is evil."

The child stopped several feet away from Judah, then looked up and stared right at him, her gaze connecting boldly with his.

"I'm not afraid of him," the child said. "He won't hurt me."

Judah smiled, impressed with her bravery.

Seasoned warriors had trembled at the very sight of Judah Ansara.

When Sidonia came forward, intending to grab the child, the little girl lifted her arm and held her tiny hand in front of the old woman, who went deadly still, immobilized by magic.

*Amazing. The child's abilities were greatly advanced for one so young.*

"You're very powerful, little one," Judah said. He had never known an Ansara or a Raintree to possess so much power at such a young age. "I don't know of any five-year-olds capable of—"

"I'm six," she told him, her shoulders straight, her head held high. A true princess.

"Hmm… But even at six, you are far more advanced than other Raintree children, aren't you?"

She nodded. "Yes. Because I am more than Raintree."

"Are you indeed?" He glanced at the stricken expression on Sidonia's partially frozen face and realized that not only had the girl immobilized the old woman's limbs, she had rendered her temporarily mute.

"You don't know who I am, do you?" the little girl asked. When she smiled at him, Judah's gut tightened. There was something strikingly familiar about her smile.

"I believe you're Mercy Raintree's child, aren't you?"

She nodded.

"Do you know who I am?" he asked, his curiosity piqued by the child's precocious nature. He sensed an unnatural strength in her…and a kinship that wasn't possible.

She nodded again, her smile widening. "Yes, I know."

This child could not possibly know who he was. He kept his true identity protected from all who were not Ansara. "If you know who I am, what is my name?"

"I don't know your name," she admitted.

Judah sighed inwardly, relieved that he had overestimated the child's abilities and had been mistaken about the momentary sense of a familial bond. Oddly drawn to the little girl, he approached her, knelt on his haunches so that they were face-to-face and said, "My name is Judah."

She held out her little hand.

He looked at her offered hand. Oddly enough, the thought of killing this child—Mercy's child—saddened him. He would make sure her death was as quick and painless as Mercy's.

He took her hand. An electrical current shot through Judah, unlike anything he had ever experienced. A raw, untamed power of recognition and possession.

"Hello, Daddy. I'm your daughter, Eve."

An earsplitting scream shook the semi-dark bedroom as Mercy Raintree woke from her healing sleep.

# THREE

The sound of her own scream resounded inside Mercy's head, and for a split second she thought she was dreaming that her worst nightmare had come true. As the echoes of her terrified scream shivered all around her, remnants of a fear beyond bearing, she awoke to the reality of her nightmare. Her eyes opened and quickly adjusted to the semidarkness around her.

"Mommy!" Eve's concerned cry prompted Mercy into immediate action. Telepathically, she called her child to her, and within seconds she rose from the bed and took her daughter into her protective embrace.

"What's wrong, Mother?" Eve asked. "You mustn't be afraid."

The moment Mercy had prayed would never come was here, descending upon them like an evil plague from the depths of hell. Judah Ansara, a true prince of darkness, stood hovering over her and Eve, his icy gray eyes staring at her, questioning her, demanding answers.

"Sidonia?" Mercy said, fearing that Judah had disposed of her beloved nanny.

"Oh!" Eve gasped, then eased out of Mercy's arms, turned and waved her hand.

Mercy followed her child's line of vision to where Sidonia's body came to life, having been released from its immobile state. "Eve, did you...?"

"I'm sorry, Mother, but Sidonia didn't want me to meet my daddy. She tried to stop me from talking to him."

Mercy's gaze reconnected with Judah's. Those cold eyes shimmered with hot anger.

*She is mine!* Judah's three unspoken words filled the room, expanding, exploding, shaking the walls and windows.

"Stop!" Mercy cried, shoving Eve behind her. "Your rage accomplishes nothing."

Judah grabbed Mercy by the shoulders, his fingers biting into her flesh. When Mercy whimpered in pain, Eve reached up and placed her hand on Judah's arm.

"You must be gentle with my mother. I know you don't want to hurt her."

Judah's tenacious hold loosened as he glanced from Mercy's face to Eve's, and then back to Mercy. "I won't harm your mother." He glanced over at Sidonia, who glared at him with bitter hatred. "Go with your nanny, child. I need to speak to your mother alone."

"But I don't want to——" Eve whined.

*Do as I tell you to do.* Mercy heard the silent message Judah issued to Eve and realized that he instinctively knew Eve would hear his thoughts.

Eve looked to her mother. Mercy nodded. "Go with Sidonia. Let her put you to bed. You and I will talk in the morning."

Eve kissed Mercy on the cheek. "Good night, Mother." Then she tugged on Judah's arm and motioned for him to bend over, which he did after releasing his hold on Mercy. Eve kissed his cheek, too. "Good night, Daddy."

Neither Mercy nor Judah spoke until Sidonia took Eve away and closed the bedroom door behind them.

The moment they were alone, Judah turned on Mercy. "The child is mine?"

Mercy stood and faced her greatest fear—her child's father. "Eve is mine. She is Raintree."

"Yes, she is Raintree," Judah replied. "But she is more. She told me so herself."

"Eve has great power that she is far too young to understand. Telling herself that she is more than Raintree helps explain these things to her so that her child's mind can accept them."

"Do you deny that she is mine?"

"I neither deny nor confirm—"

"She knew me instantly," Judah said.

Was there any way she could lie to this man and convince him that Eve was not his? For nearly seven years, since the moment she conceived Judah Ansara's child, she had kept that knowledge hidden from him and from the entire world, even from her own brothers. Only Sidonia knew the truth of Eve's paternity. Until now.

"What are you doing here on Raintree land?" Mercy asked.

He eyed her speculatively. "You don't remember?"

Unsure about what he meant, she didn't respond as she sorted through her last coherent thoughts before blacking out. It was not unusual for her to faint or to simply fall asleep after a healing, but in this instance, her restorative sleep had been far deeper than normal.

She recalled the car accident and saving the sole survivor by removing her terrible pain, then transposing enough of her own strength and healing power to keep the woman alive.

Suddenly she felt the memory of a forceful grip around her neck, cutting off her air, choking her. Mercy gasped, her gaze shooting to Judah. Taking several calming breaths, she captured those frightening moments buried deep in her subconscious and realized that someone had tried to erase those memories.

"You didn't want me to remember that someone tried to kill me."

Judah simply glared at her.

"Do you want me to think it was you who tried to strangle me?" she said. "I know it wasn't."

He said nothing.

"You won't allow me to remember my attacker. Why? And what were you doing so close to the Raintree home place at the very time it happened?"

"Coincidence." His deep baritone rumbled the one word.

"No, I don't believe you. You knew someone was going to... You came here to save me, didn't you? But I don't understand." How would Judah have known her life was in danger? And why would he bother to come to the hills of North Carolina to save her, a Raintree princess?

"Why would I not save the mother of my child?"

"You didn't know Eve existed. Not until you came here. Not until she introduced herself to you."

"Why I came here is not important," Judah said. "Not now. All that matters is the fact that you gave birth to my child and have kept her from me for six years. How could you have done that?"

Mercy laughed, the sound false and nervous. "Eve is my

child. It doesn't matter who her father is." Oh, God, if only that were true. If only...

Judah growled, the sound as bestial as the man himself. No matter what, she could never allow herself to see him as anything other than what he was—an Ansara demon. It did not matter that even now, knowing him for who and what he was, she found herself drawn to him on a purely sexual level. He possessed a power over her that she could not deny. But she could—and would—resist.

Judah scanned Mercy from head to toe, his gaze appreciative and sensual.

"The protective spell you cast over Eve must be very powerful, one that takes a great deal of your strength to keep in place."

Mercy shivered. "There is nothing I wouldn't do for Eve. She is—"

"She is an Ansara."

"Eve is a Raintree princess, the granddaughter of Dranir Michael, the daughter of Princess Mercy."

"A rare and highly unique child," Judah said. "There has been no mixing of the bloodlines for thousands of years, not since the first great battle when all Ansara and Raintree became sworn enemies. Any mixed-breed offspring have been disposed of before birth or as infants."

"If there is one drop of decency in you, you will not claim her," Mercy said. "If she is forced to choose between two heritages, it could destroy her. And you know, as well as I do, that your people would never accept her. They would try to kill her."

Judah's smile sent waves of terror through Mercy. "Then you admit that she is mine."

"I admit nothing."

Judah reached out and grabbed her by the back of her neck, his large hand clasping forcefully, his thick fingers threading through her hair. If she chose to do so, she could battle him here and now, both physically and mentally. But she had learned at a young age to choose her battles, to save her strength for the moments of greatest need. Standing her ground, neither resisting nor accepting his hold on her, Mercy faced her deadly enemy.

"When did you realize I was Ansara?" Judah asked.

"The moment I conceived your child," she admitted.

His hold tightened as he brought her closer, then lowered his head until only a hairsbreadth separated his lips from hers. "That must have been the last time we had sex. If it had been before, any of the other times, you would have left me sooner."

*I didn't leave you even then, the last time, when your seed took root within me and I knew that I would give birth to an Ansara. I stayed with you until you fell asleep, assisted by an ancient sleep spell that Sidonia had taught me. And when I knew you would not awaken for hours, I searched and found the mark of the Ansara on your neck, hidden by your long hair.*

Judah brushed her lips with his. She sucked in a deep gulp of air.

"I knew you were Raintree from the moment I saw you," he said. "I disregarded my better judgment, which told me to avoid you, that you were trouble. But I couldn't resist you. You were the most beautiful creature I'd ever seen."

*And I couldn't resist you. I wanted you the way I'd never wanted another man. You were a stranger, and yet I gave myself to you.*

*I loved you.*

Even now, Mercy found it difficult to admit the complete

truth, because it was so heinous. The very thought that she had fallen in love with an Ansara was an abomination, a betrayal of her people, an unforgivable treachery.

And if Dante and Gideon ever learned that their beloved niece was half Ansara...

"You were a delightful amusement," Judah told her, his breath hot against her lips. "But don't think that I've given you a second thought in the past seven years. You were nothing to me then, and are nothing to me now. But Eve..."

Fear boiled fiercely within Mercy, a mother's protective fear for her child. "The only way you can claim Eve is to kill me."

"I could kill you as easily as I squash an insect beneath my feet."

His words proclaimed indifference, but his actions spoke a different language. Judah took Mercy's mouth in a possessive, conquering kiss that startled her and yet stirred to life the hunger she had known only for this man. She tried to resist him but found herself powerless. Not against his strength, but against her own need.

How could she want him, knowing who he was?

When they were both breathless and aroused, Judah ended the kiss and lifted his head. "You're still mine, aren't you?" He sneered. "I could lay you down here and now and take you, and you wouldn't protest."

Mercy jerked away from him, humiliated by her own actions.

"I am Raintree. Eve is Raintree," Mercy said. "You cannot claim either of us."

Judah ran his index finger over Mercy's lips, down her chin and throat, pausing in the center of her chest, between her breasts. "You are of no importance. You were nothing more than a vessel to carry my child. But Eve is very important to me. She is Ansara, and when the time is right, I *will* claim her."

Mercy sensed a frightening truth when she caught a momentary glimpse into Judah's mind. The instant he realized she had invaded his thoughts, he cloaked them entirely, shutting her out. But not before she saw her own death. Death at the hands of her child's father.

"If you kill me, Dante and Gideon—"

"Dante and Gideon are the least of my worries at the moment."

Puzzled by his statement, she glowered at him. "If you harm me, if you try to take Eve, my brothers will fight you to the death."

"The time is not right for others to know of Eve's existence." He grasped Mercy's shoulders and shook her none too gently. "I have an enemy who would kill Eve if he knew she was my child. And many others who would take her life simply because she is a mixed-breed."

With his hands on Mercy's body, he passed currents from within him into her, a physical and mental awareness that he could not prevent.

"The protective cloak I've kept around Eve since before she was born has been penetrated," Mercy said. "This was your doing. If you truly wish to keep her safe, you have to help me form a stronger barrier around her. Now that she is aware of you and you of her, it will take both of us to protect her. Will you help me?"

"Do you actually trust me to protect her?" Judah ran his hands up and down Mercy's arms, then released her. "After all, she is half Raintree and the Ansara have sworn an oath to destroy such children."

"She is also half Ansara, and yet I love her with all my heart and would protect her with my own life."

"What makes you think that I would do the same?"

Mercy saw past the exterior steel crust to the center of Judah's soul. Not a soft or pliable soul, not one easily touched by the pain and suffering of others, but a male soul. Strong, fierce, loyal, protective and possessive. He had been unable to hide that truth from her seven years ago, and he still could not.

"Blood calls to blood," Mercy said. "It is true of mankind, but even truer of the Raintree and the Ansara."

"If you knew I wouldn't harm Eve, why keep her a secret from me all these years?"

Mercy hesitated. She felt Judah probing, trying to invade her thoughts again.

"I was afraid that you would try to take her from me," she said. "I couldn't allow that. If you had tried—if you try now—Dante and Gideon will join forces with me and stop you from taking her."

"They might try, but…"

Mercy realized that Judah had seen beyond the obvious.

Judah's lips curved downward into a speculative frown. "Dante and Gideon don't know that Eve is Ansara, do they? You were afraid of how they would react, perhaps afraid that they would kill her."

"No! My brothers would never harm Eve. The Raintree do not murder innocent children."

"Then who were you protecting by hiding the truth from them?"

"I had hoped to protect Eve from the truth," Mercy said. "I should have known that she would soon realize she was more than Raintree, and that eventually she would have sought you out and found you."

"Blood calls to blood," Judah repeated her words.

"Then we are in agreement—we will protect Eve."

"We will never be in agreement," he said. "But for the time being, yes, I will help you keep your secret. It will be difficult, now that Eve knows I am her father. Because she is so young, she doesn't have complete command of her powers, and that alone puts her in danger. Since she is unable to control her powers, we must do it for her. For her own protection."

"You are welcome to try. I've managed to subdue her powers from time to time, to keep them partially under control, but…" She hesitated to admit the truth to this man, this Ansara who could try to use their daughter's unparalleled gifts against the Raintree.

"Is her power that great?" he asked.

Mercy kept silent, afraid she had already said too much.

"Eve has equal measures of Ansara and Raintree power," Judah said in astonishment. "She inherited your powers and mine, didn't she? My God, do you realize…? Our child possesses more power than anyone in either clan."

"More than you or I." Mercy bowed her head and silently uttered an ancient incantation.

Judah grabbed her. She gasped, startled by his actions, not realizing that he had somehow figured out what she was doing.

"It won't work," he told her. "You cannot use your magic on me. Surely you know I won't allow you to—"

Mercy focused, sending a sharp mental blow to Judah's body, hitting him square in the stomach. He groaned as the shock wave hit him, then narrowed his gaze, burning through the shield around Mercy, retaliating with a searing pain that radiated from her belly. She cried out, then vanquished the fire inside her.

"Do you truly believe you are as strong as I am, that you are capable of defeating me?" he asked.

"Yes."

He stared at her, apparently skeptical, unable to believe that her power not only equaled his but might surpass it. As they stood there glaring at each other, neither backing down nor escalating the battle, Judah studied her intently.

"You're different," he told her. "And it's more than that you've matured into the premiere empath that you are today. That was always your destiny."

She held her breath, realizing that he was on the verge of understanding a truth that even she herself had not wanted to accept.

"Having my child changed you," Judah said. "Giving birth to Eve increased your powers. You, too, are more than Raintree, aren't you?"

"No, I am not—"

"Quiet!" Judah issued the order in a commanding manner. "Control your tongue and your thoughts."

"Why? Tell me—what are you so afraid of? Is this enemy of yours powerful enough to threaten your very life?"

Judah ruled the Ansara, his power unequaled by any other, not even his half brother. He, not Cael, was the superior, the mightiest of all Ansara, but he could control his brother only to a certain extent and only for brief periods of time. Cael was at this very moment fighting the spell that had quieted his telepathic abilities. His fiendish curses were bombarding Judah, who knew he could not deal with Mercy Raintree and Cael Ansara at the same time. Both were powerful creatures, each his enemy.

Cael's thoughts converged into a jumbled mass of hysteria

and rage, but as he fought Judah's spell, he revealed more of his inner self than he realized. Cael was determined to escalate the impending war, the final Ansara and Raintree battle, and he had set events into motion that could not be stopped.

Judah's head pounded with the knowledge of his brother's treachery—not only against himself but against the entire tribe. The Ansara were not ready for the final battle. Not yet. If Cael forced them to fight now, they could be defeated. And this time, they could not count on the Raintrees' benevolence. Two hundred years ago the Raintree had allowed a handful of Ansara to live, one the youngest daughter of the old Dranir. It was through her—Dranira Melisande—that the royal blood-line had survived.

"Judah?" Mercy called his name again.

"Silence!"

*Do not issue me orders,* she told him telepathically.

*If you wish to keep your child safe, protect not only your spoken words but your thoughts,* Judah warned her.

She stared at him but said nothing. Then he felt a shield lift between them. Even if Mercy knew nothing of Cael, she understood that someone—other than Judah—posed a threat to Eve.

# FOUR

"That beast is not staying the night here at the sanctuary," Sidonia said vehemently. "You cannot allow it."

"He is staying," Mercy replied. "Until we can decide how best to protect Eve."

Sidonia grabbed Mercy's arm. "He's the one you need to protect her from. He is an Ansara, the vilest creature on earth. Pure evil."

"Hush up," Mercy warned.

"I don't care if he hears me." Scrunching her wrinkled face into a frown, Sidonia spat on the floor.

"I don't want Eve to hear you. She knows Judah is her father."

"Poor little lamb." Sidonia adored Eve, would do anything for her, but she feared for the child because of her father's blood. She vigilantly watched for signs of the struggle between good and evil within Eve.

Mercy sighed heavily. "Judah will not go away meekly, and

I'm afraid that I can't force him to leave, not as long as Eve wishes him to stay. You understand what I'm saying?"

"Yes, I understand only too well—the father's and daughter's combined powers are greater than yours. And because Eve's powers are untrained, she could be dangerous without meaning to be."

Mercy nodded, then lowered her voice to a whisper. "Judah is concerned about a man who's his enemy, someone who isn't a Raintree, a man who would kill Eve if he knew of her existence. I don't know who this man is, but I'm certain he is another Ansara."

"We should have wiped their kind from the face of the earth two hundred years ago when we had the chance. Old Dranir Dante made a deadly mistake in allowing even a handful of Ansara to live."

"All that is ancient history."

"Humph." Sidonia glared at Mercy. "Why did Judah Ansara come here? And why were you with him tonight?"

"I don't know why he came to North Carolina. And as for my being with him—I don't remember everything, only that someone tried to kill me, and Judah saved me."

"Why would an Ansara save a Raintree's life?" Sidonia eyed her suspiciously. "You haven't had any contact with him since you conceived Eve, have you?"

"Of course not!"

"Hmm… There is more to this than meets the eye. I think you should contact Dante and tell him that an Ansara has shown up here at the sanctuary, that he was able to cross the boundaries of protection."

"Dante will want to know how that was possible."

"I'm sure he will."

"I can't tell him that it might have been because of Eve.... because she's half Ansara."

"You have to do what is necessary," Sidonia told Mercy.

"It's for me to decide what that is."

"That Ansara poses a threat to all of us, all who are Raintree."

"Judah poses a threat to no one but Eve," Mercy said. "He's a single Ansara, one man. What could he possibly do to harm our entire clan?"

"Call Dante."

"No."

"It's past time that you told your brothers the truth about Eve."

"No. And you won't call Dante. Do you hear me?

Sidonia nodded. "This man tricked you once, took you to his bed and gave you his child. Don't let him fool you again."

"I didn't know he was Ansara then. Now I do."

"Seven years ago, he wanted your virginity. Now he wants something far more precious. He wants *your* child."

"She's *his* child, too, as much as I wish she were not."

"I believe he knew about Eve before he came here," Sidonia said. "It's the only explanation for him coming to you after all these years. Is it possible that somehow subconsciously you...?"

"No! I've shielded myself from Judah, just as I have shielded Eve."

"You did not shield either of you when you were giving birth to Eve. You wanted him there with you. You kept calling for him."

Mercy glanced away, then turned her back on Sidonia.

Sidonia walked up beside Mercy and draped her thin arm around Mercy's shoulders. "I did my best to protect you and your child that night, because you couldn't. And if for any reason you cannot protect the two of you from him now, you must allow me to contact Dante."

"Please, go to bed and get some sleep. I need to be alone. I need time to think."

Sidonia patted Mercy on the back with tender affection. She had no children of her own and loved the royal siblings as if they were her grandchildren. As much as she loved Dante and Gideon, Mercy had always been her favorite. She had been a beautiful child. with the disposition of an angel. Even as a little girl, she had possessed a heart filled with goodness and kindness. And by the age of six—the age Eve was now—Mercy's abilities as an empath had been evident.

"I'll do as you ask," Sidonia said. "But be careful. You can't allow your heart to rule your head."

She left Mercy alone. But she didn't go to her room. Instead, she checked on Eve. The little princess lay in her antique canopy bed, her golden curls shimmering against the white embroidered pillowcase, highlighted by moonbeams streaming through the windows. Asleep, Eve was all innocence. Awake, she was a delightful little imp.

Mischievousness is not evil, Sidonia reminded herself.

*My precious darling. You must be protected. Your mother would die to keep you safe. And so would I. We have safeguarded the secret of your paternity since you were born, praying that neither you nor your father would ever learn the truth. But now that both of you know, now that Judah Ansara has come to claim you, I fear not only for your safety, but for the safety of our people. And your mother seems to have a peculiar weakness for this Ansara man that makes her vulnerable to him.*

Sidonia touched the sleeping child's cheek as she recalled the night Eve was born. Mercy had requested that no one other than Sidonia be present, acquiring a pledge of complete secrecy from Sidonia before she went into labor.

Eve had come into the world howling, as if proclaiming loud and clear, "I'm here!" Round and fat and pink, with puffs of white-blond hair and the hereditary green eyes, Eve was a perfect little Raintree. Except for the birthmark on her head, just above the uppermost tip of her spine. An indigo blue crescent moon. The mark of the Ansara.

Mercy had grasped Sidonia's hand that night and looked at her pleadingly. "You must never tell anyone. No one can know that my baby's father is Ansara."

"How is this possible? You wouldn't knowingly give yourself to one of those demons."

"I didn't know Judah was Ansara until…not until I had conceived."

"You called for him when you were in labor. Even knowing what he is, you still long for him."

Mercy had glanced away, tears in her eyes.

It was then that Sidonia knew Mercy loved her child's father. God help her.

Mercy sensed Judah's presence. Not near her, but close. Outside.

She crossed the room, drew back the lace curtain on her window and stared down at the courtyard below. Judah stood there on the stone terrace, in the moonlight, rigid as a statue, his face and body in shadowed silhouette. He had released his hair, letting it fall about his shoulders, as free and wild as the man himself. He was savagely handsome, and exuded an aura of strength and masculinity that no woman could resist.

Once *she* had been unable to resist. And for the brief span of a day and a night, she had believed his lies, had surrendered to his charm, had given herself freely and completely.

For Eve's sake, she had hoped she would never see Judah again. And for her own sake, also. As much as she despised him, she didn't hate him. Hating him would be like hating a part of Eve.

Even though she realized that he still possessed some kind of sexual hold over her, she knew Judah was her enemy. And even though he was Eve's father, he was Eve's enemy, too. Hadn't the Ansara been the ones to issue a decree that any child born of a Raintree/Ansara union would be put to death? No half-breeds allowed.

Had Judah actually come here to kill Eve?

No, that wasn't possible, was it? He had been genuinely shocked to learn of Eve's existence.

But now that he knew…

It didn't matter what he knew. He was only one Ansara, albeit a seemingly powerful wizard. But Mercy possessed equal power, didn't she? And Sidonia was not without powers, as were several Raintree now visiting the home place and staying in the surrounding cottages. There was no need to call in Dante or Gideon. If necessary, she could enlist Sidonia and the others to help her vanquish Judah…if he truly posed a threat to Eve.

If?

Was there really any doubt that Judah was a major problem? He would either claim Eve or kill her. Neither was acceptable.

As she stared outside at Judah's dark back, at his wide shoulders and flowing black hair, Mercy asked herself aloud, "How could I ever have loved you?"

It hadn't been love, she told herself. It had been infatuation.

She'd been young, a novice in the ways of the world and, in the matter of sexual attraction, a true virgin. She now knew that Judah had deliberately seduced her because he had recognized her as Raintree, and not just any Raintree, but a Raintree princess. His ability to have shielded himself from her empathic probing—something that was as natural to her as breathing— meant that either he was extremely powerful or he had been gifted with a potent spell by a mighty wizard. Instinct told her it was the former. And that led her to ask other questions.

*Just who are you, Judah Ansara? Why did you come to the sanctuary? Why did you save my life? And just how many Ansara are out there in the world now?*

The Raintree had given the Ansara clan little thought for the past two hundred years. Occasionally a Raintree would encounter a lone Ansara, but it was a rare event, leading them to believe that the Ansara had not flourished since *The Battle,* that the Ansara would never again pose a threat to the Raintree.

And there was no reason for Mercy to think otherwise. Despite Judah's tremendous power, only he posed a threat to Mercy and Eve. Whatever his reasons for coming to North Carolina, he had come alone. If he helped her protect Eve and did not betray the secret of their child's paternity...

Suddenly Judah turned around and looked up at her window—at her. Mercy gasped but did not shrink, did not turn away from his intense stare.

*Mercy.*

She heard him speak her name. Telepathically.

*Shut him out,* she told herself. *Don't listen.*

And then she heard his laughter. Deep, throaty. He was amused at her reaction.

Damn you, Judah Ansara!

Without warning, a sensation of fingertips caressing her skin enveloped Mercy. For a moment the seductive touch mesmerized her.

*Remember.*

Hearing him utter that one word broke the spell, allowing her to put up a protective barrier against temptation.

Judah turned around so that he couldn't see Mercy and walked away, farther into the backyard behind the home of the Raintree royal family. It wasn't as if the Ansara hadn't known for at least a hundred years where the Raintree sanctuary was or that it was the home of the royal family; but until Judah's generation came into power, the Ansara had not dared provoke their arch rivals. As a boy, his father had told Judah that when he became the Dranir, it was his destiny to lead his people into battle against the Raintree.

His destiny, not Cael's.

But the time was not right. It would be at least another five years before the Ansara were ready to go up against their enemy and win. If they did as Cael wanted and rushed into battle too soon, the odds were against them. And if the Ansara were defeated again, the Raintree would not be merciful. He knew this because he knew who their Dranir was—Dante Raintree, a man not unlike Judah in many ways. A fitting opponent, one who could be as savagely brutal as Judah could.

And he was Mercy's elder brother.

Judah had claimed them both as his kill. Dante because it was his right as the Ansara Dranir to do battle with the Raintree Dranir. And he had claimed Mercy because…

Because she was his, and no one else had the right to take her life.

And what of Eve?

How could he have impregnated Mercy that night? Since they had reached puberty, he and Claude had periodically gifted each other with protection. Sexual protection. If his own father had used such protection, Cael would not exist. And think how much easier life would be for all the Ansara without Cael.

Judah knew the gift of sexual protection worked with Ansara women and with human women, so why would it have failed with a Raintree woman?

Did it really matter? Eve existed. She was six years old. And she was his daughter.

She might be a tiny replica of Mercy, with the hereditary green Raintree eyes, but she was half Ansara. It was there in her spirit, in her very soul. And in her powers. Powers that would one day exceed those belonging to any Raintree or Ansara.

In days past, the Ansara had issued a decree that any child born of a tainted union would be put to death. But there had been no such child born in centuries, and as Dranir, he possessed the power to rescind the decree.

But did he want to?

Would it not simplify everything if he killed Eve now, before she came into her full powers?

*But how can I kill her? She's my child.*

If it were for the good of the Ansara clan for him to destroy his own daughter, would he? *Could* he?

Eve was a complication he had not anticipated.

A sharp pain, excruciating in its intensity, pierced Judah's mind.

Pressing his fingers against his temples, he closed his eyes and fought the pain. Cael's rage bombarded him. Curses. Threats. Dire warnings.

*How dare you freeze my telepathic powers?* Cael bellowed. *You had no right!*

*No, brother, how dare you try to usurp my authority and send Greynell to kill Mercy Raintree?*

*Greynell was like so many of our young warriors—he grew tired of waiting to confront the Raintree. If you do not strike soon, they will think you a weak leader, an old woman.*

*You have incited the young warriors, knowing we are not ready to do battle with the Raintree,* Judah said. *Your actions border on treason. Be careful that you don't force me to kill you.*

Silence.

Judah felt his brother probing, trying to lock on to Judah's thoughts. Instantly he shut Cael out. He allowed no one inside his mind, least of all a man intent upon stealing his birthright. Cael would never be satisfied until he was crowned Dranir. And Judah would never allow such an atrocity to happen. His brother would lead their people to sure and certain annihilation.

*We have much to discuss, many decisions to be made. When will you return home?* Cael asked, breaking the silence.

*In my own good time,* Judah replied, then blocked Cael, shutting him off completely, ending their telepathic conversation.

This trip to North Carolina to stop Greynell from killing Mercy and thwart Cael's machinations had not turned out as Judah had planned. He had intended to slip in and out unnoticed, leaving Mercy without any memory of his visit. But Eve's existence complicated matters.

At present, he had enough trouble without having to concern himself with a child. Keeping Cael in line had become a full-time job. And the recent attempt on his own life had cemented his brother's fate as far as Judah was concerned. He had no doubt that Cael had been behind the botched assassination. As the Ansara Dranir, it was not only his right but his duty to protect the monarchy from a toxic force such as Cael.

He should return to Terrebonne first thing in the morning. The longer he stayed away, the more chaos Cael would create.

But what about Eve?

Mercy had protected her for six years, and she would continue to protect her. No one other than the two of them—and the old nanny—knew that Eve was as much Ansara as she was Raintree.

Eve knew.

Who would protect Eve from herself?

It was only a matter of time before she would be able to override her mother's protective spells, if she so chose. And if Eve were to try to contact him, what would happen? If she were to send out vibes into the universe, there was no way to know who might intercept them.

If Cael knew of Eve's existence...he would use her against Judah.

It was at that moment Judah realized he did not want any harm to come to his daughter. Having a child made him vulnerable.

The very thought of having any weakness enraged him. But he could not turn back the clock. He could not prevent Eve's conception.

The possessive elements in his nature claimed Eve as a part of him, an Ansara, to be cared for, nurtured, trained properly, and protected at all costs. His daughter was not simply Ansara and Raintree—she was the heir to two royal bloodlines, a fact he must keep hidden. If Mercy had any idea that the Ansara had grown in strength and numbers, that they were ruled by a Dranir as powerful as her brother Dante, she would realize the danger his clan posed to hers.

When the time was right and the Raintree were vanquished, Eve would take her rightful place as an Ansara princess. In the meantime, he would leave her with Mercy. But before he left them, he had to make sure they were safe.

Yes, *they,* both mother and daughter.

Until he dealt with Cael and could be assured Eve would be safe with his people, he needed Mercy to protect their child. Once he had eliminated his brother and overturned the ancient decree to kill all half-breed children, he would take what was his.

But how could he take Eve from Mercy without killing Mercy and bringing down the wrath of hell from Dante and Gideon?

A question not easily answered, if there was an answer.

Whenever he was restless, whenever trouble weighed heavily on his shoulders, Judah would walk. Sometimes for miles. He needed the cool night air more than ever now, to clear his head and help him devise a plan before morning.

Cael threw open the doors that led outside to the deck of his beachfront home, the rage he had felt at his brother reduced to bitterness. Judah was proud and arrogant, secure in his position as Dranir. The beloved son. The chosen one.

Anger simmered a few degrees below boiling inside Cael, just enough to create rumbles of distant thunder, but not strong enough to bring lightning down or spark blazing fires.

Judah's days were numbered. Cael had spent the past few years gradually injecting the seeds of anarchy into the bloodstream of the Ansara clan. At least half the young warriors were ready for battle, eager to prove themselves. But only a handful were loyal to Cael. Judah possessed a mighty hold over the tribe.

Stripping off his robe, Cael walked down from the deck and onto the beach, then straight into the ocean. He and the water became one. Powerful beyond measure. Primeval. A force to be reckoned with. With each stroke he went farther and farther out into the sea. Fearless. Reckless.

And then he paused and willed his body to float, gliding along with the current, as much a part of the ocean as the creatures who called the earth's waters their home. Using only his mind and the more-than-human abilities he had inherited from his parents, he concentrated on transporting himself back to dry land without moving a muscle. He silently whispered ancient words his mother had taught him, adding strong magic to his supernatural skills.

His body trembled externally and internally as a current of pure energy shot through him. He felt himself lifting above the water. Even though all previous attempts to teleport himself had failed, he knew this time he would achieve his goal.

As suddenly as he had risen from the water, he fell, making a loud splash as his body shot a good ten feet down into the ocean. Forced to concentrate on making his way to the surface again, Cael focused all his energy on saving his life. After he managed to regain his composure, he swam upward and then back across the sea to the sandy beach.

He dragged himself out of the ocean, stood at the edge of water as the waves washed over his feet, and cursed the heavens. Cursed his own inabilities. How could he hope to defeat Judah unless he could surpass his brother in power and strength? The day would come—and soon—when he and Judah would face their destiny. One destiny. Winning and losing, flip sides of the same coin. Judah's defeat. Cael's triumph.

Why are you still in America, brother, still in North Carolina, near the Raintree sanctuary? What keeps you there one moment longer than necessary?

When he had conversed with Judah, Cael had picked up on a momentary flicker, just a flash of something, before Judah shut him out and protected his thoughts.

No, not a flash of something, a flash of some*one*.

A whiff of vision, there one minute, gone the next.

Green Raintree eyes.

*I have to find out what Judah is hiding from me. There is something he doesn't want me to know. A secret. A secret with green Raintree eyes.*

# FIVE

*Monday Morning, 5:00 a.m.*

Judah stood atop a low hill less than half a mile from the Raintree home, darkness surrounding him, a man alone with many decisions to make. Suddenly the small phone in the inside pocket of his jacket vibrated. He retrieved the phone and checked the lighted screen for the identity of the caller. Claude. He and his cousin occasionally communicated telepathically, but since telepathic exchanges used up precious energy, they usually simply telephoned each other. And since using telepathy also made one's thoughts susceptible to being sensed by others with the same capabilities, a secure phone was safer. The last thing he needed right now was Cael trying to listen to his private conversations.

"You're up awfully early," Judah said to his cousin.

"Where are you?" Claude asked.

"What's wrong?"

"I'm not sure. It could be nothing."

"You wouldn't contact me if you thought it was nothing. Is there a business problem or—"

"Bartholomew sent for me a short time ago," Claude said. "Sidra had a vision."

The two elderly council members had been married for over fifty years. Bartholomew possessed many powers in varying degrees, but his wife's abilities were limited to a few, one quite powerful. She was a psychic of unparalleled talent.

Judah's gut tightened. "Tell me."

"She saw fire and blood. In the center of the fire was a Dranir's crown. A Raintree Dranir. And within the pool of blood rested a gun that shot lightning."

"We know that Dante Raintree possesses many of the same skills that I do, including dominion over fire."

"Yes. That's why we assumed her vision was about him and…" Claude hesitated for a moment. "Prince Gideon works as a police detective, doesn't he? And we believe his greatest gift is connected to electrical energy and the elements, such as lightning."

"You've surmised that Sidra had a vision about the royal Raintree brothers, but you haven't told me why this is of importance to us…to the Ansara."

"The fire consuming the crown and the blood surrounding the gun both came from Cael. Sidra saw this. Before she fell into a deep sleep, she told Bartholomew that this was not a prophecy, that these events had already occurred. She believes that Cael has already struck against the Raintree Dranir and his brother."

The ground beneath Judah's feet trembled. Rage shot through him swiftly, igniting fire on each of his fingertips. Clenching his hands, he extinguished the blazes. Puffs of smoke rose from inside his closed fists.

"Cael has to be stopped," Judah said.

"He has a small but loyal following. We will have to deal with them, as well."

"We need to move quickly," Judah said. "Speak only to those you trust. Gather information. I'll be home by this evening."

"Why the delay? Sidra believes action should be taken immediately to counteract whatever Cael has done."

"There are complications here."

"Where is here?"

"I am at the Raintree sanctuary."

"*Inside* the sanctuary?"

"Yes."

"Isn't the place surrounded by a force field? How did you use your powers to get inside without alerting—"

"I'll explain more when I see you this evening."

"Do these complications involve Mercy Raintree?" Claude asked.

"What?"

"You flew to North Carolina to save her from Greynell, didn't you?"

"She was not his kill. She's mine. I thought you and everyone on the council understood my reasons for coming here to save her life."

"No one questions your right to kill her and her brother Dante in *The Battle* that is to come, but... I know you, Judah. I know you better than anyone else knows you. I have seen inside your mind."

"And I into yours, but I don't understand what you're getting at."

"I've seen Mercy Raintree in your mind on several occasions, before you were able to shut out thoughts of her."

Judah could deny Claude's accusation, but his cousin would know he was lying.

"You know that I had sex with her years ago," Judah said. "I took the Raintree princess's virginity."

"So is she what keeps you there?" Claude grunted. "No doubt she's never forgotten *you*, either."

"She is of no importance. I simply have something to settle with her before I return to Terrebonne."

"Very well," Claude replied. "I'll speak to Benedict and Bartholomew. We will call a private meeting for tonight, and make plans to stop Cael before he moves prematurely against the Raintree and brings their wrath down on all of us."

"Stay safe," Judah warned. "Don't turn your back on Cael. Not for a single moment. If he's bold enough to send an assassin to kill me, you aren't safe, either. No one who is loyal to me is safe from him."

*Monday Morning, 5:35 a.m.*

When the telephone rang, Mercy grabbed the receiver from the nightstand, sat up and kicked back the covers. She hadn't slept more than a few minutes at a time and still had her clothes on from yesterday. When she glanced down at the phone, she noted Gideon's number on the caller I.D.

"What's wrong?"

"Don't get upset," her brother said. "I'm fine. Dante's fine."

"But?"

"But there was a fire at Dante's casino."

"How bad?"

"He said it could be worse, but that it was bad enough."

"You're sure he's all right?"

"Yeah, he's okay. He phoned me a couple of hours ago and told me to call you. He didn't want either of us to read it in the newspaper or for you to see it on TV."

"The fire must have been really bad if Dante thinks it'll make the national news."

"Yeah, it probably was."

"I wish you two wouldn't shut me out all the time. If you'd—"

Gideon grumbled under his breath. "You're our little sister. We don't want you messing around inside our heads and getting involved in our private lives."

Ignoring his explanation just as she had numerous times in the past, Mercy asked, "Are you going to Reno to make sure he's all right and see what you can do to help him?" If she didn't have her hands full here at the Sanctuary, she could be on the next plane out of Asheville. But dealing with Judah Ansara was just about all she could handle right now.

"Dante said for us to stay put, that he can handle things without help from either us. But he's going to be pretty busy for the next few days, so don't worry if he's not in touch with us for a while."

"If you talk to him again, give him my love. Tell him… Gideon?"

"What's the matter?"

"Nothing," she lied. "It's just…I worry about you and Dante."

"We're big boys. We can take care of ourselves. You just keep the home fires burning and take care of Eve."

"I can do that."

"I've got to go."

"I love you," Mercy said.

"Yeah, me too."

Mercy replaced the receiver, then sighed heavily. Could she really take care of Eve now that she had to protect her from her own father? She hadn't seen Judah since late last night and had no idea where he was this morning. He wasn't in the house, that she knew for certain. She would have sensed his presence. For the time being Eve was safe from him. But where was he, and what was he doing? *Plotting against me,* Mercy thought. *He's probably making plans to take Eve.*

*Or worse.*

The Ansara were not like the Raintree, but they weren't like mere mortals, either. Given the right provocation, they could and would kill their own offspring. The evil that had taken root inside them centuries ago had altered the entire clan, making a once kindred tribe of the Raintree their sworn enemies. Judah was Ansara. He was evil. She couldn't allow herself to believe otherwise, no matter how much she wished she could.

During the past seven years, she had tried countless ways to erase her memories of the night she had spent in his arms, a willing pupil, giving herself to him completely, yearning to learn all that he could teach her. Thoughts of his lips on hers, of his large, strong hands tenderly caressing her body, his heated words of passion, tormented her, reminding her what a reckless young fool she had been. And far too trusting.

But she would not make that mistake again.

*7:00 a.m.*

"What do you mean, you don't know where he is?" Sidonia glared at Mercy. "Didn't he stay here last night?"

Mercy set the table for four, instinctively knowing Judah would join them. Wherever he was, he hadn't left the sanctuary. If he had, she would know. She felt the presence of every living creature within the boundaries of their nine hundred and ninety-nine acres. Her domain. Her responsibility.

"He didn't stay inside the house," Mercy replied. "But he is still here."

"Humph." Sidonia busied herself with meal preparations but kept glancing toward Mercy, checking on her. As Sidonia took ingredients from the cupboards, her back to Mercy, she said, "I heard the phone ring quite early this morning…"

"Gideon called. There was a fire at Dante's casino. He's fine, but apparently there was extensive damage, enough so that the fire will probably be reported on the national news."

Mercy sensed Judah's presence the moment he entered the room, only seconds after she had spoken.

"I'm surprised that one of your Raintree psychics wasn't able to predict the fire," he said.

Mercy didn't respond as she crossed the room to the pantry, removed paper napkins and laid one at each place setting. Sidonia glowered at him but also said nothing.

"We need to talk," Judah told Mercy. "Privately."

"Sidonia is preparing breakfast. Will you join us? Eve will be down soon, and I assume you would like to see her before you leave."

Judah's lips curved slightly, as if he were amused with Mercy. "Interesting. A Raintree being hospitable to an Ansara."

"Not just any Ansara. You are, after all, Eve's father."

"A fact you would prefer to forget, one that you kept secret from me and your brothers for six years."

"I can be reasonable if you can," Mercy said, finally looking directly at Judah. She wished she hadn't. He was not a man she could ignore on any level. Physical, mental…sexual…

"And being reasonable would entail...?" he asked.

"I am willing for you to visit Eve. We can arrange a——"

"No."

"If you prefer not to see her, that's——"

"I prefer to take her with me."

"I won't allow you to do that."

"I didn't say I *would* take her with me, only that it's what I'd prefer to do."

The kitchen door swung open. Wearing pink footed pajamas and carrying a seen-better-days stuffed lion in one hand, Eve bounded into the room. She rushed first to Mercy, who scooped her into her arms and gave her a good morning hug and kiss. With Eve on her hip, Mercy eyed Judah. "We will finish our discussion in private after breakfast."

"Is Daddy going to eat breakfast with us?" Eve asked.

"Yes, he is," Mercy replied.

Eve squirmed until Mercy set her on her feet, at which point she walked over to Judah and looked up at him. "Good morning."

"Good morning." Judah studied his daughter.

Eve waited. Mercy knew her child expected Judah to respond to her in some fatherly way, to ruffle her hair or kiss her or begin a conversation with her. When he didn't, Eve took matters into her own hands. She held her stuffed lion up in front of her, showing him to Judah.

"I have lots of animals and dolls," Eve said. "This one is my favorite. I picked him out myself when I was little, didn't I, Mother?" She glanced at Eve, who nodded agreement. "His name is Jasper."

Judah's expression hardened as if Eve had said something that upset him.

"Are you mad at me, Daddy?" Eve asked.

"No."

"What are you thinking?" Eve stared questioningly at Judah. "I can't read your thoughts at all, but that's okay. Mommy won't let me read hers, either."

"When I was a boy, I had a pet lion—a real one," Judah said.

"And his name was Jasper, wasn't it?" Eve beamed with delight, as if she had solved some important puzzle.

"Yes" was all Judah said.

Eve lifted her arm, reached out and grasped Judah's hand. For an instant her eyes flickered, turning from green to gold and then back to green. Mercy's heart stopped for a millisecond.

*I imagined it*, Mercy tried to tell herself. But she knew better. Something powerful had occurred between Judah and Eve, even if neither of them was aware of it.

Mercy knew. She felt it down to her bones.

All during breakfast, Eve chatted away like a little magpie, filling Judah in on her likes, her dislikes, her daily routine. Basically, she told him the story of her life. Mercy picked at her food, but Judah ate heartily.

"If you're finished, we can go into the study now," Mercy told Judah as she scooted back her chair and stood.

He glanced over his shoulder at Sidonia. "The breakfast was delicious. Thank you."

Sidonia snarled, giving him a withering glare.

He chuckled, then tossed down his napkin and stood. He waved his hand in a gentlemanly gesture and said, "After you."

Eve hopped out of her chair. "Me too."

"No," Mercy said. "You stay here with Sidonia. Judah... Your father and I need—"

"You're going to talk about me." Eve planted her hands on her hips and frowned. "I should be there so I can tell you both what I think."

"No." Mercy shook her head.

"Yes." Eve stomped her foot.

"You will stay with Sidonia."

Eve looked at Judah. "I want to go, too. Please, Daddy."

Before Judah had a chance to respond, Mercy said, "Enough, young lady. You will stay with Sidonia." She glared at Judah, daring him to contradict her.

Suddenly an empty glass flew off the table and crashed against the wall, then another and another. Within a minute, every dish, glass and cup on the table flew into the air, whirling around in a frenzy, then one by one crashed to the floor and smashed into shards of glass and pottery.

Mercy narrowed her gaze and concentrated on her daughter, using her powers to counteract Eve's and put an end to the temper tantrum. With each passing year, Eve's talents grew stronger, and Mercy knew that the day would come when her child's abilities would surpass hers. She prayed that by that time Eve would be mature enough to handle such awesome power.

"You will do as your mother requested," Judah said. "You will stay with your nanny."

Knowing she had been defeated, Eve puckered her lips into a pout and managed to squeeze a single tear from one eye.

"Sidonia, be sure that Eve cleans up the mess she made," Mercy said. "And I don't want you to help her."

"Daddy!" Eve looked to Judah to save her from her punishment.

Ignoring Eve completely, Judah grasped Mercy's arm and led

her out of the kitchen. As soon as they reached the hallway leading to her study, Mercy jerked away from him and paused to regain her composure.

"She's quite a handful, isn't she?" Judah said.

"You sound rather proud of that fact."

"Would you rather she be some sniveling, weak little mouse?"

"I imagine you were a handful when you were a child, weren't you?"

"I still am," he said, his tone teasing.

This was the Judah she remembered, a charming man with a sense of humor. If only she had known all those years ago that beneath the charm lay a wild beast, one capable of ripping out her heart. She walked away from him, down the hall to the open study door. Without looking back, she knew he had followed her. Once they entered the study, she closed the door behind them.

"Please, sit down." With the sweep of her hand, she indicated a specific chair.

He sat, lifted one leg and crossed his ankle over the opposite knee, then leaned back in the chair and looked up at her.

She sat across from him, on the sofa, and folded her hands demurely in her lap.

"Eve is my child. She is Raintree. I will not allow you to harm her, and I will never allow you to take her."

"You aren't leaving us any room for compromise."

"You're right, I'm not."

"Then let's say that—for the time being—I agree with you. I will leave Eve here with you, knowing you will continue to safeguard my child as you have done since before she was born."

Mercy didn't trust Judah. And with good reason. He had said, "for the time being." Did that mean he intended to eventually claim Eve as his?

"Eve will stay here with me until she is an adult." Mercy wanted to make sure Judah understood.

"We won't argue over details of when and what. Not now," Judah said. "I'm leaving this afternoon, and Eve will remain here with you."

"But you plan to return."

"Someday."

"Don't."

"Don't leave?" he asked, his tone light.

"Don't ever come back."

"I'd forgotten how spirited you are." His gaze raked over her. "Actually, I'd forgotten many delightful things about you."

Mercy willed herself not to react to his taunts, to show no sign of emotion. She stood slowly. "I don't see any need for you to stay a minute longer. If you'd like, I can arrange transportation for you immediately."

Judah burrowed deeper into the chair, relaxing even more. "I'll leave this afternoon. And I'll arrange my own transportation."

"Why stay?"

"I want to spend a few hours with my daughter."

"No."

"Don't make this a test of power." Judah rose to his feet and faced Mercy. "We don't want things to get nasty, do we? Not in front of our daughter."

"If I allow you time with Eve, do you promise not to harm her in any way? And that includes any kind of mental or emotional indoctrination. And will you leave here without her and never come back?"

"I promise to leave without her. And there is no need for me to try to undermine the Raintree side of Eve's nature. The Ansara part of her may, for the most part, be lying dormant inside her, but one day it will become dominant and Eve will be a true Ansara."

Mercy hated Judah for painting such a frightening picture of Eve's future, but he hadn't said anything that she hadn't thought about a thousand times since her child was born.

"You may spend a few hours with Eve, but not alone," Mercy said. "Sidonia will stay with her."

"No, not Sidonia," Judah replied. "If you don't want her to be alone with me, then *you* can stay with her. With *us*."

*Terrebonne, Monday, 10:30 a.m.*

Cael enjoyed breakfast on the terrace. Alone. Although he and Alexandria had consummated their relationship and she believed she would one day be his Dranira, he had no intention of being faithful to her now or in the future. He preferred sex with human women, because they were so easily controlled. He kept a small harem of bewitched females in a secret brothel, solely for his physical pleasure. Often he shared his whores with the young warriors he wanted to woo into his service.

As Cael drank a glass of freshly squeezed orange juice, he glanced through the open doors and into the house, his gaze locking onto the television. The all-news channel was once again showing film of the raging fire that had swept through a Reno casino. Dante Raintree's casino.

Cael smiled.

He had sent several of his most talented warriors to Reno, with one objective—Raintree destruction. Dante was still alive, but they had hit him hard. Mission at least partially accomplished. And Cael had sent a very special Ansara to Wilmington, North Carolina, to kill a very special Raintree. Tabby was such a vicious little bitch, which made her perfect for the job he had sent her to do. Before *The Battle* with the Raintree, which was now less than a week away, Cael wanted the royal siblings and a few key members of the Raintree family disposed of, by whatever means necessary. Unfortunately, the siblings were still alive—but only for the time being. At least Echo, the premiere Raintree seer, was now dead, thanks to Tabby.

Cael had cast a spell that clouded the vision of the other Raintree seers and psychics, but Echo had been too powerful for his spell to be fully effective, and so she'd had to be eliminated. Although Cael believed that the Ansara were more than ready to battle the Raintree and win, he wanted to maintain the advantage of a surprise attack. That would be more easily accomplished with Echo Raintree dead and unable to foresee the future annihilation of her people.

Revenge against the Raintree. What a sweet victory it would be.

Cael's plans were coming together nicely, although he had only a handful of faithful followers. Already it was too late to turn back, too late for Judah to stop the inevitable. With the strikes that had already been made against the Raintree, it would be only a matter of time before they realized the Ansara were responsible. The high council would see that the time to strike was before the Raintree suspected the Ansara were once again a strong and powerful clan. And Judah's pleas to wait another five years would fall on deaf ears. Even he, the seemingly invincible Dranir, would have no choice but to go into battle at Cael's side.

Judah would die in battle, of course. Cael would make certain of it. And the people would mourn Judah. But on the wings of sweet victory, Cael would be swept up into his rightful position as the new Dranir.

He couldn't allow anything to interfere with his plans. He was so close to getting what he wanted that he shouldn't allow any doubts to enter his mind and make him second-guess himself.

But he could not forget that momentary glimpse into Judah's mind last night. If only he had seen more before Judah had shut him out, but he had seen just enough to worry him. Why had Judah not returned home? What was keeping him in America?

No, not what, but who? Whoever it was, they had green Raintree eyes.

Mercy Raintree, perhaps.

Had Judah done more than save the princess's life?

Whatever Judah's secret was, Cael intended to find it out. He picked up his tiny digital phone from where it rested on the glass table and hurriedly placed a call. The moment Horace, one of his faithful minions, answered, Cael said, "I need to find out as much as possible about Mercy Raintree and anyone else living at the Raintree sanctuary. Your inquiries must be discreet. We can't risk Judah finding out. Do you understand?"

"Yes, my lord, I understand."

"I need the information immediately."

Cael laid the phone back on the table, picked up his fork and devoured the eggs Benedict his cook had prepared for him. Perfect. To his exact specifications. Once he was Dranir, everything would be done to his specifications by every person on earth. Not only every Ansara but every human, would worship him as the god he was destined to become.

# SIX

Judah had always known that, as the Ansara Dranir, he would one day be expected to provide the clan with an heir to the throne. But he hadn't actually given fatherhood a thought, and if he had, he would have seen himself as the father to a male heir. Females were different, be they human, Ansara or Raintree. A daughter needed a type of protection that a son didn't. Protection from men such as he had always been.

As he watched Eve picking wildflowers in the meadow, he thought about what she represented, not only to him, but to the Raintree. A mixed-breed child had not been born in many centuries, and none had been allowed to live beyond infancy in thousands of years. During his studies as a youth, he had thought the ancient tales of such children were little more than fabrications by the venerable Ansara scribes. Supposedly such a child possessed not only the unique abilities of each parent, making him or her more powerful than either parent alone, but if the parents were royals, the child would possess the ability to create a new and unique clan that was neither Ansara nor Raintree.

*Is that what you are, my little Eve? The mother of a new clan?*

Nonsense! The day would come when Eve would be completely Ansara, and even if he fathered other children in the future, she could still become the Ansara Dranira. It would be his choice to make.

But would Eve want to rule the clan that had wiped her mother's people from the face of the earth? Would she willingly join forces with the man who had killed her mother?

"Daddy, watch!" Eve called, as she dropped her handpicked bouquet on the ground. "I can do a somersault."

"Be careful," Mercy cautioned. "Don't show off."

Ignoring her mother, Eve bounded up on her hands and flipped over, again and again, until she moved so quickly that her little body became a whirling blur.

Judah smiled. She was most definitely showing off. For him.

"Eve! Stop that before you hurt yourself."

"Leave her alone," Judah said. "She's having fun. I used to do all sorts of things to make my parents pay attention to me."

Suddenly Eve slowed, and the force she had used to create such rapid speed came to a screeching halt, projecting her small body a good twenty feet through the air.

"Oh, my God!" Mercy cried.

Before Eve's body hit the ground, she wavered several inches above the grassy earth where she would have fallen if not for her parents' intervention. Mercy glanced at Judah and he at her, and he realized that both of them had used their powers to protect Eve.

Judah walked across the meadow while his thoughts kept Eve suspended in thin air. She turned her head sideways and smiled at him as he approached. He reached out and pulled Eve into his arms.

"Mother's angry," Eve said.

"Leave your mother to me."

Mercy came up alongside Judah and glowered at Eve. "I've warned you about doing that. You can't control your powers, and until you can, you must curtail your—"

"She has to practice, doesn't she?" Judah said as he set Eve on her feet.

Eve looked up at Judah with absolute adoration. Mercy winced.

"There are safer ways to practice," Mercy said.

Eve clutched Judah's hand, as if she knew he would protect her from her mother's displeasure. "Daddy can help me with my lessons."

"No!" Mercy all but screamed the one word response.

"Why not?" Eve whined.

"Because your father is leaving today." Mercy shot Judah a warning glare, daring him to contradict her.

"No, Daddy, please don't leave." Eve tugged on Judah's arm. "I want you to stay."

"I have to go," he told her. "I can't stay."

"You're making him go away!" Eve shouted at Mercy. "I hate you! I hate you!"

Eve clenched her teeth tightly and narrowed her gaze, concentrating on her mother. Without warning, a high wind came up and the sky turned gray. Streaks of lightning shot out of the clouds and hit in several spots surrounding Mercy.

*Stop!* Judah ordered his daughter. *I know you're angry, but you might hurt your mother. You don't want to do that, do you?*

Immediately the wind died down, though the thunder continued to rumble repeatedly. Within moments the sky cleared and the sun reappeared.

Judah began to understand his daughter's true powers. He had never known a child of six who was capable of half of what he'd seen from Eve. And he also understood Mercy's concern for their child. Untutored power such as Eve possessed most certainly could be dangerous, not only to others but to Eve herself.

With tears caught in her long, honey-gold lashes, Eve ran straight to Mercy and threw her arms around her mother's unsteady knees. "I'm sorry, Mommy. I didn't mean it. I'd never hurt you. I love you. I don't hate you."

Mercy lifted Eve into her arms and hugged her fiercely to her breast. Judah exchanged a glance with Mercy and noted the sheen of tears in her eyes.

"I know. I know." Mercy soothed her remorseful child. "You must promise me that you will try harder to control your temper and not use your powers when you're angry."

"I—I promise…I'll try." Eve clung to her mother.

Judah turned and walked away.

"Daddy!"

He paused and glanced over his shoulder. Eve was resting on her mother's hip, her bright Raintree eyes shimmering with tears. "Will you come back to see me very soon?"

"I'll come back to see you when the time is right," Judah replied.

*2:00 p.m.*

The house was unusually quiet, with Sidonia working in the herb garden and Eve taking an afternoon nap. Mercy sat alone in her study, the blinds drawn, the lights out, and thought about her predicament. Judah was gone. But for how long? He had left with nothing settled between them. In less than twenty-four hours he had saved her life, discovered he had a daughter and turned their world upside down.

Who had tried to kill her last night, and why? How could Judah have known? And why would he bother to save her life? Was it possible that like her, he had never been able to forget their brief time together?

*Stop thinking romantic nonsense!*

*Judah Ansara is no mortal man, nor is he Raintree. He doesn't love, he conquers. And that's all you were to him—a very special conquest. Never forget that he knew you were a Raintree princess before he took you to his bed.*

For all these years, she had been certain that if she ever saw Judah again, she would feel nothing except fear for her child. She was afraid, deathly afraid, of what Judah might yet do. But she wouldn't lie to herself. There was more to her feelings for him than fear.

*Sexual attraction is a powerful thing.*

She suspected that Judah was not as indifferent to her as he had proclaimed. And perhaps, if that was true, she could use it to her advantage. Just how far would she be willing to go to protect Eve? As far as was necessary, even if it meant seducing Judah and using her feminine wiles on him.

*Be totally honest with yourself. You know what has to be done.*

Yes, she knew. There was only one sure way to protect Eve

from her father. Even if Eve never forgave her, Mercy had no choice but to kill Judah.

The thought of killing the man she had once loved, or at least had believed she loved, created a tightening in her chest. She had been born to heal, not destroy. But she had also been born a Raintree princess. The blood of warriors, both male and female, flowed in her veins.

Mercy looked above the mantel over the fireplace and visually inspected the golden sword hanging on the wall. Dranira Ancelin's sword, the one she had used in *The Battle* against the Ansara. Her ancestress had also been an empath, a healer who had used her powers for good. But when called upon to defend her clan, she had fought alongside her husband. When they came to the mountains of North Carolina and built a refuge for themselves and their people, Ancelin had placed her sword above the fireplace in what had then been the living room of her home. The jewel-encrusted, golden sword had not been removed from that spot in two centuries.

"That sword has great power," her father had once told her. "It can be used for no other purpose than to defend the Raintree, and only a female descendant of Ancelin can remove it from the wall."

She had always known the sword was hers and sensed that someday she would be called upon to use it. But she had never thought that she would use it to kill her child's father.

"Judah. Oh, Judah…"

*Mercy?*

She heard Judah's voice as clearly as if he were standing at her side.

Had he heard her thoughts? Did he know that she…?

*Judah?*

*Why have you contacted me?* he asked telepathically.

*I didn't contact you. You contacted me.*

Silence.

Hurriedly, Mercy protected her thoughts, although she had believed she was already safe from anyone's mental probing.

She heard Judah's laughter.

*I don't want to talk to you,* she told him. *Go away.*

*I would if I could.*

*What do you mean by that?*

*Have a talk with our daughter. Tell her that she mustn't connect us again.*

*Eve did this?* Mercy asked. *That mischievous little... Eve, you're listening, aren't you? Cut the connection now. Your father and I do not want to—*

*Sooner or later you'll have to talk to each other again,* Eve said.

Silence. Eve had severed the connection to Judah. And to herself.

Mercy sighed, then walked across the room and stopped in front of the fireplace. She lifted her hand to Ancelin's sword and caressed the jewels glimmering in an intricate design on the hilt.

When Judah returned—and she knew that someday he would come back for Eve—she would do what any mother would do to protect her child from certain damnation. She would fight the devil for her daughter's soul.

*Beauport, on the island of Terrebonne*
*Monday Evening, 8:15*

When Judah arrived at Claude's home, half a mile from his own palatial estate, Claude's wife, Nadine, met him at the door. After bowing to him and then welcoming him with a kiss on the cheek, she escorted him into the large, open grand room of their elegant home. As instructed, Claude had assembled members of the high council whom he trusted without question. When Judah entered the room, everyone stood and bowed. Claude and Nadine were as dear to Judah as any beloved brother and sister could be. And he respected few as he did Councilman Bartholomew and Councilwoman Sidra. He quickly studied the others congregated, including Galen, Tymon, Felicia and Esther. His cousin Alexandria was conspicuously absent. Undoubtedly Claude shared Judah's suspicions, believing that Alexandria had aligned herself with Cael.

Judah looked directly at Claude. "What have you been able to find out?"

"As you know, we have several spies in Cael's camp," Claude said. "Each one reports to a different council member under the guise of trying to persuade the council member to be sympathetic to Cael's cause."

"Yes, yes," Judah said impatiently.

Claude looked to Galen, who bowed to Judah again before he spoke. "I have learned that Cael has promised Alexandria that she will be his Dranira when he becomes Dranir. There can be no doubt that she is working with Cael against you, my lord."

Judah nodded, not at all surprised to have his suspicions confirmed.

Claude turned to Tymon, who bowed before speaking to Judah. "Although we have no actual proof, we know that Cael sent Stein to kill you." Tymon glanced around the room. "We are in agreement that this crime cannot go unpunished."

"It won't," Judah assured them.

"Taking Cael down will involve others," Claude said. "A

group of young warriors, as well as Alexandria and two other council members."

"They will all be dealt with," Judah told his cousin.

"When?" Galen asked.

"Soon," Judah replied.

Galen bowed his head in a show of respect.

Claude then looked to Felicia, who walked forward, bowed, then locked her gaze with Judah's. "My lord, your brother not only sent Greynell to kill the great Raintree empath, Princess Mercy, but he ordered strikes on both of the royal brothers."

Felicia waited for a response from Judah, but when he didn't respond, she continued. "Along with hits on Dante and Gideon, Cael ordered the murder of Echo Raintree. These attempts failed. The Raintree casino in Reno was all but destroyed by fire, but Dante is alive. Tabby was sent to kill Echo and then Gideon. Unfortunately, she killed Echo's look-alike roommate instead, and now Echo has gone into hiding."

"Damn the fool." Judah's voice boomed like thunder. "Cael's actions have all but announced to the Raintree that the Ansara have regrouped after two hundred years and are now on the warpath. It can be only a matter of time before they figure out who made these strikes against them, if they have not already."

Claude placed his hand on Judah's shoulder. "I'm afraid it's far worse than we anticipated. We believe that Cael plans to strike the Raintree sanctuary very soon."

"We're not ready," Judah said. "We can't win a war against them now."

"Cael believes we *are* ready," Bartholomew said. "He doesn't plan to wait until you decide we are strong enough to defeat the Raintree. He is going to strike when *he* decides."

"And when will that be?" Judah asked.

"We don't know, but we believe it won't be long, possibly in a few months or even sooner," Bartholomew replied.

"He intends to force my hand." Judah clenched his jaw, barely managing to contain his anger. "My brother is insane if he believes we are ready to face the Raintree in battle, and unfortunately, he has infected others with his insanity."

"What are we going to do?" Sidra asked, speaking for the first time. "If you arrest Cael, his followers will rise up against us and an Ansara civil war will erupt. If you choose that path, we cannot keep our existence a secret from the Raintree. But if you choose to go into battle against the Raintree when Cael plans his attack, I see the end of our clan."

Judah walked across the room to the elderly Sidra, took both her hands in his and spoke to her as reverently as a son would speak to his aged mother. "You are our wise woman. Your visions have served us well all your life. The only two choices open to me seem to predict that the Ansara are doomed."

Tightening her hold on Judah's hands, Sidra closed her eyes and trembled from head to toe. Judah tried to pull away, but she held on to him fiercely. "The day of the Ansara is coming to an end."

Judah jerked free. Sidra opened her eyes. "You have difficult choices to make, my lord. Whatever you decide, we, your loyal subjects, will obey your commands."

Judah couldn't be sure, but he sensed that Sidra knew about Eve.

"The Dranir is tired after his trip," Claude told the others. "As Sidra said, he has difficult choices to make, decisions that require time and thought."

Within ten minutes the council members were gone and

Nadine had slipped away to her private quarters, leaving Judah alone with Claude.

"I think you need a drink," Claude said as he approached the bar area.

"No, nothing for me."

Claude paused and turned around to face Judah. "Sidra could be wrong, or she could be interpreting her visions incorrectly. She's not infallible."

"Choosing between battling Cael or going up against the Raintree on Cael's timetable is not the only decision I have to make." Judah looked deep into Claude's consciousness, needing to know if he dared share his secret with his cousin.

"Does this decision have something to do with why you were able to enter the Raintree sanctuary so easily and why you stayed there after you stopped Greynell from killing Mercy Raintree?"

"Mercy Raintree has a child, a six-year-old daughter."

Claude stared questioningly at Judah.

"My...affair with Mercy was seven years ago."

Realization dawned. "This child is yours!" Claude gasped. "She is a mixed-breed, half Ansara and half Raintree?"

"Yes, she is." Judah riveted his gaze to his cousin's. "My daughter possesses unparalleled power. She could become our secret weapon against the Raintree."

"Or she could be our downfall," Claude said.

Cael showed Horace into his home and poured his loyal subject a drink. Although he was eager to learn what this brilliant Ansara detective had unearthed about Mercy Raintree, he would play dutiful host in order to keep Horace allied with him and against Judah. He was counting on good news, a revelation of some sort that he could use against his brother. Up to this point, the first two days of this all-important week had been terribly disappointing. Stein had failed in the assassination attempt against Judah. And not only were Dante and Gideon Raintree still alive, but so was Echo. It turned out that Tabby had killed the wrong woman. Nothing had gone as he had planned.

"Sit, relax," Cael said.

"Thank you, my lord." Horace's hand trembled as he lifted the hundred-proof to his lips. After taking a sip of whiskey and gasping as the liquor slid down his throat, Horace sat, as Cael had instructed.

Hoping to put the man at ease, Cael sat across from him, doing his best not to seem overeager. "I'm pleased that you have worked so quickly to compile a report on Mercy Raintree."

Horace took a second sip of whiskey, then set the glass aside. "In the outside world, little is known of her. She seldom leaves the sanctuary, except in local emergencies and occasionally to visit her brothers."

"That is what I expected. After all, she is the Keeper of the Raintree home place."

Horace nodded. "A position she acquired when the old guardian, Gillian, died six and a half years ago. Before that time—"

"I'm really not interested in what was happening in the princess's life before then," Cael said, growing impatient.

"Very well. Where shall I start, my lord?"

"With the present," Cael said. "With this year."

Apparently perplexed, Horace stared at Cael. "As I said, little is known of her. Our psychics have tried to study her, but she has a powerful protective cloak around her, as do her brothers. We know only that she is the Keeper, the Guardian, and the greatest Raintree empath."

"She is the greatest empath alive, Raintree or Ansara," Cael corrected.

"Yes, my lord."

"Has she ventured from the sanctuary this year, other than to help in local emergencies?"

"No, my lord. She has not. Dranir Dante and Prince Gideon visited her in late March, as they do every year, but she has not visited either of them since last year. Her last trip was when she and her daughter went to Wilmington to visit Prince Gideon."

*Her daughter?* "Did you say her daughter?"

"Yes, my lord."

"Mercy Raintree has a child?"

"Yes, my lord. A six-year-old."

"And her husband?"

"I've found no evidence of a husband," Horace said.

"Are you telling me that the Raintree princess gave birth to a bastard child?"

"It would seem so."

"Who is the father?"

"I don't know."

"Hmm..."

"If you'd like, I can e-mail you the complete report." Horace fidgeted nervously.

"Before the child was born, where was Mercy living? Who were her friends? And in what hospital was the child born?"

"There is no record of the child's birth at any hospital. We assume she was born at home, at the sanctuary." Horace swallowed hard. "Princess Mercy grew up at the home place, as did her brothers. She was homeschooled. When she went away to college, several Raintree were sent with her, to protect her."

"Protect her from what? From whom? The Raintree have not considered the Ansara a threat in two hundred years."

"It is tradition that an underage princess has escorts. And just as with our empaths, any young Raintree empath must be protected from the outside world by others of her clan who can absorb the thoughts and feelings of humans before they reach the empath and flood her senses."

"Yes, of course." Cael's mind went into overdrive, processing various tidbits of information. "Do you know of any time when the princess was out in the world on her own, say seven years ago, before she became the Guardian?"

"No, my lord, but if you wish, I can dig deeper and see if I can find out for you."

"Dig deeper."

Horace nodded.

"Are there any photographs of the child?"

"No, my lord."

"What about a description?"

"No, but I can try to get that information, too, if you'd like."

"Yes, do it." When Horace started to get up, Cael motioned for him to sit. "Finish your drink before you leave, then let yourself out."

Cael stood, crossed the room and opened the doors to the patio. Until only a few moments ago, he had believed there was no Raintree heir, that if all three royal siblings were killed before the great battle, there would be a fight among the royal cousins, each possibly claiming the throne. But now he knew that Princess Mercy had a daughter, a successor.

*The child is a bastard.*

No matter. She would not be the first bastard child to become a ruler. He, too, was a bastard, and one day he would be the Dranir.

Cael was uncertain why the news of Princess Mercy's daughter concerned him so greatly. After all, the child would be killed along with her mother and uncles in *The Battle* that was to come. And once the Ansara took the sanctuary, they would prepare to go throughout the world and eliminate all Raintree everywhere.

Suddenly Cael heard a voice, as clearly as if someone were speaking nearby.

*The child...the child. She could be our downfall.*

Where had those thoughts come from? Not from him. Whose thoughts had he picked up on? Was it possible another Ansara knew about Mercy Raintree's child and was thinking about her? If so, why would anyone believe the Raintree child was a threat to the Ansara?

# SEVEN

*Monday Night, 10:30 p.m.*

Mercy looked down from her bedroom window at the patio where only last night Judah Ansara had stood. In her mind's eye she could see him glancing up at her, and she remembered the way his heated gaze raking over her body had made her feel. Desired. Ravaged. Ashamed. How could she still have feelings for such a man? Why did her traitorous body still yearn for his touch?

Until only a few moments ago, when Eve had finally fallen asleep and Sidonia had decided to rest in the adjoining room, Mercy had been too busy to think about her feelings for Judah. After he left today, she'd had to deal with Eve's tears. Her mother's heart understood her daughter's dismay over losing the father she had only just met. And there was no way Mercy could make Eve understand what sort of man Judah was. How could she tell her child that her father was an Ansara, a member of an evil clan, a deadly enemy of the Raintree?

By the time she had pacified Eve by allowing her to try out several of her powers to a limited degree—something Eve loved to do— Mercy had been faced with a Raintree crisis. Sisters Lili and Lynette had arrived at the sanctuary, both over-wrought and greatly concerned because suddenly and without warning each had lost her most powerful ability: her psychic ability to look into the future. Lili and Lynette, distant cousins to the royal family, were in their late twenties and had mastered their gifts, but neither possessed the psychic power that Echo did. Once Echo matured and learned to harness her great power, she would be the premiere Raintree seer.

After working with Lili and Lynette, Mercy's first impression had been that someone had cast a spell to blind the sisters' sight. But who would have done such an unkind thing, and for what reason? She had assigned the sisters a cabin and promised to work with them again tomorrow to help them regain their lost talent. If she couldn't heal them, then she would have no choice but to contact Dante and inform him that someone in their clan was playing wicked tricks. But she wouldn't bother her brother this week. He had enough problems of his own, dealing with the aftermath of the casino fire.

As if having to pacify Eve and begin the healing process with Lili and Lynette hadn't been enough for one afternoon, she had been called upon to deal with a human who had tried to enter the sanctuary. He had been rendered unconscious by the force field protecting the acreage, so Mercy had restored him and sent him on his way after convincing him that he had received a severe shock from an electrified fence. It had been easy enough to plant the false memory in his mind. He wasn't the first human who had tried to **trespass**, and he probably wouldn't be the last.

Mercy was mentally and emotionally weary, as well as physically tired. She doubted she would sleep much tonight. She needed to devise a plan to deal with Judah.

*You mean a plan to kill him,* an inner voice said.

But she didn't have to figure out a way to eliminate Judah tonight, did she? After all, it wasn't as if he would return for Eve tomorrow. It could be months, even years, before he came for her. *But what if it's not? What if...?*

The telephone rang. Startled, Mercy shivered and glanced at the bedside clock. A call this late in the evening was no doubt more bad news. Rushing to the telephone on the nightstand, she caught her bare toe on the wool rug and barely managed to right herself. Clumsy. She reached the phone before the fifth ring and didn't bother checking the Caller I.D.

"Hello," Mercy said.

"Hi, yourself. Are you okay? You sound out of breath."

"Echo?"

"Yeah, it's me."

"I'm fine. But you're not all right, are you?" Mercy said, sensing her young cousin's uneasiness. "Tell me what's wrong."

"Look, before you get all bent out of shape, I'm all in one piece and I'm safe."

"Safe from what?"

"Gideon didn't call you, did he?"

"He phoned early this morning to tell me about the fire at Dante's casino, but he didn't mention you."

"He didn't know about it then."

Mercy closed her eyes and concentrated, bringing her clair-empathy powers into play. She made a habit of using her lesser powers, such as her ability to sense the emotional and physical condition of others from a distance, only when necessary.

Echo was an emotional wreck but was putting up a brave front. And she was scared.

"Who are you afraid of?" Mercy asked.

"Jeez, I wish you wouldn't do that without telling me. You're probing around inside me, and I didn't give you permission to."

"You called me. I didn't call you," Mercy reminded her.

"You're right. Sorry. I'm in Charlotte, staying with a friend. Dewey. I've told you about him."

"The saxophone player?"

"Yeah, that's him. Anyway, Gideon knows where I am. As a matter of fact he sort of sent me here. You see…well… somebody killed my roommate, Sherry, last night and… well…you know how Gideon can talk to spirits and all—"

"Do you need to come to the sanctuary?" Mercy asked.

"God, no! I'm fine right here. Honest. It's just there's a possibility that whoever killed Sherry killed her by mistake. You see, she'd dyed her hair blond and pink, just like mine, and—"

"Have you had any visions recently about being in danger?"

Echo laughed nervously. "Gideon asked me the same question."

"Well?"

"Heck, I don't know. You know what it's like with me. I'm always getting these weird visions."

"Come home," Mercy said.

"Nah, I'll stay here for a few days, then we'll see."

"Echo, be careful. Just in case."

"Sure thing."

Lost in thought, Mercy held the phone for a bit too long after Echo hung up, long enough so that she heard the recorded message asking her to hang up and dial again. She placed the receiver on the base and sat on the edge of the bed. Echo was such a free spirit, so independent. Mercy worried about her because her parents didn't. They were too busy jet setting around the world.

Who would want to kill a sweet girl like Echo? Okay, so she had some really flaky friends, like Dewey the saxophone player, and she did play in a band. Musicians were notorious for taking drugs. Was it possible that Echo had heard or seen something she shouldn't have? Or could it be even more ominous? Maybe she'd had a vision that threatened someone.

Mercy didn't like the idea that three Raintree psychics—

"Mommy!"

Mercy's heart stopped when she heard Eve's terrified scream. She jumped up, yanked open her bedroom door and raced across the hall to her daughter's room. When she flung open the door and rushed into the semidarkness, she saw Sidonia trying to calm Eve, but Eve was fighting Sidonia not only with all her physical strength but with a little magical power kicking in, too. Books and dolls and stuffed animals flew around the room, whirling and spinning as if hanging from invisible wires and being propelled by a storm-force wind.

"Mommy!"

Mercy concentrated on breaking the energy that kept the objects levitated. Eve didn't fight her, so within seconds all the objects dropped to the floor, a book hitting Mercy on the arm and two stuffed animals grazing Sidonia's head. Sidonia moved aside as Mercy sat down on the side of the bed and took Eve into her arms.

"It's all right, sweetheart. Mommy's here. Mommy's here."

Eve clung to Mercy, her small body trembling uncontrollably.

"Did you have a nightmare?" Mercy asked.

"It wasn't a nightmare." Eve's voice quivered.

When Mercy smoothed Eve's long, blond curls out of her face, she realized her daughter was sweating profusely, her hair and face damp with perspiration.

"My daddy's in trouble," Eve said. "We have to help him."

Mercy exchanged a quick, concerned glance with Sidonia, then concentrated fully on her child. "It must have been a nightmare. I'm sure your father is all right."

"He wants to kill my daddy."

"Who wants to kill your father?"

"That evil man. He hates my daddy and wants to kill him."

"What?"

"I won't let him hurt my daddy." Eve grabbed Mercy's hand. "We have to help Daddy."

"All right," Mercy said. "In the morning we'll contact your father, and you can warn him that someone evil wants to harm him."

"Why can't I talk to Daddy tonight?"

Knowing how stubborn Eve was, Mercy realized that there was only one way to reassure her daughter. "If you need to contact Judah right now, then go ahead."

"No!" Sidonia cried. "What are you thinking, letting her use such powers without testing her first? And to contact that man…"

Mercy glanced over her shoulder at Sidonia. "Eve has already spoken to her father. As a matter of fact, she connected my mind and Judah's and listened in. Didn't you, my little minx?"

"Heaven help us," Sidonia mumbled.

"Go to bed in your own room," Mercy said. "I'll stay the night with Eve."

Grumbling all kinds of dire warnings, Sidonia shook her head sadly, then left mother and daughter alone.

Eve looked up at Mercy and asked, "May I talk to my daddy now?"

"Yes, you may."

Mercy didn't doubt that there was someone out there, besides herself, who wanted Judah Ansara dead. Although she knew very little about him, she did know that he was probably enormously wealthy. When they'd first met, his lifestyle had indicated he was a man with a vast fortune. He had told her that he was an international banker. Being an Ansara, he was hardly a legitimate businessman. There was no telling how many illegal deals he had bartered and how many enemies he had made over the years.

Eve closed her eyes and concentrated. While she was deep in thought, Mercy held Eve's hand and connected to her daughter's mind, sharing her consciousness.

*Daddy.*

No response.

*Daddy, can you hear me?*

Silence.

Eve opened her eyes and looked at Mercy. "He's not answering me. He won't let me in."

Mercy sensed that her child was on the verge of another psychic hissy-fit. She squeezed Eve's hand. "We'll try together."

Eve's precious smile melted her mother's heart. *Judah's smile.*

Mercy was grateful that Eve resembled her so much, with her slender frame and blond hair; and thankfully, she had been born with the Raintree eyes. Unfortunately, she also bore the Ansara blue crescent moon birthmark, which lay hidden beneath her hair. And from the first moment Eve had smiled, Mercy had known that she had inherited her father's mouth.

After Eve closed her eyes, Mercy did, too, and together they called out to the same man.

*Daddy.*

*Judah.*

*Beauport, Terrebonne, the royal palace, 11:00 p.m.*

Judah sat alone in his bedroom, unable to rest, his mind filled with thoughts of the secret council meeting earlier that evening. There had to be a way to stop Cael without plunging the Ansara into a bloody civil war. It had taken them two hundred years to regroup and rebuild after *The Battle* with the Raintree. Hiding away on this island in the Caribbean, slowly growing in size and strength until they were once again a mighty clan, the Ansara now ruled a vast economic empire, fueled by both legal and illegal activities worldwide. As far as the world of mankind knew, Judah Ansara was a banker.

*Daddy.*

*Judah.*

What the hell?

He heard Eve's voice. And Mercy's.

*Daddy, please answer me. I have to warn you.*

*Stop this now!* Judah sent the mental message with harsh force, enough to startle Mercy without harming Eve. *If you must contact me, call me on my cell phone.* He recited the number. Once. Then, using all his power, he blocked his daughter and her mother completely.

By the time Judah reached out and picked up his cell phone lying on the round table near the French doors that led outside to a second story balcony, the phone was already vibrating.

He answered immediately. "Yes?"

"Judah, Eve insists on speaking to you," Mercy said.

"You must never allow her to contact me telepathically again. Do you understand?"

"No, I don't understand," Mercy said. "Explain it to me."

Judah huffed. He was the Ansara Dranir. He explained himself to no one.

"I have enemies."

"Enemies with the ability to intercept telepathic messages?"

How did he respond? Half-truths were always best. Neither a lie nor the complete truth. "Yes. I have a half brother. We were once business partners. Now we're bitter enemies."

"Then he must be the evil man Eve believes intends to harm you."

Judah heard Eve say, "Let me tell him, Mother."

"Eve wants to talk to you."

The next voice he heard belonged to his daughter. "Daddy?"

"Yes, Eve."

"He hates you, Daddy. He wants to kill you. But I won't let him. Mother and I will help you."

Despite being slightly in awe of the child his one night of passion with Mercy Raintree had created, Judah couldn't help smiling at the thought of how Mercy must hate the fact that Eve had allied herself with him. With her father, the Ansara Dranir.

But Mercy didn't know he was the Dranir, that the Ansara had once again become a mighty clan that would soon be as powerful and plentiful as the Raintree.

"Eve, I don't want you to worry about me. I know who this man is, and I can fight him on my own. I don't need you to help me."

"You will, Daddy. You will."

"Put your mother back on the phone," Judah said.

"Be very careful," Eve cautioned.

"Judah?" Was that a hint of concern he heard in Mercy's voice? Surely not. She hated him, didn't she?

"Don't allow Eve to contact me again."

"And if I can't stop her?"

"Persuade her," Judah said.

"Maybe if you called her occasionally…"

"I thought you wanted me out of her life. Have you changed your mind?"

"No, I haven't changed my mind," Mercy told him in no uncertain terms. "But Eve is not willing to let you go and I don't want her constantly upset."

What sort of game was Mercy playing, blowing hot and cold? Go away. Come back. Never see Eve again. Call her occasionally.

"Tell Eve that I'll call her soon."

"I'll tell her. And Judah…"

"Yes?"

"You know how I feel about you."

Judah smiled. "I know. I'm Ansara and you're Raintree. We're mortal enemies."

"That's right. I just wanted to make sure we understood each other."

"Sleep well, Mercy. And dream of me."

*Tuesday, 1:45 p.m.*

Cael had been informed that Judah had returned to Terrebonne late yesterday and had spent this morning in his office, was in fact still there. Unfortunately Cael didn't have any spies among his brother's office staff, so other than relying on minions who watched the royal palace from afar, he had no knowledge of what was going on behind closed doors.

He had wasted the entire morning in fruitless efforts to discover the identity of the person whose thoughts he had overheard last night. *The child...the child. She could be our downfall.* The voice had been male and slightly familiar, yet contemplatively soft and not quite recognizable.

Frustrated by his failure, Cael had gone to the brothel an hour ago and vented his anger by beating one of his whores, then taking her savagely. Refreshed by these amusements, he was now prepared to try a different tactic in his search. If he couldn't discover who had been voicing concern about a certain child and how she could be "our" downfall, perhaps he could find the child herself.

"Who are you? Where are you?" Cael asked aloud.

The doorbell rang, but Cael ignored it. One of the servants would see to it. He didn't concern himself with mundane matters.

Was the child a threat to the Ansara? *Our downfall.* What child could possess the power to threaten the mighty Ansara?

My child? Cael thought.

But he had no children. He had made certain of that.

Judah's child?

Why would the Dranir's child pose a threat to the Ansara, especially a female child?

*Are you out there, little one?*

Do I have a niece being kept hidden away so that I cannot find her? Had Judah secretly married and fathered a child? He couldn't imagine his brother producing a bastard child.

*Bastard child. The child...the child. She—*

Mercy Raintree had a bastard child!

Could it be that this Raintree child was somehow a threat to the Ansara?

*Little Raintree princess, open your mind to me, allow me entrance.*
Nothing.
*Mercy Raintree's daughter, I wish to speak to you.*
Dead silence.
If only he knew the child's name.
*If you wish to know the names of your greatest enemies, repeat these words nine times, and nine names will appear in your mind, the last name the one you must fear the most.* Even now, after all these years, he could hear his mother's voice.

"Thank you, Mother," Cael said, then spoke the ancient words of a potent spell she had taught him when he was only a small boy.

He waited for the names to appear, until slowly as if imprinted on a puff of gray smoke, the first name appeared, and then the second, the third and the fourth. All were names of council members loyal to Judah. The fifth appeared. Nadine. Then the sixth. Claude. The seventh was Sidra. No surprises.

But the eighth name puzzled Cael.

Judah.

He believed his brother to be his greatest enemy. How could there be someone of more danger to him than the Dranir?

And then the ninth name appeared, a name Cael did not recognize.

Eve.

Who was Eve?

The spell-induced vision ended, and Cael's mind cleared.

*Eve, who are you? If you can hear me, open your mind to me.*

A vigorous surge of mental energy shot through him, bringing him to his knees. As the pain radiated through him and then quickly dispersed, he cursed loudly, damning whatever force had attacked him.

Someone did not want him contacting Eve. Could that someone be Eve herself?

*You caught me off guard,* Cael said. *I am more powerful than any Ansara. You cannot win in a fight against me. Do you hear me, Eve?*

Another blow zapped Cael, sending him flying halfway across the room and landing him in a heap against the far wall.

*Damn you! I warn you. Don't make an enemy of me. You will regret it.*

*I'm not afraid of you,* a child's voice replied. *I will not let you hurt my daddy.*

Cael's heartbeat accelerated. *Who is your father?*

*I am Eve, and I hate you!*

Tapping into the child's anger, Cael returned a psychic blow and laughed when he heard the little girl's screams.

Screaming, Eve doubled over in pain, then dropped to the ground as if she'd been hit by a giant fist. Sidonia, who had been sitting in the swing watching Eve as she raced around in the yard, playing with Magnus and Rufus, rushed to the child as quickly as her old legs would carry her. Mercy, who had been picking peaches from the lower branches of one of the many trees in the fruit orchard, saw in her mind's eye what happened to her child the instant it occurred. Someone had attacked Eve! Running as fast as possible from the orchard, Mercy sent several powerful bursts of retaliation energy, disrupting the flow attacking her child and reversing the blows so that they would strike their sender.

When Mercy reached Eve, she found her wrapped in Sidonia's comforting arms.

Her old nanny looked right at her and said, "This is Ansara evil."

"Mommy..." Eve's voice was a mere whisper.

"I'm here, baby. Mommy's here." She took Eve from Sidonia and held her close.

"He's a very evil man."

"Who is, baby? Who attacked you?"

"The man who wants to kill my daddy."

Mercy's heart sank. No! Please, God, no. How had Judah's half brother, his former business partner and now his enemy, found out about Eve? Did it really matter? Apparently this man, whatever his name was, thought he could somehow get to Judah through his daughter.

Half an hour later, when Eve had calmed somewhat, Mercy questioned her about what had happened. There was only one way anyone could have gotten past the protective barrier that Mercy kept around Eve.

Eve must have let him in.

"Why did you let him in?" Mercy asked.

"I didn't. Honest, I didn't. I just heard him call my name. He said Eve. And I knew who he was. I blasted him to make him go away, but he didn't."

No, it wasn't possible. Only someone as powerful as she, as Dante and Gideon, could have broken through such a powerful protective barrier.

"I knew who he was—my daddy's enemy—so I socked him again and again."

"Oh, Eve, you didn't."

"I did, and I warned him that I wouldn't let him hurt my daddy."

"Oh, God, Eve, what am I going to do with you?"

"He thinks he's more powerful than my daddy, but he isn't. I'll show him."

Mercy shook Eve gently. "No more communicating with this man. Do you hear me?"

"Yes, Mother." Eve hung her head.

"Now you run into the kitchen and have Sidonia get you some milk and tea cakes."

Eve grasped Mercy's hand. "You come, too, Mother. We'll have a tea party."

"You go ahead. I'll be there in a few minutes."

"All right."

As soon as Eve disappeared down the hall, Mercy headed straight for her study. After closing the door behind her, she used her cell phone to make a call.

A gruff male voice said, "Why the hell are you—"

"Your brother knows about Eve," Mercy told Judah. "Less than an hour ago, our daughter exchanged psychic blows with him."

# EIGHT

There were only two Ansara psychics loyal to Cael: Natalie, a girl of twenty, who had predicted that in the upcoming battle with the Raintree, many Ansara lives would be lost but they would not lose the battle; and Risa, older, wiser, more cautious, one of Judah's discarded lovers who now often warmed Cael's bed. Neither woman possessed half the ability that Sidra did. The old councilwoman, fiercely loyal to Judah, was the most gifted Ansara psychic. To his knowledge, the only Raintree psychic who had the potential to reach Sidra's level was Echo. But that little bitch would be dead long before she could harness and control her gifts.

At his request, Natalie and Risa, who intensely disliked each other, arrived at his home together. Cael greeted the two women cordially, then personally escorted them into the living room and offered them refreshments. After they declined his offer, they obeyed his command and took seats on the sleek leather sofa.

He stood over them, glancing back and forth from one to the other. "I need information that I cannot gain by normal methods. You understand?"

"Yes, my lord," they replied simultaneously, then glowered at each other.

"What I'm going to share with you is not to go beyond this room. If it does, there will be severe consequences."

Natalie's facial muscles tightened. "I swear my loyalty to you. I'll take an oath in blood if your require it, Dranir Cael."

Smiling, Cael reached down and caressed the blond girl's tanned cheek. She returned his smile. He slapped her. Stunned by his actions, she reeled backward and gazed at him in shock.

"I displeased you?" her voice quivered.

"Not at all," he said. "The slap was merely a test to judge your reaction."

"Yes, my lord," Natalie replied.

"I'd prefer not to be tested," Risa told him when he turned to her. "I'm your loyal servant, but I am not your doormat. You'd do well to remember that."

Cael focused directly on Risa, tall, elegantly slender, with black hair and dark blue eyes. When he was Dranir, he would prove to her that she was whatever he wanted her to be. The thought of forcing her to lie prostrate before him while he walked across her prone body brought a wide smile to his face. "I will remember," he told her.

"Why did you summon us?" Risa asked, giving Natalie another displeased sidelong glance.

"I want you to work together to find the answer to a

question. I need you to seek a child named Eve. I believe she's Mercy Raintree's daughter." Then Cael added, "The little girl has powers, so be forewarned."

"How old is the child?" Risa asked.

"Six."

Natalie laughed. "A six-year-old with powers that we should fear?"

Cael nodded. "Unusual, but not unheard of. Remember, she is a Raintree princess."

"What do you want to know about this child?" Natalie asked.

"I want to know who her father is."

"What possible interest could the paternity of a Raintree child be to you, my lord?" Risa asked.

Cael barely managed to control his anger. How dare Risa question him? But for now, he would allow her disrespect to go unpunished. He realized she was jealous that he had shown an interest in Natalie, and by summoning them to his home together, he had placed the younger psychic on an equal level with the older. For the present, he needed Risa. Once she had served her purpose…

"Why I am interested in this child is not your concern," he said. "Not at this time."

Apparently finally realizing that she had stepped over the line, Risa acquiesced without further comment. She bowed her head, then turned to Natalie. "Prepare to link your mind to my mind."

The two women sat facing each other. Risa took both Natalie's hands in hers and stared into the younger woman's eyes. "Go deep and let yourself travel across the ocean to the Raintree sanctuary, but do not project your thoughts into the future. Concentrate solely on the child named Eve."

Natalie nodded agreement.

"I will clear the path for you, so that you can reach the child's mind," Cael said, certain that if he had made contact with Eve once, he could break through the barrier surrounding her once again. He found the anticipation exhilarating.

Judah walked along the beach, Claude at his side, as he so often was. His cousin had been at his side, literally and figuratively, since they were boys. They had shared many things over the years—their first taste of liquor, their first woman, their first kill. They had left the island and gone to America to college together, and had joined the business world together as young men.

"Could it be a trick of some kind?" Claude asked.

"For what purpose? If it's not the truth, why would Mercy want me to believe that Cael knows about Eve? Why tell me that he actually exchanged psychic blows with my daughter?"

"To lure you back to North Carolina?"

"For what reason? The woman despises me and has made it perfectly clear that she doesn't want me anywhere near Eve."

"Forgive me for asking, but are you sure Eve is your daughter? Isn't it possible that—"

"She's mine." Judah was as certain of that fact as he was that the sun would rise in the East tomorrow morning.

"If Cael even suspects that this child is yours, he will try to kill her," Claude said. "And no one would stop him or judge him for his actions, because he would be obeying the ancient decree to kill any mixed-breed child."

"I'm going to call a council meeting tonight. Only those loyal to me. And I will announce that I have revoked the ancient decree. With nothing more than my signature, witnessed by two council members, I have the power to revoke any decree."

"The council will want to know why——"

"I am the Dranir. I am not obligated to answer to anyone, not even the high council."

Claude paused, laid his hand on Judah's shoulder and made direct eye contact. "Is now the time to alienate even one council member? Cael is preparing for a premature war with the Raintree. The more high council members he can turn against you, the easier it will be for him to follow through with his plans." Claude squeezed Judah's shoulder. "Your brother won't stop until he kills you or you kill him."

Judah pulled away from his cousin. "Are you saying that I shouldn't protect my daughter?"

"I'm saying that your priority should be keeping Cael in check. Only you can prevent him from destroying us."

"And you think I should be willing to sacrifice my daughter's life? Don't you believe I can protect Eve and also safeguard my people from my insane brother?"

"Why is the child so important to you? You didn't choose to father her. You didn't even know she existed until two days ago. And you can't forget that she is Raintree."

Judah seethed. "Eve is Ansara!"

"No, she isn't," Claude said. "She is only half Ansara. The other half is Raintree. And she has been reared for the past six years within the Raintree sanctuary by Princess Mercy. If your daughter had to choose between you and her mother, between the Ansara and the Raintree, who do you think she'd choose?"

Whirlwinds of sand swirled upward from the beach, shooting high into the air. Fire shot from Judah's fingertips, and the ground beneath their feet trembled.

"Enough already. I get it," Claude said. "You're pissed at me for speaking the truth."

Claude understood Judah as no one else did and accepted him without question. Instead of being irritated by Judah's hair-trigger temper, his cousin usually seemed amused. There were times when Judah envied Claude's innate calmness, an inner peace that he himself didn't possess.

As Judah's anger subsided, the whirlwinds died down one by one. He flung red-hot flashes out toward the ocean, where they sizzled and died in the salty surf. Then, when he continued walking up the beach, Claude followed, neither of them saying a word. The tropical June sun warmed them, while at the same time the breeze off the water cooled them. The Ansara lived in paradise.

"I can't claim Eve until after *The Battle,* when the Raintree are defeated," Judah said. "If I try to take her before then…"

"What will you do about Princess Mercy now that you know she gave birth to your child?"

"Nothing has changed. Mercy is still my kill on the day of *The Battle.*" Judah paused and looked out over the ocean toward the far horizon. Now that she had come into her full powers, Mercy would be a worthy adversary. She would fight him with all her strength. "As long as the Raintree exist, they will be a threat to us."

"It won't be easy to kill your child's mother."

"My father had Cael's mother put to death. He never regretted it."

"Uncle Hadar hated Nusi for what she did to your mother. Nusi was an evil sorceress, and crazy, just as her son is."

"And Mercy is Raintree. That alone is reason enough to kill her."

Before Claude could respond, they noticed one of the servants from the palace, a youth named Bru, running down the stairway that led from the palace grounds to the private beach. He waved his hands and called out for the Dranir.

When Bru reached them, he bowed hurriedly before gasping several deep breaths and saying, "Councilwoman Sidra is waiting for you, my lord. She said to tell you that you must come to her immediately. She has dire news."

Judah broke into a run, flying up the rock stairs, Claude and Bru following. Undoubtedly Sidra had experienced another vision. If she said the news was dire, it was. She never panicked, and never exaggerated the importance of her revelations.

When they reached the palace grounds, they found the old seer sitting calmly on a lower level patio, her wrinkled hands folded and resting in her lap. Her husband, Bartholomew, stood behind her, as always, her fierce guardian.

Judah went to Sidra, and when she tried to stand on unsteady legs, he helped her back into the chair and knelt at her feet. As the Dranir, he didn't bow to anyone, but Sidra was not just anyone. Not only was she their greatest soothsayer, she had been one of his mother's ladies-in-waiting and her dearest friend.

Sidra squeezed Judah's hands. "I have seen the mother of a new clan. She is a child of light. Golden hair. Golden eyes."

Judah's gut tightened. He would never forget the moment when he had seen his daughter's eyes flash golden, just for a millisecond. "The child's existence—what does it mean for the Ansara?"

"Transformation," Sidra said.

Judah looked up at Bartholomew and then over at Claude. *Transformation? Not annihilation? Not their downfall? And not their salvation.*

Sidra clasped his hands tightly once again. Judah focused on her. "If you are to save your people, you must protect the child from…" Sidra's voice grew weak, her eyelids fluttering wearily. "Guard yourself against Cael, against his evil. You must reverse the ancient decree…today." Sidra dropped off into a sudden and deep, restorative sleep, as she usually did after a powerful vision sapped her strength.

Bartholomew lifted the cloak from his shoulders and laid it across his wife, then faced Judah. "My lord, you know which ancient decree she was talking about."

Judah rose to his feet. "Yes, I know."

"Sidra believes her vision to be a true one," Bartholomew said. "If it is…there is a mixed-breed child out there somewhere, a child who is half Ansara and half Raintree."

"Yes, there is."

"You already knew of the child's existence?" Bartholomew asked.

Judah hesitated. "Yes."

"After what Sidra has seen, I agree that you have to protect the child," Claude said. "Write a new decree and sign it, with Bartholomew and me as witnesses. Revoke the ancient decree that demands the death of any mixed-breed offspring."

"Claude is right, my lord." Bartholomew glanced down lovingly at his wife. "Sidra believes Cael will try to kill the child, and you must not allow that to happen. Without her, the Ansara are doomed."

"I swear on my father's honor that I won't let anything happen to the child," Judah said. *I'll protect you, Eve. Do you hear me? No one will harm you. Now or ever.*

Mercy sensed a triad of minds searching inside the sanctuary boundaries—powerful thoughts that had combined in order to increase their strength. Instinctively, she realized the psychic exploration originated from far away. Laying aside the book that she'd been reading—an ancient script filled with spells and incantations of protection—she concentrated fully on the hostile energy. It took only a minute for her to understand the danger.

Ansara!

One mind was leading the other two, guiding them as it struggled to contact Eve.

*I won't allow it.* Closing her eyes and taking a deep, strengthening breath, she concentrated on surrounding Eve, adding extra protection to the magical boundary that already guarded her.

*It's all right, Mother. I'm not afraid of him. He can't hurt me.*

*Oh, God, Eve. Don't! Whatever you're thinking about doing, don't do it.*

*Silly Mommy.*

*You'd better listen to me, Eve Raintree!*

*No, I'm Eve Ansara.*

Striving to maintain the second level of protection around Eve, Mercy opened her eyes and ran from her study, seeking her daughter. She found Eve sitting on a cushion on the floor in the living room, surrounded by an array of stuffed animals, all marching around Eve, their little stuffed appendages bounding up and down against the wooden floor.

"Eve!"

Eve gasped. Her eyes widened as she faced Mercy and abruptly aborted the spell she had used to animate her stuffed animals.

"I was just practicing." Eve's beguiling smile pleaded for understanding.

"That man—your father's enemy—did you say or do anything—"

"Don't worry." Eve stood, shoulders straight and head held high. Self-assured in a way few six-year-olds were. A true princess.

"I sent him and the other two away," Eve said. "They wanted to know who my father was and——"

"You didn't tell them, did you?"

"Of course not." Eve stepped over a tiger and a bear as she approached Mercy. "I shut them out. It made him mad." She gazed up at Mercy, a deceptive innocence in her green Raintree eyes.

Eve had been headstrong, stubborn and not easy to control before Judah entered her life, but she was always Mercy's sweet little girl who might resist her mother's wishes but would obey in the end. Without being able to pinpoint exactly the moment it had happened, Mercy recognized that Eve was no longer under her control. Perhaps it would have happened eventually, when Eve was older, whether or not she ever met her father, but somehow meeting Judah had changed Eve. And it had forever altered Mercy's relationship with her daughter.

"I love you just as much as ever." Eve wrapped her arms around Mercy's waist, laid her head on Mercy's tummy, and hugged her.

Mercy caressed Eve's head. "I love you, too."

Eve eased away from Mercy and looked up at her. "I'm sorry you're sad because I'm an Ansara."

Mercy bit down on her bottom lip in an effort to neither cry nor scream. Sighing heavily, she looked right at Eve. "I am Raintree. You're my daughter. You are Raintree."

"Mother, Mother." Eve shook her head. "I was born into the Raintree clan, but I was born for the Ansara. For my father."

A shiver of realization chilled Mercy, sending the cold, hard truth shooting to her brain. The fear that she had kept buried deep inside her since Eve's conception came out of hiding, bursting from her in a psychic energy storm that shook the entire house.

Mercy seldom if ever lost control of her powers, but this reaction had been entirely involuntary, a knee-jerk response to suspecting that her daughter's destiny was to save the Raintree's mortal enemies.

Eve grabbed Mercy's hand, instantly calming her. For one brief instant, as mother's and daughter's powers linked, Mercy felt the immense power Eve possessed.

Once again in control of herself, Mercy said, "Your father's people, the Ansara, and my people, the Raintree, have been enemies since time immemorial. Sidonia has told you the stories of our people, how long ago we defeated the Ansara in a terrible battle and only a handful of their kind survived."

"I love it when Sidonia tells me those stories," Eve said. "She always tells me how mean and bad the Ansara are, and how good and kind the Raintree are. Does that mean *I'm* both good and bad?"

How was it possible that one minute Eve was wise and powerful beyond her years, and then the next minute she seemed to be only an adorable six-year-old?

"We are all good and bad," Mercy said.

"Even my daddy?"

"Yes, perhaps." Mercy could not bring herself to tell Eve that Judah was as wicked and evil as all his kind. *But how do you know that to be true?* a taunting inner voice asked. *Judah is the only Ansara you've ever known, the only one you've ever met.*

The Raintrees' knowledge of the Ansara came from historical accounts two hundred years old.

And from an inborn psychic instinct that Mercy could not deny.

*Tuesday, 8:45 p.m.*

Three whores from his private brothel stroked and petted and pleasured Cael as he lay on black satin sheets. Risa and Natalie had disappointed him bitterly earlier today. He had sent both women out of his sight, placing all the blame for his failure to penetrate Eve Raintree's mind squarely on the psychics' shoulders. He had spent hours fuming, the anger inside him building to an explosive point.

Needing to release his rage and find temporary ease and forgetfulness, he had sent for a diversion. Each of his whores had taken her turn under his whip, screaming and begging as his blows brought blood to their backs and buttocks. Their pain aroused Cael unbearably, adding heightened sensation to the sex act. As the redhead with the talented tongue brought him to yet another climax, Cael clutched her by the hair of her head, making her scream in pain as he shuddered with fulfillment.

As he rested there, sated and sleepy, the double doors to his bedroom suite swung open as if a gale-force wind had ripped them from the hinges. Cael laughed when he saw Alexandria storming into his private quarters. No doubt she would throw a jealous tantrum.

"Send your whores away," she said, her voice oddly calm. "I need to speak to you without an audience."

Naked and reeking of sex, Cael shoved the women aside as he eased to the side of the bed and stood to face Alexandria. When he looked her in the eye, he saw neither anger nor jealousy.

With a wave of his hand, he dismissed the whores. "Go. Leave me. Return to the brothel."

The women obeyed instantly, hurrying to put on their robes

as they exited the room. Once they were gone, Cael walked over to Alexandria and smiled at her.

"You disappoint me, my love. I had expected a jealous tantrum."

"You flatter yourself if you think I care who else you screw, now or in the future. As long as I rule at your side as the Dranira, you're welcome to keep as many whores as it takes to satisfy your sexual appetites."

Cael's smile widened. "We make a perfect couple."

"Only if you can defeat the Raintree and kill Judah."

Cael lifted his black silk robe from the floor and slipped into it. "I intend to do both very soon." He reached out and stroked Alexandria's cheek. "What brings you here tonight? You said you needed to speak with me privately."

"I have learned about a secret meeting of the Dranir and three council members."

"When?"

"This afternoon."

"Who met with Judah, and why?"

"Claude was there, along with Bartholomew and Sidra."

"Sidra?"

"I don't know who arranged the meeting, but Sidra and Bartholomew showed up at the palace and stayed for several hours."

"That old witch probably had a vision of some kind. I've been careful to protect my plans from others. That is why only I know the exact moment when we will strike the Raintree. I cannot risk Sidra seeing—"

"We have more to concern us than Sidra foreseeing your plans," Alexandria said. "Judah has done the unthinkable."

Pure fear gripped Cael. He hated the fact that his brother could evoke such terror in him. "What has he done?"

"He has revoked an ancient decree. Judah signed the nullification proclamation. Claude and Bartholomew acted as witnesses."

"Which decree was overturned?"

"The one declaring that any mixed-breed child would be put to death."

"Why would Judah...?" *The child, the child. She could be our downfall.*

"What it is?" Alexandria asked. "What do you know?"

Cael grasped Alexandria's arm and yanked her to him. Eye to eye with her, he growled. "Such a child undoubtedly exists. And for Judah to revoke a decree issued thousands of years ago, this child must be very special to him."

"Are you implying that Judah has fathered a Raintree woman's child?"

Cael snarled. "Not just any Raintree woman, but a Raintree princess. Mercy Raintree has a daughter named Eve, a little girl with extraordinary power."

*Wednesday Morning, 1:49 a.m.*

Mercy debated her options. Try to handle the situation alone. Contact Dante and tell him the truth about Eve's paternity. Trust Judah to protect Eve.

If only she had another choice.

But whatever decision she made, it needed to be made soon. No later than tomorrow morning.

Sidonia knocked before entering the study. She paused several feet away from where Mercy stood in front of the fireplace, staring up at Ancelin's sword.

"Eve is finally asleep," Sidonia said. "It's time you were in bed, too. You need rest."

"I can't rest until I decide what to do."

"Call Dante."

"As much as I dread the thought of confessing my sins to my big brother, I may have no other choice."

"He'll be angry. No doubt about that. He'll want to hunt down Judah Ansara and kill him," Sidonia said. "Is that what's stopping you? You don't want Dante to kill Judah?"

Mercy snapped around and glared at Sidonia. "It's possible that Judah could kill Dante."

"That's hardly likely. You know as well as I do that Dante has not only his own unique individual powers, but he possesses the abilities inherent in all Dranirs. Judah would be no match for him."

"We don't know what powers Judah possesses, but they must be very great for Eve to be endowed with such incredible abilities."

Sidonia walked over to the desk and picked up the telephone. "Call Dante. Do it now."

Mercy stared at the phone, a war of uncertainty being waged inside her.

The study door burst open. Wearing her pink footed pajamas, Eve bounded into the room, wide-awake and all smiles. She ran to Mercy, grabbed her hand and said, "Come on. Let's go."

"Go where?" Mercy asked.

"To the front door to meet him. My daddy's coming. I let him in."

# NINE

"Judah is…?"

"Come on. He's almost here." Eve tugged on Mercy's hand.

"Bar that black devil from this house," Sidonia said.

Ignoring Sidonia's warning, Mercy went with Eve out into the hallway that led to the foyer. Sidonia followed, grumbling her fears aloud.

Just as they reached the foyer, Eve waved her little hand and the front door whooshed open. Judah Ansara, hand raised to knock, was standing on the front porch. Surrounded by darkness, with only moonlight illuminating his silhouette, he did indeed look like the black devil Sidonia had professed him to be.

"Daddy!" Eve cried as she released Mercy's hand and ran straight to her father.

Judah stepped over the threshold, the night wind entering with him, his long hair slightly disheveled, his gaze riveted to his daughter. Without hesitation, he dropped the suitcase he held, swept Eve up into his arms and kicked the door closed behind him.

Eve wrapped her arms around his neck and planted a kiss on his cheek. "I knew you'd come back. I knew you would."

Mercy watched in awed fascination at the exchange between father and daughter. Even without her empathic abilities, she would have been able to see the bond that had already begun forming between them. And knowing she was powerless to stop what was happening frightened her.

Eve's words echoed inside Mercy's head. *I was born for the Ansara.*

Unable to completely ignore Sidonia's constant mumbling, Mercy turned, gave the old nanny a withering glare and telepathically told her to hush. Sidonia glowered at Mercy and shook her head, but she reluctantly quieted before shuffling off and making her way slowly up the stairs.

Mercy took several tentative steps toward Judah. As if only then aware of Mercy's presence, he adjusted Eve so that she rested on his hip and looked at Mercy.

She couldn't explain her feelings, not even to herself. She despised Judah, and resented his presence here at the sanctuary and in her daughter's life. But at the same time, the very fact that he was here reassured her that he cared about Eve, that he was ready to help her protect their child. Their gazes locked for a brief instant; then Judah refocused on his daughter.

"I want you to promise me something," he said to Eve.

"What do you want me to promise?"

"Promise me that until I tell you it's all right, you won't use your mind to speak with anyone except your mother and me."

With her arms clinging about Judah's neck, Eve pulled

back, cocked her head to one side and looked directly into her father's eyes. "He's a bad man, isn't he, Daddy? He wants to hurt us."

"Yes, he's a bad man." Judah frowned. "Now, give me your promise that——"

"I promise," Eve said.

As easily as that, she had agreed to do as Judah requested. Mercy sighed inwardly, fearing that Eve would never question her father's orders.

Judah set Eve on her feet. She grabbed his hand. He glanced down at her and smiled. "It's late. You should be in bed asleep."

"I was," Eve said. "But when I heard you calling to me, I woke up and let you in. That's what you wanted, wasn't it?"

Judah grunted. "Yes, it's what I wanted. But now I want you to go upstairs and hop back into bed." He glanced at Mercy. "Your mother and I have things we need to talk about."

"I want a promise, too. I want you to promise me that you won't fuss." Eve looked from one parent to the other. "Be nice, okay?."

"I'll be as nice to Mercy as she is to me," Judah said.

Eve smiled triumphantly, then eyed Judah's suitcase. "You'll be here in the morning when I get up, won't you?"

"I'll be here."

Eve bounced up the stairs, a bundle of happy energy.

Once Mercy and Judah were alone, she said, "I'll arrange for you to stay in one of the cabins."

"No, I'll stay here in the house." He approached her so quickly that she had no time to react until he grasped her upper arm. "I need to be close to Eve…and to you."

Mercy's heartbeat accelerated. *He's a master charmer,* she reminded herself. He would say whatever he thought she wanted to hear in order to get what he wanted. And she could never let herself forget for one moment that what he wanted was Eve.

"You can't stay here for very long." She forced herself to maintain eye contact, to prove to him that she wasn't afraid of him, that he had no emotional hold on her simply because she had given birth to his child. "Keeping your presence here a secret will be impossible for more than a day or two. There are other Raintree visiting the sanctuary. More than half the cottages are filled. Whatever you need to do to protect Eve from your brother, do it quickly and then leave."

"I'm afraid things are more complicated than that."

Mercy eyed him suspiciously.

Tightening his hold on her arm, he said, "You have every right to be afraid."

Mercy gazed into Judah's cold gray eyes and felt the hypnotic draw of his masculine power. The only way to free herself of this man and keep him from taking their daughter was to kill him. But not yet. Not until she knew that Eve would be safe from Judah's enemies.

He raked his gaze over her as if stripping her bare, then slowly released her. Mercy shivered.

"All you have to do is ask," Judah said, "and I'll give you what you want."

Tightening her hands into fists, Mercy willed herself not to strike out and wipe that cocky smirk off his face. "I want you dead," she told him.

"That wasn't a very nice thing to say to me."

"No it wasn't, but it's the truth."

"Only half the truth." His gaze caressed her roughly, creating an ache deep inside her. But he didn't physically touch her again. "Before you kill me, you want me to pleasure you first, to lay you beneath me and——"

"You're an egotistical bastard."

"And you're a woman hungry for what only I can give you."

"You mean no more to me than I do to you," Mercy told him. "If you weren't Eve's father——"

"But I am." He focused on her lips. "And you can never forget how it was between us the night you conceived my child. The excitement. The passion." He moved closer, until their bodies almost touched, never once removing his gaze from her lips. "I remember the way you whimpered and pleaded. The way you clung to me, shivering and moaning."

Involuntarily, as if manipulated by a force she couldn't control, Mercy reached out and laid her hand on Judah's chest, placing her palm over his heart.

"I taught you what true pleasure is," he said. "And you loved it." He glanced down at her hand. "You loved me."

Mercy jerked her hand away. "No, I never loved you," she lied—to herself and to him. She *had* loved him, if only for those few brief hours before she had learned who he really was. An Ansara.

Straightening his shoulders, Judah stood tall and aloof. "Your destiny was to give me a child. You've done that. You've served your purpose."

Mercy stared at him, suddenly realizing that she had somehow wounded him. He had switched from seductive charm to cruel indifference in a matter of seconds. Had she discovered the chink in Judah's protective armor? Male pride? Or was it something far more personal?

Storing that insight away for later use, she asked, "Will he try to harm Eve?"

"What?"

"Your brother. Will he come here to the sanctuary and try to get to Eve? That's why you're here, isn't it, to make sure he doesn't harm her?"

"My brother's days are numbered. It was inevitable that I'd be forced to kill him."

"I can't imagine hating my own brother enough to kill him."

"It's Cael's hatred that will force me to kill him. He's left me no choice."

"What about your parents? Can't they——"

"Our father is dead. And Cael's mother murdered mine."

"Oh."

Judah picked up his suitcase. "Show me to a room near Eve."

"The closest room to Eve's, other than the nanny's connecting room, is mine."

"Is that an invitation?" Judah's lips curved into a suggestive smile.

"Perhaps it is." Mercy's lips mimicked his, a smile without warmth or sincerity. "But if you come to my bed, you'll have to sleep with one eye open to prevent me from murdering you in your sleep."

"As tempting as the offer is…"

"There's a guest room at the end of the hall. You can stay there tonight."

"And tomorrow night?"

"You'll be gone," Mercy told him. "You and I will settle this matter tomorrow, and then you'll leave the sanctuary and never return."

As Judah studied her, she felt him probing her thoughts.

*Don't even try,* she warned him.

*If I show you a little bit of mine, will you show me a little bit of yours?*

*No!*

*Aren't you the least bit curious?* he asked.

*No!*

*Liar.*

"Come upstairs with me. I'll take you to your room," Mercy said aloud. "And when you wake later this morning, be sure to stay close to the house. If you venture too far away during the day, someone might see you and question who you are."

"Don't you think I could pass myself off as a Raintree?"

"Not with those ice-cold gray eyes of yours."

"Point well made," Judah said.

Mercy led him up the stairs to the second floor. He paused as they passed Eve's room, pushed open the door halfway and looked inside at his sleeping daughter.

"Why do you suppose her eyes are Raintree green?"

"Because she *is* Raintree," Mercy replied.

When Judah entered Eve's bedroom, Mercy followed but didn't try to stop him.

He halted beside the mattress, where Eve rested on her tummy, her arms thrown out on her pillow on either side of her head. He reached down and touched her long, pale hair.

Mercy held her breath. He lifted Eve's hair, then parted it with his fingers to reveal the distinct blue crescent moon birthmark that proclaimed her heritage. The brand of the Ansara.

Judah allowed Eve's hair to fall back into place. He caressed her little head, then turned, looked at Mercy and smiled. And for that one moment Mercy saw love in Judah's eyes. Love for his daughter.

*Wednesday Morning, 8:45 a.m.*

Judah's cell phone woke him from a sound sleep.

Damn! Whoever was calling had better have a good reason.

He grabbed the ringing phone from the nightstand, checked the caller I.D. and answered. "Claude?"

"Cael left Terrebonne this morning."

Judah sat straight up. "When?"

"An hour ago."

"Was he alone?"

"No."

"How many?"

"We're not sure, but Sidra says only three went with him."

"Who?" Judah asked.

"We believe he took Risa, Aron and Travis."

"They could be here in North Carolina by this afternoon."

"They can't enter the sanctuary, can they?" Claude asked.

"No, I don't think so. Not unless…"

"Unless what?"

"Unless they can somehow use Eve."

"Is that possible?"

"I have no way of knowing for sure. It's possible that her presence here has somehow compromised the shield that protects the sanctuary from the outside world."

"As you well know, that shield also protects the sanctuary from those of us who do not possess power equal to Mercy Raintree," Claude said. "If that shield has been weakened, then think how much easier it would be for us to take control of the sanctuary. With access to the Raintree home place, we could—"

"No." Judah lowered his voice. "Even with that advantage, we're still not ready to battle the Raintree."

"Not yet, but surely sooner than we had thought."

"Before we alter our plans for the timing of the next great battle, I have to make sure Eve is safe."

"That will mean killing Cael before he can harm her or find a way to use her against you."

"Yes, I know. But it's either face a possible civil war when his followers rebel or go to war with the Raintree before we're ready. Moving against Cael now is the lesser of two evils."

"Do you want me to send someone after Cael and the others?" Claude asked. "Or I can—"

"No, stay there. I need you in Terrebonne. I don't think Cael will show up here himself. He'll send Aron and Travis. When they arrive, I'll be waiting for them, and if they try to enter the sanctuary, I'll send what's left of them back to Cael in a gift box."

"Perhaps you should have waited before revoking the ancient decree," Claude said. "Once Cael heard what you'd done, he must have known there was no doubt that there was a mixed-blood child out there. A child of yours."

"I had no choice. If I hadn't revoked the ancient decree, countless Ansara would have demanded my daughter's death."

"I'm sorry I questioned your decision. If Sidra says the child must be protected, then we must protect her."

"Use whatever means necessary to keep Cael under surveillance. And it doesn't matter if he knows he's being watched. In fact, all the better if he does."

The door to Judah's bedroom swung open, and Eve sailed in, like a little morning sunbeam, bright and cheerful.

"Good morning, Daddy."

Crap! Judah slept in the nude; so here he was sitting on the side of the bed stark naked. Holding the cell phone to his ear with one hand, he grabbed the top sheet with his other and yanked it up and over, covering himself properly from waist to knees.

"Who are you talking to on the phone?" Eve bounced up on the bed and smiled at him.

He clutched the top sheet, holding it in place as she scooted closer. "Let me call you back," he told Claude.

"Don't hang up," Eve said. "I want to say hello to your friend."

Judah shook his head, then asked, "Where's your mother?"

Ignoring his question, Eve pulled herself up on her knees and reached for the cell phone. Judah gave her a stern look. She hesitated, then called loudly, "Hello, Claude. I'm Eve."

Claude chuckled. "Having a discipline problem?

"She's quite the little psychic, isn't she, to have intuitively known my name," Claude said.

"I want to talk to Claude." Eve reached for the phone.

"My daughter's talents are quite impressive," Judah admitted. "Look, just say hello to her, will you?" He handed the phone to Eve.

She smiled. "Thank you, Daddy." She put the phone to her ear and said, "Hi there. You're calling from far away, aren't you?"

Judah telepathically tuned in to the conversation.

"Yes, I am," Claude replied "How did you know?"

"I know things. I have lots of powers, but my mother won't let me use most of them 'cause I can't always make them mind me." Eve lowered her voice to a whisper. "Just like I don't always mind her."

She giggled. Claude chuckled.

"I once knew a little boy like you. He possessed great power, but when he was your age, he couldn't control his powers any more than his father could control him."

Eve giggled again. "That was my daddy, wasn't it?" She looked at Judah with pure adoration in her eyes.

Damn those green Raintree eyes!

So like Mercy's.

"Say goodbye to Cousin Claude," Judah said.

"Goodbye, Cousin Claude. I'll see you very soon."

She handed Judah the phone, then snuggled up against him as he held the sheet in place over his lower body and put in a telepathic SOS to Mercy.

"Your little Eve is quite a charmer," Claude said to Judah. "Like father, like daughter, huh?"

"Could be."

"Why does she think she'll see me very soon?" Claude asked. "Have you told her that you're bringing her to Terrebonne?"

"No. The subject hasn't come up."

Eve tapped Judah on the shoulder. Turning his head to face her, he asked, "What?"

"Tell Cousin Claude I said that I'd see him very soon because he's coming here to the sanctuary."

Judah stared at his daughter.

"Why does she think—" Claude began.

"Eve Raintree, come here right this minute!" Mercy stood in the doorway, hands on hips, a parental scowl on her face.

Eve popped off the bed and raced over to her mother. "I got to talk to Cousin Claude. He's coming to the sanctuary very soon, and we'll get to meet him."

Mercy's gaze met Judah's, the concern and puzzlement in her eyes matching his.

"We'll talk later," Judah told Claude. "Keep me posted on that matter we discussed."

He didn't wait for a reply before ending the conversation and tossing his cell phone onto the nightstand. "Eve, why don't you go with your mother while I grab a shower and get dressed?"

Mercy's glance skimmed over Judah's naked chest and shoulders, appreciating his lean body, although she wasn't consciously aware of what she was doing. He returned the admiring glance. Mercy was certainly easy on the eye. The first moment he'd seen her seven years ago, he'd been struck by how beautiful she was. Even before he looked into her striking green eyes and realized she was Raintree, he had wanted her.

Clearing her throat, Mercy clasped Eve's hand. "It isn't polite to barge into someone's room without being invited." She looked at Judah. "I'm sorry she bothered you. It won't happen again." When she pulled on Eve's hand, Eve balked.

Judah grinned.

Eve yanked on Mercy's hand and motioned for her to bend down, which Mercy did. Eve whispered loudly, "I'll go to my room and play for a while. You and Daddy need to talk about me some more."

Mercy didn't have a chance to respond before Eve scurried out of the room, lightning fast, and closed the door behind her.

"She's quite a little bossy-butt, isn't she?" Judah said.

"She's a Raintree princess. Giving orders comes naturally to her, as it should. Unfortunately, she hasn't learned the art of diplomacy yet."

"Diplomacy is an overrated art. I prefer action to talk, and I expect my daughter is the same."

"Eve does like to have her own way. But she's young, and she'll learn that she can't always have everything she wants."

Judah whipped back the sheet that covered his naked body and rose from the bed. Mercy gasped. He grinned.

"If you see anything you like, you can have it. Right now."

Mercy stared at him, drinking him in, her gaze lingering over his erection. Then she looked him square in the eyes.

"Sometimes what we want is very bad for us, and we learn from experience to avoid danger."

Judah moved toward her, one slow, provocative step at a time. She stood her ground, not backing away, keeping her eyes glued to his face.

When he reached out and caressed her cheek with the back of his hand, she closed her eyes. "You still want me."

She said nothing.

From that one brief touch, he sensed her desire. "I want you, too." He slipped his hand around her neck and lowered his head. She sighed. His breath mingled with hers. She opened her eyes, and for just an instant, unaware of her vulnerability, she let the barrier protecting her thoughts weaken.

*My God!*

He yanked her to him, pressing his sex intimately against her. If she were as naked as he was... "There hasn't been anyone else, has there? You're as much mine now as you were that night."

When he kissed her hungrily, she stood there rigid and un-responsive. But when he gentled the kiss, she whimpered. As he ravaged her mouth with tender passion, she pressed both hands against his chest and tried to shove him away.

Judah grabbed her and pulled her with him as he backed up against the bed. Taking her now would be almost like taking her for the first time. She was untouched by any other man, untutored, practically a virgin.

He toppled her into the bed and came down over her, holding her lifted arms out to either side as she struggled against his superior strength. Straddling her, his knees holding her hips in place, he stared down at her flushed face, and saw both desire and anger in her expression.

"Do you think I'll let you rape me?" she spat the words at him.

"It wouldn't be rape, and we both know it. You want me."

Breathing hard, Mercy narrowed her gaze and focused on him.

He bellowed in pain, and rolled off her and onto his side. Damn her! She'd sent a psychic punch straight to the most vulnerable area of his anatomy, the equivalent of kneeing him in the groin. While he caught his breath and mumbled curses, she got out of bed and walked to the door. Pausing, she glanced over her shoulder.

"I allow you to live only because of Eve," she said.

He shot a spray of fire arrows at her, their glowing tips outlining the space around her body. She extinguished them before they singed the door behind her.

"You may wish me dead, but you won't kill me." His cold stare pinned her to the spot. "And I won't kill you. Not until I've fucked you again."

# TEN

Judah had spent the entire morning with Eve. Under Mercy's supervision, of course. She had tried to stay in the background, at least part of the time, but she didn't trust Judah enough to leave her daughter alone with him. Watching father and daughter together exposed her to a side of Judah that she hated to admit existed. In his fascination with and adoration of his child, Judah seemed no different than any Raintree father. He played games with Eve, read to her, ate a mid-morning snack of fruit, cheese and crackers with her, and watched as she tested several of her powers. He instructed her on how to channel her abilities and use them properly. He praised her when she succeeded, and when she failed, he told her that she simply needed more practice.

Kindness, patience and the ability to love were not traits she would ever have associated with Judah Ansara. Since she had fled from his bed that morning seven years ago, she had thought of him as a charmer, a seducer, an uncaring, unfeeling son of a bitch. She had hated him for being an Ansara, a clan she had been taught from childhood were the spawn of the devil.

"Let's go on a picnic," Eve insisted when Sidonia had inquired if "that man" would be staying for lunch.

"Eve, honey, I don't think——" Mercy tried to object.

"A picnic is a great idea." Judah winked at Eve. "Why don't you and I raid the kitchen and put our picnic lunch together while your mother changes clothes."

Mercy glanced down at her attire: neat navy gabardine trousers, a tan cotton sweater, and sensible navy loafers. What was wrong with what she was wearing?

As if reading her mind—God, had he?—Judah said, "Wouldn't you be more comfortable in jeans or shorts?"

"Yeah, Mommy. Put on shorts like I've got on."

"I'll change before we leave." Mercy recognized defeat and accepted it, at least on this one issue. "For now, I'll go with y'all to kitchen and help fix our picnic lunch." In her peripheral vision, she caught a glimpse of Sidonia shaking her head disapprovingly.

Half an hour later, Mercy, in cut-off jeans and a red T-shirt, found herself sitting on an old quilt spread out under a huge oak tree in the middle of a nearby meadow. Not a single cloud marred the crisp blue sky. The afternoon June sun filtered through the tree branches, dappling golden shards of light around and over them.

Eve chattered away as she munched on her chicken salad sandwich and potato chips. Judah got a word in edgewise occasionally and seemed amused by his magpie daughter's endless babble. Several times during the meal, Mercy noticed Judah checking his wristwatch. And when he thought she wasn't looking, he stared at her. She pretended not to notice the way he was studying her.

After gobbling up two chocolate chip cookies and washing them down with milk from her thermos, Eve bounded up off the quilt and looked from Judah to Mercy. "I want to practice some more." She ran several yards away and said, "Watch, Mother. Look at me, Daddy."

Without waiting for permission, Eve concentrated very hard, and gradually her feet lifted off the ground a few inches. Then a foot. Two feet. Three feet.

"Be careful," Mercy cautioned.

"Daddy, what's this called?" Eve asked, spreading her arms and waving them up and down, as if they were wings.

"Levitation," Judah replied as Eve rose a good ten feet off the ground.

"Oh, that's right. Mother told me. Lev-i-ta-tion."

Leaning forward, intending to intervene and catch Eve if she fell, Mercy held her breath. If only Eve weren't so headstrong and adventurous.

"You're overprotective." Judah manacled Mercy's wrist. "Let her have some fun. She just wants our attention and our approval."

Mercy glowered at him. "Eve has been the center of my existence since the day she was born. But it's my job as her mother to approve of appropriate behavior and disapprove of what's inappropriate. And more than anything else, it is my duty to protect her, even if that means protecting her from herself."

Judah grunted. "You've lived in fear that the Ansara in her would come out, haven't you? Every time she's acted up, been unruly, thrown a temper tantrum, you've wondered if it was a sign of the innate evil side of her nature—the Ansara in her."

"I'm going higher," Eve called. "Watch me. Watch me!"

When Eve levitated a good twenty feet in the air, Mercy jumped up and motioned to her daughter. "That's high enough, sweetheart. That was great." She clapped several times. "Now come back down."

"Do I have to?" Eve asked. "This is fun."

"Come down, and you and I will play a game," Judah said.

Eve came sailing down, slowly and carefully, as if showing Mercy that she shouldn't be concerned. The minute her feet hit the ground, Eve ran to Judah.

"What sort of game are we going to play?"

He eyed Mercy, his look daring her to interfere. "Have you ever played with fire?"

Eve snapped around and looked up at Mercy. "Mother says I'm too young to play with fire the way Uncle Dante does. She said when I'm older—"

"If one of your abilities is psychopyresis, the younger you learn to master that skill, the better," Judah said directly to Eve as he laid his hand on Mercy's shoulder. "My father began my lessons when I was seven."

"Oh, please, Mommy, please," Eve said. "Let Daddy give me lessons."

Any decision she made might prove to be the wrong one. She couldn't be certain that a negative response wouldn't be based on her resentment toward Judah for intruding in their lives.

Mercy nodded. "All right. Just this once." She glared at Judah. "You'll have to stay in control at all times. When she was two—" Mercy hesitated to share this information with him but finally did "—Eve set the house on fire."

Judah's eyes widened in surprise; then he smiled. "She was capable of doing that when she was two?"

"I'm very gifted," Eve said. "Mother says it's 'cause I'm special."

Judah beamed with fatherly pride as he placed his hands on Eve's little shoulders. "Your mother's right—you *are* special." He grasped Eve's hand. "Come on, let's go over there by the pond and set off some fireworks. What do you say?"

Jiggling up and down with excitement, Eve grinned from ear to ear.

Despite having reservations, Mercy followed them to the pond. To watch. And to censure, if Judah allowed Eve to do anything truly dangerous...

Eve had exhausted herself practicing first one talent and then another, all under Judah's supervision. He realized that what Mercy had feared was Eve revealing to him just how truly powerful she was. And there was now no doubt in his mind that his daughter possessed the potential to be the most powerful creature on earth, more powerful than any other Ansara or Raintree.

He glanced down at Eve as she lay curled in a fetal ball on the quilt, deep in a restorative sleep. A feeling like none he'd ever known welled up from deep inside him. This was his child. Beautiful, smart and talented to the extreme. And she had instantly recognized him as her father and accepted him into her life without question.

He recalled Sidra's words: *If you are to save your people, you must protect the child.*

In that moment Judah realized that he would protect Eve for the sake of the Ansara, but more important, he would protect her because she was his child and he loved her.

He turned and gazed out over the meadow as he struggled to come to terms with what was happening to him. In his position as Dranir, he made instant life-and-death decisions without blinking an eye. His word was law. Like his father before him, he ruled supreme over his people. As a boy, he had known he would grow up to become the premiere Ansara, the most powerful member of the clan, the Dranir. He could be ruthless when the occasion called for it, but he believed he was always fair and just. He had lived his life by the Ansara code of honor, and had sworn his allegiance to his people the day he was crowned Dranir.

And he had accepted the burden that fate had placed on his shoulders: to lead his people in another great battle against the Raintree.

For most of Judah's life, Cael had been little more than a nuisance, a brother he neither loved nor hated. But gradually, Cael had proven himself to be a vile creature controlled by the evil insanity that had doomed his mother. And now he had to be stopped once and for all.

"Judah?" Mercy called quietly as she came up behind him. He glanced back at her.

"We haven't talked about the reason you returned to the sanctuary," she said. "I've allowed you time with Eve. But you can't stay here. You can't be a part of her life."

"Eve is in danger from my brother. Until she's safe from Cael, I'll remain a part of her life, with or without your permission." Narrowing his gaze, he issued a warning. "Don't try to force me to leave."

"Or you'll do what?" Mercy marched straight up to Judah and stood in front of him. Defiant. Fearless.

He wanted to tell her that he found her foolhardy but brave. Powerful men quaked in their boots if they displeased him. He had broken arms and legs, snapped off heads and sent traitors to a fiery death. He was Dranir Judah. But he could hardly proclaim himself to be the ruler of a mighty clan, not when the Raintree believed the handful of Ansara left alive after the great battle had scattered to the four corners of the earth and, for the most part, been absorbed into the human population. It was best if she continued believing that Ansara such as he were few and far between, only a handful who still possessed their ancient powers. A talented Ansara here and there could be dealt with easily; but a reborn clan of mighty warriors would pose a threat.

"We shouldn't argue," Judah said. "We have the same goal—to protect Eve."

"The only difference in our goals is that I want to protect her from you as well as your brother."

"You really think I'm the devil incarnate, don't you?"

"You're an Ansara."

"Yes, I am. And proud of the fact. But you seem to believe I should be ashamed to belong to a noble, ancient race."

"Noble? The Ansara? Hardly."

"The Raintree don't have a monopoly on nobility," Judah told her.

"If you believe that the Ansara are noble, then our definitions of the word must differ greatly."

"Loyalty to one's family and friends and clan. Using our abilities to provide for and protect the people for whom we are responsible. Revering the elderly ones who possess great knowledge. Defending ourselves against our enemies."

Mercy stared at him, a puzzled expression on her face. Had he said too much? Did she suspect he was more than just a single Ansara with power equal to any Raintree? Was she wondering just how many more like him were out there?

"The Ansara used their powers to take whatever they wanted—from humans and Raintree alike. Allowed to go unchecked, your people would have subjugated everyone on earth instead of living in harmony with the Ungifted as we Raintree do now and have done for thousands of years."

"You Raintree took it upon yourselves to become the guardians of the human race, and in doing so, you chose those who are mere mortals over those of your own kind. That decision locked our two clans into what seemed like an eternal war."

"The Ansara are not our kind," Mercy said emphatically. "Even your ancient Dranirs recognized that fact. That's why they issued the decree to kill any mixed-breed children."

*I have revoked that decree!* But Judah couldn't tell Mercy what he'd done, didn't dare reveal to her that he was the Ansara Dranir.

"Are you saying you agree with the decree?" Judah asked, deliberately baiting her. "Do you think mixed-breed children should be put to death?"

"No, of course not! How can you ask me such a question?"

"Eve is Raintree," Judah said. "She is your kind. But she is also Ansara, which means she is my kind. Her bloodline goes back over seven thousand years to those from whom both the Ansara and the Raintree came. We were once the same people."

"And for that reason, Dranir Dante and Dranira Ancelin did not annihilate all Ansara after *The Battle* two hundred years ago. The few Ansara who remained were allowed to live, in hopes that they would learn to coexist in the world with the Ungifted and find the humanity they had once shared with the Raintree thousands of years ago." She looked Judah in the eyes. "But knowing you, I see that that hope was not fulfilled. You and your brother hate each other. His mother killed your mother.

And he intends to kill you. He wants to harm Eve, and you want to take her away from me. The Ansara are still violent and cruel and uncaring and——"

Judah grabbed her by the shoulders. Mercy quieted immediately, glaring at him, her rigid stance challenging him. "You judge me without knowing me," he told her. "My half brother isn't typical of our kind, nor was his mother. Cael is insane, just as she was."

When he felt Mercy relax, he eased his hold, but he didn't release her. They stood there for several minutes, looking at each other, each trying to sense what the other was thinking. Mercy wouldn't budge, keeping her defensive barriers in place. He did the same, not daring to risk her realizing who he really was.

"Because of Eve, I'd like to believe you," Mercy said. "I'd like to know that the Ansara part of her will never turn her into someone totally alien to me. I know she's high-strung and mischievous, but——" Mercy swallowed hard. "What you did to me was cruel and uncaring. Can you deny that?"

Judah ran his hands down her arms, from shoulders to wrists; then he let her go.

"At the time, I didn't consider it cruel. I wanted you. You wanted me. We had sex several times. You gave me pleasure. I gave you pleasure. No promises were exchanged. I didn't declare my undying love."

Mercy's expression hardened; her face paled. "No, but I told you that I loved you." She bowed her head as if the sight of him caused her pain. "You must have found that amusing. Not only had you taken the Raintree princess's virginity, but she told you that she loved you."

Judah reached out and tilted her chin, forcing her to look

up at him. "I knew you weren't in love with me. You were just in love with the way I'd made you feel. Really good sex can do that to a woman when it's a new experience for her."

"If I had known you were Ansara..."

"You'd have run like hell." He grunted. "Actually, that's what you *did* do when you found out, wasn't it?" He studied her briefly, then asked, "Why didn't you abort your pregnancy? Why didn't you just get rid of my baby?"

"She was my baby, too. I could never have..."

Mercy went still as a statue. Her eyes glazed over, then rolled back in her head as she shivered. Judah realized she was experiencing some kind of trance.

"Mercy?" He had seen something similar to this with Ansara psychics, seers and empaths. He didn't touch her. He simply waited.

As quickly as she had gone under, she emerged. "Someone is testing the shield around the sanctuary. And he's not alone."

Judah hadn't thought his brother was foolish enough to actually show up at the sanctuary, knowing full well that he was here and would never let him get anywhere near Eve. But he could hear Cael calling to him. Not a challenge; simply a preliminary warning.

"It's Cael," Judah said.

"Your brother? How do you know for sure that—"

"I know."

"We have to stop him! He's trying to connect with Eve while she's sleeping."

"He's playing games," Judah told her. "He's trying to show me how vulnerable Eve is."

Mercy grabbed his forearm. "Just how vulnerable is she? How powerful is your brother?"

"Powerful enough to cause trouble." Judah removed her hand from his arm and gave it a reassuring squeeze. "You stay here and protect Eve by any method necessary. Conjure up the strongest spell you know that will guard her from Cael's attempts to enter her dreams. My brother possesses the power of oneiromancy. He can telepathically enter someone's dreams and affect their well-being."

Mercy clutched his hand. "What are you going to do?"

"I'm going to have a talk with Cael."

"I should go with you to—"

"I don't need you." Judah pulled away from her. "I can deal with my brother. You take care of Eve."

"You'll need transportation if you're going outside to meet him. There's an old truck parked in the garage. Take it," Mercy told him. "The keys are in the ignition."

They shared a moment of complete understanding, bound together in a common cause that superseded any clan rivalry or personal animosity.

Mercy reinforced the shield that protected Eve from outside forces, then placed a special guard around her dreams. Finally she cast a sleeping spell over her daughter, something mild that would keep her subdued for a short period of time without leaving any aftereffects. There was no way to know what Eve might do if she thought her parents were in danger. Then, with the utmost gentleness, Mercy lifted Eve into her arms and carried her child back to the house.

Sidonia, who was removing heavy winter quilts from the clothesline out back, looked up and saw them. She dropped the sunned quilts into the large wicker basket at her feet and scurried toward Mercy.

"What's wrong with her?" Sidonia asked. "Is she hurt? Did he—"

"She's fine. Just sleeping. I cast a mild sleeping spell over her." Mercy held out her child to Sidonia. "Here, take her, then go inside and stay there with her until I come back. I've made sure that she's well protected, but... Guard her with your life."

Sidonia took Eve into her arms, then looked squarely at Mercy. "What's happening? Where are you going?"

"To join Judah. His brother has come to the sanctuary. He's gone out to meet him, to stop him from carrying out the ancient decree."

"Dear God! That monstrous edict to kill babies." Sidonia gazed pleadingly at Mercy. "Call the others that are here at the sanctuary to help you. Don't trust Judah Ansara to save our little Eve."

"Take her inside now," Mercy said. "And don't alert anyone else. Judah and I can handle this."

"Oh, my poor girl." Sidonia tsked-tsked sadly. "You actually trust him, don't you?"

"I—I don't know, but...yes, I believe he'll protect Eve from his brother. I believe he cares for Eve as much as an Ansara is capable of caring."

Mercy rushed past Sidonia and into the house. She retrieved the keys to her Escalade from a bowl on the kitchen counter, then ran back outside and straight to the garage. She slid behind the wheel of her SUV, started the engine, backed out and headed up the road.

When she reached the entrance to the sanctuary, she saw the old truck parked just inside the iron gates, but she didn't see Judah. Her heartbeat accelerated. She pulled up behind the truck and parked, then jumped out and stopped dead in her tracks. Judah had gone outside. He was standing just beyond the closed gates, his back to her. Four strangers—three men and one woman—stood across the road, all focused on Judah. The woman, probably in her mid-thirties, stood apart from the other three. Two young men, little more than teenagers, flanked the man in the middle, the tall, lean blond with eyes as silvery cold as Judah's.

Cael. The murderous half brother.

Suddenly the woman noticed Mercy. They exchanged heated glares, and the woman zeroed in on Mercy, sending a quick telepathic zing in her direction. Mercy intercepted the mediocre attempt, added a touch more power to it and returned it to its sender. The zing knocked the woman backward so strongly that she barely managed to keep her balance.

"I see you're not alone," Cael said to Judah, who didn't move a muscle. "Your Raintree whore seems to think you need help."

Judah stood fast, not responding in any way.

Mercy walked down the road and up to the gate. She stood slightly to Judah's left, only the closed gates and less than five feet separating her from him.

"The child isn't safe," Cael said. "I can breach the shield surrounding this place, so that means others can, too. As parents, you should be watchful. You never know when someone might try to harm Eve."

"Anyone who tries to hurt my daughter will have to face me," Judah said.

Cael smiled. Cold, calculating and sinister. And filled with a bloodlust unlike anything Mercy had ever sensed in another being. She realized that this man was as unlike Judah as he was unlike Dante or Gideon. He was what she had believed all Ansara to be: pure evil.

"I don't suppose you'd like to invite me in and introduce Eve to her uncle Cael?" Judah's brother made direct eye contact with Mercy for a moment. "I see why you screwed her, brother. She's remarkably lovely. Which did you enjoy more—taking a Raintree princess's virginity or making a fool of her?"

"Leave this place," Judah said. "If you don't—"

Cael roared like a beast, the rage inside barely controlled. Ten foot flames shot up from the paved road between him and Judah. Mercy moved to open the gates, but she heard Judah telepathically telling her to stay where she was as he drew back his fist, opened it into a claw and whirled his hand in the air. From out of nowhere rain poured down in one spot, onto the flames Cael had created. The water extinguished the fire, leaving only whiffs of gray smoke.

Apparently Judah had the ability not only to create fire but to extinguish it. Dominion over fire was a talent possessed by only a few Raintree, her brother Dante to name one.

"We can end this here and now," Judah told his brother. "Is that what you want?"

Cael smiled again. "Not yet. But soon." He looked at Mercy again. "Did he tell you that he killed one of his own to save your life?"

Then, laughing, he turned and walked away toward a black limousine parked down the road. The others followed him like obedient puppy dogs lapping at their master's feet.

Judah didn't move from the spot nor did he speak until the limousine disappeared from sight. Then he turned and faced Mercy, the closed gate still between them. "Don't ask," he said.

"How can I not ask? I know someone tried to kill me Sunday, and you stopped them. How did you know? Why would you save me?"

"I told you not to ask." Judah stared at the gate. "I could enter the sanctuary without your help, but it would expend a great deal of my energy. And I don't want to disturb Eve."

Mercy opened the gate and held out her hand. Judah took her hand in his and stepped through the protective shield that separated the Raintree sanctuary from the outside world. Once inside, he didn't release her. Instead, he pulled her up to him, his gaze boring into her, chiseling through the barriers that protected her mind from intrusions. She didn't try to stop him, knowing that as he worked so feverishly to expose her thoughts, he left his own thoughts and feelings unguarded.

She sensed great worry, a deep and true concern for those he loved. Loved? Was Judah actually capable of love?

"Does that surprise you?" he asked, apparently realizing that she had picked up on his emotions.

Once again shielding herself and ending their mental connection, Mercy jerked free and turned away from him. "I want you to leave as soon as possible. You can't stay. If the others find out you're here, you won't be safe."

"You can't protect Eve now without my help," Judah said.

She whirled back around. "Then go after your brother and...and do whatever you need to do to protect our daughter. I don't understand why you didn't kill him just now."

"Because he wasn't alone," Judah said. "I could have easily dispensed with the three he had with him, but..." He hesitated, as if uncertain whether or not to share the information with her. "There were ten others—a tiny band of Ansara who are loyal to my brother—nearby, waiting for Cael to summon them. If I had challenged him to a death-fight, I would have been at a distinct disadvantage."

"I could have called for help," Mercy said, then gasped when the absurd reality of the situation hit her. "If I had called in the Raintree who are here at the Sanctuary, you would have been the enemy to them as well as to your brother."

"I had no desire to be a lone man against a small group of Ansara on one side and Raintree on the other."

"So, what do we do now?"

"We keep Eve safe."

# ELEVEN

Cael and his small band of Ansara warriors arrived at the private compound in a rural area off Interstate 40, between Asheville and the Raintree sanctuary, well before sunset. While the others ate and drank and screwed, psyching themselves up for the battle that was only days away, Cael closed himself off in his private quarters and contemplated his next move. He had leased this property over two years ago, once he had decided on a date for the Ansara attack on the Raintree home place. Slowly, cautiously, secretly, he had combed the world in search of renegade Ansara who would be willing to do his bidding and fight at his side on the chosen day. His army now exceeded a hundred warriors, small in comparison to the number Judah commanded, but adequate for the attack Cael had planned. By Saturday, they would all have arrived here at this secluded retreat, armed and ready for battle.

The element of surprise was essential to the success of his

strategy. He would lead an army of Ansara warriors against a handful of visiting Raintree and the lone guardian, Princess Mercy, the Keeper of the Sanctuary. On the day of the summer solstice. Before other Raintree could be summoned, word would already have reached Terrebonne, and all the Ansara warriors would have no choice but to join Cael in the final great battle between the two warring clans. This time the Ansara would be the victors, and they would decimate the Raintree. He would personally kill Judah and his bastard child, Eve; then he would see to it that every Raintree on earth was put to death.

He would rule supreme. His people would hail him as the conquering hero. The Ungifted would become the Ansaras' slaves and be forced to worship at his feet.

Thoughts of the future were indeed sweet. Victory. Annihilation of the Raintree. Judah slaughtered. The subjugation of mankind.

*I will be a true god.*

*But only when Judah is dead.*

Cael cursed loudly as he rammed psychic bolts through the wall, venting his frustration over years of waiting to claim what was rightfully his.

Keeping Judah in the dark about the exact date he planned to strike the sanctuary was vital to his success. His brother might suspect him of treason and probably knew he intended to go to war with the Raintree on his own timetable, but without actual proof, Judah couldn't bring him before the council and demand his execution.

How auspicious that divine providence had provided such a perfect distraction—little Eve Raintree—to keep his brother's mind occupied. Judah was the possessive, protective type. A little too noble for Cael's taste. Like his mother, Seana, that insipid empath their father had chosen as his Dranira, Judah was weak. He chose the old Ansara methods in dealing with others only when all else failed. He was far more businessman than warrior.

*Liar!* Cael's inner voice taunted. *You wish that Judah was not a true Ansara warrior, but our father trained him well in all things. A Dranir had to be a warrior, a businessman, a true leader capable of judging and executing.*

No matter. His brother might be a worthy opponent in combat, but he, Prince Cael, would prove himself superior.

Stay where you are, with your Raintree bitch, and guard little Eve day and night, dear brother. Concentrate solely on keeping her safe from me. And all the while you neglect matters on Terrebonne, I will be assembling my army and spreading anarchy among the Ansara.

We strike the sanctuary on *Alban Heruin*, when the sun is most powerful and I, too, will be filled with my ultimate strength. I will kill your child and your woman first, so I can have the pleasure of seeing you watch them die. And then I will kill *you*.

"You can't allow him to stay here!" Sidonia shouted. "No good will come of it."

"He needs to be here to protect Eve," Mercy explained.

"If he's going to kill his brother anyway, why doesn't he just go ahead and do it?"

"Lower your voice. Eve might overhear you."

Sidonia snorted. "Not likely. She's too wrapped up in spending time with her daddy to be eavesdropping."

Keeping her voice low and calm, Mercy said, "Cael has a

group of friends who guard his back, so until Cael issues Judah a one-on-one challenge, which Judah believes will happen soon, the wisest course is for Judah not to hunt his brother down."

"For all you know he's playing you for a fool. Again." Sidonia's gaze met Mercy's. "This could be some sort of ploy to ingratiate himself with you, to show himself in a favorable light, when all he's doing is buying time to bond with Eve so that when he decides to take her away, she'll go with him willingly."

"Judah *is* bonding with Eve. And he does plan to take her from me," Mercy said. "But his hatred for his brother and Cael's threats to Eve are real. I know it."

Sidonia nodded. "You've sensed this, and you are certain?"

"Yes."

Knowing that Mercy would never lie to her about such a vitally important matter, Sidonia reluctantly agreed. "Very well. Keep him here, and somehow we'll pass him off as a human visitor when the others ask. For now, you and he will stand against his brother. Then later, when the brother is no longer a threat, you'll have to fight Judah to save Eve."

"I know."

"When that time comes, you'll need Dante and Gideon."

"Probably, but not now. Not yet."

"When? You mustn't wait until it's too late."

"Eve will know when Judah decides to take her. She'll tell me when it's time."

Sidonia's gaze held numerous questions.

"Eve can't leave the sanctuary without my knowing in advance what is going to happen," Mercy said.

Sidonia gasped. "No, tell me you didn't!"

"I did. I had no choice."

"But when did you do it? You would have needed another Raintree to help."

"Eve helped me. When she was only hours old and completely dependent on me. I had no way of knowing if Judah would somehow realize I was carrying his child and come after me—either to kill her or take her. I used the old binding spell because I had no other choice. I had to be able to know at all times where Eve was."

"If only you had told your brothers who your baby's father was before she was born, we wouldn't have to deal with him or his brother now. They would have hunted Judah down and killed him." Sidonia squinted as she looked soulfully at Mercy. "You poor child. I know. I know. You loved him. You didn't want him dead."

"Enough! We've had this discussion too many times."

"You *still* love him, don't you?"

"Of course not!"

Sidonia grabbed Mercy's arm. "What if he wanted you as well as Eve? Would you go with him?"

"Shut up! Stop talking nonsense." Mercy stormed out of the kitchen and through the house, stopping only when she reached the open front door and heard Eve's laughter.

She eased open the screen door and stepped out onto the porch. Twilight had settled in around the valley, a pinkish orange glow in the evening sky, a haze of translucent clouds hugging the mountains surrounding them. Out in the middle of the grassy green yard, Judah stood holding a glass jar, holes punched in the metal lid, and watched while Eve chased fireflies. Several little captives already blinked brightly inside the jar.

Eve zeroed in on another lightning bug and caught it between her cupped palms. "I got him! I got him!" She ran to Judah, who opened the jar's lid a fraction, just enough so that Eve could drop her hostage into the glass prison.

When Eve sensed Mercy's presence, she looked at her and smiled. "Daddy's never caught lightning bugs before, not even when he was a little boy. I had to explain that I wouldn't hurt them, and that after I see how many I can catch, I'll let them all go free."

"Well, I believe it's emancipation time," Mercy said. "It's after eight. You need to take a bath before you go to bed, my little princess."

"No, not yet. Please, just another hour." Whining, Eve put her hands together in a prayer-like gesture. "Daddy and I are having so much fun." She turned to Judah. "Aren't we, Daddy? Tell her. Tell her that I don't have to go to bed right now."

Judah handed Eve the jar filled with fireflies. "Let them go."

Eve tilted her head to one side and stared up at him. "I guess this means I have to do what Mother told me to do."

He playfully ruffled her hair. "I guess it does."

Once again, Judah's actions showed him to be like any other father. How was it possible that an Ansara could be so similar to a Raintree? Perhaps Sidonia was right. Judah could be playing her for a fool, showing her what she wanted to see in him. A false impression.

Reluctantly, Eve unscrewed the lid and shook the jar gently, encouraging the lightning bugs to fly free. When the last one escaped, she walked up on the porch, handed the jar to Mercy and put on her sad face, the one she used to evoke pity.

Heaving a deep sigh, Eve said dramatically, "I'm ready to go—if I have to."

Mercy barely managed not to smile. "Go inside and let Sidonia help you with your bath. I'll be up later to kiss you good-night."

"Daddy, too?"

"Yes," Judah and Mercy replied simultaneously.

As soon as Eve went into the house, letting the screen door slam loudly behind her, Mercy set the empty Mason jar on the porch and stepped down into the yard. Judah looked up at the sky and the towering hills surrounding them, then settled his gaze on her.

"Nice evening," he said. "It's certainly peaceful here in these mountains. Don't you ever get bored?"

"I stay busy," she told him.

"Healing the bodies and hearts and minds of your fellow Raintree?"

"Yes, if and when I can. It's my job as the Keeper of the Sanctuary to use my gifts as an empathic healer to help those who come to me." Her gaze met his and held. "But then, you already knew that, didn't you? You knew the day we met that I was the appointed one."

"The moment I saw your eyes, I knew you were Raintree. I managed to see into your thoughts enough to learn you were a princess and that you were slated to become some sort of guardian," Judah admitted. "I picked up only fragments of thought before I realized that, for the most part, your thoughts were shielded."

"You used a shield, too. A powerful shield. I just didn't realize it at the time," she said. "I thought it strange that I couldn't read you at all, that when I touched you, I sensed only that I could trust you. You blocked me completely and then sent me a deceptive message."

"I did what was necessary in order to get what I wanted."

"And you wanted me."

"Very much."

Why did he make his reply sound as if he were talking about the present and not the past? Even if he did want her now, he wanted only the use of her body, just as he had that night seven years ago.

No, that wasn't the complete truth. He had wanted more than her body that night. He had wanted to take a Raintree princess's innocence and make her fall in love with him. He had done both.

"Why didn't you use protection that night?" Mercy asked.

His mouth curved upward in a sarcastic smirk. "Why didn't *you?*"

"I could say that it was because I was young and stupid and got carried away with feelings I'd never experienced. But the truth is that when I knew I was going to spend the night with you, give myself to you... I tried to conjure up a temporary protection spell. Apparently it didn't work."

"Apparently."

"So what's *your* excuse?"

"I thought I was protected," he admitted.

Her eyes widened. "You used a sexual protection spell, too?"

He nodded. "Sort of. A long-term gift that my cousin Claude and I have been exchanging since we were teenagers. It worked perfectly with Ansara and human women."

"If we were both protected, then how—oh, my God! Sexual protection spells and gifts must not work when a Raintree mates with an Ansara."

"At least not in our case," Judah agreed.

"I don't understand. They should have worked. We should have been protected."

"The only explanation I can think of is that Eve was meant to be."

"Are you saying you believe that a higher power ordained Eve's conception?"

"It's possible. Perhaps she was born for a specific reason."

Judah sounded so certain, as if he knew something she didn't. But that wasn't possible, was it? He might be a talented Ansara, with many abilities, but he was not a seer who could look into the future.

"Did someone tell you that Eve was destined to——"

"No one knew about Eve's existence, except for you and Sidonia, until three days ago. How could anyone have told me anything about her?"

"Yes, of course."

"She's an amazing child, our little Eve."

When he stared at Mercy, visually stripping her bare as he so often did, she glanced away. "If by chance you encounter any other Raintree while you're here, tell them your name is Judah Blackstone, and that you're an old friend of mine from college. We've allowed visitors to come to the sanctuary before, friends of my family who needed the peace and solitude the home place offers. No one will question you further."

"And if Eve tells someone that I'm her father, how will we handle that?"

"I'll speak to her and explain that, for the present, we need to keep that fact our little secret."

"Judah Blackstone, huh?"

"It's as good a name as any." She turned and headed toward the front porch steps. "I'm going up to say good-night to Eve. Are you coming with me?"

"Yes, I'm coming with you." He followed her onto the porch

and into the house. Once inside the foyer, he asked, "Did you have an old boyfriend named Blackstone? Do I need to be jealous?"

Taken off guard by his question, she snapped around and scowled at him.

Judah chuckled. "Don't Raintree have a sense of humor?"

"I don't see anything humorous in our relationship. You and I are enemies who find ourselves temporarily bound together in a common cause—to save our daughter. But once she is no longer in danger..." Mercy walked away from him, heading for the stairs.

He came up behind her and clutched her elbow. She stopped dead still but didn't look back at him. Now, as in the past, his touch heated her blood, warming her as if a fire had been lit deep inside her. She tilted her head and glanced over her shoulder. He was too close, his chest brushing against her back.

He leaned his head low and whispered, "When Eve is no longer in danger, you know that you and I can't share her. She will become either Ansara or Raintree, the outcome decided by which of us kills the other. That's what you were thinking, wasn't it?"

"If you would swear to go away and leave us alone, to never contact Eve again, it wouldn't have to end that way. Eve wouldn't have to grow up knowing her mother killed her father."

"Or that her father killed her mother."

Mercy closed her eyes and took a deep breath. Judah had no qualms about killing her to obtain custody of his child. If only she were as heartless. If only she could kill him without regrets.

"My sweet Mercy." Judah snaked his arm around her waist and jerked her roughly against him, her back to his chest, her buttocks to his erection.

No, this couldn't be. *Fight your feelings,* she told herself. *Don't succumb to the desire eating you alive, screaming inside you to give yourself to him.*

"I find the fact that you are capable of both saving lives and taking them extremely exciting," Judah told her, his breath hot on her neck. "You, my love, are quite the paradox, a healer and a warrior." His lips grazed her neck with a series of seductive kisses. "You love me and you hate me. You want me to live and yet you are willing to kill me to save Eve." His tongue replaced his lips as he painted a damp path from her collarbone to her ear.

Immobilized by her own need, Mercy closed her eyes, savoring this wicked man's touch. His hand crept upward from the front of her waist to her breast. She shuddered as pure electrical sensation shot through her body. While he kneaded her breast through the barriers of her blouse and bra, his fingertips worked against her nipple.

Whimpering, Mercy rested the back of her head against his shoulder.

*Put a stop to this now,* the sensible part of her brain demanded. But the needs of her woman's body overruled common sense.

While his tongue circled her ear, Judah drove his hand between Mercy's thighs and stroked her intimately through the soft cotton of her slacks and panties. "You belong to me. I own you, Mercy Raintree. You're mine."

Mercy cried out, fighting his hypnotic hold over her and her own wanton needs.

Breaking free, she fled, running away from a temptation almost too powerful to deny.

Midnight. The witching hour. And Mercy *was* bewitched. Entranced by memories of a chance meeting seven years ago.

She had never admitted to another soul how those exhilarating hours haunted her, how often, when she was alone at night, the image of Judah Ansara appeared to her. She had never hated anyone the way she hated him. Or loved anyone so deeply and passionately. In all this time, she hadn't been able to reconcile her divided feelings. Love and hate. Fear and longing. Even now, she wanted him. Knowing he was an Ansara. Knowing that he didn't love her, had never loved her. Knowing he planned to fight her—to the death—for Eve.

If only she hadn't insisted on that vacation alone. One week, all to herself, without Dante and Gideon, without Raintree friends guarding her, out from under Sidonia's watchful eye. Had that been too much to ask? Aunt Gillian had thought Mercy's request quite reasonable. As the aged guardian of the sanctuary, she'd known only too well about the great demands on Mercy's time and talents that lay ahead for her when she became the keeper of the home place.

A great empath herself, Gillian had gifted Mercy with the ability not to sense other people's thoughts and emotions on a deep level while on her vacation. Like many other gifts, that one had a nine-day shelf-life.

And so Mercy had gone out into the world alone, ready to experience life without the curse of being bombarded by the thoughts and emotions of everyone around her. For those nine days, she wouldn't be a Raintree princess. She wouldn't be a talented empath. She could enjoy being young and pretty and unguarded.

Mercy had no way of knowing that with her abilities muted, she would be unable to recognize danger when it swept her off her feet. Literally. A waiter by the pool at the resort where she was vacationing had lost his footing and plunged into a guest, who in turn set off a chain reaction, sending tables, drinks, chairs and people flying. From out of nowhere, someone had swooped Mercy up into his arms, saving her from becoming one more domino-effect casualty.

Wearing a bikini for the first time in her life, Mercy had felt naked as her flesh had pressed against the overpoweringly masculine chest belonging to the man who had rescued her. After grabbing him around the neck and clinging to him, she had gazed into his eyes—as cold and gray as a winter sky. He hadn't set her on her feet immediately, but had held her, smiling broadly, the warmth of his big, hard body heating her inside and out.

Pressing her fingertips against her temples, Mercy closed her eyes and huffed loudly. "Get out of my head, damn you, Judah Ansara."

She had tried to erase him from her memory, had even been tempted to use a spell to eliminate all thoughts of him. But she hadn't dared go to such extreme lengths. Only she and Sidonia knew that Eve was half Ansara, and Sidonia alone could not have protected Eve.

Mercy tossed back the sheet and light blanket covering her, then got out of bed, opened the door and crept quietly across the hall. Eve's door, as always, had been left open. Mercy stepped over the threshold and stood there watching her daughter sleep.

*If I had never met Judah... If we hadn't been lovers...*

Eve wouldn't exist.

She heard Judah's voice inside her head. *Eve was meant to be.*

If she believed nothing else Judah had ever said, she believed that. Their daughter's life was preordained. But for what reason?

The fact that Mercy had conceived during their one night of passionate lovemaking was practically a miracle, what with her having used a temporary sexual protection spell and Judah having been gifted with sexual protection by his cousin. With double protection, conception should have been impossible.

Gifted by his cousin. *Gifted!*

My God! Why hadn't she immediately realized the implication of the word the moment Judah had said "a long-term gift that my cousin Claude and I have been exchanging since we were teenagers"?

In the Raintree clan, only royals had the power to gift charms. Why would it be any different with the Ansara? The ability was ancient, from the time of their eldest ancestors who had lived thousands of years ago, from a time when the Raintree and Ansara had been one.

Was Judah a royal Ansara?

If he was, then she had far more to fear than just a mere Ansara male wanting to claim his child. If Judah was a prince…

No, he couldn't be. The Ansara were no longer a great clan with a powerful Dranir and Dranira, with a royal family of children, siblings, aunts, uncles and cousins. Perhaps Judah possessed royal blood, and had the Ansara won *The Battle* two hundred years ago, he might today be a mighty prince. That would explain him being able to gift charms and exchange them with a cousin.

But she didn't intend to leave anything to chance. Tomorrow she would confront him with her doubts. For Eve's sake, she had to find out the truth.

# TWELVE

Mercy waited until after breakfast before requesting a private conversation with Judah. To keep Eve occupied and away from the house, she had sent her daughter with Sidonia to take fresh baked goods to the visitors occupying the cabins. Although the kitchens in all the units were well stocked, Sidonia enjoyed sharing her homemade breads, muffins, cakes and pies with their guests. Being a gregarious, curious child, Eve liked nothing better than to meet various members of the Raintree tribe, so this Thursday morning outing with her nanny was a real treat for her.

Alone in the study with Judah, Mercy braced herself for the inevitable magnetic pull that drew her to him. If she denied their sexual connection, she would be lying to herself. What she could and would do was fight that attraction. During the years since she had seen him, she had convinced herself that what she'd felt for him during their brief time together hadn't been as passionately exciting as she remembered. But those moments on the stairs last night had proven otherwise. The extraordinary chemistry between them could still make her weak and vulnerable, two things a Raintree never wanted to be around an Ansara.

"Go ahead. Get it over with." Judah's eyes twinkled with mischievous delight, his expression similar to Eve's when she was up to no good.

Mercy squared her shoulders. "Just what do you think I'm going to say or do?"

"I assume you're going to rip into me about what happened between us last night. So go ahead and tell me that you won't allow it to happen again. Lay down the law. Show me who's boss."

She would like nothing better than to wipe that cocky grin off his face and was tempted to give him a psychic slap. But that would only prove how easily he could rile her. She certainly had no intention of giving him the satisfaction.

Ignoring his deliberate attempt to get a reaction, she asked, "How is it possible that you and your cousin are able to gift charms?"

"What?"

Well, that had wiped the smile off his face, hadn't it? She had surprised him with her question.

"Are you talking about the sexual protection that Claude and I...?"

"I'm talking about the fact that only royals have the power to gift charms. Are you a royal? If so, that means there's an Ansara royal family, right?"

He didn't respond immediately, which bothered her. He was giving serious thought to his reply. Thinking up a plausible lie? she wondered.

"You must know that there's always been a royal Ansara family. One of the old Dranir's daughters, Princess Melisande, survived *The Battle,* married, and had children and grandchildren and so forth. To answer your other questions, yes, Claude and I have royal blood, or so our parents told us."

"Are you a prince?"

"No."

Was he lying to her? Did she dare believe him?

"Where is your home?" she asked.

"Why the sudden interest in my personal life? If you're asking for Eve's sake, then I can tell you I'm strong, healthy, mentally sound and possess all the powers of a royal."

"Why are you reluctant to tell me where you live?"

"I live all over the world. I'm an international businessman, an offshore banker, with interests in numerous countries."

"And the other Ansara—how many are there? Where do the Dranir and Dranira reside? Are your people scattered throughout the world as we Raintree are?"

"What few of us there are keep a low profile," Judah told her. "We are not prepared to confront the Raintree and do nothing to call attention to ourselves."

"But you did, didn't you? Seven years ago, you deliberately seduced a Raintree princess. I'd say that's calling attention to yourself."

"But at the time, you didn't know I was Ansara. And if you had not conceived my child, you never would have known."

What he said was true enough and yet a sense of foreboding clenched her stomach muscles, creating a sick feeling in her gut. Was it possible that in only two hundred years, the Ansara had rebuilt their clan enough to actually pose a threat to the Raintree? Surely not. If the Ansara were once again a mighty people, the Raintree would know. One of the Raintrees' many psychics would have sensed the Ansaras' escalating power. Unless... Unless they had deliberately shielded themselves from detection with a mass protection spell... But was that even possible?

"What about your Dranir and Dranira?" Mercy asked.

"So many questions." Judah came toward her.

She held her ground, refusing to cower in front of him.

"The Ansara Dranir is single," Judah said. "Some consider him a playboy. He has a villa in the Caribbean and one in Italy, as well as homes and apartments in various places. He owns a yacht and a jet, and women swoon at his feet."

"Sounds like a charming guy," Mercy said sarcastically. "And you're related to him. From what you've said about him, I sense a strong similarity between you two."

"Like two peas in a pod." Judah smirked. "I also manage his money for him."

Mercy wondered why Judah was so forthcoming with information about his Dranir and his people. Either they were, as he had told her, no threat to the Raintree, or he was telling her just enough of the truth to appear open and honest. But why should a Raintree trust an Ansara?

Whenever Judah was this close, their bodies almost touching, Mercy found it difficult to concentrate, and he damn well knew it. *Ignore the fact that your heartbeat has accelerated and your nipples have hardened,* Mercy told herself. *He doesn't know that you're moist with desire, that your body yearns for his.*

"Wouldn't our brief time together be better spent not talking?" Judah leaned over just far enough so that they were nose to nose, mouth to mouth. "As I recall, neither of us needs words to express what we want."

Shivering internally, she barely managed to keep her body from shaking. Her breathing quickened. Her nostrils flared. Her feminine core clenched and unclenched.

"Why does your brother hate you enough to kill you?"

Her question acted as the deterrent she had hoped it would. Judah lifted his head and withdrew from her, at least far enough so that she could take a free breath.

"I told you that Cael's mother killed my mother. There's been bad blood between us all our lives."

"If his mother killed yours, then you should be the one who hates him, the one who wants to kill him. Why is it the other way around?"

"I'm my father's legitimate son. Cael is not. It's as simple as that. An insane mind needs little excuse to act irrationally."

Mercy told herself that she was questioning Judah to acquire needed information about the Ansara, but that was only part of her reason. Curiosity? Perhaps. All she knew was that she felt a great need to know this man, her child's father.

"How old were you when your mother died?" she asked.

Judah's jaw tensed. "My mother was murdered." He tapered his gaze until his eyes slanted almost closed.

Of its own volition, her hand reached over and spread out across the center of his chest, covering his heart. For one millisecond, while emotion made him vulnerable, Mercy absorbed his innermost thoughts. He had been an infant when his mother died, too young to remember her face or the sound of her voice. A small boy's sadness lingered deep inside Judah, both a hunger for a mother's love and a denial that he needed love from anyone.

"I'm very sorry about your mother," Mercy told him. "No child should grow up without a mother to love him unconditionally."

With his mouth twisted in a snarl, his eyes mere slits and tension etched on his features, Judah grabbed her hand and flung it off his chest. "I neither want nor need your sympathy."

Bombarded with his anger and resentment, Mercy gasped for air. The rage boiling inside him spilled over onto her, engulfing her, drowning her in its intensity. This was her fault, not his, she realized. She should have known better than offer him kindness and caring when he understood neither.

And she shouldn't have touched him.

Mercy fought to free herself from the dangerous havoc Judah's fury was creating within her. She had somehow connected to him empathically, and try as she might, she couldn't manage to sever the link. A heaviness bore down on her chest, a weight that robbed her of breath. She gasped for air, struggling for speech to demand that he release her.

Judah grabbed her shoulders. "What's wrong with you?"

She managed to expel a gasping moan.

"Mercy!" He shook her.

She felt herself growing weaker by the minute, her oxygen supply cut off as if she were being smothered. *Help me. Please, Judah, help me.*

*Tell me what to do.*

Barely conscious, Mercy swayed toward him. *Don't be angry with me. Don't hate me.*

*I did this to you?*

He caught her as her knees gave way, swooping her up in his arms. "Sweet Mercy."

Closing her eyes, she sank to a level just below consciousness. Judah lowered his head and pressed his cheek against hers as he held her securely. As swiftly as his negative energy had invaded her mind and body, it dissipated, draining from her as it drained from him. She felt a flash of concern and genuine regret before he swiftly placed a protective barrier between them.

Weak from the experience and recovering slowly, Mercy opened her eyes and met Judah's concerned gaze.

"I didn't mean for that to happen," he told her.

"It was my fault," she said. "I let my guard down."

"That's a dangerous thing to do, especially around me."

She nodded. "Would you please put me down now? I'll be all right."

"Are you sure? I could——"

"No, thank you. Just put me on my feet."

He eased her down and out of his arms, slowly, maddeningly, making sure her body skimmed over his. When he released her, she staggered, and he grabbed her upper arms to steady her.

"Should I get Sidonia?" he asked.

"No, I'll be all right. Please…" She wriggled, trying to loosen his secure grip on her arms.

He released her.

"I need to be alone for a while," she told him, then turned her back on him, afraid she would succumb to her weakness for a man who was not only dangerous to her, but to her daughter. Seconds later, the door to her study closed, and she knew Judah had left the room.

After a half hour on the phone with Claude, discussing the fact that Cael had not returned to Terrebonne and had somehow dropped off the Ansara radar, Judah had gone in search of his daughter. He needed to build a strong rapport with Eve as quickly as possible. Only if he bonded with her, if she trusted him completely, would he be able to persuade her to leave the Raintree sanctuary with him. So, he spent hours with her that Thursday morning and afternoon, every moment under the vigilant supervision of Nanny Sidonia. The old woman watched him like a hawk, as if she expected him to sprout horns and a tail. Wouldn't she be shocked if he did just that? he thought And he could. At least, he could create the illusion of horns and a tail, enough to scare the crap out of the old woman. It would serve her right if he did. But it might frighten Eve and possibly give her the wrong impression of him. He was sure the grumbling old hag had already bad-mouthed him to his child, telling her all sorts of improbable stories about the wicked Ansara.

He supposed there was some grain of truth to it. The good Raintree. The bad Ansara. But all Raintree weren't saints. And not every Ansara was the devil incarnate.

From time immemorial, the Raintree, as a people, had chosen the straight and narrow, taking the high ground, showing an emotional weakness for the welfare of the Ungifted and preferring peace to war. Wizards with far too much conscience.

The Ansara tolerated humankind, manipulated them when they were useful, disregarded them when they were not. Ansara prided themselves on their skills as warriors and defended to the death what was theirs. But they were not monsters, not evil demons. They lived and loved and cherished their families. In that respect, they were no different from the Raintree.

But there were also Ansara like Cael. A few in every generation. Depraved. Evil. True monsters. Often innate sorcerers, they possessed the ability to lure the dregs of Ansara society into their service. They killed for the pleasure of killing. Took great delight in inflicting pain, in torturing others. They were as unlike Judah and his kind as they were unlike the Raintree.

When circumstances required it, Judah had killed. To protect himself and others, or out of necessity, when killing was simply a business decision. He didn't tolerate disobedience or disrespect. As the Dranir, he possessed unequaled power among his people.

He liked power. Respected power.

He used and discarded women as it pleased him, Ansara and human alike. And once, even a Raintree princess.

Eve tugged on his hand, reminding Judah that he was tied to Mercy Raintree through their daughter, a bond that only death could break.

Sidonia's agitated voice called Eve's name.

"Hurry, Daddy, or she'll catch us." Eve urged him to walk faster as they sneaked away from Sidonia on the pretense of playing hide and seek.

Judah swept Eve up into his arms. "Hold tight," he told her.

When she wrapped her arms around his neck, Judah ran, taking his daughter away from unwanted supervision. When they were out of earshot of Sidonia's threats, Judah set Eve on her feet.

"We got away!" Grinning triumphantly, Eve clapped her hands softly. "She doesn't know where we are, and she can't find us."

"So what do you want to do, now that we're on our own?"

"Mmm..." Eve deliberated her choices for a couple of moments, then laughed excitedly. "I want to show you something really special that I can do." She looked up at him, eagerness shimmering in her eyes. Mercy's green eyes.

"Something new?" he asked. "You've already shown me how talented you are."

"It's something I've never tried before, but I know I can do it."

Judah glanced around and noted that they were not near the house or any of the cottages. Open meadow lay north and east of them, a bubbling brook to the south and a wooded area to the west. If Eve tried a new skill and it backfired, she couldn't do much harm way out here. Besides, he was with her to counteract any fallout.

"Go ahead, Princess Eve, test your powers. Try something new. Show me."

Eve smiled broadly, then stood very still and concentrated. Seconds ticked by. She focused inward, calling forth her power. The ground beneath their feet trembled.

"That's it. Command your power," Judah said. "You're in control."

The fingers on Eve's right hand twitched, moving faster and faster. A tiny circle of energy formed in her palm. An orb of golden light, shimmering like translucent diamond dust, grew larger and larger until it filled her hand.

My God! Eve had created an energy ball, the most powerful and deadliest power in any Ansara's or Raintree's arsenal. No child before had been capable of creating an energy bolt, and only a select number of adults could do it.

"Eve, be careful."

"Isn't it beautiful?"

He zoomed in on the energy bolt his daughter held in her hand, as casually as if she were holding a baseball. "It's very beautiful, but it's extremely dangerous."

"Oh." Eve's eyes widened in surprise, a hint of curiosity in her expression. "What does it do?"

Judah considered his options. He could probably dissolve the ball, but if he did, it might injure Eve's hand. He could ask her to give the ball to him, and then he could dispose of it. Or he could allow her to find out for herself, under his strict supervision, just what such power could do.

"Turn and face the woods," Judah told her. She did. "Now choose a tree."

"That one." She pointed to a towering elm.

"Aim your energy ball at the tree and whirl it through the air."

Eve swung her right arm backward, lifting it over her head, and flung the psychic energy bolt in the direction of the tree she had chosen. She and Judah watched as the blast missed the elm tree entirely, zooming past it and exploding as it hit a stand of twenty-foot pines. At least half a dozen of the evergreens splintered into minuscule shards and rained down in heavy ash particles to the forest floor.

Holy crap! His little girl had just shot one of the most powerful energy bolts Judah had ever seen, taking out not one object but six.

"I missed my tree, Daddy. I missed it." Eve puckered up, her bottom lip quivering.

He knelt down in front of her and tucked his knuckles under her chin, lifting her little face so that she looked directly at him. "You might have missed the elm tree, but look what your blast did. All you need is practice and you'll be able to hit your target every time."

Tears hung on Eve's long, golden lashes, and her eyes shimmered with moisture, but she smiled and threw her arms around Judah's neck.

"I love you, Daddy."

Judah swallowed hard. *I love you, too.*

She hugged him tighter. "Mother's coming."

"It figures."

"Huh?"

"Nothing." Judah gradually eased out of Eve's embrace as he rose to his feet. "Let me handle things, okay? When your mother finds us, she's not going to be happy, so we'll tell her that I'm the one who shot the energy bolt. That way she won't be angry with you."

"But that's lying, Daddy, and lying is wrong."

Judah groaned. Raintree logic. "Actually, it'll just be a little white lie, so you won't get in trouble."

"Mother will know that I did it. She knows everything."

Judah couldn't repress his smile. "Why don't we put her to the test and find out?"

When Eve looked up at him, he winked at her.

She winked back. "Okay."

Exactly five minutes and sixteen seconds later, Judah sensed Mercy coming up from behind as he and Eve sat on the side of the creek, their shoes off, their feet in the cool water. He glanced over his shoulder and spied her a good thirty feet away.

When he turned back around, Eve said, "Mother is very upset."

"Remember, let me do all the talking."

"I think my mother is the one who's going to do all the talking."

When Mercy approached them, Judah and Eve simultaneously turned to face her.

"Hi, Mommy. Daddy and I are just cooling off. It sure is hot today."

Mercy glared at Judah. "What did you let her do?"

Judah shrugged. "Eve didn't do anything. I did. I was showing off a little for my daughter."

"Is that right?" Mercy zeroed in on Eve.

Eve's cheeks blushed bright pink. "Uh-huh."

Mercy scanned the area in every direction. When her gaze fell on the empty spot in the woods created by the absence of six large pine trees, she gasped.

Focusing on Eve, she said, "I want the truth, young lady. Did you—" she nodded toward the woods "—do that?"

"Do what?" Eve asked.

Mercy glared at Judah. "Not only did you allow her to do something extremely dangerous, you taught her to lie."

"No, Mother, please. Don't be angry with Daddy." Eve yanked her feet from the creek and hopped up off the ground. "I did it. I zapped a whole bunch of trees. I was aiming at just one, but—" she flopped her hands open on either side of her "—my energy ball kind of went crazy, and all those trees went poof."

"Oh, God, oh, God," Mercy mumbled under her breath, then turned to Judah. "Did you help her create an energy bolt?"

Judah stood up to his full six-two height and settled his gaze on Mercy. "Our daughter didn't need any help. She was perfectly capable of creating an energy bolt all by herself. And in case you haven't realized it, she took out six trees with one bolt."

"She took out—of course she did." Mercy marched over to Judah, nostrils flared, eyes blazing. "And you're proud of her, aren't you?"

"Damn right I am. And you should be, too."

"I *am* proud of Eve, but…she could have been hurt, or hurt someone else."

"I wouldn't have let that happen."

They stood there, glaring at each, a hairsbreadth apart, the tension between them palpable. She was furious with him. He loved that about her, the passion, the fierce, protective mama tiger in her. He wanted nothing more than to take her here and now, and except for Eve's presence, he would have been sorely tempted.

She knew what he was thinking. He could see it in her eyes. And he also sensed her desire. Like animals powerless to resist the mating call, they couldn't break the visual contact or the psychic bond that held them spellbound.

Spellbound his ass! He wasn't some lovesick young fool. And he certainly wasn't in love with Mercy. Once he'd screwed her again, this fever in his blood would cool.

"Mercy!" Sidonia cried as she came across the open field, three people following her. "Is Eve all right? Did that devil…?"

"She's fine," Mercy called.

"I'm getting damn sick and tired of her calling me the devil," Judah said.

"Oh, great. Just great." Mercy heaved a deep, exasperated sigh. "She's got Brenna and Geol and Hugh with her."

"A Raintree lynch party, no doubt." Judah turned to face the approaching hangmen.

"You keep quiet." She gave Judah and Eve stern looks. "Both of you. Let me do all the talking."

Huffing and puffing, Sidonia stopped a couple of feet from Mercy. "I turned my back for two seconds, and he ran off with her."

"It's all right," Mercy said. "It won't happen again. Will it?" She looked from father to daughter.

Eve shook her head, then bowed it in a contrite manner. Totally false regret, of course.

Judah didn't respond.

"What happened over there?" Hugh, a robust, gray-haired Raintree, pointed to the wide bare spot in the nearby woods. "You aren't cutting down timber are you, Mercy?"

"Just a little psychic accident," Mercy said. "I'm completely to blame."

Hugh stepped forward, looked Judah over from head to toe, and held out his hand. "I'm Hugh Sullivan and you're...?"

"This is Judah Blackstone," Mercy said. "Judah and I went to college together. He's visiting for a few days."

Judah hesitated, then took the man's hand and exchanged a cordial shake.

Hugh studied Judah with his green Raintree eyes. "Well, you *are* a handsome devil, all right." Hugh chuckled. "I couldn't figure out why Sidonia kept referring to you as the devil."

"I'm afraid Sidonia and I got off on the wrong foot when I first arrived," Judah said, then looked right at the nanny. "I'm sorry if our little game of hide-and-seek worried you. Eve and I were having so much fun playing that it never entered my head you'd be concerned about her."

"Humph." Sidonia gave him a condemning glare.

Judah glanced at the other man and woman, who seemed as intrigued by his presence as Hugh had been. He nodded to them.

"Hello," the woman said. "I'm Brenna Drummond, a distant cousin of Mercy's."

The other man held up his hand in greeting. "I'm Geol Raintree, a not so distant cousin."

"Forgive us, Mr. Blackstone, for being so curious, but Mercy having an old boyfriend visiting is quite an event." Brenna smiled knowingly at Mercy, apparently giving her approval.

"Judah wasn't my—" Before Mercy could finish her sentence, Judah slipped his arm around her waist. She went stiff as a board.

As if on cue, Eve cuddled up to Judah's other side.

"Well, it looks as if our little Eve likes you, Mr. Blackstone," Hugh said. "It's always a good sign when a woman's child likes you."

"Hugh is grilling trout tonight, and I'm making homemade ice cream," Brenna said. "Why don't all of you come to my cabin for dinner?"

"Thank you, but I'm afraid—"

Once again, Judah cut Mercy off mid-sentence. "We'd love to, wouldn't we?"

"Yippee!" Eve shouted. "Brenna makes the best ice cream in the world."

Mercy forced a smile. After the search party went their separate ways and Mercy sent Eve back to the house with Sidonia, she confronted Judah.

"What did you think you were doing, agreeing to have dinner with my guests?"

"I was making an effort to be polite so they wouldn't suspect there was a wolf among the sheep. Wasn't that what you wanted me to do?"

"What I want you to do is disappear from my life and never return."

"If I left, you'd miss me."

"Like I'd miss the plague."

"I'll be leaving soon enough." *Going home to Terrebonne to fight and kill my brother,* he added silently.

"Once you've taken care of Cael, please don't come back here. Leave us alone. You're bad for Eve. You must know that."

"As a Raintree princess, you may be accustomed to issuing orders and having them obeyed, but I'm not one of your loyal subjects. Between us, I'm the master. And you're my willing slave."

"When hell freezes over!"

# THIRTEEN

Cael had tried unsuccessfully to crack the shield surrounding Eve Raintree's mind. All protective devices, no matter how strong, could be breached. It was simply a matter of finding the key. Every spell had a reversal spell. Every charm could be destroyed. Every power could be deflected. Given enough time, he could find a way into Eve's thoughts so he could influence her thinking, but time was one thing he didn't have. In two days he would lead his troops against the Raintree sanctuary. In two days he would kill his brother and become the Ansara Dranir. Only one thing stood in his way: little Princess Eve. She, too, had to die—along with her parents.

But the child was an unknown. Half Ansara, half Raintree. Such children possessed the talents of each parent. With Eve's parents both royals, the girl's capabilities could be uniquely powerful.

Cael laughed at his own foolishness. Eve was six. No matter what abilities she had inherited, they would be immature and untutored. Her supernatural skills couldn't possibly be a threat to him. But her being Judah's daughter could.

Projecting his thoughts, Cael directed his message to one recipient. *Can you hear me, little Eve? Are you listening? I'm your uncle Cael. Don't you want to talk to me?*

Silence.

*Talk to me, child. Tell me why I shouldn't kill your father. I'll listen to whatever you have to say. Perhaps you can change my mind.*

No response.

*You want to help Judah, don't you? If you'll talk to me, I'll listen.*

A boom of psychic energy thundered inside Cael's head, the sound deafening in its intensity as it radiated through his body and brought him to his knees. As he doubled over in pain there on the rough wooden floor of his private compound quarters, an outraged voice issued a warning.

*Stay away from my daughter,* Judah said. *She is off-limits to you. Don't try to contact her again.*

The pain stopped as quickly as it had hit him. Cael staggered to his feet, thrust his fist into the air and cursed his brother.

*Get ready. I'm coming for you. Do you hear me, Judah? And when you die, our people will rejoice that they have a true Ansara leader, one who can return them to the old days when we ruled the world.*

Judah heard Cael's threats like a distant echo as he shut out his half brother's ranting. Cael had finally crossed that thin line between instability and full-blown insanity. He wasn't surprised. It had always been a matter of when, never if.

Knowing that, sooner or later, Cael would force his hand, Judah had put off killing Cael all these years for one reason only: his father's dying request.

*"Do all you can to save your brother. Kill him only if you must."*

In his own way, their father had loved Cael and had chosen to overlook his many faults. But in his heart of hearts, he had known that the seeds of insanity needed very little nourishment to burst open, bloom and ripen.

*Kill him only if you must.*

I must, Father, to save the Ansara. To save Eve.

*Daddy?*

*No, Eve. Don't use your thoughts to speak to me.*

*I'm sorry. It's just that bad man tried to—*

*Shh . . . I'll come to you.*

Undoubtedly Eve had heard Cael's threats. Damn his brother! Damn him to hell! Hurrying downstairs, Judah took the steps two at a time.

He found Eve alone in the living room, sitting on the floor amid an array of colorful construction paper, crayons scattered all around her. She glanced up at Judah when he entered but didn't rise to meet him.

"I saw him, Daddy," Eve said. "I drew a picture of him and of where he was when he tried to talk to me. Come see."

Judah walked across the room, stood directly behind Eve and looked down at her artwork. His muscles tightened when he saw the remarkable likeness of Cael that she had sketched in crayon. She had depicted his brother standing, his fist in the air, an expression of sheer madness on his handsome face. The background appeared to be gray cinder block walls, rough wooden flooring and outdated metal furniture. Interesting.

He had never known Cael to rough it, not when it came to accommodations. His brother preferred luxury above all else.

"Amazing," Judah said, awed by his daughter's talent. "You're a remarkably gifted artist."

Eve looked up at him, smiled and laid down the yellow crayon she had used to shade Cael's hair. "Am I, Daddy? Mother says the same thing. But she told me that she has no idea where I got such talent, because she and Uncle Dante and Uncle Gideon can't draw pictures like I do."

"My mother was a renowned Ansara artist," Judah said. "The pala—" He caught himself before the word "palace" escaped his lips. "My home is filled with her paintings."

"She wasn't your brother's mommy," Eve said with certainty. "His mother was bad, just like he's bad."

"Yes, Nusi was a very bad woman."

Eve stood and looked up at Judah. "Don't worry. I won't let him hurt my mother the way Nusi hurt my grandma Seana."

Judah stared at his child, amazed anew at her keen insight. Her abilities were not only unnaturally strong for one so young, but far more numerous than those of even the most powerful members of either clan. "How did you know about what happened to my mother?"

Eve laid her left hand over her heart. "I know in here. That's all. I just know."

"What do you know?" Mercy stood in the open doorway, her features etched with concern.

Eve ran over to her mother. "Guess what? I know where I got my talent for drawing such good pictures." She beamed her radiant smile at Judah. "I got it from my grandma Seana."

Mercy shot Judah a questioning glare.

"My mother was a gifted artist," Judah said. Seana Ansara

had been the most talented Ansara artist in generations. Not only had Nusi's bitter jealousy robbed Judah of his mother and Hadar of his beloved wife, but the world of an artistic genius.

"Did you draw something for Daddy?" Mercy entered the room, Eve at her side.

"I drew a picture of that bad man, Daddy's brother." Eve rushed over, picked up her drawing and held it in front of her to show Mercy.

"When did you see this bad man?" Mercy asked, staring at the remarkably accurate portrait of Cael's madness. Judah realized she was doing her best not to reveal just how upset she was.

"He tried to talk to me again," Eve said. "He keeps calling my name and saying if I'll talk to him, he'll listen." Frowning, she threw the picture on the floor, then stomped on it. "But I didn't talk to him, and my daddy told him he'd better not ever bother me again or he'd be sorry. Didn't you, Daddy?"

Judah cleared his throat. "There's no way Cael can invade Eve's thoughts unless she willingly allows him in. The shield you've put around her will protect her."

"Yes, I know." Mercy motioned to Eve. "Come along, sweetie. Sidonia has lunch ready. Your favorite—macaroni and cheese. With fresh peaches and whipped cream for dessert."

Eve eyed her drawings, and the paper and crayons lying on the floor. "Don't I need to pick up first?"

"You can do that after lunch." Mercy exchanged a we-need-to-talk look with Judah, then gave Eve a nudge toward the door. "You run along and tell Sidonia that Judah and I will be there in just a minute."

Eve hesitated, glanced from one parent to the other, and said, "You're not going to fuss at each other again, are you?"

"No, we're not," Mercy promised.

"I hope not." Eve slumped her shoulders, sighed and ambled slowly out into the foyer.

Judah didn't wait for Mercy to attack. "He's going to come for me. Soon."

"I see." She took several steps back and closed the pocket doors. "I suppose Eve overheard him say this to you."

"She didn't tell me she heard him, but, yes, I assume she did."

"When he comes, you can't fight him here on Raintree ground."

Judah nodded. "I understand your concerns. But if he finds a way to breach the shield around the sanctuary, I'll have no choice."

"Only someone with power equal to mine or my brother Dante's—"

"Before you ask—no, Cael is not the Ansara Dranir," Judah said. "But he *is* a powerful sorcerer, with an arsenal of black magic tricks."

"When he comes here to the sanctuary and calls you out, Eve will be aware of his presence, and she'll want to do something to help you."

"We can't allow her anywhere near Cael. Somehow we have to make her understand that the fight must be between my brother and me."

"She'll listen to what we say, but whether or not she'll obey us is another thing altogether."

"I'll find a way to make her understand."

"You can certainly try."

"When the time comes, I'll need you to stay with Eve," Judah said. "If I'm distracted by trying to protect her..."

"You need to talk to Eve and explain on a level she will understand how important it is for her not to interfere."

"Would you allow me time alone with her, without her guard dog?"

"Yes. I'll tell Sidonia that you're allowed to take Eve for a walk this afternoon while I'm working."

Judah noted Mercy's frown and the weariness she couldn't hide.

"You've been gone all morning, and Sidonia refused to tell me where you were, but Eve mentioned that you were making sick people well."

"It's no secret that I'm a healer," Mercy said. "This morning, I was with two Raintree seers who can no longer see clearly into the future."

"And were you able to restore their powers?"

"No. Not yet. This happens sometimes, especially when a talent is overused or... I believe with rest and meditation, they'll be fine."

"And what will you be doing this afternoon?"

"We had a new arrival yesterday, someone who lost her husband and both children in a horrific car accident six months ago. She's in agonizing emotional pain."

"And you're going to take her pain into yourself. How can you stand it? Why put yourself through such torment when you don't have to?"

"Because it's wrong not to use the talents with which we're blessed. I'm an empathic healer. It's not just what I do, it's who I am."

"Yes, you're right. It *is* who you are. I understand." Judah wondered if Mercy would understand that their daughter had been born to save his people?

\* \* \*

Judah spoke with Claude every morning and every evening, using secure cell phones, despite their advanced telepathic abilities. Telephone communication was more difficult for Cael to intercept.

"He hasn't returned to Terrebonne," Claude said.

"Then where the hell is he?"

"I have no idea. It's as if he's vanished off the face of the earth. Even Sidra can't locate him. He's undoubtedly shielding his whereabouts."

"Eve drew a picture of him today, after he tried to talk to her."

"Could she locate him for us?"

"She might be able to," Judah said. "But I can't risk her getting that close to him. He could capture her thoughts and hypnotize her, or enter her dreams and make her deathly sick."

"Wherever he is and whatever he's doing, he's up to no good."

"What about the warriors who left Terrebonne with him? Have they returned?"

"No, and several others are unaccounted for."

"Then it's begun, hasn't it? He's gradually amassing his army."

"Let him." Claude emitted a grunting huff. "He's a fool if he believes that a few dozen renegade warriors make an army."

"He told me that he's coming for me soon."

"And when he does, you'll kill him."

"We should be there on Terrebonne for the Death Duel," Judah said. "But that could well be what he expects me to do—return home and leave Eve unprotected."

"She has protection. Her mother and—"

"Raintree protection. It's not enough for a child such as Eve."

"Then do what you have to do. Kill Cael on Raintree ground, then bring your daughter home to Terrebonne where she belongs."

After dinner with his daughter and the ever-watchful Sidonia, Judah told Eve that he was going for a walk and would see her before bedtime to say good-night. They had spent hours alone together today, and he felt he had convinced her that she could be of more help to him by not interfering in his fight with Cael than if she injected herself into the situation. He needed to find Mercy and assure her that Eve had listened to him, and that when the time came, she would obey their orders.

As he headed out the back door, Eve called, "I wish you'd go see about my mother. She's almost always home for supper, and she wasn't tonight. Meta must be terribly sick for Mommy to spend so much time with her."

"Your mother's fine." Sidonia gave Judah a warning glare. "She doesn't need anything from him. When she's done her job, she'll come home."

"Don't worry about your mother," Judah said. "I'm sure Sidonia's right and your mother's fine."

"No, she's not, Daddy. I think she needs you."

Once outside, with the sun low in the west and a warm breeze blowing, Judah thought about Eve's concern for Mercy. He had wondered what would keep Mercy from dinner with her daughter, and suspected that Eve's take on the problem was accurate. Undoubtedly the woman—Eve had called her Meta—that Mercy was counseling was seriously ill. Was this Meta the woman Mercy had told him about, the one who had lost her husband and children six months ago?

Had Mercy become so engrossed in easing this woman's pain that she had taken too much of the agony into herself and was in such bad shape that she either couldn't return home or didn't want Eve to see her in her weakened condition? Was Eve right—did Mercy need him?

Hell. What difference did it make? Why should he care if Mercy was writhing in pain, or perhaps unconscious and tortured by the suffering that rightfully belonged to someone else?

*Don't think about Mercy. Think about Cael. About finally meeting him in combat.*

*Think about Eve. About keeping her safe and taking her home to Terrebonne.*

But he couldn't help himself, and his thoughts returned to the past and the promise he'd once made.

*I'm sorry, Father. I've done all I can, tried everything possible. Cael can't be saved. He is as insane as Nusi was. Even in death, her hold on him is too strong. Forgive me, but I have no choice but to kill my brother.*

Less than an hour into his solitary walk, Judah ran into Brenna and Geol taking an evening stroll. By the way they held hands and from the mating vibes he picked up from them, he suspected that if they were not already lovers, they soon would be.

"You're out all alone?" Geol asked. "Where's Mercy?"

"She's with a new arrival to the sanctuary," Judah replied. "A woman named Meta."

"Oh, yes. Poor Meta." Brenna shook her head sadly. "She should have come to Mercy months ago. I'm afraid it may be too late for her now."

"What do you mean, 'too late'?" Judah asked.

"Did Mercy not tell you? Meta tried to kill herself and will probably try again."

"No, she didn't tell me."

"We've all been taking turns," Brenna said, then lowered her voice to a whisper. "A suicide watch."

"Where is Meta's cabin?" Judah asked, then quickly added, "I thought I'd meet Mercy and walk her home."

Brenna smiled. Lovers always assumed the whole world was in love. Brenna was young, her mind an open book, so he could read her romantic thoughts quite easily. She suspected that Judah Blackstone, Mercy's old boyfriend from college, might possibly be Eve's father, and she hoped they would rekindle their romance.

Without hesitation, she gave Judah directions; then she and Geol disappeared, arm in arm, into the advancing twilight. The sky to the west radiated with the remainder of the day's light, spreading red and orange and deep pink layers of color across the horizon.

Meta's cabin was about a quarter of a mile away, one of three structures built along the mountainside. The topmost cabin overlooked a small waterfall that trickled steadily over worn-smooth boulders, until it reached one of the creeks that ran through the Raintree property not far from the main house.

When Judah approached Meta's cabin, he noticed that the door and windows were all open, a misty green light escaping from them. Pausing to watch the unusual sight, he tried to recall if he'd ever witnessed anything similar. He hadn't. Although there were a few Ansara empaths, only two or three had actually cultivated the healing aspects of their personalities. It took a great deal of selflessness to devote your life to healing.

He had heard stories of how, in centuries past, many royal Ansara had kept empathic healers caged for the sole purpose of emptying their pain into these women as if they were waste receptacles. He could well believe that someone like Cael was capable of such an atrocity and would even take great pleasure in inflicting such torture.

Judah moved cautiously toward the open front door but stopped dead still when he saw Mercy standing over a woman sitting on the floor, each woman with her arms outstretched as if welcoming a lover into her embrace. The eerie green light came from Mercy. It surrounded her, enveloped her, poured from her like water from a free-flowing fountain. The black-haired woman Judah assumed was Meta had her eyes closed, and tears streamed down her face.

Mercy spoke softly, her words in an alien tongue. Judah, as the Dranir, possessed the unique talent of zenoglossy, the rare ability to speak and understand any language. The gift of tongues. He listened to her soothing voice as she beseeched any remaining unbearable pain to leave Meta's heart and mind and enter hers. Wisps of green vapor floated from the woman's fingertips and entered Mercy's body through her fingers.

When Mercy cried out and cursed the pain, Judah tensed. And when she moaned, shivering, writhing in agony, it took all Judah's resolve not to rush into the room and stop her. But the moment passed, and the green mist filtered through Mercy and into the air, leaving behind a tranquil turquoise glow inside the cabin. Judah heaved a deep, groaning sigh.

Mercy reached down, took Meta's outstretched hands and pulled her to her feet. Speaking in the ancient tongue once again, Mercy bestowed tranquility on Meta's mind, solace on her heart and peace on her soul, a white light passing from Mercy's body into Meta's.

Judah watched and waited.

Finally Mercy released Meta's hands and said, "Rest now.

Tomorrow you will prepare to move into the next phase of your life."

"Thank you." Meta wiped the moisture from her damp cheeks. "If you hadn't... I can never repay you for what you've done."

"Repay me by living a long and full life."

Judah could tell by how whisper soft Mercy's voice was, and by the way she wavered slightly, that she was near exhaustion. When she turned and walked toward the door, she moved slowly, as if her feet were bound with heavy weights. Judah backed out of the doorway and waited for her outside. When she stepped out into the fresh night air, she staggered and grabbed the doorframe to steady herself. As the moment of weakness passed, she closed the door behind her. Then she saw Judah.

"What are you doing here?"

"Waiting for you, to walk you home."

She glared at him.

"That was quite remarkable, what you did in there," he told her.

"How long have you been here?"

"Only a few minutes, but long enough to see what you were doing. She's going to be all right now, isn't she? She won't try to kill herself again."

"How did...? Who told you about Meta?"

"I ran into Brenna and Geol. Brenna told me about Meta, and also how to find her cabin. Did you know that Brenna thinks we were lovers and that I'm Eve's father?"

Mercy rubbed her forehead. "I'm too tired to worry about what Brenna thinks. As long as she doesn't suspect that you're Ansara..."

"She doesn't."

Mercy nodded. "Good. Now I need to go home and rest. I'm very tired. If you wanted to talk to me about something in particular, it will have to wait a few hours until I've rested."

"I really did come here just to walk you home."

She eyed him suspiciously, then started moving away from the cabin. Judah fell into step beside her but didn't say anything else. They walked a good forty yards or so in silence, the only sounds the nocturnal rural symphony coming slowly to life all around them.

Suddenly Mercy stopped. "Judah?"

"Yes?"

"I—I don't think—"

She wavered unsteadily, then spiraled downward in a slow whirl to the ground. Judah called her name as she lay at his feet, a serene angel who had spent her last ounce of energy. He knelt and lifted her into his arms; then glanced up at the mountain-side cabin nestled above the waterfall.

Waking suddenly, Mercy shot straight up, gasping for air, feeling disoriented and strangely frightened. Where was she? Not at home. She patted the surface around her. She was in a bed, just not her bed.

"How do you feel?" Judah asked.

Judah?

She turned to follow the sound of his voice. He was standing halfway across the room, near the windows, moonlight high-lighting his tall, muscular body.

"Where are we?" she asked.

"In the cabin near the waterfall."

"What happened?" She held up a restraining hand. "No, it's

all right. I remember. I felt faint and... Why did you bring me here instead of taking me home?"

He moved toward her. She scooted to the edge of the bed and stood to face him.

"I thought we needed some time alone. Without Sidonia. Without Eve."

"Eve will be concerned that we haven't come home."

"I let her know that you're all right and we're together. She's asleep now."

"I'm not staying here." Mercy took several weak, tentative steps, then faltered.

Judah reached out and caught her before she fell, keeping her on her feet as he wrapped his arms around her. "Why should we fight the inevitable? I want you, and you want me."

When she tried to free herself from his tenacious embrace, he held fast.

Tilting her head so that she could look him right in the eyes, Mercy said, "You are Ansara. I am Raintree. We hate each other. When you have killed your brother, then you and I will fight for Eve, and I will kill you."

He lowered his head, his lips hovering over hers. She tried again to break free, but without success.

"And it will bother you to have sex with me and then try to kill me. How deliciously naive you still are, sweet Mercy."

"Don't call me that."

"Why? Because that's what I called you the night you conceived Eve, the night we couldn't get enough of each other?"

"Let me go. Don't do this. Don't make me fight you tonight."

"I don't want to fight."

She struggled against his superior physical strength but couldn't overpower him. "Do you intend to try to rape me?"

He loosened his hold on her, and she pulled free, managing to make it to the door before her knees weakened. As she stumbled, she reached out and broke her fall, managing to stay upright only by leaning against the door. Judah came up behind her and gently pressed himself against her, trapping her between his muscular body and the wood. When she felt his warm breath on her neck, she trembled.

"I haven't even touched you, and you're falling apart," he told her, his voice a sensual rasp.

"I hate you."

"Hate me all you want."

Judah eased his hand across and down her shoulder, over her waist, and then he cupped her butt. Even through the cotton of her summer dress and panties, she felt the heat of his touch. And, God help her, she wanted him. All of him.

When he reached down, grasped the edge of her skirt and slowly bunched it in his hand, she closed her eyes and whimpered. His fingertips moved upward beneath the dress and over her panties.

She managed to say one word. "Don't."

"Shh..." he hissed into her ear as his fingers found the small of her back, that ultrasensitive spot just above her buttocks. "Relax, sweet Mercy. Let me pleasure you."

*Judah, please...please...*

He rubbed his index finger over her sacrum, faster and faster, harder and harder. Mercy held her breath as sensation built inside her. Suddenly a zap of electrical energy shot from Judah's fingers directly into the vertebrae in the small of her back.

Jerking uncontrollably, Mercy cried out as she climaxed.

# FOURTEEN

How could she have let this happen? She could have escaped. She could have stopped him. Why hadn't she?

*Because you wanted this. Because you want* him.

Judah eased his hand out from under her dress, letting the skirt fall back down over her legs, the hem brushing against her calves. But he kept her pinned against the cabin door, her back to his chest, his erection throbbing against her buttocks.

As the aftershocks of her orgasm faded away, Mercy fought an inner battle, her heart versus her mind. Her heart whispered soft, passionate yearnings, but every logical thought commanded her to flee.

*Fight your desires.*

*Fight Judah. Don't let him do this to you.*

"Let me go," she pleaded. "You don't want me this way, taking me against my will."

"I'll take you any way I can." He murmured the words against her neck. "And make no mistake, sweet Mercy, I intend to have you. Tonight." He shoved himself against her, grinding his erect penis against the cheeks of her ass.

Calling forth what strength the recent hours of sleep had regenerated within her, Mercy focused on overpowering Judah and gaining her release. She needed only a moment of forceful energy to take him off guard and free herself. As he ran his hands over her, his breath hot against her neck, she shot a jolt of electrical pressure from her body into his. He bellowed in pain as the shock waves hit his nerve endings.

She broke away from him, grasped the doorknob and yanked open the door.

*Run. Fast. Get away while you can.*

If only she possessed the ability to levitate, she could fly away from danger.

With her energy once again greatly depleted, Mercy made it only ten feet from the cabin before Judah caught her and whirled her around to face him. Hardened with rage over what she'd done, he focused his frigid glare on her body, raking over her from neck to toes. She felt the intensity of his gaze, a sensation of hot and then cold sliding downward, between her breasts, across her belly, between her thighs. Her dress split apart where his gaze moved over it, as did her bra and panties beneath.

Judah released her, then stepped back to view his handiwork.

Calling on what energy she had left to form a countermove, she sent a mental blast straight toward him, but he caught it midflight and crushed it as it were nothing more than spun glass. Her only hope was conjuring a spell. But did she have enough strength? And should it be a defensive or an offensive spell?

When Judah smiled, thinking himself the victor in their battle, she remained perfectly still, as if she were unable to move. But all the while she worked frantically, mentally reciting the ancient words in the tongue of her ancestors, casting a powerfully dangerous spell that would instantly infuse her with enough strength to defend herself.

Judah stopped abruptly, his big body rigid. *Do you know what you're doing? In your weakened condition, such a spell could kill you once its effects wear off.*

How did he know what she was trying to do?

He was inside her head, listening!

*How do you know the language of my ancestors?* Mercy demanded.

*Because they were my ancestors, too, and just as your elders taught you the language, my elders taught me.*

"Doesn't knowing to what lengths I'm willing to go to escape from you tell you anything?" she shouted.

Judah didn't reply.

Suddenly she felt him probing her mind. No! He was trying to erase the mystical connections she had been creating. One by one, the words disappeared. She struggled to replace them, but he worked faster than she did, removing more than she re-created, until the magic of the words exploded inside her, shattering the last of her energy and leaving her completely vulnerable.

He came toward her again, determination in every step.

"You're an animal! A brute!" She inched backward, intending to turn and run, but he was on her before she realized it, swooping down over her like a giant bird of prey capturing his quarry.

She struggled, beating her fists against his face and chest, flailing like a fish on a hook. While physically fighting him, she delved deeply inside herself, seeking the core of her strength. She might be weak and exhausted, but the essence of her powers remained. Always.

When Judah manacled her wrists in one hand and twisted her arms behind her back with the other, she kicked at him, hitting his ankles and calves. He thrust his left knee between her thighs and slid his leg around and behind hers, causing her to lose her balance. They fell together onto the ground, Mercy on her back, the wind knocked out of her, and Judah sprawled on top of her.

She gasped for breath, her chest aching as her lungs struggled for air.

He rose up just enough so that she could catch her breath, but before she had a chance to renew their sparring match, Judah plunged his hand between her thighs and ripped the torn fragments of her panties from her body. Mercy bucked up, trying to stop him, but inadvertently drew his exploring fingers into her feminine folds. He stroked his thumb across her nub as he delved two fingers inside her.

She keened softly as pure sensation spiraled through her.

He lowered his head and nudged the tattered edges of her bodice and bra apart to reveal her left breast. He lapped her nipple with the tip of his tongue, the action eliciting soft whimpers from her throat. While his thumb worked her nub and his fingers explored, his mouth covered her nipple and areola, sucking greedily.

Mercy lifted her arms and pushed against his chest, her movements weak and ineffectual. Not because she no longer had the strength to fight him, but because she no longer had the will to fight herself. She wanted Judah as much as she had wanted him seven years ago when she hadn't known he was Ansara. No, that wasn't quite true. She wanted him even more now than she had then.

She brought her right arm up and around his neck. Her fingers forked through his long, black hair, cupping the back of his head, holding him to her breast. She slipped her left hand between them and rubbed her open palm over his erection.

Judah growled like the aroused beast he was, and flung her hand aside to open his trousers and free his straining sex. When he withdrew his hand from between her thighs and lifted his head from her breast, she whimpered.

He looked down at her; their gazes locked. Passion ignited between them, shooting sparks of energy all around their bodies. While she draped her left arm across his back and yanked his shirt free of his slacks, he shoved his hands under her hips and lifted her up to meet his swift, hard push into her body. He took her with relentless force, battering her repeatedly, completely out of control. Clinging to him, she gladly took all that he gave her, as wildly hungry for him as he was for her. For every thrust, she countered. For every hot, tongue-dueling kiss, she reciprocated. For every earthy, erotic word he uttered, she replied in kind.

A passion that intense had to burn itself out quickly, otherwise it would have destroyed them. Mercy came first, spinning apart, unraveling with a pleasure that bordered on pain, a sensation she wished could go on forever. While she trembled beneath him, gasping and moaning, he climaxed so fiercely that his release caused the earth beneath them to tremble. Judah sank into her, his large, lean body a heavy weight that she held close, longing to capture this one perfect moment while they were one, their bodies still joined.

He lifted his head and gazed down at her. "Sweet, sweet Mercy."

She caressed his cheek.

He rolled off her and onto the ground beside her. When she glanced at him, she noticed that he was staring up at the starry night sky. She didn't know what to say or how to act. Had what just happened between them meant anything more to him than a sexual conquest? Now that he'd had her, would he not want her again?

"Judah?"

He didn't respond.

She lay there on the ground for several minutes, then sat up and pulled her tattered dress together, holding it at the waist. She rose to her feet, then glanced down at Judah and saw her ripped panties lying beside him. She turned from him and walked away, not caring in which direction she went.

When she reached the waterfall, she crept down the rough pathway that led to the small cave behind it. After removing the remnants of her dress and bra, she stepped beneath the cascading water and let the cool, clean spray rinse away the scent of Judah Ansara from her body.

Loving a man should bring a woman joy, not sorrow. The aftermath of lovemaking should be a time for togetherness. How could she love Judah so completely, so desperately, when he was an Ansara? How could she yearn to be with him, to lie with him, to be his woman forever, when she meant nothing to him?

Where was her pride? Her strength? Her common sense?

Without warning, Judah intruded on her shower. Totally naked, he stood under the waterfall in front of her, tilted his head and tossed his hair back over his bare shoulders. There in the moonlight, beneath the crisp, roaring water, he reached for her. She went into his arms willingly, unable to resist. He took her mouth in a kiss that spoke more distinctly than any words could have, telling her that he wanted her again, that he was far from finished with her. The kiss deepened as their desire revived, hot and overpowering. He lifted her up, his big hands cradling her buttocks. She straddled his hips as he walked them out from under the waterfall and against the boulder behind it. Balancing her against the rock surface, he buried himself inside. She gasped with the sheer pleasure of being filled so completely. He hammered into her as she clung to him, and within moments they came simultaneously. Judah eased her down and onto her feet, her naked body grazing over his slowly, his mouth on her lips, her cheeks, in her hair, on her neck, devouring her.

"I can't get enough of you." He growled the words, resentment in his tone.

"I know," she whispered, unable to move away from him. "I feel the same way. What are we going to do?"

He cupped her face with both hands. "For the rest of the night, we're going to forget who we are. You aren't Princess Mercy Raintree, and I'm not Judah Ansara. We're just a man and a woman, with no past and no future."

"And come morning?"

He didn't respond. But she knew the answer to her question. In the morning they would be enemies again, warriors in an eternal battle, tribe against tribe, Raintree against Ansara.

Judah roused at dawn, the sound of his cousin Claude's voice a wake-up call inside his head. He rolled over and felt the soft, naked body lying beside him, her arm draped across his waist. Mercy. His sweet Mercy. They had spent the night having sex again and again until they were spent. And yet just the sight of her aroused him, strengthening his morning hard-on.

*Judah, answer me,* Claude called.

*What do you want?*

*Why aren't you answering your phone?*

His phone? Damn, where was his phone?

*Give me a minute.*

Judah eased out of bed, careful not to wake Mercy, and spied his slacks lying on the floor where he'd tossed his clothes when he and Mercy had returned to the cabin after their tryst at the waterfall. He walked quietly across the room, bent over, picked up his pants and delved into the pocket to check for his phone. It was still there, vibrating away, signaling an incoming call. After slipping into his pants, he left the bedroom and went into the living room.

He put the phone to his ear. "Claude?"

"About damn time you answered."

"What's going on?" Judah asked, keeping his voice low.

"I've been trying to reach you for the past hour, and finally gave up and used telepathy, despite the risks."

"Do you know what time it is? It's not even daylight here."

"You should know I wouldn't bother you if it wasn't urgent. We've got big trouble here in Terrebonne."

"Hold on."

Judah glanced back at the open bedroom door. Mercy still slept. Moving silently so he wouldn't disturb her, he went outside and made his way a good thirty feet from the cabin.

"Okay, now tell me what's going on."

"Cael's minions have been quite busy throughout Terrebonne, spreading a rumor that Dranir Judah has sired a half-Raintree child."

"Son of a bitch," Judah cursed. "How widespread is the rumor?"

"It's just begun, but it's spreading like wildfire. By daybreak, half the island will know. By lunchtime, the other half will have heard the news. You have to know that Cael is hoping this will incite a rebellion."

"We need to do damage control right away. Call an emergency council meeting. Tell Sidra that I need her to address the people this evening and tell them about her prophecy."

"You have to come home, Judah. You need to be at Sidra's side when she confirms the rumor that you have a mixed-breed daughter."

"I can't leave Eve," Judah said. "Cael expects me to rush home when I learn of the rumors about Eve's existence. One of the reasons he's done this is to lure me back to Terrebonne, to leave Eve unprotected."

"If it comes down to a choice between Eve and your people..."

"There is no choice. Sidra has prophesied that Eve's existence is necessary for the continuation of the Ansara tribe. She told me that if I am to save my people, I must protect Eve."

"I don't know how well Sidra's prophecy will be received. She has said that Eve will be the mother of a new clan, that she will transform the Ansara."

"The people know that in her ninety years of life, Sidra's prophecies have provided us with unerring truths about the future. The Ansara revere her and believe in her prophecies."

Claude remained silent for several long moments. Judah simply waited, knowing his cousin would speak his mind after giving Judah's words more thought.

"If you feel you must stay there and protect your daughter, then I will stand at Sidra's side tonight when she addresses the Ansara kingdom," Claude said. "Since you can't return in person to Terrebonne, may I make a suggestion, my lord?"

Claude did not have to explain to Judah what he must do. He knew. "You want me to make a psychic connection to you and speak through you to my people."

"I will contact you later when our plans are finalized and the time is set for Sidra's address." Claude hesitated for a moment, then added, "These are dangerous times for the Ansara. It would be unwise to let your guard down, especially around anyone who is Raintree."

Claude hung up, leaving Judah to decipher his cryptic message. Claude could be referring to Eve, since she was half Raintree. But he suspected that the Raintree Claude believed he would be most susceptible to was Princess Mercy.

When Mercy woke at dawn to find herself alone in the cabin, she considered it a blessing. How could she have faced Judah in the cold light of day and accepted the fact that they were no longer lovers but once again bitter enemies? She crawled out of bed, dragging the top sheet with her to cover her naked body and protect her from the early morning chill. As she made her way to the bathroom, she stepped on the dress that Judah had sliced in two last night.

She would have to mend it.

As she picked up the tattered garment, just the feel of it beneath her fingertips set off her empathic powers. The cotton material held fragments of her own energy and all the emotions she had experienced when Judah's cold, penetrating glare had cut her clothes apart. Anger. Fear. Desire.

She hugged the fabric to her and buried her face in its softness as she relived the experience of Judah overpowering her and taking her savagely on the hard ground.

Carrying the dress with her, Mercy went into the bathroom, where she relieved herself, then washed her hands and splattered cold water in her face. She had the look of a woman who had spent the night making love.

*Stop thinking about Judah, about the hours of pleasure you shared, about how much you love him.*

Mercy lifted her dress from the hook on the back of the door, where she'd left it, closed the commode lid, readjusted the sheet around her chest and sat down. Fixing her gaze on the repair job at hand, she concentrated on using the heat she could generate with the touch of her hands to fuse the material together.

She had almost completed her task when she heard footsteps beyond the bathroom door. Her hand stilled. Her heartbeat accelerated.

Judah?

She flung the dress aside and opened the door. Wearing only his wrinkled trousers, Judah stood in the middle of the bedroom. They looked at each other for one heart-stopping moment; then he moved steadily, purposefully, toward her. She waited for him there in the bathroom doorway. When he reached her, he grasped the edge of the sheet where she'd tucked it across her chest, gave it a strong tug and peeled it from her body.

"It's dawn," she said.

"Then we'd better not wait. It'll be full daylight before long."

He lifted her into his arms and carried her back to bed, then stripped off his slacks and joined her. They mated with the same fury they had shared the first time they made love last night.

Would this be the final time? she wondered. Would she never lie in his arms again, never belong to him again, never possess and be possessed with such passion?

They had walked halfway back to the house together, then Mercy had gone on ahead and managed to sneak up the back stairs without getting caught. She had showered and dressed before she heard Sidonia stirring, then started her day as if everything were normal. Although Sidonia hadn't questioned her about why she hadn't returned home last night, she *had* given her several damning looks during the day, especially whenever Judah was nearby.

And to complicate matters even more, Eve apparently thought that her parents were now a couple. She was too young to understand anything about sex between adults, but she was intuitive enough, possessing some of Mercy's empathic talents as well as both her parents' basic psychic gifts, to know that things had changed between Mercy and Judah. Even if Judah didn't love her, Mercy accepted the fact that she did love him and always would. A Raintree mating with an Ansara was as improbable as a hawk mating with a tiger. But not impossible. What did seem impossible was that a Raintree truly loved an Ansara.

How would she ever be able to explain her feelings for Judah to Dante and Gideon? God help her, how would they react when she told them that Eve was half Ansara?

Dante could be stern and unforgiving, but he was always logical and usually fair. As with most people born into a position of supreme authority, he had grown up with a sense of entitlement, expecting to make all the decisions for his younger siblings. For the most part Gideon had followed in his big brother's footsteps until they grew to manhood; then he had become his own person, not always agreeing with Dante and occasionally locking horns with him.

When Mercy had told them she was pregnant, both Dante and Gideon had demanded the name of Eve's father. The fact that she had refused to name the man had enraged both her brothers, but in time they had let the subject drop. She knew that they assumed Eve's father was one of the Ungifted, or maybe a "stray," as Dante referred to humans who had developed gifts independently but were neither Raintree nor Ansara. Only with Sidonia's help had Mercy been able to keep Eve's unusually powerful abilities hidden and the truth of her paternity a secret.

But this was one secret that couldn't be hidden for much longer. Once Judah had dealt with Cael, he would try to take Eve.

No matter how much she loved Judah, she couldn't give him their child. And there was only one way to stop him.

But could she kill him?


After dinner that evening, Judah left the house without any explanation. He chose an isolated area more than a mile from the house and far from any of the guest cottages. Standing alone and insulated from all that was Raintree, he telepathically linked with Claude. He could hear what his cousin heard and see what he saw. He listened as Sidra addressed the assembled council, the highest ranking officers and many of the nobility, all congregated in the great hall at the palace. Through closed-circuit television, her message was carried to every home in Terrebonne.

"I have seen a child with golden hair and golden eyes. She

has been born for her father's people, to transform the Ansara from darkness into light. Seven thousand years of Ansara and Raintree noble blood runs through her veins."

Gasps and grumbles and cries of outrage rose from the audience.

Judah spoke through Claude. "Do you dare question Sidra's visions? Do you doubt her love for our people? Has my brother's madness infected all of you?"

Nine tenths of those assembled rose to their feet. Their shouts of faith in Sidra and allegiance to Judah completely overshadowed the handful of dissenters.

Sidra spoke again, her words of wisdom reassuring the Ansara that Judah's mixed-breed child was unlike any child ever born. "Eve is the child of our ancestors, the seed of a united people. She is more than Ansara; more than Raintree. Our fate is in her hands. Her life is more precious to me than my own."

The assembly listened with reverence, and through Claude, Judah sensed their doubts and concerns, but also their acceptance and hope.

A single request came from numerous Ansara, all wanting to know if, when Judah returned to Terrebonne, he would bring the Princess Eve home to her people.

"Princess Eve will come to Terrebonne when the time is right for her to take her place as your future Dranira," Judah replied through Claude.

When the cheers died down, a lone woman stepped forward and posed one simple question. "What of the child's mother?" Alexandria Ansara asked. "Are we to believe that Princess Mercy will simply give her daughter to you?"

A deafening silence fell over the assembly as they waited for Judah's reply.

*You must answer them, my lord,* Claude told Judah.

As he contemplated his response, Judah felt Sidra's hand on Claude's arm and sensed that she wanted to speak to him through his cousin.

*Your fate is tied to hers. Your future is her future, your life, her life. If you die, she dies. If she dies, you die.*

Every muscle in Judah's body tensed, every nerve charged with electrical energy. He understood that if Sidra could have explained further, she would have. Her prophecy was open to interpretation, but Judah knew that she spoke of Mercy, not Eve, and if he and Mercy fought over possession of their child, whichever one of them survived would die a thousand deaths during their lifetime.

"When the time comes, I will do what must be done," Judah told his people.


Sunset colored the evening sky as Mercy searched for Judah. He had left the house shortly after supper and had not returned. While she had been giving Eve her bath, Eve had stopped splashing her array of tub toys in the waist-deep, lukewarm water and grasped Mercy's hand.

"It's Daddy. Something's wrong. He's very sad."

"Are you talking to your father? Didn't he tell you not to—"

"I'm not talking to him," Eve said. "I promise."

"Then how do you know that he's sad?"

"I just know." She placed her hand over her heart. "In here. The way I sometimes just know things. He needs you, Mother. Go to him."

So here she was, sent off by her daughter on a quest of compassion. But when she found Judah, would he accept her comfort, or would he turn her away?

There was no point in wasting time taking useless routes that wouldn't lead her to Judah. She used all her senses to home in on his location. Once she picked up on his presence, she followed the energy trail left by his powerful aura.

She found him alone and lost in his own thoughts, sitting on one of several stone boulders in an isolated clearing deep within the woods.

"Judah?"

He turned his head and looked at her, but said nothing.

She took several hesitant steps toward him. "Are you all right?" she asked.

"Why are you here?"

"Eve sent me. She's concerned about you. She said you were sad."

"Go back to the house. Tell Eve that I'm fine."

"But you're not. Eve is right, something is wrong, and——"

Using a psychic thrust, Judah shoved Mercy backward, just enough to warn her off but not knock her down. She staggered for only a second.

"I get the message," she told him.

"Then leave me alone."

"Is it Cael? Has something happened? If you'll tell me, I can help."

"Leave me!" Judah shot up off the boulder, hell's fury in his eyes. "I don't want you." As he came toward her, he pinned her to the spot, and she didn't try to break through the invisible bonds that kept her from moving. "I don't need you. Damn you, Mercy Raintree!"

Judah grabbed her shoulders and shook her as frustration and anger and passion drove him hard. She felt what he felt and realized that he hated her for making him care.

"My poor Judah."

He clutched her face between his open palms and ravaged her with a possessive kiss. Swept up by the passion neither of them could deny, Mercy surrendered herself. Heart. Mind. Body.

And soul.

# FIFTEEN

Eve bounced onto the foot of Mercy's bed and whispered loudly, "I've been up for hours, Mommy. Are you and Daddy going to sleep all day?"

Mercy's eyes flew open. Startled by her daughter's cheerful greeting, she woke from a deep, sated sleep. "Eve?"

Wiggling around, making her way up the bed to position herself between Mercy and Judah, Eve spoke a bit louder now that she had roused her mother. "Sidonia told me not to disturb you, but I got tired of waiting, so I sneaked up the back stairs when she wasn't looking."

"What the hell?" Judah cracked open one eye and then the other. "Eve?" He shot straight up in bed, exposing his naked chest.

As Mercy lifted herself into a sitting position, the sheet covering her slipped, and she suddenly remembered that she was as naked as Judah. She grabbed the edge of the sheet and yanked it up to cover her breasts.

"Hi, Daddy."

"Hello, Eve." Judah glanced at Mercy, as if asking her how they were going to handle this rather awkward situation.

"You're not going to stay in bed the rest of the day, are you?" Eve looked from one parent to the other.

"No, we…er…uh…" Mercy stammered. "Why don't you go to your room or back downstairs with Sidonia, and Daddy and I will——"

Sidonia's voice bellowed, "Eve Raintree, I thought I told you not to disturb your mother. Come here right this min——" Sidonia stopped abruptly in the doorway, her eyes round and her mouth agape as she stared at the threesome in Mercy's bed. "This won't do," she muttered. "This just will not do." She shook her head disapprovingly.

"Eve, go with Sidonia," Mercy told her daughter.

Eve eyed her mother from tousled hair to bare shoulders. "Why aren't you wearing your gown?" She turned her gaze on Judah. "Daddy, are you naked, too?"

Judah cleared his throat but couldn't disguise the tilt of his lips.

How dare he find this amusing! Mercy glowered at him. He smiled.

"Come along, child." Sidonia held out her hand. "It's already summertime weather, and no doubt your mother got hot last night and removed her gown so she could cool off." If looks alone could kill, Sidonia's outraged glower would have zapped Judah. Thank goodness her old nanny didn't have the ability to shoot psychic bolts.

Making no move to leave her parents, Eve asked, "Did you get hot, too, Daddy?"

"Uh, yeah, something like that," Judah replied.

"Eve, go with Sidonia," Mercy said. *"Now."*

Puckering up as if she were on the verge of tears, Eve scooted back down to the foot of the bed, then slid off and onto her feet. "I woke you up because I needed to tell you that something's going on. I thought you and Daddy would want to know."

"Whatever it is, it can wait for a few minutes," Mercy said.

When Eve dawdled, her shoulders slumped, her head hung low, Sidonia grabbed her hand and marched her toward the door. Dragging her feet at the threshold, Eve balked. Glancing back over her shoulder, she said, "I'm going. But can I ask Daddy one question first?"

"What do you want to ask me?" Judah focused on Eve.

"Well, actually, it's two questions," Eve admitted.

When Sidonia jerked on Eve's hand, she issued her nanny a stern, warning glare.

"Ask your questions," Judah said.

"Uncle Dante doesn't have a crown even though he's a Dranir." Eve's eyes sparkled with anticipation. "I was just wondering if you have a crown?"

*What? Huh?* Mercy's mind couldn't quite comprehend her daughter's comment and question. "Eve, why would your father have a—"

"Actually, I just wanted to know if, since I'm a Raintree princess and an Ansara princess, do I get to wear two crowns? Maybe a solid gold crown and another one that's all sparkly diamonds. Or maybe just one really big crown."

Mercy snapped around and stared at Judah, who had gone deadly still. "What's she talking about?"

Unclenching his jaw, Judah ignored Mercy and answered his daughter. "I don't have a crown. But if you want a crown or two crowns or half a dozen, I'll get them for you."

Lifting her shoulders, tilting her chin and smiling like the proverbial cat that ate the canary, Eve turned around and all but pulled a stunned Sidonia out of the room.

Mercy got out of bed, found her robe lying on the floor, snatched it up and slipped into it hurriedly. Then she confronted Judah, who had gotten up, found his discarded slacks and was in the process of zipping the fly when Mercy headed toward him. She marched up to him and looked him right in the eyes.

"Why would Eve think you might have a crown, and why would she think she's an Ansara princess?"

He shrugged. "Who knows what puts ideas in a child's head?"

"Uh-uh, mister. That's not going to work with me."

"I'm starving. What about you? After the workout we had last night…all night——" he tried using that cocky, aren't-I-sexy? grin on her "——I need to rebuild my strength."

Mercy grabbed Judah's arm. "Answer my question. And so help me, you'd better tell me the truth."

He didn't try to veil his thoughts completely, allowing Mercy to momentarily use her empathic ability.

*What is the truth between us? We have a child we can't share. A life we can't share. I have never wanted another woman the way I want you, have never known such pain or such pleasure. If it were within my power to change the way things are, I would. But I cannot betray my people.*

Mercy jerked her hand away, her gaze glued to his face. "You lied to me. You *are* the Ansara Dranir."

"Yes, I am, and Eve is an Ansara princess, heir to the throne.

According to our great seer, Sidra Ansara, Eve was born for my people. That's why I rescinded the ancient decree to kill all mixed-breed children—to protect my daughter."

"No! Eve is my daughter. My baby. She's a Raintree." Eve's words echoed inside Mercy's head. *I was born for the Ansara.* "Only a few dozen Ansara were left alive after *The Battle*. Just how many Ansara are there now? Thousands? Hundreds of thousands?"

"Don't do this," Judah told her. "It serves no purpose, and it changes nothing."

"My God, how can you say that? The Raintree have believed that the Ansara were scattered over the earth and—no, no!"

She backed away from him, her eyes bright with fear. "I worried about how my giving birth to a half Ansara child would affect me, but when I saw no visible signs all these years, I assumed I was for the most part unaffected, but now..."

"You're wondering how much if any Ansara there might be in you, since you gave birth to the Ansara Dranir's child. I don't know, but my guess is none. You seem to have remained totally Raintree."

"But it's possible I was somehow affected and I'm not aware of it. When a Raintree woman takes a human mate, he does not become Raintree, but when a woman gives birth to a Raintree child, she becomes Raintree. It stands to reason that when a woman gives birth to an Ansara child, especially the child of the Dranir, it would somehow change her."

Mercy knew that she could no longer keep Eve's paternity a secret. If she had even suspected that Judah was the Ansara Dranir, she would have gone to Dante and told him the truth years ago. Was it too late now? It couldn't be coincidence that the Ansara Dranir had come to the sanctuary and saved her from one of his own. One of Cael's followers had tried to kill her, but Judah had stopped him. Why? Not because he loved her.

"Cael wants to be Dranir," Mercy said. "That's why he intends to kill you. And Eve. He can't allow your daughter to live, because even if she is half Raintree, she threatens his claim on the throne. My God, it all makes sense now. My child is at the center of an Ansara civil war."

"Don't do anything rash," Judah said. "I swear to you that keeping Eve safe is my number one priority. I won't let Cael hurt her."

"You've brought this evil here to us!" Mercy screamed. "If you'd never come to the sanctuary, if you'd stayed away…"

"You would be dead," Judah told her. "Greynell would have killed you."

"Why did you stop him from killing me?"

Judah hesitated, a look of anguish in his cold, gray eyes. "No other Ansara has the right to kill you."

Mercy couldn't breathe. Her pulse pounded in her head, and for a millisecond she thought she might faint. "I understand. Dranir Judah had already claimed me as his kill."

Sidonia's screams echoed up the stairs, down the hall and through the open door to Mercy's bedroom.

"Eve!" Mercy cried as she ran past Judah on her way out of the room.

Judah followed her down the backstairs. When they entered the kitchen, they instantly saw what had frightened Sidonia. Levitating several feet off the floor in the middle of the kitchen, Eve hung in midair, her mouth open, her little body stiff, and rotating slowly around and around. Her long, willowy hair floated straight up, parting in the back to reveal a glimpse of the blue crescent moon birthmark that branded her an

Ansara. Her eyes faded from Raintree green to shimmering yellow-brown, then back to green. Soft, golden light twinkled on each of her fingertips.

Mercy rushed toward her daughter but couldn't touch her. A barrier of some kind protected Eve, sealing her off completely from everything around her.

Judah shoved Mercy out of the way, and he, too, tried to breach the shield around Eve. "It's impenetrable."

"This has never happened to her before," Mercy said. "Is Cael doing this? Are you doing it?"

"No, I don't think this is Cael's handiwork. And I swear to you that I'm not doing it." He stared at their child, who was deep in the throes of some unknown type of transformation. "Maybe it has something to do with Sidra's prophecy."

Grabbing Judah's arm, Mercy demanded, "What about the prophecy?"

"He's trying to change her." Sidonia pointed a bony finger at Judah. "He's drawing the Raintree out of her. You see the way her eyes are going from green to gold."

"Hush, Sidonia." Mercy looked at Judah, her gaze imploring him.

"Sidra says that Eve is a child of light, born for the Ansara." Judah focused completely on Eve. "As her father, I'd die to protect her. And as the Dranir, I am sworn to protect her for the sake of my people's future."

Mercy wasn't sure what to believe. Was Judah telling her the truth, or at least a half-truth? Or was he lying to her? "We have to do something to stop this." She tried again to penetrate the force field surrounding Eve but was thrown backward from an electrical charge the shield emitted. "There has to be a way to break the barrier."

"I don't think that will be necessary," Judah said. "Look at her. She seems to be returning to normal."

Eve floated down to the floor, landing easily on her feet. Her hair fell about her shoulders, and the light on her fingertips disappeared. She glanced from Judah to Mercy, her eyes once again completely Raintree green.

"Eve? Eve, are you all right?" Mercy asked, choking back tears.

Eve ran to Mercy, her arms outstretched. Mercy lifted her daughter into her arms and held her possessively. Resting her head on Mercy's shoulder, Eve clung to her mother. When Judah approached, Mercy gave him a warning glare, all but snarling in her protective mother mode.

Suddenly Eve lifted her head and gasped. "Oh, shit!"

"What?" Mercy and Judah asked in unison.

"Where did you ever hear such an ugly word?" Sidonia, ever the grandmotherly nanny, scolded.

Eve looked at Sidonia. "I heard Uncle Dante say it. And Uncle Gideon."

Mercy grasped Eve's chin to gain her attention. "When did you hear your uncles—"

"Just a minute ago," Eve said. "I heard them both say it. Uncle Dante said it when he found out that the bad Ansara caused the fire at his casino. And Uncle Gideon said it when he found out that the person who killed Echo's friend was a very bad Ansara."

"How do you know about the fire?" Mercy asked. "And Echo's roommate?" She hadn't told Eve anything about either incident.

"I heard what Uncle Dante and Uncle Gideon were thinking when they said 'oh, shit' right before I said it."

If Eve had heard her uncles' thoughts correctly, then that

meant only one thing. "They're trying to kill us." Mercy realized the horrible truth. "The Ansara went after each of us—Dante and Gideon and me and...oh, God—Echo!" Holding Eve tightly, she started moving backward, away from Judah. "You knew what was happening, didn't you? Has it all been a lie? Are you and your brother really allies?"

"Don't jump to conclusions," Judah said. "Everything I've told you about Cael is the truth."

"Just like everything you told me about *you* was the truth?"

Judah took several steps toward her.

"Stop!" Mercy shouted. "I mean it. Don't come near me or Eve."

"Mommy, don't be mad at my daddy." Eve gazed into Mercy's eyes.

Suddenly the telephone rang.

"Answer it, Sidonia," Mercy said.

Sidonia scurried across the room and picked up the portable phone from the charger base. "Hello." She sighed. "Thank God, it's you. Yes, she's here." Sidonia brought the telephone to Mercy, all the while glaring at Judah as if she thought her evil stare could keep him at bay. "It's Dante."

"Dante?" Mercy said as she took the phone.

"Don't talk, just listen," he told her. "We're under attack from the Ansara. They were behind the fire here at the casino, and behind the attempt on Echo's life. Don't ask me any particulars. Just believe me when I say that I know it's only a matter of time before they strike the sanctuary. It'll be soon. Today would be my guess since—"

"Today is Alban Heruin." *Light of the Shore*, the summer solstice, lying between *Light of the Earth* and *Light of the Water*, the equinoctial celebrations. "The height of the sun's power."

"I've just boarded the jet, and we're leaving Reno. I'm on my way home. Gideon has already left Wilmington. We should both be there by late this afternoon."

"Dante, there's something I need to tell you." How could she explain to him that this was all her fault?

"Whatever it is, it'll have to wait."

"Please——"

"Just hold things together until we get there. Understand?"

"I understand."

"And if a woman named Lorna tries to contact you— she's mine."

The dial tone hummed in Mercy's ear. "Dante?" She flung the phone down on the kitchen counter, then turned to confront Judah.

"Daddy's gone," Eve said.

Mercy visually scanned the room. Judah *was* gone. When had he left, and where was he now?

A couple of seconds after Dante called Mercy, Judah heard Claude's telepathic message. *You're not answering your cell phone again. Damn it, Judah, all hell's broken loose and you've left me no choice but to——*

*All hell's broken loose here, too,* Judah told his cousin. *Mercy knows that I'm the Dranir.*

*That's the least of our problems right now.*

Judah ran up the back stairs. *Look, if you're about to tell me that Cael not only sent someone after Mercy but after her brothers and her cousin Echo, too, don't bother. Dante just called Mercy, and I listened in on their conversation.*

*Then they figured it out just about the same time the council did,* Claude said.

*Don't say anything else. Give me a minute. My phone's upstairs.*
*We don't have a minute to waste.*

Judah rushed into Mercy's bedroom and searched for his cell phone. He finally found it lying on the floor next to his shirt, covered with one of his socks. He picked it up and called Claude.

"What do you know that I don't?" Judah asked.

"We received information that Cael is somewhere in North Carolina," Claude said.

"That's no surprise."

"We suspect that he has up to a hundred warriors with him, and they're somewhere between Asheville and the Raintree sanctuary."

"A hundred! How the hell did he—crap! He's been recruiting these people for quite some time, hasn't he? Which isn't really a surprise."

"Well, this *will* surprise you—according to our informant, Cael is planning an all-out attack on the sanctuary sometime within the next twelve hours."

"Damn! What does Sidra say? Why didn't she see this coming?"

"She's not sure, but she suspects that Cael has somehow cloaked the details of his plan so that none of our Ansara seers were able to clearly foresee it. And he's probably put some kind of spell on all the Raintree seers, as well."

"We can't let this happen," Judah said.

"We can't stop it."

"We can try. Call in the Select Guard. Have as many as will fit on the jet come with you immediately. Have the rest follow as soon as possible. Bring them here to North Carolina. Fly into Asheville. Civilian dress for everyone. Understand?"

"Yes, my lord. We need to be as inconspicuous as possible. They can change into uniform on the way to the sanctuary."

"I'll arrange ground transportation for you, and when you arrive outside the sanctuary boundary, I'll be waiting for you," Judah said. "Contact me when you're close. In the meantime, once I'm certain Mercy can safeguard Eve during the battle, I'll make plans of my own."

"I know your first priority is to protect Princess Eve. But once she's no longer in harm's way, it will be too late to turn back. It will be all-out war between the Ansara and the Raintree. Cael has left us no choice but to fight now."

"Then we'll fight," Judah said.

"Where's my daddy?" Eve asked as Mercy knelt in front of her daughter. "Where did he go?"

"I don't know," Mercy lied. She suspected Judah had either left to join Cael or was making plans to do so. "But you mustn't worry about your father." She cupped Eve's beautiful little face with her open palms. "Listen to me, sweetheart, and do exactly what I tell you to do."

"All right," Eve said, her voice shaky. "Something really bad is wrong, isn't it?"

'Yes, something really bad is wrong. Your father's brother is going to come here and bring some other very bad men with him. So I'm going to send you with Sidonia to the Caves of Awenasa, and I'm going to invoke a cloaking spell to keep you and Sidonia safe."

"I need to be here," Eve said. "With you and Daddy. You'll need me."

Mercy choked with emotion. "You can't stay here. Your father and I can't do what we have to do if you're here. I'll be—*we'll* be too concerned about you. Please, Eve, go with Sidonia and stay there until I or Uncle Dante or Uncle Gideon comes and gets you."

Eve stared at Mercy, a soulful expression in her true Raintree green eyes.

"Tell me that you understand and that you'll do as I ask," Mercy said.

Eve put her arms around Mercy's neck and hugged her. "I'll go with Sidonia to the caves. You can go ahead and do the cloaking spell. I won't try to stop you."

Mercy heaved a deep sigh of relief. "Thank you, my sweet baby girl." She hugged Eve with the fierceness of a warrior facing possible death, knowing she might never see her child again.

When Mercy finally released Eve, she stood and turned to Sidonia. "I'm trusting you with the most precious thing in the world to me."

"You know that I'll guard her with my life."

Eve went to Sidonia and took her hand. The two waited while Mercy spoke the ancient words, invoking the most powerful cloaking spell she knew of, one that would make it difficult—hopefully impossible—for anyone to track and find Eve.

Mercy stood at the kitchen door, and watched while Sidonia led Eve across the open field and toward the higher mountain range. The Caves of Awenasa were over three miles away, deep in the forest that covered the far western mountainside. Within minutes, both Sidonia and Eve disappeared, the cloaking spell in full effect now, protecting them from detection, guarding them from harm.

Believing that Eve was safe and that she would instantly know if anyone had penetrated the cloaking spell, Mercy hurried upstairs to dress and make preparations for what was to come: battle—perhaps the final battle—with the Ansara.

Fifteen minutes later, dressed in black pants, knee-high black boots and a crimson blouse, Mercy came down the front stairs and headed for her study. Dante would contact all Raintree within driving distance first, and then word would go out to Raintree around the world. How many could actually make it to the sanctuary before the Ansara attack, she didn't know. There were only a handful visiting the home place right now— less than twenty in all, and some of them not at full strength. And her guess was that another twenty-five or so could be here within a few hours.

She also had no way of knowing how many Ansara comprised the forces Judah and Cael would bring down on the sanctuary, or exactly when the first attack would take place. Soon, certainly. Within a few hours? Before sunset?

After entering her study, she picked up the phone and dialed Hugh's cabin. He answered on the third ring. "Hugh, it's Mercy. I need you to gather up all the Raintree visiting here at the sanctuary and bring them to the house. Do this as quickly as possible."

"All right," he replied. "Can you tell me what this is about?"

"I'll tell all of you as soon as you get here."

Mercy could hardly believe what was happening. She felt like such a fool—for the second time in her life. Both times thanks to Judah Ansara. How much of what he'd told her had been lies? Part of it? All of it? One thing she didn't doubt: he wanted Eve and was willing to kill Mercy to get her.

And she also believed that he had killed one of his own people to stop the man from killing her. Because Judah had claimed her as his kill and wouldn't allow anyone else the honor of taking the Raintree princess's life. No doubt Dante was also Judah's kill. And perhaps Gideon, too.

How was it possible that she loved Judah, loved him as much as she hated him? Why had she let down her defenses, even for a few days, a few hours, a few moments?

All the while Judah had proclaimed Eve was in life-threatening danger from his brother, had it simply been a ruse, a plot the brothers had concocted together? Had Judah's purpose in staying at the sanctuary been to keep Mercy distracted?

No, it wasn't possible that he had fooled her so completely.

*Then where is he?* Why isn't he here explaining himself to me? Damn you, Judah. Damn you!

*Reno, Nevada, 9:15 a.m. (Reno time)*

Lorna hadn't taken the time to make any calls while she'd still been at Dante's house; instead, she'd grabbed his address book, checked to see that both Mercy and Gideon were listed, then run for her old Corolla. While she was on the way to the airport, she put her cell phone to use. She knew she didn't have time to fly commercial, but she didn't know how to go about renting a jet. She had a pocket full of cash and one credit card with a five-thousand-dollar limit. If that wasn't enough money, she didn't know what she would do.

The only person she knew in Reno who might be able to help her was Al Franklin, Dante's chief of security. He wasn't exactly on her favorites list, but Dante not only liked him, he trusted him—and this was an emergency.

Thank God, thank God. Al's number was listed, too. She'd been afraid Dante would have all his numbers stored on his cell phone, which he had with him. Swiftly, keeping one eye on the twisting road, she punched in the numbers.

"'Lo?"

The sleepy voice reminded her that it was—she glanced at the dashboard clock—not yet ten o'clock on a Sunday morning.

"This is Lorna Clay!" she half yelled. "Dante's gone—there's trouble at Sanctuary——he might get killed! I have to get there. How do I hire a jet?"

"Whoa! Wait—what did you say?"

"Sanctuary. There's trouble at Sanctuary. I need a jet!"

"How is Dante getting there?"

"I don't know!" Why was he playing twenty questions? Why didn't he answer *her* questions? "He just ran out. I'm about half an hour behind him, I think."

"Go to the airport," Al said swiftly. "He has two corporate jets. He'll take the bigger, faster one. I'll call and have the smaller one fueled and ready. It'll take longer— you'll have to put down somewhere for fuel—but you still won't be more than an hour, hour and a half, behind him."

"Thank you," she said, almost sobbing with relief. "I didn't think——"

"You didn't think I'd help? You said the magic word."

"'Please'?" She didn't know if she'd said "please," but she'd definitely said "thank you."

"Sanctuary," he said.

*Wilmington, North Carolina, 1:00 p.m.*

Hope Malory paced the kitchen nervously as she waited for the phone to ring. Gideon hadn't been gone much more than an hour, so she really shouldn't expect his call so soon, but still…she was anxious. He owed her a *serious* explanation.

When the phone finally did ring, she lurched forward and grabbed the receiver. "Hello?"

She held her breath as she waited for Gideon's calming, reasonable voice on the other end of the line. Her first clue that it wasn't Gideon was the lack of static.

A woman's smooth voice caused Hope's heart to drop. "Is this the Gideon Raintree residence?'

Great. An old girlfriend. A wannabe girlfriend. Maybe a telemarketer. "Yes, but he's not——"

"Not there, I know," the woman said, not quite so smoothly this time. There was an almost undetectable hint of panic in her voice. "There's no time for a proper explanation, but——"

That was the *wrong* thing to say. "I don't know who you are, but 'no time for a proper explanation' isn't going to earn you any points with me today."

Before Hope could hang up the phone, the woman laughed in a nervous but friendly way that caught her attention. "I can only imagine. I'll make this brief, then. My name is Lorna Clay. Dante and Gideon need us. I'm coming your way on a jet that's scheduled to land at Fairmont Executive Airport just west of Asheville shortly before six this evening. If you can pick me up, I'll explain all that I can while we're on our way to the Raintree home place."

Hope glanced at the clock on the kitchen wall and did some mental math, taking into account the horsepower in Gideon's Challenger. "I'll be there."

During the early afternoon, Mercy spoke to the eighteen Raintree visiting the home place, and together they began making preparations for the attack. By mid-afternoon, ten Raintree who lived within easy driving distance had arrived, including Echo, who had come flying in, tires screeching and horn honking. Her psychic abilities were powerful, but she had not yet mastered them, making her predictions a hodgepodge of sights and sounds and feelings. Mercy knew that one day soon, Echo would fulfill all the promise she now showed, including a latent empathic ability.

The moment Echo stormed into the house, she began calling Mercy's name as she ran from room to room. She shoved open the door to the study. Wild-eyed and frantic, she rushed toward Mercy and grasped her hand. "I've been going nuts all the way here. Seeing things. Hearing things. Help me, please." Echo clutched her head. "It won't stop. I had to pull off to the side of the road twice on the way here."

Mercy grasped Echo's trembling hands.

*Bloody sunset. Silent twilight. Death and destruction.* Mercy saw what Echo was seeing and understood the girl's panic. Working hurriedly, Mercy drew the fear and confusion from her young cousin's mind, and infused her with calmness and a sense of purpose. But Echo's mind fought what her subconscious perceived as interference and control.

Mercy clutched Echo by the shoulders and gave her a gentle shake. "Calm down. Now. We need you. I want you to concentrate. Can you do that?"

Echo quieted. "I—I can try."

"Good girl. Concentrate on the Ansara, think about the warriors who will soon attack the sanctuary. Try to find them."

"You mean..."

"I mean go deep and search for the Ansara who are close enough to reach the sanctuary before sunset." Mercy squeezed Eve's shoulders. "I'll be right with you every step of the way. I'll feel and see what you do."

Echo closed her eyes. "I'll do my best."

Mercy gave her shoulders another reassuring squeeze. "Concentrate on the name Cael Ansara. He's the Ansara Dranir's brother."

Echo nodded and closed her eyes again.

Mercy followed Echo, her mind and her cousin's separate and yet connected. Echo went deep within herself, while Mercy stood guard as she gently guided her cousin on a single, focused path.

*A convoy of trucks filled with men, flanked front and back by jeeps, rolled along the highway. Cael Ansara, dressed all in black, rode in the first jeep.*

Suddenly Echo saw only darkness and heard the screams of the dying. She fought to emerge from the vision, but Mercy urged her to fight her fear and follow through until the end. As if in accelerated motion, Echo's sight flashed over the faces of the Ansara warriors inside the trucks, and with Mercy's assistance, she absorbed minute traces of their emotions. The overwhelming hatred and savage bloodlust Echo sensed frightened her, and Mercy could no longer keep her focused. Realizing it was best not to force the matter, she helped Echo pull back from the vision as she took all the Ansara emotions from Echo and into herself.

"Crap!" Echo's eyes flew open, and she jerked away from Mercy. "There were at least a hundred of them. And they were all thinking about coming here, killing every Raintree in sight and capturing the home place."

Mercy staggered slightly as she struggled to dissolve the evil emotions trapped inside her. She could hear Echo talking to her, then felt her cousin shaking her, but she couldn't respond, couldn't return to the here and now, until she had disposed of the last particle of negative energy.

Several minutes later she slumped over, weak from the inner battle. Echo caught her before she hit the floor.

"Damn, that scares me," Echo said. "I've seen you do it before, but it's not an easy thing to watch."

Mercy offered her cousin a weak smile. "I'm all right."

"You saw what I saw, didn't you? There are so many of them, and they're heading here today."

"I know. We have to be as prepared for them as we can be. Dante and Gideon are on their way. I expect them to arrive sometime between five and six."

"How many Raintree do we have already here or that can make it here by the time Dante and Gideon arrive?" Echo asked.

"Not enough," Mercy said. "Not nearly enough."

*5:40 p.m.*

By late afternoon on the day of the summer solstice, a small band of Raintree were ready to go into battle to defend the sanctuary.

The clear blue sky slowly darkened with rain clouds moving in to obscure the sunlight. The rumble of distant thunder announced a brewing storm. But Mercy knew that Mother Nature had not created the impending tempest. Cael Ansara's forces had breached the protective shield around the Raintree sanctuary and were at this very moment charging toward the handful of Raintree prepared to defend their home place.

She had sent out Helene and Frederick as scouts, because of the few Raintree under her command, they possessed the strongest telepathic abilities and therefore could send her instant reports on the positions and movements of Cael's troops.

In times past, when the Raintree went into battle, their empathic healers were called upon to fight, but their primary purpose on the battlefield had been to attend to the wounded. Today Mercy had no choice but to be all warrior. Until Dante and Gideon arrived, she would lead her people against the

Ansara, and then she would fight beside her brothers, a united royal front with combined powers. Temporarily outnumbered more than two to one, the Raintree had to hold out against the invaders by any means necessary.

Reinforcements from the nearest towns and cities had joined the others who were visiting at the sanctuary, giving Mercy forty-five fighters to combat over a hundred renegade Ansara. The odds were not in their favor, but those odds would improve as more and more Raintree arrived at the home place.

Standing alone in her study, she bowed her head, closed her eyes and mediated for a few brief moments, focusing on the challenge she faced. Not only was the sanctuary threatened, but so was her daughter's life.

Mercy reached above the fireplace mantel and ran her hand over Ancelin's sword, the one the Dranira had carried on the day of *The Battle* two hundred years ago. According to legend the sword was much older, thousands of years old, and enchanted with an eternal magic spell. Only a royal empath could wield this powerful weapon, and only against great evil. If Raintree lore was correct, once Mercy used the weapon, it would then be known as Mercy's sword to future generations.

Using both hands to lift the heavy weapon from its resting place, Mercy recited the words of honor that Gillian had taught her. Once in her possession, the sword's weight lightened immediately, enabling Mercy to hold it easily in either hand.

Knowing that Eve was safely hidden in the Caves of Awenasa, protected by a cloaking spell and guarded by Sidonia, Mercy concentrated solely on leading her people against the Ansara.

Now, prepared in every possible way, she went to join her troops. When she emerged from the house, she was met with rousing shouts from those assembled, a show of respect and confidence. Twenty men and women stood before her, and the others were already strategically placed in and around the battlefield Mercy had chosen. The western meadow was protected by high mountains on all sides, and it was miles away from the Caves of Awenasa. The dozen Raintree who lay in hiding were ready to attack as Cael's troops drove farther into the sanctuary.

Mercy lifted her sword high into the air and keened the ancient battle cry. Following her lead, the others yelled in unison. The sound of their combined voices rang out across the sanctuary and mated with the late afternoon wind, carrying the Raintree call to arms far and wide.

# SIXTEEN

The hills rumbled with the clatter of battle, physical force united with psychic power, resulting in bloody bodies ripped, mangled and near death, as well as minds numbed or destroyed. The ashes of many disintegrated Raintree and Ansara covered the ground, spread across the meadow and into the hills by the force of the wind. Less than an hour since Cael's forces had set foot within the Raintree sanctuary and Mercy had lost a fourth of her people. Her only consolation was that they had destroyed more than an equal number of Ansara.

In the struggle, she had not seen Cael Ansara, nor had she caught sight of Judah. Had the brothers sent their troops into the fray while they bided their time until more Ansara could join them? She couldn't imagine Judah standing back and watching as his warriors fought and died. If she knew anything at all about Judah, she knew that he would do as she had done—take the lead and charge into battle.

So where was he?

She shouldn't be concerning herself with thoughts of Judah. He was the enemy. It was inevitable that they would meet on the battlefield and one of them would die. It didn't matter that he was Eve's father or her own lover. She couldn't allow her personal feelings to influence her, not where the Ansara Dranir was concerned.

During the battle, Mercy had employed psychic bolts sparingly, since they required a great deal of energy and she wanted to conserve as much as possible. Luckily she had encountered only two Ansara capable of the feat, and she had been able to deflect their bolts with Ancelin's sword. One of the sword's most potent magical properties was its ability to protect the woman who wielded it from all attacks, including psychic blasts, thus making her practically invincible.

Standing alone on a rock formation that jutted out of the ground, Mercy applied her telepathic powers to induce the illusion of a dozen green-eyed warriors on either side of her, battle ready and protective of their princess. To keep her magical guard in place, she would have to renew the illusion periodically or replace it with another.

As two male Ansara warriors approached, she concentrated on sending out paralyzing energy strong enough to permanently incapacitate them. Once she had dispensed with the males, she turned to the redheaded female Ansara coming toward her from the left. Mercy projected a mind-numbing mental bolt that caught the woman by surprise; she froze to the spot, then dropped into a crumpled heap. Sensing an immediate threat from her right, Mercy whirled around and swung her sword, landing a fatal blow to her attacker, a tracker with keen animal senses. Ashes to ashes. Dust to dust. As so often happened to those who died on hallowed Raintree land, his splintered body instantly returned to the earth.

Mercy noted Brenna in a fierce struggle near the creek, barely able to keep two Ansara at bay—a huge, black-bearded man and a tall, willowy blonde. After dissipating her troop of fading shadow soldiers, Mercy ran across the field, rushing to Brenna's aid. She took on the more dangerous of the two Ansara—the woman, who Mercy sensed possessed far more power than the male. The blonde turned and lifted her hand, showing Mercy the glistening energy ball floating in her palm. She smiled wickedly as she released the psychic bolt, but when she realized that Mercy's sword deflected the energy and sent it back toward her, she scrambled to get out of its path. She lunged for safety, but Mercy swooped down on her, plunging the sword through her heart. As Mercy withdrew her blade, the dripping blood vanished drop by drop, leaving the weapon shimmering and pure.

Brenna managed to take out her opponent, but not before he had pierced his poisoned dagger into her body several inches beneath her left arm. Mercy stepped over the dying blonde warrior in her haste to reach Brenna, who clutched her wounded side as blood seeped through her fingers. Mercy leaned down, lifted Brenna's hand away from the jagged slash and brushed her own fingertips over the torn flesh. The blood slowed to a trickle, then stopped altogether. Within minutes the cut would seal, and by tomorrow the wound would be completely healed.

As the pain and infection from the poison she had taken from Brenna flooded Mercy's mind and body, she doubled over in pain. She fought the agony within her, and it slowly drained away on a green mist of recycled energy carried off by the wind.

Mercy suddenly lifted her bowed head and looked due east. Her brothers were close. She sensed their nearness. For the first time since she was a child—except when they joined together yearly to renew the shield around the sanctuary— Dante and Gideon had opened their minds to her, connecting with her to give her infusions of their strength and power. The Raintree royal triad possessed an unequaled combined energy. Together, they could accomplish the impossible. They had to. The alternative was too unbearable to even consider.

More than twenty minutes later, as the battle escalated, Mercy caught her first glimpse of Dante, and shortly after that she spied Gideon. Within an hour of her brothers' arrival, more Raintree joined them, fighting alongside Dante and Gideon and Mercy. Still outnumbered, but holding their own, they called upon every resource available.

And then the moment she had anticipated and feared arrived. Cael Ansara appeared out of nowhere, his ice-cold eyes reminding her that he was indeed Judah's brother. Their gazes met across the battlefield, and Mercy heard his warning.

*Death to Dranir Dante. Death to Prince Gideon. Death to Princess Mercy. Death to all Raintree!*

Gideon shot a thin sapphire bolt of lightning at the most threatening of the three Ansara who surrounded him. Electricity danced on his skin, coloring his body and everything near him blue in the evening light, and deflecting almost all the attacks that came his way. He held a sword in his right hand, while he used his left to deliver deadly jolts of electricity.

None of these three were capable of sending psychic bolts his way, so Gideon conserved that special energy and fought with the power that was so much a part of him that it didn't require intense concentration. He would need to use psychic bolts again before the battle was over, he was sure, but he didn't need them now. The electricity he wielded was more than powerful enough for most of those he fought.

A long-haired burly Ansara whose gift was apparently one of extraordinary physical strength had twice penetrated the electrical field surrounding Gideon, leaving a deep, jagged cut on his shoulder from the small knife he'd tossed. Gideon's left thigh was sore from being slammed with a good-sized rock that had easily broken through the streams of electricity and almost knocked him down. But both injuries were healing as he fought.

The big man dropped to the ground as the lightning hit him square in the chest, but Gideon realized the bastard wasn't dead. This Ansara warrior's brute strength made it difficult to kill him with one shot, but knocking him down at least bought a little time. Gideon turned to face the other two.

These three—two men and one woman—had led him away from the others, obviously working to separate him from the siblings who gave him enhanced power. What they didn't realize was that, physically separated or not, the strength of his brother and sister remained in him, and would until the battle was over.

The female Ansara had short black hair and a gift for robbing the air of heat. She carried a sword, and had swung it at Gideon's head and neck more than once, only to have it deflected by a stream of electricity or by his own sword. The blade that had sliced his shoulder had not been poisoned, since the brutish soldier relied more on his extraordinary strength than anything as common as poison, but he suspected this woman's blade might be tainted. She'd also tried to freeze him by sucking the natural heat from the air that surrounded him, but he was generating so much energy at the moment that freezing him was impossible.

The redheaded man at her side most likely had some sort of mental power. He carried a sword in one hand and a small knife in the other but had displayed no outwardly threatening magical abilities. As he was the least menacing, Gideon turned his attention to the female Ansara, who had the audacity to smile. There had been a time when he would have hesitated to kill a woman, even an Ansara soldier, but after tangling with Tabby, he had not a single doubt about sending a deadly bolt of lightning, the strongest he could muster, into her forehead. Her head snapped back, she gasped loudly and dropped her sword. Dead, she was instantly frozen, taken by her own gift.

Her companion, the only one of the three standing at the moment, did not smile as Gideon turned to face him. The hesitant soldier lifted the sword in his hand, and Gideon did the same. He needed a moment to recharge, after putting down the more powerful two, and the remaining soldier did not look to be an immediate threat. In fact, he looked damned scared. Still, the redheaded Ansara before him had a chance to run but did not. Brave, but it sealed his fate.

There was great concentration on the Ansara's face, a wrinkling of the brow and a narrowing of eyes, and Gideon imagined the man was trying to affect him mentally in some way. Was he trying to push thoughts or emotions into Gideon's mind, or was he perhaps attempting to muster a pathetic bolt of psychic energy? Whatever he was trying didn't work, and as Gideon stepped toward him, sword in hand, the man swallowed hard.

Gideon was about to swing the sword when a sound stopped

him cold. Someone called his name in a loud, frightened, familiar voice. *Hope.*

He deflected his opponent's blade, then turned his head toward the voice that had broken through the sounds of battle and claimed his attention. Hope appeared, cresting the hill at a run, her gun in one hand, her eyes wide with shock and revulsion and all the horrors he did not want for her.

Out of the corner of his eye, Gideon saw the large, unnaturally strong warrior stand and shake off the electrical surge that should have killed him. Long brown hair fell across the Ansara soldier's face, and the muscles in his arms and chest seemed to ripple, to harden. Then the Ansara lifted his head and tossed his hair back, and his gaze fell on Hope.

"Kill her!" the man who fought Gideon screamed as he swung wildly with his sword again. "She is *his.*"

Gideon quickly killed the redheaded man, a dark psychic of some sort who had identified Hope as his woman, with a blade through the gut. He withdrew his sword smoothly and let the body fall, then spun to see the one remaining warrior running toward Hope.

Hope and Emma. They were his future, his soul, his home—and he would not allow the Ansara to take them away.

The enemy who now focused on Hope was closer to her than Gideon was. He could slow the big bastard down with another jolt, but would it be enough to stop him? Or would it be too little, too late? The Ansara warrior was too far away for Gideon to take him down with a psychic bolt, too far away for the accuracy and strength he needed. The incredibly high stakes of this battle crept higher.

"Shoot him!" Gideon screamed as he ran up the hill. "Now, Hope. Shoot!"

In getting this far, Hope had seen enough of the battle-ground to know that his order was a serious one. Before the long-haired brute reached her, she lifted her weapon and fired. Twice.

Her bullets didn't stop the Ansara, but they did slow him down. The enemy soldier staggered, looked down at the blood staining his massive chest, and appeared to be very annoyed by this unexpected resistance from a mortal woman—and Gideon knew he would now realize that she was mortal, since she'd been able to fire a gun. No Ansara or Raintree would have been able to make the weapon work on sanctuary land, and Hope wouldn't become Raintree until she gave birth to Emma.

Gideon continued to run, until at last he was close enough to do what had to be done. He formed and projected a psychic bolt, a bolt very unlike the lightning that was in his blood. Gold and glittering, it smacked into the Ansara, and in an instant, the threat to Hope was over as the Ansara warrior turned to dust.

Hope rushed toward Gideon. He let his electrical shield fall, and she threw herself into his arms.

"What the…?" she began breathlessly, her heart pounded against him. "This is not… Oh, my God… He just…" She took a deep breath and regained a bit of composure, then said, in a breathless voice, "You're bleeding again, dammit."

There was no time to explain as two Ansara warriors came into sight, rushing toward them with deadly intent. One held a sword in each hand, and the other displayed a weak flame of un-natural fire on his open palm. The firebug would have to go first.

"Stay with me," Gideon ordered as he placed Hope behind him.

As he raised his own sword and erected a barricade of pro-tective electricity that surrounded them both, she muttered, "I'm not going anywhere."

* * *

Dante whirled away from a psychic bolt of energy, and it shattered the tree trunk behind him. He threw himself as far away from the tree as he could, not even daring to look back, because if one of those massive limbs hit him, he would be dead. As he ran, he threw a bolt in retaliation, hoping to keep the Ansara ducking for cover until he himself could find a handy boulder to duck behind.

He'd lost track of Gideon and Mercy in the fierce battle, but he could still sense them there, pooling their strength with his. Together the whole was greater than the sum of the three parts, and they needed every scintilla of power they could muster. There were enough Ansara that they could almost team up three to each one of the Raintree.

An Ansara woman sprang from behind a tree and expertly threw a chain at his ankles. The chains weren't deadly, but if one wrapped around his legs he would fall, almost as helpless as a turtle on its back, and then the Ansara would make mincemeat of him. The chain flashed toward him, and less than two seconds after the weapon had left the Ansara's hand, he leaped as high as he could, drawing his legs up like an athlete on a trampoline. With silver fire the chain passed beneath him, whipping into the face of a groggy Ansara who had been trying to get to his feet. The man's face exploded in a mist of blood.

Dante threw a bolt at the woman, but she was as fast as a cheetah and bounded behind a tree.

He was tiring somewhat, taking a little longer to recharge between bolts. The Ansara had to be tiring, too, but there were more of them.

When had they gotten so strong? How could they have

rebuilt the clan undetected? Had an unusually strong Ansara escaped, two hundred years ago and somehow successfully shielded the clan from the Raintree sentinels? They must have established a home place somewhere and used it to feed their power. On a vortex, all things were possible.

Three Ansara erupted from cover, thirty yards to his left, charging him. He spun to face them and shot a bolt at the biggest one; the blast of energy hit the man in the middle of the chest, and he disintegrated from the force, but the other two raced on, and Dante didn't have time to rebuild enough energy to take both of them down.

Alarm prickled the back of his neck. He didn't stop to think, didn't wonder what was behind him; instinctively, he ducked and rolled to the right, coming back to his feet as a six-foot sword hacked the air where he'd been. A woman who had to be at least seven feet tall was wielding the sword as if it were a toothpick. Her lips pulled back in a snarl as she swung it again. He leaped back once more, but the tip sliced him diagonally from the left side of his rib cage and across his abdomen, and down to his hip.

The cut hurt like hell, but it wasn't mortal. She was too close for him to hit her with a bolt without getting caught in the back-blast, and the other two were only ten yards away now. Desperately he lowered some of the mental shields with which he held back his fire and sent a long tongue of flame licking at her. She fell backward in her haste to escape the hungry red beast. He turned his head toward the other two attackers, and they split up, going in opposite directions, flanking him but keeping a wary distance.

Fire was too dangerous to use on a battlefield. Any battle was chaotic, uncontrolled. He could send out a wall of fire at any time, but with the Raintree engaging the enemy all over the battlefield, he would be killing his own people, too. The larger the fire, the more power and energy it took to control. The risk was very real that, distracted at every turn, he would loose a monster he couldn't control. No one used fire in a battle.

The tall woman slowly got to her feet, grinning. Holding the sword in a two-handed grip, she began circling him, joining the other two as they looked for an opening.

His ass was likely dead, but he intended to take all three of them with him.

He didn't want to leave Lorna. The thought pierced him like a lance. He wished he'd told her again that he loved her, told her what to do in case he didn't make it back. She might be pregnant. The chance was small, but it existed. He would never know. He remembered the sound of her voice, full of outrage, yelling, "Where are you going?" and wished he could hear it again.

He heard her, actually heard her, so hard did he wish it.

Except she was yelling, *"What the hell are you doing?"*

Every hair on his body stood up in alarm. Aghast, he dared a quick look around and almost passed out in sheer terror. She was running headlong across the field toward him, not looking right or left, her hair flying like a dark flame. A body lay in her path, and she hurdled it without pause. "Fry their asses!" she bellowed, evidently wondering why he wasn't using his greatest gift.

He had recharged enough of the enormous energy needed for a psychic bolt, and without warning, he shot it at the tall woman. She turned, instinctively bringing up her sword to deflect the bolt as if it were another blade. The blast hit the big blade broadside, shattering it, driving needle-sharp shards of steel into her. She screamed, pierced in a hundred places from her head to her knees. One long shard protruded from her right eye. Shrieking nonstop, she instinctively put her hand to her eye and hit the shard, driving it deeper. She dropped to her knees and toppled over, much as the tree had done.

Dante spared her no more than a glance as he danced in a circle, trying to keep Lorna behind him and out of the kill zone, trying to keep the remaining two Ansara where he could see them. If he could hold them off until his energy rebuilt...

Without warning, one shot a psychic blast at him. Not all warriors could muster enough energy to wield this most powerful of gifts; most used more physical weapons, like the swords, which might be gifted with different powers but were still essentially used in traditional moves. This bastard had been hiding his light under a bushel, as it were. If their tactic had been to let Dante bleed his energy level down before unleashing their own blasts, the ploy had worked.

Lorna never stopped moving, stooping as she ran to pick up a fist-sized rock. "Fire!" she kept screaming. "Use your fire!" She was only twenty yards away, rushing headlong into the circle of death. His blood froze in his veins.

"Yeah, Raintree, use your fire!" one of the Ansara taunted, knowing he wouldn't. Then the man turned and shot a bolt at Lorna.

He miscalculated, not taking enough time to anticipate her speed. She made a furious sound and heaved her rock at the Ansara, making him duck. "Amateur," Dante muttered, firing a blast at the bastard—or trying to. He was too tired; he didn't have enough energy left.

The Ansara wolves circled closer, grinning, enjoying his helplessness as they waited for their own energy to rebuild.

They had used far less than he had; it would take only seconds more.

"Link with me!" Lorna screamed. "Link with me!"

His heart almost stopped. She *knew* what it would do to her, *knew* the agony....

There was no time for careful preparation, the gradual meshing of minds and energies. There was time only for smashing his way into her mind and tapping the deep pool of power. It fed him like water crashing into a valley after a dam collapsed, a deluge of energy that shot from both his hands in simultaneous bolts. Linked to him as they were, Mercy and Gideon both felt the enormous surge and were fed in turn.

Dante furiously fired bolt after bolt. Tears burned his eyes but never fell, the moisture evaporated by the cascade of energy running through him. *Lorna!* He could see her on the ground, lying motionless, but her power still poured into him as if there were no limit to it. He didn't need time to rebuild; the energy was there immediately, flying off his fingertips in white-hot blasts.

Faced with the killing machine he'd become, the Ansara retreated, drawing back to regroup. Agonized, Dante broke the link with Lorna's mind and charged to where she lay unmoving, her face paper white. There were bodies all around her, testament to how close the Ansara had come. If she hadn't been lying so still that they must have thought she was already dead, they would surely have killed her.

If he hadn't done the job for them, Dante thought with an inner howl of savage pain. He fell to his knees beside her, yanking her into his arms.

"Lorna!"

She managed to open her eyes a little; then her lids drooped shut again as if she didn't have the energy to hold them open.

He had drained her, turned her mind to mush. She had recovered before—but would she recover this time? Mercy and Gideon, not knowing what they did, had also been siphoning power from her. He couldn't predict the effects on her brain, because what he'd done to her—twice, now—simply hadn't been done before.

He looked up, looked around for help. The Ansara were retreating, disengaging from the battle. He felt numb, unable to make sense of everything that was happening around him. He needed Mercy. If anyone could heal Lorna, she could.

Lorna jerked in his arms, batting at him with a limp hand, and he realized he was crushing her to his chest. His heart leaped, almost choking him. Gently he laid her back on the ground, hoping against hope as he watched her swallow and try several times to speak.

"Are you okay?" he asked, but she didn't answer.

He picked up her hand and cradled it against his cheek, willing her to speak. If he could hear her talk, he would know her brain was recovering.

"Lorna, do you know who I am?"

She swallowed, nodded.

"Can you talk?"

She held up her hand like a traffic cop, telling him to slow down, to stop peppering her with questions. Slowly, laboriously, she rolled to the side and began trying to sit up. Silently he supported her, kept her from falling, as he watched her efforts. Finally she could sit, her head hanging down as she took in deep breaths. Dante rubbed her back, her arms, and asked again, "Can you talk?"

She blinked at him, then nodded, the movement as ponderous as if her head weighed fifty pounds.

Thinking she could and actually doing it were two different things. He waited for a sentence, a single word, anything, but she was silent.

In just a few minutes she got to her feet. She stood weaving, staring around her at the carnage, the sprawled bodies. He would have done anything to spare her seeing this. War was ugly, and war between the gifted clans was brutal. No one went to war and came out of it unmarked.

"Honey, please," he begged softly. "If you can, say something."

She blinked at him some more, frowning a little; then her gaze wandered back to the bodies around her. She took a deep breath, let it out, and said, "This looks like Jonestown, without the Kool-Aid."

During the relentless fighting, Mercy lost track of Cael and feared he had gone to find either Dante or Gideon, neither of whom she had seen in quite some time. But now that Dante led the Raintree, she could both fight and heal, as the situation demanded. Both were her right and her duty. She sensed Geol nearby, severely wounded and dying. If she could find him, she could save him. Following the flicker of energy left inside him, Mercy searched the ash-strewn meadow where the bloody bodies and dust particles of dead Raintree and Ansara mingled together, once again united—in death if not in life.

A large, muscular Ansara, his silver hair secured in a shoulder-length ponytail, lifted his sword in both hands as he charged toward Geol, who lay helpless on the ground. Instantly calling forth the power from deep within her, Mercy created a psychic bolt and hurled it into the attacking warrior's back. The blast exploded through him, shattering his body into dust fragments. She hurried to Geol, knelt down and laid her hands on him, drawing out his pain, healing his wounds. But as with every healing, Mercy paid a high price. Once the process of experiencing another's suffering and converting it into positive energy ended, she released that energy back into the universe, allowing it to escape from her in vapor form, a mist as green as her Raintree eyes.

When she rose from her knees, weak but revived enough to continue, Mercy sensed someone trying to connect with her. Then, without warning, she heard Eve's voice.

*Daddy's coming.*

*Eve?*

A thunderous roar shook the ground beneath her feet as hundreds of warriors in blue uniforms stormed into the vast meadow, quickly taking over the battleground. Mercy gasped in horror when she saw the man leading the massive force. Judah Ansara. He had brought reinforcements. Hundreds of Ansara men and women, armed and prepared to fight. There was no way that the Raintree who were united together here at the sanctuary could overcome such a mighty force. But they could and would figure out a way to hold out as long as possible, until more Raintree arrived to continue the battle. Tonight. Tomorrow. They would fight to their dying breaths, every man and woman defending the sacred Raintree sanctuary. This land could never belong to the Ansara.

The fighting slowed and then gradually stopped altogether. Cael reappeared, and his warriors lifted him up and onto their shoulders. He flung his arm high into the air, his sword silver bright and dripping with fresh Raintree blood.

Judah's troops formed a semicircle around their Dranir, a blue crescent moon of Ansara power. Then an elderly woman, at least as old as Sidonia, appeared at Judah's side, apparently having teleported herself into the battle, which meant she possessed a rare and powerful ability. Mercy immediately sensed a wave of respect and awe surround the woman and knew that this was Sidra, the great Ansara seer.

The battle weary Raintree followed Dante and Gideon, congregating on the opposite end of the meadow. To wait. To watch. To prepare. Mercy made her way to her brothers as quickly as possible. Knowing their thoughts, she assured them that Eve was safe.

A reverent silence fell over the valley as Raintree faced Ansara on the battlefield.

Mercy stood between Dante and Gideon. The two women with her brothers—Lorna and Hope, she had learned from reading their thoughts—stayed a good ten feet behind them. Mercy could not deny her fear. She might die today, but she feared far more for Eve than for herself. If she and her brothers did not survive this battle...

Dante made no move to initiate an attack. The Raintree continued waiting and watching, mentally preparing, psyching themselves up for what lay ahead.

Cael gestured for his men to lower him to his feet. Once on the ground, he marched toward Judah like a cocky little bantam rooster, at least four inches shorter than the Ansara Dranir. Brother faced brother.

"Hail, Dranir Judah," Cael shouted.

Cael's followers repeated his shout. Judah's warriors stood at silent attention.

"We fight together today, my brother," Cael said. "To avenge our ancestors."

Sidra laid her hand on Judah's arm, her eyes beseeching his permission to speak. With his gaze unwaveringly linked to his brother's, Judah nodded.

"Choose this day whom you will serve." Sidra's voice rang out with loud clarity, as if amplified a hundred times over, her words heard by every Ansara and Raintree within the boundaries of the sanctuary. The old seer lifted her hand and pointed at Cael. "Do you choose Cael, the son of the evil sorceress Nusi? If so, you follow him straight to hell."

When Cael lunged toward Sidra, Judah raised his arm in warning. Cael halted.

"Or do you choose Dranir Judah, son of Seana and father of Eve, the child of light, born to the Raintree princess and yet born for the Ansara tribe to provide us with the gift of transformation?"

Though Cael bristled and cursed, Mercy barely heard him over her own heartbeat, which drummed maddeningly in her ears. Sidra had shared Mercy's deepest, most carefully guarded secret with Ansara and Raintree alike—with Dante and Gideon. Her brothers glared at her, shock on Gideon's face, rage on Dante's.

"Tell me this isn't true," Dante demanded.

"I can't," Mercy replied.

"Eve is half Ansara, the daughter of their Dranir?" Gideon asked.

"Yes." Mercy answered Gideon, but her gaze never left Dante's face. "When I met him, I didn't know who he was."

"How long have you known?" Dante asked.

"That he was Ansara? Since the moment I conceived his child."

"Why didn't you tell me...tell us?"

The sound of Sidra's voice echoed off the mountains, spreading like seeds in the wind, capturing the attention of all who heard her.

"It is your choice," she said. "To live and die with honor at your Dranir's side, or be destroyed along with this madman who claims a throne that is not his!"

Shouts of allegiance rang out as the Ansara chose sides. Not one blue uniformed warrior broke formation, and only a handful of Cael's troops deserted him to join his brother's army.

"What's going on with the old Ansara seer?" Dante asked. "It's as if she's instigating war between the brothers." He looked to Mercy. "You don't seem surprised, which leads me to believe that you know what's happening, why the Ansara created this lull in the battle to iron out family differences."

Mercy realized that she did know, at least to some extent, what was occurring within the Ansara camps. "The brothers and their warriors are probably going to fight to the death."

"And you know this how?"

"How I know doesn't matter," she said. "All that matters is that we have to be prepared to fight the winner."

Within minutes, Mercy realized she had underestimated Cael's madness. The vision of brother battling against brother, Ansara renegade warriors against the Ansara army, that she had expected altered dramatically when Cael commanded his forces to attack the Raintree instead.

Taken off guard, Dante quickly recovered and started issuing orders, first to Mercy and then to his warriors. He told Mercy to search, find and heal as many of their wounded as possible, then send them back into the battle.

"If we have any hope of holding the sanctuary until rein-forcements arrive, we'll need every Raintree warrior left alive," Dante said.

As the battle raged around her, Mercy, who occasionally had to use her sword for both protection and attack, combed the battleground, searching for Raintree wounded. In all she found nine, including Echo, who had been frozen in place, and Meta, whose left arm had been hacked off. With the heat from her healing hands, Mercy thawed Echo slowly and drew the frostbite from her body. Before Mercy recovered from the healing, Echo left, rushing back into the battle.

Mercy managed to save eight of the nine wounded, including Meta, whose arm Mercy reattached, but she warned her not to use it during the battle.

"It won't be completely healed for at least twenty-four hours," Mercy cautioned.

After expending enough energy to work her healing magic on nine people, Mercy's strength was greatly depleted, so much so that she could barely stand. She desperately needed rest, hours of recuperative sleep. But there was no time.

As she continued her search, her legs grew weaker and her arms felt as if they weighed fifty pounds each. Her hands trembled. She staggered, then fell to her knees. She clutched her sword tightly but felt her grip softening.

*Hold on to Ancelin's sword! Don't let it go!*

Try as she might, she couldn't keep her eyes open, couldn't fight her body's urgent need for rest.

She toppled facedown onto the ground, Ancelin's sword slipping from her fingers. She could hear the clatter of battle and smell the scent of death all around her as she lay there in her half-conscious state, drained and defenseless.

She had to find cover, a place to hide away until she could re-energize. Forcing her eyes open, she reached to her side until her fingers encountered her sword. Clasping it loosely, she dragged it with her as she crawled toward a stand of trees less than fifteen feet in front of her. She made it halfway there before a booted foot knocked Ancelin's sword from her grasp, then stomped on her hand, flattening it against the ground. As pain radiated from her hand, along her arm and through her body, Mercy gazed up into a set of cold gray eyes.

Cael Ansara's eyes.

He lifted his foot from her broken hand, then grabbed her hair and yanked her to her feet. Realizing that in her condition she wouldn't be able to fight him, she sent out a psychic scream for help. It was all she could do.

Pressing her back against his chest, he slid a dagger beneath her chin, resting the sharp blade across her throat. He pushed his cheek against hers, and his hot, foul breath raked across her face as he laughed.

"Judah's beautiful Raintree princess." Cael licked her neck.

Mercy cringed.

"Too bad we don't have time for me to show you that I'm superior to my brother in every way." He thrust his semi-erect sex against her buttocks.

If only she could muster enough strength to command Ancelin's sword to come to her, she might be able to—

"Release her!" The commanding voice came from behind them.

Before Cael managed to turn around, the hand he held to her throat sprung open, and his dagger fell out and dropped to the ground. Startled by the appearance of a man who had been nowhere near them only seconds before, Cael momentarily focused on Mercy's rescuer and not her. While Cael was distracted, she directed her core of inner strength on one objective —freeing herself from his tenacious hold.

Just as she managed to break away from Cael, Judah reached out, grabbed Mercy's arm and pulled her to him. Cael growled with rage as Judah shoved Mercy behind him.

Where had Judah come from, and how had he gotten here so quickly? Mercy asked herself. The only explanation was teleportation, an ability she hadn't realized he possessed. But why had he appeared, and not Dante, whom she had beckoned with her silent screams?

As Judah faced Cael, he spoke telepathically to Mercy. *It wasn't Dante's name you called,* he told her. *It was mine.*

Had she actually screamed for Judah to save her and not Dante?

*How did you...?*

*Eve transported me,* Judah said. *She also heard your screams for help, so she sent me to you.*

"How touching." Cael's lips curved in a mocking smile. "You actually called for my brother to help you. You must be a fool, Princess Mercy. Don't you know the only reason he's here to fight me is because he doesn't want me to have the pleasure of killing you? That's a treat he wants for himself."

Judah didn't deny his brother's accusations. In fact, he ignored them completely. Instead he instructed Mercy to lay her hand on his shoulder. When she hesitated, he said, "Trust your instincts."

She did, and laid her hand on his shoulder. Immediately she felt a surge of Judah's strength transported into her. Not much, but enough to keep her standing, and enough to enable her to call Ancelin's sword up from the ground and into her hand.

Cael sent the first wave of mind-numbing mental bolts toward Judah, who deflected them effortlessly, then returned fire. Mercy moved backward, away from Judah, and knew he understood that she could now protect herself with the ancient power of Ancelin's sword, which left him free to concentrate completely on the Death Duel with his brother.

Cael used every weapon in his arsenal of powers and black magic to attack Judah and to counteract Judah's superior abilities. Mercy watched while the brothers fought, bloodying each other, exchanging energy bolts and optic blasts, pulverizing trees and brush and boulders within a hundred-foot radius all around them. And then they charged each other, coming together in mortal physical combat, sword against sword, might against might.

Mercy held her breath when Cael pierced Judah's side, ripping apart his shirt and slicing into the flesh beneath. Judah cursed, but the wound didn't affect his agile maneuvers as he backed Cael up farther and farther, until he managed to chop off Cael's sword hand. Howling in pain as his sword fell to the ground along with his severed hand, Cael reared up and, using all his energy, conjured a psychic bolt. Judah deflected the bolt, sending it back toward Cael, who barely managed to escape. As he hit the ground and rolled, Judah strode toward him. Before Cael could rebound and come up fighting, Judah swooped over him and plunged his sword through his half brother's heart. Cael screeched like a banshee. Judah yanked the sword from Cael's heart, and with one swift, deadly strike took off Cael's head.

Cael's body shattered, splintering into dust. Judah stood there silent and unmoving, his brother's blood coating the blade of his sword. Mercy rushed to him, her only thought to comfort and heal Judah. Holding Ancelin's sword in her left hand, she ran the fingers of her right hand over Judah's wound, then realized his body had already begun healing itself.

Judah pulled Mercy to him and slid his arm around her waist, each of them still holding their battle swords.

"Judah Ansara!" Dante Raintree called.

Gasping, Mercy lifted her gaze until it collided with her brother's.

"Release her," Dante said. "This fight is between the two of us."

Judah tightened his hold about Mercy's waist. "Do you think I intend to kill her?"

In that moment Mercy understood that Judah had no intention of harming her. He wouldn't have given her the strength to retrieve Ancelin's sword if he hadn't wanted her to live.

"He saved me from Cael when I was too weak to fight," Mercy said.

"Only to save you for himself," Dante told her. "Have you forgotten that we are at war with the Ansara?"

"Only with Cael's warriors," Judah corrected. "Or have you been too busy fighting to realize that my army was killing more of Cael's soldiers than you Raintree were? I brought my army here to defeat Cael and to save my daughter...and her mother."

Mercy's gaze met Judah's, and their minds melded for a brief moment, long enough for her to realize that Judah was telling the truth.

Dante narrowed his gaze until his eyes were mere slits. "You're lying."

Mercy sensed that her brother was not going to back down from this fight, that he had every intention of engaging Judah in battle, Raintree Dranir against Ansara Dranir. To the death. When Dante stepped forward, sword drawn, gauntlet dropped, Judah shoved Mercy aside and confronted his enemy.

"No, Dante, don't! I—I love him!" Mercy cried. When he

disregarded her completely, she turned to Judah. "Please, don't do this. He's my brother."

Both men ignored her. If only her powers hadn't been depleted to such a great extent, she might have been able to stop them, but as it stood...

As suddenly and mysteriously as Judah had appeared from out of nowhere in time to save Mercy from Cael, a bright light formed in the space between Judah and Dante. Both men froze, transfixed by the sight.

When the light dimmed, Eve was revealed, hovering several inches off the ground, her body glowing, her hair flowing high into the air, her eyes glistening a brilliant topaz gold. And her Ansara crescent moon birthmark had disappeared.

"My God!" Dante stared at his niece.

"I am Eve, daughter of Mercy and Judah, born to my mother's clan, born for my father's people. I am Rainsara."

An unnatural hush fell over the meadow, the last battlefield of an age-old war, once thought to be eternal. Raintree and Ansara alike laid down their weapons and ceased fighting, then one by one made their way to the area where Eve awaited them.

When the warriors assembled, Raintree behind Dante and Ansara behind Judah, Eve stretched out her arms on either side of her shimmering body and levitated each of her parents upward from where they stood, then brought them to her.

Judah and Mercy looked at each other and recognized the truth. Judah was no longer Ansara. His eyes were as golden as his daughter's. Mercy was no longer Raintree; her eyes, too, were burnished gold.

Eve's gaze traveled the expanse of the vast meadow, shadowing all the warriors with her light. As she passed over the

Ansara first, at least twenty of them disintegrated in puffs of sparkling dust, and all the others transformed, their eyes as golden as their Dranir's, and just as he was no longer Ansara, neither were they. When Eve turned her attention to the Raintree, a handful of them, including Sidonia, Meta and Hugh, also transformed. They were no longer Raintree.

"The Ansara are no more," Eve said. "And from this day forward, the Rainsara and Raintree will be allies."

Dante and Judah glared at each other, neither prepared to sign a peace treaty, both wise enough to know the choice was no longer theirs.

"My father is now the Dranir of the Rainsara and my mother the Dranira," Eve said. "We will go home to Terrebonne and build a new nation." She turned to her uncles. "Uncle Dante, you will rule the Raintree for many years, and your son after you. And Uncle Gideon, you won't ever have to be the Dranir."

Eve brought her parents down with her to stand on solid ground; then she led her father to her uncle and said, "The war is over, now and forever."

Neither man moved or spoke.

Simultaneously Mercy took Judah's hand and stood at his side as Lorna moved forward and grasped Dante's hand.

Judah extended his other hand. Tensing, Dante glared at Judah's hand. He hesitated for a full minute, then shook hands with his former enemy.

A reverent hush fell over the last battlefield.

*Send our people home,* Judah issued the telepathic message to his cousin. *Ask Sidra and the other council members to remain here for now. We will need to meet with Dranir Dante and his brother. In a few days, I will take my Dranira and our daughter to Terrebonne. Mercy and Eve will need time to say their goodbyes, but our people will need*

*the royal Rainsara family to guide them through the transition period
and into the future.*

Claude issued orders hurriedly. The new Rainsara clan
began their exodus from the sanctuary, heads held high, as the
Raintree rallied around Dante, Lorna, Gideon and Hope.

Judah lifted Eve off her feet and settled her on his hip, then
slipped his arm around Mercy's waist. "If you need more
time..." Judah said.

"No," Mercy replied. "I heard what you said to Claude.
You're right. Our people need us—you and me and Eve."

# EPILOGUE

Eve walked over to Hope and placed her hand on Hope's flat stomach. "Hello, Emma. I'm your cousin, Eve. You're going to like being Uncle Gideon's little princess."

The adults watched in utter fascination as Eve communicated with Gideon and Hope's unborn daughter. From hearing Eve's side of the exchange, they all realized that Eve and Emma were having quite a conversation.

Mercy had accepted the fact that her six-year-old was undoubtedly the most powerful being on earth, and that she and Judah had their work cut out for them. But they would have Sidonia and Sidra to help guide them. The two old women were already acting like rival grandmothers.

Eve gazed up at Gideon, and they smiled at each other. "It's a good thing that I got in a lot of practice with you," he said. "I just hope Emma isn't half the handful you've been."

"She won't be. I promise. Emma is going to be the Guardian

of the Sanctuary," Eve announced, then settled her gaze on Echo. "But until Emma is old enough to take over, you're going to be the keeper."

"Who, me?" Echo's eyes widened in surprise.

Eve laughed. "You really are going to have to work on controlling your abilities. You should have known that you're going to be the new keeper."

"I'm no good at seeing my own future."

Sidra placed her hand on Echo's shoulder. "Nor am I, my dear. And I count that a blessing."

In the two days since the final battle between the Ansara and the Raintree, Judah and the high council had met with Dante, Gideon, Mercy and the highest ranking Raintree in the clan. Word had come in from around the world that numerous Ansara had perished in the cleansing, but many more had been transformed, becoming members of the new clan—the Rainsara, allies of the Raintree.

There had also been another meeting, this one between Mercy and her future sisters-in-law. She had immediately liked both women and sensed that Lorna was Dante's perfect mate, as Hope was Gideon's. Mercy knew that when she left the sanctuary, she left it in Echo's capable hands. Even if the young seer questioned her ability to handle such an enormous responsibility, Mercy had no doubts. One day Echo's empathic talents would equal her abilities as a prophet. Mercy also knew that she left her brothers in the capable hands of the women they loved and who loved them. She was free to enter her new life with Judah without guilt or remorse.

"It will be some time before I'll see my brothers again," Mercy told Hope and Lorna. "At best, Dante and Gideon tolerate Judah and he them. I don't expect they'll ever be friends, but..." Mercy cleared her throat. "Our children will be friends as well as cousins, and then the Raintree and Rainsara will truly be united."

At day's end, shortly before leaving the sanctuary, Mercy tried to return her battle sword to its place of honor above the fireplace in the study, but it fell off the wall and back into her hand. The same thing occurred with her second and third attempts.

"It is now Mercy's sword," Gideon told her.

"Take it with you," Dante said. "And pray you never have to use it again."

Reaching out from where she stood behind Dante, Lorna laid her hand on his shoulder. She didn't say anything. She didn't have to. Mercy saw the immediate change in her brother, a gentling of his spirit.

Judah placed his arm possessively around Mercy's shoulders. "Are you ready to go?"

With tears glistening in her eyes and a lump of emotion caught in her throat, Mercy nodded.

When they turned to leave, Dante said, "Take good care of them."

Without looking back, Judah tightened his hold on Mercy and replied, "You have my solemn promise."

Hours later, as Judah's personal jet flew the new Rainsara royal family from Asheville, North Carolina, to Beauport, Terrebonne, in the Caribbean, Eve slept peacefully, Sidonia snoring at her side. In the quiet stillness, high above the earth, Judah took Mercy into his arms and kissed her.

"You know that I love you," she said. "I've loved you since we first met. Through all these years and everything that has happened...I never stopped loving you."

He traced his fingertips over her lips as his gaze all but worshiped her. But he didn't speak. Mercy laid her hand over his heart and connected with him.

*I won't allow you to read my thoughts, nor do I want to read yours,* he told her.

*But look inside me now and know how I feel.*

When she turned, curled up beside him and took his hand in hers, he wrapped his arms about her and held her close.

*You are mine. And I am yours. Now and forever. I need you the way I need the air I breathe. I love you, my sweet Mercy.*

*\* \* \* \* \**

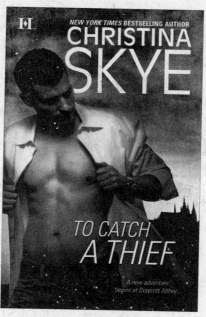

nocturne™

NEW YORK TIMES BESTSELLING AUTHOR

# SHARON SALA

## JANIS REAMES HUDSON
## DEBRA COWAN

---

# AFTERSHOCK

Three women are brought to the brink of death...
only to discover the aftershock of their trauma has
left them with unexpected and unwelcome gifts of
paranormal powers. Now each woman must learn to
accept her newfound abilities while fighting for life,
love and second chances....

*Available October wherever books are sold.*

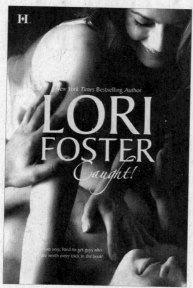

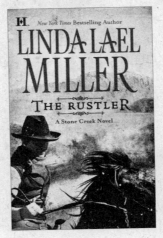